WATER MUSIC

DESCENT OF MAN

WATER MUSIC

A NOVEL

T. CORAGHESSAN BOYLE

LONDON
VICTOR GOLLANCZ LTD
1982

British Library Cataloguing in Publication Data
Boyle, T. Coraghessan
  Water music.
  I. Title
813'.54[F]   PS3552.0932
  ISBN 0 575 03068 2

Printed in Great Britain by
St Edmundsbury Press, Bury St Edmunds, Suffolk

This book is affectionately dedicated to the members of the Raconteurs' Club: Alan Arkawy, Gordon Baptiste, Neal Friedman, Scott Friedman, Rob Jordan, Russell Timothy Miller and David Needelman. It is also for you, K.K.

Listen natives of a dry place
from the harpist's fingers
rain

— W. S. MERWIN

"The Old Boast"

∾ ACKNOWLEDGMENTS

"Soft White Underbelly," "Ere Half My Days," "Corrective Surgery," "A.K.A. Katunga Oyo," "Fatima," "The Sahel," "Tantalus," "Laying It on the Line," "Plantation Song" and "New Continents, Ancient Rivers" first appeared, in slightly different form and under the title "Mungo Among the Moors," in *The Paris Review.*

"Naiad," "Glegged," "Diminishing Returns," "Apostasy" and "Cold Feet" first appeared under the title "Patience" in *Antaeus.*

"Arise!" and "Leavening" and "O That Sinking Feeling" first appeared under the title "The Fall of Ned Rise" in *The Hawaii Review.*

"Not Twist, Not Copperfield, Not Fagin Himself" first appeared in *The Iowa Review.*

"Hegira" first appeared in *The North American Review.*

"Escape!" and "Dassoud's Story" and "Escape!, Cont." first appeared under the title "Escape from the Moors" in *The Agni Review.*

The author would like to thank the National Endowment for the Arts for their financial assistance in completing this book.

✥ APOLOGIA

As the impetus behind *Water Music* is principally aesthetic rather than scholarly, I've made use of the historical background because of the joy and fascination I find in it, and not out of a desire to scrupulously dramatize or reconstruct events that are a matter of record. I have been deliberately anachronistic, I have invented language and terminology, I have strayed from and expanded upon my original sources. Where historical fact proved a barrier to the exigencies of invention, I have, with full knowledge and clear conscience, reshaped it to fit my purposes.

TCB

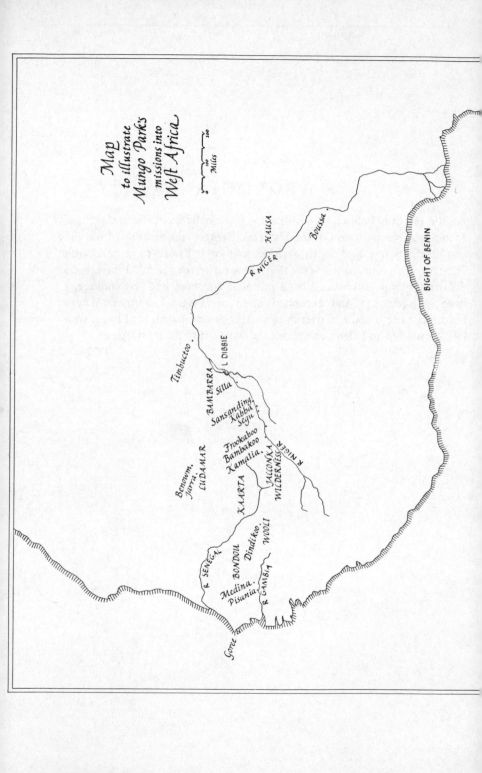

Map
to illustrate
Mungo Park's
missions into
West Africa

0   100   200
       Miles

BIGHT OF BENIN

HAUSA

R. NIGER

Boussa.

Timbuctoo.

L. DIBBIE

BAMBARRA

Silla

Sansanding.
Kabba
Segu

R. NIGER

Benowm.
Jarra.
LUDAMAR

Froohaboo
Bambakoo
Kamalia.

JALCONKA
WILDERNESS

KAARTA

BONDOU

Dindikoo

WOOLI

R. SENEGAL

Medina.
Pisunia.

R. GAMBIA

Goree

ONE

THE NIGER

❧ Na, faith ye yet! ye'll no be right ❧
Till ye've got on it—
The vera tapmost, tow'ring height
O' Miss's bonnet.

—ROBERT BURNS, "To a Louse"

⊷ SOFT WHITE UNDERBELLY ꞌ

At an age when most young Scotsmen were lifting skirts, plowing furrows and spreading seed, Mungo Park was displaying his bare buttocks to al-haj' Ali Ibn Fatoudi, Emir of Ludamar. The year was 1795. George III was dabbing the walls of Windsor Castle with his own spittle, the *Notables* were botching things in France, Goya was deaf, De Quincey a depraved preadolescent. George Bryan "Beau" Brummell was smoothing down his first starched collar, young Ludwig van Beethoven, beetle-browed and twenty-four, was wowing them in Vienna with his Piano Concerto no. 2, and Ned Rise was drinking Strip-Me-Naked with Nan Punt and Sally Sebum at the Pig & Pox Tavern in Maiden Lane.

Ali was a Moor. He sat cross-legged on a damask pillow and scrutinized the pale puckered nates with the air of an epicure examining a fly in his vichyssoise. His voice was like sand. "Turn over," he said. Mungo was a Scotsman. He knelt on a reed mat, trousers around his knees, and glanced over his shoulder at Ali. He was looking for the Niger River. "Turn over," Ali repeated.

While the explorer was congenial and quick-to-please, his Arabic was somewhat sketchy. When he failed to respond a second time, Dassoud — Ali's henchman and human jackal — stepped forward with a lash composed of the caudal appendages of half a dozen wildebeests. The tufted tails cut the air, beating on high like the wings of angels. The temperature outside Ali's tent was 127° Fahrenheit. The tent was a warp-and-woof affair, constructed of thread spun from the hair of goats. Inside it was 112°. The lash fell. Mungo turned over.

Here too he was white: white as sheets and blizzards. Ali and his circle were astonished all over again. "His mother dipped him in milk," someone said. "Count his fingers and toes!" shouted another. Women and children crowded the tent's entrance, goats bleated, camels coughed and coupled, someone was hawking figs. A hundred voices intertwined like a congeries of footpaths, walks, lowroads and highroads — which one to take? — and all in Arabic, mystifying, rapid, harsh, the language of the Prophet. "La-la-la-la-la!" a woman shrieked. The others took it up, an excoriating falsetto. "La-la-la-la-la!" Mungo's penis, also white, shrank into his body.

☙ ❧

Beyond the blank wall of the tent was the camp at Benowm, Ali's winter residence. Three hundred parched and blistered miles beyond that lay the north bank of the River Niger, a river no European had ever laid eyes upon. Not that Europeans weren't interested. Herodotus was exercised about its course five centuries Before Christ. Big, he concluded. But tributary to the Nile. Al-Idrisi populated its banks with strange and mythical creatures — the vermicular Strapfeet, who crawled rather than walked and spoke the language of serpents; the sphinx and the harpy; the manticore with its lion's torso and scorpion's tail and its nasty predilection for human flesh. Pliny the Elder painted the Niger gold and christened it black, and Alexander's scouts inflamed him with tales of the river of rivers where lords and ladies sat in gardens of lotus and drank from cups of hammered gold. And now, at the end of the Age of Enlightenment and the beginning of the Age of Imbursement, France wanted the Niger, Britain wanted it, Holland, Portugal and Denmark. According to the most recent and reliable information — Ptolemy's *Geography* — the Niger lay between Nigritia, land of the blacks, and the Great Desert. As it turned out, Ptolemy was right on target. But no one had yet been able to survive the sere blast of the Sahara or the rank fever belt of the Gambia to bear him out.

Then, in 1788, a group of distinguished geographers, botanists, philanderers and other seekers after the truth, met at the St. Alban's Tavern, Pall Mall, to form the African Association. Their purpose was to open up Africa to exploration. North Africa was a piece of cake. They had it staked out, mapped, labeled, dissected and distributed by 1790. But West Africa remained a mystery. At the heart of the mystery was the Niger. In its inaugural year the Association commissioned an expedition headed by John Ledyard. He was to begin in Egypt, traverse the Sahara, and discover the course of the Niger. Ledyard was an American. He played the violin and suffered from strabismus. He'd been across the Pacific with Cook, into the Andes, through Siberia to Yakutsk on foot. I've tramped the world under my feet, he said, laughed at fear, derided danger. Through hordes of savages, over parching deserts, the freezing north, the everlasting ice and stormy seas have I passed without harm. How good is my God! Two weeks after landing at Cairo he died of dysentery. Simon Lucas, Oriental interpreter for the Court of St. James's, was next. He landed at Tripoli, hiked a hundred miles into the desert, developed blisters, thirst and anxiety, and returned without accomplishing anything other than the expenditure of £1,250. And then there was Major Daniel Houghton. He was an Irishman, bankrupt, fifty-two years of age. He knew nothing of Africa whatever, but he came cheap. I'll do it for three hunnert pund, he said. And a case o' Scots whisky. Houghton sallied up the Gambia in a dugout canoe, drank from fetid puddles and ate monkey meat, and through sheer grit and force of intoxication survived typhus, malaria, loiasis, leprosy and yellow fever. Unfortunately, the Moors of Ludamar stripped him naked and staked him out on the crest of a dune. Where he died.

◄§ §►

Mungo stood to hitch up his pants. Dassoud knocked him down. The ululations of the women were fanning the crowd to a frenzy. "Eat pig, Christian," they shouted. "Eat pig." Mungo didn't like their attitude. Nor did he like exposing his prat in mixed company. But there was nothing to be done about it: they'd cut his throat and bleach his bones at the least show of resistance.

Suddenly Dassoud had a dirk in his hand: narrow as an ice pick, dark as blood. "Infidel dog!" he shrieked, veins tessellating his throat. Ali watched from behind the folds of his burnoose, dark and impassive. The temperature inside the tent rose to 120°. The crowd held its breath. Then Dassoud leveled the blade at the explorer, gibbering all the while, like some rabid anatomist lecturing on the eccentricities of the human form. The point of the blade drew closer, Ali spat in the sand, Dassoud exhorted the crowd, Mungo froze. Then the blade pricked him — ever so lightly — down below, where he was softest, and whitest. Dassoud laughed like a brook gone dry. The crowd whistled and shrieked. It was then that a grizzled *Bushreen* with straw in his beard and an empty eye socket burst through the press to push Dassoud aside. "The eyes!" he howled. "Look at the devil's eyes!"

Dassoud looked. The sadistic gloat gave way to a look of horror and indignation. "The eyes of a cat," he hissed. "We must put them out."

◄§ ARISE!

Ned Rise wakes with a headache. He has been drinking gin — a.k.a. Strip-Me-Naked, Blue Ruin, the Curse — enfeebler and enervator of the lower classes, clear as a souse's urine and tart as the juice of juniper. He has been drinking gin, and he is not quite sure where he is. Though he is reasonably certain that he recognizes the soleless half-boots, hairy knuckles and cinnamon-red cape that are among the first things to present themselves to his eye. Yes: that cape, those knuckles and boots, the tear in the trousers: they are familiar. Intimate, even. Yes, he concludes, they belong to Ned Rise, and thus the splintered head and staved-in eyes which perceive these phenomena, however imperfectly, must in some way be connected to them.

He sits up, and after a long pause, rises. It seems that he's been lying in a heap of discolored straw. On his hat. He bends to retrieve it, lurches forward, then regains his balance with an assertive belch. The hat is a ruin. He stands there a moment, assuming a meditative pose, something drumming in the back of his head. Then he scans the room through half-closed lids, feeling a bit like an explorer setting foot on a new continent.

He is in a cellar, no question about it. There's the dirt floor, mop in a bucket, walls of rough stone. Against the back wall, a double row of sealed casks: Madeira, port, Lisbon, claret, hock. In the corner, a shovel or two of coal. Could these be the nether regions of the Pig & Pox Tavern? At this point Ned discovers that he is not alone. Other forms, possibly human, occupy patches of straw scattered over the floor. There is the sound of snoring, a moan and gargle like rain in the gutter. The concurrent odors of urine and vomit hang heavy in the air.

"So ye're up then, are ye?" A balding crone, her face a memento mori, is addressing him from behind a plank set across a pair of hogsheads. A thin gold ring rides her lower lip like a bubble of sputum. "Well. Good mornin' to ye sir," she says. "Ha-haaa! And 'ow was yer sleep and will ye 'ave a dram to start the day off proper?" Two pewter measures the size of eggcups and a terra-cotta jug stand atop the plank in still life. A sow lies on her side beneath the makeshift bar, the swell of her jaw obscured by an overturned chamberpot. Hogarth would have loved it. Ned wonders what happened last night.

Suddenly the beldam shrieks as if she's been stuck with a dagger, a long rasping insuck of breath: "Eeeeeeeee!" The drumming in Ned's brain becomes a series of paradiddles, thunder rolls, the booming of a big bass drum. But wait. The crone isn't suffering a stroke after all: she's laughing. Coughing now, hacking and pounding the plank until a long yellow taper of phlegm appears at the corner of her mouth and makes its resilient way to the countertop. "Cat . . ." she chokes, ". . . cat got your tongue, peach fuzz?"

A sign hangs on the wall behind her, its characters scrawled in a clonic hand:

DRUNK FOR A PENNY

DEAD DRUNK FOR TUPPENCE

CLEAN STRAW, FREE

Ned bites his thumb at her. "Screw you and your mother and your hagborn dropsical brood, you scrofulous tit-sore slut!" he shouts, already beginning to feel better.

"Eeeeeeeeeeeeee!" she screeches. "Ye've no taste for Mother Geneva's 'lixir, eh? Taste enough ye had for it last night. . . . 'Ere, give Mother a look at yer manhood then — she'll find a cure for ye," lifting her skirts with a leer, the spindle legs and yellowed bush like the denouement of a Gothic tale.

Off to the left a flight of ramshackle stairs leads up to an outer door, through the chinks of which Ned can discern the chill light of dawn. He curses himself for wasting breath on the crazed hag — there's business to tend to this afternoon — and starts up the reeling stairs to the door.

"Eeeeee!" shrieks the old woman, "Mind yer gown now, fairy quean!"

Ned gives her the finger, draws the cinnamon robe tight, and swings back the door on Maiden Lane and the light of day. Behind him, from the depths, a broken shriek like a viola gone sour: "Beware, beware, beware the hangman's cravat!"

◄§ ERE HALF MY DAYS

The machine for extinguishing sight consists of two strips of brass and looks something like an inverted chastity belt. One strip circles the head at eye level, the other fits snugly over the crown. There are two screws involved: each has a convex disk attached to the working end. The device was originally fabricated in the ninth century for al-kaid Hassan Ibn Mohammed, the blind Bashaw of Tripoli. Insecure about his infirmity, the Bashaw decreed that all who desired to come into his presence must first submit to having their eyes put out. He was a very lonely man.

The machine operates on the same principle as a vise. The screws are twisted until they meet the surface of the eye, and are then tightened, crank by crank, until the cornea bursts. Simple, inexorable, final.

A hush has fallen over the crowd. A moment earlier they'd been on the brink of hysteria, razzing and gibbering like the hoi polloi at a bullbaiting or a freak show. But now: silence. Flies saw away at the hot still air, and the sound of a goat or camel making water in the sand is like the boom of a cataract. Sandals shuffle, a man scratches his beard. Many have drawn rags over their faces, as if to escape the contamination of the explorer's gaze. Dassoud and the one-eyed interloper stare down at him, arms akimbo, faces solemn.

Mungo has had difficulty grasping the gist of the proceedings. He is reasonably certain that he has pinned down one word at least — the word for eye, *unya* — which he recalls from *Ouzel's Arabic Grammar* ("We lift up our *unyas* to heaven wherein Allah resides"). But why on earth would they be nattering about eyes? And the sudden hush — he wonders about that too. But it is hot, beastly hot, and he can hardly keep his mind on anything at all. So hot in fact that it surpasses anything in his experience, with the possible exception of the Swedish Baths off Grosvenor Square. Sir Joseph Banks, Treasurer and Director of the African Association, had taken him to the baths one afternoon to iron out some of the details of Mungo's drive for the Niger. There they had been subjected to the emanations of baked stones, stones that glowed like molten lava — or so it seemed. An attendant thrashed them with birch switches and buffeted their kidneys and backbones with the sharp heels of his hands. Sir Joseph seemed to find the whole operation invigorating. The explorer nearly lost consciousness. He is beginning to experience the same sort of light-headedness at the moment, in fact. And small wonder, when you consider that not only must he contend with the sun, sand fleas, dysentery and fever, but with inanition as well. The Moors have confiscated his supplies, appropriated his horse and interpreter, and apparently decided to put him on a stringent diet. Too stringent, by his way of thinking: he hasn't seen a scrap of food in two days.

And so, despite the critical situation and the ring of strange hostile faces, Mungo begins to feel giddy — almost as if he'd drunk too much claret or gill-ale. He glances round at the furtive eyes and knitted brows, at the beards and burnooses, the prophets' robes and pilgrims' sandals, and suddenly all those hard minatory faces begin to melt, lose their contours, droop into vagueness like figures of wax. The whole thing is a masquerade, is what it is. Dassoud and One-Eye are tumblers or fire-eaters, and old Ali is only Grimaldi — Grimaldi the clown. But now they seem to be fitting something over his head . . . a helmet? Do they expect him to go to battle for them? Or have they finally come to their senses and decided to measure him for a crown?

The explorer grins stupidly beneath his brazen cap. His eyes are gray. Gray as the tentative fingers of ice that reach out over the deep pools of the Yarrow on a frosty morning. Ailie once compared them to the lovers' wells at Galashiels, and then shook the pennies from her purse and propped them against his eyelids as he lay back in the heather. Gloucester's eyes, they say, were gray. Oedipus' were black as olives. And Milton's — Milton's were like bluejays scrabbling in the snow. Dassoud knows nothing of Shakespeare, Sophocles or Milton. His rough fingers twist the screws. The explorer grins. Oblivious. The onlookers, horrified at his mad composure, turn away in panic. He can hear them rushing off, the slap of their sandals on the baked earth . . . but what's this? — he seems to have something caught in his eye . . .

◄§ CORRECTIVE SURGERY

"Stop!"

Mungo can't see a thing (the cap seems to have a visor, and every time he goes to lift it a hand seizes his wrist), but he recognizes the voice instantly. It is Johnson. Jolly old Johnson, his guide and interpreter, come to the rescue.

"Stop!" the voice of Johnson repeats, before pitching headlong into the spillway of Arabic glottals and fricatives. Dassoud answers him, then One-Eye harmonizes with a concatenation of grunts and emphatics, his voice pitched high. Johnson rebuts. And then Ali's voice sounds from the corner, harsh and grainy. There is the sound of a blow, and Johnson tumbles to the mat beside the explorer.

"Mr. Park," Johnson whispers. "What you got that thing on your head for? Don't you realize what they doin' to you?"

"Johnson, jolly old Johnson. How good to hear your voice."

"They puttin' out your eyes, Mr. Park."

"How's that?"

"The Chief Jackal here he says you got the eyes of a cat — and apparently that don't go down too good around here, as they is presently engaged in grindin' them out. If it wasn't for my fortuitous intercession I'd lay odds you'd be blind as a beggar this very minute."

Mungo's head clears like a hazy morning giving way to noon. As it does so he becomes increasingly agitated, until finally he leaps to his feet, tearing at the brazen cap and wailing like a lost calf. Dassoud knocks him down. Cracks the wildebeest whip a time or two and then calls out in Arabic for some further instrument of torture. There is the sound of padding feet, the swish of the tent flap, and then, close at hand, the cry of a human being in mortal agony. The cry seems to be emanating from Johnson. The explorer is alarmed, and tugs at the cap with renewed vigor, feeling very much like a ten-year-old with his head caught between the bars of an iron railing. "Johnson," he gasps, " — what have they done to you?"

"Nothin' yet. But they just sent out for a two-edge bilbo."

The cap finally releases its grip, heaving up from the explorer's head like the cork from a bottle of spumante. He blinks and looks round him. Ali, Dassoud and One-Eye are crouched in the far corner, jabbering and gesticulating. The mob is gone and the flap of the tent is drawn closed. A massive black man in turban and striped robe blocks the entrance, arms folded across his chest. "A bilbo? What does that mean?" Mungo whispers.

"Means we goin' to be two monkeys — see no evil, speak none either. They say I got the tongue of a shrike, Mr. Park. They goin' to cut it out."

◁§ A. K. A.   K A T U N G A   O Y O

Concerning Johnson. He is a member of the Mandingo tribe, they who inhabit the headwaters of the Gambia and Senegal rivers and most of the Niger Valley as far as the city of legend, Timbuctoo. His mother did not name him Johnson. She called him Katunga — Katunga Oyo — after his paternal grandfather. At the age of thirteen Johnson was kidnapped by Foulah herdsmen while celebrating the nubility of a tender young sylph in a cornfield just outside his native village of Dindikoo. The sylph's name was Nealee. The Foulahs didn't ask. Their chieftain, who took a fancy to Nealee's facial tattoos and to other features as well, retained her as his personal concubine. Johnson was sold to a *slatee,* or traveling slave merchant, who shackled his ankles and drove him, along with sixty-two others, to the coast. Forty-nine made it. There he was sold to an American slaver who chained him in the hold of a schooner bound for South Carolina. The boy beside him, a Bobo from Djenné, had been dead for six days when the ship landed at Charleston.

For twelve years Johnson worked as a field hand on the plantation of Sir Reginald Durfeys, Bart. Then he was promoted to house servant. Three years later Sir Reginald himself visited the Carolinas, took a liking to Johnson, and brought him back to London as his valet. This was in 1771. The Colonies had not yet broken away, slavery was still sanctioned in England, George III was already harboring the renegade porphyrins that would cost him his sanity, and Napoleon was storming the palisades of his playpen.

Johnson, as he was christened by Sir Reginald, began to educate himself in the library at Piltdown, the Durfeys' country estate. He learned Greek and Latin. He read the Ancients. He read the Moderns. He read Smollett, Ben Jonson, Molière, Swift. He spoke of Pope as if he'd known him personally, denigrated the puerility of Richardson, and was so taken with Fielding that he actually attempted a Mandingo translation of *Amelia*.

Durfeys was fascinated with him. Not only with his command of language and literature, but with his recollections of the Dark Continent as well. It got to the point where the Baronet couldn't drift off at night without a cup of hot milk and garlic, and the soothing basso profundo of Johnson's voice as he narrated a tale of thatched huts, leopards and hyenas, of volcanoes spewing fire across the sky, of thighs and buttocks glistening with sweat and black as a dream of the womb. Sir Reginald allowed him a liberal salary, and after emancipation in 1772 offered him a handsome pension to stay on as valet. Johnson considered the proposal over a glass of sherry in Sir Reginald's study. Then he grinned, and hit the Baronet for a raise

When Parliament was in session Sir Reginald moved his establishment to town, accompanied by Johnson and a pair of liveried footmen. London was a ripe tomato. Johnson was a macaroni. He strutted down Bond Street with the best of them, decked out in his top hat, wasp-waisted coat and silk hose. Soon he was frequenting the coffeehouses, engaging in repartee, learning to turn an epigram with a barb in it. One afternoon a red-faced gentleman with muttonchop whiskers called him a "damned Hottentot nigger" and invited him to fight for his life. The following morning, at dawn and in the presence of seconds, Johnson put a bullet through the gentleman's right eye. The gentleman died instantly and Johnson was incarcerated. He was subsequently sentenced to be hanged by the neck until dead. Sir Reginald exerted his influence. The sentence was commuted to transportation.

And so, in January of 1790 Johnson's legs were once again shackled, spoiling the lines of his hosiery. He was put aboard the H.M.S. *Feckless* and deposited at Goree, an island just off the west coast of Africa, where he was to serve as a private in the military. When he stepped ashore an ancient thrill went through him. He was home. Two weeks later, while on late watch, Johnson appropriated a canoe, paddled his way to shore, and melted into the black bank of the jungle. He then made his way back to Dindikoo, where he married Nealee's younger sister and settled in to repopulate the village.

He was forty-seven. His hair was salted with gray. The trees climbed into the sky and dawn came like a blanket of flowers. By night there was the shriek of the hyrax and the cough of the leopard, by day the slow drowse of the honeybee. His mother was an old woman now, her face cracked and dried like the faces of the mummified corpses he'd seen in the desert — the corpses of slaves who hadn't made it. She pressed him to her bones and clicked her tongue. It rained. Crops grew, goats fattened. He lived in a hut, went barefoot, wrapped a strip of broadcloth round his chest and loins and called it a toga. He gave himself over to sensuality.

Within five years Johnson was providing for three wives and eleven children — fourteen mouths — plus an assortment of dogs, simians, rope squirrels and skinks. Still, he wasn't exactly working himself to the bone — no, he cashed in instead on his reputation as a man of letters. Villagers would come to him with a calabash of beer or a side of kudu and ask him to scribble off a few words in return. Each wore a *saphie* — a leather pouch the size of a billfold — tied round his neck or wrist. These *saphies* were the repositories of fetishes, charms against calamity: a pickled ring finger was considered proof against the bite of the puff adder; a hank of hair guaranteed immunity from mutilation in battle; the musk gland of the civet cat prevented yaws and leprosy. But Logos was the supreme charm. The written word could bring wisdom, sexual potency, plenty in times of want. It could restore lost hair, cure cancer, attract women and kill locusts. Johnson was quick to realize the market potential of his penmanship. He would scribble off a line or two of doggerel in exchange for three pounds of honey or a month's supply of grain. Or he'd quote Pope and purchase a pair of gold anklets for his youngest bride:

> *Three catcalls be the bribe*
> *Of him, who chattering shames the Monkey tribe:*
> *And his this Drum, whose hoarse heroic bass*
> *Drowns the loud clarion of the braying Ass.*

She was fifteen, and demonstrative in her appreciation. Johnson lay back and relished, the whole thing sweet as a fiction. *Paradise Regained,* he thought.

Then one afternoon a runner came from Pisania, the British trading colony on the Gambia. He carried a letter from England sealed with the Durfeys coat-of-arms (a goat ruminant). England — the clubs, the theater, Covent Garden and Pall Mall, the sweep of the Thames, the texture of the late afternoon light in the library at Piltdown — it all rushed back on him. He tore open the envelope.

Piltdown. 21 May, 1795

My Dear Johnson:
    If this missive should reach you, I trust it finds you in good health. I must confess that the news of your elopement from Goree pleased us all immensely. I rather suspect you've "gone native" with a few of those honey-complected sirens you were forever rhapsodizing, what?
    But to business. This letter is by means of introducing one Mungo Park, the young Scot we've commissioned to penetrate to the interior of your country and discover the course of the Niger. If you will consent to act as guide and interpreter for Mr. Park, you may name your price.

    Yours in Geographical Fervor,

                              Sir Reginald Durfeys, Bart.
                              Founding Member
                              African Association

Johnson's price was the complete works of Shakespeare, in quarto volumes, just as they had appeared on the shelves of Sir Reginald's library. He packed a bag, traveled to Pisania on foot, sought out the explorer and drafted an agreement of terms of service. The explorer was twenty-four. His hair was cornsilk. He was six feet tall and walked as if a stick were strapped to his back. He took hold of Johnson's hand in his big buttery fist. "Johnson," he said, "I am truly pleased to make your acquaintance." Johnson was five four, two hundred ten pounds. His hair was a dust mop, his feet were bare, he wore a gold straight pin through his right nostril. "The pleasure is mine," he said.

They set off on foot. Upriver, at Frookaboo, the explorer stopped to purchase a horse. The horse was owned by a Mandingo salt merchant. "A real bargain," he said, "for such a frisky colt." They found the animal tethered behind a wattle hut at the far end of the village. It stood in a cluster of chickens, munching thistles and blinking at them. "Splendid teeth," said the salt merchant. The horse was no bigger than a Shetland pony, blind in one eye, and emaciated in the way that very old men are.

Open ulcers, green with flies, spangled the right flank, and a yellowish fluid, like thin porridge, drooled from the nostrils. But perhaps worst of all, the animal was given to senile farting — great gaseous exhalations that swept the sun from the sky and made all the world a sink. "Rocinante!" Johnson quipped. The allusion was lost on the explorer. He bought the horse.

Mungo rode, Johnson walked. They passed through the kingdoms of Wooli and Bondou without incident, but found on entering Kaarta that the king of that country, Tiggitty Sego, was at war with the neighboring state of Bambarra. The explorer suggested a detour to the north, through Ludamar. Two days after crossing the border they were accosted by thirty Moors on horseback. The Moors looked as if they'd just cooked and eaten their mothers. They carried muskets, dirks and scimitars — scimitars as cold and cruel as the crescent moon, weapons that hacked rather than thrust: a single blow could remove a limb, separate a shoulder, cleave a head. Their leader, a hooded giant with a hyphenated scar across the bridge of his nose, trotted forward and spat in the sand. "You will accompany us to the camp of Ali at Benowm," he said. Johnson tugged at the explorer's gaiters and whispered in his ear. The horses stamped and stuttered. Mungo looked up at the grim faces, smiled, and announced in English that he would be delighted to accept their invitation.

◄§ FATIMA

A boy bursts into the tent, double-edged bilbo in hand. Dassoud leers, Johnson shudders. Mungo scrambles to his feet, pulls up his trousers and buckles his belt. "I'd like to know just what crime we've — " he begins. Dassoud knocks him down. At that moment a second boy darts into the tent with a message for Ali. Dassoud turns back to his companions and a frenetic colloquy ensues. Fingers are shaken, arms waved, beards pulled. Through it all the explorer can make out a single word, repeated again and again, as if it were an incantation: Fatima, Fatima, Fatima. Keeping his eyes fixed on the conferees, he snakes out a hand to tug at Johnson's toga. "Johnson," he whispers. "What's up?"

Johnson's eyes are wide. "Shh!" he says.

A moment later Ali rises. One-Eye takes up the damask pillow, Dassoud flings down the bilbo in disgust, and the three stalk out of the tent.

Explorer and guide are left alone with the Nubian sentry. And the sand fleas.

"Pssst. Johnson," Mungo whispers. "What's this Fatima business they're jabbering about?"

"Beats the hell out of me. But whatever it is you can bet it's nothin' to lose your senses over."

✑ LEAVENING

Ned Rise saunters out the door of the dram shop, brushing at his clothes and boxing the collapsed hat against his thigh, when he is suddenly leveled by a blow to the nostrils. As he ripples to the pavement like a deflated balloon, fear, pain and bewilderment cloud his perceptions. Once there, however, he finds himself admiring the rich mahogany gloss of the riding boots that scuffle and rise with choreographic precision to deliver a succession of blows to his vital organs. Then he wheezes. Hacks. Pukes. The boots are affixed to the nimble feet of Daniel Mendoza, the pugilist, the Jew, the ex-Champion Fisticuffer of London, friend and associate of George Bryan "Beau" Brummell. Mendoza is dressed to the nines: starched linen collar, scarlet waistcoat, striped trousers and boots of morocco. A dandified young prig of twelve or thirteen stands beside him, folding the blue-velvet jacket across his forearm like a maître d' with a napkin. Mendoza's face is red. "So!" he shouts. "Chinee silk is it?"

From the cobblestones Ned mutters a combined apology, denial and plea for mercy.

"Dutch sateen, twelve pence the yard!" shouts Mendoza. "And you, you scum, charges Beau six pund for *a pure and original unadulterated quality Chinee silk cravat straight from the looms o' Oriental Pekin,* you says. Eh? Am I royt?"

Ned stiffens for the blow. He receives it just under the left armpit.

Mendoza is leaning over him now, knife in hand. The coatboy looks like an angel of the Lord. It is beginning to snow. "I'll just relieve you of this little trifle," Mendoza says, slicing through the strings of Ned's purse, "as a partial recompense for the 'eartache me friend 'as suffered." The toe of Mendoza's boot finds Ned's spleen — an organ he didn't even know he was possessed of — three times in quick succession. "And don't let it 'appen again, arseole. Or I'll cripple you up like I crippled Turk Nasmyth in the second round at Bartholomew Fair. 'Ear?" There is the swish of cambric against velvet, and then the tattoo of receding footsteps, two pairs. The snow sifts down like crushed bone, and the air is sharp as a bloodletter's lancet.

Ned pushes himself up from the ground and wipes his mouth with the back of his hand. He is grinning. Sick from gin, smarting about the nostrils, kidneys, spleen and armpit, a victim of assault, battery and robbery, he is grinning. Grinning over the thought of Mendoza's face when he opens the purse and finds that it contains eight ounces of river sand, two copper buttons and a pig's tooth. He passes a hand over his crotch and grins wider: the prize is secure. A strip of muslin swaddles his privates, fixed by means of pine stickum to his belly and buttocks. Nestled within, warmed and coddled by the downy flesh of his balls, are twenty-two golden guineas, the fruit of a week's frauds and chicaneries. Ned plans to invest them, and watch them grow.

◦§ §◦

At the Vole's Head Ned calls for rashers, mutton chops, wheatcakes, boiled eggs, tongue, ham, toast, pigeon pie and marmalade — "and a pint of bitter for lubrication." Then he sends a boy out to one of the pawnshops across from White's Gaming House to pick him up a suit of clothes, "as what a gentleman would wear," from pumps to cravat to topper. The boy's feet are wrapped in rags, his eyes, mouth and ears are running, and he's lost all his teeth to scurvy. Ned gives him half a crown for his trouble.

The landlord at the Vole's Head is one Nelson Smirke. Smirke is a big man, scabious, with bald patches along either side of his head and a mad electric growth of hair across the crown. The overall effect is vegetal: he looks like nothing so much as a colossal turnip. "Ah, Smirke!" says Ned over his pigeon pie. "Draw up a chair, my friend — I've got a proposition for you." Smirke sits and folds his massive hands on the table. "I'll give it to you straight," says Ned. "I want to let the Reamer Room for tonight, from eight to maybe three or four in the morning. I'll give you two guineas and no questions asked."

"Wot's it, a party then?"

"That's right. A party."

"Yer not plannin' to tear up the cushings and piss in the tea service like ye done last time, is ye?"

"Smirke, Smirke, Smirke," says Ned, clucking his tongue. "Have you got no confidence in me? This is a gathering of gentlemen." The head of a buck hangs on the wall behind him. Coals glow in the grate. Ned lays his fork aside and thrusts a hand into his trousers, plumbing for gold. He takes a deep breath, tears the muslin (and hair) from his abdomen, and digs into the hoard.

"Gennelmen, my arse," says Smirke. "I know the sort of turks and derelicts and 'uman garbage wot calls you friend, Ned Rise." Two guineas clank down on the table, sweet music. Smirke covers them with a fat fist. Ned looks into the landlord's eyes, then rams down a wheatcake, champing like a refugee. He folds a slice of ham and wads it in on top, then slips a boiled egg up inside his cheek. "Three," says Smirke, "and it's a deal." Ned chokes briefly, something caught up the windpipe, then spins the third coin across the table. Smirke rises. Points a thick finger between the entrepreneur's eyes and snarls: "There'll be no trouble in my house or be Gad I'll 'ave yer liver out."

᠊ᡃᡃᢀ ᢀᡃᡃ᠊

Seven-thirty. Ned stands at the door of the Reamer Room, decked out like a young lord. From a distance, and in the murk of the hallway, he could almost pass for a solid citizen. Up close the illusion fades. First, there is the matter of his face. No matter how you look at it, from whatever angle, in light or shade, extremity or repose, it is at bottom the face of a wiseguy. The face of the young lout who lolls in the classroom with his boots on the desk, sets fire to old ladies and drinks ink. The face of the teenager who saunters and slouches and terrorizes the fruit seller, smoking opium, bathing in gin, making a chamberpot of the world. The face of the young panderer arranging something improper, scurrilous even, outside the door of the Reamer Room at the Vole's Head Tavern, the Strand. Then there's the matter of his clothes. The pin-striped trousers and engagé jacket droop like a tailor's nightmare, and the collar, maculated with sherry, gravy, ketchup and Worcestershire until it resembles the hide of some howling jungle beast, has already gone limp as a bathtowel. The gold watch chain? Buffed copper. The bulge in his waistcoat pocket? A stone impersonating a pocketwatch. The stockings are cut from a pair of wool socks and the boutonniere is a scrap of colored paper. But all this is nothing when compared to the cape, white stars on a cinnamon background, which billows round the impresario's shoulders like a gypsy encampment.

Nevertheless, Ned is doing a brisk business. Gentlemen, in pairs or trios or even individually, make their way down the narrow hallway, press golden guineas and silver sovereigns into his palm, and pass through the doorway of the Reamer Room. Ned deposits these coins in the Bank of the Bulge. And grins the grin of a burgher. Inside, the sounds of revelry: clinking glasses, squealing chairs, yar-hars and yo-hos. Smirke's cue. He appears at the far end of the passageway, a tray of drinks hoisted in one meaty hand, a pair of barmaids sweeping along before him like bubbles riding the crest of a breaker. "Get yer merrytricious arses in there now and keep the spirits flowin' or be Jozachar they'll tear the fookin' joists down," he roars. The girls giggle past Ned and into the room to a burst of applause, catcalls and rabid whistling. Smirke pauses at the doorway. "I'll 'and it to ye, Ned — ye've got yerself an audience of drinkin' gennelmen wot's already been through half a cask of Scots whisky and fifty-three bottles of the grape."

Ned's grin is sleek and wide. "Told you so, didn't I Smirke? Leave it to Neddy. You'll be rich."

A stentorian voice, the voice of a temperamental mountain, calls from within: "Drink! Goddamn and curse the virgin for a whore, drink!" "Booza!" shouts another. "Yaaaaar!" The shouts are like hot wires applied to Smirke's spine. He shudders, stiffens, twitches, his muscles gone clonic, the glasses teetering on the rim of the tray. Then he throws back the door like a soldier and takes the full blast of a sirocco redolent of sweat, sperm, spilled beer and urine. His eyes are like peas. "Be gad this show better be good Ned Rise or I'll, I'll — "

"Have me liver out?"

"Fricasseed!" he roars, and offers himself up to the din.

Ned slams the door and takes a pull at his flask. It's been a bitch of day. First there was the business of the carpenters and the stage. Then the advertisements. Shorthanded, he'd painted up the sandwich boards himself:

FOR THE BLOOD WHAT'S BOARD WITH PATIENCE
A New Entertainment
The Vole's Head. 8 P.M. Tonight.

TITILLATION.
The V.'s Head. Tonight.

COME TO THE VOYEER'S BALL
The Vole's Head. 8 P.M. Tonight.

Then he had to pay Billy Boyles and two other reprobates a shilling each to display them outside the gaming houses and gentlemen's shops. They were to answer inquiries sotto voce and fill in the details as delicately as possible. But if he knew Boyles, the flaming ass would be coarse-mouthing it up and

down the street till every Charlie and magistrate in town got wind of it.
Worries on worries. But that was just the beginning. Throughout the
afternoon, in the midst of placating Smirke and hounding the carpenters,
he'd had to keep Nan and Sally at a fine pitch of intoxication — soused
enough to stay happy and yet not too far gone to perform. And then there
was the biggest headache of all: leasing Jutta Jim, the black nigger of the
Congo, from his master/employer, Lord Twit. Twit wanted three guineas
and a firm assurance that his precious manservant would be returned
before dawn, "sweet energies intact." Shit. The whole thing — the hassles,
the tension, the long hours of enforced sobriety — it's nearly crippled him.
His head is a suppurating blister and gin is the only tonic.

And so he is standing there in the dim hallway, pulling at the flask,
dreaming, caressing the golden bulge at his crotch (thirty-two new guineas
so far) . . . when suddenly he finds himself pinned up against the wood-
work. There is a fist beneath his chin, iron fingers at his throat. A smell of
lavender, ruffled shirtsleeve. Mendoza.

"The entertainment better be stimulatin', sucker, or I'll snap off yer legs
and arms as if they was matchsticks. You see, I've brung Beau along with
me and I'm bleedin' anxious the boy should be uplifted and edyfied by wot
'ee's about to see, understand?" The fingers relax their grip, and the
impresario's chin — assisted by the gravitational pull of the planet
— regains its customary plane. Ned clears his eyes and looks past the
Champion Fisticuffer to where a young dandy of seventeen or eighteen
stands sneering at him. The dandy's hair is curled like a gilded poodle's, his
eyes are the color of honey. His linen is so pure it glows. "Leave the sorry
turd alone, Danny," he says in his nasal whine. He pauses to float a
jeweled snuffbox from his pocket, dab a pinch on the back of his hand and
inhale it with an elegant toss of his head. When he looks up his eyes cut into
Ned like lamb skewers. "There'll be no charge for friends, will there
Rise?"

Ned grins till his gums ache. "No," he says. "No charge at all."

Mendoza throws back the door and Beau steps into the room like a swan
lighting on a mountain pond. "Cocksuckers," Ned mutters, so low and so
far back in his throat he's not even sure he heard it himself. The door slams
shut. Ned pulls the stone from his pocket and glances at it. The stone is flat,
smooth, two inches in diameter. Someone has painted a clockface on its
surface. Eight o'clock, it reads. Showtime.

◦§ §◦

Sally Sebum and Jutta Jim are onstage, performing. Nan Punt, in a
broadcloth dressing gown, stands beside Ned, awaiting her cue. "Uh-uh-

uh-uh-uh," says Sally. "Uh-aah, Aaah! AAaaahhh!" Jutta Jim backs off
from her, bare-assed, buck black naked, his member slick and hard in the
light from the oil lamps. Spikes of etiolated bone jut from his nostrils,
quills pierce his earlobes, whorled cicatrices vein his torso like a relief map
of the moon. The audience is hushed. He turns to them, slow, silent,
methodical, and begins to pound at the hogshead of his chest. "That's my
cue," whispers Nan, slipping out of the gown and tripping daintily onto the
stage, drunk as a sow. After parading around and rubbing her bosoms a bit
for the audience, she puts Jim's cock in her mouth. The onlookers — they
who a moment before had been stomping and whistling and throwing
socks, hats, napkins and silverware — suddenly fall silent. Meanwhile,
Sally peels herself from the stage's only prop — a green-velvet confidante
— and staggers off into the wings. Ned holds the robe open for her.
"Whew," she puffs, "the black cannibal like to've swived me to death."
She's running sweat, her makeup a swamp, the rich black curls plastered to
her cheeks and throat. Her breasts are red and white. They strain at the
robe like vegetables in a sack. "And his breath! Like a fookin' chamberpot.
He's got a tool on 'im, though — I'll say that for the beast."
   "Glad you enjoyed it, Sal."
   "Enjoyed it?" Indignant, hands on hips. "You think I enjoys being
grunted over and slobbered upon by a stink-mouth nigger bebarian?" But
then she winks. "Easiest four quid I ever made since Lord Dalhousie's milk
punch got the better of 'im and 'ee fumbled 'is purse down the front of me
sateen dress."
   Ned laughs. "Just the beginning, Sal. I've got another show lined up
here for Thursday and then one for Saturday at the Pig & Pox. And I'll tell
you what — if you get back out there and do your histrionical best I'll give
you another two crowns on top of it."
   She's about to remark how her mum always wanted her to pursue a
career on the stage, but peeps out at the crowd and giggles instead. "Ned,"
she whispers, "come have a look at this." Ned looks. The entire audience
— lords and Garterees, naval officers, shopkeepers, footpads and clerics,
even Smirke himself — is caught up in a trance, their mouths hanging
open, chins and beards wet with spittle. Jim is stretched out supine now,
stage front, Nan riding him like a jockey, leaping the dikes, fences and
water hazards of orgasm, panting and gibbering all the way. There's not a
whisper from the patrons, not a cough or snuffle, a golly or gee — they
wouldn't have looked up if Halley's Comet had torn the roof off the place.
Some are twitching in face and limb, others grip their hats and walking
sticks as if they were grasping at twigs on the brink of a precipice. Here and

there a handkerchief swabs a brow, restive teeth chew at the back of a chair, feet tap and knees knock. "Yahooo!" shouts Nan at the peak of a pure gallop, and poor Smirke pitches forward in a typhoon of crunching glass. No one notices.

Sally helps herself to a pull at Ned's flask. Then she laughs. Laughs till she has to put a hand to her ribs.

"What's the joke?" asks Ned.

"Well," she manages, between bursts of giggles, "either they've took to wearin' codpieces again or I'll swear somebody's put yeast in all them trowsers out there."

◆§ THE SAHEL

The Sahel is a strip of semi-arid land girding West Africa like a waistband, stretching from the Atlantic coast in the west to Lake Chad in the east. Above it lies the Great Desert; below, the rain forests of tropical Africa. Its northernmost fringes give way to steppe, baked and blanched, and then to the dunes and ergs of the Great Desert itself. To the south, the Sahel becomes savanna, lush with seas of blue-green grass from June to October, the months of the monsoon. During these months al-haj' Ali Ibn Fatoudi moves his herds of goats and cattle, his people, tents, wives and milk-fed horses to the north, pressing the green line to its limits. From November to June he moves southward as the fierce harmattan winds shriek out of the desert with claws of flying sand, leaching the moisture from the air, the shrubs, the eyes and throats of his herds and his tribesmen. The sad truth is, Ali's herds overgraze the northern Sahel. His cows crop the grass before it's had a chance to germinate, his goats tear it up by the roots. Each year Ali drifts farther south, a mile here, a mile there. In two hundred years Benowm will be desert. The great ergs, Iguidi and Ehech, flow with the wind, drifting, stretching out tongues, fingers and arms, beckoning and beleaguering.

It's no picnic, life on the Sahel, let's face it. Talk of scarcity and want, whims of nature: welcome to them. Talk of years when the rains won't come and the sweet bleating herds build monuments of bone to the sun. Or a well that goes salt, sandstorms that shear the whiskers from your cheeks. Then there are the hyenas — making off in the night with kids and goats, disemboweling them and leaving the pissed-on remains for vultures and jackals. And then there's the push south: the farther you go, the greater the risk of a sneak attack by the Foulahs or the Serawoolis. That'd be a fine thing. Your people in chains, cattle butchered, horses raped, kouskous devoured. Of necessity, life is lean. And portable. The entire camp at Benowm — all three hundred tents — could be gone in an hour, fata morgana.

Because he lives under the gun, Ali puts his stock in movable wealth, wealth on the hoof — camels, horses, goats, oxen, slaves. If you inventory his material possessions he's practically a beggar. The Emir of Ludamar, ruler of thousands, hegemon of an area the size of Wales, man of the Book and descendant of the Prophet, actually owns fewer things than a Chelsea chambermaid. A goat-hair tent, a change of *jubbah,* a pot, a cookstove, two muskets, a leaky hookah and a blunt-edged saber that once belonged to Major Houghton — that's about it. Ah, but his horses — moon-white, marbled with muscle, their tails red as an open vein (he dyes them). And his women! If Ali is to be envied, it is for his women. Any one of his four wives could launch a thousand ships — if they knew what ships were.

Chief among them — in influence and beauty both — is Fatima of Jafnoo, daughter of the shereef of the Al-Mu'ta tribe, Boo Khaloom. Fatima's erotic charms are predicated entirely on a single feature: her bulk. In a bone-thin society, what more appropriate ideal of human perfection? Fatima weighs three hundred and eighty-two pounds. To move from one corner of the tent to another requires the assistance of two slaves. On the sixty-mile trip to Deena, in the north, she once prostrated a pair of camels and a bullock, and finally had to be transported on a litter drawn by six oxen. Ali comes in off the desert, blood and sand in his eyes, and plunges into the moist fecundity of her flesh. She is a spring, a well, an oasis. She is milk overspilling the bowl, a movable feast, green pasture and a side of beef. She is gold. She is rain.

Fatima was not always a beauty queen. As a girl she was a mere slip of a thing — big-boned and with enormous potential, yes — but nonetheless something of a slim and dark-eyed ugly duckling. Boo Khaloom took her in hand. He stepped into the tent one evening with a rush mat and a pillow. He spread the mat in a corner, set the pillow atop it, and commanded his daughter to sit. He then called for camel's milk and kouskous. Fatima was puzzled: the remains of the evening meal — wooden bowls black with flies, an overturned pitcher — still lay in the corner. All at once she became aware of shadows playing over the walls of the tent, as if a number of people were milling around outside. She asked her father if he was planning to meet with his counselors. He told her to shut her hole. Suddenly the flap was thrown back and a man entered the tent. It was

Mohammed Bello, sixty-three years old, her father's closest friend and advisor. He was naked. Fatima was mortified. She'd never seen a man's legs before, let alone those puckered wattles squirming against the old man's leg like some freak of nature. She thought of the spineless struggling things caught in the muck of a dying waterhole. She was eleven years old. She burst into tears.

Mohammed Bello was not alone. The flap swished and eight other men, naked as babes, stepped silently into the tent. Zib Sahman, her godfather, was among them. And Akbar al-Akbar, the oldest man of the tribe. When they were all assembled, a slave entered with a bowl the size of a birdbath. The bowl contained camel's milk, a week's supply at least. He was followed by a second slave carrying an even larger bowl filled to the rim with kouskous. The bowls were set before her. Camel's milk is sweet, and rich with nutrients. Kouskous, a sort of porridge made of boiled and pounded wheat, is the staple of the Moors' diet. It is not at all unpalatable, but all things have their limits. "Eat," said Boo Khaloom.

At first she didn't understand. Surely all this food must be for her father's guests. Did he expect her to serve them? But then she remembered that they were all naked and she began blubbering anew. Her father was shouting. "Eat, I said!" he roared. "Don't you understand Arabic? Have you lost your hearing? Eat!"

She glanced up at the eight venerables. They sat in a semicircle, watching her. They were still naked. And then came the biggest jolt of all: her father was stepping out of his *jubbah!* All her life — through meals, bedtime, on the road — she never glimpsed anything more than his face, hands and toes. Now suddenly here he was — naked — and equipped with the same rubbery wattles as the others. She was terrified. "Eat," he repeated. She was dazed. It was then that the switch appeared in his hand. He struck her twice across the face. She cried out. He struck her again. And then again. "Eat," he said.

She put her lips to the milk and drank between sobs. She took a fistful of kouskous and forced it into her mouth. But she wasn't hungry. She'd just eaten — and eaten more than usual. Her mother had been nagging her about her bones, her coarseness, how no husband would want her, a girl who looked like a desert ostrich. And so she had made an effort to eat more. Now she was full: another bite and she'd puke. The porridge caught in her throat.

Boo Khaloom was deranged. He whipped and shouted till his arm throbbed and his throat went raw. "No more cat's cradle with the other girls, no more lessons, no weaving — nothing. You will sit here, on this pillow, and eat until you come of age. You will eat and you will grow. You will be beautiful. Do you hear? Beautiful!" Mohammed Bello and the others watched. From time to time one of them would nod approvingly. Fatima ate. Wept and ate. "And when you come of age you will continue to eat — day and night. That is your duty. To your father, and to your husband. He will have a rod!" her father shouted. "A rod like this one. And he will thrash you as I am thrashing you now and as I will thrash you tomorrow and the next day and the day after that!" Suddenly the venerables were on their feet, as if this were some sort of signal. Fatima looked up, her cheeks swollen with mush, and gasped: a hideous unnatural change had come over them. Where before they'd been flaccid, now they were hard. Wizened old turkey cocks, their members engorged, they closed in on her. "Thrash you!" her father shrieked and they began pumping at themselves, milking their rods with a whack and thwap, their faces strained and distant, beatific even. Fatima felt as if she were made of wax. Her head was light. She was falling, tumbling down through the eons, chasms in the earth, the abyss. It was then that she felt the first few random drops, like rain.

After that excoriating and traumatic night, she ate. She ate prodigiously, furiously, she couldn't get enough. Sugar dates, mutton, yogurt, slabs of salt, kouskous and dried fish, kouskous and nuts, kouskous and kouskous. There was fruit in the south — tamarind, cassava, watermelon — flat loaves of bread, jars of wild honey, yams, rice, maize, butter and milk, milk, always milk. Goat's milk, cow's milk, camel's milk — she even suckled like an infant at the breast of a nursing slave. She was insatiable. She ate for fear, she ate for vengeance. She ate for beauty.

◄§ TANTALUS

He is perishing, winding down the long tunnel of waste and death, hurtling toward completion in the dust of generations gone down. He is perishing, quite simply, of thirst. Of hunger too — but the thirst is more immediate. At night, when they remember, the Moors give him a handful of kouskous and half a cup of yellow swill. Tonight they forget. His stomach contracts on air, cells wither and die like jellyfish washed up on the beach. Then the temperature drops and he lies huddled in his jacket, shivering and sweating, the fever an internal weather valve, on and off, sun and sleet. Outside, beyond the circle of tents, jackals shriek like a knife in the heart and hyenas gather to intimidate the moon. There will be weeping and sorrowing and the gnashing of teeth, he thinks. Then he closes his eyes. The explorer's dream is immediate and vivid. He is out on the Great Desert in the heat of midday, the sun a torch, his mouth full of sand. There are men behind him, strangers — burned faces, beards, tattered clothes. They trail out over the horizon like ants. In his hand, a forked stick. At his side, Zander — wally old Zander — Ailie's brother. They used to fish together. "Where is she when we need her?" asks Mungo. "At home," says Zander. "Waiting." A man gags and pitches forward. The explorer turns him over and then starts back: the eye sockets are empty, the gums drawn back from the teeth, the skin crusty as a glazed ham. At that moment a pewter dipper appears overhead, its belly frosted with dew — and then another, and another — a procession of them, dippers full of water, floating overhead like gulls riding an updraft. A feeble huzza goes up from the men. They stretch out their arms and smack their gummy lips — but the dippers hang there, just out of reach. Frantic, they scramble over one another's shoulders, their fingers raking the sky. The dippers are coy, wriggling and sashaying, flirting with the outstretched fingers: but they won't give up a drop. The men despair, dashing their heads against stones and shrubs and rocky crags. "Do something!" they implore. "Help us!" Just then the forked stick begins to twitch. Mungo cocks his ear to the wind. He hears something: faint and distant, lilting and lyrical. A wet trickle of sound, like a flute or a harp. Can it be? He is quick, firm, decisive. "Follow me!" he shouts, and begins jogging toward the swelling sound of it, the roar, the hiss, the sweet syncopation of water rushing over a bed of stones. Dazed, the men stagger to their feet and hobble after him. Across a plain, up a rise and there, there it is! The Niger, clear and cold as an October morning, neat lawns clipped along its banks, punts, coots and great silent swans coasting over the dimpled surface, salmon leaping, cool ferns and leafy elms fanning the shore. He plunges in, the men whooping at his heels, ecstatic, redeemed, alive. But when he turns round, they've vanished. Waves lap, swans duck their heads: he's alone with his triumph. But no matter, he's having such a time, churning up waves, blowing bubbles and gulping, swallowing, sucking up the smooth, tooth-chilling current till he can drink no more.

He wakes with a stone in his throat. His tongue is dry. His palate is dry. His uvula. What he needs is a drink. Water. Ice. Blood. A cup of tea. Glass of milk. Mug of beer. He tiptoes to the entranceway and peers out. The three guards are asleep, chewing at their beards and snoring like drunken lords. But here's the rub: they're stretched out across the entrance, shoulder to shoulder, the near man flush with the flap of the tent. He d have to broad-jump the three of them to get clear — and even assuming he could make it, there's still the thump of his descent to contend with. Why they'd be up like starved wolves at even the hint of a sound, cursing and clutching at their daggers. He hesitates.

But then, miracle of miracles, the man in the center rolls over, exposing a few inches of open ground. It's now or never. The explorer eases out of his boots, takes a deep breath, and steps over the first man. The air is still. Somewhere a bird cries out. But the guard sleeps on, stertorous, lips smacking and lids twitching. Mungo shifts his weight to the front foot and begins to swing the left leg over when suddenly he feels a bit woozy, his mind for some reason flashing on the high-wire artist at Bartholomew Fair. It was years ago. The young explorer stood in the crowd, Kewpie doll under his arm, and watched the man negotiate a wire strung two hundred feet from the ground. The man was in the process of balancing a barge pole in one hand and juggling half a dozen apples in the other, when a pigeon landed at the tip of the pole. The man fell.

Mungo blinks his eyes and finds himself seated on the chest of the first guard. The guard mutters something in Arabic, slow as syrup, and then begins rubbing the explorer's hand against his bristling cheek. The sensation, considering the circumstances, is not at all unpleasant. *"Yummah,"* groans the guard, as passionately as a lover, *"Yibbah!"* But then he drops the explorer's hand and segues into the stertor of sleep while Mungo steals off into the night.

◄§ §►

For more than a month now the explorer has been a captive of the Moors. He is held in solitary confinement. His horse and goods have been appropriated. He has not been charged with any crime. The question of snubbing out his eyes has, praise to Allah, been shelved for the time being. It seems that Fatima, Ali's principal wife, has sent word from Deena that she insists on examining the freak intact — evil eye and all. (In London they flock to see the human caterpillar and the man with three noses; in Ludamar it's albino mutants.) Still, the explorer's life has been anything but idyllic. He's been held against his will, harassed as an infidel, threatened with death and mutilation, starved, bullied, tormented, bored, deprived of conversation, intellectual stimulus and water. And he hasn't laid eyes on his interpreter for a week. When he last saw him, Johnson was still keeping a tongue — civil or otherwise — in his head. Ali had found that flap of muscle and fatty tissue a sine qua non when interrogating the explorer about the arcana of his dress and baggage: the shoes and stockings, the buttons of his coat and trousers, his compass, watch and razor. "How does this work? And this?" Ali inquired, directing his questions to Johnson while his sullen dark eyes fixed on the explorer's face. Eventually, he made the explorer step in and out of his clothes thirty-seven times so that successive groups of rubberneckers could marvel at the ingenuity of it. After the thirty-seventh demonstration, Ali expressed a curiosity as to why Mungo had come to the Sahel in the first place: if he wasn't a trader he must be a spy. "I'm looking for the River Niger," Mungo told him. Ali studied his great toe for a moment and then looked up. "There are no rivers in your country?"

◄§ §►

Down a gentle rise from the encampment — no more than three hundred yards — are the wells. Mungo can hear the lowing of the cattle as they crowd round the troughs for their nightly irrigation. When he gets closer he can make out the rounded humps and the wild spiked horns jabbing at the sky like a forest in motion. The cows — more like overweight gazelles than beef on the hoof — stamp and push and bellow for water. He could bellow along with them. He could cry and screech and out-howl all the demons in hell he's so thirsty. But what's this? Something moving in the stand of acacias up ahead. The explorer sidles up for a closer look.

Six or seven slaves, muffled in their burnooses, are lounging around an open fire, passing a pipe and laughing. Every once in a while one of them dips a bucket in the well and sloshes its contents into a trough, where the cattle snort and shove to get at it. Mungo steps out of the shadows and goes down on his knees to them. "Water," he begs. "Give me water." And then in English: "A drop, a taste, a spoonful!"

At first they're startled. But then, looking down at the wasted wretch prostrating himself in the cowshit, they begin to laugh. Their eyes are glossy and veined with red. They stagger, whoop, hold their sides, their laughter echoing into the night — "Yee-ha-ha-ha-haa!" — laughter like the throttling of birds. Then one of them steps forward, pipe in hand. His eyes are tiny, pig's eyes, and his brow swells out over his face like an eroded riverbank. "Water!" cries Mungo. The man bends, drawing on the pipe, and blows a lungful of smoke in the explorer's face. The odor is strong, aromatic, viscous: are they smoking incense? Mungo coughs. Then the man rocks back on his heels and calls out to his companions: "*Nazarini* wants water?" They laugh. "Give him water, Sidi!"

Sidi turns back to the explorer and hisses: "*La illah el allah, Mahomet rasowl Allahi.*" Mungo recognizes the phrase: There is only one God, and

Mohammed is his prophet. They make him repeat it a hundred times a day. "Okay," he says. "Okay," and mutters a quick Lord's Prayer, begging extenuating circumstances. Sidi kicks him. *"La illah el allah, Mahomet rasowl Allahi,"* says Mungo. "Water!" shout the others. "Give the *Nazarini* water, Sidi. Give him holy water!"

The hocks of the cattle rise and fall. Dust settles on the explorer like a parched snow. It is up his nose, down his throat. He can hear them, the stupid beasts, drooling over the troughs in mindless contentment, the precious silken droplets tumbling from their muzzles, catching like jewels at the tips of their whiskers. "You want water?" Sidi says. Mungo nods. And then suddenly, without warning, the slave throws back his *jubbah* and pisses on him — quick and salt, the hot urine runs down his collar, through his fingers, soaks deep into the fabric of his waistcoat. The explorer leaps up in a frenzy, desperate and homicidal, but Sidi has backed off, laughing, and now the others are bending for stones and bits of wood. Mungo stands there, weak and stinking, as the herdsmen begin to pelt him. "Drink piss, Christian!" they jeer. He turns heel and jogs off into the night.

It is quiet. The stars fan out across the heavens like spilled milk; mosquitoes whine in the trees. He is turned away from the next three wells in succession, pummeled with fists and sticks. At the last well, an ancient brackish pit set apart from the others, an old slave and his son, a boy of eight or nine, are watering their master's herd by torchlight. Mungo begs them for a drink. The old man eyes him suspiciously for a moment, then dips a bucket of water from the well. *"Salaam, salaam, salaam,"* says Mungo, reaching out for it, when the boy tugs at his father's sleeve. *"Nazarini,"* says the boy. The old man hesitates, looking first at the bucket, then at the well. He is concerned about contamination, hexes, a well gone dry in the night. "Please," the explorer says, "I beg you." The old man shuffles to the trough, empties the bucket and points a weathered finger. Mungo doesn't have to be asked twice. He throws himself forward, wedging his head between the big horned skulls of a pair of heifers.

The trough looks like a gutter on a rainy day, the water like sewage, twigs and straw and bits of offal swirling on the surface. The explorer buries his face and drinks, but the competition is fierce, the stream already a puddle, cattle slavering, their great pink tongues like sponges lapping up the last few drops. He turns to the old man. "More!" he shouts. "More!" A piebald cow, its eyes big as pocketwatches, bowls him over. And then suddenly a gunshot barks out, loud as a thunderclap. Then another. The cattle fall back, confused, butting shoulders, snouts and flanks, panicky, running blind. *Ka-bomb, Ka-bomb, Ka-bomb,* they boom off into the night.

When the dust settles, Mungo finds himself looking up at three horsemen. One of them is Dassoud, the hyphenated scar glistening in the torchlight. There is a pistol in his hand. He steadies his mount, levels the pistol at the explorer's head and pulls the trigger. Nothing happens. Mungo sits there in the dust and cattle droppings, his heart frozen, nerves shot, wondering how on earth to conciliate this madman with the gun. *"La illah el allah, Mahomet rasowl Allahi,"* he says, taking a stab at it. Dassoud is pouring a fresh charge into the priming pan, all the while growling like a dog at an intruder's pantleg. The horses stamp and whinny, the old man and his son cower. Then Dassoud raises the gun a second time, shouts something in Arabic, squeezes the trigger. A flash of light, a sound like hot coals dropped in a tub of water. The pistol has misfired. "What have I done?" the explorer pleads, edging away. Dassoud curses, flings down the pistol, and calls over his shoulder for another. "Hua!" shouts the man at his back, tossing him a fresh weapon. Dassoud snatches it out of the air, cocks the hammer, and aims at a constellation of freckles just to the left of the explorer's nose.

"Mr. Park!" Johnson, skirts aflap, bursts into the circle of light like a character out of the commedia dell'arte. His chest is heaving and his jowls are streaked with sweat. "Mr. Park, you crazy? Get up on your feet and double-time it back to that tent before they shoot you dead on the spot. You got the whole place in a uproar. They think you tryin' to escape."

Mungo looks up. Fires blaze on the hillside. Horsemen ride off into the night with torches. There are shouts and curses, random gunshots. Mungo rises. Dassoud lowers the pistol.

◄§ NAIAD

Outside, beyond the lace curtains and leaded windows, a lazy fat-flake snow settles over the trees and gardens of Selkirk, smoothing corners, blurring distinctions, inundating the mileposts along the Edinburgh road. There are no footpaths, no flowerbeds, no lawns; the azaleas are bowed and the evergreens stagger at the edge of the field. It has been snowing for two days now. Drifts darken the lower panes and lean against the door, saddle horses go without exercise and wagons lose their bones in soft sculpture. There is ice in the well. Up on the rooftop the weather vane grinds round its axis.

Here in the kitchen, it's another world. Thick and sultry, the atmosphere steams like an island in the Pacific. The windows perspire and drip, the hand mirror fogs over, bath towels go heavy with damp. In the hearth: a holiday fire. Mounds of glowing coals, a crosshatch of split oak and the low sucking moan of the flames. Two blackened cauldrons hang over the fire, suspended from hooks driven into the stone a century ago. Vapor spews from them, thick as a mist over the moors. On the table, dark leafy ferns glow with wet, and dace and shiners flash at breadcrumbs behind the beaded glass of the aquarium. From the corner, lost somewhere in the banks of rising steam, the turtle doves imitate a flute caught in the lower register.

It is February second, the anniversary of her engagement to Mungo Park. Ailie Anderson is commemorating the occasion with a bath — a rare luxury in these pinched times. She glides round the room, arranging her bath things, humming, occasionally fanning the fire with a blast from the bellows. Dr. Philby's green soap stands ready on the table, beside her comb and tortoiseshell brush; the Bain des Fleurs dangles from her fingertips. Luxury or no, she'll have her bath today. She'll lie back in the steamed-up kitchen surrounded by her menagerie and the sounds and scents of nature, and dream of Mungo fighting his way through the dripping jungles of the Dark Continent. Her father allows but one bath a month. "I canna spare the hardwood and the coal," he says. No matter. She'll have her bath today and stink till March. After all, this is no mere rub and scrub, this is ritual purification.

Ailie is twenty-two, and patient as Penelope. She was fourteen when she first met Mungo Park. He came to live with them, her father's apprentice. Eight years ago. When he left for the university he asked her to wait for him. Leaves were turning in the trees. She cried for joy and confusion. After two years at Edinburgh he kissed her brow and signed on as ship's surgeon on a spicer bound for Djakarta. She waited. When he returned he was morose and restive. They were to be married. But then, out of nowhere, there was a letter from London, from Mungo's brother-in-law. Would he accept a commission from the African Association to explore West Africa with the object of locating the Niger River? She could read the answer in his eyes. Two weeks later, his bags packed, he stood at the door of the London coach. "I'm going to make a mark in the world, Ailie," he said. "Wait for me?"

She's been waiting ever since.

Of course, there isn't a man in the Borderlands can hold a candle to him. They're all a bunch of plowboys and fops, with about as much adventure in them as a sick housedog. Look at Gleg — her father's current apprentice — he's no more than a tadpole compared to Mungo. He wouldn't know adventure if it took hold of one of his great flapping ears and bit into it. Ailie sighs, sets the bath oil beside the hairbrush, and then calls out to her brother. "Zander! Help me haul the tub out, would you?"

Alexander Anderson is in the parlor, alternately staring down at Southey's *Joan of Arc,* which lies open in his lap, and gazing out at the languid feathery flakes drifting past the window. He is savoring the storm, and the quiet, glad for the respite from the comings and goings of medicine. Glad too for the presence of Gleg. Ever since the spring, when he left the university, his father has been dragging him along on housecalls, thrusting splints and scalpels at him, blustering, cajoling, imploring him to take up the standard of a country physician. "What's with ye, lad?" the old man would boom. "Ye plan to loll about lickin' yer hinder parts like ye was some sheep o' the field for the rest o' yer days? — or are ye going to find yerself some God's work for yer idle hands as befits a mon and an Anderson? Eh? Speak up, lad — I canna hear ye for all the anger and puzzlement belaborin' the runnels o' me brain."

But Zander has no desire to set up as a country doctor. He loathes the smell of the sickroom, the blackened lips and foul breath. There's a man pinned beneath a cart, the ribs like pink stakes driven into his chest; an infant hacking in the night, blood on her chin; bones breaking, vessels rupturing, hearts seizing. He wants no part of it. Mortality is a cancer, a running sore — does he need to stare it in the face ten times a day? Drunken men, pregnant women and filthy children with their ruptures and boils, their poxes and plagues — they strike him with terror, not compassion. He doesn't want to probe wounds or let blood or tamp poultices round tumors and lesions — he wants to vomit, he wants to run.

Thank God for Gleg. He may be awkward and two-faced, gangling and graceless, an alien and obtrusive presence in the house, but he lives and breathes, walks on two feet and provides a clear and unmistakable target for the old man's enthusiasm. Since Gleg arrived, the pressure's been off. When there are horses to be hitched, bones to be set, herbs to be gathered and pounded, it's Gleg who gets the call. When there's moralizing to be listened to, or carping about prices, weather, powdered hair or the "grate Kraut King," it's Gleg who must bow his head and look attentive. This is not to say that the good doctor has been neglecting his only son — not by any means. He still scolds and lectures, berates him for his dreaminess, his

lack of ambition, his clothes and hairstyle and opinions, and he still drags
him out into the cutting winds to make the odd housecall. No, that will
never change — so long as Zander is under his father's roof. But at least
Gleg has diverted the old man for the time being. Zander can breathe. He
can sit back and sip sherry before the fire. Play patience, read a book of
poetry. Or wrap a scarf round his throat, wander the blighted hills and
wonder what in God's name he's going to do with his life.

"Zander!" Ailie is in the doorway, a bathtowel in her hand. "Help me
with the tub?"

Zander looks up from his book. Outside the snow has begun to change
to sleet. "A bath?" he says. "In this weather?"

•§ §•

The tub is an heirloom. Dark and massive, smelling of the sea, of rancid
soap, of wet hair and mold and age. Euan Anderson, Ailie's grandfather,
bathed in it after the battle of Culloden. Her great-grandmother, Emma
Oronsay, was kicking up a fine froth of soap bubbles as Handel coasted
down the Thames on a barge, and Godfrey Anderson, great-uncle on her
father's side, was found dead in it, the water gone red, his wrists cut
through to the bone. Ghosts and echoes. Ailie's last memory of her mother
is bound up in the feel and smell of the thing. A warm light from the
candles, kettles singing, she and Zander kicking and splashing, and that
woman with the sad and suffering eyes, with the hair like a field in bloom,
that woman, her mother, reaching out soft hands to scrub their backs and
ears and the spaces between their thighs. She disappeared one day. Left for
a weekend in Glasgow and never returned.

Euphemia Anderson, née St. Onge, was a devotee of astrology. She
charted the heavens, spoke of stars in ascendancy and planets in conjunction. "Buy into the grain market, James," she would tell her husband, "the
time is ripe." Or: "The mare will foal tonight. It'll be a bay stallion with a
bad hind leg." She was a Gemini. "My twin is an Arabian Princess," she
would say. "Out in the wide world. I will never know her."

Her daughter was born in June, nine and a half minutes before her son.
Alice and Alexander. Twins. She dressed them identically, now in short
pants, now in skirts. She would stop people on the street to introduce her
darlin' little daughters one day, and her bold little sons the next. Obsessed
with the concept of twins — twin bodies, twin minds, twin fingers and toes
and ears and eyes — she was incapable of accepting the momentous and
wrenching disparity indicated by so trifling a thing as a cleft or a wrinkled
flap of skin no bigger than her thumbnail. It offended her sense of
proportion. When she left for Glasgow, Dr. Anderson took the twins in

hand. Zander was sent to boarding school and Ailie fell into the lap of a governess.

She was six when Mrs. Alloway arrived. Mrs. Alloway explained to her that ladies were meant for hoops and finery, for accomplishment in verse and music and other anodynic arts, that ladies above all else were ladies, the fleece and plumage of society. Ailie cut her hair at the shoulder in protest. She's worn it that way ever since.

But now her mother is a memory, indistinct, loose at the edges, and Mrs. Alloway has shrunk into insignificance, an old woman, her bulk loose on the bone, death's pensioner in a leaking cottage. There's always an homage to pay to this old tub, memories caught in a scent or the feel of the roughened wood, but today is a celebration of life, and she squeezes her eyes shut and summons Mungo, his face drifting in a thousand guises, smiling, winking, the pitch of his upper lip as he begins a funny story, the look of befuddlement as he steps in a bucket or tumbles from his horse. The water is hot, comforting and sensuous. It flushes her skin. She's in Iceland, Norway. A hot spring, snowflakes melting on the water and a figure looming through the mist, naked and athletic, her name on his lips — but dammit, she's forgotten the washcloth. It crouches on the table, just out of reach.

The water sucks back as she rises, her breasts boyish and tight, body glowing with wet, the dark bush like a hole cut through her. At that moment the door swings back and her father bursts into the room, dogged by his apprentice, Georgie Gleg. She freezes for an instant, then drops into the water like a stone. Incidental waves break over the lip of the tub to slosh the floorboards.

"Bairns!" her father shouts, blustering to hide his embarrassment. "Bairns, bairns, bairns! They maun crawl out of the womb in a blizzard." He is at the closet already, shrugging into his mackintosh and boots. "The third call! Third! Two months it's been since I've delivered a child and now Beelzebub himself has got hold of the weather they're birthing all over the county."

She is up to her neck in hot water. Her ears are red. Gleg, lank and unctuous, two years her junior, his teeth like the teeth of a horse, stands mooning at a spot over the tub as if he'd just caught a glimpse of a burning bush or a ladder dropped from the sky. His mouth hangs open, his nostrils quiver.

"Gleg!" her father roars. "Stop gaping like a hyena and get into your coat, boy. We've got a housecall to make!"

Gleg flings himself at the closet as if he were flinging himself over a cliff, fumbles into his greatcoat and begins grappling with the doorlatch.

Impatient, Dr. Anderson sweeps the door open and shoves him through. The door slams. There is the sound of scuffling on the back porch, then the wheeze of the outer door, and they're gone.

The fish stir in their tank. The turtle doves preen their wings. The fire hisses. And Ailie, buoyed up by the penetrating warmth of the bath, begins to rub at her legs with the washcloth, her mind gone blank, rubbing and scrubbing, working at the process of purification.

❦ NOT TWIST, NOT COPPERFIELD, NOT FAGIN HIMSELF

Not Twist, not Copperfield, not Fagin himself had a childhood to compare with Ned Rise's. He was unwashed, untutored, unloved, battered, abused, harassed, deprived, starved, mutilated and orphaned, a victim of poverty, ignorance, ill-luck, class prejudice, lack of opportunity, malicious fate and gin. His was a childhood so totally depraved even a Zola would shudder to think of it.

He was born out back of a twopenny flophouse in what the wags called "The Holy Land" — cribs of straw that went for a penny a night. The year was 1771, the month February. His mother didn't have the price of a bed, and so she crept into the outbuilding, the labor pains coming like blows to the groin, a bottle of clear white Knock-Me-Down clutched in her fist. The straw was dirty. Pigeons dropped excrement from the rafters. It was so cold even the lice were sluggish. She selected a crib in the rear because of its proximity to the horses and what little warmth they generated. Then she settled down with her bottle.

She was a souse, Ned's mother. A sister in the great sorority of the sorrows of gin. At this time in British history, the sorority — and its brother fraternity — were flourishing. When gin was first introduced in England at the close of the seventeenth century (some claim it was brought over from Holland by William III, others say it was distilled from bone and marrow by the Devil himself), it became an overnight sensation among the lower classes. It was cheap as piss, potent as a kick in the head. They went mad for it: after all, why swill beer all night when you can get yourself crazed in half an hour — for a penny? By 1710 the streets were littered with drunks, some stripped naked, others stiff as tombstones. When Sir Joseph Jekyll, Master of the Rolls, introduced legislation to curb the pernicious influence of gin through licensing and taxation, a mob gathered to stone his house and chew the wheels from his carriage. There was no stopping it. Gin was a palliative for hard times, it was sleep and poetry, it was life itself. Aqua vitae. Ned's mother was a second-generation ginsoak. Her father was a tanner. He drank two pints a day and flayed hides. He sold her into service at nine, she was out on the streets at thirteen, a mother at fourteen. She died of cirrhosis, brain fever, consumption and green sickness before she reached twenty.

There were three other lodgers in the Holy Land that drear winter's night. The first was a tribeless patriarch who coughed like dice in a box and died before first light. The landlord discovered him next morning: clots of blood frozen to his lips, his neck, buried deep in the sere white nest of his beard. Then there was the stone mason — granite monuments and markers — on the tail end of a three-day drunk. He retched in the straw and lay down to sleep in it. Lastly, there was the old woman wrapped in tattered skirts like a dressmaker's dummy, who scraped in after midnight and pitched headlong into the next crib over from the pregnant girl. She lay there, the old woman, her breathing like the friction of rusted gears, listening to the moans of Ned's mother. Moans. They were nothing new. She closed her eyes. But then there was a cry, and then another. The old woman sat up. In the next crib lay a girl of fourteen or fifteen. Her brow was wet. The neck of a bottle peeked out from her jacket. She was in labor.

The harridan crept closer, snatched up the bottle and held it to her lips. " 'Ere," she keaked. "Wot's the trouble, little cheese: birfin' a babe, is it?" The girl looked up, heart in mouth.

"Ee-eeeee!" screeched the old woman, scattering the pigeons in the rafters. "I've done it meself, done it meself, oh yes. There was a time the babbies dropped from these old loins like pippins from a tree." Her face was a shed snakeskin, ageless. Who could say how much flesh she'd molded within her? Or count the years she'd languished in a Turkish seraglio or a Berber hut? Who could guess what twisted paths and dark alleys she'd been down, or what she was thinking when that ring of hammered gold was struck through her lip?

" 'Elp me," the girl whispered.

◄§ §►

It was a breech birth. First the wrinkled legs and buttocks, then the shoulders and chin, the smooth slick dome of the head. The hour of the wolf came and went, and the old woman yanked Ned from his mother's womb. Her fingers were dry and crabbed. She tied off the cord and slapped him. He wailed. Then she wiped the blood and mucus from his body with the hem of her skirt and tucked him inside her coat. She glanced round, sly and secretive, then made for the door. Babysnatch!

Ned's mother propped herself on one elbow and felt round her, first for the child and then for the bottle. Both were gone. She focused on the pinched shoulders of the old woman receding into the gloom at the far end of the barn and then she began to scream, scream like sandstorms on the desert, like the death of the universe. The crone hurried for the door, the girl's screams at her back, the horses kicking blindly in their stalls. The bearded patriarch did not wake. But the stonecutter did. He was in his mid-twenties. He flung slabs of granite about as if they were newsprint, day in and day out. "Stop 'er!" the girl cried. "She's got my baby!"

He vaulted the railing and jogged the length of the stable just as the harridan was squeezing through the door. She spun around on him, a rusted scissor in hand. "Get back!" she hissed. The blow came like a seizure, secretive and brutal. He caught her in the shoulder and she collapsed like a bundle of twigs. Beneath her, there was the sound of shattering glass. And the keen of an infant.

◆§ §◆

The stonecutter's name was Edward Pin. They called him Ned for short. He took the girl and her child to his lodgings in Wapping, a fierce hangover raging behind his eyes. She'd washed him in tears and he felt like a hero, no matter how much his head ached. The infant, it seemed, had been gashed across the chest when the bottle broke. Pin lit a few sticks of wood and a handful of coal to take the chill off the room. The girl's hair hung loose as she bent over the baby to dress his wounds. Her name was Sarah Colquhoun. She was drunk. "I'm going to name 'im Ned," she slurred. "After 'is deliverer." Pin beamed. But then a change came over his face and he took hold of her hair. "Don't you go callin' 'im Pin, you slut. 'Ee's none of mine."

"Rise I'm callin' 'im!" she shouted back. "Ned Rise, you son of a bitch." It was the metaphoric expression of a hope. "You know why? . . . Cause he's going to rise above all this shit 'is mother has had to eat since I could barely say me own name."

"Ha!" he sneered. "Baptized in blood. And gin. And with a ginswill of a whorin' mother. I bleedin' doubt it."

◆§ §◆

Ned's memories of his mother are sketchy. A drawn face, all cheekbone and brow, the skin stretched tight as leather on a last. A persistent hacking in the night. Phthisic pallor. Too much green round the gills. She was dead before he was six. Pin, needless to say, was a violent drunkard with the temperament of a cat set afire. When he worked, he came home white with stone dust, his eyes bleeding alcohol. Then he would settle down to torture the boy for the sheer joy of it, like a ten-year-old with a frog or rat. He tied Ned's feet together and hung him out the third-story window like a pair of wet pants. He clamped the chamberpot over Ned's ears, stropped a razor on his back, submerged his head in a tub of water for sixty seconds at a time. "Drown you like a rat, I will!" he growled.

When the boy was seven the stonecutter decided it was time he earned his keep. He appeared in the doorway one night with a fistful of baling twine, caught the boy round the neck, pinned him down and trussed up his leg at the knee. Then he cut Ned's trousers high up the shin, fashioned a crutch from a broomstick, and set him out on the street to beg. It was cold in the wind, and the bindings chewed at the boy's flesh. No matter. Seven years old, shrink-bellied and filth-faced, he teetered like a drunken stork and pleaded for pennies in Russell Square, Drury Lane, Covent Garden. But mendicity was a popular profession in those days and the competition was fierce. An army of amputees, lepers, pinheads, paralytics, gibberers, slaverers and whiners lined the streets shoulder to shoulder. There was the legless man planted in a chamberpot who hopped round on his knuckles like an ape; the limbless woman who polished boots with her tongue; the man-dog with a withered tail and spiked yellow teeth hanging over his lip. Ned didn't have a chance.

There were twenty shillings in a pound, twelve pence in a shilling, four farthings in a penny. When Ned came home with two farthings the first day, Pin thrashed him. The following day, after sixteen hours of entreating, imploring and beseeching, Ned had nothing to show but a bit of string, three chestnuts and a brass button. Pin drubbed him again, this time giving special consideration to the nose, mouth and cheekbones. As a result, Ned's face took on the color and consistency of a fermenting plum. This development improved the take somewhat, but then there was always the necessity of raising fresh welts each day. After a month of it, Pin pulled something in his thrashing arm. There's got to be a better way, he thought. Then he hit on it. "Ned," he called. "Come over 'ere."

Pin was sitting at the table with a tumbler of gin. The floor was ankle-deep in rags and papers, the bones of chops and chickens, scraps of wood, fragments of glass, smashed earthenware, feathers. Ned was in the corner, feigning invisibility. The stone mason jerked his head round. "Come over 'ere, I said." Ned came. A meat cleaver lay on the table, cold and tarnished. When Ned saw it he began to blubber. "Shet yer 'ole!"

roared Pin, forcing the boy's right hand down on the table. His own grimy fist smothered it like a hood. Trembling, vulnerable, the boy's fingers lay there on the block, pale as sacrificial lambs. There were black semicircles under the nails. The cleaver fell.

With his arm in a sling to display the mutilated hand to advantage (Pin had excised the first joint of each finger, thumb included), Ned's take began to improve. In a month or two he was pulling in seven or eight shillings a day: a small fortune. Pin gave up the lapidary profession to sit through the long afternoons in taverns and coffeehouses, bolting duck with orange sauce, swilling wine and laying his broad callused palms across the bosoms and backsides of women of pleasure. Ned froze his ass off on the street, choked on crusts and cabbage soup, the loss of his fingertips an ongoing horror to him, a waking nightmare. He wanted to run off. He wanted to die. But Pin kept him tractable with blows to the back of the head and threats of further mutilation. "Like to lose the rest of them nubbins? Or the 'and maybe? Or 'ow bout the 'ole arm, eh?" Then he would laugh.

One grim afternoon, as the ex-stonecutter was reeling across the street from the Magpie and Stump to inspect his ward's pockets, a landau drawn by four handsome bays dashed him to the pavement. He became involved in the rear spring mechanism and was dragged about a hundred yards up the street. A woman screamed. He was dead.

◦§ §◦

For the next several years Ned lived on the streets: begging, filching, eating garbage, occasionally finding shelter with a loon or pederast or axe murderer. It was a tough life. No hand to comfort, no voice to praise. He grew up like an aborigine.

Then, when he was twelve, his luck turned. He was at Vauxhall Gardens one morning, picking pockets and stripping bark from the trees, when he was arrested by a sound trembling on the warm still air, an unearthly fluting like something out of a dream. It seemed to be coming from beyond the fountain, near the flowerbeds. When he got there he found a scattering of parkgoers — rakes and gallants, ladies and tarts, nurses with infants, fops, cutpurses, itinerant hawkers — all gathered round a man blowing into a wooden instrument. The man was bald, his face and crown red as a ham, his cheeks puffed. Jollops of flesh hung over his collar and quivered in sympathetic response to the keening vibrato of the instrument. He was dressed like a gentleman.

Ned watched the clean athletic fingers lick up and down the keys, lighting here, pausing there, lifting, darting and pouncing like young animals at play. The pansies and jonquils were in bloom. Forget-me-nots and peonies. He sat in the grass and listened, the music reedy and sweet, like birds gargling with honey. The man's foot tapped as he played. Some of the listeners began to tap along with him, the buckled pumps and slippers and wooden clogs rising and falling in unison, as if manipulated by a string. One woman swayed her head in a soft glowing arc, almost imperceptible, the sun firing an aureole of curls round her face. Ned's foot began to tap. He couldn't remember a happier moment.

When the musician took a break, the crowd dispersed. Ned lingered to watch him. The man twisted the mouthpiece from his instrument, unfastened the reed and balanced it like a wafer on the tip of his tongue. From a leather-bound case he produced a brush, with which he swabbed first the mouthpiece and then the hollowed body of the instrument itself. The keys flashed in the sun. "You find all this stimulating, do you?" the man said. He was addressing Ned.

Ned sat there, chewing at a blade of grass, ragged as a field gone to seed. He'd lived his life in the muck of the streets, pissed in the Thames, scavenged his clothes from dustbins, comatose drunks, the stiffened corpses stacked like firewood beneath the bridges. He couldn't have been wilder and filthier had he been raised by wolves. "What of it?" he spat.

The man drew the reed from his mouth, examined it, then slipped it back between his lips. There were ten thousand shit-faced orphans like this one out on the streets. They were at his elbows everywhere he went, insinuating themselves, offering their mouths and bodies, whining for coppers, bread and beer. But something in this one appealed to him: what it was he couldn't say. He made an effort. "I don't know — it just seemed as if you appreciated my little performance . . . the tunes, I mean."

Ned softened. "I did," he admitted.

The man held up the instrument. "You know what this is?"

"A fife?"

"Clarinet," said the man.

Ned wanted to know how the sound was made. The man showed him. Could he learn to play? Ned asked. The man stared down at Ned's hand, then asked him if he was hungry.

◄§ §►

Prentiss Barrenboyne owned a block of houses in Mayfair. He was in his mid-fifties. He'd never been married. His mother, a fierce and acerbic empiricist with whom he'd lived all his life, had died a month earlier. He brought the boy home that night and let him sleep in the coal cellar. In the morning he instructed his housekeeper to wash and feed him. It was a foot in the door. By the end of the week Ned Rise had become a habit. Officially he was established in the house as a servant, but Barrenboyne, won over by the lad's ingenuous and consuming enthusiasm for the clarinet, came to treat him more like a member of the family. He bought him clothes, gave him milk and chops and drippings, taught him to read and how to balance a teacup on his knee. There were trips to the concert hall, the theater, the shipyard and the zoo. A tutor was engaged. Ned acquired the rudiments of orthography, geometry, piscatology, a phrase or two of French, and a profound loathing for the Classics. He was no Eliza Doolittle. His progress — if the bimonthly absorption of a date or sum merits the appellation — was as leisurely as the drift of continents. The tutor was beside himself. He looked at Ned's face and saw the face of a wiseacre. He accused him of drinking ink and flogged his backside as he flogged his memory. Ned bore it with patience and humility. There were no tantrums, no fits, no funks. He did what was expected of him, sang hosannas to his redeemer and polished his prospects. He knew a good thing when he saw one.

Seven years passed. In France they were sending out invitations to a beheading, across the Atlantic they were knocking down forests and bludgeoning Indians, in the East End they nabbed the misogynist known as "The Monster" who for two years had been goring women's backsides in the street, and in Mayfair Ned Rise was eating three meals a day, sleeping in a bed, bathing at least once a fortnight, and stepping into clean underwear each and every morning. Seven years. The memory of the streets had begun to fade. He'd never eaten offal, witnessed perversion, theft, arson and worse, never huddled over ash pits with ice crusting his lashes and a cold fist clenching at his lungs — not Ned Rise, pride of the Barrenboynes.

Over the years Ned and his guardian had grown as close as palate and reed, wedded by their love for music. A week after the old man took him in the music lessons began. His face and crown suffused with blood, the hoary mutton chops bristling, Barrenboyne grinned his way into the room one night, a wooden case in hand. Inside was an ancient C clarinet, the one he himself had played as a boy. He handed it to Ned. Within the year Ned was playing passably in spite of his handicap, capable of sight-reading practically anything by the following summer, and in five years' time proficient enough to accompany his mentor to the park for his public debut. They sat there on the very bench on which Ned had first seen the old man, he with his C clarinet, Barrenboyne with his B-flat, and played airs from Estienne Rogers' tunebook. People gathered round, tapped their feet, swayed their bodies, while Mozart, dying in Vienna, composed his great Requiem Mass. Ned rose to the occasion.

◄§ §►

One morning, just before dawn, Barrenboyne stepped into Ned's room and shook him by the shoulder. "Get up, Ned," he whispered. "I need you." His voice trembled. His face and jowls were redder than Ned had ever seen them, red as tomatoes, flags, the jackets of the King's Hussars. Ned was nineteen. "What's the matter?" he asked. No answer. Birds began to whistle from beyond the windows. The old man was breathing like a locomotive. "Get dressed and meet me out front," he said.

Barrenboyne was waiting at the gate. He was dressed in the suit he'd bought for his mother's funeral, beaver top hat, silk surtout. Under his arm, a leather case, the rippled skin of some exotic reptile. A new clarinet? thought Ned. He'd never seen it before. They walked at a brisk pace: through Grosvenor Square, down Brook Street, across Park Lane and then into the soft green demesne of the park itself. The place was deserted. Fog, like milk in an atomizer, hung low over the wet grass. A crow jeered from a treebranch. "You know what a second is?" Barrenboyne said.

It was a slap in the face. "A second? You're not —?"

The old man took hold of his sleeve. "Just take it easy now," he said. "You're a grown man, Ned Rise. Prove it."

Two men — figures out of the gloom — were waiting for them by the edge of the Serpentine. One of them was a blackamoor, short, fat as a sow. He wore a feather in his hat, doeskin breeches, lisle hose and an iridescent waistcoat. A real buck. Barrenboyne strode up to them, bowed, and presented the leather case. It was seventy degrees at least, but the negro was shivering. His second, who kept inhaling snuff from an enamel box and sneezing into his handkerchief, took the leather case and opened it, between sneezes, for the negro. The negro selected a pistol. There was liquor on his breath. Then the sneezer offered the case to Barrenboyne. The old man lifted the weapon from its case as gently as if he were unpacking his clarinet for a breezy concert on the green. It began to drizzle.

The sneezer was snuffing snuff in a paroxysm of nervous energy, snapping open the box, pinching a nostril, gasping and slobbering into his handkerchief, all the while jerking his limbs and shuddering like an epileptic. The negro dropped his gun. The drizzle turned to rain. Barrenboyne's wattles began to vibrate as if he were exploring the upper register of the clarinet, and Ned found himself trembling in sympathetic response. Finally the sneezer managed to walk off twenty paces and set the principals on their marks. "Ready!" he bawled. Two harsh metallic clicks echoed over the field, one in imitation of the other. "Take aim!" Barrenboyne and the negro slowly raised their arms, as if saluting one another or taking part in the opening movement of a revolutionary new dance routine. Ned could picture them, jetéing over the greensward to leap through one another's arms. "Ffff — " came the aborted command, tailed by a septum-wrenching sneeze. There was a flash and a snap. Birds cried out at the far end of the field. The negro's pistol was smoking and his eyes were still buried in the crook of his elbow. Barrenboyne lay on the ground. Dead as a pharaoh.

◄§ LAYING IT ON THE LINE

Dawn. The sun breaks over the Sahel like a cracked egg and takes up where it left off the day before — scalding, incinerating, searing the life from everything within its compass. Carrion sniffers and night-roving reptiles creep back to their dens, and the big battered Nubian vultures sail out over the plain to check out the leavings. Rocks begin to expand, stunted shrubs dig deeper into the earth, mimosas fold up their leaves like parasols. By eight in the morning the horizon is shirred.

Mungo Park lies motionless on his back, watching a millipede trace a series of blind circles across the roof of his tent. Since the night of his "attempted escape" things have gone hard on him. Six men now doze outside his tent each night, and his food and water ration has been cut by half. It begins to occur to him that he may not make it after all, that he might just lie here and waste away, dauntless discoverer of the interior walls of a Moorish tent. He will join Ledyard, Lucas and Houghton in the ranks of failure and ignominy. He will never again lay eyes on Ailie, nor his mother, nor the bonny banks of the Yarrow. His bones will dry and crack and fall to dust under the alien sun and the wheeling strange colossi of misplaced constellations. He begins to feel daunted.

Suddenly the flaps part and Johnson ducks into the tent. In his hand a goatskin waterbag, known as a *guerba* in these parts. The explorer lies there, racked with fever, riddled with worms, his stomach shrunken, sphincter open wide, barely able to raise his eyes. He is weak and stinking, tabescent, at the far edge of hope. Johnson kneels beside him and feeds the leather nipple into his mouth. His lips grope, pulse quickens. It is water, cold and clear, water dipped from the shifting porous depths of the earth.

It stirs the roots of his hair, firms his toenails, sings to his brittle bones. "I'm saved!" he gasps, and then vomits.

"It's all right, Mr. Park. Take it easy: you got the whole thing to yourself."

"Wha?" The explorer's eyes are crusted and yellow, cheeks drawn, his beard a playground for ticks, fleas, lice and maggots.

"You heard me right. Chief Jackal, he tells me to come in here and give you the waterbag and then a pan of milk and kouskous."

"Milk? Kouskous?" Johnson might just as well have announced haggis, finnan haddie and sheep's-head soup. Mungo goes into peristaltic shock, then jerks himself up, clutching at the *guerba* and ransacking the tent with his eyes. "Where?" he pants, struggling to his feet. "Where? Tell me for God's sake!"

At that moment a boy enters with a wooden bowl. Milk and kouskous. The boy makes as if to lay it at the explorer's feet, but Mungo snatches it from him and buries his face in the thick ropy paste with all the desperation of a man stranded on the desert for forty days and forty nights. Which is precisely what he is.

Afterward, he pats his abdomen. "Johnson," he says. "Oh-ho, Johnson, Johnson, Johnson, how I needed that . . ." But wait! What has he done? The bowl's been scraped clean and here's his faithful guide and interpreter languishing before his eyes! "Johnson," he stammers, staring down at the ground, ". . . can you ever, can you ever forgive me? I'm afraid I went into a bit of a frenzy there . . . I—I forgot all about you."

Johnson holds up his palm. "Oh they been feedin' me right along, don't you worry about that. Got to. Else how am I goin' to bust my ass for them? Fetch this, mend that. Scrub this pot, milk them goats, oil up Akbar's sandals and skim some cream for the horses. Shit. It's like bein' back on the plantation again. Sometimes I wish they'd just let me lie here and languish along with you."

Mungo strokes the soggy grain from his beard and systematically licks the kernels from his fingers, then takes a long pull at the waterbag. Color trickles back into his cheeks. "So what's up?" he says. "What's made the bloody camel drivers so charitable all of a sudden?"

"Fatima."

Fatima. The syllables flow like wind on water. First she'd saved his eyes, and now the rest of him. Hope glimmers. "She wants to see me?"

Johnson nods. "Ali says you got to be fed, washed up and made presentable. He won't have his wife examinin' a unwashed Christian.

And he gave me this too," handing the explorer a pale folded garment.

"What is it?"

"*Jubbah.* Ali says you got to cover up your legs — he finds your trousers objectionable, high-quality nankeen or no." Johnson laughs. "You ever get back to London you can sweep all the beaux and noodles under the table, start a craze: skirts for gentlemen." Mungo laughs along with him, drunk on food and water. The two chuckle and wheeze, wiping tears from their eyes. Then Johnson looks up, suddenly serious. "She'll be here tomorrow night," he says. "Don't blow it."

✑ PLANTATION SONG

On this sub-Saharan evening awash with pale light and tapering shadow, Mungo Park, for the first time in nearly three months, finds himself out of the tent and back in the saddle again. His horse has been restored to him (cachectic as ever, looking like one of the gutted nags the Druids used to impale for decoration), his beard, locks and loins cleansed and anointed, his rags exchanged for a spanking white *jubbah*. On his head, a battered top hat; round his shoulders, the blue velvet jacket he wore while addressing the African Association at St. Alban's Tavern, Pall Mall. Ali and Dassoud flank him on their chargers. Ali's mount is white, Dassoud's so absolutely black it cuts a hole in the horizon (an illusion he enhances by blackening the animal's hoofs and anus, and staining its teeth). Johnson brings up the rear on an Abyssinian ass.

They are bound for Fatima's tent at the far edge of the encampment, a distance of perhaps six or seven hundred yards. Ali and Dassoud are silent, while Mungo, sotto voce, rehearses phrases from his Arabic grammar: "I am honored to bask in your presence." "Allow me to make obeisance to the undersides of your feet." "Hot, isn't it?" As they pass through the heart of the camp, dogs dart out to yap at the Christian's stirrups, children gather to bombard him with nuggets of camel dung, adults step from their tents to squint up at him and denigrate his race, creed and color. "I piss in your mother's hole!" a man yells. But then Ali holds up his hand and the voices fall silent, the children run to their mothers, the dogs vanish. "Thanks," says Mungo. Ali's face is impassive. His gesture has had nothing whatever to do with compassion or fellow feeling — he just doesn't want his wife inspecting a washed Christian in a shit-stained *jubbah*, that's all.

⋙ ⋘

Fatima's tent is two or three times the size of any of the others in camp, and distinguished by broad bands of color: gray, beige, indigo. Mungo recognizes the huge Nubian out front. The Nubian stands there, on guard, flexing the black bulges between his elbow and shoulder. Off to the right a woman squats in the dust, busily milking four or five she-goats. The explorer observes the pale soles of her feet, the yellow torpedoes of the goats' teats. A fly lands on the explorer's nose. The sun touches the horizon.

"Dismount!" shouts Ali, as he and Dassoud spring from their steeds like a pair of Russian tumblers. Johnson, ambling up on his ass, relays the command to his employer, while the Nubian steps forward to take charge of the animals.

It should be said that the explorer's mind is laboring under a Sisyphean strain at this juncture: he is keyed up, jittery, aquiver with apprehension and doubt. The success of his mission — yea, his life itself — may depend on the impression he makes in his forthcoming interview with the Queen. His stomach sinks with the same nauseated, socked-in-the-kidney feeling that used to assail him at school before end-of-term exams. Butterflies, they used to call it. Stage fright. Heebie-jeebies. The Choke.

And so, sweating like a marathon runner, he steps down out of the saddle, catches his left foot in the stirrup and slaps to the ground in a storm of dust and goat hair. He lies there a moment, thinking Christ in Heaven what have I done now, while Dassoud and Ali exchange glances and Johnson rushes to his aid. After steadying the horse, loosening the stirrup and finally thinking to remove the explorer's boot, Johnson succeeds in extricating him. But this is just the beginning. The ground here, it seems, is a mecca for the costive denizens of the Sahel, an unspoiled latrine for Mother Nature and all her feathered, furred and squamate creation. Goat turds lie here, cheek by jowl with hyena ordure; grainy bars of camel dung, dogshit, cowshit and sheepshit coil round the withered ropy leavings of adders and skinks; there's even a stray ibex turd or two. Mungo rises from this morass, brushing at his *jubbah* and dusting his hat. "Sorry about that," he says. Ali shrugs. Then gestures for him to follow, and disappears through the soft contiguous flaps of Fatima's tent and into the mystery beyond. Mungo, reeking like a zoo, his back an abstract collage of mauves, siennas and dun yellows, the representative of King George III and all of England, follows the Emir of Ludamar into the sanctum of the Queen.

꙳ ꙳

It is dark inside, a pair of oil lamps burning fitfully. There are tapestries, mats, urns, a perch on which two birds of prey — saker falcons — are calmly disemboweling a jerboa. The explorer glances up just as one of them finds a long strand of intestine and begins to tug at it, like a robin with a worm. *"Salaam aleichem,"* says Ali, and there she is, seated on a pillow the size of a double bed. The explorer is stunned. He'd expected a big woman — but this . . . this is impossible! She is gargantuan, elephantine, her great bundled turban and glowing *jubbah* like a pair of circus tents, her shadow leaping and swelling in the uncertain light until it engulfs the room. Her attendants — two girls in billowy pantaloons and a hoary old woman — sit at her feet like olives flanking a cantaloupe in a surreal still life.

Mungo cannot make out her face, which is concealed behind a *yashmak* — the double horsehair veil worn by Muslim women in public — but he is immediately struck by her feet and hands. Petite and delicate, they float at the tips of her bloated extremities like ducks on a pond. He is fascinated. Each of her digits is ornamented with a ring, and for some reason — perhaps to draw attention to their charms — her hands and feet have been stained saffron. The effect is dazzling. When finally she turns her head toward him she gasps, and gives out a faint squeal. Ali rushes to her, jabbering in Arabic. When she answers him, her voice is soft and sensual as a sunshower.

Mungo nudges his interpreter.

"She says she's afraid," Johnson whispers.

"Afraid? I'm the one whose giblets are on the line here."

"You're a Christian. To her that's like bein' a cannibal or a werewolf or somethin'."

"What about you?"

"Don't look at me, brother — I'm a Animist. Shhh . . . now she's bitchin' about the smell . . . 'Do they all smell like that?' "

Suddenly Ali barks out a command. "He wants us on our knees," says Johnson, easing himself down and burying his forehead in the sand. The explorer follows suit. They pose like this for a long while ("I'm beginning to feel like a ostrich," Johnson quips), until a high nasal voice begins yodeling out the evening prayers. It is the *muezzin,* stationed somewhere outside the tent. Ali and Dassoud likewise prostrate themselves, and Fatima comes down off her throne like a thundercloud rolling down the side of a mountain. As she tilts her forehead to the earth, the explorer can feel her rich black eyes upon him.

When the prayers are finally finished, Fatima lumbers back to her pillow, settles herself primly, and softly dismisses Dassoud and her husband. She then turns to Mungo and his interpreter, and asks them to be seated. Behind them, the Nubian edges into the tent, scimitar in hand. For a long while the room is silent, Fatima and her attendants ocularly feasting on this blond apparition in the blue velvet jacket. Finally the Queen addresses him, a single sentence, her voice rising as if on the crest of a question. Mungo looks at Johnson.

"She wants you to stand up and take your jacket off."

Mungo complies, and one of the girls slips up to take the garment from him and deliver it to the Queen. Fatima regards the jacket silently, running her hand over the material against the nap, taking one of the brass buttons between her teeth. The explorer stands there in his *jubbah* like a child in a nightgown. "Give it to her," Johnson whispers.

The explorer clears his throat, and in his best Arabic offers her the jacket. She looks up at him and politely declines, but does appropriate two of the brass buttons. "For earrings," she explains, holding them up to the corners of her *yashmak*. From the shadows one of the falcons begins to crow: ca-ha! ca-ha! Fatima wets her lips. "Does he want any pork?" she asks.

"Tell her no," says Johnson.

At that moment One-Eye appears with a bushpig on a leash. The bushpig has an elongated snout randomly disfigured with lumps and ridges, several yellowed tusks, and a nasty look in its eye. With a leer, One-Eye offers Mungo the pig. "Snark-snark," says the pig.

"Look disgusted," Johnson coaches.

The explorer does his best to express horror and loathing, knowing full well how deeply the Moors abhor pork. He backs away, fingers atremble, slapping his forehead and tugging at his lip while the bushpig, squealing like an accordion, stamps and stutters and jerks at its leash. The performance seems to be reassuring Fatima, and so the explorer gyrates even more wildly — really hamming it up — until he accidentally stumbles into the falcons' perch. This, he immediately realizes, is a mistake. At the touch of his elbow the birds rear up and shriek in his face, their beaks and talons like scissors, wings beating round his ears. Then the larger of the two springs onto his shoulder. He is terrified. In his anxiety to brush it away he ducks directly into the path of the bushpig, who has been waiting for just such a chance. In a flash the pig lurches forward and savagely bites the explorer six or seven times in rapid succession. During the panic that ensues, the explorer somehow manages to collapse half the tent and wind up spread-eagled across the Queen's voluminous lap. The Nubian eunuch intercedes to behead the pig with one swipe of his scimitar, while One-Eye and the pantaloon girls try to dislodge the shit-caked and bleeding explorer from the Queen's person. Through it all, Mungo can hear the strains of Johnson's voice raised in song — it seems almost as if he's singing a dirge, downhearted and mournful, one of the old plantation songs Johnson likes to call "the blues."

"You done blowed it now," he's singing. "Blowed it now. Lord God Almighty, you done blowed it now."

❧ O THAT SINKING FEELING

February, 1796. Wordsworth has been in and out of France and Annette Vallon, Bonaparte has put the screws to Babeuf and is vigorously pounding at Joséphine's gate, Goethe is living in sin with Christiane Vulpius, and Burns is dying. In Edinburgh Walter Scott fights a losing battle for the hand of Williamina Belches, while in Manchester a snot-nosed De Quincey wanders the streets and wonders what a whore is. In Moscow it's snowing. In Paris they're plugging holes with *assignats* for lack of anything better to do with them. And in Soho, at the Vole's Head Tavern, they're sucking and fucking. Onstage.

Ned couldn't be more pleased. Jutta Jim's been going strong for better than an hour now (if you discount the two brief intermissions during which he chanted tribal lays and quaffed a pint of chicken's blood to keep his spirits up), Nan and Sally have enlarged their roles admirably, and the audience has been too preoccupied to wreak mayhem or piss on the carpet. What's more, Ned's throat, limbs, liver and lights haven't been threatened in over an hour (Smirke's been running round with a hard-on all night, peddling drinks like an oasis owner in Araby, and Mendoza hasn't said boo since Jim strutted out onstage), and his gross take has far exceeded his rosiest estimate (nearly thirty-six pounds against an outlay of twenty-three and two, which includes a new suit of clothes, tips, and refreshment for himself and his cast). And all of it tucked snugly away in the Bank of the Bulge.

So why all this anxiety? He's been through a flask and a half of gin already, smoked three pipes and paced the room twenty-two times, and he's still jittery as a case of rat-bite fever. He can't understand it. He's even starting to develop an itch in the missing joint of his pinky. Of course, deep down, he already knows the answer — things are going too well. And that means he'd better dodge, duck and flinch, because when things start going too well that's when the Powers That Be swoop down on you like a dozen hurricanes and leave you buried under half a ton of flotsam and jetsam.

It reminds him of the time at Bartholomew Fair when he and Billy Boyles just couldn't lose at the gaming tables, had themselves a couple of tarts for nothing, then fell into the way of a champion fighting cock worth fifty quid easy. And then, as they were skulking off the fairgrounds with their booty, there it was — Zeppo the Eleusinian's star-spangled cape — just hanging out to dry like a gift from the gods. On the way back Boyles led him down a lampless lane, and sure enough, a pair of dacoits pounced on them. "Stand and deliver!" a voice growled, and Ned found that the barrel of a pistol had been inserted in his ear. "I'll jest disburden yer of yer loose coin," the voice rasped, "while me accomplice 'ere bleeds yer pal."

The accomplice was a dwarf, no more than three feet high, with a carroty mass of hair flaming round his cheeks and crown like a brush fire. Ned handed over his purse and watched as the dwarf limped from the shadows, ordered Boyles to sit in the road, and began probing his rags with the point of a dagger. " 'Ere!" the dwarf exclaimed. "Wot's this then?" It was the fighting cock, nestled in Boyles' breast, its legs and beak bound with strips of blue ribbon. The dwarf plucked the bird from its cachette, throttled it with a twist of his knotty hands, and held it up for the gunman to admire. "A bit of somefin for the pot, then, 'ey Will?"

"Good show, Ginger," growled the gunman. "Now strip the beggar raw and see if 'ee's got any coin of the realm about 'im." Down with the trousers, up with the shirt: Billy Boyles was naked as a jay inside of ten seconds. "Now you, pretty boy," the gunman said.

Ned appealed to the gunman's compassion and sense of fair play. "But I already gave you my purse," he sniveled, " — have a heart, will you?"

"Ha!" the gunman laughed. "Think I doesn't know river sand when I feels it? Wot yer take me for, a dyspeptic baboon or somefin? Off with yer drawers, sucker!"

The game was up. Ned dropped his trousers and there it was, glowing in the moonlight like a luminescent diaper — the strip of muslin stuffed with the day's winnings. The dwarf tore it from his abdomen and coins rained to the ground. "Hoo-hoo!" he sang. "We've 'it the buggerin' jackpot this time, 'asn't we, Will?"

Just as the dwarf was scooping up the last of the coins, a coach-and-four rumbled round the corner and the muggers vanished. Boyles crouched against the wall *in puris naturalibus,* while Ned wrapped the magician's cape around his bare legs and flagged down the coach. "Ho!" bellowed the driver. The coach came to a stop with a rattle and screech. "We've been robbed!" Ned shouted. The door shot back. Inside was Sir Euston Filigree, magistrate and gamecock fancier. Beside him sat an officer of the law with a cocked pistol. "What a coincidence," said Sir Euston. "I've been robbed too."

"Get in," said the officer.

"Three months at hard labor," said the judge.

It never fails. Whenever things start to look up, whenever fantasy begins to jell into possibility, the Hand of Fate intercedes to slap you back to your senses. Frightening. Enough to make you paranoid. Ned takes another pull at the bung and glances round him like a lamb at a convocation of wolves. Up onstage Jim, Sally and Nan are approaching the climactic finale — an impossible, multi-limbed, sinew-straining, tour de force feat of sexual acrobatics — heads, tongues and hips undulating in a quickening tempo, *allegro di molto,* the audience spilling from chairs, upsetting tables, panting like a dogshow in mid-July. The moment suspends here, ticking along at the edge of release, sublimely attuned to the functions of the body and the sway of the planet — when suddenly the door flies back and the voice of authority booms through the chamber: "CEASE AND DESIST IN THE NAME OF GOD ALMIGHTY AND ALL YE HOLD DECENT!"

The gilded youth is the first to react. "Holy shit! It's the constabulary!"

"It's a raid!" someone shouts, and the room erupts in confusion. Regimental commanders trip over their swords, baronets and shopkeepers collide, clergymen hit the floor, while rogues, rakes, noodles, beaux, bucks and bloods make for the rear exit, Ned Rise leading them by a length. Up onstage Jim vacates Sally and Sally strips herself from Nan who in turn releases Jim and reaches for her gin and water. "SEIZE THE PROPRI-ETOR!" bellows an officer, and Ned, already at the door, looks back to see poor Smirke in the grip of two burly Charlies. " 'Ee's the one!" roars Smirke, pointing a thick finger at the entrepreneur as he squeezes through the door. "The clown in the cape!"

"AFTER HIM LADS!" booms the coordinating officer.

Ned is in the alley already, off like a fox at the first woof of the hounds, passing bucks and bloods as if they were standing still, the gin coming up in him, feet flying, the cape beating round his shoulders like the wings of the Furies. Unable to flee in their high-heeled pumps, the bucks and bloods fall easy prey to the pursuing officers — the dread Bow Street Runners — and shout curses at Ned's retreating back. "You slimy weevil, Rise — you'll pay for this!"

"Gallowsbait!"

"Clystermonger!"

Ned pays them no mind. He is caught up in the pure frenzied ecstasy of flight, in the astonishing coordination of heart, lungs, joints and feet, in this fearsome momentum fueled by alcohol and driven by panic. Down the street to his left, over the cobbles — just a blur — and into the dark close on the far side. The shouts and curses receding now, almost safe. But what's this? Footsteps at his back, regular as a drumbeat. He turns to look over his shoulder and an icy dagger punches at his ribs: two grim and athletic Runners pad along the alley, barely winded, confidently working into the easy loping stride of marathon men. Good God, he doesn't stand a chance. These Bow Street Runners are relentless, tireless. Word has it they've even run down men on horseback.

He gives it all he's got, heading for the river. His chest is heaving, there's a fire in his lungs, the coins dig at his crotch. "STOP IN THE NAME OF THE LAW!" Never. The law's a joke and only losers get nabbed. His feet slap on the pavement. Now he's rounding the corner into Villiers — and there's the river! If he can just make the cover of the docks or jump one of the boats . . . but they're gaining on him, the bleeding jocks, and *chink-chink,* there go the first two coins. He grits his teeth. Churns harder. And then suddenly the boards of Charing Cross Pier resound under his feet, nowhere to go, the jocks thumping at his heels — a hand on his collar — and then he's free, plummeting through the dank night air. There's a crust of ice, the coins like a ship's anchor, the water an icy cudgel. SLOOSH! And he's gone.

The Runners stand at the edge of the pier, plumbing the shadows. The ice is the color of slate, the water black. Nothing moves. "Well Nick, I guess that's that," says the grimmer of the two.

"Right you are, Dick," comes the reply. "Case closed."

⊷ NEW CONTINENTS, ANCIENT RIVERS

But he hadn't blown it. Not by a long shot. In fact, as things turned out, the Queen didn't seem at all indisposed by the presence of a porcipophagic albino infidel in her lap — perhaps, in a strange way, she even welcomed it. The explorer's first intimation of this came almost immediately. As he lay there, stunned and bleeding, cradled in the trembling aqueous flux of her lap like a ship come to harbor, he felt he detected a movement deep within

her. A ripple, a swell. An undulation as soft and inevitable as the rings
which fan out over the waters of a pond after a stone has broken its surface.
Was she laughing? Tittering deep in the omphalos of that magnificent flesh
factory? Was he a hit, after all? Unfortunately he had no chance to find
out, for Dassoud, murder in his eye, was already hacking at the deflated
wall of the tent. Mungo sprang from the Queen's nave and planted his
brow in the earth, following Johnson's example. *"La illah el allah,"* he
chanted by way of amends, *"Mahomet rasowl Allahi."*

There was the shriek of rending goat hair — *zit! zat! zoot!* — and
Dassoud leaped into the tent, inflamed with the notion that the Queen was
in danger, thirsting to exact a hasty and savage retribution. "Aaarrrr!" he
growled, whirling his terrible swift sword — but then he stopped in his
tracks. What was going on here? The handmaidens were in hysterics, tent
poles shattered, blood spewed and feathers strewn from one end of the
place to the other . . . and yet there sat Fatima, just as he'd left her, while
the *Nazarini* and his slave lay quailing on the ground, One-Eye and the
Nubian standing over them like executioners. "What in the name of Allah
is going on here?" he demanded.

The Nubian, who had never spoken a word in his life, said nothing.

The pig sprawled in the corner, still quivering, gouts of blood issuing
from its severed throat. Its head lay at the Nubian's feet.

"Lord have mercy!" whimpered Johnson, addressing the sand.

Finally the handmaidens' lamentations wound down to an easy gagging
mewl, and One-Eye launched a rapid-fire narration of what had transpired,
playing down his own involvement as best he could and emphasizing the
reckless and irresponsible behavior of the *Nazarini* and his slave. Dassoud
listened impatiently, rocking on his feet, twisting the saber in his hand,
until finally he cut the story short and insisted that the transgressors be led
out into the dunes and disemboweled. At this point Fatima cleared her
throat. Dassoud fell silent. Her tone was firm, her diction spare. The sense
of it blew right by the explorer, but the upshot of the whole thing was that
he and Johnson were led back to his tent, where a seventh comatose guard
was summoned to complement the six men tried and true who were
already dozing before the entranceway.

An hour later an unwonted aroma charged the air. It was lingering and
piquant, redolent of hearths and basting and relishes. It was the smell of
meat. The explorer swallowed twice. "Johnson — do you smell what I
smell?"

"Prime rib. I'd know it anywhere."

Just then the flaps parted and the savory rich aura filled the tent. It was one of the pantaloon girls. In her hand, the haunch of an addax, still hissing from the spit. She gave it to the explorer. "For you," she said. "From Fatima." Then she winked and disappeared into the night.

Mungo tore a mouthful from the bone, then passed the joint to his interpreter. He was laughing. "We're home free now, old fellow — guess I must have done something right after all."

"Maybe she's big on slapstick," Johnson suggested.

"Who knows? But one thing's for sure: she's an angel. First the *guerba*, then the milk and kouskous — and now this!"

"Yeah," said Johnson, chewing. "It was big of her."

◂§ §▸

The next morning she sent him a dish of yogurt and bittersweet hoona berries; in the evening it was scrambled brains and rice. He was astonished. After two months of water and mush, here was something he could sink his teeth into. And this was only the beginning. In the ensuing days Fatima's girls brought him sheep's liver, camel's hump (braised), a stew of chickpeas and sweetbreads, buttermilk pudding, three dozen bustard giblets and a whole roast kid. "Soul food," Johnson called it. "It's your inner man that's got her worked up — never mind your disreputable and shit-caked outer man." Inner man, outer man — what difference did it make? Red meat fed them both. Why, he must have dropped a good four stone since he left Portsmouth. He glanced down at his yellowed toes and drawn ankles, the sticks of his forearms: couldn't weigh much more than ten right now. But then he grinned, and muttered a little prayer. If this kept up he'd put it back on in no time. And then — who knows? — maybe he'd be strong enough to make a run for it.

There were other changes too. He was allowed to wander round the camp at will (shadowed by his seven keepers, of course), spend as much time as he liked with Johnson, and even have a firsthand look at some of the Moors' customs and ceremonies. This last, above all else, lifted his spirits. After all, he *was* an explorer — and here he was, exploring. He witnessed two circumcisions, a funeral, the death of a dog that had lifted its leg against Ali's tent. He watched the slaves pounding millet, tanning hides, churning butter in a *guerba* suspended between two sticks; he watched them reciting prayers, defecating, throwing pots, chewing roots, tattooing infants and dogs. It was all very illuminating. But ephemeral. He couldn't keep track of things from one day to the next.

Then one morning, as he sat watching a slave tie up the nipples of a camel to keep its calf from suckling in the heat of day, an idea hit him like a blow to the back of the head: he'd write a book! He'd write a book and be famous like Marco Polo or Gulliver or Richard Jobson. Why not? Here he was, seeing and smelling and tasting things no white man had ever dreamed of — it would be criminal to miss his chance to document it. He marched back to the tent, tore the leaves from his pocket Bible, and began writing, filling sheet after sheet with his impressions of the climate, the flora, the fauna, the geological formations, the habits and physiognomies of the blackamoors, Mandingoes, Serawoolis and Foulahs. He described Ali's beard, Dassoud's scowl, the heat of midday, the solitude of the baobab. Talked of Fatima's graciousness, the tang of the hoona berry, woodsmoke on the night air. He filled thirty sheets that first day, and secreted them in the crown of his hat.

One evening he witnessed a wedding. It was strikingly similar to the funeral he'd attended: keening hags, howling dogs, a solemn procession. The bride was a walking shroud, veiled from head to foot, even her eyes invisible. He wondered how she was able to see where she was going. The keening women followed her, their stride measured by the beat of a *tabala*. The groom wore slippers with upturned toes. He was accompanied by a retinue of Mussulmen in embroidered burnooses and a cordon of slaves leading goats and bullocks, and carrying a tent. At an appointed spot the tent was struck, the goats and bullocks slaughtered, a fire ignited in a depression in the earth. There was a feast. Beef and mutton, songbirds, roasted larvae and other delicacies. There was dancing, songs were sung and tales told. And then there was the pièce de résistance: a whole baked camel.

BAKED CAMEL (STUFFED)

Serves 400

500 dates
200 plover eggs
20 two-pound carp
4 bustards, cleaned and plucked
2 sheep
1 large camel
seasonings

Dig trench. Reduce inferno to hot coals, three feet in depth. Separately hard-cook eggs. Scale carp and stuff with shelled eggs and dates. Season bustards and stuff with stuffed carp. Stuff stuffed bustards into sheep and stuffed sheep into camel. Singe camel. Then wrap in leaves of doum palm and bury in pit. Bake two days. Serve with rice.

A regular feature of this expansive period were the explorer's daily meetings with the Queen. Each afternoon — immediately following the *dhuhur* or midday prayers — he was summoned to Fatima's tent for a question-and-answer period. She questioned, he answered. Insatiable, she never tired of quizzing him. She was an anthropologist, a sociologist, a comparative anatomist. She wanted to dissect and absorb his habits, thoughts and beliefs; she wanted to taste his food, wear his clothes, sit at his box in the theater. England, Europe, the vast and uncertain oceans — she wanted them built of words, words supple and evocative, words that would calcify in her imagination. She wanted visions. She wanted the memories behind his eyes. She wanted to digest him. Why had he come to Ludamar? How did his father manage the herds without him? Why did he wear so asinine (*jalab*) a covering on his head? Did all Christians have cat's eyes? What was the sea like? Had he ever been crucified? The explorer, grinning like a monkey and trying his clumsy best to radiate wit and charm, answered her questions as fully and patiently as he was able.

One afternoon she asked if the *Nazarini* practiced circumcision. "Certainly," Mungo replied. She wanted to see for herself. The explorer looked at Johnson. "What do I do now?" he whispered.

"Tell her you'll be more than happy to demonstrate — but it'll have to be in private. Then toss your eyebrows a couple of times."

Mungo told her. He tossed his eyebrows. For a moment the tent was as silent as the dark side of the moon. The Queen's black eyes burned over the fringe of her *yashmak*. Then she slapped her thigh and tittered.

That night the explorer ate leg of lamb.

◦◦◦

On this particular morning, three and a half weeks since his first meeting with Fatima, the explorer is sitting in the shade of an acacia, writing. *The Moorish women,* he writes, *wear their hair in nine plaits, which they divide as follows: two on either side of the face, six thinner braids over the crown, and one stout coil at the base of the neck. The hair is washed and oiled once a month, dressed and replaited weekly. For sanitary reasons, and because it tends to bleach the hair somewhat, the women prefer a rinse of camel's urine, which is collected for this purpose. (One can always see a slave or two, cup in hand, pursuing a micturating camel about the camp.) The urine is a powerful astringent, and serves to destroy vermin and other parasites. Indeed, I have had the opportunity to assess its efficacy personally, as my pubes, axillae, side-whiskers and locks were infested with lice and desert mites. I found it refreshing, if somewhat mephitic . . .*

There is a bloom on the explorer's cheek. A clarity in his eye. Worms, grippe, scabies, the fever and racheting cough — they're things of the past. Nasty memories. He's a meat eater now, a man of broth and blood, as befits a Scotsman, and gaining strength day by day. The heat enervates him, of course, and he still suffers attacks of confusion — but all in all the change in diet and the fresh air have gone a long way toward resurrecting him. And the peace and quiet have had something to do with it too. Just a month ago it would have been impossible for him to sit here: the very sight of him drove the average Mussulman into a frenzy. Within seconds he would have been beleaguered by a stinking, spittle-spewing mob of Moslem zealots. Now it's different. They know he's under Fatima's protection, and aside from isolated incidents (some unseen adversary walloped him in the side of the head with a pig's pizzle not more than twenty minutes ago), he is left to himself.

The Moorish men, on the other hand, never bathe. They do, however, have a biannual ceremony known as asíla má, *during which they bury themselves in hot sand for some forty-five minutes to an hour just prior to sunset. They are then disinterred, rubbed down with the sweat of an estruating mare and thrashed with the underbranches of the* seríf *bush. I am told that the operation is congenial to long life and sexual vigor.*

As the explorer looks up to wet his quill, he is startled to discover that he is not alone. Standing there before him, her chocolate eyes following the dip and rush of the pen, is the plumper of the pantaloon girls. "What is it?" he says.

"Fatima says you must come to her."

Come to her? At ten A.M.? What could she possibly want with him at this hour? "All right," he says, getting to his feet. "I'll fetch Johnson."

"No," says the girl. "Fatima says he will not be needed."

The explorer shrugs. "Lead the way," he says.

◦§ ¿◦

As he pushes through the flaps and into the tent he is instantly engulfed in darkness. Blue spheres pulsate before his eyes, yellow cartwheels drift off into space. He can see nothing. There are the familiar odors of frankincense and camel urine, and from the corner, the rasp of the saker falcons chewing at their wings. But why hasn't she lighted a lamp? And where's that damned girl gone off to? Ah, well. No matter. May as well ride with the current. "*Salaam aleichem,*" he says, addressing the shadows.

"*Aleichem as salaam,*" comes the reply, soft as the beat of a moth's wing.

He jumps. She's sitting right beside him — he could have stumbled over her . . . Christ it's dark. Can't very well move for fear of upsetting something. "Braaaaak!" says one of the falcons. Maybe he should ask her to light a taper — but then how in the name of God do you say "taper"? He settles for *"Kaif halkum?"* — how are you?

"Bishára," she answers, which he takes to mean she has no complaints. Silence.

He shuffles his feet, picks his ear and jerks at his knuckles, wondering if he should risk taking a seat. It's an awkward moment. After ten or twenty seconds of ear picking, he makes a stab at conversation, hoping to express how pleasant it is to see her again — though he can barely make her out. Unfortunately, what he actually says is: "My sight is rabid pleasure."

Fatima titters.

Encouraged, he goes on, addressing the shadowy bulk before him. Battling case endings, syntax, verb tenses and a spotty vocabulary, the explorer waxes eloquent as Antony, Demosthenes and the Speaker of the House all rolled into one, telling her how much he's appreciated the attention she's given him, not to mention the jellied calves' feet and puréed mung beans. At that moment, however, the elderly attendant enters with a taper and the explorer discovers that he's been addressing a hand loom. The Queen is actually seated on the far side of the tent, rising up out of her enormous pillow like an Alp rising from the foothills. The explorer is bewildered. "Come over here," she says.

At the sound of Fatima's voice the old woman starts, then hurries about her business. She fixes the candle in the upturned palm of an ivory figurine, gathers her skirts and sweeps past the explorer with a lickerish grin. Mungo starts forward, but then hesitates. Something is wrong here — but what? Suddenly it hits him: Fatima's head is bare, the thick braids fanning out over her shoulders like the runners of a plant. He's never glimpsed so much as a single hair before — unless you count her eyebrows. "Come here," she repeats.

The explorer steps up to her and bows, trying to think of something witty to say. She pats the pillow. "Up here," she motions. Mungo shrugs. Then scales the pillow and sinks into its vastness. The old woman is nowhere to be seen. Nor is there any trace of the pantaloon girls. It occurs to him that he has never before been alone with the Queen. But now the pillow has begun to quake, flowing along its length like a wind-driven sea. He looks up. The Queen is pulling the *jubbah* up over her head, grunting daintily as she labors with the flashing fields of cloth. Beneath the *jubbah:* naked flesh. The explorer begins to get the idea.

"Help me," she moans, the gown smothering her head and upper torso.

Mungo leans forward and seizes the nape of the stupendous garment, thinking of sheets and flags and circus tents' He tugs, she grunts. Her arms ripple beneath the cloth like animals in a sack, she gasps, and then suddenly her breasts jog free, shuddering mightily with the concussion, colossal orbs, heavenly bodies. They come to rest over the multiple folds of her abdomen like the twin moons of Mars. The explorer is suddenly stung with hurry and necessity. He jerks at the recalcitrant cloth with all the meat-eating fervor he can rouse, panting and moaning, until all at once the *jubbah* gives as if it were made of paper. He falls back, and there she is — the Queen — naked and ineluctable as the great wide fathomless sea. *"Yudhkul,"* she whispers. *"Yudhkul alaiha."*

He flings the boots, paws at the buttons, jerks at his *jubbah.* Moist and mountainous, she waits for him, eyes aglow, veil lowered, her flesh smoldering like Vesuvius. He wheezes with haste and anticipation. It's a dream, an attack of fever: no mere mortal could approach this magnificence! He scrambles atop her, feeling for toeholds — so much terrain to explore — mountains, valleys and rifts, new continents, ancient rivers.

◄§ GLEGGED

She's a fortress under siege, is what she is. Ramparts manned, oil hot to scathe, gates shut tight as a drum. Since the day he surprised her in the tub she hasn't had a moment's respite. It's been Gleg to the right of her, Gleg to the left. Gleg at the window, Gleg at the door, Gleg in the closet when she reaches for her wrap, Gleg in the garden when she goes out for a stroll. He's inescapable, inexorable. In the morning he brings her flowers — great bundles of dead men's fingers and pepperwort, then waits on the stairs while she dresses. At breakfast she finds love lyrics tucked between her oatcakes or folded into her napkin:

> *How should I love my best?*
> *What though my love unto that height be grown,*
> *That taking joy in you alone*
> *I utterly this world detest,*
> *Should I not love it yet as th' only place*
> *Where Beauty hath his perfect grace,*
> *And is possest?*

She can't crack an egg without hearing about the "Blushing Morn" of her cheeks or the "Foaming Billows" of her breasts. Lovelorn sighs punctuate each sip of tea, while the scraping of her toast is, he protests, like the rasp of a file along the ridges of his heart. As the chairs shriek back and Zander and her father shuffle out of the room, Gleg leans toward her and whispers: "Had we but World enough, and Time, / This coyness Lady were no crime." And then adds with a wink, "But we haven't. And it is."

Gleg, Gleg, she's been Glegged to the gills. He is ubiquitous, unshakable, a flea under the collar, a fly in the ointment. In the evening he sits beneath her window, alternately dribbling into a recorder and howling at the treetops like a cat in heat. During the intervals between "airs" he composes poetry and tosses pebbles at the windowpane. One morning she stepped out of her room to find him mooning over the chamberpot she'd left in the hall. Another time she caught him stuffing his pockets with bits of fat and gristle in the hope of ingratiating himself with Douce Davie, her border terrier. She was adamantine. The dog was a pushover.

For today, though, she can let down the drawbridge and air out the battlements — she's free of him till supper. Just after breakfast he and Zander went off with her father to roam the countryside draining pustules, letting blood and applying leeches to lumps and goiters and yellowing contusions. She watched them amble up the lane on their horses, Zander rhythmic and graceful, Gleg as ungainly as a mantis astride a beetle. At the top of the lane he turned to wave his handkerchief at her. The simp. She wanted to thumb her teeth at him, but he was so relentlessly absurd she actually found herself grinning. Which encouraged him all the more. The handkerchief flapped like a jib in a crosswind. He was a beaming boy, she was a blushing beauty. No doubt about it, there'd be poetry at supper tonight — "My heart's a red running ulcer, / Putrefact, till your love's sweet lance / Should cauterize and console her" — but it's a small price to pay to be rid of him for a whole afternoon.

The first thing she does is throw open the window. Outside the grass has gone from yellow to green, feathers flash in the trees, and the rich raw odor of sodden earth hangs in the air. "Cheep-cheep," call the mavises, chaffinches and whinchats, anathematizing one another from the rooftops and hedges. A breeze bellies the curtains and the sun throws rhomboids on the floor. Behind her the fish stir in their tank. She begins to feel restless. She feeds her doves and dace, waters her plants. Starts a book, walks the dog, pulls out her sketchpad. Makes a tongue sandwich, bakes some scones. Sits at her spinet and tears through an up-tempo version of "Edom

O'Gordon." Stares at the clock. Finally she goes to her desk, unlocks the drawer, removes a letter and tucks it into her dress. Then slips out of the room like a thief. Into the vestibule, down the front steps, across the morass of the lane and into the wood beyond.

Ferns line the path like sentinels, clots of shadow gather beneath the bushes. The air is a transfusion. From the pond, the falsetto trill of the spring peepers calling for creeks-creeks-creeks. She's seen them there, bug-eyed and blistered, trailing coils of mucus, crawling atop one another, foaming, seething, humping. Her feet pad over coupling earthworms, sprouting seeds, the hem of her dress tousles wild geranium and saxifrage, toadflax and meadow rue, gathering pollen, dispersing it. The letter is from Mungo. His last. She's read it through a dozen times, and she'll read it through again, on a bluff above the Yarrow, slugs and bugs and grubs mounting one another at her feet, larks twittering overhead, doing it on the wing, the whole world going at it in the slow persistent grind of beating blood and thirsting tissue.

> Pisania, The Gambia.
> 14 July, 1795

My Life,

   A touch of the fever, some worms, emaciation, hair loss — nothing to worry over. I am fit and fine so far as outward appearances go. But oh what an ache in my heart! Leeches, flies, food fit for dogs — I endure it all gladly for the fleetingest memory of you. You who sweeten my dreams here in this place of heat and rot, you who give me courage to forge on, you who give me a reason to survive where no other could. Ailie: I'll sniff out the Niger and be back by spring. Will you wait for me?

   When I'm at my lowest ebb, when it seems as if the rains will never let up and I'll be stuck in this hole eternally, I think of you. And then my heart stirs and I think of da Gama rounding the Cape, Balboa gazing on the Pacific, and I know this is the life!

   I remain your faithful and affectionate scaler of peaks, forder of rivers and plumber of the Unknown,

> Mungo

P.S. Have met and engaged Johnson, a fine stalwart fellow, intelligent and articulate, a credit to the Negro race. It is his expectation that we shall encounter no real impediment so long as we avoid Ludamar, the Moorish kingdom.

The sun is a weight. She closes her eyes. Mungo is seventeen, hair like spilled barley, muscles hammered into his shoulders, her father's apprentice. From the far end of the dinner table she grins at him. He lifts his head from the soup, grins back. They have a secret. She's fourteen. Her chest is flat as a child's. In the fields, she raises her blouse for him.

When she wakes it's nearly dark. A rabbit crouches in a pocket of grass, ears pressed back, watching her. She sits up, folds the letter with all the reverence of a votary folding up the Shroud of Turin, and slips it back into her pocket. At home they're waiting supper. Gleg bats his eyes at her through the kidney pie, fowl, collops and pease pottage, while her father dissertates on the approved method of removing a gangrenous limb. Afterward, the old man takes her aside. "You're a grown woman of two and twenty," he says, "and you maun be findin' yourself a mate. Gleg's as good as any, by my way of thinkin', even if he be a bit of a shit-for-brains."

"You know I'm waiting for Mungo," she says.

The old man stares at the floor for a long moment, the lines in his face gradually marshaling themselves into the stern, pious and pitiless expression he puts on when breaking bad news to his patients. I'm afraid it's a cancer. Brain fever. Vitriolic liver. His eyebrows knit until he begins to look like God's uncle. "Much as I hate to say it," he whispers, "I'm afraid you canna count overmuch on the lad's returnin'."

◆§ ᘒᕽ

That night she finds a locket on her pillow. Gold, in the shape of a heart, Cupids jessant round the perimeter. She flips it open. There is a portrait inside. She recognizes herself, naked to the waist. Beside her, his arm stretched across her chest in a gesture of protective modesty, is Gleg. Naturally.

◆§ NITTY-GRITTY

They come for him in the dead of night, like demons or apparitions. Three of them. Daggers, dirks, falchions, muskets. "Get up, slave." The voice is throaty, remorseless. "Ali wants you." He'd been dreaming of Scotland, of emerald slopes and glacial lakes, of silver salmon cakewalking up the falls where the Gala soughs into the Tweed. And now he's wrenched from sleep like an infant from the womb, a sudden deep primordial panic beating at his ribs. Fatima, he thinks. The jig is up. He is instantly seized with attacks of perspiration, indigestion, gas, guilt and fear. Will they try him by fire? Brand his chest with an *A*? No, of course not. The dark ages reign out here. Justice and retribution are synonymous, swift and sudden. No time for such niceties as peer pressure, no room in the system for rehabilitation. They cut out the tongue of a liar, hack the hand from a thief . . . And an adulterer?

There are hands under his armpits. He is jerked roughly to his feet and shoved through the flaps of the tent, propelling him over the supine forms of the seven narcoleptic guards in the entranceway. *"Wallah!"* they cry. *"Shaitan!"* "Son of a bitch!" The night air is dry as an oatcake, and surprisingly cold. He finds himself trembling. Behind him, his escort joke in low tones, feet hissing through the sand, weapons jangling and clanking like an armory in motion. Should he run for it? — or buck up and face the music? When he was eight he and his brother set fire to the henhouse. Adam denied it. Mungo faced the music — and took a thrashing that would have melted iron and fused rock. Even now the memory of that thrashing tingles in his thighs and buttocks, implanted deep in the nerve fibers and knotted cords of muscle, a memory beyond words, beyond reason. All at once it hits him: he'll run for it.

Unfortunately, however, the men at his heels are members of Ali's elite cavalry, known for their courage, decision and quickness of reflex. Before he can so much as spring from the block a musket is introduced between his legs and he finds himself face down in the sand. The hands grope beneath his armpits again, hoist him up as if he were a drunk or a toddler learning to walk, and steer him through the still, silent camp — past tethered horses, sleeping dogs and ghostly blocks of canvas — right on up to the cookfire snarling before Ali's tent.

Ali is surrounded by counselors and courtiers. Dassoud is there. One-Eye. The Nubian. He is squatting beside the fire, dirk in hand, toasting bits of meat. The leaping garish light plays off the hook of his nose, cuts into the cheekbones, narrows his deadly eyes. Crouching there before the fire, testy and watchful, greedily gobbling up the kill at his feet, he looks like a colossal bird of prey, something terrible and leathery left over from the Saurian Age. The explorer expects the worst.

Ali blows at a piece of meat, takes a sip of hoona tea. Then bares his teeth, drawing the morsel into his mouth. He gestures at the explorer with the point of his knife. "Saddle — " he begins, breaking off to gnash at a piece of gristle, "saddle your . . . horse." He swallows with a click and grunt, then turns back to the fire with another hunk of raw flesh. "We leave for Jarra in an hour."

Mungo is stunned. Jarra! Why that must be sixty or seventy miles south of here! For weeks, as the monsoon season drew closer and Ali's withdrawal to the north more imminent, the explorer had been begging

Fatima to intercede in his favor — to petition for his release, or at least for the opportunity to make short forays from Benowm. He shuddered to think what would happen if he were still a prisoner when Ali gathered his herds and tents and horses for the summer migration to the skirts of the Great Desert. They'd skin and disembowel him. Cut his throat. Stake him out on the dunes to shrivel up like a fig. His bones would whiten in the sun like the sad remains of the slaves Johnson had told him of, like Houghton's bones, shattered by the years, no longer Irish, Celtic, Caucasian — merely bones, the bones of a man, the bones of an animal. He has a quick image of his own skull, wind-burnished, half buried in sand, and the slink and shuffle of a spotted hyena, its face blank and stupid, raising an unhurried leg to piss in the empty eyesocket. The explorer blinks, shakes his head as if to clear it — and then realizes that they're all watching him. Jarra! He grabs for the hem of Ali's burnoose, thinking to kiss it, but Dassoud slaps his hand away. *"An' am Allah 'alaik,"* blurts Mungo, thanking the Emir profusely amid a flurry of bows and curtsies. Ali, impassive as a stone, stares into the fire, and chews.

◄ε ϧ►

It is said that when a Sahelian Moor dies and finds himself amidst the searing fires of hell, his spirit invariably returns to earth — for a blanket. Mungo can believe it. They've been on the road for nearly eight hours now, and the sun is directly overhead. It must be a hundred and forty degrees in the shade — if there were any shade. The creatures who live here — the golden gopher, the white lady spider, various beetles, bugs and stinging things, scorpions, skinks and mole rats — are of course buried deep in the sand. Mungo, in his beaver top hat, nankeen trousers and blue frockcoat, is out in the sun, traveling, the swollen bundles of his restored tradegoods rattling at his back. He is hemmed in by scrub and cactus, sandbur and euphorbia, a landscape of the palest green and a thousand shades of brown, from khaki to ecru to russet. The hills are pale and scoured, ribbed like the remains of antediluvian beasts stretched across the horizon. There are baboons in these hills, purple-assed, crew-cut, short of brow, long of tooth. "Yeek-a-yeek-a-yeek!" they screech. "Chip-chip-chip!"

In a month it will be green here. There will be rivers, ponds, puddles. Deadly cobras will part the grass side by side with three-step adders and the crested lizard called tomorrow-never-comes. Duikers will appear, skirting from shade to shade. Pangolins, guibas, caracals and chamas. Wood storks, gaunt as refugees, secretary birds with their ragged braids and hawk's legs and partiality for cold-blooded lunches. Addax, puku, eland and oribi. Aoudads, korins, mhorrs and mambas. Hartebeests. Wild asses. Rats the size of piglets . . .

But for now, it's pretty bleak. And dry. So dry the saddles crack with a groan, hairs fall like leaves, a stream of urine evaporates in mid-arc. This is where the business of exploring gets down to the nitty-gritty. Sitting at the foot of the big mahogany table in St. Alban's Tavern and gazing up into the rapt, florid and bewhiskered faces of the African Association, the explorer never dreamed it would be like this — so confused, so demeaning. And so hot. He had pictured himself astride a handsome mount, his coat pressed and linen snowy, leading a group of local wogs and half-wits and kings to the verdant banks of the river of legend. Yet here he is, not at the head, but somewhere toward the rear of the serpentine queue wending its way through all this parch, a prisoner for all intents and purposes, his horse wheezing and farting, his underwear binding at the crotch. Is there no sense of proportion in the world?

Half a mile ahead, spatters of white and black, Ali and Dassoud undulate over the plain on their chargers. The two hundred members of the elite cavalry, mounted on equine panthers and lions, fan out behind them for nearly a mile. Some of the younger and more enthusiastic horsemen make forays into the scrub to run down the occasional monitor or skink, lop a bush here, a succulent there. For the others, despite the heat, the whole thing is nothing more than a party on the hoof. They're busy passing pipes and *guerbas,* telling dirty tales about camels and veils and virgins, jolting the solemn hills with explosions of laughter.

The explorer turns to survey the scene behind him, trying to decide whether he's part of a military expedition or a foxhunt, when a sudden flash of light catches his eye in the far distance. It is Johnson, mounted on his doleful blue ass (an animal remarkable for its lugubrious length of muzzle and ear), just now making his way over the lip of the horizon. The explorer raises his arm and waves. And there! — a movement inveigled by the distance and the rippling corrugations of the air — Johnson is waving back!

◄ AEOLIAN

Jarra is a town of a thousand wattle huts, give or take a few. It lies just south of the Sahel, on the border of Ludamar, Kaarta and Bambarra. One approaches the town through a series of gentle yeasty hills rising out of the

plain like bubbles in batter. This time of year the hills are pocked with
blackened stubble, a consequence of the villagers' burn-and-bloom philosophy. Fires raged here a month ago. Bands of flame coruscating along the
dark line of the earth, roiling billows darkening the sky. It went particularly hard on the rats. Legions of them, like migrant lemmings, foaming out of
the holocaust and into the path of the entire assembled village. The Jarrans
lifted rakes and hoes and cudgels, bursting rats like so much wet pottery.
They harvested blood.

These are the grazing lands, broken here and there by close stands of
wood — karite, kapioka and two-ball nitta, doum palm and acacia. Beyond
them, cultivated fields fan out round the village walls like the upturned
palms of sleeping giants, etched and furrowed, patiently waiting to snatch
up the first random drops from the sky. There is a river too — the
Woobah — now just a succession of puddles seething with tails and scales.
It slinks out of the woods as if ashamed of itself, meanders through the
village like a drunk, then disappears in the grassland beyond. The rest is
just about what you'd expect. Dusty streets, consumptive cattle, women
with haunted eyes and children with distended bellies and hunger-bleached
hair. These are the hard times, the long lingering days before the rains.
Udders dry, grain reserves shot — even the insipid nitta pods in short
supply.

Ali and his retinue boom onto the scene in a storm of white dust,
scowling and black-bearded, fierce and vain. Villages like this are fair game
for the Moors — for Kafirs live here, unbelievers, and not only is it the
sacred duty of all good Muslims to spread the word of Allah, but Kafirs are
notoriously feeble at defending themselves. Hence: fair game. The illiterate blacks of Jarra — Mandingoes for the most part — fall conveniently
into the Kafir category, though nearly all of them have informally adopted
the tenets of Islam. The Moors glance down at the prayer rugs, sandals,
jubbahs, and then up at the flat black faces. They're not fooled. To them
the Jarrans are a sort of inferior subspecies, nonhuman really, a race
designed by Allah to milk the goats and butter the bread of the Chosen
People, namely themselves. Thus, Kafir cattle, Kafir children, Kafir
women, grain, jewelry, huts, the very clothes on their backs, are considered as properly belonging to the Moors. When Ali's boys thunder into
town, you can be sure it's not just to see the sights.

On this occasion, however, rapine and plunder are not foremost in Ali's
mind. He has long since established a system of extortion with Jarra and
other Kafir towns within his compass. He sells them protection, assessing
so much produce and so many bolts of cloth in return. If he gets what he

asks, he leaves them alone. If not, he hacks half the villagers to pieces and takes twice as much. The reason for the present visit has nothing to do with protecting the Jarrans from himself, but with protecting them from the Kaartans. A simple case of power politics. Yambo II, the headman of Jarra, had sided with Bambarra in the ongoing conflict between Tiggitty Sego of Kaarta and Mansong of Bambarra. At the time it seemed the expeditious thing to do: Mansong was really tearing them up, hewing to the right, gouging to the left. But since then there had been a number of reversals, the Bambarrans had fallen back, and Tiggitty Sego, mother-murdering mad over the Jarrans' defection, was now advancing on the town to chastise them. And so Yambo, at the cost of three hundred head of cattle and nineteen virgins under the age of twelve, had hired Ali to bail him out.

◦ ◦

Long after the dust has settled, the explorer makes his grand entrance. On foot. He is limping slightly, and leading his horse by the rein. During the course of the journey the animal has drooled steadily, bled from the anus, vomited, pitched forward into the dirt twice, and gone lame in three of its four legs. The upshot is that the explorer has had to hoof it himself for the last twenty miles or so. As he hobbles into town, the Jarrans come out to line the streets and scrutinize him. Colorful people: faces like licorice, big hoop earrings, strings of beads and cowrie shells winking in their hair, skirts and sashes pulsing red, yellow and orange like a thousand flags. Colorful, but quiet. There's not a stir through the entire crowd, not a whisper, not a grin. The meditation room at a Carthusian monastery would have been noisy by comparison. The explorer, thinking he may have overawed them, does his best to look harmless and unassuming. At his side, Johnson bobs along on the blue ass, fat and serene as a potentate. From time to time he raises a chubby palm to salute one of the sirens in the crowd or swat at a fly. Bringing up the rear is Dassoud, strutting along on a charger the size of a park statue. Keeping an eye on things.

The explorer's immediate desires are pretty basic: a mug of water, a plate of mush, a mat on which to throw his weary bones. Under normal circumstances he would have been provided with all this and more. For the Mandingoes of Jarra are a friendly and hospitable people — they've already groomed and watered Ali's thundering herd, and slaughtered eight bullocks for his dinner. But just as Mungo draws into town, the wind begins kicking up. Kicking up violently in fact. The coattails fly up over his head, his hat lifts off like a kite on an updraft and his ears begin to roar as if someone has suddenly clapped seashells to them. Behind him, the horse whinnies and farts, its mane foaming round its ears. Suddenly a wall collapses with a groan, and a thatched roof takes off like a flock of vultures flushed from the kill. This is wind!

"Whooo!" he says, turning to Johnson. But Johnson, along with Dassoud and everyone else in sight, is bolting headlong in the opposite direction. He stands there, puzzled. "What's the rush?" he shouts. "It's nothing but a little breeze." The wind whistles. The sky goes dark. A hut skitters by. And then he hears it — a harsh sibilance, a spitting ticking release of air, as if all Edinburgh, Glasgow and the Borderlands had turned out to hiss the villain in a melodrama. All at once he's terrified. He takes to his legs — but too late! WHOMP! The horse blows down. And then he is himself knocked to his knees, suddenly stung in every pore of his body as if he'd blundered into a hive of bees. Sand! It's a sandstorm!

He scrambles to his feet, the jacket beating round his head like the wings of the devil and all his legions. There is sand in his eyes, his ears, up his nose, down his throat. Suddenly an airborne goat cracks him across the shoulderblades and down he goes again. He fights up, staggering, and an empty calabash rebounds off his head like an asteroid, and then — SLAP! — a guinea hen catches him flush in the face and he's down for the count. Up again, down again. This is getting serious. "Help!" he screams. SSSSSS-SSSShhhhhhhhhhhhhh! hushes the sand. He can't breathe, his lungs are filled with it; he's gone blind, crawling over wind-strewn refuse, minidunes, kettles and spoons, tattered blankets, the corpses of goats or milch cows. Where to go? Is this the way it ends? But then he feels a pressure on the back of his neck, a hand there, an arm. He grabs at the hand and follows it along the ground, creeping like a rodent, the shriek in his ears, things batting at his head, the wild wind clutching at his lungs like a pair of hot tongs . . .

◄§ §►

'Hey, Mr. Park," rumbles the voice of Johnson, "don't you know enough to come in out of the sand?"

The explorer, fighting the dry heaves, does not respond. His eyes are crusted over and someone has been building sand castles in his ears. He has no idea where he is.

"You coulda had the hide confricated right off you, you know that? I mean a sandstorm is nothin' to fuck around with."

The explorer is groggy. He doesn't know where he is or how he got here, and he can't see a damned thing. Is it night already? There is the sound of wind, the hiss of sand. "Johnson," he says, " — is that you?"

Instead of answering, Johnson's voice slips into Mandingo, and the explorer is startled to hear laughter blooming in the darkness around him. What is going on here? "Johnson?"

"*Obo weebo jalla 'imsta, kootatamballa,*" says Johnson, and the laughter bursts out afresh. And then: "Don't you worry, Mr. Park — we're in safe hands."

"But where are we? And how did we get here?"

"Root cellar. I walked, you was dragged."

So that's it. He must have been unconscious all this time. But whose voices are these, and why this impenetrable, godawful darkness? He detects a whisper, somewhere close by, followed by a giggle. And then the maddening swish and tinkle of liquid swirled in a jar. "Johnson," he calls. "Couldn't we do with a little light in here?"

"I think it can be arranged," says Johnson, whose voice abruptly changes direction, and in resonant, jocular tones wades through a muddle of Mandingo *m*'s and *k*'s and long smooth double *o*'s. Other voices — grunts really — answer from the void. After a moment or two the explorer becomes aware of a low, barely distinguishable sound from the far side of the room: a murmur, a rustle, the gentle soughing of treebranches rubbing in the wind. He is puzzled at first, but then it comes to him: sticks. They're chafing sticks! A second later there's a spark, and then a hungry flame swelling from a handful of shavings to illuminate the room.

What he sees is this: five men, black and knobby, sitting against the earthen wall passing a calabash and holding it to their lips. One of them is Johnson. The others are Jarran Mandingoes, feet splayed, baggy knees, noses pushed back into their heads. Each wears a white toque set atop his crown like a mushroom, and a variegated sash that runs from shoulder to crotch and back again. The soles of their feet are the color of smoked salmon. The gentleman closest to the explorer, a toothless relic with a concave chest, offers up the calabash. Mungo takes it gladly. As he tips his head back, the fire winks out — but no matter, he's more concerned with the business at hand than with peering into crannies. He gulps and guzzles, flushing the sand out from under his gums and between his teeth. He rinses, gargles, drinks deep, the dark a comfort, his thirst boundless, all thought, sensation and reflex held in abeyance to this single-faceted ecstasy, this pouring of liquid into the buccal cavity and down the esophagus. But then a weathered hand makes contact with his own, and he's forced to give up the calabash. "Damned good stuff, Johnson," he murmurs, addressing the darkness and hiccoughing between syllables. "Reminds me of a good Irish stout."

From the corner, the voice of Johnson, muttering. "Good as anythin' them potato pluckers ever come up with. Better. That's *sooloo* beer you drinkin' there, Mr. Park. *Sooloo* beer. Black-roasted sorghum malt and the purest spring water, aged and krausened in strict accord with a ancient and closely guarded tribal formula. Hey — this is the cradle of civilization here, Mr. Park. Who you think was around this planet first anyway — us — or them bleached-out Hibernians? This is beer, brother."

There is something unfamiliar in Johnson's delivery. His words are sluggish and chewed-over, his tone combative. And his pitch deeper than ever — the sort of thing you'd expect from the banks of a pond on a summer's night. Could it be that he's had one pull too many at the calabash? "Are you drunk, Johnson?"

"Drunk?" he repeats, his basso scraping bottom. "Hell, yes. Drunk as a emir."

At that moment an exceptionally virulent gust rattles the cane-and-earthen floor above them, and a quantity of sand explodes across their faces like buckshot.

"Blow, winds, and crack your cheeks!" bellows Johnson. "Rage! Blow!"

An idea had been forming in the explorer's head — something to do with the fact that this was the first time in nearly six months that he's been left unguarded. But the sudden gust and Johnson's exclamation have driven it right out of his head. Besides, someone has just passed him the calabash.

✺ YOU CAN'T KEEP A GOOD MAN DOWN

When they first spotted him they thought he'd been dead for days. His hands and chin were fast-frozen to a block of ice and the fluid in his eyes had turned to slush. He was bobbing there like a piece of driftwood, the black waters of the Thames lapping round his shoulders and ears.

"Wa' is it, Liam?"

"Doan't know, Shem: looks like a dead mon, and drownded."

Shem Leggotty and Liam McClure were fishermen. Six days a week they set their gill nets for salmon and sturgeon coming upriver with the tide. The fish would blunder into these nets, catch their gills in the three-inch mesh, thrash about and drown. Sometimes they would thrash about and escape. It was all in the cards. This night, as the men tugged at the net, it felt somehow different, peculiar. It wasn't the weight — a good sturgeon could go ten feet long and five hundred pounds — it was just the feel of the thing.

A bitter wind stabbed at the back of their throats. Their hands were raw. Was it an ice floe? A log? When Shem lit a lantern to investigate, there he was, riding the swell like a man three days dead.

"So it's a drownded mon, then. And froze."

"That it is."

"Well then. Let's cut the poor beggar loose and be on with it. He's no consarn of ours."

They tugged at the net. As the drowned man came into contact with the bow of the boat, his head knocked against the planks with a crack, wood on wood. "Ik," he said.

"Wa' was that, Liam?"

"I didna say nothin', Shem."

The drowned man bobbed at their feet as they worked to disentangle him. His mouth was frozen open and the tongue welded to his teeth. "Ik," he said.

"Sweet Jaysus, the mon's aloive! Here, help me get him into the boat, Shem." Liam's breath hung in the air in clumps. He was a monument of sinew and brawn, case-hardened by years of hauling nets and brawling on the docks. He bent his back to the drowned man and heaved him up into the skiff, ice floe and all. The drowned man was naked from the waist down and wrapped in a sodden cape.

"Get some blankets round him, Shem. And hand me the usquebaugh."

"The usquebaugh? That's as like to kill him off as bring him round."

It was a home brew, potent as fire. Liam poured it down the man's throat while Shem pried his chin and fingers from the block of ice. The effect was almost instantaneous — the dead man lifted his head, vomited and fell unconscious. "Ik-ik," he said.

⌘ CHICHIKOV'S CHOICE

Fishstink. For the past three months it's been fishstink, day and night. The oily stink of eels taken from the green water among the pilings, the salt-stench of skate and mackerel, the cold mud reek of pouters and perch and carp. He's snuffed them all — tench and bream and saury pike, bearded ling, gouty blowfish, alewives, hake and haddock — plucked out their entrails, whacked off their heads, set the air afire with their flashing translucent scales. It's a grim, stinking, thankless job.

But safe. And safety is everything. That and invisibility. He'd made a lot of enemies that fateful night — Smirke, who was fined and sentenced to three hours in the pillory; Mendoza, Brummell and the others, whose names appeared in the paper the following afternoon; Nan and Sal, who wound up in Bridewell until they were bailed out by the Forlorn Female Fund of Mercy; and Lord Twit, who was publicly upbraided for consenting to the moral corruption of his black nigger servant. A lot of enemies — but none of them suspected he'd risen from the dead. And Ned Rise was not about to disabuse them.

So here he is, in the Leggotty Brothers' fish shop, Southwark, breathing fishstink, hacking away at cold bloodless flesh in a welter of dumb-staring eyes. They pulled him from the river, Shem and McClure, three-quarters dead, and then nursed him for a week till he came round. He was penniless, having jettisoned pants, boots and bulge in a frantic effort to stay afloat. They offered him a job and a place to sleep. Fish chowder and black bread twice a day. Liam loaned him a pair of trousers. "All right," said Ned.

It's not that he's ungrateful — he just isn't cut out to be a fisherman. The nets slip through his hands, the oarlocks have a mind of their own, he's afraid of the water, boats, oars, docks, the smell of fish turns his stomach. He can hardly swim. What's more, he's fed up with their dull talk and duller lives ("Aye," says Liam, sucking at his pipe like a sage, "a storm'll either take 'em or bring 'em"), and he longs for the gaming tables, the coffeehouses, the Pig & Pox and the Vole's Head. Southwark is nothing but a festering slum, the hind end of the earth. How can you expect to rise in the world if you're stuck in a fish shop in Southwark? He hacks at the heads and fins. He grows despondent.

Then one afternoon, as he's stripping the scutes and hide from a shortnose sturgeon, an idea hits him. A modest idea, but one that combines invisibility and profit both. He looks round for someone to break the news to. Shem and Liam are out back in the alley, passing a jug and spitting in the dirt.

"You know wha' they got over there in Africa, Liam?"

"Hamadryads?"

"Nope. They got river perch six hunnert pund."

"Go on."

"It's true. Ned read it to me out of the *Evenin' Post*."

"Six hunnert pund?"

"In the River Nigel. There's this young Scotsman disappeared up there tryin' to bring one back."

"Go on."

Ned wipes the blood and fishslime from his hands and steps through the doorway. "I've got an idea," he says.

Liam salutes him with the jug. "Well then lad, have yerself a snootful o' mother's finest and tell the old graybeards all about it."

Ned takes a slug, pounds his breastbone and asks them if they've ever heard of caviar.

"That's Latin, isn't it?" says Liam.

"What I'm talking about is fish roe — sturgeon's eggs. Here we are throwing away fistfuls of the stuff, when all the nobs over in the West End are paying the Russians three pounds a jar for it."

"Three pund a jar? For offal?"

"It's na offal, Liam — the Swedes eat it."

"Bah, the iggorant squareheads. They gobble up pickled heering too, doan't they?"

"Leave it to me," says Ned. "I'll strain it and salt it myself, undercut the Empress by half and peddle it door-to-door from Tottenham Court to Mayfair. You watch: we'll be rich inside of a month."

◄§ §►

A month later, Ned Rise strolls across Westminster Bridge in false nose and spectacles, white periwig, silk hose and brocaded waistcoat, a rich man. Or comparatively so. Chichikov's Choice (named after a whaling companion of Shem's brother Japheth) is selling like lemonade at a track meet. Gentlemen's clubs, coffeehouses, taverns, inns and even private residences are buying up Ned's caviar as fast as he can bottle it. "The finest Russian caviar," he tells them, his voice lingering over the double s and the final rumbling r, " — at half the price." It gets them every time. From parlormaids to head cooks to the white-capped chefs at Brooke's or White's. He pitches, they buy. Within the month, half the haut monde is spreading its crackers with Chichikov's Choice.

And the beauty of the whole thing, Ned reflects, as he strides along with a basket of fish roe under his arm, is that the stuff is practically free to begin with. It's like bottling air and selling it for one and ten the bottle. There is an outlay, it's true — he gives Liam and Shem two shillings a fish out of gratitude, pays a penny the dozen for terra-cotta jars and labels, and sixpence a day to a pair of street kids who strain and salt the stuff for him. But that's nothing. A good fish will hold twenty or thirty pounds of roe — so for an outlay of a few shillings here and there he'll recoup thirty or forty quid. It's like a dream. Of course, he can't count on its lasting forever — he knows that. For one thing, sturgeon only breed for two months out of the year — April and May — and so his egg supply will be tapering off soon enough. Then too, Shem and Liam are bound to wise up and ask for a bigger cut . . . But for now, Ned Rise is riding an updraft: the Bank of the Bulge is solvent again, and under the bed of his new lodgings in Bear Lane an iron chest is slowly turning to silver.

On this particular morning — a morning struck through with sun and birds and bloom — Ned is off to try his luck on some of the households round Berkeley and Soho squares. As he traverses the grim dark line of the bridge, he breaks into an energetic whistle and begins twirling his cane. The wind off the river ruffles his wig. A gull coasts by overhead. "Ah! The glory of life!" he thinks, striding along like a young lord on his way to an afternoon at croquet. But when he reaches the far side of the bridge, a sudden change comes over him. It's as if the God of the Spastics has touched him with his crooked wand: his limbs contort, tongue goes awry, neck falls loose. Suddenly he's round-shouldered and stooped, dragging his leg as if it were cut from a tree — and now there's a tic under his left eye and his shoulder has begun to buckle. Is it an attack? Convulsions? Tic douloureux? Ned smirks with satisfaction as passersby back away from him in alarm. "Gah," he says to them, chewing at his tongue and holding up his mutilated hand like a badge. "Gah," he says, lurching up the street like a dog with a broken back. All this of course is part of his design to escape detection — he likes to think of it as his "mantle of invisibility." The false nose and spectacles, the outmoded dress, the tics and twitches, the palsied walk — why he's just another harelipped cripple peddling fish eggs in the street. God Himself, come Judgment Day, wouldn't recognize him in this getup.

He crabwalks up Great George Street, through St. James's Park and across the Mall, limping and scraping like a terminal syphilitic, when suddenly he hears a voice call out behind him. "Ned Rise! Ned Rise! Wait up a minute there!"

It's Boyles, the ass, his face flushed with drink and hurry. "Ned!" he puffs, jogging up to him. "We thought you was dead. Drownded in the river. Why, when I seen you roundin' the corner back there I couldn't hardly believe me eyes."

Ned shrinks into his jacket and pulls the three-cornered hat down over his brow. His head and limbs are flapping like wash in the wind. A battery of tics surges across his face.

Boyles has a hand on his sleeve. "But wot's the anty-quated weeds for? And all this limpin' and cringin'? Did you catch the ague or is it just a bit of play-actin'?"

The world is coming down round his ears, a piece of the sky has broken off and clapped him in the back of the head. He can't think. His hands are trembling. Twit, Smirke, Mendoza — they'll be down on him like hounds. "Ohhhh — I gets it. You're in disguise, then. Am I royt? Eh, Ned? Am I royt? Layin' low, is it?"

Ned glances round, takes hold of Boyles' arm and leads him down a back alley. A dead dog lies in the dirt beside a broken parasol. Out on the Mall, people of ton clip by in carriages. "How did you know it was me, Billy?"

"You kiddin'? I'd spot you a mile off, Ned Rise. A little foot-draggin' and a false nose isn't goin' to help you any. I conned you plain as day."

So much for the mantle of invisibility. "Listen, Billy. You can't let on that you've seen me. If Mendoza and Smirke and the rest found out about it — "

"They'd eat you alive, Neddy. Mendoza come lookin' for you the next mornin', and Smirke cursed you up and down for a week after his public yoomiliation. Ha! You should of seen that, Ned — Smirke in the pillory. I let him have it with half a dozen rotted turnips and a dead cat. Gorry, it was good fun."

But Ned's not listening. He turns his back preoccupied, and digs deep in his knee breeches, fumbling about for crown and shilling, fishing for hush money.

"I'll say this for him, though," Boyles coughs, blowing a wad of bloody sputum into a rag of a handkerchief, "he felt heartsore about cursin' you after he found out you was drownded. He set up the house for you, Ned — three times! And Nan and Sal — you should of seen 'em carry on. The two of 'em went out and nicked black bonnets and screens and all to sorrify their faces, and then they threw a armful of geraniums into the river for memory of you . . . no, you didn't go to your grave unmourned, be assured of that, Neddy."

Ned swings round and holds up a coin. "For you, Billy," he says. "For your discretion. You never saw me, right? I'm dead and gone, right?"

"You can count on me, Ned. I won't breathe a word."

◄§ ESCAPE!

Mungo wakes with a headache. He has been drinking *sooloo* beer — a.k.a. *bobootoo das* — juggler of legs, scrambler of minds. He has been drinking *sooloo* beer and he is not quite certain where he is. A cellar certainly. He recognizes the yellow earthen walls, the roots and rhizomes, the cane ceiling, the ladder. Yes. No doubt about it. A cellar. He raises himself wearily to his elbows and discovers an empty calabash between his legs and a flocculent head across his ankle. The head belongs to Johnson, who is sprawled over the floor with his cronies in a farrago of limbs and feet, his great belly rising and falling like some elemental force of nature. All five are snoring serenely, teeth whistling, lips vibrating, tonsils flapping in the breeze.

It occurs to him that it must be morning, since the blackness he experienced earlier has now given way to the sort of soupy crepuscular light one expects of crypts, wine cellars and other damp and unsalubrious places. He rubs at a spot on his neck where something has bitten him during the night, and glances up as a glossy black scarab struggles across the floor with a ball of dung the size of an apple. He is sitting there, propped on his elbows, watching the beetle and waiting patiently for his head to clear, when the first cry sounds from above. It's more a gasp actually, an insuck of surprise, tailed almost immediately by a prolonged wail, plaintive and despairing. Then a hurried exchange of voices — monosyllables thrown back and forth like tennis balls — the sound of feet rushing on the bamboo floor above, silence. The explorer cocks his head and gradually becomes aware of a whole undercurrent of noise emanating from beyond the house, out in the streets. A hum, building now to a roar — it seems as if the very earth is alive with it. He's puzzled. Is it an earthquake? Stampede? Another sandstorm?

Ever curious, the explorer rises and crosses to the ladder, Johnson's head slapping down behind him with a dull thump. Just as he steps on the first rung, however, a flap opens in the ceiling above and he finds himself confronted with a bony posterior and a pair of naked soles, descending. The explorer backs off as a shrunken little man makes his way down the ladder, slow and oblivious, dangling in the air like an arthritic spider. At the base of the ladder the little man plants his feet, turns round, and then starts back violently at the sight of the explorer.

He is old, this little man — ancient, antediluvian. His hair is white and corrugated, his face lined like a river delta. He is five foot nothing, ninety-five pounds, looks as if he's been carved from a shadow. Around his neck a throttled chicken, stiff with rigor mortis, dangles from a cord. There is an awkward moment as explorer and gnome stand there toe to toe, the little man turning his big slow rolling eyes to the explorer, then looking away again, something between astonishment and indignation caught in the web of his face. He looks up once more, then turns away as if dismissing an apparition, bends to one of the sleeping men and begins piping in his ear. "*M'bolo rita Sego!*" he hoots. "*M'bolo bolo Sego!*"

The effect is instantaneous: Johnson and his retinue start up in unison, clutching at their chests and bugging their eyes, while the old man claps his hands and narrates a shrill tale of doom (Mungo is no linguist, but he can pick up repeated phrases like "cannibal," "child-skinner" and "Tiggitty Sego"). An instant later the five beer-drinkers are wringing their hands, running into one another and fighting for the ladder.

In his anxiety to escape, Johnson brushes past the explorer, who takes the opportunity to seize his arm. "What's up, Johnson? Is it Sego?"

The others are licking up the ladder like ants on a stick, while the old man teeters round the room scattering feathers. From above: the roar of cumulative panic.

"Quick!" shouts Johnson, tearing away like a crazed beast and clambering over the old man. "He's going to put Jarra to the torch!" Johnson hesitates at the top of the ladder. "No prisoners," he whispers.

◄§ §►

Outside, it's a scene from Milton or Dante: weeping and wailing, self-flagellation, misdirection, panic, loss of faith. Mothers run childless, children motherless. There is smoke and dust in the air, the rush of blood. One old man stands in the street whipping his ancient milch cow because it cannot heave up from the ground under the weight of the panniers slung over its shoulders. Another carries his wife, who carries her dog, who carries a scrap of cloth in its mouth. All over people are running and shouting, a mad urgency in the atmosphere, kicking through the drifts and rubble left by the storm, gathering sacks of grain, driving cattle: fleeing the little mud-walled village on the Woobah, the village where they were born.

The explorer, always somewhat slow to react (something in the genes), stands in the midst of all this sorrow and confusion wondering what to do. He can't very well join the exodus, as his horse and bags (restored to him at Fatima's insistence) were lost in the storm — and how far could he get on foot? Besides, Johnson's disappeared, and the Moors certainly wouldn't . . . but wait a minute — where are the Moors? It suddenly occurs to him that he hasn't laid eyes on a Mussulman in the last twelve hours at least . . . and then, even more suddenly, an insidious thought begins poking at the periphery of his brain — the very thought that was about to step out of the wings and announce itself last night when a weathered hand passed him the calabash: here at long last is his chance!

◄§ §►

What has transpired in Jarra is really quite elementary as the politics of war go. Ali, at some time during the night, experienced a crisis of divided priorities: his own best interest came into conflict with that of the Jarrans, who are, after all, merely Kafirs. After an evening of feasting and good-natured raping and extorting, he ordered ten of his men to select the three hundred fattest cattle from among the Jarran herds and to drive them into the wood where they'd be sheltered from the storm. This, he reasoned, was in his own best interest — merely protecting his investment. The Jarrans felt that Ali's move was ultimately in their best interest as well, as it constituted his acceptance of their payment in advance for his services. Three hundred cattle are alot to lose, but not when you consider the alternative — i.e., losing the entire herd, as well as your goats, crops, huts and daughters to the raging and mindless Tiggitty Sego, known far and wide for his bloodlusting and vindictive nature.

But late that night, after the storm had abated, another factor entered the equation: Ali learned that Sego's armies, taking advantage of the weather, had marched to within striking distance of Jarra, and that from there they planned an early morning attack. This intelligence precipitated Ali's crisis of priority. Since he'd already collected his virgins and his cattle, he reasoned that he was satisfied — and that by fighting the Kaartans he would certainly derive no further satisfaction, and in fact ran the risk of losing what he'd already gained. He didn't agonize long over the decision. Within minutes the tents were struck, his men mounted. They rode through the night, nineteen ex-virgins under their arms, driving the cattle before them. By the following evening they would be back at Benowm.

◆§ §◆

"Free at last!" thinks the explorer, jubilant in a slough of despond. A woman scuttles by, her life balanced in the earthen jar perched on her forehead. Mungo wants to dance with her, sing a song of deliverance, roar like a lion burst from his cage. "Hee-hee!" he laughs, tossing his hat as a group of stunted children dart past, swift, dark and furtive as rats. He kicks up his heels and begins whistling "Oh whare hae ye been a' day, my bonnie wee croodlin' dow?" as an old woman claws at the door of her hut, sobbing and pleading with the two men who tug at her arms. He flows along with the crowd, a silly grin on his face, as children cry for their mothers, cripples grope in the dust and women frantically snatch up provisions for the road. His plan is to head east with the refugees — horse or no horse — toward Bambarra. And the Niger.

On the far side of the village his conscience catches up with him, and he suddenly finds himself hoisting children, loading litters, pounding grain, prodding goats. The Jarrans, too harried and distraught to think twice, accept his hands and shoulders and then look up at him as if he were transparent. A cow here, a lost child there, wives and husbands reuinted on the road, they begin to move — passing the eastern gates, fording the Woobah, struggling up the distant rise, the town lying desolate at their backs. Things are beginning to run smoothly, the stragglers closing ranks, the whiners and shriekers running short of breath, when suddenly a fearsome rumor shoots through the crowd: Sego is coming! Sego! The crowd falls silent, momentarily stunned, while a heavyset woman in a babushka pushes her way through, broadcasting the news: "He burned Wassiboo during the night! Roasted children! Drank blood!"

This information is followed by a series of gasps and moans, and then finally by a long generalized screech like the screech of hogs scenting the butcher's block. Then they're off like the start of a marathon: heels and hoofs flying, dust rising in billows till it filters out the sun. "So this is mass hysteria," thinks Mungo, drawing back from the scene, until suddenly, as if he'd just wakened from a dream of falling, it seizes him. His pupils dilate, his breath comes in bursts. And then all at once he's running, bolting like a spooked mare, throwing aside the lame and halt, kicking at livestock, clawing for position. When he thinks to look back the field is already behind him and he's steaming up a hill past the fleetest of the teenage boys, loping athletes and spear carriers, running for his life, running for his liberty, running for all he's worth.

But then he rounds a bend and stops dead in his tracks — there, mounted astride his stallion like a colossus, is Dassoud, the reins of the explorer's horse in his hand. Beside him, perched dolefully on the doleful blue ass, is Johnson. Johnson shrugs his shoulders.

Dassoud gestures toward the waiting saddle, then slips the scimitar from his belt and points northward — in the direction of Benowm.

"Better climb aboard," says Johnson.

The explorer hesitates, crestfallen. The cries of the refugees echo round him; he can't seem to catch his breath.

"I'm tellin' you, Mr. Park, he means business."

As if on cue, Dassoud cuts the air with a titanic swipe of his sword. Something like a grin creases his lips.

Mungo mounts the horse.

᳹ ᳺ

An hour later, and miles from the road to Bambarra, the three horsemen are picking their way down a rocky slope littered with the remains of oryx and bushbuck, when suddenly Johnson reaches into his toga, produces a

silver-plated dueling pistol and shoots Dassoud's charger in the left eye.
The horse rears back, beating its head from side to side as if it were trying
to clear its ears, and collapses atop the Chief Jackal. "Let's make tracks!"
shouts Johnson, frantically lashing the backside of his ass as Dassoud
heaves up from beneath the dead horse. The explorer doesn't have to be
asked twice. He kicks his heels deep into Rocinante's flanks and the animal
breaks into a half-hearted canter, its lungs heaving like a bellows filled with
water. Meanwhile, Dassoud strips off his sandals and *jubbah,* touches his
toes four or five times, and takes off after them, scimitar clenched in his
teeth.

Johnson jogs over the rocks on his balky blue ass, Mungo bears down on
his stumbling nag. Ahead, an unbroken plain studded with scrub. Behind,
Dassoud, leaping hazards like a panther. "If we can m-m-make the p-plain
we'll hav-have him!" Johnson cries. Mungo holds on, and prays. Dassoud
is no more than twenty feet away, running like a bandit. Ten feet,
five — but now the smooth, hard-packed earth of the plain drums under
hoof and they begin to draw away from him. He falls back twenty feet, then
fifty, and Mungo begins to cheer. Johnson looks worried. "Why so glum?"
the explorer calls.

"You see the way that sucker is runnin'?"

Mungo glances over his shoulder. Dassoud has dropped back nearly a
hundred yards now. His face is set, the light fixed in his eyes. He is a naked
man, muscled like a statue, running against his heart and lungs, the sun
and the plain. "What of it?"

"He goin' to catch up with us, that's what."

The explorer's horse gears down from a canter to a walk, staggering
from one lame leg to another, the saddlebags clacking like maracas. The
ass cranes its neck to snap at Johnson's knee. Mungo is suddenly alarmed.
"Don't be ridiculous," he says. "We're mounted."

They jog along in silence. Dassoud pumps his arms, holding steady at a
hundred yards. The sun, of course, is like a freshly stoked smelting
furnace.

Johnson squints up at him, a sad and suffering look in his eye. "You
mean to tell me you never heard the stories about this maniac?"

"Unnhhhh," says the horse, slowing to a brisk amble. The ass sways
along beside it, ears in motion. Clotta-clot, clotta-clot, clot.

"No," says Mungo, something tightening in his groin. "I never heard."

ᴥ DASSOUD'S STORY

He was born at Az-Zawiya, on the Mediterranean coast of Libya, third son of a Berber sultan. When he was six he was caught in a stampede. Sharp black hoofs pounded over him for a quarter of an hour. He wasn't even bruised. At fourteen he joined his father in a punitive expedition against a party of Debbab Arabs. The Arabs were camped at the oasis of Al-Aziziyah, fires strung across the plain like a fallen constellation. Dassoud, at fourteen, was already over six feet tall. The firelight was lurid, there were the screams of the women. A man came at him with a pike. He disengaged the man's leg with a swipe of his scimitar, then crushed his collarbone and severed his head. The man retaliated by spurting blood in his face. Dassoud leaped back, shocked and dazed, his pulse pounding, the raw salt taste of blood on his lips . . . then went looking for more. Two days later his father was murdered. Sixteen Debbab renegades rode off across the desert for the bleak plateau of Al-Hammada al-Hamra. Dassoud followed them. One by one they died in the night.

When he was twenty he led a caravan across the Great Desert. Their destination was Timbuctoo, on the River Niger, sixteen hundred miles to the south. It was a difficult crossing. Sandstorms swallowed them, camels evaporated, wells ran dry. By the time they reached Ghat they'd lost nearly half their number. The sun rippled the horizon, dunes rolled off into the sky like waves on an iron sea. When the wells at Tamanrasset failed them, they fell on one another. Dassoud stood six feet four inches tall, two hundred thirty-five pounds. He was one of the survivors. The other twelve crowded round him. "We'll make for Taoudenni, in the northern reaches of Ludamar," he said. "It's our only chance."

The oasis of Taoudenni was set in a pocket of basaltic hills that rose up out of the sands like the molars of a half-buried giant. It had been the principal watering stop on the trip from Tamanrasset to Jarra since the days of the Prophet. Its wells were said to be inexhaustible. When the caravan drew within sight of the oasis they had been without water for three days, their eyelids swollen, throats raw. The trade goods — Persian rugs, salt, muskets, kif — trailed out behind them over the dunes, still lashed to the backs of rotting animals. As they approached the wells, the sole surviving camel stumbled and fell, its hoofs pedaling the void. One of the men cried out: impaled on the animal's foreleg was a human ribcage. The bones clacked and rattled, dice in a cup. The merchants looked round. There were hummocks in the sand — hundreds of them — a hand reaching out here, the back of a skull glistening there. Taoudenni was dry.

Dassoud claimed the camel. Two men challenged him. He killed them both. Then he bled the animal, drinking deep from the open artery and draining the excess into a *guerba*. He ate the inner organs, the lining of the stomach, moist and raw. When he last saw the others, they were huddled round a crack in the rock where there had once been water.

He traveled by night, unearthing insect larvae, scorpions and beetles by day. He crunched them like nuts, scanning the wind-scrawled dunes, his head gone light, his life at the far end of its tether. This amused him. The more hopeless it became, the stronger he felt. One night, alone in the universe and hopelessly lost, the *guerba* empty, his tongue sucking at the shell of a scorpion, he realized that he was enjoying himself. The desert was hard. He was harder. If the whim had taken him, he could have turned round and strolled back to Libya.

Two weeks after leaving Taoudenni, Dassoud stumbled across the well at Tarra. He drew a *guerba* from the depths and drank till he vomited. While vomiting he became aware of a shadow which had fallen over him, a shadow cast by three of Ali's elite horsemen. They were pointing their muskets at him as he knelt in the sand. Poaching from a well was as heinous a crime among the Moors as kidnapping or having sex with one's neighbor's livestock. The penalty was death. Dassoud listened to the click of the hammers. He was starved, dehydrated, exhausted, unarmed. The first man shot him through the elbow, the second brought a scimitar down across his face, the third was easy. When he finished with them he tore the leg from one of the horses, devoured it, and lay down to sleep. The following morning he rode into Benowm, thundered up to Ali's tent, and offered his services as henchman and human jackal.

◄§ ESCAPE! (CONT.)

"Well Jesus Christ, Mary, Joseph and All the Saints," says Mungo, glancing over his shoulder, "couldn't you have aimed a little higher?"

"Against my principles." Johnson is pounding along beside the ass now, his toga soaked through with sweat. "Shot," he wheezes, "a man once . . . back in London. Broke a boy's heart, uff-uff, never . . . forgive myself."

"Principles?" the explorer echoes, wondering how far principles go toward meliorating an early death.

Behind them, Dassoud shows no sign of letting up. In fact, for the past hour or so he's been hurling epithets at the explorer's back, his blade slashing in the sun as if to underscore his meaning. "Uncircumcised!" he roars. "Pig eater!"

Mungo pulls the hat down over his eyes, and has a vision of the kitchen at Selkirk: fresh-cut flowers, cold ham, Ailie smiling up at him. "You ever notice that fellow seems to have it in for me?"

"Ha!" says Johnson, rumbling along. "He hates you. Hates you the way a . . . beard hates a . . . razor or a balloon hates a . . . pin. It's nature. You . . . come onto the scene with your . . . your wheaty hair and catty eyes, a freak and a wonder," he puffs, gasping for breath. "Where you think that leaves him? You might just as well . . . expect a trash-yard cur to put up with a lapdog."

"Oh," says Mungo.

⋯⋯

The day wears on, Johnson silent and morose, the muzzle of the explorer's horse flecked with blood, Dassoud padding along with the grim determination of a wolf running down its quarry. The horse is a problem. The explorer has been sparing it as much as possible by periodically dismounting and jogging the odd mile or two, but for all his effort the animal has been teetering on the verge of collapse for the better part of the afternoon—at one point he had to set its tail afire to keep it going. And Johnson's ass hasn't done much better, feigning lameness, bucking and biting, braying like a calliope. No doubt about it—it's only a matter of time before one animal or the other gives out and Dassoud overtakes them. And then: goodbye Niger, goodbye Africa, so long mortal coil.

But then, just when things look bleakest, Johnson sings out like a shipwrecked sailor descrying a mast on the horizon. "Look!" he crows. "Up there, through the trees!" The explorer looks. There, winding over the wooded hill before them like an erratic seam, is the road to Bambarra. But what's this? A funnel of dust seems to be hugging the road, the tapered end narrowing away from them. The explorer's first thought is dustmen —thousands of them—sweeping along the road, but then, like an epiphany, it comes to him: the refugees! They've doubled back! "Johnson!" he cries. "You're a genius!"

This new development, however, has not been lost on Dassoud. The Chief Jackal begins pouring it on, surging at them like a sprinter making for the tape. The gap closes to fifty yards, then forty, Johnson beats the ass, Mungo whips his horse, the gap closes to thirty yards. Then Johnson does a peculiar thing. "An old Mandingo trick," he shouts, stuffing the ass's right ear into his mouth and champing down as if he were lashing into an overcooked chop. The ass lets out a screech, bucks twice and then takes off like a three-year-old at the start of the steeplechase. Mungo follows suit, the horse's ear like a strip of felt laid against his tongue, biting down till he tastes blood. And sure enough, the nag comes to life, galvanizing its last inner resources in a furious scramble of fetlock and hoof.

Johnson and Mungo, ass and nag, rocket over the stony ground through a stand of trees and up onto the road, Johnson shouting out in Mandingo to the ghostly figures emerging from the gloom. Then the ass slashes into the thick of it, neck and neck with the explorer's mount. Weary refugees leap aside, the hoofs rain on the road, chickens take to the air. A moment later the riders emerge on the far side, galloping along parallel to the roadway. Johnson kicks at the ass, his elbows flapping as if he were trying to take off, the trees a blur, the explorer fighting to keep up. "Now!" shouts Johnson, and they plunge back into the talcum gloom. This time they upset a litter and bowl over a village dignitary with a graven idol tucked under his arm, Johnson all the while jabbering away at the astonished faces: "Slow him down! Stop the Moor!" Twice more they skew from side to side at breakneck speed, pebbles flying, dust raveling out behind them, until Johnson rattles off the road and plunges into the woods, the explorer hot on his heels.

"Shhhh!" warns Johnson, dismounting in a tangle of burrs and glossy black thorns. The explorer's heart is drumming at his ribs. He climbs down from the wheezing nag and crouches in the vegetation. "Think we lost him?" he whispers.

Out on the road the slow fuliginous procession rumbles past. The explorer makes out a leg here, a head there, the back end of a goat or sheep. The din is steady, broken now and again by a curse or shout. There is no sign of Dassoud. And then suddenly — a bogey leaping out at a sleeping child — there he is! Tireless, fixated, trotting along the roadway and pccring into the dustcloud, his eyes so swollen with rage they look like hard-cooked eggs. His shins seem battered and bruised, his calves veined with blood. He never even turns his head.

Deep in the bushes, Johnson holds out his hands, palms up.

The explorer looks him in the eye, a silly euphoric grin creeping across his face, then reaches out and brushes the upturned palms with his own.

◀§ THE STREETS OF LONDON

At this time in history the streets of London were as foul, feculent and disease-ridden as a series of interconnected dunghills, twice as dangerous as a battlefield, and as infrequently maintained as the lower cells of an asylum dungeon. It was pretty rough. Drunks lay sprawled across the footpaths, some dead and stinking and blanketed with crows. Whole families squatted on streetcorners and begged for bread. Murders were committed in the alleys. There were yellowed newspapers clinging to the lampposts, smashed crocks and bottles underfoot, bits of produce and the bones of gamebirds and fowls moldering in the corners. There was pigeonshit. Mud, coal dust, ashes, dead cats, dogs, rats, scraps of cloth stained with excrement, and worst of all, open sewers. "We live, Sir, like a colony of Hottentots," complained Lord Tyrconnel, addressing the House. "And our streets abound with such heaps of filth as even a savage would look on with amaze." Others agreed. A society for Civic Salubrity was formed, a Clean Air Club. They held regular meetings, followed Bledsoe's *Rules of Parliamentary Procedure,* aired complaints, accomplished nothing.

There were a few private nightsoil collectors, it's true, and a handful of dustmen. But the nightsoil collectors built festering mounds of muck in their backyards and the dustmen merely created smoldering dumps. And this still left the overwhelming majority of the city's residents with no means of sewage disposal save their own backyards and the choked gutters which bisected the streets like running wounds. Grim shopkeepers trudged out into the roadway to dump their chamberpots, barmen limed the walls outside their establishments to deaden the reek of urine, housekeepers flung buckets of nightsoil from second- and third-story windows. "Gardy loo!" the chambermaid would shout, and a dark clot of it would arch out over the walkway to slap down in the street, there to ooze inch by inch toward the fetid gutter. Of course, this was inconvenient for the passerby, who might already be limping and brushing at his clothes as a result of tumbling into an open cellar or blundering across one of the several thousand mad dogs that roamed the city at will. And as if that weren't enough, the gutters were generally clogged with horsedung, pigs' ears and other offal, causing the sewage to back up in dark rills and steamy swamps — not only was the pedestrian up to his ankles in human waste, he also found himself dodging the airborne clods thrown up by the wheels of passing carriages.

Because the streets were so unpleasant, people of means took to raveling from place to place by coach or sedan chair. The sedan chair was particularly well adapted to its time and place, providing comfort and security for the privileged and a means of employment for some few of the starving masses. It consisted of an enclosed compartment attached to a pair of parallel bars. These bars were hoisted on the shoulders of the chairmen, one fore and one aft. The chairmen, impoverished inbreeds with harelips and misshapen heads, made a few pennies; the lady going out to tea could arrive with a petticoat free of shit smears. Advantages all around. But there was a further advantage to the sedan chair: once inside, one was invisible. Merely pull the curtains and peep through the cracks. See, and remain unseen.

What better means of conveyance for an invisible man?

◆§ THE BALLAD OF JACK HALL

With a sinking feeling, Ned watches Boyles' pinched shoulders and flat-bottomed head recede into the crowd. He looks round furtively, feeling naked and vulnerable, a crab without a shell. Up the street, a chairstand. Ned hobbles up to the first chair, hands the chairman a coin and disappears within. The curtains are drawn. It is dark as a womb. Ned's mind rushes with schemes and ruses and counterschemes. His own voice surprises him. "Monmouth Street," he calls. "Rose's Old Clothes."

◆§ ६◆

Rose's Old Clothes is a secondhand shop specializing in women's attire and highly recommended by Sally Sebum ("She's got the keenest bargains in town, Rose does"). It is one of a dozen shops of the rag-and-bone variety squeezed into a two-block span, all of which cater to the servants of the rich (selling), the wives of frugal burghers (buying), and the poor (just looking). The grimy bow windows out front are heaped with the strata of fashion: hoops, hats and whalebone corsets; petticoats, parasols, caps, bonnets and bustles. A cockeyed sign hangs over the door:

WE LAWNDERS ALL GARMINTS
PRIOR TO SELLING

Ned's chair scrapes down outside the shop. "Monmouth Street," announces the chairman, swinging back the door.

In the dark, jostling through the crowded streets, Ned's mind has been active. Boyles, he realizes, is totally untrustworthy. As soon as he gets a few drinks in him he'll blab the whole thing: *Ned Rise is alive! I talked to him. Had me hand on his arm!* The rumor spreads like ink in water, passes round barrooms, served up with the soup, until finally it whispers in the ears of Mendoza, Smirke, Twit and the rest. Two weeks. That's all he needs. If he can get through two weeks more he'll have cleared five hundred pounds on Chichikov's Choice and he can get out of town altogether. Try his luck on the Continent maybe. Paris, The Hague, Leghorn.

"Monmouth Street," the chairman repeats.

Ned straightens his nose and adjusts his wig, then limps out into the street. He hands the chairman half a crown. "Wait here," he says, "and keep an eye on my basket of fish eggs, will you?"

·~§ §~·

An anemic bell murmurs over the door as Ned steps into the shop. He finds himself in a foul-smelling room lit only by the odd strands of light that seep in through the avalanche of ladies' apparel heaped up round the windows. The smell is of clothes tight at the groin and under the armpit, clothes worn without washing for years on end, clothes harboring all the vermin and disease known to man. He looks round for the proprietor. "Shopkeeper!" he calls. The place seems deserted.

But then, in the far corner, a bundle of rags disengages itself from the general disarray and begins shuffling toward him. The bundle of rags turns out to be an old woman wrapped in a moth-eaten cloak. She looks as if she feeds on nothing but thousand-year-old eggs. "Yes?" she cackles, her voice full of rust. "Wot'll it be? Buyin' or gapin'?"

"A woman's outfit," Ned says. "The whole works: skirts and gloves and shoulderknots, a cap that ties under the chin and the biggest bonnet you've got."

"EEE-ee-eeeee!" cackles the proprietress. "A bit o' finery for the littul mistress, 'ey?" She nudges him with her elbow and winks.

Ned is suddenly seized with a sense of déjà vu.

"Ye've got 'er nekked up in some garret then, ain't ye? Tore the threads right off 'er, didn't ye, ye wicked beast? Eeeee-eeeee!" she laughs, nudging him again.

Ned steps back a pace. The woman's face is fleshless, skin stretched over bone. She is half bald. Something glitters on her lower lip.

" 'Ow'll this be, then?" she puffs, bending to pluck a bundle of flowered skirts from the floor. "And this?" She reaches up for a veiled bonnet piled high with artificial fruit and gilded dromaderies.

"F-fine," Ned stutters, his arms heaped with cotton, muslin, wool and chintz. He seems to have lost command of the situation, taken aback by the old slut, wrestling with the feeling that he's been through all this before.

"Petticoats?" the old woman leers. "Undies?"

Ned heaps his clothes atop the makeshift counter — a plank stretched between two barrels. The proprietress produces a filthy scrap of paper and a pencil, and begins scrawling figures across the page. She is humming. No: singing. He recognizes the tune. *The Ballad of Jack Hall.*

"Oh, it's a swingin' I must go, I must go," she moans, scraping away at the octaves like a saw cutting through a wet log. "It's a swingin' I must go-o-o." Then she leers up at him. "Four shillin's, tuppence, Lothario," she cackles. "Eeeeeee!"

"Have you got a back room?" Ned asks.

"Back room? Can't ye wait till ye gets 'ome to yer own mizzable lodgin's? Wot are ye, anyway: one o' them perverty types wot runs around jackin' off on ladies' garmints like a cat in 'eat? Eh? Eh? That wot it is, peach fuzz?"

Ned lays another shilling on the counter. "Just point it out, will you?"

The old woman points, then looks down to count her money. "Takes all kinds," she mutters. "Eeeeeee!"

❧ ☙

Ten minutes later he steps from the back room, a blushing beauty. The skirts are soiled, and they reek a bit, but you'd never know it from a distance. He's tied a white cap under his chin, letting his own hair fall down his back, and crowned the whole thing with the foot-high bonnet.

The old woman perches on a stool behind the counter, a pewter cup and a jug before her. When she throws back her head with the cup, she catches sight of him and begins gargling out her weird laugh. "Ye didn't tell me it was 'alloween," she chokes, pounding the plank and hooting. "Or is it the faggots' ball ye're going to? Hee-eeee! Eeeeeee!"

Ned draws up his skirts and swishes past her, too uneasy to trade insults. There's something about the old slut that rushes back to his earliest memories, pokes at him like a nightmare in the womb. He shudders as he hurries out of the shop, the splintered old voice ringing in his ears:

> *Oh, it's a swingin' I must go, I must go,*
> *It's a swingin' I must go-o-o;*
> *I must hang until I'm dead, dead, dead,*
> *I must hang until I'm de-e-ad;*
> *I must hang until I'm dead, 'cause I killed a man,*
> *And I left him layin' on the cold, cold ground.*

◄§ INBREEDING

"Soho Square," says Ned.

The chairman eyes the bonnet, skirts, flounces. He is a tall and singularly ugly fellow, his head close-cropped and disproportionately small. There are tufts of hair growing out of his ears. "Oy'm sowwy, Madame, but this conweyance is spoken for," he says.

"You stupid ass," growls Ned. "Can't you see it's me?"

The man takes hold of Ned's arm, preventing him from stepping into the compartment. "Me 'oo?"

"Me. The gentleman what owns them fish eggs on the seat there."

The chairman looks hard at Ned's bustline, the frilly ribbon tied under his chin, the curls trailing down his back. Then he glances at the basket of fish eggs and back again. He looks confused. " 'Ey Bob," he calls, and his co-worker peeks out from behind the rear of the conveyance. "Was it a gennelman we 'auled over 'ere from St. James's, or am Oy in fear of me sanity?"

Bob is short and moonfaced, with high-set ears and a fringe of orange hair that gives him the look of a neutered cat. "That's royt," he says. "An elderly gent, somewhat lame. 'Ee was all decked out in a three-corner 'at and wig and such — like they useter wear in me granddad's day."

"Ye see?" says the crophead. "It's like Oy told ye, Madame — the conweyance is otherwise occupied."

A carriage rattles up the street and splashes the side of the compartment with dung. Two blocks down a baby falls from a window.

"But that's what I'm trying to tell you!" shouts Ned. "That gentleman is me."

Bob looks suspicious, crophead puzzled.

"I've changed my clothes in the shop, don't you see?"

No response.

"Look: think of it this way. A man is invited to a costume ball. He hires a sedan chair — "

"Aye," says crophead, nodding vigorously.

" — in St. James's Square, and takes it over to Monmouth Street — Rose's Old Clothes, to be exact — gives the chairman half a crown to mind his basket, then enters the shop, purchases a lady's outfit, changes into it, and hops back in the sedan chair ready to shoot off to the costume ball — disguised as a lady."

"Gawn!" scoffs Bob.

"Yeah," adds crophead. " 'Oo'd do a thing like that?"

"All right: fuck you both, then," Ned snarls, lashing out with his parasol and springing into the compartment.

"But Mistress," pleads the crophead, "Oy appeals to yer sense o' fair play. A gennelman give us arf a crown to 'old the chair for 'im and to mind 'is basket o' fish eggs. Now wot are we going to tell that gennelman should 'ee come out o' the shop and see that ye've 'propriated 'is eggs and 'is conweyance both?"

Ned motions the man closer, takes hold of his elbow and whispers in his ear. "I'll level with you," he says " — this is a very delicate situation here. You see, I'm the lady friend of the gentleman in the shop, and we don't want to be seen together for fear his wife should hear of it. Now: he's left these fish eggs as a special present for me and he's slipped on out the back way to meet me at his flat for what the French call an assignation."

The man scratches his head.

"We call it 'dipping the wick.' "

The man breaks out in a grin. "Woy didn't ye say so? . . . . 'Ey Bob — she says she's 'is konkabine then."

Bob's voice is distant and faint, emanating from somewhere on the far side of the chair. "Well, I guess it's all royt then."

"Aye," says crophead. "Guess it's all royt."

"Soho Square," says Ned.

◆§ THE HEART OF DARKNESS

The woods. Dark and deep. Two figures squat over an anemic flame, roasting meat. Lions roar, and lightning plays over the horizon like the flicker of ideas.

"So tell me, Mr. Park, if I ain't gettin' too personal, just what it is you see in this explorin' business anyhow? I mean you been starved and abused, sick with the ague and the fever, your clothes is in rags, half your goods is gone and your horse is layin' over there in the bushes like it ain't never goin' to get up again."

"I'm glad you asked me that, Johnson. You see — my lord that smells good. What did you say it was?"

"Paw pads of the jackal. Only thing the vultures won't touch."

"Hmp. Learn something new every day. . . . Anyway, I'm the eighth of thirteen. Know what that means?"

Johnson looks up from the skewered bits of meat. "You're consumed with a almost demonic obsession to prove yourself?"

"Exactly."

"And all the regular avenues is closed — you bein' a Scotsman and your father only a crofter. So you can't enter politics or take a commission in the army or hobnob with the elite in their drawin' rooms and clubs — "

"Uh-huh."

"So what else is there? You rely on your courage and stamina and you go off to fathom the unknown and then come back a hero. Right?"

"Yes — but there's more to it than that. I want to know the unknowable, see the unseen, scale mountains and look behind the stars. I want to fill in the maps, lecture the geographers, hold up a torch for the academicians. The Niger . . . think of it, Johnson. No white man has ever laid eyes upon it. I'll have seen what none of them have — not the Laird of Dumfries, nor Charles Fox, nor the King himself."

"All well and good," shouts Johnson over the protestations of a nearby lion. "But you got to get to it first, and then you got to backtrack all this long way we come already — with all your notes and faculties intact, not to mention your lights and limbs . . ."

But wait: what's all this noise in the bushes? They've been so engrossed in their discussion they haven't paid it any mind — but yes, come to mention it, bushes *have* been swaying and leaves rattling — steadily — for the past few minutes now. The realization grips them like a seizure: words choke in their throats, their limbs go heavy, ears leap. A twig snaps, the leaves rush, and suddenly explorer and guide are on their feet, the one clenching a thorny cudgel, and the other brandishing an engraved dueling pistol. There's a moment of silence, and then the movement begins again — unmistakable — coming right for them. Leopard, lion, wolf, they think. Or worse: Dassoud! "Come on out of there!" Mungo shouts. "Be you man or hyena!"

Lightning breaks the sky, thunder rolls in the hills. Johnson swallows hard and tries to steady the pistol. And then, with a sudden dramatic swish, the bushes part — to reveal the stooped and wizened old soothsayer from Jarra. The dead guinea hen still hangs from his neck, half plucked, limp and stinking. "*Wamba reebo jekenek,*" he says, his bags and wrinkles attempting a sort of grin. "*Bobo keemboo.*"

A moment later the old man is squatting between explorer and guide, bony knees and cracked feet, snuffing the skewer and jabbering like an ape come down from the trees. "What a night! Lions trying to chase the moon. Hear that one? Close by, eh? Hee-hee. Hm, meat smells good. I know how o cook meat, bet your life. Used to, anyway. Now I'm alone and friendless, terrible calamity. Did you know? Going my way by any chance?"

"What calamity?" Johnson asks, and the old man, waiting his opening, launches a windy narrative embellished by the geriatric gesture and punctuated by the creak of rusted joints. His name, it seems, is Abah Eboe — or Ebah Aboe — the explorer can't decide which. He had been separated from the other refugees during a skirmish with Mansong's army. On hearing that the fugitive Jarrans had crossed into Bambarra seeking asylum, Mansong had apparently decided that the time was ripe for collecting a little tribute — a squatter's fee. He appeared around a bend in the road, enormous, mounted on a baby elephant and surrounded by eighty or a hundred potbellied warriors in leopard skins and ostrich plumes. A *jilli kea,* or singing man, preceded him, howling out his demands. The long queue of refugees came to a halt. Yambo, the Jarran chieftain, made his way to the front and protested that his people had been loyal to Mansong during the war with Tiggitty Sego and that the loss of their village and all their goods was calamity enough. They threw themselves on the mercy of the wise and charitable potentate of Bambarra.

Mansong's scepter was capped with a human skull. He adjusted his proud fat belly and repeated his demands. It was at this point that the soothsayer had interceded. (Here the old man becomes violently animated, flailing the twigs of his arms and pounding his chest.) He had shoved his way angrily through the crowd and hobbled up beside Yambo. Then he raised his fists in the air and began castigating the Bambarran king. If Sego was a tyrant, the old man had squawked, then Mansong was an ogre conceived of queers and jackals. Mansong smeared himself in dung and sucked the seed from his warriors. He was a thief and a woman — only look to his great sagging tits for proof. For a moment, both parties were stunned silent. Then, with a shout, Mansong's army fell on the defenseless Jarrans. Two hundred were killed, mostly women and children. The rest were led off in shackles.

"And how did you manage to escape?" the explorer asks in his halting patois.

The old man glances up, his features lost in a grin. A noiseless laugh shakes at the bones of his chest. "*Mojo,*" he says.

The explorer looks at Johnson.

"The man says he's got his *mojo* workin'," says Johnson, twirling the meat on the skewer. "You know: magic, black arts, hoodoo and voodoo. Nobody messes with a witch doctor."

"Witch doctor?"

"Of course — what do you think he's doin' runnin' around with that chicken tucked under his chin?"

The explorer leaps to his feet. "Can he — can he tell fortunes?" Johnson's lids are thick as a crocodile's. He looks up at the explorer and sighs. "Well he's no gypsy, if that's what you mean . . . But listen, you sure you want your signs and portents conjured with, Mr. Park? Here and now? I mean, it's one thing to have some old white lady take a look at your tea leaves in her front parlor up in Edinburgh or London or someplace — but hey, this is *Africa,* man. The eye of the needle, mother of mystery, heart of darkness. And this old naked black man here with his feet all crusted up and his penis danglin' in the mud — he don't fool around."

"Don't be silly, Johnson. I've got the luck of the Scots with me. There's renown in my future, I know it. Laurels, and a book. And Ailie. Are you kidding: I'll die in front of the hearth with a cat in my lap."

"All right. Don't say I didn't warn you."

Overhead, lightning tesselates the sky until it glows like an illuminated map of some celestial river and its tributaries. Off in the distance, harsh dyspeptic rumbles of thunder can be heard. Johnson turns to the old man and mumbles something in Mandingo. The effect on Eboe (or Aboe) is instantaneous. The grin vanishes, crow's-feet rush out from the eyesockets and corners of the mouth, furrows drop and lines vein the cheeks and chin until he's transformed, unrecognizable, a great drooping bloodhound, a ball of wax, an unthrown pot. He rises shakily and takes hold of the explorer's hand, scrutinizing it as if it were a text or a painting. His leathery old fingers play over the knuckles and joints, a wild bolt lights the sky, thunder steps down like a giant walking the earth. The soothsayer spits in Mungo's palm, then pricks his finger with a vulture's talon, blending blood and spittle and now a bit of clay, all the while working it into the lines of the palm and muttering some antediluvian formula over and over, *mojo-mojo-mojo,* his eyes pinched shut, the thunder beating like tribal drums. Finally he looks down into the huge white palm and his eyes go wide. He is stung, stricken. Utters a cry like a wounded beast and clutches at his breast.

A hyena laughs in the night. The wind tastes of sand. Mungo is frightened. "Well?" he says, his voice a pinched vibrato. "What do you see?"

But the old man doesn't answer. Already he's edging away from the explorer, hands held up to his face, his stooped black form a shadow among shadows. CRACK! Lightning blanches the clearing and the old man is a ghost. CRACK! Johnson is pale as milk. "*Obi-lo-bojóto,*" the seer intones. "*Obi-lo-bojóto.*"

"Johnson! What's he saying?"

Johnson stares into the fire.

"Johnson!"

The guide's head cranks round, slow as a plant turning to the sun. All the beasts of the plain are howling in unison and the sky is lit like a ballroom. "He says you got nice hands."

"Nice hands!? What the — "

Question or exclamation, it remains forever unformed. Because at that moment the heavens part, the first fat drops plummeting like stones, pounding at the parched earth and withered trees.

The rains have begun.

◄§ EUREKA!

Four days later, in the drool and drizzle of an intermittent rain, explorer, guide and soothsayer — closely tailed by nag and ass — can be found plodding along the road to Segu, capital of Bambarra. Actually they are headed for Segu Korro, westernmost of the four towns that comprise Segu proper (the others being Segu Boo, Soo Korro and Segu See Korro). According to old Eboe, who twice visited the city in his youth, it's a wide-open place, awash in palm wine, mead and *sooloo* beer, the streets ringing with wanton laughter, snatches of song, the shriek of cockfights, the alleys packed full of whores with brass rings round their necks and skin like the bottom of a well. There are jugglers and dwarfs and acrobats, men who bite the heads from chickens, marvels untold. Water flows uphill in Segu. People speak backward. There is lewdness in the streets, in the alleys, in the dens of iniquity. Jewels are like gravel. They pave their streets with marble, tradesmen eat from gilded plates, food is for the asking: fowls and poached fish, eggs, mutton, rice. And the bazaar — the bazaar is boundless, infinite, a catalogue of human needs, human dreams, inhuman desires. "Get anything you want," the old man croaks, licking his lips. "Daggers, slave girls, talking monkeys, hashish." The explorer's palms are sweating. Yes, after so many dead dull months in the desert, the prospect of a town — a negro town — excites him. But that's only part of it. Cities

he's seen. What makes his blood race and organs palpitate is that this city —
unlike any other known to Western man through all recorded history — this
city sits squarely on the west bank of the river of legend, the River Niger.
The Niger! It stuns him to think of it. Caesar, Alexander, Houghton,
·Ledyard — none of them even came close. He's suffered for it, denied
himself, ruined his digestion and deserted the woman he loves. The Niger.
It fills his dreams, sours his morning tea, etches its course in his imagination. And now, at long last, it's within reach.

Or almost. For the moment though, things are pretty bleak. All three of
them are starving, bone-tired, chilled — and limping like a charity ward in
motion. The seer with his cracked feet, arthritic knees; the explorer with
blisters and bunions and rotted boots; Johnson with fat brown leeches
between his toes and up his toga. Nag and ass are hobbling too, all but
useless. Behind them the landscape rises and sinks, rough and broken,
pitted as a cheek ravaged with acne. Up ahead: more of the same. There
are sudden declivities, hills and valleys, ridges, gullies. Stands of ciboa
darken the valleys, and massive tabbas, wide around as Big Ben, transfix
the hilltops. Underfoot, wilted guinea grass and a furze thick with burr and
briar. Snakes lie in wait, scorpions, spiders the size of omelets. Wild dogs
howl behind banks of layered succulents, while vultures, bald-headed and
black-winged, hunch in the trees like graverobbers at a concert. The road,
if you can call it that, isn't much more than a cowpath.

The rain, falling harder now, drills at them. When it first began, they
were ecstatic. They cut capers and did cartwheels. They rolled in it, opened
their mouths and shirts to it, clapped and hooted and danced like pardoned
criminals. They slept in muck, woke laughing, rain in their faces, the sweet
scent of it in the trees. When they slipped and fell on the rain-slick road,
they laughed. Suddenly the universe was benign. They were in love with it.

But that was five days ago. Enough is enough. The puddles are up to
their knees in places. Mud sucks at their feet. Their chests are congested,
noses running, ears plugged up. The mornings are blotted out by mist and
fog, everything indistinct, dreamlike, the air dank and fetid. Great gray
phantoms spring up before them and clatter off into nothingness
— whinnying and squealing, hissing, roaring. The strain is beginning to tell
on them. At one point, late in the afternoon, the explorer cannot summon
the strength to go on. After struggling for half an hour to drag his horse
through a ravine neck-deep in foaming yellow water, he throws himself
down, exhausted, at the side of the road. The old man drops beside him,
and Johnson, hawking up a ball of sputum, follows suit. Nag and ass
collapse like paper bags.

"Much — farther?" Mungo chokes, his voice thick with catarrh. Johnson spits again, then blows his nose in the soggy folds of his toga. "Don't ask me — I never been here before neither."

The two turn to Eboe. He sits there, lined, sagging and naked, hunched like a gargoyle under a bush. The guinea hen, one of its wings lost to deterioration, still hangs from his neck, its feathers heavy with wet and maggots. "*Woko baba das,*" he croaks.

"Ten miles," Johnson grunts. "Be there in the mornin' "

The morning comes like a slap in the face, harsh and brilliant. Johnson is already up, gathering berries and mushrooms, when the explorer suddenly jerks awake to a cloudless sky and the slow drift and wheel of a pair of kites. He is puzzled at first, disoriented, but then it hits him: today is the day! Instantly he's on his feet, gathering up his things, swatting the horse's flank with a stick, calling out to Johnson, shaking Eboe's spindly shoulders. "Wake up, Eboe — time to hit the road!"

The old man, nestled beneath his bush, sleeps on. Deathly still. His mouth hangs open, the pink bud of his gums and palate an hors d'oeuvre for the huge green flies that hover round the putrefact chicken. A column of ants has been using his foot as a highway, mosquitoes tattoo his cheeks and eyelids. Looking down at him, so frail and motionless, his bones in stark relief against the yellow muck, a terrible realization comes over the explorer. Old Eboe, last of the Jarrans, is dead.

Mungo backs away, still crouching, and calls out to Johnson again — his voice pitched higher this time. Up the road, Johnson emerges from the bush, his jaws working, a pouch full of herbs, nuts, berries and fungi swinging at his waist. In his arms: half a dozen gnarled tubers. "It's the old man," shouts Mungo. "I think he's had it."

The tubers fall to the road with an obscene plop, and Johnson takes off at a trot, chest and belly heaving beneath the toga. He drops to his knees beside the old man, pressing his ear to the fissured chest. When he looks up, his expression is glum. " 'Fraid you're right, Mr. Park," he says. "You want to bury him or leave him for nature's sanitation squad?"

The explorer is shocked. "Why — bury him of course."

Johnson, still kneeling, squints up at him. "Goin' to be a scorcher today. Humid. Ten miles up the road is that river you been pissin' and moanin' to get to. And a big town full of marvels and wonders, nubile women and alcoholic beverages. You sure?"

But the explorer hasn't time to answer, as Johnson, reaching out to cut the dead bird from the old man's neck, is arrested by a bony clasp. Slow as syrup, the old man's lids pull back. He stretches, yawns, sits up. Then wags an admonishing finger at Johnson. "Eboe thinks we are friends," he says. "Yet you try to steal his *mojo*-hen?"

Johnson backs off, his face slack. "But we thought —"

The old man is on his feet now, tottering slightly, a fly caught in the bubble of saliva on his lip. He staggers toward the guide, body quivering with rage or infirmity, his crabbed fingers picking at the leather thong until finally he grasps it and eases the bird up over his head. It dangles from his fingers, slack, drooling, coated with insects. "You want?" The old man's Mandingo is thick as a sleeping potion.

"No!" pleads Johnson. "No!"

Then, suddenly, with a motion so quick and smooth it defies the eye, Eboe loops the grisly thing through the air. A flutter of feathers, and it catches Johnson's neck like a noose. FOOMP! The bird strikes his chest, and dangles. Maggots wriggle in the folds of his belly. Flies orbit his head. His face makes the Pietà look like a portrait of joy.

The explorer is mystified, mouth agape, witness to some primitive rite. "Johnson," he says, astonished. "Cut it loose. Toss it in the bushes."

Old Eboe is grinning ear to ear.

Johnson hangs his head. "I can't," he whispers.

◅❧ ❧▻

The mud crusts underfoot, remugient beasts stir up the undergrowth, Johnson attracts flies: greenflies, blowflies, blackflies, crutflies. The road has begun to widen now, and from time to time habitations can be seen crouching beneath trees or perching atop mounds of red clay. Outside the huts: bare-breasted women, men in baggy shorts, striped shirts and conical hats, apathetic dogs. The men suck on long-stemmed pipes, the women chew roots and spit from between blackened teeth. Palms wave overhead. Goats shuffle about in pens. The scent of urine curdles the air.

As they reach the crest of each hill the explorer darts on ahead, stretching his neck like a sightseer, unable to contain himself. He shouts and waves his hat against the horizon, gesturing frantically toward a white blur in the distance. "Is that it?" he calls, dancing in place. "Is that it?"

At the top of the eighteenth hill old Eboe pauses to sniff the breeze. Mungo catches his breath. There is certainly something out there, towers maybe, the sudden flash of a window catching the sun. The shrunken soothsayer stoops to pluck a round white stone from the mud. He rubs it briefly between his leathery fingers, then slips it into his mouth. The gerontic eyelids drop like curtains, the lips purse, sucking reflectively.

Eternities pass, the world cranks round on its axis, constellations heave in the firmament. "Well?" Mungo demands. Eboe lifts his lids. Spits out the stone. The buzz of Johnson's flies is loud as a drumroll. "Well?" Slow and deliberate, Eboe raises his arm, points a crooked finger. "Segu Korro," he croaks.

For one brief fraction of a second the explorer stands transfixed, and then he's off like a sprinter. Starvation, weakness, disease, nails pricking through the soles of his boots, the sun scorching the water from his eyes — none of it matters: his goal is in sight. His feet pound the yellow clay, erasing the footsteps of those who came before him, as Johnson, Eboe, nag and ass recede in the distance and the glorious golden walls of the city come into focus before him. Huts flash by, traffic on the road. Women balancing jugs, boys driving goats with long supple switches, laden asses, litters of produce, spangled birds in wicker cages. All a blur. He stops for no one, dashing through the massive gates now, shoving his way past astonished faces, down congested streets, alleyways, frantic for the river, feet pounding, stunned Bambarrans gathering at his back like children at a parade, dirt streets, a dead dog, hawkers and tradesmen, a flash of color and movement — and there, there it is! Wide across as the Thames, brown as a gutter, cluttered with rafts and dugouts, the shore a riot of splashing children, rooting pigs, washerwomen in white caps. He doesn't turn at the roar behind him — doesn't even notice — leaping crates and cages, bowling over children and old women, stiff-arming farmers and fishermen, a strange primordial squeal of triumph burning in his throat. The bamboo dock sways under his feet, a boatman ducks out of the way, flinching as if to ward off a blow, and the explorer is airborne. His legs and arms flail for a brief delicious instant, suspended there in all his glory, mindless as a hatter, shouting out some Greek exclamation until the dark steaming water envelops him like a mother's embrace.

ᐊ§ HERODOTUS BE HANGED

"What, Sir? You doubt Herodotus?"

"Herodotus be hanged. And Pliny along with him. How can you actually sit there and expect a rational being to accept all this folderol about tribes that squeal like bats and outrace horses? Or pygmies, leprechauns — whatever you call them — tripping about the jungle like nursery children in

Mayfair? It's myth I tell you. Folklore. Timbuctoo no more exists than the land of the Laestrygonians."

Sir Joseph Banks, President of the Royal Society, Treasurer and Director of the African Association for Promoting Exploration, sits at the head of the mahogany table in his library at No. 32, Soho Square. Before him, a glass of Madeira. It is July, the windows are open, moths bat about the lamps. On the back wall, Desceliers' sixteenth-century map of Africa. Sir Joseph regards it glumly, barely attentive to the debate going on around him. A pretty piece of work, Desceliers' map. Colorful. Imaginative. But it is of course nothing more than an outline, a perimeter pricked with place names — the vast uncharted interior artfully concealed behind a dribble of imaginary rivers and a host of mythical beasts, six-armed maidens and limbless Cyclopeans. Sir Joseph sighs, takes a lugubrious sip at his wine. Now, two centuries later, children of the Enlightenment, he and his colleagues know little more than Desceliers.

"You forget, my good fellow, that while Homer may have been enamored of Euterpe, Herodotus was an historian. His object was not to divert us with fictions, but to edify us with facts." The Bishop of Llandaff, though a charter member of the Association, is tonight attending his second meeting since its inception eight years ago. He is chiefly remarkable for the salience of his cartilaginous features, and the coldness of his tiny, misaligned eyes (his family, the Rathbones, have been heralded since the fourteenth century for their sloping foreheads, majestic beaks and pale fleshy ears — beaks so majestic and ears so fleshy as almost to suggest the development of new species and keener functions). For the better part of an hour he has been defending the sacred and unshakable authority of the Ancients. Sir Reginald Durfeys, William Fordyce and Lord Twit, soured by their public school experience, have opposed him, while Edwards and Pultney have for the most part remained silent.

"And what is history, pray tell, if not a fiction?" Twit, known in the Lords for his reedy, lisping orations, pauses for effect. "You presume to call Herodotus' suppositions fact? How were these 'facts' obtained? Thirdhand? Fifthhand? I ask you, Sir."

Llandaff's ears are suffused with color. He begins to pull on his white calfskin gloves, thinks better of it, downs a glass of brandy instead. "You dare to impugn the Ancients? Why, our whole system of Modern Thought — "

Twit holds up his palm. "Excuse me. I haven't finished. I mean to say that all our cherished histories — from those of the Greeks to that of our late departed colleague Mr. Gibbon — are at best a concoction of hearsay, thirdhand reports, purposeful distortions and outright fictions invented by the self-aggrandizing participants and their sympathizers. And as if that weren't enough, this hodgepodge of misrepresentation and prevarication is then further distorted through the darkling lens of the historian himself." Twit, lips painted and cheeks rouged, is in his glory — he revels in his reputation as iconoclast, intellectual outlaw and assailer of priggery. Twit the Wit, they call him. After a pause for the application of two pinches of snuff, he continues. "What happened at Culloden — do you know, Sir? And what then of Tangier and Timbuctoo? At least my own knowledge of the African continent is no worse than second-hand."

Llandaff has been waiting for this. "Yes, Twit," he grins, ever so slowly whitening his palm with salt from the shaker, "we've all had occasion to read of your rigorous excursions into the blacker holes of Africa — incidentally, how is the nigger slave getting on these days?"

Pultney sniggers.

"Hear, hear!" shouts Edwards. "A blow for the Ancients!"

"Gentlemen, please." A bulky, florid form has risen at the far end of the table. Sir Reginald Durfeys, Bart., now on the threshold of his eighth decade, has yet to begin the long slide toward the grave that has crabbed and disfigured so many of his coevals. At sixty-eight, he is as pink and fat as a baby, ingenuous as a teenager. He gives to charity, loves a glass of port, takes his postprandial exercise on the boulevard each evening. He has never married. "While I cannot agree with our distinguished confrere that the Niger is merely imaginary," he begins, the great silver bush of his head all but blotting Desceliers' map from view, "neither can I accept with any sanguinity the Bishop's asseverations that the information gathered by the Greeks is our most reliable. No. I feel we must look to our modern cartographers — to Major Rennell and D'anville." He leans forward, pressing his fists to the table. "Gentlemen: it is my belief that the Niger flows *eastward*, toward the heart of the continent — "

"Oh piffle, Durfeys — it flows to the westward and disembogues along the Pepper Coast."

" — flows *eastward*, I repeat, and feeds the great lake called Chad, where its waters are given to evaporation in the blistering temperatures of the mid-Sahara."

"Come off it, old man," Edwards interjects. "If it flows to the eastward, then Llandaff and Herodotus must be vindicated — what else could it then do but join with the Nile in the Nubian foothills?"

"Rubbish!" shouts Twit, his eyes watering from an excessive dose of snuff. "It's all a fantasy, I tell you. A dream. No more substantial than Atlantis or the land of the sugarplum fairy."

Durfeys, still standing, begins to stammer from confusion. "But, but gentlemen . . . I had it . . . had it from Johnson — "

"Pfffff, Johnson." Llandaff's face is slashed by the line of his nose, cut in two like a halved apple; his ears look as if they're about to flap up off his head. "Another voice of obfuscation from the Dark Continent. Trigger-happy and swell-headed. A black nigger cannibal in a two-guinea wig. Let's all consult our charwomen and gardeners next time we need a cartographer."

"Yes, Reginald — what of your precious Johnson?" says Edwards. "What's he accomplished for us thus far — the loss of yet another explorer?"

At that moment Sir Joseph Banks clears his throat. Durfeys, reddening, sinks back into his seat. Six pairs of eyes fasten on the Director. "The term, Mr. Beaufoy, is 'geographical missionary,' and yes, I am chagrined to report that we must now begin to think of casting about for another man to undertake the illumination of the Niger region. There has been no word from the young Scot for nearly eight months now." The Director stares down at his glass, running a thoughtful finger round its rim. "In point of fact, gentlemen, the indications are a good deal worse than you might imagine. I have before me a recent communication from our factor on the Gambia, Dr. Laidley." Sir Joseph breaks off, and then slowly raises his head. His eyes are distant and unfocused, as if he were just then waking from a dream. On the far wall, dancing under the lamplight, Desceliers' figures seem to swell and recede, twitching their multiple arms and headless shoulders, beckoning, teasing, mocking.

"Yes?" Llandaff prompts.

Sir Joseph snaps to attention, focuses on Durfeys. "It's all up, I'm afraid. Park has fallen into the hands of the Moors."

◄§ LIKE A CLOUD SWALLOWING
A FLOCK OF IBIS

As Johnson limps through the gates of Segu Korro, trailing flies, a nag and an ass, a walking stick in his hand and a revitalized Eboe at his side, he is astonished to find the streets all but deserted. Windows shuttered, stalls left unattended, pack animals — still laden with swollen *guerbas* and panniers of produce — calmly dipping their heads into baskets of onions, yams and cassavas. A smithy's forge sputters and roars beneath a spreading fig, lumps of wet clay harden in the sun beside finished pots. Tools lie where they've been dropped, goats call out to be milked, a monitor lizard, staked out for sale, stubbornly thrashes round and round its cord. From somewhere, the smell of burning bread. Johnson feels uneasy. It's strange, eerie: like something out of a fairy tale. Red Rose and Snow White. Sleeping Beauty. When he spots a pair of eyes glaring out from behind a bamboo screen, he turns to Eboe. "What you suppose is goin' on here?"

The old man, buoyant and oblivious, is strutting along like a teenager on his way to a dance. He stops in his tracks. "Going on?" he says, slapping Johnson's back and exploding in a burst of harsh wheezing giggles. "It's a holiday, is what it is. Wine, women and song."

Johnson merely stares.

"Can't you feel it?"

"Feels more like a cholera epidemic to me."

Eboe winks. "Follow me," he says.

They turn down a street lined with tamarind and raffia palm. The houses, built of whitewashed clay, are almost picturesque. There are patches of vegetables, trellises, even a flower or two. No paradise on earth, perhaps, but pleasant — very pleasant — all the same. It occurs to Johnson that this is the biggest town he's seen since leaving London. Pisania was a sink compared to it, and Dindikoo, for all its charm, is just a hamlet in the sticks. Suddenly he finds himself thinking of *sooloo* beer — and mutton.

Round the next corner they stumble over a drunk stretched out in the road. "Baaaa," says the drunk. "Urp." Johnson bends over him, the guinea hen describing a wide arc and coming to rest, at a dangle, just under the drunk's chin. "What's goin' on here?" Johnson asks.

The man looks up at him, eyes red, lips slack. "Drunk," he mutters.

"No. I mean in the town. What's goin' on in this place? Where is everybody?"

"White," slurs the drunk. "White as . . " he chokes off to tap his sternum and spit in the dirt. "White as a salted ghost. White, white, white. Like a cloud swallowing a flock of ibis."

Johnson has begun to get the idea. "Where is he?"

"White as cotton, white as day. White as fangs and bones and moonlight in a clearing." The drunk is sitting up now, his voice a nursery-school rhyme, vapid, singsong, endless and repetitive.

Johnson staggers up, breathing hard. The explorer is an innocent, a holy fool. They'll cook him alive, crucify him. He's got to find him. "Eboe!" he shouts, whirling around. "We got to find Mr. Park."

But Eboe is already half a block away, standing stock-still, nostrils flared, snuffing the breeze. Then all at once he's grinning and stamping, waving his arms like a juggler with nine plates in the air. "This way," he motions. "Hurry!"

Johnson tugs at the leather strap, and nag and ass mechanically plod off at his heels. "White as teeth!" the drunk shouts. "Whiter than a dead mud turtle!"

Eboe drifts like a somnambulist, following his nose. Two blocks to the left, then back to the right, through the abandoned marketplace, down a street shabby with garbage and yellowed reed huts that could pass for outhouses. There are rats and snails in the gutters, snakes in the eaves. "Eboe!" Johnson calls, struggling to catch up, but the old man hurries on as if he hasn't heard. The ground is soggy underfoot, banks of bamboo rise from between the huts now, birds flit through the trees. Finally the old man stops across from a sprawling, ramshackle hut propped up on stilts. Johnson, bringing up the rear, can make out the dim form of three or four women in the deep shade beneath the house. He is puzzled. He'd been under the impression that Eboe, recognizing the emergency, had been leading him to the explorer. Now he sees that he's been misled.

Meanwhile, Eboe stands there, gazing into the shadows: still snuffing. The women are large, middle-aged at best. Their dugs are pendulous, gravid, balloons filled with water. If they can boast twenty teeth between them, they're lucky. "Eboe!" shouts Johnson, but the women are doing fascinating things beneath their skirts, then holding up their fingers and licking them. The old necromancer can stand it no longer. He cracks a withered grin, gives Johnson the thumbs-up sign, and saunters into the shadows.

Johnson is stunned. Disappointed. Disgusted. Envious. He wants a beer, a plate of meat and rice, a woman, a bed. Here he is, a man of dignity and education, well past the age of retirement, a man with wives and children and a happy home — and what does he do? Wanders all over the continent, risking life and limb to bail out some half-witted, glory-hungry son of a crofter. He heaves a great wet sigh of despair and resignation, and turns to mount the balky blue ass, trying his level best to ignore the big flat-faced woman who dances out into the street and lifts her skirt for him.

◦◦

Fifteen minutes later (after following his hunches first, and then, as he draws closer, his ears), Johnson finally manages to locate the explorer.

Emerging from a maze of narrow earthen streets into a sort of square fronting the riverbank, he is all at once confronted with an extraordinary scene. People — packed in like bees in a hive — as far as the eye can see. There must be three or four thousand of them, hanging from windows, treetops, roofs, perched on shoulders, the backs of camels, straining on tiptoe. The banks of the river are black with them, scores in water up to their ankles, knees, necks, scores more bobbing in pirogues and coracles. All gathered to stand hushed and appalled while this impossible, inexplicable presence, this man in the moon fallen to earth, this white demon from hell chants, screeches, laughs, gibbers and sings, churning up the water, cursing the crops, bringing the sky down, and who knows what else.

Johnson, lost somewhere in the rear of the press, steadies the blue ass and gingerly raises himself atop the washboard of its back until he is able to stand erect. From his eminence he can see the woolly expanse of four thousand heads. Closer to the river (the Niger — how about that? he thinks), the heads are more congested, like thick stands of papyrus reed. Way up front, just off the lip of a rickety bamboo dock, Mungo Park is kicking up a froth and singing "God Save the King" at the top of his lungs. The Bambarrans seem mesmerized, stunned — as silent and sober as the awestruck crowds that slowly filed past the bier of George II.

But then, as is often the case in a world of action and reaction, things begin to lose their center. The explorer, totally oblivious to the audience gathered round him, suddenly slashes toward the dock in a moment of enthusiasm. His object is a yellow gourd attached to a fishing net; his intention, to set it adrift and thereby determine for the western world and all the generations of posterity the true direction of flow of the River Niger. Unfortunately, however, those Bambarrans closest to him misinterpret his motive and fall back with a shriek. In an instant the shriek is universal: the panic has begun.

Johnson is knocked from the ass and trampled. Lepers drop fingers and toes, the blind run into walls. There are shouts and curses, cries of pain and surprise, the drum of footsteps and the wail of lost children. The crowd surges against the mud-walled buildings like a river in flood, gushing through into streets and alleys, washing off with the undertow. Two minutes later the square is deserted, the banks empty, the river stripped of boats. All that remain are Johnson, a crumpled ass and nag, and the amphibious explorer. In the distance: the sound of hubbub and turmoil, voices raised, doors slammed.

Meanwhile, the yellow gourd has been drifting — inexorably and beyond a doubt — to the eastward. The explorer, momentarily distracted by the clamor of the Bambarran withdrawal, turns back to his experiment with a shout of exhilaration. "Pip!" he shouts. "Pip-pip!"

Johnson raises himself from the dust with a groan and wearily hobbles down the the water's edge. "Mr. Park," he calls. "Come on out of there and let's pay our respects to Mansong the Potentate before he sends his army out after us."

The explorer looks up, dripping, mats of algae caught in his beard and hair. The river parts round his waist, the current sluggish. He focuses on Johnson like a man waking from a deep sleep.

Straddling the dock now, arms akimbo, Johnson presents his case. "Look: if we get it together and offer him some gifts and trinkets and whatnot, he could just treat us like visitin' dignitaries. And that means food and drink, a roof, maybe even some female companionship. I don't know about you, but I'm damn sick and tired of sleepin' on the ground, eatin' thistles and makin' love to my hand."

The explorer sloshes toward him, his eyes gone buttery, arms outstretched in a wide, vacant embrace. "Johnson—we've done it! The Niger, Johnson." He pauses to flail his arm in the direction of the far bank. "Look at it, will you? Wide across as the Thames at Westminster. And to think: through all the ages, from the time of Creation till this very minute, it's tumbled along in ignorance and legend. It took *me,* old boy. It took *me* to uncover it."

Johnson glances back over his shoulder at the ranks of whitewashed buildings clustered on the hillside, the bamboo docks ranged along the shoreline, the dugouts bobbing at their tethers. "I can appreciate that, Mr. Park, and I extend my sincere congratulations. But if we don't get our asses over to the Mansa's palace and start grovelin' at his feet, we just might not live to tell about it."

The sun beats at them like a fist, the baked earth of the square throws up a shimmer of heat, somewhere a dog whimpers. Everything seems to steam and stink. Malignant odors hang in the air, corrosive, thick with rot. They tell of fishheads, human waste, blackening leaves, muck. All at once the explorer begins to feel queasy. Overpowered, actually. Things are slowing down, anticlimactic, and his senses are gradually reawakening to the realities of hammering sun, putrid water, festering riverbank. He reaches for Johnson's hand and pulls himself from the river.

"You're right, Johnson. We can celebrate when we get back to Pisania. But for now we've got a job to do." The explorer's voice catches and stutters, his body seized with a sudden shiver. The blue velvet coat hangs limp, black and shapeless, duckweed spots his shirt, his boots are fishponds. A huge water strider, enmeshed in the tangle of his beard, waves its ungainly legs.

Behind him, the beaver top hat — stuffed with notes on manners and mores, distances, temperatures and topographic curiosities — perches on the edge of the dock like some strange fungal growth. High and dry. Johnson dusts it against his leg.

"Mansa's palace?" suggests Mungo.

Johnson hands him the hat. "Mansa's palace."

◄§ MANSONG

The potentate of Bambarra, having just finished an enormous breakfast (baked plantain, four varieties of melon, boiled rice with spinach, fried cichlids, sorghum pudding, palm wine), is in the process of slaking his lust with the aid of two prepubescent boys singled out from among the Jarran refugees, when news of the explorer's arrival reaches him. His initial reaction is a protracted belch. Naked, big-bellied, indolent, he is stretched out beneath the sycamore fig in the inner courtyard of his townhouse, still as a sunning crocodile. Sandalwood sweetens the air, caged birds warble of peace and solitude, the cool of the rain forest. The royal flyswatters, scrawny old men in loincloths, are busily at work, the soft swish-swish of their whisks like footsteps in a dream. Mansong sucks meditatively at the hookah, its bowl glowing with *mutokuane,** thinking "Ah, ah," while his twenty grim and devoted bodyguards, each manipulating a long-stemmed fan, stir up a bit of a breeze. His senses reel. The younger of the boys is gently fellating him, while the other licks at his face, running a stiff probing tongue over his lips and nose and eyelids, as if he were lapping milk from a bowl. The whole thing is so blissful and sensual, such an orgasm of neuron and synapse — such a trip — that at first the runner's words don't register. Blanched demon? Cat's eyes? Mass hysteria? But then, like pinpricks, the words begin to penetrate: outside the gate, white horror, begging admittance. This. Very. Minute.

Mansong jerks up, slapping the boys aside. "What?" he roars. The fans drop with a hiss as the bodyguards snatch up their spears, the birds fall silent, the royal swatters redouble their efforts. Mansong is up out of his

---

*A sort of tobacco made from the cured leaves of the hemp plant, *Cannabis sativa,* which the natives smoke in order to enhance sexual performance and induce dreams.

hammock now, huge, terrible, champing his jaws like a river horse startled up from the muck. One bulbous fist is already closing round the messenger's throat, the other poised to deliver a blow. "What are these lies?" he bellows.

"No lies — truth," says the messenger, prostrating himself. "A demon, white as mother's milk, burst through the gates of the city and threw himself into the river, curdling its waters. Then he hounded the people from the streets, chanting and jabbering in a harsh alien tongue. And now he has come to speak with you, Mansa."

Mansong removes his foot from the back of the man's neck. He suddenly looks as if he's about to cry. "With me?" he whispers.

The prostrate messenger strains his eyes upward, as if consulting a note pinned to his forehead. "That's what he says."

"Jackal! You're lying!" The foot comes down again, grinding the messenger's cheek into the dirt. "You just got through telling me this demon speaks in a harsh alien tongue. How then can he ask to see me?"

The runner's face is twisted out of proportion by the weight of Mansong's foot, his lips puckered like the lips of a fish. "He speaks Mandingo."

Mansong staggers back as if he's been shot. Speaks Mandingo? It's all up. They've sent a zombie from the nether world to take his throne. They'll chain his ankles and lead him down through caverns in the earth, through the festering holes where the walking dead gibber and moan, down, ever deeper, to the world of shadows. He scans the faces of his bodyguards, men who could pull charging lions inside out, and sees terror in their eyes. He wants to run, hide himself, leave the country, burrow into the ground. "You say . . . he's out there . . . now?"

"Yes, Mansa. Out there now."

The potentate backs away, eyes rushing. The sun is gone, the fig tree, nis guards — he can see nothing but the transparent figures of his victims, legions of them, disemboweled warriors, charred women, children holding out their severed limbs to him. "No!" he whispers, backpedaling still, his lips and tongue working, on the verge of crying out — shrieking till his throat goes raw, howling like the hidden hopeless things that die night after night in the black fastness of the jungle.

But at that moment a calm dignified little man steps into the courtyard, walking briskly. Businesslike, each step a minute lost, he strides up to the chief, a huge black object tucked under his arm. There is an air of expectancy about him, of intrigue, of upper-echelon wheelings and dealings. He could be a high-powered attorney, Secretary of Foreign Affairs, the Prime Minister. "Calm yourself, Mannie," he says. "I'll take charge here."

His name is Wokoko, the tribal necromancer. He is dressed in a costume composed of the spare parts of a pack of hyenas — claws, teeth and matted yellow fur — and the feathers from a flock of marabous. The object under his arm is a carved wooden mask so relentlessly hideous in every detail as to put any ten demons in their place. With a snap of his fingers he orders half the guards to the front gate, then addresses the still-prostrate messenger. "Tell the demon," he says, in his judicious tones, "that the omnipotent Mansong, throttler of the lion and tamer of the bull, cannot see him now . . . he has a headache."

◈ FIFTY THOUSAND COWRIES

Mansong's palace is a rambling, haphazard structure built of notched timber and the rocklike red clay from which termites construct their mounds. The flow of the building is interrupted by an involuted series of walled walkways and courtyards. Tapering palms sway over these court-yards like antennae, and the crown of a huge sycamore fig can be seen rising in canopy from the center of the compound. Each of the buildings and interior walls has been whitewashed with a mixture of bone powder, starch and water. Inadequate to the task, the wash has left the walls a soft pastel pink; in places the red glares through in streaks like clawmarks in the flank of a sacrificial cow. The whole is enclosed behind a ten-foot wall of clay and pointed stakes surmounted by blue-black thorns an inch in length. There is only one gate. The door is made of fasces of bamboo lashed tightly together. It is three feet thick.

Explorer and guide have been standing before this gate for nearly three hours. At periodic intervals Johnson cups his hands to his mouth and delivers a stentorian plea to the effect that he is but a humble Mandingo from Dindikoo who has brought with him a harmless white man (*hon-kee*) from beyond Bambouk, the Jallonka Wilderness and the great salt sea, and that this white man has come expressly to pay obeisance to Mansong, slayer of lions and throttler of bulls, whose fame has blossomed like the spreading lotus until it has come to incorporate the wide world.

Thus far there has been no response.

The heat of course is oppressive. Nag and ass lie in the shade of the wall, bundles of bone. The explorer has been alternately shivering and sweating, his nose is running and his joints feel as if spikes have been driven into them. Johnson bats at flies.

"Tell me, Johnson," the explorer begins conversationally, squatting now in the dust, "why is it that you feel compelled to wear that damned bit of carrion round your neck?"

The guinea hen has by this time lost its head and the remaining wing. Ribs, stippled with bits of pink flesh and blue vein, have begun to emerge from the mat of feathers, and maggots foam from the body cavity like paste squeezed from a tube. It would be redundant to talk of flies.

"Convention," says Johnson.

"Convention?"

Johnson sighs. "It's no big deal. When the Jarrans heard that Tiggitty Sego was advancin' on them they went to Eboe. As village necromancer it was his duty to appease Chakalla, god of violated taboos, by assumin' all the sins of the townspeople in the hope that Chakalla would then turn back Sego's army. So Eboe he mixes his potions and mutters his incantations until all the sins of the village are transferred to the guinea hen. From there it's child's play: bleed the hen and hang it round your neck until the flesh drops off. And voilà: Sego is stopped in his tracks."

The explorer looks as if he's just swallowed a fork. "But you're joking. You don't mean to say you believe all that mumbo jumbo?"

"No more unreasonable than believin' in virgin births or ladders to heaven."

"You mean — you question the Bible?" Mungo is shocked to his roots. Lord, they're savages, he's thinking. Dress them up, educate them, do what you will. Their minds are in the jungle.

Johnson remains silent, arms folded, eyes fixed on the gate.

"All right. If it's so bloody effective, all this damned guinea hen business, then what happened at Jarra?"

"See for yourself: the hen ain't rotted yet. Eboe was too late, that's all. Simple as that." He grins. "You know the old saw: a stitch in time — "

Mungo waves the back of his hand at him. "Okay. I'll grant it all — black magic and witchcraft and the whole works. But you still haven't answered me: why should *you* have to go around wearing the bloody thing?"

Johnson's face falls. He looks like a hound caught slipping a chop from the table. "Well, I figured — well, you know, we was starvin' — "

"You don't mean — ?"

Johnson nods. "I was goin' to cook it up with the mushrooms and tomberong berries and all. Shit: I thought he was dead. What harm would it have done?"

"So now — you've got all those sins on *your* head?" Despite himself, somewhere deep in his superstitious soul, the explorer is beginning to feel the clutch of a nameless dread. Ghoulies and ghosties and things that go bump in the night.

"'Cause I reached for it. Like a fool. And Eboe was just lyin' there waitin', holdin' his breath — playin' possum, the old artificer." Johnson fiddles with his toga, sighs. "So now I've got to answer to Chakalla for every little broken taboo in the history of that godforsaken backwater hamlet. Every time a pregnant woman eats a egg or a boy copulates with a pangolin. Every time a young girl walks backward under a crescent moon, rubs her face with hoona sap or plucks her pubic hair with her right hand. And that's just the start. Then there's the bird taboos, the fecal taboos, the mandibular taboos. Did you know you're not allowed to touch your chin with the index finger while sittin' on the north side of a campfire?

"It all devolves on me now. Chakalla's out to flay the sin out of my hide. If I can stay out of trouble till there's nothin' left of this damned bird but desiccated bone, I'll live to dance on Eboe's grave. If not — well, bury me deep."

Their conversation is interrupted at this juncture by a shuffling sound on the far side of the gate. A moment later the gate cracks open and a servant pokes his head out. "Mansong can't see you now. Come back next year." And that's that. The head disappears, the massive door begins to creak shut.

Mungo is dumbfounded, immobilized by surprise. But Johnson, always alert, springs forward and jams his foot in the door. "Look," he says, fighting for ground, "we got to see the Mansa right away. This minute. It's been a long, hard road and we figure we're entitled to a little hospitality. Besides: we got presents for him."

The servant's head reappears. "Presents?" Lines break across his brow. "One minute, please," he says before vanishing again. From behind the door, the sound of conferring voices. Minutes tick by. A pair of opalescent lizards chase one another up the wall. The explorer picks a bit of duckweed from his coat and looks forlornly at the sack of trade goods lashed to the nag's concave back. "Lavish presents," Johnson calls. "Exotic, magical things — fit for a god and a emperor."

All at once the door swings back and the servant, shrunken with worry, gestures for them to enter. Guide and explorer step through the gate and into a walled courtyard bristling with armed guards. Giants, six and a half or seven feet tall, pectorals like iron, knives, spears, darts and arrows glinting out from the black shadows of their bodies. They wear loincloths of leopard skin, plumes and anklets of ostrich feathers. Any one of them could clear the floor of Parliament in thirty seconds flat.

But as the explorer brushes by, he notices that they avert their eyes and clutch at their *saphies,* thick lips moving as if in prayer. "Hot dog," Johnson whispers, falling back on one of his arcane colonial expressions. "You've got them awestruck."

Wringing his hands and tugging at lip and ear, the servant leads them through a succession of identical rooms, walkways and courtyards. The rooms are uniformly low of ceiling, decorated with a Persian rug or tapestry, reed mats on the floor, a tumble of earthenware pottery; the courtyards feature wispy palms, water troughs alive with weed and insect, caged birds, goats, chickens, lizards, dust. It seems as if they've been walking for miles. In and out of rooms, down pathways so narrow the explorer has to hug his shoulders. Through a courtyard with six palms, another with two. Eight chickens here, four there. Here a goat, there a cow. Finally, the servant, who has begun to quake like an epileptic at the onset of a seizure, motions for them to wait at the entrance of a long narrow walkway. They watch the pale flash of the soles of his feet as he hurries toward the point at which the walls seem to converge. They watch as he falls to his knees, presses his forehead to the earth. They hear themselves announced: white demon and black sorcerer.

The explorer stumbles twice and finds himself in an expansive courtyard, two or three times the size of the others. The whole is brooded over by an enormous snaking fig tree that casts a bit of shade in even the farthest corners. As he looks closer, the explorer is chilled to discover that the tree is festooned with human skulls, and a number of carved figures depicting unnatural acts: autofellatio, pederasty, the eating of excrement. The most arresting statue, its features greedily distorted, shows a pregnant woman with the multiple dugs of a dog either swallowing or regurgitating a serpent, which is in turn either swallowing or regurgitating the head of an infant.

At the base of the tree, obscured in deepest shadow, there is a sort of throne, rough-hewn wood with a glitter of paint. Beside the throne, a white dog lies asleep in a cloud of flies. When he turns to look behind him, the explorer sees that the narrow walkway is choked with armed guards, black giants identical to those who barred the front gate. He begins to feel somewhat ill at ease.

Suddenly a masked figure springs out from behind the tree with a primordial shriek. "Wo-ya-ya-yaaa!" the figure screams, pounding bare feet in the dust and brandishing a scepter topped with a polished skull.

Mungo, taken by surprise, steps back a pace or two and finds himself standing in a low trough filled with a dark, nasty-looking liquid. There are splashes of it on his boots and the legs of his pants. Wet and red. Bloody red. And now suddenly the dog is on its feet, howling, yabbering, foam on its muzzle. "Wo-ya-ya-ya-yeee!" the masked man thunders, apocalyptic, whirling toward him in a blur of feather and bone, and now all at once the sound of drumming, doom-baba-doom, doom-baba-doom, and the guards taking up the refrain: "ya-ya, ya-ya, YEEE!" The explorer is stricken, paralyzed, his legs and feet encased in lead, inner voices screaming for self-preservation, exhorting him to run, flee, bolt, scratch, bite, kill.

But then a familiar hand closes round his elbow. "Stay cool," Johnson whispers. "They're terrified of you."

Terrified? he thinks. Of me? Yet already the din has begun to subside, the guards chanting under their breath, the dog easing back on its haunches, the drumming a whisper. The masked man, swathed in fur and feather, settles into the throne and with a wave of the scepter commands silence. The explorer takes advantage of the lull to step from the trough, and Johnson, bowing low to the ground, approaches the man in the mask and spreads the gifts before him. Sunlight dapples the dust beneath the tree. The gifts, chosen in London by Sir Joseph Banks and calculated to win the savage heart, glow like the treasury of the gods. An appreciative gasp escapes one of the guards, but the man in the mask remains impassive, arms folded across his chest.

Johnson bows again, and then launches his presentation speech. "O Mansong, terror of mountain and plain, widowmaker, grappler with spirits and demiurges, vanquisher of eland and elephant, I present these strange and wonderful gifts to you in the name of my liege and protector, this mild, inoffensive and saintly white man, who has traveled immeasurable distances in order to prostrate himself before your eminence." At the word "prostrate," Johnson turns to the explorer and indicates the ground. Mungo falls to his knees, then stretches himself prone in the dust.

While lying there, nose to the ground, he becomes aware of an intermittent movement in the farthest recess of the courtyard. He concentrates on the movement, a blur of shuffling feet, and from the corner of his eye observes this: a screen of woven grass, black feet, fleshy toes wriggling beneath it. And there: the servant, looking harried, ducking behind the screen and then jerking back again, as if his head were on a string. He seems to be conferring with someone, a hidden presence, the articulator of those curled and bloated toes. Here's another mystery, thinks Mungo, slightly feverish, somewhat fearful, totally lost in reverie. But then he becomes aware of Johnson's voice, in English now, floating above him like a nest of hornets. "Okay," a sting in the tone. "Okay, already. Get up."

The explorer rises, dusting at his clothes. He adjusts his tattered collar, finger-combs his beard and slicks back his eyebrows with spittle. But then he realizes that no one is paying the slightest bit of attention to him — all eyes are fixed on a new cynosure: the presents. The servant is hunched over them now, reverentially handing piece by precious piece to the masked man for his examination. First the silver salver. Then the table service for ten, a pair of ivory cufflinks. An umbrella. Ten plugs of tobacco and a jar of orange marmalade. A dozen inkwells, a corset, a wig. And finally, the pièce de résistance: a miniature of King George.

So taken is the presumptive monarch by the glitter and novelty of these gifts that he lets his defenses down: in a single fluid motion he slips the mask up over his head in order to enjoy a better perspective of them. The explorer is stunned. He'd expected a monster, but this fellow, with his quick sharp eyes and sleek little bulb of a head, is more like a ferret, a chicken thief, a sneaky skulking thing of tall grass and shadows. As the little man gingerly bites down on the silver salver, Mungo can't help wondering about Eboe's description of Mansong as a brute of a man with chins and bellies and a head like a melon. Could this fellow be an imposter?

It is then that the explorer becomes aware of the traffic between the throne and the screen in the corner. The original servant, abetted now by a smaller, shrunken, and if possible even more tentative colleague, is scurrying between throne and screen with the treasures. For the explorer, it is an epiphany. "Johnson," he whispers. "You see that screen back there?"

"Shhhh." Johnson looks edgy. "Don't pay it no mind," he hisses. "And whatever you do, don't stare at it. Don't even glance at it. That screen don't exist. Get me?"

At that moment the second servant, a youngish man with a face as puckered and wrinkled as the foreleg of an iguana, sidles up to the explorer. Clenched in his hand, the umbrella. Shrinking back, he holds it out to Mungo at arm's length. Then says something in Mandingo that sounds like "rub-a-dub-dub." Mungo stares at him, blank.

"They want you to open the thing up for them," Johnson prompts.

The umbrella is pink and nacreous, like the stuff of ladies' underwear. An artist has rendered the Tower of London, in red and black, across the top. The explorer releases the catch, and unfurls the parasol with a flourish. This, he realizes too late, is a mistake. At the first rustle of silk, the servant backs off with a gasp; when the umbrella bursts into flower, pandemonium erupts. The guards drop their spears and bolt for the exit, the presumptive monarch grabs frantically for the mask and the white dog lunges for the explorer, while perhaps worst of all, there is a stricken cry from the corner as the screen topples with a rush of air. Behind the screen, now exposed for all to see, is a titanic bull of a man seated in the lotus position, his stomach like a medicine ball, broad skull bowed as he scribbles furiously in the dirt. Though the explorer has no way of realizing it, the big man's scribbling represents the frantic geometry of voodoo — vectors and tangents, catenaries and triangles — charms to ward off evil. The potentate is terrified.

In the confusion, the explorer collapses the umbrella, more as a means of defending himself from the dog than as a gesture of conciliation. The effect is immediate and tranquilizing: the guards pause, elbow one another, grin sheepishly; the imposter calls off the dog with a single harsh command; the servants hurriedly reerect the fallen screen. Johnson has all the while been chattering away in Mandingo, too fast for the explorer's grasp, but in a tone that seems reassuring, jocular even. Now he puts together a string of six or seven phrases, the whole thing timed as if leading up to a punchline. He breaks off with a hearty laugh, then nudges the explorer. "Heh-heh," Mungo says.

The imposter, mask in hand, ducks his head twice and shows his teeth in a weird, strained facial expression partway between grimace and grin. He looks as if he's just been punched in the bladder after watching a hundred fat women slip on banana peels. After donning the mask once again, he commands the servant to bring him the parasol. The servant handles it as if it were a sleeping cobra.

Five minutes later, the masked man is busily engaged in dipping his finger into the marmalade and emitting short cries of epicurean delight as he licks the goo from his fingertip, while from behind the screen can be heard the soft rustle of silk. From time to time the pink flash of the parasol shows itself coquettishly over the top of the screen. The dog is asleep, its muzzle buried in the portrait of King George, as if in olfactory contemplation of that great and distant monarch.

Finally, after a lengthy conference with the man behind the screen, the imposter steps forward and begins a rambling acceptance speech. The voice emanating from behind the mask is crisp and animated, but for all that the explorer finds the dialect difficult to follow. At first he makes a concerted effort at interpretation, pinning the words down one by one, translating them in his head, coming to understand that his homage has been accepted by the gracious and puissant Mansong, Mansa of Waboo, M'butta-butta, Wonda, and about two hundred other places. But he soon begins to develop a migraine from the sheer force of concentration all this requires, and after awhile simply assumes an interested expression and lets his mind wander. Ten minutes into the speech he is distracted from his mental peregrinations by a series of odd, muffled sounds which seem to be coming from the adjoining courtyard. Sounds of a scuffle perhaps, stifled cries, a sussurus that recalls a barnyard in Selkirk and the butchering of chickens for the pot. He taps Johnson's shoulder. "What's going on next door?"

Johnson's eyes are pinned deep in their sockets. "Better you don't know."

"— the magnanimous Mansong — " drones the man in the mask.

"Tell me. That's an order." ·

"Well, they're impressed." Johnson glances up quickly, then looks down at his feet. The masked man drones on. "Mansong is disembowelin' thirty-seven slaves in your honor."

"Mother of God." Nothing could prepare him for this. Nothing. He grits his teeth and tries to think of Scotland, of barbered hills, open white faces, safety and sanity. But there's no time to think, the worry-worn servant at his elbow, holding out some sort of sack and a cup of dark liquid, wine or beer — and what do they want with him now?

"Take it," Johnson hisses.

Shaken, the explorer reaches out for sack and cup.

"Fifty thousand cowrie shells," Johnson whispers. "That's enough cash to support a village like Dindikoo for the next ten years. Smile, you fool. Nod and grin. That's it." Johnson is rubbing his hands together like a shopkeeper sitting down to his evening meal. "Now we can buy bed and board in any village up and down the river. Women. Beer. Meat. No more sleepin' in the bushes."

"But . . . those damned bloody heathen aborigines are taking thirty-seven lives right under our noses — in our honor nonetheless. Thirty-seven rational beings. . . . Take the money and we condone it."

"Hey, Mr. Park. This is no time to get sanctimonious. So long as we don't wind up as number thirty-eight and thirty-nine I figure we're doin' just fine."

The masked man seems to be winding down now, his phrases growing long and languorous; the explorer, shuddering at each gag and wheeze from the adjoining courtyard, picks up random phrases: "prosperous journey," "too bad you can't stay longer," "riches untold — downriver."

Finally the little man throws off the mask. There is a cup in his hand. He raises it, as if saluting the explorer.

Mungo stares numbly at his own hand. He is almost surprised to see that he is holding an identical cup. "Raise the cup," Johnson coaches. There is a burbling sound from beyond the wall, a flatulent groan, as if the air had been forced from a mammoth bellows. "Drink!"

The explorer raises his cup as if toasting the little man in hyena skins. He puts it to his lips, the smell of it firing his nostrils, gamey, somehow reminiscent of moor and wood, out shooting with his father, the taste of it now, warm and faintly salt, roast beef, liver and duck: he doesn't think, doesn't want to think. Just drains the cup and wipes his mouth with the back of his hand.

⊰ DIMINISHING RETURNS

Ailie Anderson lifts the teacup to her lips, vapor rising, the dark earthy aroma of pot-brewed coffee firing her nostrils. Like steamed acorns, she thinks, sipping. Or a good black stout. Some of the church elders have gotten up tracts against coffee, tracts that show how it leads to moral decay while it upsets the body's equilibrium and tampers with the Lord's design for the regulation of appetite, but she doesn't pay them much mind. She likes her cup of a crisp morning. Likes the smell and the bitterness and the lift it gives her.

Gleg and her father, traditionalists, take tea with their bannocks and brose. The two of them are strangely silent this morning, as if they've been conspiring — they sit there, slumped over their saucers, champing at their oatcakes like horses in a stable. The resulting lipsmack, and the ring of a spoon in a cup, are the only sounds. Zander's place is empty. He was up before sunrise, restless, out wandering the hills somewhere.

Gleg, as usual, had showered her with "good mornings" and semilascivious compliments on the fit of her dress, the color in her cheeks, the trim of her waist. But now, sleep in his eye, he's settled down to the steady, serious business of cramming his maw. Her father, shaggy and unkempt, has emitted six syllables since taking his place at the table: "The bannocks is burnt, lass." His head is bent to fork and plate in a way that strikes her as common, inappropriate to his station. A streak of scalp shows naked and pink through the white mass of his hair.

Yes, the bannocks are burned. She'll be the first to admit it. She was distracted — and it's his fault really. Two months back, when the sun was strewing wildflowers over the hills, he'd brought her back a present from Edinburgh. Something to amuse her, take her mind off the deeps of Africa and the tedious progression of days and weeks and months. He slipped through the front door, a smirk on his face, his right hand buried deep in the pocket of his greatcoat. She was a child again, his little girl. What is it, tell me?

It was a microscope. Wooden stand, brass cylinder, glass lens. Nothing to wear, nothing to eat. He hadn't brought her a scarf, or a pendant, or a box of pralines. No news of fashions, no perfumes, not even a copy of *The Lady's Magazine* or *The Monthly Review*. A microscope. She couldn't hide her disappointment.

It sat in the front vestibule for two weeks. Gleg simpered after her, while her father seemed to encourage him. Her closest friend, Katlin Gibbie, married and moved to an outlying farm, and Zander became increasingly withdrawn, absorbed in his own problems. There had been no news of Mungo. She was bored. One afternoon she magnified a piece of newsprint and was astonished to see that each letter was composed of myriad black specks. A bit of thread was a boatman's cable, the dog's hair a thicket, a flea a monster. She ransacked the house, exploring everything she could lay her hands on — the weave of her skirts, the topography of a piece of rag paper, the impossible, delicate tension that held a drop of milk in suspension. Then she turned to the yard. Leaves, bark, the petals of roses, insects. She marveled at the grid of a fly's wing, the downy froth that beads a moth's antennae, the cruel cusp of an ant's mandible. She tore spider webs from the eaves, plucked feathers from her doves. One morning she took a dace from the aquarium and pinned it down to examine the fine mesh of its scales, overlapping like waves on a beach. She was enthralled. The void Mungo had left began to diminish as the objects of her scrutiny grew beneath the lens. There was a center to her days. She watched it expand.

Her sketches, charcoal and ink, banished the walls. Here the veins of a leaf, there the whorls of a fingerprint. An eyelash like a spar, the minatory serrations of a beetle's leg. She found a copy of Hooke's *Micrographia* in her father's library and devoured it as if it were a three-volume novel. Hooke had magnified a bit of cork and discovered its hidden superstructure: it was composed of tiny interlocking units, cubicles invisible to the eye, unsuspected by the imagination. Cells, he called them, because they reminded him of the compartments in a monastery. Ailie took the stopper from a bottle of port, sliced a wafer-thin shaving from it with her father's razor, and screwed it into focus. She saw nothing but pits and fissures. That night she went to bed deflated, dreaming of worlds beyond the scope of the eye, beyond the scope of screwbarrel and lens, worlds ever smaller, worlds within worlds within worlds.

Then she discovered van Leeuwenhoek.

She came across a reference to his work in one of her father's medical journals. Nearly a hundred years earlier, with the aid of the extraordinarily powerful lenses he ground himself, Leeuwenhoek had debunked the Aristotelian notion of spontaneous generation. He described the life cycles of the flea and the grain weevil, asserting that they arose from fertilized eggs rather than sand or grain itself, as had been previously supposed. As Francesco Redi had connected the growth of maggots and the eggs of houseflies, so Leeuwenhoek demonstrated that even the lowliest creatures, hardly visible to the naked eye themselves, similarly arose from creatures that had preceded them. For Ailie, who had labored for days making crude sketches of the fleas she plucked from beneath her dog's collar, it was a revelation.

Her father's library was spotty, but his old friend and colleague, Dr. Donald Dinwoodie of Kelso, had a complete set of the Royal Society's *Philsophical Transactions,* to which Leeuwenhoek had contributed for the last fifty years of his life. Ailie packed her microscope and sketchpads, saddled the mare and rode the thirty miles to Kelso. She boarded with Dinwoodie for a month, poring over his books. Leeuwenhoek, she discovered, had seen "animalcules" teeming in a drop of water, the trembling globular components of human blood, the thrashing swarm of spermatozoa in the semen of insects, cattle and men. Worlds within worlds. Quaking with excitement, she went to the rain barrel, removed a vial of water and examined a drop of it beneath her lens. She saw nothing. Her simple apparatus didn't have the power. She pricked her finger and scrutinized a drop of blood. Again, nothing. For the semen, she thought, she would wait for Mungo.

Back at Selkirk, she continued her studies, but her enthusiasm was waning. What was the sense? No one knew Leeuwenhoek's secrets — how he had managed to grind lenses that magnified an object from fifty to three hundred times its actual size, or how he had enhanced that magnification with mirrors and lights to attain an even greater amplification. Her screwbarrel scope was a toy. She was disgusted. But then, one morning, Gleg had sidled into the kitchen, grinning like a frog, hands hidden behind his back. "I missed you," he said, lingering over the syllables as if each were a slice of toast to be buttered. "My heart bled each morn at your absence, and swounded each even when the sun set without you."

She was kneading dough. She glanced up at him and was startled at the expression on his face. His head was bobbing, his ears wagging, while his impossible slippery grin hoisted his cheeks, dropped his nose and exposed his yellowed teeth like a row of tombstones. Suddenly it hit her: he was having an attack. She started up from her stool, hands white with flour: "Georgie — are you all right?"

He stood there, beaming, stuffed to bursting with the news and the rustle of paper behind his back. "Here," he said, producing a package wrapped in brown paper, "for you. With all my love and esteem."

She wiped her hands on her apron, grinning despite herself, and reached out for the package. "For me?" she said, tearing at the paper. She caught her breath. It was a book, leather cover, gilt lettering. *Essays on the Microscope* by George Adams the Younger, 1787. The latest word on microscopy. She threw her arms out for pure joy — but Gleg held up his lank palm.

Grinning still, trembling, bursting, an otter with a fish in his mouth, he produced a second package from behind his back. She tore off the paper. A wooden box. Heavy. She took it to the counter and pried it open with a kitchen knife — the gleam of metal — could it be?

It was a new W. & S. Jones microscope, three times as powerful as her screwbarrel. "But Georgie, how — ?"

"My aunt," he said. "Auntie MacKinnon. She's dead of the dropsy and left me a modest inheritance. Or rather," his face was flushed, "left it to you — to do with as you wish. All I have is yours."

Drums, there were drums beating in her chest. She spun round the room, skipping, then took hold of his frayed flapping sleeves and kissed him.

◆§ §◆

And so, the bannocks are burned. It's the fault of both of them really. She'd been up at first light, peering into the gilded aperture, overseeing a ballet of animalcules, hundreds to the head of a pin, whirling things, translucent, their edges furred with the shades of chromatic distortion. There were cylindrical things, and oblong things that propelled themselves with hairs or tails, things that joined and split and joined again. And then there were the amorphous things, looking as if they'd been dropped from a height, their boundaries crenellated, a great dark spot hovering over them like the yolk of a frying egg. How could they expect her to think of oatcakes and milk brose when she was lambent with the thrill of discovery?

Even now, at the breakfast table, Gleg patting his lips with the napkin and throwing her lovelorn glances, her father belching over his tea, she can't put down her dog-eared copy of the Adams book. She wants one thing only: for them to get up and go off to their doctoring so she can be at peace with her sketchpads and her tools of surveillance.

Her father clears his throat, pushes his chair back from the table. "Gleg," he mutters, his voice thick with catarrh, "get out and harness the horses, will ye? We've got a call to make out Fowlshiels way."

Gleg stands, awkward, his knee cracking the table like a hammerblow, then shuffles out the door.

There is sun now, tapering blades stabbing in over the curtains, setting the olc man's head afire. He sips at his tea, noisily. Then clears his throat agair. a sound like the dredging of rivers. "I see Katlin Gibbie's got herself nuptialed, eh?"

Ailie looks up from her book. "That's right, father. It wasn't two weeks ago that you yourself washed the bride's feet, broke bannocks over her head, finished off a jug of whisky and danced a Highland reel atop her dining table singing 'Hey tuttie taitie' at the top of your lungs — if I'm not mistaken."

The old man is grinning — gentle, paternal and boyish all at once. "I seem to recall something of the like."

"So why do you ask?"

"Well —" he scratches at the bristle under his chin, locks his fingers and stretches, then looks her dead in the eye. "She was sixteen, wasn't she?"

Ailie nods.

"You're no gettin' any younger, lass."

"I know it, father."

"There's a young mon round here that dotes on every breath that passes your lips."

She looks away, closes her book and lays it on the sideboard. When she turns back to him he's still staring at her, sage and slow, patient and persuasive. Her voice catches in her throat. "I know it, father."

⊰ FROM THE EXPLORER'S NOTEBOOK

Immediately following the discovery of this storied and magnificent river, which is to my way of thinking in all respects superior to the Thames or even the Rhine, my factotum and I made our way to the palace of the local sovereign, Mansong of Bambarra. There we were greeted with a warmth and civility that made our hearts glad after grappling so long with inanition and the merciless depredations of the desert Moor. Though Mansong kept no lions on gilded chains, nor were his streets paved with that precious metal, his rooms and grounds were nonetheless the very picture of opulence. There were open courtyards in the Iberian style, flowing fountains and exotic gardens laden with every sort of fruit and bud imaginable. We were led through a succession of these courtyards to the inner sanctum itself, where Mansong awaited us.

The potentate was a big-boned man of cheerful countenance, seated on a golden throne and surrounded by his fierce elite guard, savages built like racehorses and standing six and a half or seven feet from the ground. I made my obeisance, and then presented him with the gifts I had carried with me from England. Of these, he seemed most taken with the portrait of his counterpart on the far side of the world, our own son of Hanover, His Majesty King George III. He sat and contemplated the face and figure of that august monarch for some time, his own features glowing with the incandescence of enlightenment.

After thanking me profusely, Mansong made me a munificent present in return, with his heartfelt hope that it would aid me in the pursuit of my quest for knowledge. He rose heavily from his throne, embraced me like a lost son, and handed me a leather sack filled to bursting with cowrie shells — over fifty thousand in all. Imagine my gratitude at so selfless a gesture on the part of this rude but true prince of the jungle, who had just given over a small fortune to me — a fortune that would allow me to pursue my journey upriver to Timbuctoo, and from thence to the termination of the mighty Niger itself!

Though he urged us to stay, offering up the most princely accommodations and a feast of loaves, viands and local delicacies his servants had prepared in anticipation of our coming, we were anxious to press on, and left that very night, after sharing a firm handclasp and a ceremonial drink . .

✍ ALL THE KING'S MEN

"But this is the purest of bullshit," says Johnson, handing the slip of paper back to the explorer. "A distortion and a lie. About the only thing that's accurate is the seven-foot guards. And the cash."

Mungo rides on in silence, something like a superior smirk tugging at his lip. He and Johnson have just passed the last sagging hut along the road out of Segu. They are headed for Kabba, four miles downriver, where they plan to purchase food and lodging for the night, and from there to make their way to Sansanding, a Moorish trading town on the road to Timbuctoo.

The immensity of the forest broods over them, dense and thick-ribbed, close as a glove. Colossal dripping leaves hang out over the path like greatcoats draped over sticks, there is a stench of decay, of muck, of slow heat and decomposition. Hidden things rush off in the vegetation as they approach. A hyrax screeches from its perch, leopards cough. It has begun to get dark.

The explorer twists in his saddle to look back at Johnson. "Exactly," he says, folding up the scrap of paper and working it under his hatband. "Can you imagine how unutterably dull it would be if I stuck strictly to bald bare facts — without a hint of embellishment? The good citizens of London and Edinburgh don't want to read about misery and wretchedness and thirty-seven slaves disemboweled, old boy — their lives are grim enough as it is. No, they want a little glamor, a touch of the exotic and the out-of-the-way. And what's the harm of giving it to them?"

Johnson weaves along on his ass, parting leaf and stem like a swimmer parting the waves. He is shaking his head. "But you're suppose to be an explorer. The first white man to come in here and tell it like it is. A myth-breaker, iconoclast, recorder of reality. If you ain't absolutely rigorous, down to the tiniest detail, you're a sham, and I'm sorry to say it." Johnson's voice is raised. He swats angrily at the festering guinea hen, and a bit of it drops to the path beside him. "A sham," he repeats. "No better than Herodotus or Desceliers or any of them other armchair heroes that charted out the interior of Africa from behind the four walls of their book-lined studies."

"Now Johnson, you're not being fair at all. I'm giving them facts — of course. About the geography, the culture, the flora and fauna. Of course I am. That's what I'm here for. But to stick to facts and nothing but — why the English reading public wouldn't stand for it. They can read Hansard if they want facts. Or the *Times* obituaries. When they read about Africa they want adventure, they want amaze. They want stories like Bruce and Jobson gave them. And that's what *I* intend to give them. Stories."

"All right, look Mr. Park: sorry I mentioned it. Actually, it's no skin off my ass what you do with your book. No chance I'll ever see it anyway. All I care about right now is that we're ploddin' along here jawin' away while the sun is sinkin' into the trees and there sure as hell ain't no place to spend all them cowries out here in the bush — so maybe we ought to concentrate on the road and gettin' to the next town up the line, huh?"

"No need to get huffy about it. Just thought you'd like to see what I'd been scratching away at the last mile or so, that's all."

After this exchange, a raw nagging silence sets in, full of bitter sniffing and aggressive flyswatting, as the two jostle along the weed-choked path in growing darkness. Soon a dreary insistent rain begins to fall, as if the hunger, discomfort and general irritation weren't enough. They plod on, the silence rankling. Trees drift by, trees upon trees, as they work their way deeper into the green maw of the forest. Up ahead a towering vine-draped ciboa looms in the mist, and the explorer is just about to suggest that they take shelter beneath it when suddenly a violent blow catches him under the chin and he is catapulted from his horse into a sodden welter of leaves.

He lies there a moment, taking stock of the situation, while predatory insects scoot up his pantleg and down his collar. Then he hears Johnson's cry. It begins as a screech that could curdle milk, modulates down through six or eight octaves and ends in an abrupt gasp. At this point, the explorer is not overly anxious to discover what it was that hit him, but he stands up anyway, fumbling in a vague way for the knife he sometimes keeps at his belt. What he sees is this: a clutch of six-and-a-half or seven-foot giants pounding away at Johnson's inert form with cudgels the size of railway ties, while another of their party drops the nag with a single bone-crunching blow. There is a surprised, interrogatory whinny, and then the thundering crash of the animal's fall.

Then one of the cudgel wielders suddenly looks up, points a finger at the explorer and shouts: "*Tobaubo!*" At this, the man who'd dispatched the horse starts up violently from the carcass (where he'd been plundering the saddlebags). Mungo is no more than ten feet from him. He can see the sweat on the man's upper lip, the points of his filed teeth, the black leather sack of cowries clenched in his fist. Almost as a reflex the explorer draws his knife, and the man is on him like a great leaping mastiff, a blow to the solar plexus, another to the crotch and then a stunning crack just beneath the left ear, and now there are hands under his armpits, on his boots, hands tugging at the buttons of his trousers . . .

It is dark and still. Rain sifts through the trees with a whisper. The horse is dead, the ass gone. There is no sound from Johnson. Mungo is lying supine in the ooze of the forest floor, naked as the day he was born, broken it seems in any number of places, and feeling very weary indeed. Very weary of exploring, very weary of Africa. And very weary of being alone here in the dark, defenseless and afraid. He props himself on his elbows, wincing with the effort, and looks around. Nothing. The dark is so absolute and impenetrable it's as if the earth has been turned inside out. But what was that? A movement in the bush, a rustle of leaves. "Johnson?"

No answer.

He tries again. "Johnson — is that you?"

This time he gets a response, but not what he'd hoped for. A snarl, low and ominous, punctuates the night. A snarl as savage and arbitrary as the forest itself, rasping and harsh as the birth of evil.

◄§ FANNY BRUNCH

One grim afternoon, as the rain slashed across the panes at No. 32, Soho Square, and Sir Joseph Banks, his spine still leaping from the thrashing he'd taken at the Swedish baths, wearily ascended the front steps, the upper house parlormaid — a thick-ankled old bird of a woman who had been in his employ for twenty-seven years — succumbed to a swift and sudden attack of brain fever. She was serving tea to Lady Banks and Miss Sarah Sophia in the drawing room. The tea had been brewed in a silver pot, which rested on a silver salver. The cups and saucers were of Sèvres china. As poor Betty Smoot bent over her mistress with the teapot, she suddenly jerked up as if she'd been bitten in the rear, sang two verses of a filthy drinking song at the top of her lungs, and keeled over dead.

Two days later Lady Banks was well enough to discuss the situation with her husband. "Jos," she said, "what we need is a new upper house parlormaid."

Sir Joseph was scanning the newspaper for word of the Portuguese expedition in the Bight of Benin.

"Cook has a cousin in Hertfordshire. Or a sister or something. They've got a girl there who's anxious for a place. I believe she's Cook's cousin's daughter. Or sister's. Well, she's young. Seventeen. But as I said to Cook, a little youth wouldn't hurt around here"

Sir Joseph glanced up. "The girl's name?"

"Brunch," said Lady B. "Fanny Brunch."

◆§ ৪►

Fanny Brunch was fresh from the creamery. Her breath was hot with the smell of milk, and it whispered of cribs and nipples and the darkness of the womb. Her skin was cream, her breasts cheeses, there was butter in her smile. When she was fifteen two country louts hacked one another to death over her. With hoes. The following year the local squire abducted her and bound her to his bed. They found him in his nightshirt, the bed a sea of feathers, red welts stippling Fanny's buttocks. It was then that her parents, hardworking paupers who believed in the goodness of man and the kingdom of God on earth, decided that she should be put into service for her own protection. The death of Betty Smoot was a godsend.

Fanny was good-natured and ingenuous. She grinned like wheatfields in the sun, stole round the house on soft celestial feet. Lady Banks, after twenty-seven years of Smoot, called her a breath of springtime. Sir Joseph, occupied as he was with the African Association and the latest of his vanished explorers, hardly noticed her. Which was just as well — the last thing she needed was to have to do battle with an old satyr in his lair. Cook worshipped her. The butler, Byron Bount, tried to lick her forearm one afternoon when she had her sleeves rolled up, but Cook cured him by saltpetering his fried tomatoes. There was one unfortunate incident: a houseguest of the Banks', a melancholy young poet with black circles round his eyes, threw himself from the third-story window for love of her. He broke nine ribs, both legs and lost an ear. But aside from that, things had been quiet, and Fanny Brunch was well on her way to becoming an institution at No. 32, Soho Square.

Then she met Ned Rise.

◆§ THE SEVEN CITIES OF GOLD

It was fated. Or so she thought looking back on it. How else explain the combination of circumstances that found her strolling up Soho Square on the very June afternoon that Ned Rise was peddling his caviar? As it happened, Sir Joseph was expecting a luncheon visit from one of his African associates, Sir Reginald Durfeys. On his previous visit to No. 32, Soho Square, Durfeys had been so taken with Fanny that he'd torn her dress in three places, destroyed a pair of Ming vases and suffered a mild dropsical fit that left him speechless for the better part of a week. Sir Joseph, a man known in Parliament for his good cigars, sound judgment and foresight, felt that on the present occasion it might be prudent to remove the source of temptation. "Fanny," he said, pressing a coin into her palm, "why don't you take the afternoon off and enjoy yourself?"

She was thrilled. Her first half day in better than three months with Sir Joseph and Lady B. She looked in at shop windows, bought herself a tart, watched a man juggle half a dozen hedgehogs while his sidekick, a ginger-headed dwarf in short pants and turban, played nose flute, contra-bassoon and 'cello in unison. She ate saltwater taffy, tumbled into a cellar, narrowly avoided a mad dog and sat in the park brooding about the lack of poignancy and sweet surrender in her life. When the sun dipped into the trees, she headed home.

❧ ❦

Ned on the other hand thinks of fate as a purely negative force. In accordance with Rise's Law (all things that rise must contain yeast), he's been expecting a fall. Little does he realize, as he settles back in the soothing clasp of the sedan chair, secure in his disguise and reapproaching equilibrium for the first time since Boyles howled out his name in the street, that he is about to soar. Nor does he have an inkling, as he hawks his wares up and down Soho Square, that he is teetering on the verge of a momentous discovery. No: his thoughts are purely mercenary. Debits and credits, pounds and shillings. Jars sold against passage to Amsterdam and a fat nest egg. Yes, Amsterdam, he's thinking — canals and tulips and frazzle-headed fräuleins. Dutch genever. Hans Brinker. Paris is definitely out. What with all the beheadings and Jacobins and reigns of terror . . . he's had enough terror right here in London. No, Paris is out. The celebrated whores and full-bodied wines (or is it the other way around?) will have to stay corked — for the time being, anyway.

At No. 14 the cook takes three jars and invites him in for a cup of tea. The cook compliments him on his bonnet. He compliments the cook on her pans. Two doors up a scullerymaid shuts the door in his face. At No. 19 a dog bites him in the thigh. But the sun is sitting atop the trees like a big round cheddar, the breeze is full of petal and blossom, and in spite of being dead, depressed and exiled, trussed up in a woman's foundations and haunted by shadows, Ned Rise throws back his head and bursts into song:

> *As I was going to Derby,*
> *Upon a market day,*
> *I saw the biggest lamb, sir,*

> That ever was fed with hay,
> That ever was fed with hay.
>
> The lamb was fat behind, sir,
> The lamb was fat before —

But then, right in the middle of the verse, the world stands him on his ears and rearranges his senses: a voice, pitched high and pure and ringing with the conviction that there is after all peace and plenitude on earth, has suddenly joined him:

> She measured ten yards round, sir,
> I think it was no more.

Ned wheels around, his skirts crepitating like a hidden audience. There before him, wicker basket tucked under her arm, stands a girl of seventeen or eighteen. White mobcap, blond ringlets. A chocolate frock over her white stiff tucker. A parlormaid, thinks Ned, as she launches into the next verse as casually as if she were singing before the hearth:

> The wool grew on her back, sir,
> It reachèd to the sky,
> And there the eagles built their nest,
> I heard the young ones cry.
>
> The wool grew on her belly, sir,
> And reachèd to the ground,
> 'Twas sold in Derby town, sir,
> For forty thousand pound.

He's amazed. Staggered. She's something out of a Renaissance painting. Mary the milkmaid, sun firing the nimbus of her ringlets, a basket of fresh eggs and a jar of cream cradled like an infant Messiah in the crook of her arm. Innocence, beauty, sweetness and light: the combination is breathtaking. Without thinking he leaps right into the next verse and plays his tenor against her wavering contralto:

> And all the boys in Derby, sir,
> Came begging for her eyes,
> To kick about the streets, sir,
> As any good football flies.

The mutton that lamb made
Gave the whole army meat,
And what was left, I'm told, sir,
Was served out to the fleet.

And now she's laughing, her teeth perfect, head thrown back, a little dollop of flesh under her chin. "Quite a voice you've got there, Mistress," she laughs.

Ned is grinning like a shark. "I may not be all that I seem, Mistress."

"A wolf in sheep's clothing?"

"Not exactly," replies Ned, tearing off cap and bonnet.

She claps her hands and giggles. "A Mister-Mistress!"

"Actually," says Ned, "I've just come from a costume ball. Very elaborate affair. Glass punchbowls cut in the shape of elephants, melon balls, iced caviar."

"Oh!" she says, "what fun!"

Ned clicks his heels and nods his head. "Ned Rise, at your service."

Her name is Fanny Brunch. She's house parlormaid at No. 32, the residence of Sir Joseph and Lady Dorothea Banks. She doesn't mind if he walks her home.

The street is deserted. Sun dapples the trees, birds flit from branch to branch. Ned takes her arm and shuffles off down the avenue, his skirts massaging hers. "You know," he says, "I'm beginning to feel like Pizarro when he stumbled across the Seven Cities of Gold."

◄§ FALLING

What could he do? His life was transformed.

He woke with Fanny on his mind, hawked fish eggs and thought of nothing else, tumbled into bed with an ache like hunger gnawing at him, swollen and empty at the same time, and dreamed of Fanny, Fanny, Fanny. Women he'd had. Dozens of them. Whores and barmaids, farmgirls, shopgirls, flowergirls, the daughters of fishmongers and tinkers, nurses, nannies, souses and sluts — the Nan Punts and Sally Sebums of the world. A matter of exercising his organ, as simple as that. You put it in, you take it out. But this, this was different. This time his heart was involved. And his mind.

The day after he met her he haunted Soho Square — disguised as a piano tuner. It was raining. Drizzling, actually. His false mustache drooped, the dye ran out of his hair, his sack of tuning forks, pewter hammers and whisk brooms grew sodden. Sir Joseph glanced out the library window and saw him leaning against the iron pickets, soggy and forlorn. Lady Banks passed him by on her way to Mrs. Coutts' for whist. A stray cat urinated on his stockings. At one point a scowling clerk from J. Kirkman & Sons, Piano Forte Makers, stepped from the shop at No. 38 and asked him to move along. Fanny never knew he was there.

The following day was no better. He hired a coach, set the driver in back, took the reins himself and trotted up and down the square from dawn till dusk. His eyes strained to catch a hint of movement behind the windows at No. 32, but aside from two partial glimpses of Byron Bount and a full frontal of Lady B.'s pug, he saw nothing. On ensuing days he dressed as a seaman, bellows mender, furmety woman, floorwipe, terminal syphilitic and King's guard. Fanny hadn't been out of the house in over a week. Pounds were slipping through his fingers. The caviar business was languishing.

Then one evening, as he skulked about the shadows arrayed in the torn and soot-blackened weeds of a chimney sweep, the front door swung open and a female form — jerked by a pug on a silver leash — descended the steps. Ned moved in, heart pounding, simultaneously formulating a greeting — should he whistle a few bars of "The Derby Ram"? — and an inspired excuse for the way he was dressed. "Fanny," he whispered, his voice hoarse with passion.

" 'Ey? Wot's 'at?" came the reply in a voice that could scour the streets. He was staring into a face crusted over with eczema, and a milky, leering eye. The pug growled.

"Begging your pardon, Mistress," he said, bowing. "I thought you would be Fanny Brunch."

" 'Oo? Fanny 'oo? Nivir 'eard of 'er."

He was speaking with Barbara Dewfly, the scullery maid. Half a crown later she recalled that Fanny was " 'at young trollop wot washes 'is Lordship's socks," and added that "there'd be 'ell to pay if ennybody was seen bringin' 'er a message or the like." Ned pressed another coin into her palm along with a hastily scrawled note: *Meet me out back at Midnight, Yr. Hmble. & Obdt. Servt. Who Wishes To Know You Better, Ned Rise.* The dog dropped a turd in the walkway, Dewfly gathered her stained skirts, mounted the stairs and was gone.

It should be remarked at this juncture that the life of a servant in

Georgian England was not one that allowed for a wide range of social intercourse. Servants, if they were fortunate enough to pass muster, were taken on for life. They were expected to give up their families, interests and former ties, their sex lives and the expectation of marriage. From the moment they were hired they lived entirely for the comfort and benefit of their employers, worker bees fussing round idle drones and swollen, helpless queens. The reward? Six or seven pounds per annum, a warm grate, a dry bed, and — most importantly — three square meals a day. At a time when the streets were lined with thieves and beggars, prices were soaring as a result of the war with France, housing was inadequate or nonexistent, and truckloads of spindly hollow-chested men and women were dropping dead of hunger each day, a position as chambermaid or footman was nothing to sneeze at. And a loss of self-determination seemed a small price to pay.

So it was with Fanny. She'd gone from a hand-to-mouth existence in the country (milking cows, shoveling shit, gruel three times a day) to a life of relative ease and plenty, from her parents' dominion to Lady B.'s. On her first day in the Banks household she was taken aside by Lady Banks, warned of the horror and degradation of the sex act and the slavery of motherhood, given a prayerbook and told that she must now devote herself to higher things. She had a position to maintain. From now on she was upper house parlormaid to Sir Joseph Banks, one of the truly great men of his time, and she must do nothing to embarrass him or his household. When she was finished, Lady B. had smiled a grandmotherly smile and asked Fanny if she understood. Fanny had nodded solemnly.

Still, when the crier cried twelve, she was out in the garden all the same.

◈ ◈

After that first furtive assignation (during which hands were pressed and vows exchanged), Ned Rise prowled Sir Joseph's garden nightly. Sometimes he and Fanny would sit there whispering and necking for hours, other times they'd sneak off to an inn for a meal and more comfortable lovemaking. They ate caviar on toast. They drank wine. Fanny told Ned of her days on the farm, of Squire Trelawney and the hoe duel. Ned told her of his own miserable beginnings and his struggle to rise above it and establish himself in the world of commerce. Which he had done, finally and brilliantly. He was a businessman of independent means, he told her, privileged to move among the aristocracy and their hangers-on, a familiar to the likes of Lord Twit and Beau Brummell. Her eyes widened at the mention of these exalted names. She pressed him for details. He invented them. Then, one night, as they lay in the long plush grass beneath Sir

Joseph's lime, he asked her to run off with him. The moon hung in the branches like an ornament. Soft and low, a bird began to sing. She agreed. Ned was moved. Here was a beginning, a center, a new key to which he could tune his life. He thought of his clarinet. Of buds opening in dark places. Of a little inn in Holland or Switzerland maybe, a stone hearth, a dog, Fanny at his side. The following morning he retrieved his clarinet from the pawnbroker and booked passage for two to The Hague, via Gravesend. Later he took Fanny out to Lamb's Conduit Fields and played her a clarion version of "Greensleeves" while Venus rode across the sky. In two weeks they would be gone.

Still, he was troubled. All this heartbreak and ecstasy, delicious though it was, had deflected him from his work. Sixty-three jars of Chichikov's Choice were backed up on him in the cellars at Bear Lane. The sturgeon had quit on him long ago, all bred out for the season, he'd laid off his street urchins and given Shem and Liam five-pound bonuses — but he hadn't sold a jar of caviar in nearly a month. Yes, the iron chest under his bed was brimming — nearly three hundred and fifty pounds — but he'd gone through quite an outlay wooing Fanny and it would be a shame, a criminal shame to let those last sixty-three jars go to waste. Besides, they'd need every farthing to set themselves up in the Netherlands what with all those sharp-nosed Hollanders running around.

He went back to the streets, peddling his caviar with an evangelical fervor, wheeling and dealing. Two for the price of one, one for the price of two. Catherine herself eats it, he told the head chef at White's. Washes it down with frozen vodka and steins of kvass. He held up a jar for the little man's inspection. The label featured an amorphous building identified in block letters as "The Kremlin," and a wolfhound that looked like an epileptic seal. The chef took six jars. Lord Stavordale, profoundly drunk outside Boodle's Club after dropping eleven hundred pounds at whist, bought a jar and consumed it on the spot. Lady Courtenay sent two jars to her maiden aunt in Bath; Messieurs Grebe and Parsley of Bond Street had a jar with crackers for luncheon; Rose Elderberry, companion to the P.M.'s wife, used it as a facial restorative. Apparently the chic of Chichikov's Choice had grown in proportion to its scarcity. Ned sold out his stock inside of a week.

He tallied up his earnings, minus expenses (disguises, jars, labels, salt, sedan chairs and the like), and found that he'd added over a hundred pounds to his nest egg. He was elated. But why stop here? Herring were running. Shem and Liam were hauling them out of the river by the cartload. He'd salt up the eggs, darken them a bit with shoe blacking, bottle and label them and who'd know the difference? And what if they did? — he'd be in Holland in a week. He concocted twenty-six jars of the stuff, falling back on frog's eggs when the herring supply ran short, got himself up as a Russian balalaika master and sold them in an afternoon. Fifty-two pounds more went into the iron chest, and every penny of it for Fanny.

But then one night, with less than a week to go, Fanny failed to show up at the hour appointed for their liaison. Ned was stunned, distraught, buried under a weight of suspicion and gloom. He paced beneath the darkened windows for three hours, stomach churning, oaths and resolutions and speeches running through his head, until finally he vented his frustration on a bed of peonies and clambered up over the back wall, defeated. As he reached the top, however, he became aware of a sound emanating from the direction of the house. A sort of hiss or rasp, the sound of a fly trapped against a windowpane. He held his breath. There it was again: pssssssssst.

He dropped back down into the garden and warily approached the house. It loomed above him: shutters drawn, dark as a grave, three stories and an attic. Clumps of shadow designated bushes, rock gardens, benches and birdbaths. When he reached the lime tree he saw that the shutters of a second-story window were slightly ajar. "Fanny?" he whispered.

Her voice came back, pinched and susurrant. "Ned, Ned — where are you, Ned?"

"Here," he whispered, stepping out of the shadows. "What's the matter?" He could see her face now, a pale oval set against the deep black of the interior like an inverted egg.

"Shhhhh! Lady B. is on to us. Or at least she suspects something. She's locked all the doors and taken the key to bed with her."

"But no. She couldn't." The news manifests itself as a sharp stab to his groin, the hopeful erection that had sprung up with the sound of her voice already fading, giving way to a bottomless ache of longing and disappointment. "The bitch," he mutters, and suddenly finds himself clawing at the thin wisps of ivy that striate the lower wall of the house. He'll climb up to her, that's what he'll do.

"Ned!" she hisses. "You'll wake the house."

She's right. Sixty or seventy limp strands of ivy droop round him, and he hasn't got a foot off the ground yet. He brushes the leaves from his face, steps back a pace or two and demands an explanation — what's gone wrong?

She tells it as quickly as she can, her voice pitched low. It was her lack of sleep that gave her away. Lady B. commented on her sluggishness, the slowness of her smile — was she getting enough to eat? Feeling ill? Then Sir Joseph caught her dozing in the library, feather duster in hand. He asked her if she wasn't staying up late, giggling with the other girls and reading those scandalous novels by Horace Walpole and Mrs. Radcliffe. She denied it. But then the next evening she nodded off while serving at table and scalded his Lordship with the hare soup. Lady B. ordered her from the room. Later, she was called into the parlor for a full-scale interrogation. No, there was no man in her life, she asserted tearfully. No assignations. Please ma'am, what you must think of me! It's just that she was restless at night, homesick for the country, and had taken to sitting in the garden till all hours, listening to the crickets and the nightingale. She didn't know there was any harm in it. Lady B. looked like an executioner with indigestion. She called Fanny's behavior "irregular" and prescribed a week in the kitchen, fixing vegetables and trimming meats. That ought to tire you out, dear, she said, and then ordered Alice to go round and lock the doors.

Ned cursed at the thought of it. Fanny in the kitchen. A prisoner. "All right," he said. "We'll fix her. Tomorrow night, two A.M., I'll be here with a ladder. You can come stay at my place till Saturday, and then we'll catch the boat for Holland."

"Ned," she whispered, her voice soft as a featherbed. "I love you."

He was about to give her the standard lovers' reply, *con gusto,* when all at once the pug started yapping somewhere in the darkened house, yapping as if its tail had been yanked out by the roots. The shutters closed with a click. Ned took to his feet but there was someone at the back door with a lantern — Bount or Sir Joseph — and now the pug was out the door, flying across the lawn like a puff of hair in a gale, a shrill insistent yip-yipping at his heels. There was a flash and the sound of a gunshot, then he was over the wall and gone.

◆§ §◆

Ned slipped through the dark side streets and back alleys with the slow grace and intuitive assurance of a cat. The streets were unlighted and dangerous at this hour, haunted by footpads, cutpurses, drunks and murderers. Ned kept a low profile. Dodging in and out of shadows, keeping to the base of walls, cutting through yards where possible, he scrupulously avoided all human contact as he made his way back to Southwark. He'd had a close shave back in the garden — if old Sir Jos hadn't been such a rotten shot, who knows? Anyway, it was a bad sign. They could be waiting for him tomorrow night when he came round with the ladder. He wondered if he should borrow Liam's rusted harquebus.

When he finally turned up Bear Lane, nearly an hour later, he was beat. An afternoon of peddling fish eggs and a long and frustrating night in Sir Joseph's garden had taken their toll. He would sleep till dark, see about a coach, a ladder and maybe a pistol, then go and fetch his Fanny. The thought exhilarated him as he mounted the steps to his room: tomorrow night he'd have her beside him — in his bed — secure, safe and private. No more sneaking about in the dark, no more abbreviated lovemaking, no more wet grass and thorny hedges. There was a stirring in his trousers as he turned the key and stepped into the room.

He didn't even bother to light the taper. Just shrugged out of his jacket, tore off the false beard and flung himself down on the bed. But wait — what was this? There was someone in his bed! His first glancing thought was of Fanny, but then a far more likely and chilling explanation came to him . . .

At that moment a match flared on the far side of the room and illuminated the ruddy acromegalic features of Smirke — then the taper took hold and the room rushed with light. Ned shrank back. The room, he saw, was crowded. Twit and Jutta Jim were leaning against the chest of drawers; Mendoza sat on the washstand beside the angelic young prig who'd held his jacket for him on a day Ned would prefer to forget. Then there was Smirke. Towering, round-shouldered, grinning a tiny expectant grin like a black bear in heat. In the bed, snoring soundly, was Boyles.

"Well, well, Ned," Twit began in his reedy nasal tones, "what a pleasure and a surprise it is to see you again."

Mendoza was slapping a stocking full of sand against the base of the washstand: thwack . . . thwack . . . thwack . . .

"Yes, a real pleasure. But why you didn't invite us over sooner, I'll never know. We could have capitalized on your miraculous ascension from the dead. The Papists would have eaten it up." His voice dropped to a snarl. "The thieves they hung alongside Christ should have been so lucky."

"I'll fookin' tear yer face off," Smirke rumbled.

It was then that Ned noticed the iron strongbox. It was sitting on the table, the lock ravaged, lid twisted back on its hinges. Empty. "What have you done with my money, you bastards?" Ned was on his feet. Boyles, very drunk, sat up in bed and rubbed his eyes.

"Let's call it compensation for the yoomiliation wot ye've cost us, ye scum," Mendoza hissed.

"Neddy!" Boyles had hold of his sleeve. "I didn't mean to tell 'em — they forced it out o' me."

Ned felt the rage rising in him. There would be no elopement now, damn them, and he was going to take a beating. A savage beating. Suddenly he snatched up the iron box, flung it in the face of the young prig and broke for the door. Mendoza was there. The blackjack caught him across the cheekbone, twice in quick succession — and then it was Smirke's turn.

Smirke hit him as he was rebounding from Mendoza's blow. The first punch staggered him; the force of the second drove him back toward the window, Smirke in pursuit, arms flailing, another blow and another, and then he was going down, reeling back into someone — Twit? — there was the sound of splintering glass and a cry followed by a sort of hopeless, unbelieving, enraged shriek — the sound a pig makes when the sticking knife pierces its throat.

Ned was on the floor in a sea of glass. Smirke and Mendoza were hanging out the window. The young prig sat in the corner, wiping the blood from his cheek and sniveling. "I'm scarred," he whimpered. "I'm scarred." Then Mendoza's voice, shaken. "Sweet Jesus, 'ee's stuck 'imself."

Ned staggered to his feet and took a look. Twit lay contorted below, impaled on the iron pickets. A crowd was gathering. Two men bent over him with a torch. " 'Ee's dead," one of them said.

Mendoza's face was ashen. Suddenly he had hold of Ned's arm. "It's murder then," he shouted. "Call out the watch."

◄§ A SHOT IN THE DARK

For a moment there is nothing, no sound at all, the black of the forest and the slow drip of the rain. The dark is so absolute and impenetrable, so much an absence, he might as well be blind. This is what it's like to live in a cave, he thinks, to live without fire and candlewax, this is what it's like when you reach the seventh circle of hell. And then it begins again: a branch displaced, the tentative footfall, the low soughing snarl like a tocsin: I am afraid but I will kill.

In the leaves and mold, Mungo frantically casts about for a rock or treebranch, a bit of root, the jawbone of an ass, anything he could lift up to his face when the growling thing comes at him in a rush of tooth and claw. The loam beneath his fingers is rich and saturated, like coffee grounds or the black muck at the bottom of a grave; wormlike things slip through his fingers, a spider runs up his arm. But there, he has something, a stick certainly — no, it's thicker and heavier, the size of a club. He tugs to dislodge it, but it seems to be stuck. And now all of a sudden the snarling grows more animated, as if his reaching for the stick were a provocation. Coming closer, warning, threatening, cursing, the hot breath of it, the spitting and hissing. He jerks at the stick for his very life, in a fever, the snarling thing nearly beside him now, growls turned to roars, blood-starved, maddened, raaaaaaaaooowwwwwwww!

But of course the darkest hour comes just before the dawn. At that moment the scene is lit by the flash of a pistol, inundated by the report. There is an instant of revelation — the carcass of the horse, its stiffened leg in his hand, the searing venomous eyes and curled lips of the beast dissolving into the night — and then the black pall drops again, the gunshot echoes in the trees.

"Mr. Park — you okay?"

What can he say? Naked, bludgeoned, beggared and horseless — yet not mauled and devoured? Lost, but not alone? "Johnson," he says.

Johnson's voice comes back at him from nowhere, disembodied. "You got any bones broke?" It's like playing hide-and-seek in a coal cellar.

"Where are you?"

He starts at the touch of Johnson's hand. "Right here, Mr. Park. Right here."

Now he says it like a lover: "Johnson." And then: "What about you — you all right?"

There is a concatenation of violent respiratory sounds — throat clearing, spitting, hacking and drooling — followed by a series of groans and wheezes. "I am about as tore up as it is possible to be without being laid out for the undertaker — and that's no lie."

A wave of depression crests up out of the void and washes over the explorer. His shoulders are slumped, his privates chilled, ribs shrieking for attention. And his left knee. It seems to be out of joint. When he speaks, his voice is nearly inaudible: "What now?"

"Say what?"

"What do we do now?"

"Find a tree."

"A tree?"

"Climb up and wait for light. You don't want to be hanging around down here when that cat comes back for his horsemeat, do you?"

Mungo considers this for a minute. Things have begun to chirrup a bit, crickets or frogs or something. "Actually," he says finally, "I don't know. At least it would be quicker down here."

◄§ HOW DOES IT FEEL
TO BE DEAD?

In the morning Mungo wakes with a start, and finds a tiny bald-headed monkey staring at him out of eyes the size of golf balls. When he moves to shoo it away the branch dips violently, then springs back to jar him loose. There is a moment of pure weightlessness — ethereal, almost exhilarating in its detachment — immediately succeeded by a gut-wrenching panic and a quick but focused image of the high-wire artist at Bartholomew Fair. The first branch slaps him in the face, the next gives way; but finally, after a drop of twenty feet or so, he manages to ram a projecting limb into his armpit and stabilize himself. Grunting, cursing his mother, his Maker and the African Association, he works his way along the length of the branch until he reaches the trunk. Which he embraces like a lost lover. But then he detects a movement out of the corner of his eye — just above him, dangling by its left arm, is the monkey. The wizened little creature gives him a quizzical look, then reaches out a cautious finger and touches him, soft as a kiss, on the brow.

The explorer works his way, limb by limb, to the ground. Johnson is sitting there beneath the tree, waiting for him. He is wrapped in his toga, but his sandals are missing. It is, given the fact of the rainy season in the rain belt, raining. Mungo stands there a moment in his shirt — feet, legs and buttocks bare. His pubic hair is the color of mashed turnips. "I was going to say good morning," he says, "but under the circumstances it would be an obscenity."

Johnson grunts. His right eye is swollen closed and there is blood caked in the hair over his ear. "You look terrible," Mungo observes.

"I feel like I been dragged behind the London mail from Bristol to Covent Garden — and then pounded with mallets on top of it." He licks his split lip and spits between his teeth. The spittle is red. "Here," he says, producing the crushed top hat from behind his back. "They left this behind. Wasn't worth the trouble."

"Worth the trouble? All my notes are crammed in here."

"That's what I mean."

"I see they left you your toga."

"It ain't worth nothin' either. Took my sandals though, the bastards. And my ass."

At the mention of the ass, the explorer wheels round, a look of disbelief on his face. "But — where's the horse?"

Johnson shakes his head.

"You don't mean to tell me that one leopard put away a whole horse — in a single night?"

"Look close, Mr. Park. You can see where he drug it away."

The explorer looks. A swath has been cut through the vegetation, as if someone had dragged a rowboat across it: shoots and tendrils crushed, branches snapped off, plants flattened. "Well don't just sit there, man — let's go after it. I haven't had a joint to gnaw on for days, weeks."

"Can't. He's gone and hauled it up a tree someplace. Common practice with leopards. They eat what they can hold, then stash the rest way up high where the dogs and hyenas and such can't get at it. When I was a kid we was asleep in the hut one night when a leopard carried off my aunt Tota. Next day we went out lookin'. Nine years old, I found her. She was stuffed up a tree, half-eat away, her eyes all covered over with flies. It was her head I saw first — hangin' there like a melon or somethin'."

"All right, I get the picture. So what do we do — starve?"

"What we do is we get on down that road to Kabba and beg us some alms, then decide how we are goin' to get ourselves back to Dindikoo."

"Back? Without completing my mission?"

"Hey, let's face it. You almost finished it right here. With the rains it's goin' to be about three shades of impossible to travel anywhere — shit, we might not even *be* able to get back. Plus you got the Moors to contend with the farther up you go. Sansanding's a Moorish town, from what Eboe says. And Timbuctoo too. They'll *Nazarini* you alive up there. That what you want?"

The explorer's jaw is set. His voice is shot through with emotion. "I'll chart the course of this river if I have to dance naked in hell first."

"Uh, forgive my mentionin' it, Mr. Park — but you already are naked, and this is about as close to hell as you better hope you ever get." Johnson pauses to grin till his molars show. "So start dancin'."

◆§ ξ◆

In Kabba, a collection of fifty or so clay huts whitewashed to a dazzle, Johnson approaches the *Dooty*,* throws himself on the ground and begins pouring handfuls of dust over his head. The explorer, totally naked save for his hat and the strips of shirt-cambric swaddling his privates like a colossal diaper, stands off at a distance. "Alms!" cries Johnson in a piteous voice. "We are respectable merchants set upon by dacoits, raped of our goods and clothing and left for dead in the forest." The *Dooty* looks doubtfully at

---

*Chief magistrate of a town or province, responsible for overseeing the communal granary. He is instantly recognizable as the fat man in a cluster of ambulatory sticks.

Mungo, his gaze riding up the splotched white legs to the diaper, the bare chest, tangled beard and freakish eyes, and then finally coming to rest on the accordioned top hat. Johnson catches at the man's robe, and drives his voice down to a quaking, heartrending rumble: "We-we haven't had anything bu⁺ bark and grass for two weeks. A crumb, I beg of you, a crumb."

The *Dooty* steps into his hut, returns a moment later with a dog at the end of a tether. The dog is tall at the shoulder, solid of bone. It has massive, disproportionate jaws, a smallish skull, and a mane reminiscent of the hyena. At first the explorer thinks the man means to give them the dog, and he conjures up images of those meaty haunches crisping on the spit, stuffed with yams, foundering in rice, etc. But then the *Dooty* does a curious thing. He reaches behind his back and produces a dart, the sort of thing you'd associate with hazy barrooms and pints of porter, a splinter of bone honed like a shiv and capped with a burst of feathers. Quick as a magician, he jabs the dog in the flank three or four times. This has the effect of instantaneously arousing the animal to a pitch of malignant hysteria, its whole being concentrated in scrambling paws and champing incisors. Only the leash restrains it from falling on Johnson and tearing him to pieces. "Two minutes," the man shouts over the remonstrations of the dog, "and I let him go."

Half a mile up the road, the explorer collapses beneath a tree. "I can't go on, Johnson. I'm just too sick and too beat and too discouraged." A hundred yards off, cloaked in reeds and rushes, is the Niger, as brown and indifferent as all the eyes in all the faces of Africa.

Touracos squawk in the trees. A red river hog grunts from the muck at the water's edge, flushing a great crowned crane in an explosion of gold and soapstone gray. The explorer watches the bird lift into the sky, wings beating like a drumroll, spindly legs trailing behind, watches it soar until it vanishes in the clouds. As his eyes drop he is startled by a pair of vultures, circling low, humping along under their leathery necks, patient as undertakers.

"Well, as I see it we got two alternatives," Johnson sighs, easing down beside his employer. "We can sit here and starve to death, or we can turn back."

The explorer doesn't answer, but this time a softer expression creeps into his eyes, less inflexible, an expression suggesting that at long last the voice of reason has begun to whisper in his ear. "If we do turn back," he says finally, his voice nearly inaudible, "what are we going to do about food and shelter? Clothes?" He looks down at his feet, blistered and bare. "Shoes even? Am I going to walk a thousand miles barefooted?"

"What else you goin' to do? How would you get to Timbuctoo — fly? And if you did get there — then what? No, listen. We got a much better chance getting charity from the Mandingoes back the way we come than from these people around here. That *Dooty*. He was no Kafir — he was a convert. A true believer — and I'm talkin' about a blood now, a animist — he won't let you starve. It's these damned apostates that wouldn't give you a stick to chew on if you was the last man on earth."

Suddenly a whistle sounds from the forest, soft and low. The two start, ready for anything, expecting the worst. Nothing there. Canopy, shadow, a billion trunks knotted with vine. "What was that," the explorer says, "a bird?" Unconsciously, Johnson strokes the yellow lump over his eye. "That was no bird," he says.

There it is again: long and low, wind in a drainpipe. "Who is it?" Johnson shouts, first in Mandingo, then in Arabic.

A shadow detaches itself from the general gloom and starts tentatively for them. The explorer, starving and stinking, peers up out of eyes dulled with fatigue and resignation, almost too far gone to care, as the shadow becomes a tall black woman gliding through the foliage like an apparition. When she gets within ten feet of them, she stops, poised for flight like a deer surprised in the garden. There is a calabash in her hand, and a disk of unleavened bread. "We won't hurt you, sister," Johnson says, and then she's bending over them, offering bread and *sooloo* beer.

Her name is Aisha. The hair pulls back from her head in a topknot, gold hoops dangle from her ears. She looks to be about thirty, dressed in a striped tunic and sandals. She'd followed them from the village where she'd seen them turned away by the *Dooty*. He was a criminal. Heartless. Would they accept her hospitality?

Walking beside her, a bit dizzy from the sudden impact of the bread and beer, the explorer finds himself studying her profile: the tapering neck, jutting jaw, ears so small and delicate he wonders if they might somehow have been shrunk. While pondering this strange and absorbing phenomenon, he notices the cicatrices, faint pinkish welts that trace the line of her jaw and spiral elegantly across her cheek, and then the blue paste dabbed over her eyelids, and finally the recalcitrant hairs fanning out in an almost transparent aureole round her skull. Unaccountably, he finds himself thinking of gerenuks and gazelles. As they walk, she keeps her eyes averted, but tells them that her father has always believed that white men existed, spirits of the dead, bleached of their souls and the color of the skin, and that if ever one appeared she should treat him with courtesy and respect, for he had come a long terrible way looking for his village and the skin he had lost. Mungo, interrupted periodically by his own belches and a barrage of kicks from Johnson, assures her that all this is nonsense, and that he is as alive as she, and that furthermore he is perfectly content with the color of his skin and sees no necessity of improving on it. Her only reaction is to glance up shyly at him and grin, as if she'd heard that one before.

Aisha leads them back toward Kabba, but to a separate compound outside the walls of the town proper. It consists of three huts enclosed within a palisade of sharpened stakes grown over with thorns and flowering vines. There they are introduced to her infirm and astonished parents, a succession of sisters whose ages are difficult to ascertain as a result of wrinkles and toothlessness, a brother and his wife and a pair of sorry-looking watchdogs. Aisha herself is a presumptive widow. Her husband, a relative of the *Dooty,* had gone north sixteen months ago to track a band of Moors who had kidnapped his youngest sister. She understood that it was his duty to go, but felt deserted nonetheless. He hasn't been heard from since.

But for the present there is goat's milk and cheese. Something in a pot with spinach and fish heads. Aisha spreads mats for them in her parents' hut. Johnson scrapes the pot. The explorer, feeling a bit under the weather, retires early. Throughout the night he is awakened at intervals by the awestruck old patriarch, Aisha's father, who plies him with questions about the afterlife. How can a spirit hold sustenance? Will his skin blacken of itself, or must he wait for someone to die, someone old perhaps, so that he can slip into that person's skin? Mungo looks up at the puzzled, frightened, hopeful face in the firelight, so exhausted he can barely mutter, the questions fading into dreams, mounting in his head like the rungs of a ladder, why and when and where, and how does it feel to be dead?

✑ MO O MO INTA ALLO

During their week-long stay in Kabba's suburbs, a dramatic change comes over Johnson's guinea hen: where once there was putrid flesh and scraps of feather, now there is naked bone, bleached and dried like a goose's wishbone hung up over the mantel. Though still a bit pink and damp in the joints, essentially the thing has been transformed into a crusted, frozen skeleton, relatively inoffensive, devoid of interest for all but the least discerning flies. "Looks pretty good," Mungo says. Johnson glances down, running his fingers over the brittle bones, examining the joints. "Still wet in the seams. But you're right: I may have this thing beat yet." He beams like a kid with a lollipop. "Three or four more days, that's all it'll take."

The two have agreed, after hours of debate, that the only course of action left to them is to turn back, tracing the line of the Niger to the southwest, and then angling up through the Jallonka Wilderness to Dindikoo. Aisha has provided the explorer with a toga of some coarse material (banana yellow with splashes of red and aniline orange), a pair of sandals and a bag of peanuts for the road. Her father, who hasn't left his side since he stepped through the front gate, presents him with a walking stick, intricately carved to represent the changing of skins after death. When Mungo asks what he can do to repay them, the old man begs for a lock of hair for a charm; Aisha averts her face and tugs nervously at her earring, then turns to him, her eyes dark and full, lips trembling.

This time, Johnson doesn't have to nudge him.

◦§ ६◦

On the day of their departure, Johnson borrows a scrap of paper from the explorer, dashes off some couplets from Herrick and Donne, and distributes them to Aisha's family for their *saphies*. Mungo looks on, incredulous, the right half of his head cropped to the roots. " 'Julia's Clothes'? You mean . . . all you have to do is scratch off a couple lines of nonsense in exchange for a week's food and lodging — and they'll settle for it?"

"You'd be amazed at the power of the written word, Mr. Park."

Aisha has prepared a dish of raw eggs, millet and yogurt for their final breakfast, with bits of tamarind added for acid and bamboo seeds for bulk. As the explorer eats, she sits beside him, holding his hand, running her fingers through the remains of his hair. The old man sits nearly as close, gaping at him as if he were all seven wonders of the world wrapped up in one and the grandson of the demiurge to boot. In a voice like last year's cornshucks the old man pursues his eschatological inquiry: Where does this world end and the other begin? Why must we die? Is the soul, once removed from the body, still hungry for sex? Between mouthfuls, the explorer answers the old man as patiently and imaginatively as he can, until finally, the meal finished, he rises to leave.

But then, just as he and Johnson are gathering their things, one of Aisha's sisters leads a blind woman into the hut, a woman so crabbed and blasted by age she makes Aisha's father look as if he's just been pulled from the womb. The woman is Djanna-geo of Djenné, and she has come to consult the explorer about *Tobaubo doo** and the afterlife, and to tell him of the geography and society of the eastern Niger. The explorer had offered hanks of his hair to anyone who could give him information concerning the course of the lower Niger and the inhabitants of its banks — and there had been plenty of takers. One man told him that the river ran to the world's end. Another that it ended in a violent whirlpool that sucked all things down into the waiting maw of a sea-beast called Karib-dish. Still another that it enclosed the Mountains of the Moon and had its tributaries in the Kingdom of Kong, a land interdicted for its cannibals and the giant apes that roam its cloud-hung massifs.

Others, notably a pair of brothers in the salt trade, gave him what seemed more reliable information. Past Sansanding, they said, was a town called Silla, twelve days' journey from Timbuctoo. It was a Mandingo settlement, but Moors congregated there for commerce. To the north of Silla was the kingdom of Masina, inhabited by Foulah herdsmen. Down-river, to the northeast, was a swampy lake — Dibbie, or the dark water — so immense that while traversing it you lost sight of land for an entire day. Beyond this, on the north shore, was Timbuctoo, a place where noblemen lived in palaces and shat bars of gold. The king of Timbuctoo was Abu Abrahima, and he was a Mohammedan zealot. On their first trip to his city the brothers had taken a room in a sort of public inn, and the landlord, on showing them to their hut, had produced a length of rope. If you are Mussulmen, he said, sit down and make yourselves comfortable — but if you're Kafirs you are my slaves and with this length of rope I will lead you to market like a pair of heifers. *La illah el allah, Mahomet rasowl Allahi,* the brothers chanted.

Still, no one has yet been able to give him anything concrete about the progress of the Niger — or Joliba, as they call it — once it leaves Timbuctoo. His final hope totters before him in the person of this deformed and very probably deranged old blind woman. He poises, pen in hand, and waits for her to speak. With difficulty, her legs like sticks, the right side of her body withered from some nameless disease, the old woman settles herself on the mat. Aisha brings her a cup of *sooloo* beer, which she quaffs as if she were a coal miner coming off an eight-hour shift. She smacks her lips, casts her empty eyes round the room, and announces that she has to relieve herself.

---

*Land of the *hon-kees*.

When she hobbles back into the hut, clutching at the dress of Aisha's sister with all the desperation of a child abandoned on the edge of a cliff, she calls for another beer in a stentorian voice, then shouts that she wants to smell the white man and feel his hair before she'll strike a bargain to reveal her secrets. The explorer crouches beside her, the cool dry fingers roaming his scalp, the busy nostrils snuffing at the side of his face. Finally, after three or four minutes of kneading and snuffing, she appears satisfied. "*Tobaubo*," she says, and lets out a sort of giggle.

She talks for an hour, her voice as clear and resonant as a carnival barker's. Born in Djenné, she was abducted by slavers and sold to a merchant from the kingdom of Hausa, which lies beyond Timbuctoo, far beyond — beyond Kabara and Ansongo and a dozen other places neither Aisha nor her father has ever heard of. After eight years in the merchant's seraglio she escaped along with a man named Ibo Mmo, a Mandingo from Kaarta. Two weeks later he was killed and sectioned by a party of *maddummulo* — man-eaters — while she lay in the bed of a shallow stream buried in mud and breathing through a reed. It took her six years to work her way back to Djenné, supporting herself by exchanging favors for food and shelter.

Periodically during the course of this recitation, Djanna-geo stops abruptly, releases two or three booming eructations and shouts for more beer. At one point she lifts her dead cracked face to the explorer and lowers her voice to a hiss. "There is a place on the river called Boussa," she says, her index finger gliding before her face as if to reconstruct it in the air. "A place of jagged rocks and white water, where the river forks like the tongues of a thousand snakes. It is a very dangerous place. Beware it." Then she sits back and demands a hank of hair.

The explorer, able to follow most of what she's told him, is quaking with excitement, hardly capable of gripping the pen, his mind flooded with the course of the Niger and the names of faraway places: Kabara, Yaour, Boussa. Here, at last, is the voice of experience. He clumsily hacks off a lock of hair with the bone knife Aisha has given him as a going-away present, and presses it into the old woman's hand, the ultimate question trembling on his lips. "But where does the Joliba flow from there — below Boussa, beyond Hausa?"

The glabrous old head cranks round on him, stiff and slow, until the clouded eyes draw level with his own. He can feel her breath on his face. "*Mo o mo inta allo*," she whispers.

"What was that?" The explorer's voice leaps out at her. "I don't understand."

She grins, silent, the cat that swallowed the canary, belching softly to herself. The explorer turns to Johnson. "What did she say?"

"She said 'mo o mo inta allo' — no man knows."

◆ ON A FIRST-NAME BASIS

The rivers are pregnant, jumping banks, fanning down trees, giving birth to torrents. The rain falls in sheets like panes of glass, splintering into shards and nuggets as it hits the ground. Monsoon winds howl, trees hang their heads. Where before there was a gully, now there's a river, rushing and brown, studded with splintered trunks, drowned livestock, the staved-in roofs of native huts. Fields are inundated, waist-deep in water, swamps are bottomless. The frogs think they were meant to inherit the earth.

After a long wet day of wading through swamps and gagging on soggy peanuts, the explorer and his interpreter have been stopped at what once was a fording place on the River Toolumbo, a minor tributary of the Niger. A cluster of miserable, waterlogged huts crouches on a barren hillock at the juncture of the two rivers. This is Bammako, or Wash-A-Crocodile, and the name seems appropriate, as the Toolumbo sweeps along near the crest of the hillock, tickling the timbers of the crude fences thrown up round each hut. The two mendicants are turned away from the first three huts in short order, but at the fourth they are advised by a toothless teenager sucking at a pipe that the far hut is temporarily unoccupied. Its owner, a goatherd, can be seen in the distance, mechanically beating his head against a rock in an attempt to assuage the loss of his goats to the rising waters.

There is firewood inside, neatly stacked in the corner. After half an hour of chafing and puffing, Johnson manages to get a blaze going. Then he borrows the explorer's quill pen and a sheet of paper, secretes them in his toga, and ducks out into the rain. Ten minutes later he's back, grinning, a calabash of beer in one hand, a shriveled, cancerous-looking chicken in the other.

◆ ◆

Later, the two share a pipe of the local tobacco, a heady sweet stuff that makes the eyes fix and the mind wander. For the first time since they left Kabba their clothes are dry and their stomachs full.

"You know," Mungo says finally, "after all we've been through together don't really see the necessity of your calling me Mr. Park any longer, do 'ou?"

Johnson shakes his head. "Force of habit, Mr. Park."

"Please." The explorer stretches out his hand. "Call me Mungo."

A shy smile steals over Johnson's lips. He looks immensely pleased with nimself as he takes the explorer's hand and murmurs, "Okay . . . Mungo."

CROCODYLUS NILOTICUS

The Nile crocodile (*Crocodylus niloticus*) is pandemic over the African continent, found from Madagascar to South Africa in the east, and throughout the Niger basin in the west. It is one of the largest and most feared of crocodilians, swift, savage and inexorable. The largest specimens are known to reach twenty feet in length and two thousand five hundred pounds. Young crocodiles, under optimum conditions, will grow a foot a year, but as the animal reaches its upward age of fifty years, its constant growth is directed toward an increase in girth and overall body weight rather than length. Thus, the difference in weight between the average fifteen- and sixteen-foot specimens is about two hundred and eighty pounds, or the full weight of a nine-foot specimen.

Characteristically, *Crocodylus niloticus* feeds on fish, but it is an active hunter and will devour anything it can catch, including baboons, gazelles, waterbirds, other crocodiles, leopards, turtles and men. Smaller prey is swallowed whole. Larger animals are seized and held beneath the surface until drowned, then dismembered and devoured at leisure. Like other reptiles, the crocodilians are incapable of mastication.

The Egyptian fear of the crocodile grew over the centuries into a fetishistic worship — the cult of the crocodile — and large specimens were mummified and interred in the tombs of pharaohs. A ritual among the Igbo Ukwu tribe was the regular sacrifice of goats to the river deities, combined with the semiannual feeding of virgins to a pair of slack-bellied crocodiles kept for that purpose in a walled enclosure. In the fourth century B.C., Perdiccas' troops were decimated by crocodiles while crossing the Nile at Memphis — nearly a thousand men were lost. A century later, the Greek poet Callicles is said to have lost a lyre to a crocodile one afternoon while extemporizing verses on a barge in the Nile. The following day, hearing music, he went down to the shore and was astonished to see a gargantuan

green head rise up from the water with the instrument lodged in its mouth.
He leaned forward to retrieve it. Foolishly.

⋖ IN MEMORIAM, K. O. J.

The world is a shock of green, as brilliant and intense as a tennis lawn
artificially lit against the night; the morning sky, dirty and lowering, gives
no hint of the sun. From the trees comes the doleful cry of the black-faced
dioch, and the weary rustle of galagos creeping back to their nests after a
meticulous night's prowl. The odor of fish hangs in the air like a tale of
waste and carnage.

Mungo rolls off his mat, shivering, and steps outside to survey the scene.
The river sweeps along, unimpressed, still scraping away at the village's
perimeter, its waters choked with uprooted trees, swollen carcasses
— roots, hoofs and antlers stabbing at the surface, veering off, swirling on
themselves and vanishing as if jerked under by some invisible force. As he
stands there pissing against the outer wall, a section of it suddenly leans
back and tumbles into the river, hitting the water with a slap that flings
froth in his beard, resaturates his toga and rinses his feet to the knee. And
then it's gone — like a cracker in a cup of café au lait. Wet member in
hand, he continues standing there, half-awake, a bit befuddled, his eyes
scanning the quick, muscular surface of the Toolumbo. But wait — there it
is, lurching up from the depths, eight feet across, dipping, bobbing,
uncertain as an adolescent eagle trying its wings. He watches as it spins out
into the current, rough-hewn palisades still bound together with thorn and
creeper, watches as finally it steadies itself and begins to float . . . float
like . . . like a raft!

⋖ ⋗

Half an hour later, equipped with long supple poles hacked from a stand
of bamboo, explorer and guide are assiduously punting their way across the
angry Toolumbo, sky threatening to inundate them from above, snags and
obstructions from below. It's a nightmare. Like trying to conquer the
Himalayas on roller skates or swim the English Channel lashed to a
cannon.

The moment they push off from the bank the current seizes them with a
jolt and sends the raft spinning crazily from the brink of disaster to the
edge of annihilation. A twisted black branch sweeps up on them like a claw
and nearly rakes the explorer into the seething flood, two logs the size of

Corinthian columns kiss just off the bow with a volcanic crush while three of the palisades suddenly part company with the rest and shoot off under their own initiative, and an out-of-sorts baboon, soaked through and champing his incisors, tries to climb up out of the torrent while Johnson frantically plunges at him with the bamboo pole . . . leaving the raft open on the left to the onslaught of a drowning leopard with two mongeese and a monitor lizard clinging to its back and a single black slab the size of Mont Blanc rushing up on them like a runaway carriage . . . which the explorer at the last minute deftly avoids by thrusting his pole forward with a crack of splintering bamboo and a violent lurch of the raft that sends baboon, leopard, mongeese, monitor and Johnson reeling off into the current, heads dashed and bobbed, the baboon gone, Johnson fighting his way to a passing logjam, the raft ramming it from behind and Mungo bending to haul him aboard . . . only to be assaulted an instant later by a school of tiny, slick, leaflike fish that crests over the floorboards like an attack of the falling sickness, upending explorer and guide and putting an end to any further pretense of piloting the craft, the two of them clinging helplessly to the hoary palisades while the raft hurtles from one dunking to the next . . .

◄§ ६►

Much later, and some distance downstream — far beyond the juncture of the Toolumbo and the Niger — the raft runs aground in the upper branches of a grove of tabba trees. The time has come to abandon ship. Explorer and guide slip into the water and dog-paddle from treetop to treetop until they close in on the river's outer verge, where flotsam-plastered trunks begin to emerge from the swirling yellow current. Finally, weary and waterlogged, they find their feet and start wading toward higher ground. Neither has spoken a word for the last hour or so — it was all they could do to hang on, grim, fighting for survival, no initiative left for such an extravagance as forcing air through the larynx. The explorer is the first to comment on the situation. "I think we made it," he pants.

Johnson, belly-deep in fetid water, is about to reply, but doubles over and vomits instead. The guinea hen, so nearly exsiccated a few days earlier, dangles limp once again, as wet as if it had been freshly slaughtered.

They wade on. The forest hangs round them like a theater curtain, mist rising from the water, half-drowned things — jackals, monkeys, pottos, bushpigs — wading along with them, looking dazed and bearish. As they slosh on, avoiding arrow-headed snakes and poisonous tree frogs, their hips begin to emerge from the water. Then their thighs, their knees, and finally their ankles. "Hallelujah," Johnson mutters.

They've reached a rise of sorts, so closely overgrown with bamboo they have to hack their way through it to make any headway. A grim sodden line of honey badgers, rats and hairy-legged spiders follows in their wake. Suddenly Johnson stops hacking and stands frozen for a moment, sniffing the air. "Stew," he says, and begins laying into the foliage with renewed vigor.

Five minutes later they are standing before a cookpot crammed to the rim with choice bits of drowned herbivore. A family of flood refugees — a narrow-shouldered little man with disks in his earlobes, his pregnant wife and six sticklike children — are gathered round the pot, feeding the fire and gnashing away at ribs and joints. The man gestures for them to have a seat and help themselves. "There's plenty here," he grunts, nodding at the bloated carcasses of two hartebeests and a sitatunga. "They'll be rotted past all use in a day or so."

Johnson rubs his hands and starts for the pot, thinking to warm himself with a cup of broth for starters — but instead of fragrant steam, a thick black smoke has begun to rise from the pot. "Hey, you need some more water here," he observes, fanning at the smoke.

The little man, sitting cross-legged against a stump, asks Johnson if he would mind fetching a calabash of water from down below. Johnson turns round and sees that this side of the hill is relatively clear — a few big-boled trees and hothouse plants, the river no more than forty or fifty yards away. "My pleasure," he says, snatching up a calabash and heading down the slope, his mood dramatically improved by the prospect of a hot meal.

"Need any help, old fellow?" the explorer calls.

"No — you just take it easy, Mr. Park — Mungo — and I'll be back in a trice."

Unknown to any of the participants in this scene, however, is the very crucial fact that a colossal old riverine crocodile — nearly eighteen feet in length — has followed the rising waters deep into the recesses of the jungle in the hope of picking up an easy meal at the expense of some half-drowned, warm-blooded creature making its miserable way to higher ground. He lies concealed in a tangle of flood-run debris at the base of the hill, in water no more than a foot or two deep. He has been lurking here for better than three hours now, the scent of the tainted carcasses and stew and tender little children whetting his appetite, his dead-keen saurian eyes fixed on the group gathered round the cookpot. Things have gone splashing past him — easy marks — wretched, wet, vomiting things creeping out of the water unawares — but he's ignored them. A mandrill dragging a broken leg and a buttery fat bushpig that normally would have made an exquisite entrée were especially hard to pass up, but he has his heart set on the regnant woman, a sort of two-in-one treat. Or the stringy little man. Or hat strange, pale newcomer. And he knows, as he's known all along, that ooner or later one of them will come fumbling down that bank to fetch a :alabash of water.

As Johnson steps into the stream the beast is ready for him. There is no warning — no reverential hush of the parrots, touracos and weaverbirds — just an explosion. The bush parting to reveal eighteen feet of brute ravenous power, the children shrieking, Mungo dumb with horror, the :alabash in orbit and Johnson, poor Johnson, snapped up like a cocktail olive and wedged between the awesome snaggle-toothed jaws. Without hesitation the explorer is on his feet, leaping down the hill with his knife drawn, a hero to the core . . . but the croc, its great jagged tail and dragon's claws churning up the muck, is already bolting for deeper water, Johnson clamped firmly in its jaws. The explorer flies through the water like a hurdler, self-sacrifice pounding at his ribcage, but it's too late, too late, and he watches, helpless, as Johnson's eyes cry out to him and the grim Mesozoic beast sinks into the ooze.

NEWGATE

The walls are of stone, blocks of granite smudged and scrawled over with paint and ink and the imprints of a hundred thousand chapped and hopeless hands.

ROGER PEMBROKE, 1786.

Nan Featherstone, Slut, Buried Her
Soar Heart Under the Wait of
These Unyeelding Walls

VENI, VIDI, VICI. TOM THUMP.

Ned Rise has a good close look at these walls in the dawn's early light. An intimate look, in fact. For he is chained to them, the impossible crushing weight of the shackles cutting off the circulation in his ankles and feet. His feet feel as if they've been thrust into a bucket of ice, while his ankles, traumatized by the pressure, seem to have been pinned beneath the cornerstone of some monumental edifice — Westminster Abbey or the Great Pyramid at Giza. But that's not the worst of it. Unable to pay garnish or to bribe even the lowliest turnkey, he has been stripped naked and pushed into this, the deepest, darkest, foulest hole in Newgate Prison.

There are no flagstones here, no straw, no sawdust even — nothing bu
mud. One part soil, two parts human excrement. Mud. The stink i
appalling. There are rats of course, and fleas, lice, protozoans, bacteria
molds, viruses. Things that breed in secret holes and thrive in corruption
things that fester the life from you and gnaw you down to a convenient
digestible form. Half of those awaiting trial in this chamber never surviv
to see the inside of a courtroom. Typhus claims them, or smallpox
dysentery, pneumonia, consumption, inanition, exposure. This is it, think:
Ned. This is it.

Suddenly there is a rattling of chains beside him, and what he at firs
took to be a sort of low bench or heap of rags begins to compose itself intc
a fallen chest, ratty beard and luminous eyes. "Wot ye in for?" rasps a
voice in the gloom.

"Nothing," says Ned. "Except being an honest businessman, maybe.
Trying to get ahead. Live decent."

"Ye're the murderer they drug in last night, ain't ye? Killed a lord,
wasn't it? Didn't give 'im no quarter, neither, the way I 'ears it."

"Wait a damned minute, friend — I'm innocent. It was an accident."

"All I can say is more power to ye. I'd like to kill a lord meself. Ten of
'em. A thousand. Bring 'em in 'ere right now, all the lords and ladies in the
county, and I'd choke 'em to death one by one and take as great a pleasure
in it as if I was banqueting on Portugee wine and oysters, I would."

"I tell you: I didn't do it. They bore false witness against me — my
enemies did."

"No sir, ye're a desperado and a true 'ero of the people. I can tell by the
lay of yer ears. No sense in denyin' a crime of passion — a savage and
courageous one at that — by Jesus I wisht I'd a killed me a lord or two
when I 'ad the chance. . . . Nope. They'll 'ang ye as sure as linen gets gray
and a gin bottle empty, 'ang ye high. My advice to ye, young bucko, is to
take it like a man and drop yer drawers in their prissy, lavender-scented
faces just as they goes to hoist yer up. That's the ticket."

"Shut up, you old loon. Shut up or I'll — "

"Tell me. 'Ow'd ye do it? Throttle 'im? Stick 'im in the ribs? Or'd ye just
blarst the inbred degennerit in the back of the 'ead? 'Ey?"

Ned doesn't answer. The full realization of all that's transpired in the
past few hours has begun to seep into his consciousness, depress his
stomach and worry the moisture from his throat. There will bè no
elopement now, no Dutch inn, no Fanny . . . there won't even be another
court of sessions for six weeks so he can plead his case. By then he'll be

lead of the stink. With a little money, prison doesn't have to be all that
bad. You can have a private room, a fire, irons as light as drawstrings
— and then only at night. You can send out for your meals, a bottle, a
big-bosomed whore, have your cronies in to dine and play at cards, hire
jugglers and musicians, keep a cat, sniff snuff, drink geneva and sleep
between silken sheets. But come to prison penniless and they'll strip the
clothes from your back and mew you up in the dungeon, where day and
night meld into one and dinner consists of a stale crust washed down with a
cup of standing water that looks and smells like cow's piss.

"I think I woulda drowned 'im in a pig trough," the loon says. "Or
maybe just tie the bleeder to a pole and 'orsewhip 'im till the bones poke
through 'is haristycratic 'ide."

Mendoza. He's the one. He got Smirke and the young prig to give
depositions against him, then talked and bribed, talked and bribed, until
the magistrate agreed to march the prisoner across the river and over to
Newgate — "Southwark Prison isn't foul enough for the likes of 'im,"
Mendoza had argued. "Besides, why make 'is late lordship's 'igh-placed
friends and relations travel all the way over 'ere to see the filthy beggar get
'is deserts?" And so, after Ned's pockets had been picked and his mouth
stopped with a dirty rag, the magistrate had laid half a ton of chains on him
and remanded him to Newgate.

"Lords. Bah. Leeches is wot they is. Never done me a bit of good in me
'ole life — and plenty of 'arm, I'll tell ye. Lookit Jock over there — 'Ey
Jock! Jock! — hee, hee, 'ee's been dead three days, and don't nobody
know it yet but me. And you. Know wot Jock was in for?"

Ned shakes his head.

"Nipped tuppence from the waistcoat pocket of one of yer lords out on
King's High Street. Tuppence. Can ye believe that? 'Ee was a cobbler,
Jock was. I knew 'im well. Three babbies squawlin' in their craddle all
night and day for an empty stomach and so Jock goes and dips 'is fingers
into the precious pocket of some addle-'eaded lord. And wot does 'ee get
for it? Tuppence. And tuppence ain't no capital offense, as well ye knows,
me bucko. But 'ee paid capital for it, din'ee?"

"Yeah," says Ned, distant. His ankles have gone to sleep. He tries to
shift position, but the shackles won't budge. "So what did he die of then?"

"Die of? Why ye young ass, don't ye know?"

"Know? How should I?"

The old loon snorts. "Ye'll know soon enough, I warrant. Jock died of
the cholerer."

∽ SHOCK AND OUTRAGE

Sir Joseph Banks drops the afternoon paper with a shout and springs
to his feet, upsetting a decanter of sherry and a humidor packed with
Virginia tobacco. "Dorothea!" he bellows, lunging through the library
at the expense of an elephant's foot umbrella stand, the tea tray and
a japanned cabinet half buried in stationery, envelopes and sealing
wax.

Fanny, who has been dusting in the hallway, is nearly bowled over as her
employer bursts from the library and leaps at the stairs like a wounded
stag, bellowing "Dorothea! Dorothea!" as if it were a battlecry. Startled,
she turns to gaze after him as he slams up the steps and vanishes round the
corner, the sound of his footsteps hammering overhead, another shout
and then the curt rap of his knuckles on Lady B.'s door.

He'd caught her daydreaming, Fanny, staring into space and rubbing
away at a bust of Lycurgus as if she were a cog in a machine. She's been like
this all day. Bount attributed it to the excitement of the previous night
("what with the burglar and all"), while Cook took her aside and asked if
her monthly flow might be especially troublesome owing to the new moon.
To think of their simplicity! Fanny smiles, filled with a delicious sense of
anticipation, intoxicated with the thought of the coming night and her
elopement with Ned. Holland! She can barely believe it. She'll buy herself
a collar of Dutch lace, and one of those white mobcaps with the little wings
and a pair of wooden clogs. They'll live in a windmill, maybe, or on a
barge — hah! She'll be mistress of her own household, with a servant to
bring her tea and cut flowers . . . no more kowtowing to Lady B. or wiping
up pug's turds in the foyer.

From upstairs, Lady B.'s voice: "Jos — what is it?"

"It's Graeme! Graeme Twit. They've killed him!"

"Killed him? Whatever are you talking about?"

Sir Joseph's voice is pinched with emotion. "It's an outrage, is what it is.
A shock and an outrage. By God — "

Absently, already losing interest in the turmoil upstairs — Twit? Where
has she heard that name? — Fanny turns to the open library door and the
chaos within. Muttering to herself, she rights the japanned cabinet, and
squats to pluck fragments of china from the carpet. The newspaper and
humidor lie on the floor too, at the base of Sir Jos' armchair.

" — no, Dorothea, don't try to calm me!" Sir Joseph thunders from
above. "I don't want to be calmed."

Fanny cups the loose tobacco in her hands and restores it to the humidor.

:hen picks up the paper, smooths and folds it, and is about to lay it across :he arm of the chair when she is arrested by the headline:

LORD TWIT MURDERED IN SOUTHWARK

She reads on, strangely compelled, stumbling over the words, *Suspect in custody,* reconstructing a dark night in a poor section of London and the darker motives of the criminal mind, *willful, premeditated and unprovoked act of savagery.* And then she comes to the two words that stop her heart: *Ned Rise. Ned Rise, the assassin.*

Upstairs, like a vengeful, triumphant horn sweeping up the scale to conclude an *allegro furioso* in a burst of power and vituperation, Sir Joseph's voice rings out: "I'll see him flayed alive and strung up for the dogs to piss on — by God I swear an oath I will."

ᵉ⁵ QUID PRO QUO

At this juncture in the history of manners, it was considered *de rigueur* for a heroine to faint dead away when confronted with so sudden and devastat-ing a turn of events. But Fanny was made of sterner stuff. After a short but cathartic cry, she retired to her closet at the rear of the kitchen — pleading illness — and began racking her brain for a means of helping her lover out of his predicament. It seemed hopeless. She had no more than a pound or two herself (and that hoarded up over a period of months, penny by penny), her parents were ragged paupers, her friends milkmaids and servants — and clearly she couldn't turn to Sir Joseph. She thought of extorting money from Cook's household funds or of making off with Lady B.'s plate and silver . . . but no, she couldn't do that. What then? Innocent or not, Ned had to be saved — no matter what it took. All at once it hit her: Adonais Brooks! Of course. She remembered the look on his face when he goosed her in the hallway and threatened to throw himself from the window if she spurned his advances. Sallow, round-shouldered, something sick in his eyes. Go ahead and jump, she'd said. He jumped. Adonais Brooks. Walks with a cane now. She smiled a grim and calculating smile. Adonais Brooks. Horny as a tomcat.

She tiptoed from her room. The house was quiet. Sir Joseph had roared off to his club in a storm of threats and imprecations, and Lady B. was confined with a headache. Fanny stole a look at Lady B.'s address book, wrapped herself up in a shawl and slipped out the front door.

For a time, when he was eighteen or nineteen, Adonais Brooks had insisted that his friends call him Werther, so affected was he by Goethe's portrayal of that sad and neurotic youth. During the ensuing years he had discovered Collins, Smart, Cowper and Gray. The *Oriental Eclogues* sat on his shelf beside Macpherson's Ossian poems and Thomas Percy's *Reliques of Ancient English Poetry*. He cultivated ballads and cultural primitivism, sported red trousers and black velvet jackets. At the bimonthly meetings of the West End Poetry Club, of which he was then secretary, he championed passion over precision, sensibility over wit. One evening, in the middle of "Demitasse and Spoon," an elegant satire by Blythe Bender, he rose to his feet and shouted: "Enough of Pope, Addison and Steele! Enough of wit and urbanity and the heroic couplet! Where is life, where is blood, where is the grave?" A shocked silence fell over the hall — never before had a reading been interrupted, never before had there been such a breach of taste and decorum. He was shouted down by his fellow members, and later asked to resign from the club.

Now, at twenty-six, he wandered the dismal foggy streets with tears in his eyes, thrived on electrical storms and blasts of wind, dreamed of mountains, wounds, derring-do and sex — thrilling, voluptuous and morbid sex. Sex in churchyards and catafalques, sex in shackles, galleys, dungeons. He kept four servants and a carriage. He believed in witches and revenants, and lived in decadent splendor on Great George Street. There was still a lingering pain in his ribs — especially when he coughed or breathed too deeply — and the shattered bones of his right leg, though healed, hadn't quite knit properly. He secretly thrilled at the loss of his ear.

When Fanny came to the door he was toiling away at his "Elegy on the Demise of Our Afric Explorers" ("O Ledyard, O Lucas, O Houghton and Park, / Must I count you among the dear departed, / And Timbuctoo still languishing in the dark?"). Bellows, his manservant, announced her in stentorian tones. "Fanny Brunch, Sir."

He was stunned. How many times had he pictured her here? How many times, alone in his bedchamber, had he . . . et cetera? He leaped to his feet, shaking like a wet spaniel, licked his palms and smoothed back his hair — and then she was there, standing before him like a vision in a dream. "Fanny!" he ejaculated, rushing forward to offer her a chair. But what was this? Tears on her cheeks?

"I've come, begging your pardon, Sir, to entreat a favor," she began, her breast palpitating. He listened, sucking at the vision of her like a vampire: her ankles, hips, hair. The sound of her voice was an aphrodisiac, apples and oysters, a feather tickling at his crotch. He wanted to plunge at her, sink himself into her — but he listened, twitching, an uncomfortable projection straining against his trousers. When she was finished he took hold of her hand. "I'll help you," he said, his voice so strained it was almost a whistle. "God knows I'll help you, do anything you ask, anything . . . mortify my flesh, tear out my eyes, open a vein — do you want proof of it? Right now? I'll do it, I will. Anything you ask." Then he looked her in the eye, cold as a knife. "But you must understand . . . there has to be a quid pro quo."

"A what, Sir?"

"An exchange. A tit for tat."

Fanny lowered her eyes. "I knows that, Sir — what else has a poor girl got to offer? But you don't have to get vulgar about it."

⊷ ⊷

The next morning Fanny visited Newgate. She held a scented handkerchief to her nose and followed the turnkey down the winding stairwell to the dungeon, her footsteps echoing like gunfire in a well. When the massive iron door swung back on its hinges, the stink nearly knocked her to her knees. Inside the atmosphere was rank and caliginous: fumes rose from puddles, groans sifted through the shadows. She started forward gingerly, her pupils widening in the gloom. Muck pulled at her shoes, twisted claws reached out for her, the reek of urine stung her eyes. "Hey Mistress big-arse, come sit on me face," growled a voice. "Titties," called another, "titties, titties, titties." A stark animal terror came over her — a fear of being buried alive, mewed up in a wall, sucked down through the hole in the latrine, down, down to the slick and steaming intestines of the earth where demons picked the flesh from your bones and howling beasts snuffed up your soul and shat it out in hard black pellets. Fanny pulled back with a cry, but the turnkey took her by the elbow. "It's all right, Mistress," he said. "Don't mind them . . . look now, there's yer friend up ahead."

Ned was delirious, gibbering about fish heads and pots of gold, lying in his own waste, naked and shivering. An old man, the gums drawn back from his teeth, lay dead beside him. Fanny pressed a half crown into the turnkey's hand and he unshackled Ned's legs, wrapped him in a blanket and carried him from the room. Later, in a private cell, Fanny sponged her lover down with vinegar and made him a hot broth. She held the steaming cup to his lips and kissed him. He vomited. Looked into her eyes and didn't seem to recognize her. By the time the surgeon arrived he was running sweat and beating his head against the wall. "What is it, Sir?" Fanny begged. "What's wrong with him?" The surgeon was seventy or eighty years old, dressed in the tight trousers and periwig of a young rake. His nostrils flared as he opened a vein in the patient's leg and drew blood until Ned lay still. "Gaol fever," the surgeon said matter-of-factly. "He'll either pull through it or he'll die like a dog. Flip a coin if it'll make you feel any better."

の ご

The following day Lady B. demanded an explanation of Fanny's failure to answer the bell. Byron Bount stood on the carpet before her, heels locked, staring down at his feet. "Well, speak up Bount — is the girl still indisposed? Should I have the medico come round?" Bount answered, begging his ladyship's pardon, that Fanny was not in the house. "Not in the — did you say not in the house?" That's what he'd said. But where was she then? Bount cleared his throat. "It's anybody's guess, Ma'am." Lady B.'s face hardened past simple petrification, through the igneous phase, the metamorphic and beyond.

The upshot of all this is that when Fanny returned from the prison that evening, her dress smudged and heart heavy, she found Byron Bount waiting for her on the front steps. Beside him lay two bundles of clothing and a crude oil portrait of Fanny's mother. Bount folded his arms and looked down on her like a carrion bird.

Did she really have a choice?

"Great George Street," she said to the cabbie.

⤳ APOSTASY

Alexander Anderson was at war with himself. His father had been pressuring him to have a talk with Ailie about her marital status, and he couldn't decide which side he was on. "There's nobody in the world closer to her than you are lad, not even her old Da'," his father coaxed. "Talk some sense into her." There had been no word of Mungo in nearly two years: the old man wanted her to marry Gleg.

The idea would have been anathema to him at one time. But now he wasn't so sure. Gleg was still something of an ass — but an infinitely more tolerable ass than he'd been when he first came to Selkirk. And there was no question that he was devoted to Ailie — he'd been fawning at her feet and showering her with gifts and poems and off-key ballads ever since he'd laid eyes on her. The thing that hung Zander up was that by embracing Gleg he'd be turning his back on Mungo — worse, he'd be admitting that

Mungo had failed, that he was dead and gone, buried in a shallow grave or stewing in the intestines of some slow-haunching beast. And yet, painful as such an admission might be, was there really any doubt? What was the sense of nurturing false hopes? Could he stand to see his sister pining away interminably, waiting on, hope curdling until it tasted of despair, her back humped with disappointment, the barren years aging her prematurely as she shuffled in and out of the kirk muttering over a string of prayer beads?

Gleg wasn't so bad. He had his faults — he ate like a drayhorse and laughed like a hyena, his teeth were bad and his breath worse . . . he was clumsy, long-nosed, ugly as a dog . . . and yet his heart was good and he'd doubtless make something of himself in the world . . .

Zander poured himself a whisky and ambled into the parlor, where Ailie was bent over her microscope and notepad. Gleg and the old man were out on a housecall, doing what they could to relieve old Malcolm McMurtry, who was dying of the bloody flux. Christmas was two weeks off. Wreaths of holly and groundpine hung in the windows. Outside the wind tore through the trees.

Zander sat on the edge of the table and studied his sister's profile for a moment: the slope of the neck, the retroussé nose, the clipped black hair. "Ails," he said finally, "I've been mulling it over, trying to be rational, and I don't think — well, I don't think you can count on Mungo coming back." She didn't look up from her work. "I mean — isn't it about time we faced up to it and began to think of a future without him?" He took a sip of whisky; she was sketching something, going from microscope to notepad and back again. "I haven't told you this . . . but I'll be leaving Selkirk before too much longer, you know — as soon as I can get myself together. I can't stay here till the cows come home, mooching off the old man." Still she didn't respond. "And what about you? The old man isn't going to live forever. Shouldn't you be making plans?"

Ailie turned and looked up at him. "Et tu, Zander?"

He laughed. "Yes, me too. The old man wants you to marry Georgie. He asked me to talk to you. And you know, really, I don't think it's such a bad idea."

"You don't want me to be a spinster."

"Something like that."

"And Mungo?"

Zander left his drink and stirred up the coals in the hearth. Ailie's doves started up a mournful duet, a sort of threnody, and then abruptly cut off in midnote. "We've got to face up to it, Ails," he said, his back to her. "Two years and no word. What other conclusion is there?" When he turned round, she was peering into the microscope again. "Well?" His voice was gentle, a whisper. "Do you think there's any hope?"

"I do not love Georgie Gleg," she said.

ఆకీ ៛ా

Two weeks later, on Christmas Day, after they'd drunk a toast and exchanged presents, there was dancing. (Ailie had been inundated with gifts from Gleg—a box of sweetmeats; three yards of green muslin store-bought in Edinburgh; the two volumes of Pierre Menard's new study of protozoan life, *Le Monde Secret;* a dipnet and half a dozen sketchpads; scented handkerchiefs; a bottle of lilac water. She gave him a pocketknife in return.) Neighbors and cousins tramped over the floorboards, Kathy Kelpie and uncle Darroch, Nell Gwynn, Robbie Campbell and all the Motherwell Andersons. Godfrey MacAlpin shrieked and moaned through his pipes, Zander struck in with a fife and old man Deans sawed away at a fiddle. There was milk punch and spiced whisky, a smell of goose and maukin roasting on the spit. Katlin Gibbie came in late, cheeks flushed, her new husband on her arm and a conspicuous bulge beneath her coat. Gleg asked Ailie for a dance.

Later, when everyone had settled down for the meal, Dr. Anderson raised his glass and shouted that Ailie had an announcement to make. She rose unsteadily from the table, Gleg beamed up at her, Zander looked puzzled. "You all know," she began, "that I've lost my betrothed in the wilds of Africa. I have every hope that he will one day walk through that door . . . every hope . . . but the days and minutes and hours are like venom to me and I . . ." she was sniffling. Old man Deans offered her his handkerchief. "Another man, kind and gentle, has been growing in my esteem . . ." She fumbled for her glass, drained it in a gulp. "What I mean to say is this: if there has come no word from Mungo to stop it, I will give my hand to Georgie Gleg in this very room one year from today, so help me God."

✒ HORRIPILATION

Days became weeks, weeks months. Ned, miraculously recovered but with a tendency to fall asleep in midsentence, drank gill ale in his private cell and toasted kidneys over the grate. Outside it was snowing. He could see the hard white pellets swirling beyond the bars of his window like gravel in a stream.

Billy Boyles sat on a stool in the corner, a pot of ale in his hand. Visiting. He crossed his bony legs, took a long swallow and wiped his mouth. "Gettin' nervous, Neddy?"

"Nervous? Why should I? I'm innocent, ain't I?"

"That's right, Neddy. I was there."

The court of assizes met in the Old Bailey (a courthouse conveniently adjoining the prison) eight times a year, or every six weeks or so. Ned had been arrested in early August, but his barrister, Neville Thorogood of the high-powered firm of Jaggers & Jaggers, had managed to procure three postponements on the grounds of ill health. Thorogood was one of the premiere criminal lawyers of his day, retained for Ned on the strength of Adonais Brooks' bank account. But good as he was, he was no miracle worker. Ned Rise was to stand in the dock at ten o'clock the following morning.

◦§ §◦

Fanny was so keyed up she couldn't eat her dinner. "But Fanny," Brooks protested, "you've got to keep your strength up. Have a bit of raw veal — or an onion and porridge at least." No: she couldn't touch a thing. Really. Brooks arched his eyebrows and gestured toward the bedroom. "A bit of a tumble, then? To take your mind off it?"

The months at Great George Street had been a trial. Not that Brooks hadn't been kind — and more than generous. It was his sexual demands. They were implacable. Never-ceasing. Strange and bestial. He'd dismiss the servants and strap her to the bannister in the downstairs hallway, take her from the rear and use her upturned buttocks for an ashtray. Or he'd lash her to the cook's worktable — spread-eagled — and probe her orifices with carrots, cucumbers, zucchini, sausages. Then scramble half a dozen eggs in her navel and lap them up raw, take impressions of her breasts for gelatin molds, bury her in cole slaw. One afternoon he pinned her down and branded his initials in her left buttock; another time he came home with a terrier and a box of rats, and made furious love to her while the dog scrambled about the room throttling rodents and growling like a two-man saw. Terrified rats sprang onto the bed, clicking and squealing, burrowing into the bedclothes, the mute insistent *snap, snap, snap* of their companions' necks driving them like a whip. Fanny went into shock. Adonais never missed a stroke.

It was difficult. But it was either submit, or watch Ned die a lingering death in the muck of Newgate. The history of love was full of such sacrifices — Pyramus and Thisbe, Venus and Adonis, George and Martha Washington. If they could do it, so could she. As she lay in Ned's arms behind the cold stone walls of Newgate, too sore and exhausted to move, her lips swollen and eyes wet with tears, she felt herself lifted into the airy solitudes of the Christian martyrs, into the realm of Ignatius, Polycarp, Joan of Arc — of Christ Himself. This was martyrdom. This was love.

Ned did his best to lighten the load. He soothed her, massaged her welts and bruises, tried to smooth away the calligraphic blot on her backside with creams and unguents — all the while swearing he'd get revenge, make it up to her, take her off to some island in the Mediterranean and raise an altar to her. She let him talk on, his voice an anodyne. The walls were of granite, the gate of cast iron. He was penniless, powerless, emasculated by a system that crushed the downtrodden and rewarded perjurers and thieves. She never reminded him. Never undermined his hopes, never burdened his flights with the ballast of reality, and above all, never alluded to the trial that hung over their heads like the wicked flashing blade of a guillotine.

But now the moment was at hand. Ned would be acquitted and she could turn her back on Brooks to live with her lover in poverty and ecstasy. Or else —

She steeled herself. Thisbe's example had not been lost on her.

☙ THE BLACK CAP

The day of the trial dawned like an infection, the sky low and pus-colored, the sun a crusted eye. A few sickly pigeons flapped over the prison walls like newspapers lifted on the wind. From the street below came the pathogenic roar of the mob gathered outside the courthouse. Ned Rise felt sick to his stomach.

The mob was a ruly one for the most part, composed of shopkeepers, clergymen, budding industrialists and the wives of M.P.'s — the very heart, lungs and marrow of the middle class. They had been convened largely through the efforts of Sir Joseph Banks. Tirelessly, throughout the fall and early winter, he had led a campaign in the press and in the drawing rooms of Soho and Mayfair to make a public example of this case, to "lay its bloated carcass before the public eye and nostril till the very sight and stink of it drives them to rise up and exterminate the human vermin that infest our streets and threaten the life, liberty — and yes, property — of our good citizens." He was stung by the wanton act of violence against his old friend and African associate and maddened to the brink of aneurysm by the revelation that his own ex-servant was connected — in the most odious way — with the evildoer. One thing and one thing only had brought him to the Old Bailey: to see Ned Rise sentenced to hang.

Inside, the gallery was packed. Charles Fox was there, Sir Reginald Durfeys, the Duke of Omnium and Lady Bledsoe. Countess Binbotta, Twit's sister, was in from Leghorn with her husband Rudolfo. The African Association was out in force. Carlotta Meninges was there, and Bishop Erkenwald. So too was Beau Brummell, now an intimate of the Prince of Wales, and well on his way to becoming the preeminent cravat folder of the age. Twit's death had come as a jolt to all of them, nagging as it did at the heels of their own vulnerability. Who hadn't lost a purse in the street or been robbed at gunpoint in one's own coach? Or come home to find his rooms ransacked and jewelry absconded with? But this — this was something else again.

There were nearly two hundred capital offenses on the books during that winter of '96–'97, including such heinous crimes as: *stealing linen from a bleaching ground; shooting at a Revenue Officer; pulling down houses, churches, etc.; cutting hop binds; setting fire to corn or coal mines; stabbing a person unarmed if he die in six months; sending threatening letters; riots by twelve or more, and not dispersing in one hour after proclamation; breaking down a fish pond where fish may be lost; stealing woollen clothes from tenter grounds; stealing from a ship in distress; privy councillors, attempting to kill, etc.; sacrilege; turnpikes or bridges, destroying.* With so many felonies to choose from this poor idiot had to go ahead and murder a nobleman. It was more than a crime. It was an outrage, a violation of the rules, a challenge to the system. Let them murder a Lord today, they'll be raping a Lady tomorrow. It was unthinkable. Burghers and haut monde alike had turned out in protest. They'd come to see the prisoner get his deserts. They'd come to see the judge put on his black cap.

◆§ ৡ◆

The entire cast was assembled when Ned Rise was led into the courtroom, chains tintinnabulating at his wrists and ankles. The jurors had taken their oaths, kissed the ancient lip-blackened Bible and settled themselves in their box; the counselors were shuffling papers and grinning over some private joke; the judges — the Lord Mayor, the alderman, the sheriffs and the Chief Justice of the Court of Common Pleas — were arranging their robes and coughing into their fists, the ebb and flow of their plethoric wigs like a flock of sheep on the run. Clank-clank, echoed the chains. The faces in the gallery looked up from newspapers, knitting, flasks of brandy, keen as weasels on the scent of a stricken bird. Ned, shoulders slumped, looking apologetic, clanked into the dock.

The Chief Justice wiped his spectacles and rubbed the bridge of his nose while Ned scanned the room for a friendly face. None was readily apparent. The judges looked bilious and sour, as if just awakened from naps; the members of the jury sat stiff as fence posts, some wigged, others not, their faces hammered from granite; the prosecutor gnashed his teeth. Ned's glance shot from face to face in the gallery, lighting on Sir Joseph Banks' Vesuvian cheeks and brow, the Countess Binbotta's rapierlike nose, Reginald Durfeys' fluff of silver hair, and then finally, with a sigh of relief, on Fanny's sad and wistful smile. At least *she* was here, thank God. But who was that beside her, in the scarlet jacket and beestung lips? Was *that* Brooks? And even worse, who was that tattered hag in the front row — the one with the ring struck through her lip? There was something about her that made his blood run cold, something strange and terrible, something that reached back to his earliest memories and whispered *lost, lost, all lost.*

"Clerk!" thundered the Chief Justice. "Read the indictment."

The clerk's voice was pitched like a bassoon, deep and mellifluous. "It is charged," he read, "that the prisoner, one Ned Rise, did willfully and with malice aforethought take the life of Lord Graeme Eustace Twit in a violent manner on the night of August 11, 1796, after having lured his late lordship to the prisoner's own foul and disreputable lodgings in Southwark, and there defenestrating him to his great bodily harm and subsequent demise."

"The indictment has been read," observed the Chief Justice in his sonorous tones. "How does the prisoner plead?"

Something caught in Ned's throat. "Not — " he choked, seized by a sudden coughing spasm, drooling and wheezing for breath while the bailiff thumped his back and the spectators sniffed at jars of vinegar and crumbled sprigs of rue to ward off contagion. Finally, eyes tearing, Ned managed to squeak out his plea. "Not guilty, Your — Worship."

There was a hiss from the gallery. The Chief Justice pounded the table with his gavel. "Call the first witness!" he roared.

The first witness was Mendoza. The Champion Fisticuffer strode across the room to a murmur of approval, resplendent in a pristine cravat, charcoal-gray jacket and black velvet trousers. His hair, lightly powdered, was tied back at the nape with a bit of ribbon that coordinated with his pants in the most delicate and felicitous way. He told his story in a clear, forthright voice, occasionally choked off by a flood of emotion when forced by the prosecutor to dwell on the more unpleasant details of the crime. Everyone agreed that he acquitted himself well.

Ned felt a rush of relief when his counsel, Neville Thorogood, rose to cross-examine the witness. Thorogood was bland and corpulent, a man whose reputation rested as much on the fact that he had once consumed thirteen roasted hens in one sitting as on his juridical prowess. He stepped forward impressively, a stern and commanding look ironed into his bloated features, the immensity of his black-robed figure blotting half the room from view. Unfortunately, his voice had the high thin pitch of a choirboy's, and there were titters from the gallery as he began his questioning. "Mr. Mendoza," he piped, "can you tell the gentlemen of the jury just what you were doing in the defendant's lodgings at four o'clock in the morning on August eleven of this year?"

Mendoza didn't bat an eye. "The prisoner went and advised us that 'ee 'ad some silver plate and certain hancient paintin's and hairlooms for sale, Yer Honor, and knowin' that Lady Tuppenham 'ad lately been deprived of such, we agreed to rondyvoo with the prisoner for the purpose of recoverin' the property and 'oldin' 'im till the authorities could be called."

There was a flurry of applause from the gallery.

The Lord Mayor congratulated the witness on his keen sense of civic duty.

Ned was stunned. "But that's a lie!" he shouted. "A barefaced lie!"

The Chief Justice thumped his gavel and ordered the bailiff to restrain the prisoner. A sharp blow to the kidneys doubled Ned over, and he began to cough again. When he recovered he lifted his head and gazed steadily at Mendoza. "You were there to rob me," he said.

At this point the prosecutor rose from his seat. "Your Honor," he began, "I beg you to consider that at the time of his apprehension the accused was a fugitive from justice, implicated as the prime mover in the sordid Vole's Head Tavern affair that so shocked us all a few months back. Furthermore, I submit that it is a patent absurdity to accuse a man who left an estate valued at some sixty thousand pounds of attempting to . . . *rob* a wretched Southwark pauper." Here he paused gravidly. "And beyond its inherent absurdity, this wild and desperate tale constitutes a callous profanation of the memory of a great and noble Englishman who, but for the hand of that blackguard there, would be among us today to defend himself from the sting of such calumny."

"Bravo!" called Rudolfo Binbotta.

The Chief Justice, ignoring Binbotta's outburst, looked down at the prisoner as if he were examining a bit of offal. "I quite agree, Counselor." The gavel came down. "Next witness!"

The next witness was Smirke. He lumbered up to the stand, all feet and thumbs, and told his tale. Ned Rise was a thief and a liar. A scoundrel who had tricked him into besmirching the good name of the Vole's Head, and then ducked out of sight to avoid "payin' the piper." On the night of August eleven, Smirke testified, he had gone over to Southwark with "the majestic pugilist, 'is late lordship and the black nigger slave to recover wot properties the prisoner 'ad nipped from an 'igh-placed lady and to see that 'ee got wot was comin' to 'im. There I witnessed 'im backin' up like a cornered rat and viciously shovin' 'is late lordship out the window to 'is untoimely death."

When Ned protested, the bailiff stuffed a rag in his mouth.

Jutta Jim was called in next as a corroborative witness. Because his English fell somewhere in the range between nonexistent and prerudimentary, he conveyed his recollections by means of sign language and pantomime. While describing his performance at the Vole's Head, for instance, he made a circle of the thumb and forefinger of his left hand, through which he repeatedly thrust the stiffened index finger of his right. *"Mojo-jojo,"* he grinned. "Scroo." When it came to depicting the fatal night, he crept round the courtroom with his teeth bared to indicate the stealth and savagery of the prisoner, then flopped over on his back in imitation of his dead employer. He ended the performance in tears.

The prosecutor rested his case and Neville Thorogood rose to call his first and only witness: Billy Boyles.

Boyles, the back of his head flat as a book, lurched into the courtroom from the hallway beyond. His clothes were limp and shredded, his face and scrag of a beard plastered with dirt; he stank of halfpenny gin. For a long moment he stood there in the center of the room, dazed and uncertain. All eyes were upon him. He shook his head twice, as if to clear it, took a step forward and stumbled over the court recorder. "Bailiff!" boomed the judge, "help this man to the witness stand."

Thorogood demurred. "But Your Honor—the witness is inebriated." "Nonsense."

By this time Boyles had been helped from the floor, and was clutching at the sides of the witness stand as he dragged himself up into the box. "Are you inebriated, sir?" asked the Chief Justice.

Boyles found his seat and looked up at him. "Wot was 'at?"

"Are you inebriated, sir?"

No response.

The Lord Mayor whispered in the ear of the Chief Justice. The Justice rephrased his question. "Drunk, sir. Are you drunk?"

This seemed to register, and Boyles' face blanched. "Who, me? Not a bit of it. I may have had a drop or two in my day, but for a sacred event like this one I wouldn't . . ." (here he paused to fight back a belch and pound at his breastbone) ". . . wouldn't dream of it."

The Chief Justice sat back in his chair. "The witness is yours, Counselor."

Thorogood blew out a long exasperated breath, then turned to the witness and asked him if he knew Ned Rise to be an honest man.

"Honest?" Boyles barked. "Why he's honest as a rogue could be wot must live by his wits."

Someone laughed in the gallery. Boyles winked at Ned.

The counselor then asked Boyles for the particulars of the encounter in Southwark on the night of August eleven.

Boyles seemed perplexed. "August eleven? Why I can barely remember back a week — how am I supposed to know wot went on five, six months ago, eh?"

"The night of Lord Twit's demise," piped Thorogood.

"Ohhhhh," said Boyles, as if this cast a whole new light on things. "That was the night, was it? August eleven? You sure?" He picked his nose thoughtfully for a moment, and then began his story. "Well, I tells you. I was present for the whole thing and I says that Neddy Rise is innocent as a babby." (This prompted a protest from the gallery, to which Boyles responded with an obscene gesture.) "You see they got me drunk," he continued, "and forced me to find out Neddy's lodgin's for 'em, though Neddy was dead and drownded five months before. So we goes up to his lodgin's and waits for him, me and Twit and the rest . . . and the rest . . ."

"Yes," shrilled Thorogood, "go on."

But Boyles could not go on. His head had come to rest on the rail before him and he had begun to breathe through his nose with a low racheting sound. The Chief Justice ordered the bailiff to shake him, but it was no use: he was out cold. "Remove the witness!" boomed the judge. And then: "Have you any more witnesses to call, Mr. Thorogood?"

"No, your honor," whined Ned's counselor, "but — "

"Mr. Prosecutor — you may address the jury."

In his summation, the prosecutor drew on the Classics, Shakespeare and the Bible. He quoted poetry, marshaled evidence, spoke of sin and corruption, the sad state of London's streets, of inbreeding and the criminal mentality. He spoke glowingly of torture and the gallows, of the deterrent effect of public execution. Ned Rise, he asserted, was a fiend and a libertine. A Jack the Ripper, an Ethan Allen, a Robespierre. He was filth, vermin, disease. To stamp him out would be patriotic, Christian — as close as the English public could come to asserting their identification with Jesus of Nazareth and their loathing for Satan and his vile minions on earth. "I implore you," he concluded, "no — I command you in the name of King George and the Lord in Heaven to eliminate this cancerous growth, this bubo, this Ned Rise, before he swells up to consume us all!" The prosecutor was bathed in sweat. His final words rang out like the trumpets of the archangels warming up for Judgment Day. The gallery burst into spontaneous applause.

And then it was Ned's turn. The rag was removed from his mouth, and he prepared to make his final plea to the jury. (At this point in the history of English jurisprudence, counsel for the defense was prohibited from addressing the jury — that privilege was reserved for the defendant alone. Often as not the defendant was half-starved, ignorant, intimidated by the proceedings, incapable of weighing evidence or of reasoning clearly. But that was his lookout.)

Ned took a deep breath, turned to face the jury, and gave it his best shot. "Gentlemen of the jury," he began, "there are two sides to every story, and I beg you now to take heed of mine. First, everything you have heard here today is a lie." There were boos and catcalls from the gallery; the judge rapped for order. "All I wanted was to live decent. I put aside a few pounds so I could be married and open a tavern or some other respectable business. I worked hard and saved my money. But these men came in the dead of night to beat and rob me — Smirke, Mendoza, and yes, Lord Twit, God rest his soul."

"Infamy!" shouted Sir Joseph Banks.

"It's a lie!" shrieked the Countess Binbotta.

Ned held up his shackled hands for silence. "Where would the likes of me get the near five hundred pounds that was stole from me that night? Simple. It was I, who by the sweat of my brow, bottled — er, imported — the renowned caviar, Chichikov's Choice — "

There was an angry rumble at the mention of the brand name; Ned began to feel he'd made a mistake, but blundered on nonetheless. "Chichikov's Choice, which I sold at a sacrifice so the good people of London could enjoy the finest — "

"Frog's eggs and shoe blacking!" shouted an angry juror.

"Poison!" shouted another.

"String him up!"

The bailiff had to restrain one of the jurors, red in the face, who was attempting to climb over the rail and assault the prisoner. The gallery was in riot, Ned ducking shoes and bits of rotten fruit, the Chief Justice and Lord Mayor pounding the table with their gavels. "Order!" called the clerk. "Order!"

When the courtroom had settled down, the Chief Justice glared angrily at Ned. "Bailiff," he roared, "the prisoner is inciting to riot. Muffle him." The rag was reinserted in Ned's mouth and the Chief Justice charged the jury to deliberate and pronounce their verdict.

The foreman rose. He was a rangy, dyspeptic-looking fellow whose face was creased with scowl lines. "There is no need for deliberation, your honor. Our decision is unanimous. We find the defendant guilty as charged." He made as if to sit, but then thought better of it. "And if I may say so, Your Honor, I think hangin's too good for him."

The Chief Justice looked down the row of his colleagues — the sheriffs, the alderman, the Lord Mayor — while the court held its breath. Then, with a grim terrible look, he reached beneath the table, produced the black cap and set it atop his wig. "Ned Rise," he called in a voice that would wake the dead. "Face the court and hear our doom." He paused to blow his nose mightily. "After weighing the evidence we find you guilty as charged and sentence you to hang by the neck until you are dead, dead, dead."

As the Chief Justice delivered the sentence, the bailiff slipped a string about the prisoner's thumb and pulled it tight to illustrate his words. Ned was dazed. He looked round him and saw that the entire courtroom was on its feet, people were applauding and whistling, razzing and jeering — Fanny was nowhere to be seen. The bailiff took him by the arm and led him across the room toward the door that communicated with the prison. Through all the noise of the crowd one sound rang in his ears, filled his being, made his flesh crawl as if all the corpses in the world had risen up to rake their nails across a monstrous blackboard: "Eeeeeee!" it grated. "Eeeeeee! Eeeeeee-eeeeee!"

⋅§ HEGIRA

The loss of Johnson hit the explorer like a hammerblow. If before the situation was grim, now it was desperate. Not only was he half-naked, starved, febrile, nauseated, penniless and lost, he suddenly found himself on his own in an alien and hostile environment — without guide, companion or fellow sufferer. Life with the Moors was a lark by comparison.

As he watched Johnson's brow sink into the muck, he lost control of himself, carrying on like a Greek housewife at the funeral of her eldest son, or a federalist, forced by luck of the draw to inscribe his name last on a historic and revolutionary document. Purely and simply, he gave way to despair. Sat down in the water and began tearing at his hair, wailing, sobbing and moaning, gnashing his teeth, rending his skin, flailing at the water with his useless knife and cursing, blaspheming, crying out against the senseless mechanism of the universe and the black arbitrary heart that oversees it. This went on for ten minutes or so, until he felt a hand on his arm. It was the refugee. Behind, up to their knees in water, stood the little man's wife and stunted children, their faces stung with anxiety. "Come on," the man said. "There's nothing you can do here — except maybe attract another crocodile."

The man's name was Jemafoo Momadoo. Like many of the Mandingoes of the region he was a Moslem, having converted to Mohammedanism under pressure from the Moors. He bowed to Mecca twice a day, abstained from pork and named his first son Ismail — but he was no fanatic. Until the deluge he had been a tenant farmer in the village of Sooha, scraping away at the dusty soil from dawn till dusk, yanking at the desiccated yellow teats of his goats, boiling the meat from the bones of snakes, toads and rats. A week of steady rain flooded the fields around Sooha to a depth of three and a half feet. He and his wife and their wisps of children were asleep in their cane hut when the Niger swept down on them, seething and booming. The flood waters took his goats, two sons, his hut, tools and meager stock of dried legumes and rice. In return it gave him the bloated carcasses of two hartebeests and a sitatunga.

He led the explorer back up the rise to where the pot was once again simmering over the fire. The clearing was so green it ached. "Would you like a cup of broth?" he asked.

                                    ◄§ §►

Mungo accompanied the Momadoos to the village of Song, where Jemafoo's father-in-law was the *Dooty*. It was a two-day trek. Jemafoo was hoping to participate in the reduction of his father-in-law's larder, while Mungo, still reeling under the shock of Johnson's sudden demise and shaken with the onset of fever, welcomed the opportunity to travel anywhere, so long as it was in the right direction. (He had discovered, much to his dismay, that the failed attempt to cross the Toolumbo had resulted in his landing on the far side of the Niger, *twenty miles downriver from the point at which he'd started*. The discovery came as no surprise, actually — it was just another link in a concatenation of major setbacks and bitter disappointments that had begun with the disappearance of his sea-trunk ten minutes after landing at Goree, and that had continued unabated ever since.)

The Momadoos, *en famille*, trooped into Song just after dawn, the explorer bringing up the rear. Cook fires smoldered under the light drizzle, dogs yapped, guinea hens pecked in the dirt. There was no one to be seen. Madame Momadoo, eight-and-a-half months pregnant and a native of the village, was puzzled. She peered into this hut or that, called out a time or two, and then turned to her husband and shrugged her shoulders. But then she caught her breath and stood stock-still, listening. Her broad face broke into a grin. *"Mola lave akombo,"* she said. "They're singing. Listen."

The sound was faint and distant, a static in the air, a hum of the sort that announces a massing of insects — or a gathering of armies. The explorer strained his ears: it seemed to be coming from the direction of the river. He started toward it automatically, without thinking, almost as if he were under a spell. Human voices, raised in song. How long had it been? Bass and contralto, counterpoint, soaring sopranos — the sweep of voices took him back to the cavernous cathedrals of Edinburgh and the simple oak-beamed chapel of his boyhood at Fowlshiels. He found himself returning Madame Momadoo's grin.

The muddy path wound through a series of vegetable plots already burgeoning with yellow gourds, incipient watermelons, yams, cassavas, Indian corn and peanuts, then dipped down a short incline to follow an earthen levee across what appeared to be a flooded rice paddy. The children scampered on ahead, thin as featherless birds, while Madame Momadoo hurried after them, her great belly jogging in time to the flash of her elbows. Mungo picked his way along carefully, quizzing Jemafoo about the local power structure, agricultural techniques, initiation rites. The music swelled in his ears.

They passed through a dark clot of vegetation that hemmed them in on all sides, then came round a bend and caught their breath — there was the Niger stretched out before them, oceanic, gray with mist. Trees stood in the water like women lifting their skirts, and the riverbank was crowded with people. Brooding over the scene were masses of shrieking, squabbling birds. Jemafoo's face lit up. "The *akeena* are running!" he shouted, bounding forward like a hound on the scent.

No one even glanced up when the explorer joined the crowd on the riverbank. They were too busy hauling at ropes, collectively drawing a huge seine across the bay before them — and singing their hearts out.

"Wo-habba-wo!" chanted the men in a basso that shook the earth, dipping forward on the *"habba,"* leaning back into the rope on the upbeat. *"Weema-woppa, weema-woppa,"* sang the women and children, while an old man, ribby but muscular, wove a snaking melody above it with all the fire and ice of a tenor at the Royal Opera.

Mungo looked round. Madame Momadoo had joined one of the rope gangs behind her eldest son. Jemafoo stood by a mound of silver fish, each the size of a sardine, and flailed a stick at the terns and pelicans that plunged toward the seething mass and then shot off into the sky. Each villager had his task — from the old women who tended the bonfires to the boys who ran off dogs and jackals with a barrage of stones — and yet each was attuned to the other through the rhythmic insistency of the song. Order and harmony, sang the voices, cooperation and prosperity, heave and ho. The explorer stood there like a mannequin, intent on the struggle with the net, until he began to detect a change in the intensity of the music. It seemed as if the voices were about to explode, rumbling away like a stampede, when a woman's voice rushed up the scale in a burst of Dionysian energy, searing and triumphant, the rhythm pulsing quicker now, driving toward a climax, thunderous — and suddenly Mungo was at the rope, tugging for all he was worth, oblivious to fever, hunger, sorrow, caught up in the emotional sweep of the thing.

The net was closing like a throat, squeezing off into a U, then a V, and all at once the water was alive with thrashing fish. Thousands leaped the net, hundreds of thousands more went deep, tangled in the mesh, and pounded the water to foam. Men waded in up to their waists, clubbing at the escaping fish, children scooped the stunned transgressors from the surface, the crowd pulled, and then it was over. The net was beached, colossal, a river of flesh.

Snakes and eels slithered for the water, fish flapped across the mudbank like acrobats. But for every potential escapee there was a quick scrawny Mandingo boy with a club. Thud-thud went the clubs, and a new song began, less insistent in its beat, slower-paced, methodical: a killing song. Not a fish escaped. Already the drying fires were roaring as women strung the little silver fish on lines and hung them out to toast. There was a perch in the catch that must have weighed over a hundred pounds, and a catfish-looking thing that could have swallowed it whole. Two men held up a terrapin the size of a wagon wheel, another dragged a twelve-foot python up the bank and headed off in the direction of the village. Within minutes the terrapin was shelled, dismembered and bubbling away in a pot; the perch and catfish were gutted, wrapped in leaves and tossed into a smoldering pit while a pair of marabou storks fought over the remains. Jemafoo tapped the explorer's shoulder. "Here," he said, offering one of the three-inch fish that flashed and writhed in his hand. "*Akeena*." He was grinning encouragement, having learned from experience that all distress is food-related. "Watch — like this," he demonstrated, putting his lips to the fish's vent and squeezing it lengthwise to draw out the roe. "Go ahead, try it."

Birds were shrieking, a thick greasy smoke hung in the air. The voices of the chorus swelled and sank. Mungo lifted the fish to his lips, but when he tried to squeeze it he found that he didn't have the energy. His temples were pounding, his legs gone to rubber. He sat down and dreamed of blackness.

◆§ ?◆

The fever came on with a vengeance. It left him enervated and delirious, and it was accompanied by an excoriating diarrhea that so debilitated him he couldn't even muster the energy to clean himself. For two weeks he lay on a mat in the father-in-law's hut, sweating and stinking, waking from jarring nightmares to the stark actuality of four walls on an alien planet. At intervals someone bent over him with a damp cloth, or put a wooden spoon in his mouth. An old woman offered him a potion of hammered bark: her face was Dassoud's. Demons howled, strange melodies chanted in his ears. He saw the net that holds up the stars, dug to the center of the earth, floundered about the icy black depths of the sea. Rain hissed at the thatched roof, centipedes and crimson spiders crept over him, sucked at his organs, nested in his eyes. He screamed until he was hoarse. And then — as suddenly as it had come on — it left him. He could see and hear. He knew who he was.

The hut was crowded: children and adults, dogs, poultry, an old leper. Sheets of rain obscured the doorway, there was a smell of gutter and bilge. Jemafoo and his father-in-law were arguing.

"You throw all your burdens on me."

"What choice do I have? Starve your daughter and grandchildren?"

"What about him?"

"You can't turn your back on a guest."

"I didn't invite him. Nor you for that matter."

The explorer stirred, raised himself to his elbows. "I'm better now," he croaked. "Really." He stood shakily. There was nothing left of him but eyes. "If you could just give me a bite for the road . . ."

At that moment there was a cry from the far corner, an unearthly screech, a protest from another world. Madame Momadoo was surrounded by women. One of them held up a newborn infant, slick and red. It was a boy. He screeched again, a strange primal squeal compounded of terror, rage and bewilderment. But there was something else in it too: a demand. "I can give you nothing," the father-in-law said.

The explorer gathered up his things — the top hat stuffed with notes, his walking staff, a water gourd and battered compass — and started for the door. Jemafoo stopped him and handed him a bag of dried fish, grain and tobacco.

"Yaaaaaaaaaaaaaaaaaaaaaa!" shrieked the baby, as if his teeth had been pulled.

The explorer stepped out into the rain.

≈§ §≈

Half a mile up the road he began to feel dizzy, sought out shelter in a lean-to fashioned from leaves the size of overcoats, and fell asleep. When he woke, the sun was shining. He'd been told that the next town over was called Frookaboo, and that for twenty cowries you could get a Frookaboo-an to paddle you across the river in a dugout. So he had a choice. He could lie there in a heap of rotting leaves, or force down some dried fish and hobble up the road to Frookaboo. Indomitable, he chose to hobble.

At Frookaboo he applied to the *Dooty* for food, shelter and passage across the river. He was a scribe, he said, and could pay for his lodging by inditing potent and efficacious *safies*. Then he fell asleep. The *Dooty* shook him and asked him if he was a Moor. Mungo considered the question a moment, his lids at half-mast. His beard hung below his breastbone, he was dressed in a tattered toga and sandals, his skin was yellow from sun and jaundice. He squinted up at the *Dooty*. "*La illah el allah,*" he said, "*Mahomet rasowl Allahi.*"

The explorer spent three days at Frookaboo, a guest of the *Dooty*. He ate well, slept in a dry hut, bowed to Mecca. The fever drew off a pace or two, and he began to regain some of his strength. He even found energy, for the first time in weeks, to take some notes. *I repaid the* Dooty, *he wrote, by scribbling out the Lord's Prayer for him on a bit of slate. The man was a strict Mohammedan, and thought I was writing in Arabic. I felt it expedient not to disabuse him. When I had finished, he wiped the slate clean with a wet cloth, wrung the cloth out over a cup and drank down its contents, thereby assuring himself of the maximum benefit of my words. Afterward he offered me a pipe of* mutokuane *and a peep beneath his wife's veil.*

On the afternoon of the third day Mungo thanked his host, scribbled off a final blessing, and limped down to the river, where he found a number of ferrymen perched like water spiders in the prows of their canoes. He struck a bargain with a sloe-eyed Bobo whose skin was the color of a Concord grape: six lines of inspired calligraphy in exchange for passage to Sibidooloo, on the far side of the river. The explorer felt that something out of Virgil might be appropriate — inscribed to the Charon of the Niger — but he couldn't remember a word of Latin and wound up giving him an abridged version of "The Owl and the Pussycat" instead.

There were four goats, a parrot and a cage full of monkeys in the canoe, in addition to six other passengers and a dozen earthenware jars of produce. When Mungo asked what the monkeys were for, the ferryman grinned to display a gleaming mouthful of teeth. "Bake them," he said. "Make monkey bread."

◄§ §►

Sibidooloo lay directly across the river from Frookaboo. It was, according to the ferryman, a trading town of about a thousand people. From there, he said, it was perhaps seventy-five miles to Kamalia, a slave market situated on the edge of the Jallonka Wilderness. If the explorer could make Kamalia he might be able to hook up with a slave coffle heading for the coast. It was a hope. He would have preferred a coach and four back to Pisania, but at least now he knew that there *was* a way back. The explorer landed at Sibidooloo in high spirits. His plan was to spend the night and leave the next morning for Kamalia. If the fever held off and the road wasn't too muddy, he should be able to make it in three or four days.

But first to the business at hand: finding some shelter for the night. The sky had begun to darken, clouds scudding low and smoky over the thatched roofs and whitewashed walls of the town. Thunder rumbled in the distance, and the air had suddenly cooled. It was probably raining in Frookaboo already. The explorer hurried up a narrow street of well-kept mud-and-wattle huts, occasionally looking in at a doorway and asking for shelter. After two or three rebuffs, he stopped before a hut where a woman in kerchief and hoop earrings was suckling an infant and preparing kouskous with bits of *akeena*. He greeted her, then pulled a slip of paper from his hat, dashed off a couple of lines from *Abercrombie's Art of Divine Converse*, and handed it to her. She glanced up suspiciously. "You a *marabout?*"

He didn't know what to say. *Marabouts* were Moslem holy men who traveled from town to town, dispensing learning. It seemed like a good thing to admit to, yet why the strange look? He opted for insincerity. "That I am," he said.

She put the infant down, and called to someone in the hut. "Flancharee," she said. "Come here."

A tall Mandingo in a pair of baggy shorts stepped from the hut, flanked by two Moors. Mungo's heart sank. The Moors were dressed in dirty white *jubbahs* and *tagilmusts*. Somehow, one of them looked familiar. "This man claims to be a *marabout*," the woman said. "Look what he wrote on this paper."

Flancharee and the Moors squinted at the quotation from Abercrombie. Then one of the Moors looked the explorer dead in the eye and said something in Arabic. Mungo didn't know what to answer. The Moor repeated himself. It sounded as if he were saying "Your mother eats pig."

"He's no *marabout*," Flancharee said in Mandingo.

The second Moor stepped forward. His skin was baked to leather, his nose twisted like a scythe — but worst of all, the explorer realized with a cold shock of recognition, his left eye socket was empty. "No Mussulman," the Moor hissed in broken Mandingo. "*Nazarini!*"

"Imposter!" rumbled the woman.

Flancharee took hold of the explorer's arm.

"He's a thief," the first Moor said. "He stole from Ali and crawled off in the night like a dog. Dassoud is offering four prime slaves for him, enough to make a man rich."

"*Nazarini!*" shrieked One-Eye.

Flancharee looked at the explorer as he might look at a snake that had just lashed out at his ankle. "Chain him up," he said.

◦§ §◦

That night the rain came like an explosion in a glass factory. It tore the leaves from the trees, the trees from the ground. Light fractured the sky, thunder thrashed the hills like an open hand. The explorer was not without shelter through all of this, though it was less than he could have hoped for. His cage sat in the middle of a square of sorts, exposed on all sides to the violence of the storm. Sometime during the night there was a sudden heart-stopping crack as of a hundred muskets fired in unison, and a raffia palm, its leaves the size of canoes, slammed down beside the cage, lifting the wooden box three feet in the air and startling the explorer from a despondency that bordered on the catatonic. After all his triumphs, narrow escapes and quickening hopes, falling back into the hands of the Moors has been too much for him. He'd gone into shock.

He sat up and looked round him. What he saw was no cause for joy: wooden bars, insects, a crazed sky, and a dark silent bank of huts. The cage in which he found himself had been built of hardwood and bamboo to accommodate a rogue lion that had burst through the roof of a hut, killed and devoured the occupants, and then apparently found himself too bloated to abscond. The villagers found him sleeping atop a pile of half-eaten corpses the following morning. While a pair of daredevils stood at the door with their spears, others hastily constructed the cage, which was then forced against the opening. On awakening, the lion had break-fasted briefly and then lumbered out the door and into the cage before he realized that something was amiss. For a month or so the man-eater had been the drawing card of Sibidooloo, but had recently been presented to Moosee, King of Gotto, as a peace offering. When One-Eye and Flancha-ree found that all the irons available were already employed in restraining slaves collected for the trek to Kamalia, they hit upon the cage as a convenient place to shut up the explorer. And so he had spent the evening there, in a heap of lion dung, thinking the blackest thoughts.

The collapse of the tree came as something of a blessing. It jolted him from his torpor, and he began to probe the enclosure for a means of escape. He crept round on his hands and knees in the dark as dry scuttling things backed away from his fingers and the rain slashed through the bars to awaken the dormant odor of lion piss. Smelling salts couldn't have cleared his head more effectively. He gasped and gagged, his eyes tearing, hands frantically pawing over every nook and joint of his cell. The first time round he found nothing — the native joiners had done their work well. But then, on closer examination, he discovered a rough spot in the upper right-hand corner where the planks of the ceiling met the corner-piece. The wood was abraded where the lion had persistently gnawed at it during the weeks of his captivity. Mungo's blood pressure rose: here was a chance! But how to take advantage of it? Instinctively he applied his teeth to the gnawed wood, but managed only to collect the odd splinter in his lips. Then he gouged at it until his fingernails began to bleed. Still nothing. Finally, he frisked the ground outside the cage until he came up with a sliver of stone that chewed away at the weak spot like a saw.

Three hours later the first of the bars gave way with a snap of protest. He held his breath and glanced round. The rain beat down with a steady mechanical roar. There was no light anywhere. He went back to work, bent over the wooden struts like a huge sedulous rodent. It took him two hours more to carve himself free. The final bar snapped and he slipped out into the deluge, working the hat down over his brow. Nothing stirred in Sibidooloo — not even a dog — as he leaned into the storm and headed up the road for Kamalia.

◄§ §►

It took him six days to get there. He traveled by night, holing up in the forest during the day, drinking from puddles, chewing at roots, picking leeches from his skin. He was startled awake on the afternoon of the second day by the clatter of hoofs, and peered out from his cover to observe One-Eye and his companion hurrying up the road. At dawn on the fourth day he came across a tiny cluster of huts beside the road. He hadn't eaten in days: what little strength he had was ebbing. Desperate, he woke the *Dooty* and offered to write charms in exchange for a bite to eat. The *Dooty* said that there was no food in town for the likes of him, a common thief. "All right," the explorer said, squatting outside the door. "I'll sit here until I've starved to death. And I'll curse you and your crops and your descendants and their crops through all eternity and in the name of Mansa King George III of England." Twenty minutes later the *Dooty*'s wife appeared in the doorway with a bowl of kouskous.

At Kamalia he traded a half-written letter to Ailie for a cup of milk and a platter of *boo*, a dish which was made from corn husks and tasted like sand. When he asked his host about the possibility of joining a slave coffle for the coast, the man directed him to Karfa Taura's house on the far side of town. The month was September. Mist rose from the streets and everywhere there was the insidious clank of chains as slavers gathered their wares against the end of the rainy season and the march to the sea. The explorer kept his head down.

Taura's house, a four- or five-room affair built of clay and stone, dominated a hill in the center of town. There was a well, a shade tree or two and an expanse of muddy red earth pocked with goat tracks. Out back were a number of cane huts and a corral fenced round with thorn. The explorer presented himself at the door, suffering from fatigue, starvation, mental duress, emaciation, jungle rot, blisters, hemorrhoids, various local infections, hepatitis, diarrhea and a febrile body temperature of one hundred and one degrees. His toga had degenerated to a web of knotted strips, his hat looked like a byproduct of cat-skinning, and he was barefooted. Twenty-five years old, he could easily have passed for sixty. "Tell your master," he croaked at the incredulous black face at the door, "that I am a white man desirous of traveling to the Gambia with one of his slave coffles. Tell him . . ." here he lost his train of thought, "tell him . . . I . . . I failed Greek but could kick a football the length of the field."

A moment later he was led through the house to the *baloon*, a large airy room reserved for guests. There he found Karfa Taura sharing a pipe of tobacco with a number of *slatees** who had come to join his coffle. Taura

*Free Mandingoes, generally Muslim converts, whose stock-in-trade is human flesh.

was wearing a tarboosh and a lustrous blue robe. A gray parrot perched on his shoulder, peeling a berry. "So," he said, "you claim to be a white man from the west. I have never seen a white man, though as a boy I once saw two Portugee in Medina." Taura was Mandingo by birth, Muslim by conversion. He was also filthy rich. "It's funny," he continued after a pause, "but you don't look white. I expected something, well — brighter. Like the belly of a frog."

One of the *slatees* spoke up. He was a murderous-looking character with corrosive eyes. "He's no white man."

"Never," spat another. "I've seen white men at Pisania and Goree, and their skin is as white as the pages of this book." He held up a copy of the Koran.

The explorer felt woozy. He found it difficult to remain standing. "Give me a football," he shouted, lapsing into English, "and I'll show you who's white."

This outburst seemed to startle his interrogators for a moment, and they stared up at him with renewed interest. "What's that he said?" But then the first *slatee* growled, "Aaaah, he's just a pariah Moor down on his luck, coming round here on false pretenses in the hope of getting a handout."

"Mad is what he is," his cohort said. "Mad as a hyena. Look at his rags — and that hat!"

Karfa Taura held up his palm. "Suleiman," he said to the man with the book, "give the newcomer your book."

Suleiman handed the book to the explorer.

"Can you read the Koran?" Taura asked.

Mungo tried, straining to remember *Ouzel's Grammar* and how those arcane dots and slashes related to letters and words. After staring at the book a moment he raised his head and mumbled, "No, I can't read it."

"Illiterate!" shouted the first *slatee*.

"Kafir!" muttered another.

Taura whispered something to his servant and the man left the room to return again in a moment with a second book in his hand. As the servant handed it to the explorer, Taura's voice, calm and patient, purred over the prickling silence: "Perhaps you can read this?"

The leather binding was splotched with mold, there were fingerprints in the dust on the cover. The explorer opened the book and tried to concentrate on the black printed letters that swam before his eyes like sunspots. He couldn't focus. The *slatees* were shouting out insults. "You cannot?" Taura asked.

Then all at once the letters came into focus and he was reading, reading like a man at the breakfast table with a copy of *The Monthly Review* spread out before him:

Good Christian People, I bid your prayers for Christ's Holy Catholic Church, the blessed company of all faithful people . . .

It was *The Book of Common Prayer.*
"Niyazi," Taura called out to the servant, "sweep out the back hut for the white man."

◄§ §►

The next time the explorer became fully cognizant of his surroundings it was November, and the sere harmattan winds had begun to sweep in off the desert. In the interval, he had tossed on his pallet in the back hut, sweating and hallucinating. Karfa Taura had seen him through the worst of it, spoon-feeding him chicken broth and hot milk and garlic, rubbing his body with healing herbs, letting blood. During one of his lucid moments Mungo had promised Taura the value of one prime slave in return, deliverable upon reaching Pisania and the factory of Dr. Laidley. Taura thought it a pretty good deal, as he would have nursed the explorer in any case, fascinated as he was by this strange mythical being whose hair grew blonder and skin whiter by the day.

At Taura's table one evening, as they were sharing a bowl of kouskous and mashed chick-peas, the explorer brought up the subject of the slave coffle: when would it depart for the Gambia? Outside, the crickets suddenly left off their cheeping. A host of faces looked first at the explorer, and then at Taura, seated at the head of the mat which served as a table. (There were many more *slatees* present now, most of them dependent upon Taura for their current expenses — he would be reimbursed when the slaves were sold at Medina.) Taura smiled at the explorer as he might have smiled at a six-year-old who'd asked why the stars didn't fall from the sky. "Well, my friend," he began, "I'll tell you. There are six swollen rivers to cross between here and Dindikoo on the far side of the Jallonka Wilderness. In between there are seas of grass, taller than a man's head. If we wait a month or so — till late December or early January — the rivers will have subsided and the villagers will have burned away much of the grass. I know you are anxious to get back to *Tobaubo doo,* but to travel now would be impossible."

On December nineteenth Taura collected all his local debts and set out up the Niger to the town of Kancaba, in order to purchase slaves for the trip to the Gambia. He returned a month later with a new wife (his fourth) and thirteen reasonably marketable slaves, all of whom had the requisite number of limbs and eyes. The explorer was overjoyed when his benefactor stepped through the door. He'd been counting the days, impatient, his every waking moment devoted to thoughts of Ailie and the African Association. He pictured himself dressed to the nines in a sparkling muslin cravat and a new sergdusoy jacket, lecturing Sir Joseph Banks and Durfeys and the rest, a legend in his own time. The suffering and privation were over. In two months he'd be the toast of London. Karfa Taura wrapped an arm around his shoulder. "The rivers are down," he said, "the grass burned off, the *slatees* have gathered their wares. We depart on the first of February."

But the first of February came and went. Sulciman had gone off to Sibidooloo to collect some trifling debt; Hamid and Madi Konko didn't have their dry provisions ready; the moon was in the wrong corner of the sky. Excuses. The month wore away with them. And now, with March coming on, the *slatees* argued that they should postpone traveling until Rhamadan was over. March became April, the fast moon prevailed. Then one night in the middle of the month all of Kamalia turned out at the open-air mosque to watch for the new moon, the appearance of which would signal the end of the Rhamadan fast and offer an auspicious omen for travelers. The explorer stood amidst the throng of chanting Mandingoes and looked up with disgust at the clouded night sky. Hours passed. A number of villagers gave up and returned to their huts, determined to fast another day. But then, at midnight, the clouds began to pull back in shreds and the new moon poked its horns through to a chorus of hoots, cheers and pistol shots: Rhamadan was ended.

Like everyone else, Karfa Taura was caught up in the excitement. He threw dignity to the wind, jogging up and down like a cheerleader. Fires lit the sky, pandemonium crested like a wave. Karfa took the explorer by the arm and shouted in his ear: "We leave at dawn tomorrow!"

✧ ❧

Light was working its way across the night sky in a series of barely perceptible leaps when the coffle began to gather outside Karfa Taura's house. Seventy-three people and six asses shuffled their feet in the dust, waiting for the sun to break over the hills. Thirty-five of these were slaves, bound for sale on the coast. The rest were itinerant merchants, *slatees,* their wives and domestic servants. Rounding out the group were Mungo and six *jilli keas* (singing men), whose vocalizing came in handy as a diversion from the hardships of the road and in smoothing the coffle's reception at villages along the way. As the first pale rays illuminated the treetops there was a flurry of cinching and uncinching, coughing into fists, rechecking of final details and idle ear-pulling. Then they were off, leaving Kamalia in an orderly line of march, preceded by Karfa Taura, Suleiman and the singing men. When they reached the summit of a hill two miles from town, all the travelers were ordered to sit down, half the group facing westward, half looking back on Kamalia. Suleiman then delivered a solemn, nasal and interminable prayer, after which two of the other *slatees* circled the coffle three times, making impressions in the earth with the butts of their spears and muttering something unintelligible by way of a traveling charm.

When they got under way again, the explorer noticed that some of the slaves were having trouble walking. They staggered under their loads, bow-legged and uncertain, tottering from foot to foot like worn-out drunks. Karfa Taura shook his head. It was a pity, he said, but some of them had been in shackles for years, and the unwonted exertion of taking a full stride wrought havoc on disused muscles, tendons and joints. It was a pity, he repeated, but an accident of the trade. Slaves had a tendency to run off, and so the accepted manner of confining them was to bind the ankles of two of them together, making it impossible for either to move independently. In order to merely scrape about like the losing entry in a three-legged race, one of the slaves had to raise the heavy shackles above the ankles by means of an attached chain. Then, with mincing deliberate steps, the pair would rattle forward. While traveling to market the leg shackles were removed, and the slaves were bound together in fours by a rope looped round their necks. A man armed with a spear marched between each group of four, to discourage any thoughts of wandering. When the coffle settled down for the night the leg irons were refastened, along with a heavy-link chain that replaced the rope round each slave's neck.

"But these are human beings," the explorer said.

Karfa Taura adjusted his tarboosh. "True," he said. His tone was matter-of-fact, as if he were discussing nuts and bolts or a herd of sheep. "But they are also trade goods."

Despite the limping and groaning of the slaves (which was lessened from time to time by the application of the lash), the coffle made the walled village of Marraboo by midafternoon, rested briefly, then marched on to Bala, where they spent the night. The following day's trek brought them to

Worumbang, on the border of Manding and Jallonkadoo. It was the last outpost of civilization for a hundred miles — beyond Worumbang lay the Jallonka Wilderness.

The Jallonka Wilderness was an atavism — ten thousand square miles of uninhabited jungles, hills and grasslands, as pristine and primitive as the world before man. Within its reaches were six rivers that had to be forded, three of them upper tributaries of the Senegal. There was no food to be had along the way, nor any shelter. Predators roamed the brakes and forests as they had for eons, and bandits lay in wait along the borders. It was a dangerous and inhospitable place — a place of shadow and legend, of bad luck and sudden death — and Karfa Taura, his fingers crossed, was anxious to get through it as expeditiously as possible.

Accordingly, the coffle left Worumbang at dawn and marched until nightfall without a break. The slaves carried bundles of trade goods on their heads, the sun was like a whip, the whip like a bad dream. One of them, a middle-aged woman whose facial cicatrices indicated that she had once aspired to a higher station in life, constantly fell out of line. At one point she lay down and refused to go any farther until Suleiman applied the lash to the soles of her feet and she staggered up and continued on in a sort of trance. The explorer was appalled — but knew he was powerless to do anything about it. He was excess baggage himself, and besides, given his debilitated condition it was all he could do to keep up with even the weakest of the slaves.

When the coffle stopped at a stream called Co-meissang for the night, Mungo shuffled over to where the slaves had been confined and looked for her among the sullen black faces. He found her at the end of the queue, stretched out on her back. Her eyes were wide, staring up at nothing, and she was breathing as if she'd just broken the tape in a footrace. The explorer bent over her and offered her a drink of water. She said nothing. Just lay there, staring at the sky, breathing hard. He asked her name, his voice hushed and sympathetic. Somehow he felt a need to comfort her, tell her it would all work out, though he knew it wouldn't.

"Her name is Nealee," whispered the slave beside her. A crude iron band pinched his ankle to hers. "She's got a sickness, her blood won't warm her feet."

Nealee. The explorer looked down at her. Where had he heard that name before?

"You going to eat her?" the voice rasped.

"Eat her? What do you mean?"

The man's lips were cracked. There was a rope burn across his adam's apple. *"Maddummulo,"* he said. "The black man puts his slave to work, the white man eats him."

Mungo was astonished at the misconception, offended by the accusation. "Nonsense."

"No one ever comes back."

"Well that's because they put you in a boat to take you to another land, a land like this one, where you work in the fields and — "

"Tobaubo fonnio," the slave said, "a white man's lie." His voice was flat and emotionless. "There is no other land. They take you to where the water goes on forever and hack you to pieces. The fires flare through the night, the kettles boil. They pick at your bones."

≈§ §≈

Nealee wouldn't eat the following morning. It was cold, gray, half an hour before sunrise. Quick piliginous things flashed through the undergrowth, birds nattered, a breath of stagnation soured the air. Karfa Taura intoned a general benediction, after which everyone in the party was given a cup of watery gruel. Nealee sat up painfully, took the cup from Suleiman's domestic, and flung it in his face. When Madi Konko laid into her with his switch, she rolled over and began vomiting. Someone cursed. She'd been eating clay. "Eating clay?" the explorer said.

"She wants to die," said the man shackled to her.

After morning prayers the coffle reassembled. Nealee refused to stand and Suleiman was forced to uncoil his braided whip. She lay there, face down in the dust, and bore the first two or three strokes patiently, then rose shakily and started off. It was immediately apparent that something was wrong: she lurched forward and reeled back again, as if she were being tugged apart by some invisible force. Suleiman ordered one of his men to cut her from the tether and take up her load. The *slatee* then marched behind her himself, prodding her from time to time with the butt of his spear.

Just before noon there was a minor disaster. One of the singing men blundered into a hive of fierce, irascible West African bees — killer bees, as the locals called them. Through the millennia these insects had developed a swift, effective and inexorable means of dealing with the honey badgers and sweet-toothed hominids that assaulted their nests: at the slightest provocation they swarmed out en masse and stung the offender to death. Each bee was programmed to fly into a suicidal stinging frenzy at the release of an alarm chemical, which also served to direct the bee to its target. If a man was stung within a hundred yards of the nest, he could expect to be inundated by a foaming mass of insects in less than a minute. Needless to say, the encounter more often than not proved fatal.

In the case of Geo, the singing man, it wasn't as bad as it might have been. The first sting prompted him to drop his flute and plunge headlong into a bog beside the path, where he burrowed into the muck like an amphibian. Two or three of his quick-witted companions followed suit, while the rest — free men, slaves and *slatees* alike — took to their heels. The bees, confused over the loss of the primary target, divided their forces in pursuit of the seventy-two secondary targets. Strategically, it was a mistake. As it turned out, no one in the party took more than fifteen or twenty stings, and some — the explorer included — escaped unscathed. But when the coffle was regrouped it was discovered that Nealee was missing. Immediately the *slatees* broke out the irons and shackled the slaves together, while armed guards ran off to track her down. After setting fire to the brush in order to drive off the bees, they found her beside a shallow stream, swollen with scores of beestings. She had apparently attempted to elude the insects by splashing water over herself. It hadn't worked.

This time the whip was ineffective: she could not get up. Karfa Taura shook his head. "Strap her to the ass," Suleiman shouted. The panniers were removed from one of the asses and Nealee was laid across the animal's back, her hands and feet lashed together underneath. From the first the animal was intractable. It bucked and kicked until finally the straps gave way and Nealee was tossed into the bushes where she lay like a rag doll.

Over two hours had been lost. The members of the party, spooked by the wildness of the place and the hair-raising legends surrounding it, were anxious to move on. A cry went up and down the length of the coffle: *"Kang-tegi, kang-tegi."* Cut her throat, cut her throat. The sun scraped across the sky. A man stepped forward with a knife. Suleiman nodded at him, then ordered the coffle forward. Half an hour later the man rejoined the party, Nealee's dress tied round his waist.

◦§ §◦

The remainder of the journey was uneventful. The coffle proceeded in a series of forced marches, from dawn till dusk. Twenty miles a day, over mounds of splintered rock and hills haunted with shadow, through copses cluttered with fallen trees and strangling lianas, bogs that sucked the shoes from your feet, silt-clogged rivers darkened by clouds of insects and churning with fish and reptiles. It was all Mungo could do to keep up, weakened as he was by his bout with fever and starvation. He threw away his spear, his water gourd, the bone knife Aisha had given him. The straps of his sandals bit into his feet like wire and the sun crashed down on his head until all he could hear was the frenzied pshh-pshh-pshh of cymbals slashing away at the denouement of some opera or other. But he made it. First to Dindikoo, where he broke the bad news to Johnson's three wives and eleven children, and then to Pisania, where he drifted up the front steps of Dr. Laidley's log piazza like a ghost.

Dr. Laidley was fat and florid. He wore a dress shirt in one-hundred-ten-degree heat and ninety-nine-percent humidity. With his tonsure and wire-rimmed spectacles he looked like a caricature of Ben Franklin. "Park?" he shouted, thundering across the floorboards, his pudgy hand outstretched in wonder and greeting. "Mungo Park?"

◆§ ౭◆

Mungo was in luck. He arrived in Pisania on June 12, 1797, with one thought in mind: booking passage to England on any boat that would have him. But the monsoon season was settling in with its rot and pestilence, and he was afraid he'd have to wait it out before another boat landed on the Gambia. It could be months. He drew a bill on the African Association through Dr. Laidley, paid Karfa Taura handsomely, and settled in for a long, anticlimactic wait. But on the third day of his vigil, by purest coincidence, an American slaver sailed up the river to exchange a cargo of rum and tobacco for men, women, and children. *The Charlestown* was bound for South Carolina, departing on the seventeenth. Without hesitating, the explorer signed on: better to take a circuitous route home than wait out the rains in a leaky back room in Pisania. After two years on the Dark Continent, he was aching for some light.

On the morning of the seventeenth the explorer shaved, slipped into the clothes Dr. Laidley had provided him, and climbed aboard *The Charlestown*. The deck creaked under his feet as he set his valise down and tried to ascertain where his cabin might be located. He could see nothing. Fog hovered over the water like the underside of a dream, catching at the rigging, dissolving the quarterdeck. Vague forms glided ghostlike through the haze, mosquitoes whined. It was hot as an iron foundry. Puzzled, the explorer stood rooted to the deck and watched two figures gesticulating like Punch and Judy through a curtain of mist.

"We got to wait till the soup clears off, Cap'n," said the shorter of the two.

"Draw the anchor, Mr. Frip. We sail immediately."

"But — " (there was the sound of mosquito slapping and a guttural, heartfelt curse).

"But me no buts, Mister. Stay here in this fetid shithole another ten minutes and half the crew'll be down with the shivers and the black vomit. Haul that anchor, I say!"

The smaller figure drew off into the gloom, mumbling and swatting: "Can't even find the fuckin' thing in this shit . . . Ouch! Sonofabitchin' moskeeters . . ."

It took two weeks to get down the river to Fort Goree, held up as they were by heavy fog, snags and contradictory winds. Four seaman, the ship's surgeon and three slaves died of fever along the way. At Goree the Captain informed Mungo that the ship would be unavoidably detained because he was unable to obtain provisions for the crossing. "Detained?" said Mungo, his heart sinking. For two months now — lying at Kamalia, struggling through the Jallonka Wilderness — he had been sustained by visions of the eager, attentive faces ranged round the conference table in Soho Square, of Ailie in her underwear, of his book and burgeoning celebrity. He'd survived disease, humiliation, exhaustion and despair, and now he was ready to reap his reward. "For how long?" he asked.

The Captain pulled on his dogskin gloves and offered the explorer a Raleigh cigar. "There's a relief boat due in at Goree in mid-September," he said. "We can stock up then and be on our way."

Mid-September! He couldn't believe it. Three months more in this pest-ridden hole, three months more bobbing in a rotten berth off of a last-chance garrison maintained by the dregs of London. He may as well have stayed at Pisania, with Dr. Laidley. There at least he could have had a glass of wine, some intelligent conversation, a room to himself. Here he had convicts for companions, a hold full of moribund black faces, cockroaches longer than a man's finger, and the incessant creeping rot that made Goree one of the world's more pestilential spots. So near and yet so far. He gave way to depression, lay in his berth and watched the ship rot around him.

The Charlestown finally set sail on October first, the explorer having been pressed into assuming the role of the late surgeon. He hadn't made much use of his medical knowledge in the interior, but summoned up all Dr. Anderson had taught him in order to deal with the frightening conditions aboard ship. The American slavers, because their crews were smaller, were far less humane than the British. For fear of mutiny the slaves were kept in irons throughout the voyage. They lived in the dark, damp and cold, wallowing in their own waste, prey to consumption, typhus, hepatitis, racked with malarial fevers. The irons wore the flesh from wrists and ankles; maggots hatched in the wounds. Mungo did his best. He let blood, applied leeches, forced vinegar down their throats. Eight died at Goree, eleven more at sea. The stiffened corpses were dragged from their irons and tossed into the spume, where quick pelagic sharks fought over the remains.

The crew didn't fare much better. Three died at Goree, another two at sea. But as it turned out, this was the least of the Captain's worries. A far more pressing problem was the leaks that had developed in the hull while the ship sat at anchor off Goree. Now, on the high seas, these leaks had become critical. So critical in fact that the most able-bodied slaves were released from their irons in order to man the pumps. Fourteen-hour shifts, the whip cracking over their heads. They pumped, fainted from exhaustion, were lashed to consciousness, and pumped again. Still, the boat was taking on so much water it became clear that it would never make South Carolina. It became clear to some, that is.

"Cap'n — you've got to make for the West Indies or before you know it we'll be treading water in the company of them sharks out there."

"You're an educated man, Mr. Frip. Take a look over the gunwale and read me what's writ along the bow: I think you'll find that it says *The Charlestown,* does it not? Well, Sir, that's where I've been paid to take her and that's where she'll go."

"Begging your pardon, Cap'n, Sir, but me and the crew has been talking amongst ourselves, Sir, and we've unanimously decided to break out our seamen's dirks and ventilate your domineering hide till you look like one of them fountains in downtown Richmond, Sir, if you don't change course for Antigua within thirty seconds by my pocketwatch, with all due respect, Sir."

≈§ §≈

From Antigua, the explorer was able to catch the Chesterfield Packet, which had stopped at St. John's for the mail on the return voyage from the Leeward Islands. The ship sailed on the twenty-fourth of November, and drew within sight of Falmouth on the morning of December twenty-second, 1797. Shorebirds wheeled in the sky, the wind flung spray over the decks. There was ice on the rail, and a thin watery snow added sting to the gusts. The crew was invisible, the Captain in bed, the cook's terrier huddled beneath the stove. But Mungo Park, after two years and seven months in exile, stood beside the helmsman with a grin on his face as the distant rocky isle rode up over the waves.

ᵆ COLD FEET

A year is nothing: a feather in the breeze, a breath of air. Turn around and it's gone. Ice, bud, leaf, twig. Geese on the pond, stubble in the field. Three hundred sixty-five mornings, three hundred sixty-five nights. Minor lacerations, a sprained ankle, runny nose, the death of a distant relative. There's a squirrel in the attic, a tree down in a storm. The clock in the hallway cranks round seven hundred and thirty times. Windows are raised, shades drawn, dishes, cups and spoons dirtied and scrubbed, dirtied and scrubbed. Thunder hits the hills like a mallet, snow climbs the fenceposts, sunlight burnishes the windows like copper. A year. One of how many: fifty? sixty? The days chew away at it, insidious.

ᵆ ᵇᵉ

Ailie huddles in the corner of her bed, head buried in her hands. The window is gray with dawn and the cold slashing rain that began just after dark. Katlin Gibbie lies beside her, breathing easily, her nine-month-old boy curled into her breast. Betty Deatcher, a cousin from Kelso, snores on a pallet in the corner. The coals in the fireplace have turned to ash.

Christmas morning, but Ailie feels no leap of the spirit or good will toward men. The year is out, and today she redeems her promise: by nightfall she'll be Ailie Gleg. Something tightens in her at the thought of it. She never imagined she'd have to live up to her vow, never doubted that Mungo — like some galloping cavalier out of a medieval romance — would turn up to save her from the dragon. A year had seemed so far off — he could have been back by New Year's or Easter. How was she to know? She had settled in and waited. Waited with a sinking in the pit of her stomach, through spring planting, Whitsuntide, Midsummer's Eve, through Michaelmas, Martinmas, the harvest ball, and right on up until the night before Christmas, when she finally gave in and let the bridesmaids stain her feet with henna and throw the traditional cow's hide over her and Georgie. But even now, at the eleventh hour, she's still not resigned to it. And she still hasn't given up hope. She's got till three P.M., hasn't she? Maybe he'll burst through the door as she stands before the altar, tall and commanding, his face sunburned, a wild look in his eye . . .

But stop. How could she even think it? She's given her word, her father has killed a calf and a pig and sent out the invitations and white kid gloves, her friends and relations have come miles through bitter winds, ice and sleet — how could she rob them of their pleasure? Worse: how could she steal Georgie's heart and run off with it? No: she should prepare herself, wake up, accept the way of the world. One man has been taken from her, and another offered in his place. So what if he isn't perfect? So what if he's lop-eared, oafish, as sexless as a plucked rooster? He loves her, that's all that counts. And he's got a good heart . . .

Her reverie is suddenly broken by the sound of whistling: pitched high and lively, it echoes eerily through the still house. The tune drifts in and out of hearing, she can't be certain, but yes — yes, it's a tune Mungo used to sing to her years ago, the words as much a part of her memory of him as the drift of his voice:

> Now a' ye that in England are,
>   Or are in England born,
> Come ne'er to Scotland to court a lass,
>   Or else ye'll get the scorn.
>
> They haik ye up and settle ye by,
>   Till on your wedding day,
> And gie ye frogs instead of fish,
>   And play ye foul, foul play.

Could it be? Mother of God, could it? She leaps from the bed, still in her dressing gown, her feet the color of Valencia oranges, blood beating quick, the whistling louder now, just outside the door, oh Mungo, Mungo, Mungo, she whispers, flinging the door back in a paroxysm of blind hope — and there he is — Georgie Gleg. In fresh linen, top hat, silk coat. His eyes are butter-soft. "Good morning, love," he says, handing her a holly wreath molded in the shape of a heart. "Today's the big day."

Disappointment creases her face. "Thank . . . you," she stammers, a bit confused and embarrassed, awkward in the role of sacrificial lamb. When she reaches out to take the wreath, she pricks her finger. A spot of blood wells up almost instantly.

"Here," he says, snatching up her hand. "Let me suck it."

And so she stands there, feeling foolish in her orange feet and rumpled dressing gown, while the rain gargles in the gutters and her husband-to-be bends over her and sucks at her thumb like a baby at his mother's breast.

◆§ §◆

Ten minutes later, the door closed and latched, she tiptoes around the room, stuffing things into a black leather satchel. Her mouth is set, her movements fluid and furtive. When Katlin turns over in bed she freezes in midstep and waits a long silent moment for her friend's breathing to settle back into the gentle soughing rhythm of sleep. In the hallway she digs out

her gloves, hat, scarf. She can hear her father and uncle snoring like a
gristmill in the back room as she eases through the kitchen and out the
door.

The rain is steady and sonorous. There is a smell of purity and renewal in
the air, as if the earth has been washed clean. Up ahead the slick bare
trunks glow with wet; behind, the house sinks into the mist. Bent low, she
fades into the trees like a thief.

⊷ HAIL THE CONQUERING HERO

Should he get down on his knees and kiss the earth? No. Too theatrical.
But what a rush it is to tread the old sod once again! What a thrill to hear
the English tongue, gaze on English faces, bonnets, churchtowers and
shingled cottages! Overwhelming! He can't resist, he must . . . get down
on his knees this . . . instant . . .

As the repatriated explorer dodges down to buss the earth — or rather
the slick, weed-strewn planks of the Falmouth docks — he is so thoroughly
caught up in the rhapsody of the moment that he fails to take account of
the traffic behind him. The other passengers, anxious to disembark and be
on their way, pile up at his back — one of them, Colonel Messing, colliding
with the man in front of him and dipping awkwardly to one knee. The
Colonel, just returned from an inspection of his estates in the West Indies,
is a man of unimpeachable personal dignity. He rises to his feet, dusts his
stockings and raps his cane smartly across the explorer's upturned buttocks. "Out of the way, you impudent young dog."

⊷ ও⊷

An inauspicious homecoming, to say the least — but then all of Great
Britain thinks he's gone the same route as Houghton and Ledyard and the
rest. No one recognizes him, no one expects him. At the Dog & Duck
Tavern, Falmouth, he glances up from his eggs and drippings to scan the
ruddy faces and long noses at the bar, pregnant with his secret, savoring
the quiet incubation of his celebrity. If they only knew. He stifles a sudden
impulse to shout it out, dance on the tables, set it to music and sing it to
them, emblazon it on great drooping banners like bellying sails: I DID IT. I
ALONE. I'VE BEEN WHERE NO OTHER MAN HAS BEEN AND
I'VE SEEN WHAT NO OTHER MAN HAS SEEN AND I'M HERE TO
TELL ABOUT IT. But no, let them read it in the London papers and

crowd round this very bar, stunned and amazed: "Gorry — 'ee was 'ere. In this very room. The chance of lifetime and Oy nivir so much as lifted me 'ead. But 'oo was to know?" Who indeed? But there's one who should know — and without a moment's delay. The explorer calls for pen and paper and scratches off the good news, as excited as the day he won his first football match:

> Dog & Duck, Falmouth
> 22 December, 1797
>
> My Love:
> I am alive and well and my mission has been an unqualified success. Know that the great and glorious Niger flows *eastward* and that I am rushing home to your arms.
>
> *M.*

The following morning he books a place on the packet boat to Southampton, and from there finds himself squeezed into the tiny compartment of a coach-and-four bound for London. His fellow passengers turn out to be a Mrs. Higgenbotham, on the rebound from a visit to her niece in Portsmouth, a pair of disreputable-looking drummers selling "the latest in stickless frying pans and guaranteed runless hose for gennelmen," and Colonel Messing, of the short temper and long cane. Another three passengers are perched atop the convex roof: two young girls and a cleric in formal dress. Fortunately, Colonel Messing does not seem to recognize the explorer. After an hour or so of jostling along in silence he leans forward confidentially and tells Mungo that he shouldn't mind the tear in the knee of his breeches. "You see," he explains, "I'm just back from Antigua and all my things are gone ahead in the wagon. And damn me if I didn't have a bit of an accident before I ever set foot on shore. Some histrionic young ass was bent over double kissing the bleeding dock, if you can believe it, as if we'd been at sea three years instead of a month — and it cost me a good tumble."

Mungo makes a sympathetic noise in the back of his throat, and the Colonel suddenly stiffens up and gives him a penetrating stare.

"That's quite a skin color you got there, lad. If I didn't know you was English by the sand of your hair, I'd swear you was a Chinaman. Where you coming from, anyways?"

꧁ ꧂

One night at an inn along the way, and the next — Christmas Eve — jostling through the dark countryside, through Newington, St. George's

Fields and Southwark, across the Blackfriars Bridge and right on up to the White Swan on Farringdon Street. Christmas morning, 6:00 A.M., a cold drizzle hangs on the air like a washcloth, the Colonel snoring over a pint of brandy. The explorer steps down from the coach, his legs stiff, shoulders his satchel and starts off down the street. But then stops short, as if jerked by a rope. Where to? His sister Effie's? But she'd be asleep at this hour. If it were ten or eleven he could take a cab to Soho Square and astonish Sir Joseph. Walk in as blithely as if he'd just strolled round the block and rewrite the map of Africa. "Well, Sir, I'm back. Back from the Niger. I've seen it, tasted it, swum in it. It's no myth, believe me. Magnificent. Dwarfs the Nile, the Thames, the Mississippi . . . riches untold . . . a thriving civilization crowding its shores. And oh yes: it flows, most decidedly, to the *eastward*."

But at 6:00 A.M., on a holiday?

Suddenly it hits him. Effie's husband, Charles Dickson. He'll be at the British Museum at this hour, tending the plants. It was Dickson who'd launched the whole Niger venture in the first place, through his botanical association with Sir Joseph. Of course. He should be the first to know — especially since he's the only one likely to be stirring at this hour. The explorer turns around and starts off for the museum. But then stops dead again. Will he be there on Christmas Day? Mungo pictures his brother-in-law bent over mounds of dried specimens in a white smock; feeding, watering and pruning his indoor collection; winterizing the arboretum; pinching off stamens and anthers; living and breathing horticulture till it must burgeon in his dreams like the thickest Gambian rain forests . . . and knows he'll be there.

There are no cabs at this hour, but it's a short walk up to High Holborn and from there to Great Russell Street and Montague House, where the museum had been relocated six months before he left for Africa. Fingers of light are beginning to take hold of the eastern sky. There are wreaths on the doors, pine cones and red ribbon. The explorer feels as if he's just been handed a million pounds. He flings the satchel in the air, claps his hands twice and catches it on the way down without breaking stride. Then launches into a hearty whistle, a Christmas carol. The wet cobblestones echo with it, glad of heart, soaring, heroic, until he modulates into another key and slides into "Now a' ye that in England are," thinking of Ailie.

He turns into Great Russell Street, and the dark imposing building springs up before him, a monument to the stone quarry. At that moment the drizzle begins to whiten, changing to snow. The wet crystals fly into his jacket and dissolve, the soles of his boots tap at the pavement, pigeons rustle their wings. All is silence, the streets deserted. It's as if the entire world were holding its breath.

The arboretum gate is unlatched. Mungo slips in like a cat, playing for the surprise. Round a corner, through a stand of dwarf fruit trees — and what's this? Up ahead, bent over a mulberry with strips of protective sacking, is a form in cloth coat, gloves, fur cap. A Dicksonish form. "Dix," is all the explorer needs to say.

Charles Dickson turns around on a ghost. His breath hangs in the air, snow whitens his shoulders. A figure stands before him, eerie and incongruous in this place, on this day, at this hour. A figure out of the past — wasted, sallow, the gray of his eyes flecked with red — a figure dead and buried, so long hoped for that hope has become a habit. The botanist drops the sacking and wipes his spectacles on the sleeve of his coat before breaking into a wide wet grin. "Is it really you," he stammers, "or some wraith come back to haunt us?"

◄§ PEACE ON EARTH, GOOD WILL TO MEN

Prior to 1784, public executions in London were held at a place called Tyburn Tree, opposite the Marble Arch. An elaborate ritual was involved, and a good deal of hoopla as well. The condemned prisoners would ride through the streets on a cart, their elbows pinioned, the plain pine caskets beside them. Thousands turned out for the parade, bleachers were erected round the gallows, and makeshift stalls sold everything from small beer to gin, mackerel, muffins, gingerbread and tongue sandwiches. Hawkers did a brisk business in lurid confessions detailing the prisoners' crimes, or tear-jerk letters ostensibly written to their sweethearts at the eleventh hour. All too frequently the condemned were small fry — sniveling forgers, starving women convicted of shoplifting, fifteen-year-old pickpockets — and when this was the case the crowd was merciless, jeering and spitting, pelting them with stones and offal. But when a highwayman was executed — particularly a striking and notorious one — they were in ecstasy. Invariably he would be decked out in silks, his hair fluffed and curled, the gold buckles of his pumps flashing defiance. He would bow to the women, shake hands with the boys who ran beside the cart, even sign autographs. He went to the gallows a hero, a martyr, and when the cart trundled off and left him swinging, his friends would rush forward to hang on his legs, anxious to expedite the inevitable and spare him the pain and ignominy of the slow process of strangulation.

But in 1784, despite the protests of a throng of people, not the least of whom was Dr. Johnson himself, the "Tyburn March" was done away with, and criminals were subsequently hanged just outside the walls of the prison itself. The idea was to eliminate the carnival atmosphere surrounding the executions, in the hope of intensifying their deterrent effect. The crowd that gathered for the first Newgate hangings was shocked and dismayed — the prisoners were led out, a short prayer was said, and they were hanged. No parade, no fanfare, no glory, no dignity. Just meat, twisting slowly round the rope in the cold glare of the sun.

❦

Ned Rise isn't particular about the details. Fanfare or no fanfare, he doesn't want to die. But it seems that now, after nearly a year of delays and hard-won postponements, he is going to do just that — die, croak, kick the bucket, part the pale — and there's nothing anyone short of the King can do about it. And the King, as everyone knows, is mad as a hatter. Thorogood, backed by the Brooks fortune, had performed feats of prestidigitation — stretching days to weeks, weeks to months, months to a year. And he'd fought tenaciously for yet another postponement, but Sir Joseph Banks had fought just as tenaciously to see the thing consummated.

"But on Christmas Day, my lord?" Thorogood had squeaked at the Lord Mayor.

"Christmas falls on a Monday, Counselor — a regular hanging day."

"What about 'Peace on Earth' and all of that?"

Banks was in the background, pulling strings. He'd talked to Pitt, the Prince, the Lord Chamberlain, protesting that so long a delay in so heinous a case was unconscionable, reprehensible — the courts were derelict in their duty. In their majestic, inscrutable, planetary way, these luminaries were moved to agree. The word came down from on high, and the Lord Mayor was deaf to further pleas. He squinted down at Thorogood. "We have two thieves and a murderer to hang, Counselor — I should think that their extermination will give the honest citizens of this nation a great deal of peace indeed."

❦

Ned is alone, pacing off the final minutes in his cell. It is Christmas morning, gray, the drizzle turning to snow. The night before, Boyles had been in to pay his last respects, drunk as a hoot owl. He sang a couple of maudlin Irish tunes in a quavering baritone, took hold of Ned's hand and told him he hoped to see him in a better world, then passed out in the corner. And Fanny had been in too — for the final farewells. Bruises like fermenting plums maculated her thighs, chafe marks gnawed at her wrists. There was a tattoo behind her ear (a Jolly Roger, in green), a fresh welt across her cheekbone, the lingering impressions of human teeth perforating her buttocks. She looked worn. Ned no longer cared. He flung himself into her with all the desperation of the doomed, his every cell crying out for survival, for the wedding of sperm and egg, for the sweet posthumous incubation of life. She left him at dawn, her face puffed with despair.

Quarter of seven. Fifteen minutes to go. He smokes his thirtieth pipe — panic beating at his ribs, his hand shaking — takes another pull at the bottle of gin Boyles left him, and bends to wipe a speck of dust from his shoes. Outside in the courtyard, the other prisoners are taking their exercise, huddled forms pressed to the walls and gathered in the corners like conspirators. Lucky bastards, he thinks, choked by a wave of self-pity. Absurdly, the strains of a Christmas carol keep pulsing through his head — "All is calm, all is bright" — and though he's nearly polished off the bottle he feels as sober as a . . . a judge. He laughs at the thought, a booming belly laugh that somehow gets out of control and pinches off into a shriek, crazed and bloodcurdling, the wail of an animal caught in a trap. "AAA-aaaa-aaaaaaah!" he shrieks, "AAA-aaaa-aaaaaaah!" But wait: what's this? Footsteps?

They're coming for him.

All at once he goes loose — his limbs heavy as wet mortar, spine slumping, eyelids drooping, feet splayed. A soothing serenity creeps over him, gripping him like a warm mitten. Now that the moment has actually come, he feels as calm as the average butcher or bootblack waking from his bed to the smells of holiday goose and figgy pudding. Got to die well, Ned Rise, he tells himself.

The turnkey stands at the door, flanked by two men with muskets. Ned throws his shoulders back and steps forward with all the composure of a prince gliding off to his coronation. Apart from an incipient pallor about the cheeks, he looks fit and trim, almost bubbling with health — thanks to Fanny he's been well provided for. His hair is tied back with a bit of silver galloon, and he is dressed with panache in a blue velvet jacket, white silk hose, buckled pumps. Stay calm, he tells himself — don't give in. But then another voice starts up in his head, a voice that keeps repeating, "But I'm going to die / But I'm going to die" like a litany. Die, die, die, echoes the blood pounding in his temples.

⤙ ⫶⤚

A spotty crowd is gathered outside the wall for the executions — mainly hyenas and degenerates, and agents for dissectors hoping to claim the corpses. There is a small contingent of the gentility as well, fronted by Sir Joseph Banks and the Countess Binbotta. They sit in coaches parked along the street, or stand discreetly in the rear, lured from their hearths and wassail bowls by the grim logic of an eye for an eye. If any of them see any incongruity in attending an execution on Christmas Day, their faces — stern and wire-jawed — don't show it.

By now the snow is coming down in earnest: nearly two inches of fine white powder smooths the muddy earth, softens the harsh lines of the gallows. The empty nooses are frosted like cakes, liveried footmen hurry to throw blankets over the backs of their masters' horses, the spectators pull shawls and mufflers tight round their throats and close in on the gallows for better visibility. Thick as paste, the big wet flakes swirl out of the sky.

His elbows pinioned and knees unsteady, Ned stands at the main gate waiting for the ceremony to begin. Beside him, dressed in rags, are the two thieves condemned to hang with him. One of them is a tall, brutal-looking character, his hair cropped close, nose broken. There are tears on his face and he seems to be muttering prayers under his breath. He clutches a prayerbook in his sweaty fist as if it were a life preserver. The other unfortunate, Ned realizes with about as much surprise as a prospective hangee can muster, is a dwarf. Three feet high, with a carroty mass of hair flaming round his cheeks and crown like a brushfire. Without warning the dwarf suddenly turns and delivers a vicious kick to the lower leg of his companion.

"Cut yer blubberin' and 'ail Maryin', arse'ole. Die like a man."

"Lay off me, Ginger," the big man pleads. "Ye've 'ounded me into a life of crime — ain't that damage enough?"

The dwarf turns his head away to spit on the cold stone floor. "Me 'ounded you, eh? And 'oo was it wanted to roll Lord Lovat when 'ee come out of White's gamblin' 'ouse, eh? And wot about the brilliant idea of peelin' the gold-leaf paper off the inside of the Duke of Bedford's coach? I don't 'ear you, pea brain," the dwarf snarls, kicking the tall man a second time.

"Ye twisted little 'omunculus!" the big man explodes, dropping his prayerbook and snatching at the dwarf's coiffure with both hands, "I'll show ye 'oo corrupted 'oo." Though the pinions severely restrict his maneuverability, he manages to come up with two fistfuls of bright orange hair, one on each side of the dwarf's head. "Son of a bitch!" he roars, shaking the little man as if he were a sack of feathers, while the dwarf in his turn tries to get a purchase on his antagonist's groin.

At that moment however the gates draw back with an apocalyptic screech and the two combatants go limp, looking sheepish as the chaplain appears from a back stairway to lead the solemn procession out into the blue-white glare of the street. The driven snow rakes at Ned's face, harsh and stinging, but he doesn't turn his head or narrow his eyes, welcoming this little prick of sensation, this wonderful automatic quirk of the organism. In a few minutes there will be a final and absolute end to all sensation — to pleasure and pain, taste and smell, the soft pressure of Fanny's lips, to hunger, bitterness, cold. Behind him the thieves have fallen silent, absorbed in their own reflections, awed by the shadowy prospect of death. As soon as they'd opened their mouths a corresponding channel had opened in Ned's brain, and he recognized them as the bastards who'd robbed him and Boyles after the Bartholomew Fair. Somehow, the fact that they'll soon get what's coming to them seems a small consolation.

The sight of the three gibbets looming up out of the storm is a shock: save me, Ned prays, save me. I haven't lived yet. Give me one more chance — just one more chance. But then he focuses on the immense black-hooded figure standing silent beneath the apparatus, and he knows it's no use praying. The hangman's grip is like a vise as he helps Ned up onto the box, center stage. A special high-rise platform has been built to accommodate the dwarf — he curses when the hangman hoists him under the armpits and sets him atop the box as if he were a mannequin. The big man is whimpering like a puppy: at the first sign of his weakness the rabble comes alive, spewing taunts and epithets. He has to be prodded before he'll mount the box, and when the hangman secures the noose he cries out as if he's been burned. The spectators seem to find this amusing, and a nervous titter works its way through their ranks.

"You men, poor sinners," begins the chaplain, "bow your heads and beg forgiveness of Jesus Christ Our Lord. You will soon appear before the judgment seat of your Creator, there to give an account of all things done in this life, and to suffer eternal torment for your sins committed against Him, unless by your hearty and unfeigned repentance you obtain mercy — "

The chaplain's words are lost on Ned. They're nothing but random noises that prolong his life a precious moment more: he doesn't even hear them. Nor does he have any clear perception of the crowd before him. He doesn't notice Banks, Mendoza or Smirke, nor Billy Boyles, Adonais Brooks' footman or the old harridan who's haunted him since he drew his first breath in a cold crib of straw. He is looking back at his tracks in the snow, the last physical evidence of his willed existence, already filling with fresh white powder.

"— through the merits and death and passion of Jesus Christ — "

Ned closes his eyes, fighting for control. He thinks of Fanny, Barrenboyne, the clarinet. Music, color and movement. Of running, bursting his bonds, leaping a horse and charging off down the street, the wind in his hair . . .

"— Lord have mercy upon you, Lord have mercy upon you all."

. . . where is he now? They've cut the horse down, their hands round his throat, but Boyles — yes, Boyles — fires into the crowd and Ned is up again, legs pumping, carrying him up and away from the dismal walls of Newgate and the shadow of the gibbet . . .

But Ned Rise is not running. He is hanging. Choking on his own vomit as it rises, catches in his throat and drops back to constrict his lungs. Below him, sorrily, futilely, Billy Boyles swings from his legs, crying like a baby, while somewhere off to the left the dwarf shouts out: "Fuck the Virgin Mary!" And then all is calm, and all is dark.

◄§ WATER MUSIC

Christmas, 1797.

It's been a year of victory and defeat, of bold offensives and timely retreats. Thus, Napoleon has whipped the Austrians and annexed the major part of Italy, while Walter Scott has thrown in the towel with Williamina Belches and nuptialed Margaret Charpentier on the rebound. In Hampshire, Jane Austen, disappointed by the rejection of "First Impressions" (should she retitle it?), has churned out a gothic tale, "Northanger Abbey," and begun a little didactic romance called "Eleanor and Marianne." Horatio Nelson has been knighted and promoted to the rank of admiral for his part in the crippling of the Spanish fleet at Cape St Vincent, and John Wilkes, the fire breather, is succumbing to the weight of the world and will be dead inside of twenty-four hours. The Dutch have been prevented from landing a French army in Ireland, but the Irish are insurrecting nonetheless, and Pitt, desperately trying to effect a consolidation of England and Ireland, is exciting his monarch's ire over the question of Catholic emancipation. In the midst of all this, Coleridge and Wordsworth are quietly putting together a book that will break the back of neoclassicism as neatly as a gourmand breaks a breadstick.

But this evening, despite the turmoil of the times, the *beau monde* has gathered at Covent Garden for a Christmas concert featuring selections from Handel's *Messiah*. Outside, the snow lies thick on the cobblestones, in the gutter, in the branches of the trees; inside, the nobs of London bask in the glow of their own sunny faces. King George is there of course, accompanied by Queen Charlotte and their daughters. He has not been looking well of late, and his ministers fear that he may once again be falling prey to the madness that put him out of commission in '88 (a madness that prompted him at one point to attempt to throttle the Prince of Wales over the question of succession to the throne). In another box, the Prince is entertaining one of his father's greatest antagonists, Charles Fox, and the young arbiter of fashion, Beau Brummell. Behind them, the hall is packed. Fanny Burney is there, the Duke of York, Peg Woffington, Lord Hobart. Wilberforce the Abolitionist settles himself in the back row, along with the Bishop of Llandaff, member *in absentia* of the African Association, while the Countess Binbotta, as sleek and smug as a full-bellied shark, makes a show of offering her heartfelt thanks to William Pitt and the Lord Mayor. Throughout the hall there is a rustle of silks and ornamental swords, the sound of subdued chatter, sniffling, discreet coughs. The scents of lilac water and eau de cologne thicken the air.

Mungo Park, seated at the right hand of Sir Joseph Banks, is feeling a bit giddy. From the moment he took his brother-in-law's hand in the predawn quiet of the museum gardens, he has been thrust into a vortex of activity, a constantly accelerating round of good cheer, congratulations, beefy faces and raised glasses. Roast goose with Dickson and Effie, punch, Yorkshire pudding and rum cake with Sir Reginald Durfeys, a tree full of candles, snatches of forgotten song, three slices of mince pie and brandy at Sir Joseph's, a welter of parties, coaches, snowy streets, slapped backs and extended hands — and now this. He is delighted, upset, comforted, dyspeptic, exhausted, exhilarated. As soon as the word got out, the members of the African Association had flocked to him, eager as schoolboys at a rugby match, probing with their animated faces and thousand-and-one questions. Did the negroes slice steaks from living cattle and eat them on the spot? Were the cities made of gold or dung? How wide was the river? Was it commercially viable? Were the hippogriffs a problem?

This is what he's wanted, this is what he's dreamed of. He's the talk of London, a sensation, the cynosure in this galaxy of pole stars. But he is tired, bone-tired. Banks is at his elbow with yet another introduction, and he can barely hold his head up. "Oh Mungo, have you met the Duke of

Portland?" the languid aristocratic tones bathing the name in syrup. "This is the fellow I was telling you about, Duke — been to the Niger and back . . . this morning . . . east! Flows east!"

But then, mercifully, the lights dim, the conductor mounts his podium and the opening strains of the "Sinfonia" sift through the hall. The effect on the explorer is instantaneous. The sound of strings, organ and trumpet is an anodyne, washing him in the sweetness and light of civilization, whispering of precision and control, of the Enlightenment, of St. Paul's and Pall Mall, of the comfortable operation of cause and effect, statement and resolution. He is back, at long last he is back. Back in a society where the forms are observed and love of culture is a way of life, a society that nurtures Shakespeares, Wrens, Miltons and Cooks. Hail Britannia, yes indeed.

When he looks up, the bass soloist is fulminating against "The people that walked in darkness," and Mungo thinks of Ali, Eboe, Mansong, the chaos and barbarity of Africa. But then the chorus comes in like a thunderbolt to drive back the darkness with the joy and intensity of "For unto us a child is born" and he feels that he's never heard anything so beautiful. And now the soprano is opening up, soaring like an angel, the pageant unfolding, a venerable old story of shepherds in their fields and the glad tidings of mankind's redemption. When the alto steps forward to begin her recitative, "Then shall the eyes of the blind be opened," Mungo finds himself thinking of Ailie. The soloist is slight, built like a boy, her black hair coiled in a chignon. Mungo's eyes are closed, there are children on the undersides of his lids, a stone house, Ailie at the door — but then he's jolted back to consciousness by a grating cacaphony, some disturbance in the front row, someone . . . someone shouting down the soloist!

It is the King, on his feet, calling out the name of a composition like a drunkard in a tavern. The audience is stunned; the courageous little alto falters but continues, her voice ringing out over the harsh persistent cries of the King. His Royal Highness seems to be calling for an earlier piece, a favorite of his great-grandfather, and now the Queen is on her feet tugging at his sleeve, and Pitt is running down the aisle, the orchestra losing heart as the red-faced man in the silver wig keeps shouting for "Water Music, Water Music, Water Music!"

TWO

THE YARROW

❦ "What Yarrow but a river bare, ❧
That glides the dark hills under?
There are a thousand such elsewhere
As worthy of your wonder."

— WILLIAM WORDSWORTH, "Yarrow Unvisited"

✎ LAZARUS

Muttering darkly as he trudges through the drifts heaped up around the steps of St. Bartholomew's Hospital, Dr. D. W. Delp is in no mood for miracles. In fact, if a miracle sat up and slapped him in the face over his small beer and muffin he'd shout it down and chase it right back where it came from, and then possibly, if he felt insulted enough, dissertate in Latin on the experiential impossibility of its existence. He is in a funk this morning, a screaming blue funk, rankled to the quick by what he perceives as a failure of government — or rather, the impossibly inconsistent and unpredictable judicial system upon which it rests. The idea of hanging a man on Christmas Day! Shocking. Barbaric. Worse than that: inconsiderate. He swipes angrily at the iron handrail, misses, catches a pool of dead gray ice with his left foot, and goes down cursing on the hospital steps.

"Where the bloody hell is that porter?" he shouts, slamming through the door and shocking the nurses out of their bonnets. "Do we pay him his five shillings a week to remove the frost around here or don't we? Well, where is he? Malingering by the fire and warming his lazy arse no doubt, eh? Sucking at a pot of beer, eh?"

The porter peeks out from the broom closet, sheepish, while patients in nightcaps, splints and yellowed wrappings sink into themselves, momentarily hushed by the doctor's outburst. Delp stands there a moment in his greatcoat, muffler and beaver hat, snorting through his mustache. And then an elderly patient, his leg withered and eyes clouded with cataracts, calls out in a feeble voice: "Doctor, it's me lungs — me lungs is stopped up till I don't know whether I'm dead or alive."

That's all it takes: the spell is broken, the pall lifts. Like supplicants before the oracle they crowd in on him with their arthritic hands and gouty legs, bleating *Doctor, Doctor, Doctor.*

But Delp has neither time nor inclination for them. He shoulders his way through the press, long legs kicking out impatiently, and makes his way up the corridor to his laboratory. No, it's not sprains, rheumatism and goiters that have gotten him out of bed this morning. Suppurating sores and compound fractures are quotidian, unremarkable — hardly the sort of thing that would make a man forgo his holiday excursion to Bath on the day after Christmas, a trip planned long in advance to coincide with his son's vacation from classes at Oxford and his daughter's arrival, amidst trunks and boxes, from Miss Creamer's boarding school. Oh, no. The only thing that could draw Delp to the hospital on such a day as this·is scientific curiosity — the consuming désire for knowledge, the chance to extend the limits of anatomical understanding, the chance to perform a pedagogical dissection on a pair of cadavers obtained from the hangman the previous day.

The doctor pauses by the bust of Vesalius to blow out a long sigh of resignation, the columns and cornices of Bath and his children's disappointed faces already receding into the far corners of his consciousness and the problem at hand emerging like a coach hurtling out of the mist. You've got to take them when you can get them, he knows that. Christmas, anniversaries, the first golden day of spring — if Quiddle comes round and says he's got a corpse on ice, then it's an operating day. No two ways about it. There's been a real dearth of cadavers these past few years, and the competition has been fierce for the few clean and unmutilated specimens that do turn up. Everybody's getting into the act. The Royal College of Physicians, Oxford University, St. Thomas's Hospital, St. George's, Guy's, Westminster, Middlesex. The earth doesn't even have time to settle over half the churchyards in London before someone's dug up the late dear departed and sold off his moldering remains to the highest bidder. But what's a man of science to do? Look at Philpott, over at the Royal College. He was so hard up for bodies he dissected his own three-year-old son, dead of the whooping cough, before a class of unsuspecting anatomy students.

"Decius!" Quiddle is waiting for him outside the door of the amphitheater. "How are you this morning? Have a good holiday?"

Delp fixes his assistant with a fishy stare. "What do they look like?"

"The one's a beauty, laid out like a dead angel. The other — "

"Yes?"

"The other's a dwarf."

"A dwarf? Damnation. He came cheap I suppose?"

"Thirty-five quid for the sound one, twenty for the dwarf. Agent for Middlesex Hospital beat me to the first one — a pity too. He was a real corker, that one. A giant. Six-two or -three, at least."

Delp, absorbed in the process of unbuttoning his greatcoat and ducking

out of his muffler, looks up sharply. "You mean that son of a bitch Crump
s selling them off to Middlesex now — after all the business we've given
him?"

" 'They goes to the 'ighest bidder,' that's what he told me."

The doctor shrugs angrily out of his coat, tears off the muffler, fumbles
for a match and then throws the whole box of them down in disgust. The
corridor is haunted with shadows, early morning, underlit, a cold wind
humming at the walls. "Well, let's have a look at them then."

•§ §•

In his garret on Paternoster Row, Dirk Crump warms his hands over the
grate and counts through the pile of coins on the table before him — nearly
a hundred pounds. Not bad for a day's work. The real stroke was to get
that old hag in there to claim the murderer's body. What hangman is going
to deny the poor unfortunate's dear old mom? The dwarf was up for grabs,
of course — where would you find a hoary old midget to play the bereaved
father anyway? But the big one, he was easy. Just hand over five shillings
to Tall Bob, the apothecary's assistant, and have him run over his lines
twenty or thirty times: I'm Will's brother, come over from Southwark. Da'
sent me to fetch 'im 'ome in the cart.

Bob blew his lines, but there was nobody there to care much about it,
and the old lady — she was perfect. Absolutely deranged with grief. He'll
have to see if she wants to work for him on a regular basis. There were two
or three friends or relatives or whatever pressing the hangman to give up
the body to them, but the old lady shoved her way through the throng,
screeching and blubbering like the mother of Christ come to haul him
down from the cross. The only problem was she didn't want to give up the
body once she'd got it into her cart and hustled round the corner. Even
now it makes him shudder to think of the look in her eyes as she sat
perched atop the donkey cart in her black tatters like a ghoul or zombie or
something. "Eeeee-eeeee!" she shrieked, " 'ee's sleepin' sound now I'll
warrant. Five pund and 'ee's yours."

She had him over a barrel: he knew he could get thirty easy. He counted
the coins out into her twisted claw, tossed the corpse in with the other two
and trundled up Paternoster Row. Then settled down in a chair by the
grate and waited for Quiddle and Babbo and the rest of them to come
round and bid up the price. What am I bid? he asked Quiddle, leering
across the table. Eh? What am I bid?

•§ §•

The operating theater is close and warm. The two students from Leyden
are there, bent over drawing pads and notebooks; behind them Delp

recognizes Freischütz, the serious young German with the long nose and frazzled hair. Dr. Abernathy is there of course, seated in the front row, ever curious about the mysteries of the organism. In the back: four strangers, one of whom is a lady. Quiddle had arranged it. Society people with a scientific bent and a pocketful of guineas. They've come for the frisson.

Delp bows curtly to his audience before drawing on the calfskin gloves he customarily dons when delving into the body corporeal. He then clears his throat and fixes his gaze on Dr. Abernathy's stockings: "Today we will begin with an examination of the principal sanguiferous conduits of the leg . . . Quiddle?"

Quiddle, in white smock and cravat, strides briskly to the center of the room, where the two cadavers, large and small, lie side by side on a massive slate-topped table. With a flourish, he uncovers the smaller of the two. There is a murmur from the back row, tailed by a soft ladylike gasp. The doctor turns to the corpse, pointer in hand, and frowns. One of the dwarf's hands, rigid as a claw, is frozen at the neck, his body the size of a child's, his face an accusation — twisted with rage and agony, eyes locked, lips drawn back from the teeth in a wild desperate grin — monstrous and absurd all at once. "No, no," Delp whispers, "let's begin with the other one."

Obedient and efficient factotum that he is, Quiddle pulls the sheet up over the dwarf's ears and the audience breathes a sigh of relief. As he bends to expose the second cadaver, the apprehension is palpable — the lady's fingers dart to her mouth, ready to stifle a cry, the students from Leyden are suddenly struck with the architecture of the ceiling, young Freischütz sucks at his pen until his lips turn black. But as it turns out, there's no cause for alarm: the body is at rest, arms at its sides, face clear and untroubled, a white towel swaddling the groin. If it weren't for the rope burns and broken blood vessels discoloring the throat, one would never guess that the fellow had died an agonizing and premature death — he could be sleeping, playacting, posing for a diorama of Adonis slain by the boar. A hush falls over the room, all eyes fixed on the limp and pallid form on the operating table.

The dry cutting voice of Dr. Delp is almost an intrusion. "As I was saying, today we will begin with an investigation into the blood vessels of the leg . . . ah . . . Quiddle, if you please?"

As Quiddle's scalpel deftly lays open the dermis of the lower leg in order to expose the anterior tibial artery, a strange and wonderful thing happens: a rush of blood — forceful as a geyser — leaps up from the incision to spatter his chest, face and hands, coloring the smock as if it were a canvas.

"The anterior tibial artery," Delp intones, his back to the table, "branches off at the patella from the posterior tibial artery, which in turn branches off to form the peroneal artery — " He cuts off in midsentence, wondering what has gone wrong. Abernathy is on his feet, speechless, the students from Leyden have dropped their notebooks with a clatter, the faces of the society people are ashen . . . and then, as chilling as a summons from beyond the grave comes the groan at his back, subhuman, riveting, terrible.

"Doc-Doctor — " Quiddle stammers.

Delp swings around on a fountain of blood, the drained face of his assistant, and worst of all the trembling eyelids and fitfully clenching fists of the corpse on the table. His mouth falls open, the pointer drops to the floor. With the clear unreasoning instinct of a hunted animal he staggers back, turns, and bolts for the door.

"Stop! Stop! Stop!" screams Abernathy, leaping the rail and springing to the floor like a geriatric acrobat. "He's alive! The fellow's alive! Stop that blood, man!"

Quiddle is the first to come out of it. Corpses don't spring to life, he tells himself. Vampires, zombies, ghouls — a patient is bleeding to death. No time for thought, surprise, terror, his fingers are at the wound, pinching off the sheared vessels, and now Abernathy and Delp are at his side, trembling with the urgency of it, shouting for ligature and cautery.

In the gallery, the shock is not so easily overcome. Freischütz has fainted dead away, the students from Leyden are under the seats, the society gentlemen on their feet, as mad and uncertain as horses caught in a burning barn. Beside them, the lady sits rooted to her seat, eyes glazed with shock and incomprehension. But then a new look creeps into her face, a look of certainty and joy. Silently, reverently, she slips to her knees and clasps her hands in prayer. "Blessed be the Lord," she murmurs. "It's a miracle."

Down on the floor, in the midst of the flurry round the slate-topped table — hands and instruments and terse panting commands — Ned Rise lifts his head and opens his eyes on Resurrection Day and the shifting lights and colors of life.

◂§ THE LOTOS-EATER

"We thought you were dead."

"Yes, old boy, sorry to say it, we did."

"Well, I mean, no word in two years' time — and then that devastating news from Laidley about your Moorish captivity . . . Tell me, confidentially now, do they really take their women from behind?"

Another reception, another round of drinks, another bank of faces. As best the explorer can ascertain, this is the twentieth bash thrown in his honor since he got back a month ago — or is it the twenty-first? The pace is killing. But exhilarating: He goes from one lecture to the next, one drawing room to another. One night he meets a duchess, the next an earl. Mungo Park, son of a crofter, rubbing elbows with the high and mighty — and not twenty-seven yet. Heady, is what it is.

No. 12, St. James's Place

The Baroness von Kalibzo requests the
honor of your presence at a reception for
Mr. Mungo Park, geographical luminary and
discoverer of the River Niger.
9:00 P.M.

28 January, 1798

Sir Joseph, who isn't much for these affairs, had warned him about the Baroness. Though she was cousin-german to the King, and of the highest rank and precedence in her own country, her reputation in London was somewhat unsavory. Sir Joseph would only say that she had been "guilty of excess," and he advised the explorer to decline the invitation. But when it became apparent that Mungo was to be the guest of honor, Sir Joseph agreed that he should attend, if only for an hour or two.

So here he is, basking in the adulation of his social superiors, sipping at his fourth glass of wine, munching crackers smeared with Russian caviar and experiencing the distinct sensation that all is right with the world. Blackamoor servants in periwigs and Cluny lace scurry about, bare-bosomed statuary and portraits by Bonifacio, Titian and Fra Bartolommeo line the walls, a nine-piece orchestra softens the atmosphere. And what's more, every time he opens his mouth, people in evening dress crowd round him. Is this paradise, or what?

At the moment, Sir Ralph Sotheby-Harp and two other wealthy subscribers to the African Association have worked him into a corner beside a potted fern. They are excited, their faces lambent with the ardor of

ure and disinterested scientific inquiry as they press him for details
ertaining to the sexual preferences of the various tribes, while the
explorer, usually reticent in such situations, finds himself waxing glib under
the influence of the wine. "The Foulahs, so I'm told, often have sex while
mounted on their camels, and the Serawoolis —" here he lowers his
voice while a blackamoor servant refills his glass and his auditors lean
forward, "— the Serawoolis actually prefer prepubescent ewes to their
women — "

"How unutterably dull." The Baroness has appeared from nowhere, her
head a mass of curls, neckline plunging to the point of no return. "To
reduce so vital and transcendent an act as luff to mere lubricity, I mean.
Don't you tink, Mr. Park?"

"I — I — uh . . ."

"Come," she says, locking arms with him, "I haff some odder guests you
maybe would like to meet. Gentlemen, you'll excuse us pleese?"

⁓ ❧

A few hours later the explorer is three sheets to the wind and leading the
Baroness through a vigorous and semispastic reel while the other dancers
clear the floor and the violin strains away at the upper end of the
fingerboard. Chandeliers flash by overhead, plants, statues, paintings and
astonished faces melding in a vertiginous blur, the Baroness looming and
receding like a vision in a dream. She kicks up her heels, spins like a
dervish, hair falling down her back in loops, bosoms jogging, petticoats
aflutter. Inspired, the explorer attempts a sort of grand jeté, springing
across the room like an antelope, leaping a writing desk and spinning
toward his partner in a series of widening spirals. He feels so good he could
shout for joy, roar like a lion, beat his chest and howl like some elemental
force of nature. Unfortunately, he loses his balance at the last moment and
pitches headlong into the Baroness, driving her back against a Pembroke
table and blasting it to splinters. She lies there a moment, pinned beneath
him, forty years old and feeling twenty. "You're quite a dancer, Mr. Park,"
she murmurs finally, her long-fingered hands spread across his back.

A moment later the two terpsichoreans are back on their feet, grinning,
a knot of anxious guests crowding round to survey the damage. "More
champagne!" calls the Baroness. "Strike up the orchestra!"

Dutifully, the musicians launch another tune, and a few couples edge
timidly out onto the floor. Someone is telling a joke in the corner, the wave
of chatter swells again, the incident already forgotten. The Baroness
smooths her bodice, plumps her bosoms and adjusts the ruffles of her skirt,
while the explorer brushes at his frock coat, momentarily at a loss for

words. "Mein Gott, dat was fun," she says finally. And then: "May I offer you anodder glass of champagne, Mr. Park?"

"Yes — yes, of course. And please: call me Mungo."

While the servant refills their glasses, she looks up at him in a wide-eyed, cattish sort of way. "Iss dere anyting else at all you might want of me — Mungo?"

The explorer stands there, swaying back on his heels, grinning like an idiot, lost in contemplative admiration of the front of her dress.

"Maybe yóu would be interested to see the rest of the house — the sitting room, library . . . my bedchambers?"

He watches her sip at her wine, the tip of her tongue like a bud, rich and pink and moist "And uh," he stammers, fighting for nonchalance, "the Baron . . . uh, I don't believe I've had the pleasure yet — "

"Ach!" she says, taking his arm. "Didn't I tell you? The poor man succumbed t'ree years ago."

✑ DOWN AND UP AND DOWN AGAIN

It's been a shattering month. A month of trial and vindication, doubt giving way to certainty, crisis to resolution. And then this sudden deflation, the rush of joy and affirmation superseded by a new and malignant sense of incomprehension and hurt, lingering, persistent, dull. Like having a tooth pulled, the same tooth, twenty-four hours a day, thirty days running.

Mungo's letter reached Selkirk on the twenty-ninth of December. Ailie was not there to receive it. She was in Kelso, in a brick house just outside of town, sitting before the fire and scrutinizing her emotions as closely as she'd ever scrutinized hydra or paramecium beneath the ground and polished lens of her microscope. The brick house belonged to Dr. Dinwoodie. She could think of no one else to turn to. Her father, the relations, Katlin — even Zander was against her in this. Dinwoodie was bald, semi-invalid, sixty-three years old. His hobby was taxidermy. I dunna understand it, he said when he answered the door, ye're a wild and wicked gull. But of course ye can stay with me. Of course ye can. Glad for the company.

On Christmas night she sent a message to her father via Dugald Struthers, who was riding into Selkirk to be with his mother for the holidays. *Dear father,* she wrote, *don't worry yourself. I'm at Dr. Din-*

woodie's, sorting things out. I just couldn't go through with it, I hope you'll understand. Won't you?

The following morning, 6:00 A.M., the old man was beating at Dinwoodie's door. With his shoe. A frozen rain was falling, gray as a dead lake, starlings stirred in the hedge, the world was sunk in glass. "Dinwoodie!" the old man thundered. "Open this door, be gad, open it this minute or I'll put me shoulder to it!"

Ailie was upstairs in the guest room. She'd spent a sleepless night, racked with guilt and uncertainty. Staring up at the rafters, listening to the drum of the ice pellets on the roof as the snow turned to sleet, sick at heart over the absence of Mungo and the unforgivable thing she'd done to Georgie Gleg and her family. One minute she would think that she'd run back and marry him despite herself, the next she would know it was impossible. And at dawn, just before she dozed off, she knew, in a sudden flash of intuition, that waiting for Mungo was equally impossible. He was lost. She would never see him again.

The sound of her father's voice startled her. She sat up in bed and listened to him storming around downstairs. "Where is she, the jezebel?" he shouted. "Be gad I'll drag her back by the nape of her neck, spank her disrespectful bottom till it blisters, horsewhip her if need be!" And then the calm soothing tones of Dr. Dinwoodie, offering a cup of tea with a bit of brandy, going on about things psychological, the effect that Mungo's loss has had on her, the need for time to heal the wounds. "Surely you don't want to force the gull into marriage, Jamie."

"Force her? She give her word. Give her word, Donald. It gars me greet to think on it. An Anderson, and she broke her solemn vow. Ye should hear the gossip —"

Then Dinwoodie, mumbling something about the new generation.

"New generation, my arse!" Her father's voice shot back like a rally in a tennis match. "She's twenty-three years of age. A growed woman. And she maun get married. Get her down here, the hussy — get her down here before I lose me self-control and thrash her out of bed before me oldest friend's eyes."

"Jamie, get a hold on yourself —"

"The devil with gettin' a hold on — this is a time for action!"

There was the sound of a scuffle, crockery shattering, Dinwoodie's voice, louder now, angrier, but with an edge of resignation to it: "All right, all right, keep your sark on — I'll fetch her." And then the scrape of the old doctor's footsteps on the stairs.

Ten minutes later she was standing before the fire in the parlor, wincing down at the cup of tea Dinwoodie had brewed her, weathering her father's tirade. Behind her on the mantel was one of the old doctor's taxidermic triumphs: a badger and two stoats, erect, dressed in kilt and tam o'shanter, playing at viol and fife. She transferred her gaze to the grinning badger as her father raged and spat round the room. The old man had a magnificent pair of lungs, but eventually he had to pause for breath.

"Are you done?" she asked, and before he could start up again she cut him off. "Because whether you are or not it's time I had my say. Georgie Gleg is odious to me. He always has been. For all his good heart he's a coof and a simp. There's no magic between us, and I'll not have him now nor ever."

Her father's mouth dropped. "Not have him — ? But ye give your word, gull."

"You'll see me in the nunnery first."

"All right!" the old man bellowed. "All right then — suit yourself," slapping his hand down on the table. "I'll bring the cart round and drag ye to the Abbey meself." He fumbled angrily into his coat and slammed out the door, muttering "no daughter of mine," over and over, as if he were rehearsing it.

That was on the twenty-sixth. Three days later he was back, vaulting the picket fence on his winded mare, plowing through evergreens and dormant flowerbeds, galloping right on up to the doorstep, and all the while sputtering through a bugle like some kind of madman. Ailie had heard the sound of the horn in the far distance and had come to the window, puzzled. Dinwoodie was in the midst of stuffing a pair of hedgehogs, which he'd dressed to resemble the parson and his wife, when he heard the commotion and thought for one wild moment that they were under attack. The confusion was short-lived. The next instant Ailie's father was careening through the door, no time to knock, bellowing at the top of his lungs. "He's alive, lassie," the old man was shouting as he bounded up the stairs. It took a moment for his words to sink in — was it possible? — then she was up and out the door, rushing down the hallway to meet him. He swooped her up in his arms, whiskery and red-faced, rabid with the news, a letter flapping loose in his hand. "He's done it lass. He's back. Your mon's come home!"

After that it was easy. The years of waiting, the trouble about the wedding, breaking her vow: it was all forgiven her. People began to talk about premonition, clairvoyance, a sign that had come to her at the last minute. How had she known? They came from miles around to congratuate her, to look at her, touch her, hear the sound of her voice. It's a miracle, is what it is, they said. A love made in heaven. Ailie was vindicated. She felt as if she'd just won the lottery, restored Bonnie Prince Charlie to the throne, taken her seat at the right hand of God.

But now, back in Selkirk, the walls have come tumbling down again. A month passes, and no further word from Mungo. He's alive, thank God, she'll always have that — and yet where is he? The coach takes four days from London, five ownin' for bad weather, her father says. Where is he then? Where is this boy that's so hot to see his betrothed, eh? Where is he? Talk starts up again. He's back, all right, but he's deserted her — just as she had deserted Gleg. Serves her right. It goes on like this, worse each day, until finally, on the day after the anniversary of their engagement, the second letter comes.

> The George & Blue Boar, Holborn
> 29 January, 1798

My Dearest Ailie:

I am unavoidably delayed in London over the issue of preparing a shortened account of my travels for dissemination to members and subscribers of the African Association. With the aid of Mr. Bryan Edwards, Secretary of the Association, I expect I should have it completed in a few months' time — after which I shall fly to your arms. Think of it, my dearest friend and wife-to-be: once this minor impediment is out of the way, we shall be together always. At least while I'm at Fowlshiels working on the manuscript of my book, to be called "Travels in the Interior Districts of Africa, 1795–97." Isn't that exciting? Too, too much? I'm to be a literary man!

But of course, I languish till I feel your touch.

> Yrs., *Et Cetera,*
> *Mungo*

A few months' time? She's waited an eternity already. Badgered and beleaguered, fighting off the wide world for faith in him. And now he's too busy to see her? Too involved with his book to come up to Selkirk for a week and tell her he's missed her as she has so painfully and vitally missed him? She crumples the letter in disgust, suddenly filled with remorse for what she's done to Georgie Gleg. It hits her like an epiphany: poor Georgie, he must feel as hurt and bewildered as I do now.

But that's another story.

⋅§ GLEG'S STORY
(BORN UNDER A BAD SIGN)

Georgie Gleg was born at Galashiels, second son of the local laird. As the
moment of parturition approached, a golden eagle coasted down out of the
haze, flapped its great dark wings a time or two, and settled lightly on the
weathervane atop the Gleg house. The locals were astonished. People
came running from shops and fields to stand in the courtyard and gawk at
it.

"It's a sign," someone said.

"Aye," said another, "but is it auspicious or no?"

A debate started up, right there beneath the windows of the laird's
house, Georgie's mother crying out in pain, the eagle preening its wings as
calmly as if it were perched high in its aerie.

"It's the devil's own hand laid on, I tell you," insisted a man in an
oversized hat.

"You're a blatherin' fool," countered another. "It's a benediction out of
the heavens is what it is."

Almost immediately a fistfight erupted. Women screamed, horses whinnied, someone broke out a bottle of whisky. Factions were already
forming, and there were indications that the controversy could develop
into a full-scale brawl, when suddenly Davie Linlithgow put an end to it.
He raised his musket and took the bird's head off in a blast of fire and
smoke. Spastic, the big-feathered torso pitched forward and slathered the
tiles with blood.

The crowd fell silent, the combatants held their punches. Upstairs, thin
and harsh as a penny whistle, the voice of Georgie Gleg was heard for the
first time on earth.

⋅§ ễ⋅

If there were any doubts as to the meaning of the events surrounding
Gleg's birth, they were unequivocally dispelled as he grew into boyhood.
Without question the appearance of the great bird had been ominous, its
slaying a disaster: misfortune settled on the boy's shoulders like a winged
apparition. When he was six his father was killed in a hunting accident, and
his sister Effie — the darling of the family — was kidnapped by gypsies and
nailed to a tree in the wood beyond the north pasture. Anthrax decimated
the flocks that year and three of five milch cows went dry. Inexplicably, the
hens began laying yolkless eggs. There was a fire in the barn. Hailstones
the size of goiters wiped out the wheat crop, and Georgie's elder brother
was struck by lightning. Poor Simon. They found him laid out in the

heather as limp as some soft boneless thing washed up out of the sea.

Two years later Georgie's mother remarried. Tyrone Quaggus, the new man of the house, was a gambling fool. Skeet shooting, tea drinking, a stroll in the garden — any human activity was occasion for a wager. I'll bet you can't put away twenty cups of tea in half an hour, vicar, he would say. Ten pund says I can make it around the garden in two minutes flat. See that jay out in the hedge? Five'll get you ten he raps on this windowpane before noon. By the time Gleg was twelve, Quaggus had squandered the boy's patrimony and three quarters of the estate as well. The family was in deep trouble.

But as if that weren't enough, the blight touched Georgie in a far more subtle and insidious way: it made him a pariah. People shied away from him as if he were a leper, dogs snarled at him, his coevals kept him at a distance with sticks and stones. He was a toad, a worm, a freit — not fit for human company. And what made matters worse is that Gleg so clearly looked the part. He grew thin and ribby, with narrow shoulders and a breast like a plucked chicken. His feet were huge, his hands chapped. Talk had it that the high arched beak of his nose was the mark of the bird on him. His eyes too — they were tiny and close-set, flecked with yellow and red, pushed far back in his head and rimmed with flesh the color of liver. Bird's eyes.

At school he was the object of taunts, epithets, practical jokes, inhuman pranks, outright mockery and patent disdain. He was ten years old, homely as a horse, and the best Latin scholar in the Selkirk grammar school. This last was the kiss of death as far as his classmates were concerned. If they could forgive him his strangeness, his flapping ears and lack of coordination, they could never forgive the way the declensions rolled off his tongue, effortlessly, while they sat agonizing over the ratlike scrawlings in their battered copybooks. The older boys were particularly incensed. They'd been at it, day and night, for four years — only to be shown up by a sniveling little wimp of a bejan. They decided to get even.

As school let out one evening, four of the older scholars — the Park brothers, Finn Macpherson and Colin Raeburn — took a detour on their way home and met at Ballindalloch Glen. The air was crisp and dry, the snow crepitated under their feet. Adam and Mungo had a fire going by the time the others arrived, uncertain shadows emerging from the black screen of the woods. They greeted each other silently, grimly; Finn slipped the jar of whisky from his pocket as if it were a dirk. No one mentioned Meg Munro. There was no talk of football or shinty, there were no jokes. This was serious business. This was a council of war.

Gleg had done the unthinkable — he'd won the Hogmanay prize for accomplishment in the scholarly tongue by outdoing his classmates in a sight translation from the *Eclogues*. The prize was half a crown, donated each year by Mrs. Monboddo, a widow with an enormous bosom and a taste for culture. Never before had a first-year boy won the prize.

"This is the straw that broke the camel's back," Adam said. "We've got to teach the little bastard a lesson."

Finn passed the jar to Mungo, wiped his mouth with the back of his hand and assented. "I'm for layin' his ears back."

"No, no. We've got to be more subtle, trip him up with the old man." Adam, at fourteen, was the leader among them, though Mungo and Colin were a year older and set to graduate at the end of the term. Mungo, in fact, wasn't much interested in the whole affair — he'd come along merely to show solidarity. It wasn't so much that he liked or disliked Gleg — of course he disliked him — it was simply that he couldn't be bothered with such petty concerns. At fifteen, Mungo was something of a golden boy: an average scholar, but the best athlete in school, despite a tendency toward clumsiness. He was already six feet tall, and he had the musculature of a grown man. "I'm with Finn," he said.

Adam took his turn at the jar. "Hear me out," he said, and leaned forward to outline his plan. It was fiendish in its simplicity, and what's more it involved Gleg in a major transgression of school discipline:

Since the raison d'être of the local grammar school was to inculcate an understanding of Latin, all students were interdicted from speaking Scots — at work or play — during the hours that school was in session. This rule was enforced through the use of spies or "private clandestine captors," who would report violations to the schoolmaster. The first offense was punishable by a public upbraiding and a fine of two shillings, the second by a whipping before the class. The older boys, of course, knew who the spies were and bought their silence in one way or another. Of the six or seven finks operating in a class of thirty-seven, Robbie Monboddo was the most dependable. They'd simply have him give the schoolmaster a false report on his star pupil. Mr. Tullochgorm. I've a boy to report, Sir. Young Gleg. Profaning the Lord — and in broad Scots, Sir.

❧ ☙

Two days later Gleg was summoned to the front of the classroom. Peat glowed in the stone fireplace, a slow steady drip of meltwater puddled the earthen floor. The place had formerly housed dairy cattle, and the air was stung with the odor of urine and soured milk. Frost silvered the slats of the inner walls, the scholars' candles flickered fitfully in the gloom, rodents

ustled in the thatch overhead. "George Peter Gleg," Tullochgorm in-
oned, "come forward."

The thirty-seven scholars froze at their makeshift desks. All eyes were
on Tullochgorm as Gleg apprehensively rose from his seat and started up
he aisle. Since the schoolmaster's face never varied in expression, it was
difficult to assess his mood at this juncture — was he angry or merely
dyspeptic? Was Gleg to be chastised or praised? It was anyone's guess
— though Adam and Mungo, among others, had a pretty good idea.

Tullochgorm's totem was the cat-o'-nine-tails that cut an ominous slash
n the wall behind him. He liked no one and no thing. Words like wonder,
beauty and life were foreign to his lexicon. He was impoverished and
embittered, a mere grind dependent upon the niggardly salary the town-
ship raised for him, and on the charity of his students. *"Venit summa dies et
ineluctabile tempus,"* he snarled, lashing out at each syllable as if it were a
log to be kicked.

Gleg stood before the schoolmaster's massive oak table, his head bowed.
He answered in Latin: "I — I don't understand, Sir."

"What! *Nil conscire sibi, nulla pallescere culpa,* you young Turk."

"But — "

"Silence!" Tullochgorm was on his feet now, delivering the customary
lecture about disobedience, lack of discipline, those insidious few who
circumvent the established rules of society and weaken the fiber of the
Empire. When he was finished he seized Gleg by the scruff of the neck and
shook him till the snot ran from his nose. "Two shillings!" shrieked the
schoolmaster. "Two shillings! *Quamprimum!"*

A week later Gleg was called before the class for the second time. Adam
smirked at Finn and Colin as the room fell silent and the wind moaned in
the thatch. The younger boys blanched, clutching at the edges of their
desks till their knuckles turned white. Tullochgorm was livid, Gleg
frightened and confused. Mungo merely glanced up, absently finger-
combed his hair, and then turned back to the dog-eared copy of Jobson's
African adventures he'd concealed beneath his Latin grammar. *"Bonis
nocet quisquis pepercerit malis!"* roared Tullochgorm. And then: "Bend
over the desk, reprobate."

◄§ §►

Adam Park and his cohorts had achieved their end: Gleg was toppled. In
the space of seven short days he'd gone from first scholar to thirty-seventh.
But it didn't end there. How could it, after all, when Gleg was so clearly
marked, so conspicuously pathetic, so obvious a target he might as well
have painted a black spot between his eyebrows? Adam and his friends had

found the quintessential whipping boy. The more he suffered, the more they despised him — and the more determined they became to annihilate him, devastate him, squash him as they would have squashed a slug or spider. Adam took his brother aside. "Let's have him expelled," he whispered.

The following morning, at dawn, the scholars of Selkirk were gathered outside the schoolhouse awaiting the arrival of Tullochgorm. It was cold, and a number of them were huddled round the doorway, wringing their hands and stamping their feet. Adam and Finn were there, hands in pockets, copybooks tucked under their arms. They grinned at one another like Casca and Metellus Cimber on the front steps of the Senate House. Mungo and a few of the hardier types were out on the glazed-over duckpond, keeping warm with a round of curling. The big forty-pound stones hissed out over the ice like a long insuck of breath, the players panting along beside them with their whisks, the echo of the collisions bludgeoning the sharp morning air. From time to time a shout of triumph would ring out — in Latin, of course.

Gleg was late. He hurried along the path, bent over double, his copybook stuffed down the front of his jacket, a pot of ale cradled in his arms. Today was a tuition day, and each of the scholars was required to contribute a specified item to the schoolmaster's larder, in lieu of pecuniary considerations. Colin had brought a boll of wheat, Mungo a basket of potatoes. Others had been asked for neeps or butter or a stewing chicken. Gleg's assignment was to bring a pot of ale for the schoolmaster's lunch each day for the next two weeks.

As Georgie beat his way around the pond, Mungo turned and called to him. "Hey Gleg — you want to sweep for me?" Georgie was stunned. He couldn't have been more disoriented had he been hit in the back of the head with a shovel. Sweep for Mungo Park? He couldn't believe it. Never before had anyone invited him to participate in anything. Though he wanted nothing more. Though he sat for hours and watched them at shinty, football, golf, dying for a chance at it, praying that the goaltender would break a leg and they'd turn to him, Georgie Gleg, slap his back, see him in a new light.

"Well: what do you say? You want to or not?"

He nodded, nodded emphatically, his heart beating against his ribs like a bird fighting to burst free. "I've just got — just got to drop off the ale — " he stammered, already loping across the lot to the schoolhouse, too caught up in it to be suspicious.

He rushed up to the door, out of breath, twin streams of mucus depending from his nostrils. It took no more than five seconds — he set the pot of ale down among the other offerings, slid his copybook into a chink in the wall, and shot back up the path.

His fate was sealed.

Adam grabbed up the tankard as soon as Gleg turned his back, flipped back the lid and took a long hard swallow. He wiped his mouth and took another swig. Then handed the jar to Finn. Finn drank deep, passed the jar to Robbie Monboddo, who took his turn and passed it on. A moment later Adam drained it. And then, with Colin looking out for Tullochgorm, he unbuttoned his trousers and pissed into the neck of the jar, fighting for every last drop, pushing, pushing, his face red with the strain. Finn was next. And then Robbie, Colin and the rest. At first Colin couldn't make his water come and the others coached and cajoled him, talking it up as if they were out on the football field and this were a shot on goal. Tullochgorm had been sighted, the jar wasn't full yet. Come on, come on: you can do it. Finally, with less than a minute to spare, Colin let loose, sweet music, and filled the jar to the rim. A cheer went up. Tullochgorm thought it was for him, and tipped his hat as he stepped past them to open the door.

In the winter, sessions began at dawn and ran through till sundown, with a half-hour break for refreshment at noon. During the break the boys sat at their desks, shivering, and nibbled at a bit of cold porridge, or took advantage of the free time to skate or curl on the pond. On this particular day, no one left the room. There was a low murmur of lunchtime chatter, Mungo chewed at a cold potato, Colin warmed a crust over the fire. Furtively, they all watched Tullochgorm.

The schoolmaster had turned his chair in order to face the side wall. He'd laid up his rod — for thirty minutes at least — and had already begun to shut out the scene around him, already begun to forget the slate board, the dreary room, the unwashed faces at his elbow. There was a book open on the desk before him — the *Bellum Grammaticale* — and he was alternately skimming through it, massaging his feet and dicing a raw turnip into a dish of groats. Fascinated, the scholars hung on his every move, as if they'd never before seen a man scratch his feet and spoon up porridge at the same time. When he reached for his pot of ale the room was electric with tension, a wave of quiet hysteria cresting and then as quickly subsiding. It was a false alarm. Abstracted, the schoolmaster put the tankard down again and took a spoonful of cereal instead, his eyes all the while fixed on the pages of his book. Finn Macpherson nearly leaped from his seat. Adam couldn't resist a low nervous chuckle. Colin wiped his nose expectantly. Only Gleg was oblivious to it, scribbling away in his copybook as if he were immune to the nasty little surprises of life, poor dull unlucky Gleg, the sacrificial lamb blindly nosing round the pillars of the blood-stained altar itself.

Then, like the punchline of a bad joke, the moment passed into history. Tullochgorm lifted the tankard to his lips and took a long thirsty gulp. No reaction. He turned the pages of his book. There followed an instant during which he looked down at the pot of yellow liquid, took a puzzled experimental sip, and then spewed it all out like a whale coming up for air. Thirty-six heads dropped, suddenly absorbed in the intricacies of Latin grammar. Georgie Gleg looked up. The schoolmaster was having a fit of some sort, gasping and retching, pounding on the desk with the flat of his hand, blood vessels bursting in his face like a fireworks display. Georgie was awed, puzzled and frightened at the same time. But if he was surprised, the surprise was short-lived. For Tullochgorm was staring at him. Not staring exactly — glaring. Looking daggers. A froth of saliva and partially digested food on his chin, his eyes piglike with rage and hatred, Tullochgorm was glaring at him.

Georgie Gleg, ten years old, began to feel very small indeed.

◄§ §►

It was all downhill after that. There were peaks and valleys, of course, but essentially the plane of Gleg's life inclined toward the nether pole. The immediate result of the incident with Tullochgorm was expulsion, followed by a tripartite thrashing at the hands of Georgie's mother, Quaggus and the schoolmaster. For the next two weeks Gleg was forced to take a cup of his own urine with each meal, and to stand in the town pillory, erected ad hoc, for half an hour each afternoon. At the end of the two-week period he was unceremoniously booted from the house at the long end of Quaggus' foot, and sent up to Edinburgh, where he was to live with his uncle Silas and attend the local school.

Surprisingly, Edinburgh wasn't all that bad. For one thing, no one knew him in the big city. No one knew of the slain eagle and the tiles slathered with blood, no one accused him of harboring the evil eye or of curdling milk by his mere presence. To his schoolmates he was just another gangling, flap-eared object of ridicule — nothing special. Through the hail of abuse he even managed to nurture a friend or two — other misfits, of course — but it was a start. For another thing, Silas Gleg took an active interest in his nephew. He dressed him properly, hired a tutor, gave him an allowance — Georgie began to develop as a laird's son should. He graduated with high honors.

At this point, Quaggus stepped in. Since there was really no estate left to manage nor any patrimony to speak of, he argued, the boy should set himself up in a professional way, earn a living, learn to maintain himself. Silas Gleg reluctantly agreed. Georgie was first apprenticed to an apothecary, and then later, when the druggist unexpectedly passed on, to Silas Gleg's old friend, Dr. James Anderson of Selkirk. There he met Ailie, and his life developed into something worthwhile, something beautiful, something that for the first time approached the sublime. When she agreed to marry him he felt as if he'd conquered the world. Alexander, Caesar, Attila the Hun — they were pikers by comparison.

But then, just when life was opening up to him like an orchid in bloom, it snapped shut again, deadly, vituperative, rotten at the core. She left him. Crept off in the shadows as if he were some beast she couldn't face in the light of day. The relatives and neighbors had gathered. Quaggus and his mother. Uncle Silas. It was to have been the crowning moment of his life.

He left Selkirk the day after Christmas. There were no explanations, no apologies, no farewells. Stoop-backed, valise in hand, he headed off in the direction of Edinburgh. It was cold. The wind swept down out of the north with a sound like the keening of birds, and the crusted branches rattled like chandeliers at a wake. If he'd bothered to lift his head he would have looked out on a ripple of cropped gray hills, sorry gashes of erosion, trees stark beyond any hope of renewal. He didn't bother. Hunched against the wind, Gleg struggled on, weary and disconsolate, limping along the roadway like some half-dazed footsoldier beating a retreat from an enemy he could neither subdue nor comprehend.

◅ LIFE AFTER DEATH

"It's happened before, I tell you. An obstruction in the windpipe, shock and coma, the premature pronouncement of death. Good Lord, man, it was snowing to beat all hell — and Christmas morning on top of it. Who's to blame the hangman for maybe rushing things just a bit?"

With the slow, steady persistence of grains accumulating in an inverted hourglass, the voice of reason is beginning to have its effect on Quiddle. Still, he resists. "He dangled twenty minutes, didn't he?"

"Psssh," Delp waves his hand contemptuously. "Need I remind you that the human animal is infinitely various, and that what will dispatch one quite neatly may not necessarily, inexorably and in all cases do the trick for another. A Fiji Islander might not last more than five minutes in the waters off Greenland, but what of an Eskimo? Or better yet — take your average greengrocer. He'd go up like a wad of paper if you sent him through a bed of hot coals, and yet the Indies are swarming with fakirs who do it three and four times a day — for a lark. Use your sense, man. Who's to say that twenty or thirty or even sixty minutes' hang time is sufficient to choke out a human life without first taking into consideration the vagaries of time and place, weather conditions, the type of knot and quality of rope, the endurance of the individual and any of a thousand other intangibles?"

"I don't care how you explain it, I still think it's a miracle that that man in there is alive. Whether it's the hand of the Almighty or just a ripple of the law of averages, I'll wager it's the most extraordinary thing to happen round here since Queen Elizabeth's handmaid got hit by lightning and sprouted a beard."

Delp's eyes have gone cold with exasperation. "Wager away," he grunts, pulling the pipe from his mouth as if he were unplugging a drain, "but I'll tell you this — I want that character out of here in a week's time. Chafe his neck, let some blood, feed him broth — whatever it takes — but get him on his feet and out that door." Here he pauses to strike a match and suck the yellow flame over the bowl of his pipe. "I have no objection to your parading him around a bit, incidentally. There's been a lot of folderol about the miracle of modern science and all that, the patients looking on it with a certain degree of awe and so on. Walk him around. I don't think it would hurt us a bit — if you know what I mean."

✥ ❧

The door swings back and scatters light through the little room. In the doorway, Quiddle. A tray in his hands. Pewter mug, golden crust, steam rising from a bowl. "Well, you're awake then," he booms in a jaunty, whistling-in-the-churchyard sort of voice.

Ned Rise lies on a pallet in the corner, a dirty blanket pulled up to his neck. The room is dank and windowless: earthen walls, brick floor, deal planks overhead. A cellar of course, crude and unfinished, and yet not without its amenities: a washstand and tub of water, fireplace carved out of the wall, bucket of coal, framed mirror. Beside the door, a tottering rack of clothes and an upended grocer's basket cluttered with books (medical texts and religious tracts) and the refuse of quotidian life: apple cores, cheese rinds, loose tobacco, the stumps of deceased candles. Someone has painted a window on the far wall and framed it with a fluff of soiled yellow curtain.

"So — how are you feeling?" Quiddle hollers, edging into the room and making motions toward the low table at the foot of the bed.

Ned says nothing. He lies there, unshaven, hair matted, the red rope burn a reproof round his neck. His eyes stick out like swords.

Quiddle sets the tray down with a quick athletic motion and springs back a step or two, keeping his distance, wary, light on his feet. He folds his hands behind his back. "Heh-heh," he says. And then: "Listen, you do know where you are and all that, don't you? I mean, this isn't heaven or anything. You've been saved — you've lived through it. The hanging I mean." Quiddle looks down at his shoes. "What I mean is you're alive, man — alive as the King himself!" He ends with a burst of nervous laughter, as if he's just told a joke in a tavern.

Ned says nothing. He knows perfectly well what's happened. He's had nearly a day and a half to sort it out, savor it, run the emotional gamut from initial bewilderment to religious ecstasy to pure animal joy. Besides, he's been eavesdropping on the conversation in the hallway.

"Well, listen — if you don't feel like talking just yet . . ."

Ned's eyes are fixed on Quiddle's perspiring face. He has made an effort to keep from blinking since his benefactor stepped into the room. And it is an effort. Especially since he's starving. The smell of the beef broth or oxtail soup or whatever it is has been setting off a whole battery of involuntary responses: a hollow thumping in the pit of the stomach, pursing of the lips, a clenching of the salivary glands. But he's got to play this for all it's worth.

"I can understand," Quiddle says, backing toward the door. "It must be very hard for you. Just rest. You're all right now. We'll have you on your feet in a day or two and you can start life over, put it all behind you, make new associations, new — " His voice has become a whisper, soothing, motherly.

An instant later the door pulls shut and Ned falls on the tray like a pack of wolves.

◦§ §◦

For the next several days Ned is led round the hospital in a white smock, nodding at the sick and dying, laying hands on crippled children, patiently exposing himself to the astonished probing fingers of surgeons, physicians and students. His leg hurts like a son of a bitch and his neck feels twisted out of joint, but Quiddle has found him a bottle of laudanum and the barber has been in to scrape his cheeks and powder his hair. Ned knows what's expected of him. He limps round the corridors like a wounded seraph, the rope burn artfully concealed beneath a white cravat, a fervent messianic look in his eye. Whenever he's addressed he turns round and raises a sorrowful finger to his throat.

Quiddle's opinion is that the larynx has been crushed, while Delp insists that there is no evidence of physical damage whatever. After a painstaking examination of Ned's vocal apparatus, Abernathy is forced to concur with Delp, but suggests that the crux of the problem may be mental rather than physical. In support of his diagnosis he adduces the case of Lucy Minor. Some years back she had been brought to the hospital after an accident in which she was run down by a drunken coachman. The horses bore down on her; she stumbled. When the coach had passed, bystanders rushed to her aid and were astonished to see that she had escaped injury — miraculously the flying hoofs and churning wheels had run wide of her. She was helped to her feet, someone dusted her dress, she was given a glass of brandy — but when she turned to thank the man who'd helped her up, she found that she couldn't speak. Doctors were baffled. Abernathy himself tried every remedy he could think of, from leeches to hot poultices to binding the throat. He bled her until she blanched. Nothing. Now, twelve years later, Lucy Minor devotes most of her time to charity work with the deaf and dumb. No sound has passed her lips in all that time.

Dr. Maitland, who has been practicing at St. Bartholomew's for nearly half a century, admits Abernathy's point, but cites a glaring disparity between the two cases: the fact of constriction. "It's a simple question of blockage," he insists, "plain as the nose on your face. Purgatives is what the man needs. Give him a dose or two of croton oil, bleed him twice, and follow it up with an enema of antimony and foxglove." Runder, a strict Brunonian, has his own theory. "Clearly it's an asthenic disorder — treat the fellow with alcohol and he'll be jabbering like a myna inside of a week." Delp demurs. "He's a fraud I tell you. I say we let the other patients have a look at him and then boot him out in the street. Or better yet, send him back to the hangman." Finally, after a debate that consumes two dinner hours, three ribs of beef, eight capons, half a wheel of cheese and fifteen bottles of port, it is decided that Ned Rise's initial week will be extended to two, and that Abernathy will contact Mrs. Minor in order to have her instruct the patient in the science of communicating by signs. At the end of the two-week period, the patient will be removed from the premises.

Ned's reaction to all this is elemental. He sleeps in Quiddle's bed, eats Quiddle's food, drinks Quiddle's laudanum. He pours Maitland's croton oil down the hole in the outhouse, quaffs Runder's alcohol, spends two hours a day waving his fingers at an earnest Mrs. Minor, and scrupulously avoids Delp. He continues to wander about the halls, his eyes stricken, hair tastefully arranged, lips sealed. Of all the theories put forward to account for his affliction, he privately concurs with only one: Dr. Delp's.

Oh, he was hoarse for a day or two — who wouldn't be? He lay there in the dark, grinning, the words dropping off his tongue like bits of solder as he rehearsed the miracle of his resurrection and the fevered ecstatic version he would deliver to Fanny. In person. He would stride up the steps at Brooks' house, shove his way past the astonished butler and burst into the parlor, a ragged noose dangling from his neck. "I've come back from the grave to exact my vengeance, you pervert!" he'd shout, and bring Brooks to his knees with a single blow. Then he'd take Fanny in his arms, whisper that she shouldn't be frightened and then reveal the whole story. Brooks would be moved, write them a check, call a carriage, and off they'd go. Or something like that.

But for now Ned is lying low. Licking his wounds, getting his strength back, trying to grapple with the horror he's been through. Every time he closes his eyes it's there, pitiless, unrelenting — the gallows looming over him like some gigantic carnivorous insect, the snow sifting down like ash, the dead cold gaze of the hangman and the inescapable sense that the black hood conceals some nameless inhuman terror. Awake or asleep, it haunts him. He shudders and writhes on Quiddle's narrow pallet, the nightmare descending, noose poised, and then he starts up in a sweat thinking, What if they come for me again? What if Banks or Mendoza or Twit's sister gets word of it? Sinking, he can feel the whole nasty cycle beginning again, the wheel creeping round on him, exquisite torture, slow and redundant. He wants to shout out, screech till the walls shatter — but he doesn't. Silence is the key. Keep them guessing. Just a day or two more and the leg will be healed, a day or two more and —

The door cracks open. Quiddle. Sidling in with a tray: cold chicken, kidney pie, a mug of ale. But wait: this isn't Quiddle. It's someone taller, broader — who?

Decius William Delp stands over the bed, tray in hand. As he bends to set it down, Ned instinctively draws back. For a long moment the tray sits there between them, steam feebly rising from the meat pie. Delp's eyes are locked on Ned's. Ned looks away.

"Feeling better, I take it — huh, Sleeping Beauty?" Delp says finally. He is a big-boned man, very pale, with black hairs on the back of his hands. "Well — aren't you going to sample the offering for the day . . . Ned?"

Ned sits up as if he's been slapped. "How — ?"

Delp is smiling — a cold merciless sort of smile that digs deep into his face, flattens his ears and reveals his ravaged teeth. "Suddenly recovered the use of your tongue, have you? . . . Well, speak up, I can't hear you — Ned. Ned Rise, isn't it?"

Suddenly Ned is up and breaking for the door, but Delp takes hold of his arm and flings him back down as if he were a disobedient child. "I'm not finished yet, friend." The doctor pauses to light his pipe, the smoke squinting his eyes and riding up over his head like a hood. "I've been on to you from the beginning, you know. I'm no pushover like that ass Quiddle and the rest — I know you for what you are: a con man and a murderer. My first impulse was to toss you back to the hangman after the novelty wore off, but then another alternative occurred to me. It occurred to me that you've eat pretty well here, that you might even want to stick around, take a new name, lie low for awhile. Soft living and anonymity, eh?" Delp is pacing now — striding up and down in front of the door, head bent, pipe streaming. He looks like a bear in the pit just before they throw the dogs in. "I really see no reason why people like Sir Joseph Banks should need to know about your ah, recovery, do you?"

Ned is slouched against the wall, knees cocked under him. For the first time his eyes make contact with Delp's. His voice is weary with resignation. "All right," he says. "What do you want me to do?"

◄§ THINGS THAT GO BUMP IN THE NIGHT

The lights have winked out in the last cottage along the New Road, the sky is moonless and cold as a stone, roofs are white with frost, doors latched, the healthy, sane and wise snoring in their beds or nodding before the fire. Out on the highway the stillness is broken by the slow plod of a mare's hoofs and the barely perceptible snick-snick-snick of a rusted wheel. Ned Rise hunches in the bed of the creeping cart, huddled, muffled, gloved and hatted, while up front Quiddle keeps a numbed grip on the reins. Trails of vapor stream from their nostrils and their eyes water with the cold. The smell of the horse mingles with the faint acrid aroma of woodsmoke and the clean antiseptic bite of the air. Overhead, leafless trees claw at the sky.

Suddenly Quiddle pulls back on the reins and clucks softly to the horse, the wheels grab with a screech and the cart jerks to a halt beside the road. "This is it," he whispers, securing the reins and springing down from the cart.

Ned looks round him glumly. He can't make out much, objects drifting in and out of focus, murky, phantasmagoric, identifiable only as dense clots of darkness against an impenetrable backdrop. No more than a yard away is the black slash of a stone wall, the gray or white of individual stones aligned in a shifting ghostly grid. And there, beyond the wall, the silhouette of an enormous crippled yew snaking out into the night. The church steeple is invisible, black on black, a massive erasure in the corner of the sky. "I don't like it," Ned says.

"Shhhhhh, keep it down." Quiddle lifts a pair of shovels from the back of the cart and hoists himself to the top of the wall. "Come on," he whispers, "follow me."

◄§ ৡ►

After Delp left him that night, Ned lit a pipe and lay back on his pallet to sort things out. He'd kept his ears open around the hospital and knew that Delp needed cadavers badly — desperately even. The new term was starting, the other hospitals were in competition with him, his former source — Crump — had proved unreliable. And furthermore, society was against him — dissection was verboten, taboo, as unthinkable as cannibalism. If the afterlife was seen as corporeal as well as spiritual, how could a man enjoy his eternal bliss or suffer the torments of his damnation if he were in sixty-eight pieces? Accordingly, the public coffers provided for the interment of all those who expired in a given parish — vagrants, paupers and half-wits included. The only legal means of obtaining specimens was to visit the hangman and hope that one of his victims would go unclaimed by friends or relatives. All this, Ned realized, made Delp a very dangerous antagonist indeed. He was desperate. Manipulative, unscrupulous — and he held a knife to Ned's throat. All he need do was drop a word — a single word — and Ned would find himself back in prison, dangling from a rope, dead meat on the dissector's table.

When Delp came for his answer the following morning, Ned managed a smile and held out his hand. "I'll do your bodysnatching for three shillings a week," he said. Delp slapped the hand aside and pointed an admonitory finger at him. "You'll do it for two. Another word out of you and you'll do my bidding gratis, understand?" Ned understood. Of course, what he neglected to tell Delp was that he had no intention of doing anything whatever for him. He was merely buying time. As soon as his leg could take the strain he'd slip out and go to Fanny. She'd have something. And if she didn't he'd force it out of Brooks — God knows she had earned it. Then they'd disappear and Delp be hanged.

Unfortunately, there was a hitch in the plan.

Ned was up before dawn one morning, past the slumbering porter and out the door. Quiddle had given him a suit of ragged clothes, and the suppurating slash in his leg had transformed itself into a long thin scar the color of calf's liver. He made his way to Great George Street, slowly, painfully, the cold stiffening his leg, the thought of Fanny spurring him on. He pictured the expression on her face when she saw him there at the door, remembered the careful white precision of her teeth, the cool slip of her arms, the way she laughed and made it sound like a symphony. But as he turned into Great George Street, he felt that something was wrong. There was Brooks' house, imposing with its portico, Palladian windows and steep-pitched roof, but it looked closed up — as if — as if the occupants had gone out of town.

It couldn't be. Ned bolted across the street, the pain an irrelevance, clumsily leaped the palings and found himself in the still, leaf-spattered yard. There was no sound from the house, no sign of life. No servants, delivery boys, gardeners. Surreptitious, a shadow among shadows, he peered through the shutters and saw the furniture draped in cloth coverings, the dark squares on the walls where the pictures had once hung, the cold soot-blackened hearth. Later, out on the street, he made some casual inquiries. After a rebuff or two he came across a loquacious housemaid walking a pair of Gordon setters. "Oh yes," she said, "bless me if I can say wot's moved 'im to it, but Mr. Brooks 'as gone off to It'ly and Greece for a spell. At least that's 'ow the gossip 'as it."

Ned's stomach contracted. Hope was out of reach, he knew it, felt it slipping away like a leaf in a windstorm. The question was on his lips — Fanny, what of Fanny? — but he didn't know how to phrase it.

The maid was picking thoughtfully at a mole on her chin. "They say 'ee's took 'is trollop with 'im too . . . Oh don't look so mortified, goldilocks — it was common knowledge up and down the block. A scandal it was, a reg'lar scandal. Keepin' a woman and 'im a bachelor. Ha! I could tell you a thing or two about these society people, believe you me."

The dogs were pissing, sniffing, nosing one another in the rear. Ned became aware of a sudden chill in the air. He shuddered along the length of his body, as if the cold had stabbed him in the base of the spine, then turned and wandered off, the woman shouting something at his back. Up the block he found a sheltered spot to sit down and think it out. Fanny was gone. Indefinitely. Delp suddenly loomed in his mind. If Ned wasn't back at the hospital when the doctor walked through those doors there would be hell to pay. Literally. He'd turn the hounds loose in a second, the bastard. Then what?

Ned sat there, chilled through, watching the pigeons scrabble in the gutter. After awhile he picked himself up wearily and started down the street. For St. Bartholomew's.

ᕶᔥ ᔥᕶ

"Come on," Quiddle hisses, "let's get it over with." And then he disappears behind the wall, the brief sharp clatter of the shovels like a hole poked through the night.

Reluctantly, Ned slides out of the cart, flapping his arms to keep warm. There is the scent of freshly turned earth on the air, and something else too — something like the smell of wet leaves or earthworms drowned in a rainstorm. The absolute blackness of the night is appalling. Ned shuffles around a minute, squinting into the gloom and fighting an impulse to whistle. The skin around his eyes and ears seems to have shrunk, tugging back at his hairline as if it were elastic. Good God, he thinks, and then he's up and over the wall.

There had been a funeral in the Islington churchyard earlier that day. A family of four. Murder/suicide. In despair over a life of rags and potatoes, the Mrs. had seasoned her spouse's porridge with arsenic trioxide and then smothered the children as they lay sleeping on their shuck mattresses. She kept a vigil over the bodies until dawn, and then forced the blade of a wood saw over her wrists, time and again, until she lay down beside them and bled to death. Delp had read about it in the morning paper.

If anything, it's even darker on the far side of the wall. What now? Ned wonders, when Quiddle's voice suddenly leaps out of the void at him — "Pssst: over here" — and he finds himself diving for the shrubbery, rattled to the bone, a stray branch whipping at his face, the crush of dead weed, and then that terrible stillness again. Lying there in the dark, feeling foolish, he begins to feel more strongly than ever that there are better ways of spending a cold winter's night. His inner eye briefly flashes on white arms, sleeping dogs, mugs of ale and wild leaping extravagant fires. But to the business at hand: slowly, cautiously, as if a thousand eyes were on him, he rises to his feet and is startled half out of his wits by the shovel thrust into his hands. "Knock off your fooling and let's get on with it," Quiddle rasps, and then they're moving, Ned concentrating on the vague glint of baldness at the back of Quiddle's head as they make their way between pale headstones and looming dark monuments, crucified Christs and wingspread angels of death.

"Horace," Ned whispers, "this is ridiculous. It's ghoulish, unchristian, against all the laws of God and man. Couldn't we tell Delp we got lost and never found the place?"

The bald spot moves on, dipping here, bobbing there. Quiddle's only response is a sort of chuckle, so low and throaty it would frighten a hyena.

Then all at once they're stopping, Quiddle down on one knee it seems, scratching about in the half-frozen earth. "This is it," he says, his voice wrestling with nerves, susurrus and a tendency to crack into falsetto. "Try not to make too much noise with the shovel."

Ned tries not to. He gingerly slips the spade into the pool of blackness at his feet, feeling for soft earth. Quiddle is beside him, shoveling stealthily — Ned can hear the whisper and whine of his shovel and the accelerated chuff-chuff-chuff of his breathing. They work in silence for a long while, dipping deeper for their loads, Quiddle periodically kneeling to strike a match and check their progress. Finally, with a dull thud, Ned's shovel makes contact with something solid. "That'll be it," Quiddle whispers, digging harder now, sweeping along the length of the coffin with the edge of his shovel.

Ned has stopped digging. At the first touch of metal and wood an involuntary shudder galvanized his body, as if the handle of the spade were a lightning rod and the rough planks charged with electricity. He stands there, looking into nothing, temples pounding, throat dry, listening to Quiddle's knife as it pries at the lid of the coffin, thinking what next, what next, and waiting with a dumb stricken revulsion for his companion to light the next match. He can see them already, the poisoned husband, the smothered children, the mutilated wife sitting up in her bloody shroud and shrieking out with a wild desperate laugh.

But wait: is he hearing things? A rustling in the bushes at the base of the wall? Muffled footsteps? The walking dead? "Horace: what was that?"

Quiddle, breathing hard, forces back the lid of the coffin, wood splintering with a groan of protest: eeeeeeee. "What was what?"

"That sound. Out there."

Quiddle pauses, the bald spot motionless in the dark. A profound silence settles over the churchyard. Nothing moves. It is as still and dark and bleak as the back side of the moon. "Listen," Quiddle says finally, "you keep it up and we'll both be in a state. Now get on down here and give me a hand with this stiff."

Ned drops the shovel with a clatter and eases down at the edge of the pit, feeling his way gingerly, catching his breath in case there's an odor, his whole body revolting against the task at hand. Quiddle has propped the corpse up, stiff as a log, and is struggling to maneuver it toward Ned when suddenly a great crashing weight descends on Ned from the rear and impels him face forward into the coffin. Quiddle sprawls, the corpse totters, Ned cries out and the presence at his back — it is warm, possessed of arms and legs — grunts like a rooting pig. And then all at once a blinding light is shining in their faces and a voice snarling: "That's royt: dig away, Quiddle. It'll spare me the effort."

Dirk Crump is standing over the pit, a lantern in one hand, pistol in the other. His accomplice is atop Ned, Ned is atop Quiddle, and Quiddle is wedged into the corner with the cadaver. As if in protest, the corpse's hand is thrust straight out of its shroud, the raw ragged gashes slanting across the wrist, flesh gone gray, nails battered and black. "All royt Billy, ye've done well," Crump says, " — come out of it now."

It is then that Ned gets his first look at the accomplice and realizes with a start that he's staring into the pale green unbelieving eyes of Billy Boyles. "Billy?" he says. But Boyles is backing away from him, his face working, eyes collapsed in on themselves with terror and disbelief. Then his mouth opens, a hole black as the night. "Run!" he shrieks, alternately clawing at the edge of the coffin and blessing himself, Ned reaching out to pacify him and Boyles screaming again, his voice pinched and raw with terror, the voice of spitted babes and animals skinned alive. Crump drops the lamp in shock and bewilderment, light dashing out on the ground in a spray of hot oil and the quick inevitable night rushing in to swallow it. There is the sound of scrambling, hands and feet tearing at the earth, Crump shouting out an obscenity and then Boyles' traumatized shriek again: "Run for God's sake, run — it's a haunt!"

The snarl of the pistol is almost anticlimactic.

◆§ WORDS

Sir Joseph Banks, at fifty-five, is a hub of power and influence. President of the Royal Society for the past twenty years, Honorary Director of the Royal Botanic Gardens, Knight Commander of the Bath and member of the Privy Council, he is the doyen of the British scientific community, a distinguished botanist whose collection ranks among the best in Europe, founding member of the African Association, former explorer and eponym of a number of South Pacific landmarks, the man to whom the government turns for consultation on nearly every scientific matter, from the most effective way of preserving breadfruit on the H.M.S. *Bounty* to the disposition of explorers in the Tropics.

Though born to wealth and privilege, it was in the role of explorer that he first caught the public eye. In the late sixties and early seventies he circumnavigated the globe with Captain Cook, and was so successful in promoting his own role in the expedition that he was named President of the Royal Society shortly thereafter. He is self-righteous and proper, autocratic, insatiably curious, a manipulator, collector, seedsman, hobnobber, pacesetter, publicity hound — but above all else an explorer grown too old for exploring. And so, like the ex-athlete turned to coaching, he is mentor to his geographical missionaries. He is a man of taste, refinement and connection, a man of dedication and perseverance, a man who can make the entire country sit up and listen. At the moment, however, it is all he can do to keep from shouting.

"What's this I hear from Edwards?" he says, each word cutting like a sword. He is sitting at the head of the big conference table in his study, shoulders hunched, chin jutting forward, looking for all the world like a bulldog straining at an invisible leash.

"Sir?" Mungo is flushed to the ears. He looks up quickly and then drops his gaze to the glass of claret in his hand.

"Don't play games with me, boy — you know damned well what I'm talking about."

"If you mean the Baroness — "

"The Baroness," Sir Joseph mocks, hanging on each syllable as if it were smeared with excrement. "The woman's a disgrace. She's an immoralist, a vampire."

Mungo looks up as if he's been slapped. "You're not being fair — she has her good points."

"A pair of boobs, Mungo, a pair of boobs. That's all." He holds up a palm to forestall any further argument. "I'm not going to debate the subject. I want you to stay away from her. Period. You're not just some hick from the Borderlands anymore, son — you're a celebrity, you've got a position to maintain. And I'll be damned if one of my geographical missionaries is going to run around town like some lower primate with an itch in his testicles.

"You've been at it for two weeks now — to the detriment of your work on the book, so Mr. Edwards tells me." Banks' expression softens a bit. "We have subscribers to account to, Mungo. The good people who put up the money to buy you this glory that's gone so quickly to your head. Isn't it about time you sat down and repaid them?"

He pushes himself up from the table and shuffles over to the sideboard to refill his glass. Then adds, almost as an afterthought, "After all, it's only words they want."

❧ ❧

Words. They haunt him night and day, through his rewrite sessions with Edwards, through breakfast, tea and dinner, words masticated over plaice and fowl, lucubrated at the hour of the wolf, pried from the recesses of his memory like bits of hardened molding . . . words that fight one another like instruments out of tune, arhythmic, cacophonic, words that snarl sentences and tangle thoughts until he flings the pen down in rage and despair. He never imagined the book would be such drudgery. After the stark physical challenge of Africa and the heady swirl of celebrity, the last thing he wants is to sit at a desk and push words around like a professional scrabble player.

Of course he does have Edwards. Bryan Edwards, Secretary of the African Association, has been looking out for him at Sir Joseph's request. Precise, logical and thorough, he is constantly at the explorer's side, coaching, cajoling, editing, sometimes sleeping the night on a cot in the spare room (Mungo has taken lodgings in London at the Association's insistence and expense). And yet, no matter how eager and helpful his amanuensis is, Mungo still can't seem to get himself out of bed in the morning. Every cell of his body resists it. He lies there, feeling hollowed out, a husk, drained and sucked dry. It's an old but familiar feeling, the terrible devastating Weltschmerz of the boy who wakes with the knowledge that he hasn't finished his Latin assignment.

One afternoon, the weak winter sun spilling into the room like milk, he turns to Edwards and bares his teeth. "I've had it," he says, pushing back the chair and leaping up to pace round the room. "I don't give a damn if they strip away my salary and boot me out into the street, I can't write another word."

Edwards is sitting at a table heaped with an accumulation of torn and yellowed scraps of paper that could only have come from an overturned wastebasket. He is wearing spectacles, and has the thin-lipped, watery-eyed look of the scrivener. At the moment he is sifting through this heap of crumpled paper — Mungo's original hat-sequestered notes — looking for a reference to Tiggitty Sego's cousin's wife that Mungo insists is there.

"I tell you," the explorer shouts, "I'd rather be tortured by the Moors again, flayed with whips and scourges and shackled face down in my own vomit, than have to spend the rest of the evening here like some damned copyboy."

Edwards peers over the spectacles and fixes him with a wet, bloodshot eye. "May as well resign yourself, old man, you're a celebrity now and you've got public responsibilities. You know as well as I do that great discoveries are as much a product of a good warm study as they are of deserts and jungles. Besides," pulling a pocketwatch from his waistcoat, "we'll knock off for tea in an hour or so."

At that moment there is a rap at the door. The servant enters with a card on a tray. "The Baroness von Kalibzo."

Edwards blanches at the name. The explorer, on the other hand, begins to breathe more rapidly, and his face undergoes a telling transformation — pupils receding, nostrils dilating, a muscle twitching at the base of his jaw — until he looks like a demented stallion sniffing out a mare in estrus.

Suddenly Edwards is at the door. He takes hold of the servant's elbow for emphasis and announces in a clear authoritative tone that Mr. Park is not at home.

"Not at home? This is — this is too much, Bryan. The lady's a friend of mine, and — and an aristocrat." Mungo is standing beside his collaborator now, panting a bit, his face reddening. The servant stares at the floor. "Do you know what you're asking?"

Edwards looks him in the eye, corporation man to the core. "I'm not asking." Then he turns back to the servant. "You are to inform the lady that Mr. Park is not at home."

The door closes with a soft click and the explorer stands there a moment, hands at his sides, studying the flat dull grain of the wood. He looks up at Edwards, who has moved a step closer to the door as if to block it, then strides across the room, flings himself down at the desk, and begins scratching away at the sheet before him with the desperate manic ferocity of the damned.

❧ ❧

And so it goes, week after week, month after month, invitations refused, lectures declined, friends and relatives snubbed. Mungo has become a prisoner to pen and ink, his fingers blotched like a leper's, face pale, spine curved until it looks like an odd piece of punctuation. Day after day he stares at the page before him, eyes watering, progress testudineous, thinking he should never have left Selkirk, never challenged his place in life, never set foot in Africa. The man of action reduced to the man of recollection like some chatty doddering old veteran of foreign wars. It's disgusting. Not at all what he'd thought it would be. A book. It's a thing on a shelf, complete, ordered, rational — not an ongoing ache and deprivation. After walking nearly fifteen hundred miles he barely stretches his legs anymore. The only time he leaves his desk is to take his daily constitutional — with Edwards at his side, of course — or to make the occasional public appearance under Sir Joseph's aegis. And when he bridles, Edwards is always there to remind him of his duty.

The target date is June. That's when they'll have the shortened version done and he'll be free to visit Selkirk — and Ailie. Ailie. She looms in his mind like an island in the sea, an oasis in the desert. She is love and life and moral goodness, a buffer against the long African night and the seductive whirlpool of celebrity. How could he have forgotten her? The thought haunts him as he suffers through his London captivity, slave to the desk, the page, the word. Her letters have been increasingly cold and distant, his less frequent than they might be (after sifting through a jumble of words day and night, who has time for letters?). He knows he has hurt and offended her, duty before pleasure and all that, and he burns with a secret shame over his dalliance with the Baroness. He feels like a dog, some loping beast of dark desire and rutting instincts, some jism-addled hyena running with the pack. But then, insidious, the image of the Baroness cuts through his thoughts like a whiff of Eros, her breasts and bush, the hair under her arms, legs spread wide. The Baroness with Ailie's face, Ailie with the Baroness's face — can he even remember what Ailie looks like?

It's an agony. But an agony that must end, will end — is ending, page by page. He looks up from his work, the fantasy playing before him, Ailie at the door of her father's house, a stirring in his trousers, taking her now out into the garden, flowers and the scent of lilac . . . but then it all dissolves and he's gazing down at the sheet before him, letters coming into focus, dotted *i*'s and slithering *s*'s, words running across the page like troops, forming ranks, recalcitrant and hostile, boxing him in, staring him down, defeating him.

∽§ THE HOMECOMING

The London coach, on the last leg of its journey to Edinburgh, rattles into Selkirk at 4:00 P.M., in a vortex of swirling leaves, dust and hair. Flowers flash beside gates and walls, sheep step out of the way and gaze up with their stupid baffled sheep faces, moths and butterflies scatter like confetti, an ancient dog lifts his head and then slaps it back down in the dirt, volitionless. For a moment everything is still, as if held in suspension. The sun hangs overhead like a lantern, the essence of new grass and apple blossom narcotizes the air, the clack and whir of the wheels have a quelling, hypnotic effect on the passengers.

Mungo breathes deep, craning his neck to peer out the window over the accumulated bulk of an Edinburgh-bound matron and her antediluvian but robust mother. What he sees, in snatches, is endlessly fascinating. Three and a half years of change, both subtle and arresting — cracks in foundations, new walls and hayricks, hedges trimmed back from the road, a barn charred by fire. He leans farther, mesmerized, nostalgia sweeping him up as each landmark leaps out at him like a silent benediction — the old Hogg place set in a clump of birch, alderman's gate, the Russells' pea patch — his eyes gone soft with it all, leaning and looking until he's literally hanging over matron and mother like some sort of molester. "I say there, what's the matter with you? You, Sir — back off or I'll holler out to the coachman." Three and a half years.

The mood carries him into town, houses glancing by as if in a dream, trellises hung with ivy, the MacInnes girl bent over the well in a sunburst of daffodil and tulip, bees humming, cats napping, everything as orderly and serene as a page out of Oliver Goldsmith. But then a mongrel bitch with a strange stiff mane darts out of an open gate and throws herself at the wheels in a paroxysm of ferocity, yabbering at the coach as if it were packed with raw meat. The driver cracks his whip at the animal and she backs off, whimpering, but already the coach is going too fast, horses spooked, pedestrians shouting, disaster in the air. The accident is abrupt as a scissor cut: the coach veers close to a man on horseback, the horse shies, the rider is thrown. Two hundred feet up the street, nearly in the dead center of the village square, the coachman gets his team under control and brings the vehicle to a halt.

The first on the scene are smudge-faced boys, a horde of them, running with abandon, converging like flies on a shattered cider jug. Next the passersby, and shopkeepers, then just about everyone within earshot — crofters, wetnurses, sweeps and charwomen, cobblers, flaneurs, the Reverend MacNibbit. It seems that the rider — an old man in kilt and tam o'shanter — has been flung into the middle of a cart full of trout and salmon wrapped in wet leaves. The fishmonger is beside himself with shock and grief, the old man in tartans is cursing like a professional, and the fishmonger's wife has begun a high-pitched tirade against exorbitant taxes, the price of coal and the Presbyterian Church. There is a moment of confusion punctuated by angry shouts and catcalls, and then a bearded man catches the horse by the bridle and calms it, while another helps the old man from the fishcart. Someone laughs. Willie Baillie, drunk as usual, declaims a few snatches of a dirty limerick. And then, inevitably, someone spots Mungo.

It is old Cranstoun, his face raptured and keen, hurrying along the street with his cane, straining forward to get some sense of what all the commotion is about. He bobs past the stalled coach in a sort of three-legged canter, but then suddenly pulls up stock-still and turns to gawk at the vehicle as if he's just seen an apparition. For a long moment he just stands there, the milky old eyes taking in the matron, her voluminous mother and the tall fair-haired hero peering out the window behind them. Slowly, degree by degree, the old man's expression works itself round from surprise to elation, and then he's hustling for the door of the coach, all the while bellowing like some sort of mental defective with his hair set afire: "Be gad if it isn't the explorer! It's Mungo! Mungo Park come home to his people!"

Mungo had hoped to slip into town as inconspicuously as possible. He hadn't written Ailie for a month. No one knew he was coming. His plan, impulsively formulated, was to surprise her. The work on the abridged version of *Travels in the Interior Districts of Africa* had finally been completed — after a period of protracted torture that seemed Alighierian in its proportions — and he was free to spend the next several months in Scotland, relaxing, fishing, preparing the final version of the book, making love. He was particularly enthusiastic about this last prospect. Since he'd seen the error of his ways and given up the Baroness, his passion for Ailie had grown hotter and hotter. So hot in fact that he'd had trouble sleeping through the misty London nights. Spring came and went. Edwards badgered him. Sir Joseph ruled him with an iron hand. Then it was June. The abstract was finished on schedule and he was on his way to Scotland to lighten his fiancée's heart.

But life isn't always so simple.

For one thing, the crowd gathers round the coach so precipitously you'd think old Cranstoun had yelled: "Guineas! Fresh-minted guineas, free for the taking!" For another, the look in their eyes says that they're not about to let Mungo off with anything less than a full-scale celebration and the good, rousing, whisky-washed, old-time hullabaloo the occasion demands. There is rapture on every face. Wondering hands reach out for the explorer, the matron and her mother look puzzled and offended, old Cranstoun stands at the open door like a footman. "Huzza!" shouts the crowd as a geyser of hats and wigs shoots high into the air, and now Jamie Hume is leading them in "For He's a Jolly Good Fellow" and Nat Cubbie is calling for a speech.

Mungo steps down from the coach to a roar of applause. He looks every inch the martyred hero, sallow, still a bit gaunt, the imprint of suffering and the indomitable will to conquer etched into his face. If anything, the past few months at his desk have taken more out of him than all the hopeless disease-ridden months of privation in Africa. But who's to know that? All the crowd sees is their darling, grinning shyly, one of the greatest men Selkirkshire has ever produced, discoverer of the Niger, conqueror of Africa, why they watched him grow up! "Mungo!" they howl. And: "Speech!"

The explorer raises his hands on a roar and brings them down to a hush of expectation. There must be three hundred people in the street and more coming. Old friends, faces he grew up with. Finn Macpherson in a cobbler's apron, grinning as if he's just been named next in line for the Crown, Mistress Tullochgorm, Robbie Monboddo in a cleric's collar, Georgie Scott. He doesn't want to give a speech. He wants to burst in on Ailie, sweep her up in his arms. He wants to hike up to Fowlshiels and show his mother what her son has made of himself. But here are all these expectant faces looking up at him as if he could change water to wine or raise the dead or something. "All right," he shouts, and then in a lower voice: "I'll do my best."

Immediately a call goes up from the rear of the press. "Speak up, lad: we canna hear ye."

"I said that I'll say a few words," the explorer shouts, already at a loss for what to say next. A hush falls over the crowd. The explorer can hear the hurried footsteps of the latecomers, stifled shouts, doors slamming in the distance. "I — I'm glad to be back home at Selkirk" — a cheer goes up — "among my friends, and I — "

"Tell us about the black nigger cannibals!" someone shouts.

"Aye!" adds another. "Did they torture ye?"

"Cattul!" a powerful voice peals. "Wot sort o' cattul has they got over there?"

" — I really hadn't intended to make a speech," Mungo stammers to a renewed roar, beginning to feel as if he were running for office, ". . . you see I'd been meaning to come in quiet like so as to see my loved ones first . . ."

"Hoooo! He's a hot-blooded mon, all right!"

"It's Ailie he'll be wantin' to see, no mistaking."

The hoi polloi take up the refrain, joyous, mindless, pullulating with excitement — "Ailie! Ailie! Ailie!" — and the next moment the explorer is swept up on their shoulders and carted off in triumph. Through the square and down the street, the crowd swelling, dogs barking, someone strangling a set of pipes and another beating a snare drum. And all the while the crowd chanting "Ailie! Ailie! Ailie!"

Before he can resist or even fully comprehend what's happening, he finds himself set down before the gate at Dr. Anderson's house, his bags at his feet, fifty or sixty people cheering at his back. Suddenly the front door swings open and there she is, Ailie, in a bonnet and housedress, sleeves rolled up, staring out in bewilderment at the brouhaha in her front yard. The crowd lets loose at the sight of her, surging toward an emotional orgasm, some primitive hysterical sense of completion demanding that they join the two principals. Arms are raised, the cheers are deafening, the pipes turn to a strathspey and a whole section of the crowd launches into a mad jig.

The gate has been unlatched. There's an arm on Mungo's shoulder, someone gives him a gentle nudge and then he's walking up the path toward her, the cheers like waves breaking on a beach, Ailie tiny, silken-haired, her lips and eyes beckoning like the promise of water at the far end of an expanse of desert. Three and a half years, all those nights of scorching need and seductive dream, his feet on the front steps, something else in her eyes now, some amalgam of recognition, hurt and surprise, something proud and belligerent in the face of the crowd. "Ailie," he whispers, at the summit of the steps, his arms spread wide.

"Take her up in yer arms, lad!"

"Kiss her!"

The noise is tumultuous, apocalyptic.

He looks into her eyes. They say no. They say I've waited too long. They say Penelope be damned.

She shuts the door in his face.

◄ THE LONG ARM

He gets drunk that first night back. Stinking, puking drunk. Somebody has to send up to Fowlshiels for his brother Adam to come on down and take him home. The next morning he wakes in the back room of his boyhood home in a welter of younger brothers and sisters. He has a violent headache. His bones feel hollow. He thinks of Ailie and feels sick. Suddenly the door bursts open and his mother swoops into the room and buries herself in his arms, crying over him as if he were a corpse. His brother stands in the doorway, a short, dark-haired figure beside him. For one wild moment he thinks it's Ailie — Ailie softened by a night's reflection, Ailie come back to him. It is Zander.

After a breakfast of milk brose, bannocks, fried eggs and rashers, fresh-baked bread, finnan haddie, potatoes, onions, small beer and tea (his mother thought he was looking peaked), he trundles his way down to the river with Zander and settles himself in the long grass opposite Newark Castle. It is warm. The sun hits the river with a slap before it is filtered to softness in the trees. A grasshopper balances on every blade of grass, a butterfly on every flower. Mungo plucks a heather leaf and chews it. After awhile he turns to Zander. They've been talking village gossip — who'd married whom, who'd died, got rich, went off to fight the French. Neither has mentioned Africa, or Ailie. "So she thinks I've deserted her?"

Zander is sifting pebbles through his fingers. He answers without looking up. "She does. She went through an awful lot when you were lost in Africa and nobody'd heard from you — a hell of an awful lot. But then when you came back to London and never made it up to see her . . . well, she felt you didn't care."

"But I had no choice in the matter — surely she can see that?"

"She's not a man, Mungo. What does she know of duty and commitment? But listen, give her time — she'll come around. She loves you."

The explorer looks up glumly at the ruined walls of the castle. He knows every chink and crevice. As boys, he and Adam refought the Border Wars there, capturing the battlements, putting the invisible enemy to flight, dreaming dreams of glory. "I went through alot too, Zander. Death and disease, starvation, imprisonment. I watched my guide die before my eyes and I was powerless to do a thing."

"We know it, Mungo. And it's only natural you should have a period of readjustment. But she told me if you want her you've got to start at the beginning."

"Court her all over again?"

Zander nods. Then he turns to the explorer, his face suddenly animated. "But listen. Tell me what it was like over there."

❦ ❧

That afternoon, head splitting, throat dry and stomach broiling with acid, the explorer again mounts the front steps of the Anderson house. He is wearing a freshly starched cravat and a new sergdusoy jacket, his boots are polished and he carries a clumsily wrapped package under his arm. A maid in apron and clogs answers his knock and shows him in. She must be new, he is thinking, when Douce Davie comes bounding up the hallway. The explorer goes down on one knee and holds his hand out. "Here Davie," he calls, clucking his tongue, "good boy." The dog pulls up short, inhales a snarl or two and shows his teeth. Slam, the maid is gone. Mungo rises awkwardly. The dog begins to bark.

There is the sound of hurried footsteps, then a door opening at the far end of the hallway. It is Dr. Anderson, big, wide-nostriled, a new beard appended to his face like some lush species of aquatic growth. He wraps his arms around the explorer like a lover and presses him to his body. "Mungo!" he whispers, his voice·quavering, "ye've come back to us then."

The explorer is embarrassed. When the doctor loosens his grip, Mungo backs off a pace and nods his head. "Aye," he mumbles. This sets off a renewed paroxysm of hugging, patting and hand pumping on the doctor's part, while the terrier paws at the explorer's legs, yipping in protest. Mungo feels as if he's just taken the ball downfield and drilled the winning goal into the net. "Well, well," the doctor booms, "step into the parlor and let's have a look at ye."

Mungo follows him into the familiar room, a wave of warmth and nostalgia washing over him, and then stops short. What is this? The walls are cluttered with odd black-and-white drawings — squares and rectangles in a beehive arrangement, oblate spheroids, circles within circles — drawings that approach a crude geometry, as if the artist has intended something that falls midway between the aesthetically pleasing and the mathematically precise. Then he notices the cherrywood desk in the corner. A new Cuff microscope stands in its center, gleaming like an icon. Mungo is about to ask his old friend and mentor if he's taken up microscopy when the doctor turns to hand him a glass of claret. "Bon santé!" he barks, "and me hearty congratulations. Ye've brung fame and glory to Selkirkshire and I'm damned proud of ye for it."

And then the doctor is off, flitting round the room, refilling the glasses, offering cigars, oatcakes, kippered herring, jars of preserves, jerking books from the shelves and all the while jabbering about a case of impetigo he's been treating in an Abbotsford lady. "Horseradish!" he shouts. "Five parts. Put that against two parts menstrual blood and three parts bezoar stone and the sores'll disappear as if ye'd touched 'em with a wand. Blast homeotherapy. I say stick with the tried and true." The doctor pauses and turns round to look at the explorer as if he were seeing him for the first time. "But I guess ye've heard enough out of me. It's me daughter ye've come about, isn't it?"

Mungo takes the doctor's hand. "I want to marry her."

"Marry her?" Dr. Anderson shouts. "Of course ye want to marry her. Did ye not ask the gull to wait for ye while ye was off riskin' life and limb amongst the niggers and Hottentots? And don't ye call that an engagement — even if ye never give her no ring?"

"I — I've got a ring right — " the explorer stammers, fumbling through his pockets, "right — "

"And don't an engagement mean a holy troth to be married before the eyes of the Laird and man?" Somehow the doctor has worked himself up into a sort of stentorian rage. His last words echo through the room like the voice of judgment, setting up sympathetic vibrations in the glassware on the shelves.

The explorer is no less puzzled at the excess of emotion than at the line of questioning. "Well, yes — "

"Ye're deuced right, lad," the doctors bawls, red to the eyes. "Marry her then," he roars, then lowers his voice abruptly — is he winking or is there something caught in his eye? — "but treat her right, lad, treat her right." And then he's gone, the door engaging the frame like distant thunder.

◆§ ॐ◆

Ten minutes later the door swings open with a whisper. The explorer has been sitting in the big armchair by the window trying to make sense of the esoteric drawings that paper the walls. Is it some new craze of Zander's? he wonders, when the soft click of the latch strikes at his nervous system like a sudden ferment of churchbells. He leaps up from the chair as Ailie slips into the room and gently closes the door behind her. He doesn't know what to say. Awkward, harried by his emotions, his confidence shattered by yesterday's debacle, he can only gape at her.

She too is silent. But her lower lip is unsteady and her eyes are gorged with green, the pupils drawn in on themselves, pinpoints, hard and cold with resentment, determination, anger. Aside from those eyes and lips and the turned-up nose, he hardly recognizes her. She's been transformed. The country girl in a white cotton dress and clogs is standing before him looking like a London socialite, turned out à la mode in a free-flowing gown of English velvet with gold brocade scrawled across the bodice, the velvet a shade of green so rich and dark it could carpet a forest floor. Her clipped black hair is swept back beneath a matching green cap, her face is powdered, feet elegantly slippered. Perched on her forearm, as cool and gray as rainclouds, are the turtle doves.

"Well," she says finally, "father says you wanted to see me."

"I did. I do," he answers, starting toward her and then hesitating, the package held out before him like an offering. "I want — " he begins, the words marshaling themselves at the tip of his tongue, words to express simple emotions and expectations, love, marriage, family — but something interferes, some sudden and stunning mindblock, a function of his debilitated condition, the night of drinking, nerves at a pitch, the quick rise from the chair. He'd had six or seven attacks while in London, the malarial curse reaching a long arm from the coast of Africa to muddle his thoughts and rock his knees. Once he'd lost his train of thought while addressing the Ladies' Equestrian and Geopolitical Society of Chelsea, and Sir Joseph had had to step in and finish for him. Another time he blacked out at the Baroness' after a single glass of champagne. Now he inexplicably finds himself on his knees, a good twenty feet from Ailie, wondering what he was about to say.

"Yes?" she prompts, her face softening in anticipation.

"I uh . . . uh . . . I . . ."

"Yes?" She moves a step or two closer, alarmed at the expression on her lover's face — has she been too hard on him? "Is it the package you want to give me?" she whispers, as if talking to a child. "Is the package for me?"

Mungo shakes his head to clear it, down on all fours now like a dog come in from the rain. He looks down at the package as if he's never seen it before. "I want . . . want . . . uh . . . I want to . . . uh . . ."

Good God, what have they done to him? Mortified, she drops her arm and the startled doves take wing, careening into the walls, flapping against the ceiling in a panic . . . and then she's on the floor beside him, cupping his face in her hands and trying desperately to make sense of his eyes. "Mungo? Mungo: are you all right?"

He turns his head to kiss her hand and then stretches out prone on the floor, the package at his side. "Uh-uh-uh-uh," he says, and suddenly she's on her feet and out the door shouting for her father.

An instant later Dr. Anderson bursts into the room, white-faced, the new apprentice at his side. "Quick boy: salts! And bring me my bag — we're going to have to bleed him!"

The salts bring the explorer around — enough so that doctor and assistant can prop him up in the chair and make an incision in his forearm. Ailie is there, equal to the occasion, gritting her teeth and holding the gleaming porcelain bowl while her fiancé's blood runs fresh and wet between her hands and leaps to spatter her dress. The apprentice, a boy of sixteen with a wandering eye, turns his head and then excuses himself to vomit in the fireplace while the old man thunders and the doves coo from the mantel.

◄§ §►

Later, much later, Ailie stands before the mirror in her room, unfastening her earrings, releasing the clasp of her necklace. It is past three in the morning. Mungo is sleeping soundly in the guest room, a bit pale from loss of blood and running a slight fever, but over the worst of it. She and

Zander have been sitting up with him through the night. When she left for bed Zander was nodding in a straight-backed chair, a glass of brandy jammed between his legs.

She pulls the dress up over her head and lays it across the bed, smoothing back the creases. The blood has dried black against the green, hardly noticeable, and yet she runs her hand over the spatters thinking how stubborn they are and at the same time wondering what they'd look like under the microscope. She pictures herself by the window, pinning down a section of the dress and screwing it into focus, a patch of something organic freckling the material, fibers that clot and draw a wound together like fingers, fibers inextricably bound up in the calculated weave of the fabric. Dried blood. Frangible, no more than dust — and yet the stain will persist through half a dozen washings.

On the edge of the bed now, in her underthings, she waits a long tired moment before reaching to remove her shoes and stockings. She's exhausted and exhilarated, empty and fulfilled. No more games, no more waiting. She'd been acting like a schoolgirl. Her man is back, and he needs her — that's all that matters. The shoes drop to the floor, first the left, then the right, when suddenly the package on the dressing table catches her attention. Bulky, crudely wrapped. He'd been trying to give it to her when the attack came on. Something from London?

Moths bat round the oil lamp. A cricket rubs its legs together somewhere in the far corner of the room. Outside, beyond the lace curtains, a thousand others respond until the night crepitates with an airy whistling cacophony that sounds like an army of babies shaking their rattles. Ailie gets up from the bed, arms and legs bare, glides to the dressing table and hefts the package in one hand. Heavy. Solid. What an odd shape. She wants to tear it open, but no, she can't do that — Mungo would want to see her surprise. Resolute, she sets it down again. And begins unlacing her stays. A moment later she slips out of the corset, drops her underthings to the floor, and is about to start for the wardrobe when the package again catches her eye. She lifts it a second time, puzzling, and then — before she can think — she's shredding the paper with her nails.

Now she's even more puzzled.

It seems to be some sort of carving — wood or stone. She turns it over in her hands. Smooth, black. So black it seems to drink in light and swallow it. At first she can make no sense of the thing, but then as she traces the thickly carved lines it comes to her: a woman. Ponderous, disproportionate, her head the size of an acorn, sagging dugs, abdomen and nates distended to cruelly absurd proportions. She looks closer. The woman's feet are like trees, each toe a bole. And what's this? Tortuous, secretive, black on black, a snake winds its way up her leg.

Ailie stares down at the figurine for a long while, lost in the pure rich glossy blackness of it, and then she begins to shiver. A night breeze lifts the curtains. Naked, she sets it down on the table and moves for the wardrobe and her nightgown. Outside the crickets stir.

◆§ CHILD OF THE CENTURY

In the summer of 1799, while Napoleon was slipping out of Egypt and Nelson was embroiled in Italian politics, Ailie Anderson changed her surname to Park. Less than a year later — in June of 1800 — her first child was born. Dr. Dinwoodie performed the delivery, her father and Mungo sharing a nervous pint of whisky in the front room. It was a boy. So big he nearly split her in two. They named him Thomas.

Mungo held the infant in his arm, the eyes yellow with mucus, fingers creased and reddened as if they'd washed ten thousand dishes, the head a slick bulb of vein and tissue. Ailie's father proposed a toast. "To the child of the century!"

Ailie couldn't quite believe the whole thing. After all those years of fear and uncertainty, all the interminable days and weeks and months of waiting, he was back. Less than two years after he'd appeared on her front porch, all but a stranger, she was Mrs. Mungo Park, mother of his child. Each morning she woke beside him, each night sat down with him to supper. He was hers. She was absorbed with the thought of it, saturated to the very tips of her fingers with pride and satisfaction. The microscope gathered dust.

Of course, they had had their problems.

The first year after his return had been an admixture of hope and disillusionment, in equal parts. For six months Mungo lived at Fowlshiels, working on his book from morning till late in the afternoon. Then he would ride into Selkirk and spend the evening with her. They strolled along the river and watched the leaves spin down from the trees, rode out to visit Katlin Gibbie and danced a strathspey in her parlor, built a fire in the woods and roasted salmon on a spit. They grew to know one another again. It was like it once was.

But then the pull of Africa exerted its influence yet again. At Christmas Mungo took the coach to London and was gone five and a half months—

while he and Edwards put the finishing touches to *Travels in the Interior Districts of Africa*. The book came out in May. It was an immediate and resounding success. A second edition was ordered. And then a third. African clubs and associations sprang up all over the continent. He wrote her every day.

In August she married a famous man. Packed up her books and microscope and moved to Fowlshiels — temporarily. Mungo was up in the air. Offers were coming in so fast it took half his time and energy just to reject them. The government wanted him to survey Australia, Banks was holding out for a second expedition to West Africa, others wanted him to lecture, write articles, collect plants, head up expeditions to Greenland, Borneo, Belize. "I don't want to settle down in our own place just yet," he told her.

She asked him what he meant.

"I mean I don't know where we're going to be. We could just get moved in and then have to pack up and leave."

She'd been afraid of something like this all along. "You don't mean to say you're going to leave a wife pregnant with your first child and go off and disappear for another three and a half years? Disappear and maybe never come back? Good God, man, we're just married and already you want to leave me a widow?"

"Ailie. *We,* I said *we.* Sir Joseph has been talking about the government's setting up a colony on the Niger — we've got to, if we're going to beat the French to it. They'd want me — us — to run the place. Think of it." His eyes had gone out of focus, distant and hazy. "Think of what we could do if we lived right there on the Niger — think of the territory I could cover, the discoveries I could make!"

"I do not want to live in Africa," she said, but he wasn't listening, didn't hear a word, didn't even see her. No, he was talking to someone else, talking to himself, selling Africa, a place of color and life and extravagant nature, where the rivers were choked with gold and the earth was so fertile you didn't even need to cultivate it.

Nine months later, when Thomas was born, they were still at Fowlshiels.

◆§ §◆

Now, the first child weaned and a second on the way, she sits on the porch at that same Fowlshiels, sipping at a cup of coffee, an open book in her lap. Summer, 1801. Nothing has changed. There's a war on with France. Prices have gone crazy. People are emigrating in droves. Mungo is still waiting.

Since he finished the book he's had alot of time on his hands. Two years' worth. He fishes. He hunts. He takes long solitary hikes through the hills, sometimes spends an overnight in the woods with Zander. Since his father's death and Adam's move to India, he helps his brother Archie look after the farm. He is silent, morose. Once he didn't show up for dinner and she found him down by the river, staring into the water. He was dropping pebbles in, one at a time, and counting to himself—one thousand, two thousand, three thousand. It's how I used to figure the depth of streams in Africa, he said. Then he smiled for the first time in a week: Important to know when you've got to wade across them. He wakes in a sweat sometimes, shouting out in a strange language. His sexual appetite is astonishing. He says he's happy.

Still, when the London mail comes in, he's first in line. Looking for an envelope with the government seal—or Sir Joseph's. Inevitably he is disappointed. The news has been bad. The government has diverted its attention to the war, Sir Joseph feels that the time is not right to go ahead with a second expedition, the French are making inroads in West Africa . . .

Ailie is worried. What will happen if the war ends or Sir Joseph reconsiders or the French stop making inroads? She looks up at the steady green sweep of the hills and sees instead a seething jungle. The fetus moves inside her. Somewhere, from deep in the house, the child of the century begins to cry.

◆§ PEEBLES

Peebles.

There's no other answer for it.

Yes, Peebles. She'll speak to him when he gets back.

◆§ §◆

It is late afternoon when she spots him emerging from a stand of larches at the far end of the field, Zander at his side. The sun is low in the sky, cold and milky, and shadows ravel out from the trees. Deep, menacing, blue-black shadows, stretching across the field like fingers, reaching out as if reluctant to give up the burden of her husband and brother. She loses them for a moment, but there—the flash of Mungo's hair as he glances into the sun, the familiar loping stride, Zander struggling to keep up. A moment later they're coming up the cart path.

"Hello," she calls.

They wave in response.

"Thirsty?"

"Aye."

By the time they reach the porch she has two tankards of ale set out for them. They fling themselves down on the wooden chairs with the easy animal grace of men who have just performed some prodigious feat. Zander's collar is soaked through with sweat. His nose is sunburned.

"So where've you been today?"

"Out to Ancrum Moor," Zander replies.

"Ancrum Moor? It must be fourteen miles there and back."

"Seventeen."

"And I suppose you talked of nothing but crocodiles and Mandingoes the whole way?"

Zander grins. The baby, who has been playing in the dirt, cries out in infantine rapture, and Mungo turns to look down at his son in an abstracted sort of way, as if he doesn't recognize him. Thomas regards his father steadily, then sticks a bit of offal in his mouth. His chin is slick with a film of dirt and saliva.

There is a moment of silence, the men concentrating on their ale. Ailie picks up her knitting. "Father was out today," she says.

No response.

"He told me of a place open at Peebles. A doctor's place — and a fine old house with it. What do you think?"

Mungo looks up from his ale. "Peebles? But that's a day's ride from here."

"It'd mean leaving our family and friends. But we can't hang around here forever — waiting. Can we?"

Zander has been waiting all his life. He sets his tankard down. "I don't see why not. Better to wait on the chance of going off on a new adventure than get mired down in the life of a country physician. Look what it's done to the old man."

Mungo gives her a doleful look. "I don't know," he says.

Suddenly Zander laughs out loud. "What is it they say about Peebles?"

"What do you mean?"

"You know, that expression old man Ferguson used to come out with all the time — "

The explorer's face lights with recognition. "Yes, yes — I remember. 'It was an unco still night,' he'd say, 'quiet as the grave — or Peebles.' "

✑ GRAVE BUSINESS

The mourners lining the front steps are professionals, in black suits and scarves, their eyes fixed solemnly on the ground or gazing off into space with an expression of profound grief and bewilderment. Each stands rigidly at attention, holding a long ebony mourner's pole at half-mast before him, the black-plumed tips crossed like swords. A fine doleful drizzle beads on their top hats and muttonchop whiskers. They are waiting patiently, professionally, for the funeral procession to begin, after which they look forward to falling on the remains of the funeral supper and drinking themselves into a stupor. The procession is scheduled for 9:00 P.M.

Throughout the afternoon, a succession of carriages has pulled up at the gate and discharged various groups of sober-faced men, stricken women and sniveling children. Relatives mostly, earning their inheritances. They are gathered in the house now, weeping and moaning. At quarter past eight a gleaming phaeton lurches up to the gate and a gentleman in black swings back the door and leaps into the street, too distraught to concern himself with ceremony. An instant later he is at the door, out of breath, his hair perfect, face radiant with tears.

The gentleman is Ned Rise. Dressed in a suit of black Genoan velvet, gloves and scarf dyed in printer's ink, even the soles of his shoes blackened for the occasion. In his pocket, a black silk handkerchief soaked in vinegar. He presses it to his face as he enters the house.

A lugubrious old man with a pitted nose sits at the door passing out sprigs of rue and gold rings engraved with the deceased's name and dates. Walls, windows and ceiling are draped in black crape and candles in sconces light the place like a chapel. From the room beyond, the sound of hushed voices and a steady sonorous undercurrent of mewling and nose blowing. Already in tears, Ned takes a fortifying whiff of his handkerchief and is about to plunge into the front room in a state of hyperaqueous hysteria, when he feels a hand on his arm. He turns round and finds himself staring at the trembling lower lip of a young woman — a girl, actually, no more than seventeen or eighteen. Her hair falls to her waist in two sheets, her eyes are like pools of oil, there is a mole on her left breast. "Claude?" she says.

Who in Christ's name? Ned is thinking. The cousin? Yes, of course. Blinded by tears, he takes her hand and sniffs: "Cousin?"

She nods, her eyes filling.

May as well start here, he thinks, tucking the handkerchief away. "Oh cousin!" he cries, and buries his nose in her hair.

꿋 ꙮ

Since that chaotic night in the Islington churchyard three and a half years ago, Ned's life has followed as circumscribed a course as rainwater in a sluice — a sluice designed by Dr. Decius William Delp, man of science, husband, father, blackmailer, ghoul . . . Delp, the eminently respectable professor-surgeon who takes a glass of Madeira with my lord or a hand at whist with my lady, and then sends his confederates round to rob their graves before the fluids have had a chance to settle.

Given the conditions, Ned had little choice. He was a survivor. He'd survived brutality, mutilation, drowning, the stink of fish, Newgate, the gallows. He looked back on it all as the pistol flashed in the utter desolation of the Islington churchyard and knew he could bloody well survive anything — the witches' sabbath, an insurrection of the walking dead, the full onslaught of Delp, Banks, Mendoza and Napoleon himself. Besides, there was just a single shot fired and the ball missed him by a good two yards, striking Quiddle in the thigh and shattering the bone. The bullet hit with a dull slap, like the sound a good pig stunner makes when he brings his cudgel down in that clean, fluid, killing swipe that buckles the animal's legs and pitches it limp to the ground — a sharp sound, almost immediately soaked up in the sponge of meat and gristle. There was a moment of surprised silence, as if no one had really meant to take things so far, and then the tattoo of Crump's retreating footsteps and another outcry from Boyles. Quiddle said nothing.

Ned's first impulse was to run. Shove the whole thing and run till his lungs burst — but then he remembered how Quiddle had stuck by him, nursing him, giving up his bed, defending him against Delp. "Horace," he whispered. "You all right?" No answer. Blackness. Nothing. Ned began to feel his way round the open grave, fearing the worst. If Quiddle was dead, Delp would expect five bodies — and his former assistant would be cut up like the rest, so many feet of intestine, so many ounces of this organ or that, sausage, tripe, headcheese. The thought was so vivid and arresting that Ned nearly collapsed when Quiddle suddenly seized his hand.

Quiddle's grip was a vise. His voice was hoarse. Between gasps he instructed Ned in the use of a tourniquet and emphasized the need for haste — both on his own account and because Crump's indiscretion would bring the constables down on them. Ned understood perfectly. He bound the wound and dragged Quiddle to the base of the wall — but didn't have the strength to get him over. "Hold on," he whispered, and went off in search of Boyles.

Boyles was hunched behind a grave marker, gibbering and moaning to himself. He'd always had something of the Irish peasant's fascination with elves and ogres and banshees — but this was the real thing. Not five minutes ago he'd come face to face with an impossibility. Call it specter, phantom, shade — it was real, a walking, talking dead man. He was shaken. Half-drunk, it's true, but shaken nonetheless. Ned had to tackle him, pin him down, slap him forty or fifty times and twice run through the story of his escape from the hangman before he could convince Billy to get up and help him lift Quiddle over the wall.

Boyles sat up in the cart and sucked at Ned's flask like a man in a dream. Quiddle bled and moaned. From time to time he would complain of the cold. Ned whipped the horse till his shoulder went numb in the socket, and back at St. Bartholomew's Delp himself performed the operation, taking the leg off just below the hip and cauterizing the wound with the blade of a shovel held over the fire till it glowed.

With Quiddle out of commission, Delp came to rely heavily on Ned. And Ned, with few if any options left him, gradually overcame his resistance to the job and began to exercise his wits in competing with Crump and others for the short supply of cadavers in the precincts of London. For a gallon and a half of gin a week he was able to hire Boyles as his assistant, and the two soon became as familiar with catafalques and churchyards as they were with hogsheads and taverns. Within the year Ned was providing all the specimens Delp could handle, and doing a bit of free-lancing on the side. The following year he was able to move out of St. Bartholomew's and take up lodgings in Limehouse. He began to dress with a degree of elegance. Dine out. Think about a trip to the Continent to track down his lost love.

He was alive. He was adapting. Despite the dangers and unsavory conditions of his new trade, he was infused with a guarded sense of optimism. Delp loomed on the one hand, demanding and unscrupulous, and Crump, rankled over the incursion into his sphere of influence, threatened on the other. But Ned was tiptoeing a fine line between them, and very gradually, with a steady, slow, incremental force, his star was rising.

✐ ﺑ✐

And so, like the mourners on the front steps and the old man distributing sprigs of rue, Ned is interested in the deceased on a purely professional basis only. The previous morning, while scanning the obituaries, he had come across the following notice:

The City will sorely feel the passing of Mr. Claude Messenger Osprey, manufacturer of fine porcelain and china, dead of the quinsy at the age of fifty-seven this eighth day of June, eighteen hundred and one. Mr. Osprey was perhaps best known for his determined and innovative work in the manufacture of porcelain chamberpots. He was the first to conceive of the personalized *pot de chambre,* and he employed a number of inspired artisans whose refreshing clover-leaf and willow designs are intimately known to us all. Mr. Osprey is survived by a brother, Drummond, of Cheapside, and a son, Claude junior, the Bristol china merchant. The deceased will lie in state at the residence of his brother this evening and throughout the day tomorrow. The funeral service is scheduled for nine o'clock tomorrow evening.

A few inquiries among the bereaved Osprey household staff turned up a rather intriguing bit of information: Claude junior, now en route from Bristol, was remembered only as a small boy. Due to a rift between the senior Osprey and his wife, the boy had been sent away to school at the age of nine, matriculated through the university, married, and had taken control of the Bristol branch of the family business without ever having returned to London. None of the London Ospreys had laid eyes on him in nearly twenty years.

That evening, Ned, Quiddle and Billy Boyles were waiting for the Bristol mail when it rolled up in front of the Gloucester Coffee House. Boyles, in livery, swung back the door of the coach before it had come to a stop and called out the young Osprey's name in a voice thick with grief and anxiety. He introduced himself as footman to the late Osprey senior, and led the young heir up the street to a waiting carriage. Inside the carriage, like house spiders anticipating a visitor, Ned and Quiddle toyed with lengths of rope and sturdy strips of cotton. Osprey didn't have a chance.

᳐ᣔ ᣗ᳐

"You know," the cousin sniffs, "I recognized you the instant you stepped through the door."

Ned emits a mournful whimper or two, then blows his nose and looks up at her out of grief-stricken eyes. "Oh? How was that?"

"You . . . you . . ." here she falls into his arms again, blubbering like a drowning dog, "you look so much like him."

The rest is easy. A few ponderous aunts, quaking uncles, sour in-laws, cousins thrice removed, a suspicious old nursemaid. No widow, thank god. (Ned can't be sure, but thinks he recalls snatching a Mrs. Tillie Marsh Osprey from a churchyard in the West End nearly two years back.) Meanwhile, expressions of sympathy fall around him like brick buildings collapsing in an earthquake. Someone proposes a toast. And then another. More tears, back-patting, the reek of perfume and alcohol, a kiss and a squeeze, and then they're out in the street, wrapped in black capes, torches held high, treading with stately tread behind the massive horse-drawn hearse. Over the cobbles and down the street, around a corner and into the churchyard. The glittering weasel eyes of the parson, dust to dust. And then Ned flinging himself on the coffin, biting at the ankles of the gravediggers, inconsolable, fighting off a host of soothers and sympathizers in the pure fierce outflowing of his grief. He grovels, he whines, out-Hamlets Hamlet. And finally, tearfully, begs them to leave him with his sorrow and his burning compulsion to bury this great and noble man, his father, with his own caring hands.

Ten minutes later the cemetery is deserted as the sleek phaeton draws up at the gate, Quiddle at the reins. A thin, flat-headed figure slips out and joins Ned beside the grave. There is a movement in the dark, a grunt or groan perhaps, some brief hint of nefarious activity. Then the carriage moves off and the final torch is snuffed in the cemetery.

ᵉᶨ ALL THINGS THAT RISE
MUST CONTAIN YEAST

As dawn stretches her rosy fingers over the rooftops of London, a harelipped match girl stumbles upon the writhing form of Claude M. Osprey, Jr. The heir to the Osprey fortune, bound hand and foot, is methodically inching his way up a soot-blackened alley, dragging a small ridge of detritus along with him. His face is a grid of scratches thin as cut hair, and a dirty cravat has been stuffed in his mouth. "Mmmff," he says. "Mmmmmmmmff!" The girl cocks her head and looks at him alertly, like a setter responding to its master's cluck, then bends to sift through his pockets. Half an hour later a butcher's boy happens by, does a double take, and then slouches up to hang over the young heir as if the appearance of a bound and gagged man in a back alley presented a dilemma of Aristotelian proportions. Osprey's eyes widen above the gag in rage and exasperation. The boy's mouth drops open. He starts up the alley, ducks his head, turns and comes back again. Finally he squats down and cautiously removes the cravat from Osprey's mouth.

The bound man works his jaw as if it were a newly created part of his anatomy. "Cut me loose," he demands.

The boy tucks the cravat away in his pockets. He digs a sliver of wax from his ear and then examines it thoughtfully at the edge of a blackened fingernail. "Wot's in it for me?"

"Half a crown."

"Make it a crown and yer on."

"A crown then. Cut the cords."

"Ten shillings."

"Help!" Osprey shouts. "Murder! Help!"

"All royt, all royt." In a single practiced motion the knife appears from the boy's ragged sleeve and the hemp cords fall to the ground.

Osprey sits up and frees his ankles, then reaches up a hand for support. The boy helps him to his feet. "Idiot!" the young heir hisses, and slaps the boy against the wall. Then he's out of the alley and running for a hackney cab.

◆§ §◆

They are stunned in Cheapside. Bowled over. "But, but — why would anyone want to do such a thing?" the uncle stammers.

"The grave!" shouts Osprey.

The authorities are called in. The parson. The cousin with her eyes of pitch. The aunts and uncles. The in-laws. When the earth is turned back from the grave and the casket revealed, they breathe a sigh of relief. "Open it!" shouts the heir. "Open it!" he insists, over a murmur of protest. The gravedigger pries open the lid. The casket is empty. Some gasp. Others faint. That afternoon the following handbill is distributed throughout the city:

> *Claude M. Osprey, Jr., offers a reward of £100 for information leading to the apprehension of three men, a one-legged man among them, who committed a heinous act of depravity against God and Nature in the St. Paul's churchyard on the night of June the eighth. Information held strictly confidential. Great Wood St., Cheapside.*

There are thirty-seven respondents. One after another they slouch into the study of the house on Great Wood Street. Bearded, one-eyed, pockmarked, drooling and stinking, each has a story for the young heir. He listens to semicoherent tales of murder, cannibalism, rape, robbery and mayhem. He hears of kidnapping and mutilation, fellatio, buggery, gypsies, blackamoors and Jews. The carpets are soiled and the spitoon full when a rangy man of about forty is led into the room, his biceps as lean as a side of bacon. A beard of three or four days' growth darkens his chin, and he reaches up to stroke it from time to time with quick nervous fingers. His eyes are bright as bits of blue glass. "My name's Crump," he says, his voice flayed and harsh. "I knows the men ye want. Graverobbers."

Osprey motions for him to sit.

"They're a vicious lot, in league with the divil. It's un'oly wot they done. Inyooman."

Tight-lipped, seductive, Osprey rattles a bag of coins. His eyes hold the other man like pincers. "Where are they?"

"The gimpy one, 'ee's Quiddle. Ye'll find 'im at St. Bartholomew's. The other one, the one with the flat 'ead, they calls 'im Boyles, Billy Boyles. 'Ee's a drunk. Sleeps in sheds and carts and such. But 'oo you wants is the ringleader, the brains behind it all." Crump pauses to wipe his mouth on his sleeve. "That's a hunnert pund yer offerin', init?"

Osprey rattles the bag, slow and sweet.

" 'Is name's Ned. Ned is all I knows 'im by. 'Ee's a subtle snake, 'ee is. Slippery. But I've watched 'im and I've followed 'im like a terrier after a rat. I can tell ye where 'is lodgins is at. In Lime'ouse. Upstairs from the Mermaid Tavern." Crump pauses to lick his cracked lips. "Go now," he whispers, "and catch 'im while it's light."

◄§ THE HOUND OF EARTH

Experience has taught Ned Rise a good many things — nearly all of them unpleasant. One thing it has taught him is to keep his assets liquid. Another is to wear a life jacket if you're expecting heavy seas. He has also come to understand that the prudent homme des affaires never removes his shoes, keeps one eye propped open in repose, and never under any circumstances allows himself to enter a room with only one door.

And so, when Osprey and a pair of armed lieutenants burst in upon him entirely unannounced and unexpected, Ned is only partially surprised. Though he is in bed asleep when they kick in the door of the front room, he has vanished by the time they reach the bedroom. As the front door splinters there is a moment of recognition during which the young heir, armed to the teeth, stares directly into the eyes of the bodysnatcher, startled awake in his bed. Not fifteen feet away. Through the doorframe, in the back room, under the bedclothes. Osprey has already begun to smile a wicked vengeful smile when Ned simply turns over in bed and disappears. One minute he is there, flesh and blood, and the next he has been drunk up by the air, trompe l'oeil, like a blacksnake vanishing into a stone wall.

Ned has planned for such contingencies. When he rented the modest apartment from the landlord of the *Mermaid,* he also took charge of a small room on the floor directly below it — a room no bigger than a closet actually — explaining to the landlord that he was an itinerant merchant and that he needed the extra space to store his wares. The landlord said he didn't give a great blue damn who he was or what he did with his rooms, so long as there was no destruction done and he paid his rent on time. Ned smiled, and counted out the first week's rent in advance. Then he appropriated Delp's bone saw, waited until a fresh boatload of tars and salts began drinking, shouting, breaking glass and howling out sea chanties downstairs, and cut a neat round hole in the floor of his bedroom. The hole communicated directly with the closet on the floor below. It was the work of a minute to slide the bed across the room and conceal his handiwork. Add to this the fact that Ned always slept fully dressed, with his life savings tied up in a sock round his neck, and it is understandable that he was able to elude his would-be captors.

For the time being, at any rate.

For Osprey was not so easily discouraged. He seemed quite willing to let the chamberpot business languish in the hands of underlings while he pursued his present affair to its conclusion. The outrage to his father's remains would have been reason enough to hunt the perpetrators to the far corners of the earth, but when coupled with the outrage to himself, the very existence of these thieves, kidnappers and crypt gougers was intolerable, rankling, a blot on society, and their extermination took on the nature of a sacred mission. Dogged, indefatigable, he was mad for vengeance, his mouth bitter with the taste of bile, his dreams puddled with blood.

The first to go was Quiddle. He was apprehended at St. Bartholomew's, imprisoned, tried and eventually hanged. The only evidence against him was a deposition by the junior Osprey. It was enough. Delp, of course, denied everything. He did attend the execution though — seeing that Quiddle had no next of kin. Afterward, in a gesture that touched nearly everyone present, he stepped forward and announced that he himself would take charge of the body.

Boyles was another story altogether. He was none too bright, and dead drunk about three quarters of the time. But where he might be from moment to moment was hard to say. He had no lodgings. No friends. No job. No prospects. He slept in doorways, kitchens, ginshops. Osprey hired a dozen men to roam the alleys and taverns in the neighborhood of the hospital and to keep a watch in Limehouse. But to no avail: Ned Rise found him first. He was down on Hermitage Dock, taking in the sun and watching a swarm of skinny-legged boys dive into the Thames while seabirds dangled from the sky and three-masted schooners ran with the breeze like great white swans. He had a lemon, a potato and a bottle of gin with him, and he was sucking at them in slow succession — first the gin, then the lemon, and finally the potato. When Ned spotted the familiar flat head and tattered overcoat, he felt a rush of relief. Boyles turned his glittery green eyes and long nose to him as he sat down. "Neddy! Wot's up? Another job?"

"We're in trouble, Billy."

Boyles didn't want to hear it. He looked out over the gray sudsing waves like Napoleon surveying the Channel. "Lookit the way them gulls hangs in the air, like somebody was runnin' a Punch and Judy show out o' the sky," he murmured. There was a fragment of lemon pulp stuffed up his nostril.

"They got Quiddle."

"Who got 'im?"

"Osprey."

There was no change in Boyles' expression. He looked at Ned blank as a baby.

"The one we dumped two nights back — the chamberpot king."

Boyles' face fell. He began to look queasy, as if his recollection of the fire-eyed young heir had suddenly cast him into stormy seas or swamped his potato in stomach acid.

"They're going to hang him, Billy."

Boyles absorbed this information with the same half-thoughtful, half-bilious look. His face gradually went white and he reached clumsily for his mouth. Then he vomited potato, lemon and gin all over the dock.

Ned took the bottle from him and flung it into the river. "Come on, Billy," he said, "get up. We've got to go get ourselves lost."

◆§ §◆

That was in the summer, when days were long and nights as soft as a mother's breast.

Now, with two months of winter and the New Year behind them, things are getting rough. For one thing, they are out of money. Boyles had all of six shillings on him when they decided to melt into the shadows, and Ned's seventy-four pounds (an amount accruing in large part from the sale of the elder Osprey's remains on the open market and the appropriation of the junior Osprey's wallet and other effects) has been exhausted by the demands of lodging by the night in order to keep on the move. For another thing, the weather has turned against them. A cold wave is sweeping in off the North Sea with a frightening intensity, cracking foundations, smoothing over the Thames, spreading ague, pneumonia and influenza in its wake. While pigeons fall from the sky like stones and workhorses stiffen and die in their stalls, Rise and Boyles have had to make do with cold porridge and a bed in the straw. Still worse, Osprey has refused to give up the chase, sniffing them out of every hole they manage to crawl into, setting up a fierce bloodthirsty baying at their backs, ruining their digestion, assailing their peace of mind, hiding a bogey in every bush and making a gibbet of every streetlamp.

Currently they are huddled over a fire beneath the Blackfriars Bridge, muffled and miserable, noses plugged with mucus, feet numb, stomachs growling. They sit there for nearly half an hour, hugging their sides and staring into the flames, before Ned turns to his companion and whispers in his ear. Ten other vagrants are shivering round the fire. None even bothers to look up. Out on the river the shifting ice groans like a chorus of drowned men.

"There's a woman buried tonight up at St. Paul's," Ned says.

"Wot, with the ground froze?"

Ned grins. "That makes it all the easier for us, don't you see? She'll be just lying there atop the grave for a few days till the gravedigger can open it up for her."

Boyles' nose is running. His eyes have sunk deep in their sockets, like two feverish little creatures retreating into their burrows. His voice is reproachful. "You got me into this, Neddy."

"Crump did."

Boyles turns back to the fire, carefully clears each nostril, and lets the idea drift through the gin-impaired circuits of his brain for a minute or two. "I could sure use a cup of negus and maybe some hot soup," he sniffs. "And I wouldn't mind passin' the night on a bench in a inn someplace neither." He pauses to cough up a clot of white serum. "But can we risk it?"

"Shit. We'll freeze to death if we don't."

<ag ĝ>

It is past three in the morning when they slip into the cemetery. The night sky is a cauldron of clouds, white, black, a hundred shades of gray. There is wind, and that numbing, headaching cold that penetrates every cell and whispers death in your ears. Ned is in a hurry. Trembling with the cold, thinking only to snatch the corpse, stash it someplace and find a ginshop where they can sleep on the floor for a farthing, already envisioning Bluestone the surgeon counting the notes out in his hand and the bed and supper they'll have by this time tomorrow. Osprey? He tries not to think of him, need rationalizing fear — how could anyone, even the devil himself, carry a grudge so far as to keep watch in a cemetery on a deathly cold night eight months after the fact? No, if he were Osprey he'd be in bed now, with a woman to keep him warm and a fire that lit the room like Guy Fawkes Day . . .

There is a sudden sharp sound at his back and he spins around, tense as a cat, until he realizes it's only Boyles stumbling over the gate. He waits for his accomplice to come loping up out of the shadows, then motions for him to stay put. Ned slips off, the brief scare snapping him out of his rapture, suffusing him with blood and adrenalin, his heart turning over like a machine. Five minutes later he locates the coffin — a plain deal box set between a pair of grave markers at the far end of the churchyard. He crouches low and watches for a full sixty seconds or more, the wind hanging in the vacant trees, the cold creeping up his legs, then starts forward.

But then there's another sound — off to his left — a rippling or snapping like wash on a line. He hesitates, all his instincts shouting *watch out, watch out,* the cold prodding him on, whispering it's all right, make the snatch, get warm, stay alive. He takes a tentative step forward. There it is again. Ripple, flap. Something is wrong. Dead wrong. Crouching, he slips off to his left, breath sucked back, heart churning, every muscle strung tight against the bone.

The sound becomes more insistent as he draws closer, its rhythm geared to the rise and fall of the wind. Spooked, he pictures a host of the dead standing silent atop their tombs, cerements rustling in the breeze, skeletal hands reaching out in mute appeal. But no, there must be a rational explanation . . . He moves closer, ripple, flap. There: the sound seems to be emanating from the bank of shadow up ahead — a sepulcher, isn't it? Yes, a sepulcher, oblong, massive, looming over the dark ranks of headstones like the passageway to the underworld. He moves closer still, and is startled to realize that the whole thing seems to be moving, undulating somehow with the slow soft wash of a gentle sea. Too dark to see, he reaches out a hand to touch it — and comes up with a handful of cloth. Strange. Someone has draped the entire thing in black muslin. In Memoriam? Another nob laid to rest?

He doesn't have time to puzzle over it. The cold speaks to him again and he is about to turn back to his task, satisfied, when another sound, far more arresting, takes hold of him like a clenched fist and freezes every muscle in his body. Faint and muffled, a sound of voices — from inside the tomb!

This is too much. For all his recent experience in darkened graveyards he wants to piss his pants, take to his heels, creep back to Blackfriars Bridge and lie down to die of the cold. But then a sudden gust lifts the sheets and a sliver of light cuts the darkness. A new fear comes over him, far more terrible than any thought of ghosts and goblins. His joints tremble with it. He is beginning to understand.

Carefully, carefully, he slips beneath the black sheet and huddles over the stone door that gives onto the tomb. It is ever so slightly ajar. He puts his eye to the opening.

Inside, by the dim glow of an oil lamp, three men in furs are sitting round a coffin, playing cards. Their feet are propped up on iron bed warmers; clouds of suspended breath dog their movements. Ned's view is partially obstructed by the back of the man nearest him, but when the man sits up to look at his hand Ned realizes with a start that the cardplayer in the far corner is Osprey. Suddenly Osprey throws in his cards. "Hadn't you better be making your rounds, Mr. Crump?" he says to the figure with his back turned.

"Aww, 'ave a 'eart, Claude. There ain't nobody goin' to be out on a night like this, not the divil nor 'is dam."

All the light from the lamp is puddled in Osprey's eyes until they seem to glow with a preternatural light. He sighs, and casually draws a pistol from the lining of his coat. "I said: hadn't you better be making your rounds, Mr. Crump?"

◄§ §►

Back at the gate Ned claps one hand over Boyles' mouth, the other round his shoulder. He leads him from the cemetery and up a side street at a jog. Three blocks later a winded Boyles stops and spins his friend round by the arm. "Wot's up, Neddy? Where we headed?"

Ned's face is veiled in shadow. His voice is harsh, nagged at by the cold, muffled in the scarf drawn over his mouth and nose. "Hertford," he whispers.

"Hertford?" Boyles' chin drops. "But that's outside Lunnon, init?"

A light goes on in a window up the street, throwing a pale flicker over Ned's face. His look is so fierce and bitter Boyles steps back, but Ned grabs hold of his companion's coat and draws him up close. His voice is clear, unmistakable. "That's right," he hisses.

✣ ILLUSORY CHEESES

Ned turned his back on London without a second thought. It was the winter of 1802, and he was thirty-one years old. He was tired. He'd had thirty-one years of creeping through the shit and grime of the streets, thirty-one years of having his knuckles rapped and the ladder jerked out from under him every time he managed to step up a rung. Thirty-one years of torment and degradation, prejudice, abuse, and cruel and unusual punishment, mitigated only by the charity of Barrenboyne and the precious few months he'd had with Fanny. Now, at the end of all those blighted years, all those dark hollow years that had been drawn from him one by one like deeply embedded splinters, he was no better off than when Barrenboyne had first taken him in. He was broke. He had no lodgings, no possessions, no family. As far as friends were concerned, he was taking them all with him, in the flat-headed, pinch-shouldered person of Billy Boyles, drunkard and half-wit. Quiddle was dead, Fanny had vanished, Shem and Liam were up to their ears in fish and scales somewhere on the far side of the river — in any case, he hadn't seen them in four and a half years. For the rest, they were faceless multitudes, hard as stones, ready to strip the clothes from your back as you lay dying or run you down in the streets with their phaetons and landaus. And if they weren't strangers, they were sworn enemies. Banks, Mendoza, Brummell, Smirke, Delp — and the most venomous of all, Osprey. Orestes couldn't have had it worse.

So he was off to Hertford. The country. Like Boyles, Ned had never been out of London, and had no idea what to expect. He had a vague image of great wheels of cheese, slabs of fresh-baked bread slathered with butter and honey, cattle at their cuds, the lazy sizzle of sun showers on a thatched roof. He and Billy could get jobs as fieldhands or shepherds or something. The air would be good for them.

Beyond all this, another factor entered the equation: Fanny. She'd been born and raised in Hertfordshire, and had served her apprenticeship there as milkmaid to a certain Squire Trelawney. Ned would look up her family. Perhaps they'd heard from her or knew where she could be found. After four and a half years of scouring the streets, he was at a loss. She wasn't in London, as best he could determine, and with Osprey dogging him he had no chance of raising the money to go off to the Continent. Brooks' house had long since been boarded up. Letters went unanswered. It was rumored that he was dead. If so, where was Fanny?

What Ned couldn't know, as he trudged up the deserted turnpike in the cold vague light of dawn, was that the question no longer held any meaning.

◄§ SUSPIRIA DE PROFUNDIS

Fanny Brunch left London early Christmas morning, 1797, in a state of shock. She wouldn't be back for nearly four years.

It was snowing that morning, trembling little gouts of white spinning down out of the caliginous sky. She hardly noticed. When she finally emerged from the prison it was past five in the morning, and Brooks' footman was waiting outside the gate. She looked right through him as he handed her into the coach, his touch the touch of a doomed man, flesh, blood, sinew, bone. All the way to Gravesend she watched the trees emerge from the darkness and turn to gibbets, the snow clinging to the naked branches like shreds of flesh, nests of dried leaves suddenly transforming themselves into kicking, writhing human forms. She felt light-headed, disconnected from her body. There was a smell of meat in her nostrils, nagging and persistent. At one point the smell of it was so strong she had to ask the coachman to pull off to the side of the road so she could be sick in the weeds.

Brooks gave her a dose of laudanum for the trip to Bremerhaven, then a second, third and fourth dose to calm her nerves as they continued on from there to Cuxhaven and Hamburg. She lay dreaming on her narrow bunk as the ship lurched through a storm in the North Sea, her pupils reduced to slits, the wind soothing her with a chorus of voices. Her nostrils cleared, the fetor of decaying flesh giving way to a breath of the outdoors, azalea and hyacinth, spring in Hertfordshire. Above her, the darkened rafters began to shift and blend, faces clustered like grapes in the shadows, the candle guttering wildly as the ship pitched like a carriage with a thrown wheel. She saw her father, a spring they'd visited in the chalk hills, the clean-swept kitchen of their stone-and-thatch cottage. She was awake one moment, dreaming the next. She vomited and enjoyed it. There were roses in her nostrils. Toward the end she saw Ned, lying in some dark place — a cave — his throat chafed, a linen garment folded across his loins. She saw the gallows again, just as flash, and then Ned was on his feet, gliding toward the mouth of the cave. The light was blinding. There was singing. And then she found herself in Hamburg, at a hotel, sitting across the table from Brooks in a new white silk gown.

"Fanny," he was saying. "Fanny. Will you look at me, please?"

She looked. He was standing now. There was a man at his side, tall and erect, his mustaches combed out from his face. His eyes were close-set, half the normal size. He was peering at her through a lorgnette.

"This is the gentleman I was telling you about—the one I met over cards last night?"

The man leaned forward and took her hand. "Karl Erasmus von Pölkler," he said.

She smiled like all the fields of clover in Hertfordshire, she smiled like an idiot. She was thinking of something else.

≫ ≪

Two nights later she opened her eyes again and found that she was seated at a massive walnut dining table set in the center of a high-vaulted room. The walls were of stone and mortar, softened at intervals by a gloomy portrait or an oriental tapestry. A chandelier blazing with a hundred candles depended from the ceiling like a fragment of the sun. For a moment she was disoriented, the opium settling a deep fog over the backroads of her mind, but then she glanced up at the head of the table and saw von Pölkler raising a glass of wine in toast. Six other guests, Brooks among them, raised their glasses in unison while von Pölkler intoned something in German and seven pairs of eyes fastened on Fanny. Reddening, she stared down at the white tablecloth. A jeweled bracelet flashed on her wrist.

They ate Erbsensuppe, Beuschel and Gnagi, Bratkartoffeln, Fleischvögel and Hasenbraten. There were mounds of shredded cabbage and beets. A dozen bottles of Rüdesheimer. The conversation, in honor of the principal guests, was in a halting, consonant-choked English. "Ve haff . . . wery great honor to place . . . to place such charmed English mens and vomens here at Geesthacht," von Pölkler sputtered, the ridge of his high forehead glistening under the chandelier. Fanny bowed her head and ate with a mechanical precision: two bites and a dab at the lips with her napkin. By the time the girl in pigtails and apron brought around the Schwarzwälder Kirsch, Fanny was floating. Brooks, drunk as a skunk, limp from laudanum and semi-articulate as a result of sharing two pipefuls of their host's oriental tobacco, fell asleep in a puddle of gravy.

After dinner Fanny excused herself. The girl in the apron helped her up to her room. She lay on the bed for a long while, thinking of Ned, her family, the place she'd given up at Sir Joseph's, the dismal prospect—like wriggling down through an interminable tunnel—of a life with Brooks. She reached for bottle and spoon. Tincture of opium. The stuff was magical, soothing, it was her friend and counselor. She took it like the medicine it was.

Fanny lay back and dreamed. The candle became the light of the sun, the room spun twice and suddenly she was in a deep lush canyon. Golden fish drifted through transparent pools, pleasure domes sprang up on precipices overlooking the sea, larks floated in the sky and the clouds pursed their lips and whispered nonsense rhymes in her ear. She dreamed. But the breath on her pillow was von Pölkler's.

◄§ §►

On the surface, Brooks' motive in getting Fanny out of London was purely compassionate — he meant to spare her the agony of her lover's execution. The con artist's death was a fait accompli. They'd done all they could. Now she must forget. But in point of fact, he hungered to stand at her side while the rope twitched and Ned Rise gagged his last. He burned for it; there was no scene in the world he'd rather witness. The whole thing was so deliciously morbid, so painfully exciting — the doomed lovers parted forever, torn from one another's arms by the brooding implacable force of the hangman, the distraught heroine throwing herself on the corpse while the crowd casually remarked on the execution like drama critics strolling from the theater. "Aaaah, 'ee was nothin', this one. Remember Jack Tate? — kicked like a bleedin' 'orse for arf an hour and then made them 'orrible noises in 'is throat?" Brooks was titillated, no doubt about it. He desperately wanted to watch her watching the execution. But even more desperately, he was afraid of losing her. Once Ned Rise had passed beyond the pale she would no longer have any use for the Brooks fortune — or the Brooks proclivities. As soon as it hit her, she'd be gone. He knew it.

And so he dosed her with laudanum and hustled her off to Germany before she could have any real awareness of what was going on. Penniless, and unable to speak the language, she would be more than ever dependent upon him. And that was just what he wanted. Fanny Brunch was the most desirable woman he had ever laid eyes on — he was mad for her. She had the soft, pure, angelic sort of beauty that spoke to every fiber of his algolagniac's heart. With her it wasn't the mere momentary pleasure of sex, it was an ongoing process of erotic defilement, it was pissing in the pews, jerking off on the altar. She was made for him.

Germany was the obvious place to take her. With the war on, France was out. Ditto Italy. He thought of Greece, but the Mediterranean was nothing less than a floating battlefield — why risk it? No, Germany was the place. Fatherland of the few truly heroic men of the age — Goethe,

Schelling, Tieck, Schiller, the Schlegels. And all of them gathered at Jena, the Athens of the modern age. It was too simple. They would travel up the Elbe, through Magdeburg, Halle and Weissenfels, and settle at Jena. He would write great poems that celebrated love, death and pain. He could have Goethe over to tea. Tell Schiller how wrong he was to have let Karl Moor give in — far better to be an outlaw, spitting in the face of bourgeois society. The thought of it — he, Adonais Brooks, an intimate of the great minds of his time, helping mold a canon of drama, poetry and philosophical speculation incandescent with scenes of pain and loss, windswept peaks and tortured youth, a canon of work that would once and for all lay to rest the precious claptrap they'd been heralding in England for the past fifty years. Brooks could feel himself teetering on the verge of a great and emotional future. Then he met von Pölkler.

"You must come out to the estate at Geesthacht," the Margrave said. "Rest up for awhile." The German tucked his lorgnette away and looked Brooks dead in the eye, as if he could see through to the inner man behind the flat blue eyes and hint of a smile. "I tink we haff alot in common."

◆§ §◆

As the weeks passed, each day more hopeless and humiliating than the last, Fanny lost the ability to care. About anything. Life, love, food, drink, sex, the functions of the body and mind. The only thing that pricked her interest was the blue bottle that stood on the shelf beside her bed. Laudanum helped her to dream, to forget what was happening to her, where she was, who these people were. Sex came like an avalanche, smothered in wine and opium. Sex with Brooks, von Pölkler, the girl in pigtails, beet-faced guests, a dog. Legs and arms flailed, smoke rose to the ceiling. Fanny reached for the blue bottle.

After three months at Geesthacht, she realized that she was pregnant. Strange things were happening to her body. She was sick before breakfast. Her liver was tender. Her blood no longer flowed in secret accord with the cycles of the moon. She reached for bottle and spoon, but before the glow came up she felt a stirring in some deep intuitive pocket of her mind, a burgeoning cellular knowledge that suddenly hit her with all the force of certainty: she was carrying Ned's child. That final desperate night at Newgate came back to her in a flash of revelation, Ned driving at her with a frantic relentless fury as if he could somehow transcend his fate through the urgency of his lovemaking, while she lay there, sorrowing, cradling him in her arms as if he were a lost infant. She looked up at the stone walls of her apartment at Geesthacht. The drug was in her stomach, in her head. She leaned back on her pillow and smiled.

It was a boy, of course. Born on the twenty-fifth of September, 1798. At Geesthacht. Von Pölkler was delighted. He spoke of a system of education he had devised, a system that would inscribe the clean slate of the boy's mind with precise, orderly strokes, a system that would allow him to achieve an intensely realized state of transcendent native freedom through the rigid application of drill and regimen. He would be instructed in the only two disciplines that mattered: philosophy and the martial arts. This was no ordinary boy, and he would have no ordinary education. No, he was destined to become a new man, a hero for the coming century, the Anglo-German Napoleon. Von Pölkler named the boy Karl. Privately, Fanny called him Ned.

Brooks viewed the whole thing with suspicion and distaste. While it was true that the child may have been his own, despite von Pölkler's insistence to the contrary, the fact was that it deprived him of Fanny's company much of the time. At first, of course, the prospect of Fanny's motherhood excited him, and he did make an effort to explore the various erotic avenues that Madonna and child opened to him — balancing the baby's cap on his erect member, suckling at the breast, strapping Fanny to the cradle and ravishing her from the rear, making love to a pair of village fräuleins dressed in diapers — but he soon grew bored with the whole thing. Gurgling, baby talk, rattles, the insufferable cuteness of it all. This wasn't the way heroes lived. He became depressed. Stopped writing. Spent his time arranging cockfights or lying in bed with a bottle of laudanum and a fist-sized chunk of the Margrave's oriental tobacco. He plumbed the depths of his host's wine cellar, played billiards until he wore a hole in the felt. His eyes drooped, the beestung lips became so impossibly swollen he looked as if he were perpetually pouting over some imagined injustice, and he developed a habit of tugging at his missing ear. One night he and von Pölkler got stinking drunk and slit one another's cheeks with a razor — strictly for cosmetic purposes. They wore their thin scars like chevrons.

≈§ §∞

On the eve of the child's third birthday, von Pölkler arranged a gala celebration: the boy would begin his formal education the following morning. The Mayor of Hamburg was invited, various local dignitaries and minor aristocrats, bankers and shopkeepers. Most declined the invitation, as a means of registering disapproval of the Margrave's life-style. But those who did come were regaled with dancing, chamber music, a feast of roast suckling pig with plum sauce and Weinkraut, home-brewed black beer, flagons of wine and whatever else they had the imagination to desire. A select few were invited to join the Margrave in a lower chamber once used as a dungeon and still fitted out with all the accoutrements of bondage and torture. There they tasted French champagne, swallowed opium, stripped off their gowns and dinner jackets and let their impulses guide them.

Fanny did not attend the party. She lay in bed, the child at her side, counting out drops of laudanum. It was now nearly four years since she'd stepped through the gates at Geesthacht, four years that had accumulated all her loneliness, despair and self-contempt until the combined force of it lashed her like a whip day and night, four years that constituted her season in hell. She was a prisoner. Her future had been throttled on the gallows, her present was a blight.

At first, the child had revitalized her. She came out of her haze, made demands of Brooks and von Pölkler, tried to cut back her intake of medicine. Her keepers acceded to her demands — she was given a degree of autonomy and left alone much of the time — but the laudanum had a hold over her that struck far deeper than any influence either of them could assert. Without it, her dreams turned sour. She saw Ned in his grave, the cerements creeping with worms and insects; she saw her boy, son of a whore, grown into a beast under von Pölkler's tutelage; she watched herself writhing in the cold dark muck of a riverbed, the current swirling over her like a stormy sky. She started up in bed, wet with perspiration, and was immediately racked with shivers. Her throat was dry, a thousand bright-eyed rodents dug at her insides with quick sharp movements of tooth and claw. She reached for the blue bottle.

Now it was a matter of course. She took seven thousand drops a day, and her dreams were easier. The child slept better for it too. When she first took him off the breast he couldn't keep his food down and would toss in his cradle, colicky and restless. Frau Grunewald, the ancient midwife who had tended von Pölkler in his infancy, suggested a drop or two of medicine in the boy's porridge. It worked. And now the medicine was as much a part of the child's life as it was of Fanny's own. She didn't like it. She sensed that the child was starting out at a disadvantage, a cripple, saddled with a special need and a special craving to satisfy it. But then what did it matter? Von Pölkler would take her son away and indoctrinate him until he became a stranger to her. She was powerless to stop him.

As she lay there brooding over it, the laudanum stroking her abdomen with firm hot fingers, the door swung back, and Brooks staggered into the room. His clothes were torn, his face smeared, the eyes drilled into his head. He lurched for the bed, missed his mark and fell headlong into the corner. A moment later there was the sound of gagging — and then he was still.

Fanny cautiously lifted herself from the bed and bent over him. He did not seem to be breathing. She turned him over and listened for a heartbeat. There was none. She crawled back into bed and took a spoonful of medicine to clear her head. Very gradually, something began to bloom there, something compounded equally of fear and exhilaration. Two hours later, when Brooks had grown cold and a faint gray light had begun to peer in at the windows, Fanny lifted a fistful of currency from his waistcoat pocket, dressed the child and crept out into the hallway.

The place was silent. Stone corridors stretched off into darkness, arrases shadowed the walls. She tiptoed down the steps and into the main hall, afraid that von Pölkler might still be at it, red-eyed from debauch — he would stop her for certain, mother of his child. She'd have to reach Cuxhaven — no, be aboard a smack in the North Sea — before she'd be clear of him. But for the moment, all was well: there was no sign of him.

The main hall was a shambles. Littered with smashed furniture, overturned tables, scraps of food, the shards of bottles. There was a sound of snoring. Somewhere, someone was groaning. To her left, propped up against the wall, was Herr Meinfuss, the stablekeeper. Another man was asleep in his lap. Beyond them a dark shadow lay frozen against the floor. It was Bruno, von Pölkler's Alsatian. The dog had been eviscerated, its intestines trailing from the rictus of the body cavity like rotten sausage. Fanny led her son around the carcass and out into the gray light of morning.

Her Hertfordshire upbringing served her in good stead when she reached the stables. It was nothing to saddle the Margrave's finest horse — an Arabian gray — seat the boy across the pommel and head out over the fields for the Hamburg road. At a gallop. In Hamburg she was able to dispose of the horse to a suspicious but profit-loving dealer after she explained in her rudimentary German that her husband had been injured in Oldenburg, and that she needed to raise money so she could rush to his aid. The horse trader flashed a complicitous, full-toothed grin, gave her a fifth the animal's worth and wished her husband well.

By nightfall she was at Cuxhaven. A boat was leaving for London, via The Hague, at six the following morning. She had just enough to cover her fare after purchasing two bottles of laudanum from the chemist and some milk and groats for her son. All night she sat huddled on the dock, jumping at every sound, expecting von Pölkler to swoop down on them at any moment. Finally, at dawn, the passengers were taken aboard, the captain weighed anchor and the schooner moved out into the bay. Fanny stood at the rail and watched the shore recede as a tall, mustachioed figure on horseback thundered out onto the dock, fist raised in anger. The commotion was sudden and violent. There was the sound of a gunshot, voices carrying across the water like the cries of the damned. But just then the wind came up and took hold of the sails like a great gloved hand, and the shore was lost in the gray wash of the waves.

◆§ ξ◆

If there was triumph in that escape, a feeling that she had been able to react in a crisis and marshal her inner resources to outmaneuver a vastly superior force, the grimness of her homecoming all but annihilated it. There was no one to meet her, no one who cared whether she was alive or dead, returned safe to England or forever trapped in exile. Ned was gone, her parents would bolt the door and latch the windows against a fallen woman, Cook, Bount and the Bankses would sooner run naked through the streets than look at her. She was even cheated of the little patriotic jump of the heart that a first glimpse of the Tower or the spires of St. Paul's might have given her — the German vessel put in at Gravesend, and she had no money even to hire a fisherman's smack to take her up the river. As it was, she had to beg a ride with a man hauling a cartload of chickens to market. The cart jostled, a cold rain fell, the child cried, the chickens stank of scale and excrement, the man put a hand on her thigh.

They wound their way into London through the stinking slums of the East End. Soot hung in the air. Children were begging on the streetcorners, women lay drunk in the alleys. Two pigs gorged on the offal in the gutter, a madman was selling invisible Bibles, a woman with cancer of the throat offered to drink a gallon of water and vomit it up for a penny. After the carter let her down in Poultry Lane, Fanny wandered the streets for hours, aimless, the child tugging at her arm. She had nothing but a few worthless pfennigs in her pocket, no place to stay, nothing to eat, and what was worse, she was down to her last few drops of laudanum. She'd been pacing herself, trying to make it last, but already her stomach was beginning to crawl. The rain fell like fire and brimstone.

Sometime that night or the next, she found herself on Monmouth Street, grimly plodding through the rain, looking for medicine, food, shelter, warmth, medicine, medicine, medicine. The child had been crying steadily for hours, pulling back at her hand, tugging at her skirts, whining that he wanted to lie down and sleep. Her own legs felt like lead and her back ached as if she'd been hauling pails of milk all night or laboring over the butter churn. She had the dry heaves. Her throat burned with a raw desperate thirst that no amount of water could quell.

She finally stopped outside an old clothes shop to sift through a pile of refuse in the hope of coming up with something to quiet the child. There, in the midst of fouled rags and fragments of glass, lay a fish head, slick with wet and trailing a pale bubble of bladder and intestine. Her stomach turned, but the boy snatched for it. He crammed it in his mouth as if it were a crumpet or sugar bun and she began to scream, scream with disgust and despair and a mounting hysteria that fed on the thought that she had finally given way and would never be whole again, when the door behind her fell open and a pale stream of light trickled out over the cobblestones.

" 'Ere, 'ere, wot's the matter?" a rusty voice creaked at her back.

The massive wooden sign heaved on its hinges: Rose's Old Clothes, it said, moving in the wind. Rose's Old Clothes. An aged woman stood in the doorway. She was withered with years, her spine frozen at an angle, a bunch of skinless knuckles clutching at the head of a cane. Fanny's screams caught in her throat. The child sat in a puddle and worked at the fish head with quick fingers and teeth. " 'Ere," the old woman repeated. "Come in now and warm yerselfs by the fire. It ain't much, but it'll do ye better than the wet of the streets."

Inside, Fanny and the boy hunched before the fire, dark mountains of clothes heaped up around them. The old woman shuffled out from the back room with a handful of coal and a bowl of crowdie for the boy. While the boy ate she settled herself beside Fanny and looked up at her with a knowing eye. Fanny was trembling, Saint Vitus' dance and tic douloureux. She couldn't hold the cup of broth the old woman forced into her hand. "Like a tumbler o' Mother genever, dearie? Or is it somethin' stronger ye'll be wantin'?"

Fanny hung her head and asked for laudanum — if the old woman could spare it. "I've got a stomach problem," she added, sotto voce.

The old woman clawed her way up from the floor and trundled off into a darkened corner where she rummaged through a mound of soiled garments for what seemed like hours. When she finally hobbled back to the fire, the breath whistling through her lungs, she clutched a blue bottle in her hand. "Tincture," she read from the label, "of opium. That wot ye want, dearie?" The old woman was grinning. Suddenly a crazed primordial squeal flew from her lips: "Eeeee!" she cackled. "Eeeee-eeeee!"

Fanny grabbed the bottle from her and held it to her lips. Almost immediately the tightness in her throat was gone. The rodents stopped gnawing at her stomach, the blinding pain in her head began to soften, dissipate, finally losing itself in a pool of numbness. She took another drink, then another. After awhile she lay back and watched the ceiling revolve in an accelerating whirl of planets and satellites, fiery suns and the cold black reaches of space.

※ ❧

She woke at dawn. A man and a woman were standing over her. The man sported a yellowish blood blister on the tip of his nose, the woman clutched a broom to her chest as if it were a shield. "Wot the bloody 'ell you think you're doing in my shop?" the man said.

Fanny sat up, dazed, and felt around her for the child. The child was gone.

"Well, speak up, you slattern," the woman hissed.

Fanny felt as if she'd been thrown down a flight of stairs and hit with a mallet. Panic was beating at her ribs. "I — I . . . the old woman — "

"Old woman?" the man said.

"She's daft," the woman spat, edging closer with the broom.

"No, no — you don't understand. She's got my boy. Right here, last night, she — "

"Out of it," the man snapped. "Out before I calls the constable. 'Ear? Get out."

※ ❧

She haunted the streets for a week, slept outside the shop on Monmouth Street every night. She ate nothing. The laudanum gave out. She lay in the alleyway back of the store, gasping for breath, her stomach punctured, heart torn out. She was a whore, an opium eater, a childless mother. All her beauty, all her stamina, all her resourcefulness had brought her to this. It was the nineteenth century. What else was a heroine to do but make her way to the river?

The month was October, the year 1801 — but she hardly knew it. Napoleon was lulling the British with the Peace of Amiens, De Quincey was sixteen and bridling under the regimen at the Manchester Grammar School, Ned Rise was busy ducking Osprey and looking, with a sort of hopeless resignation for his lost love, for her, Fanny. Fanny, however, was looking for no one. Her son was gone, Ned was a memory. She made her way to Blackfriars Bridge one foggy night, pulled herself over the railing and toppled into the mist below. The flat dark water closed over her like a curtain drawn across a stage.

❧ NAIAD, YES INDEED

The river is a murmur, a pulse, a dream of the body, schools of dace and shiners ebbing like blood, the tick-tick-tick of an arrested branch as persistent as a heartbeat. From down here, on a level with it, the surface seems to break into a thousand fingers, each one probing for direction, smoothing channels, skirting the worn black rocks that seem to dip and swell like shoulderblades as the current washes over them. Mungo leans back in the stiff high grass that overspills the bank, his face to the sun, the tip of his cane pole propped up against an overhanging branch. He is on holiday, at Fowlshiels, the playful cries of his children and the murmur of his wife's chatter washing over him like balm. The earth breathes in and breathes out again. Beside him, Alexander Anderson lazily thumbs through an account of the West African slave trade and sips at a pint of porter.

After awhile the explorer props himself on an elbow and glances up the bank to where Ailie stands knee-deep in the cold swirling water while Thomas and Mungo junior play in the mud and grandmother Park rocks the baby in her cradle. Ailie catches his eye, a smile and a wave, and then she's gone, slashing into the current like an arrow. The month is September, the year 1803. Two years have dragged by since the move to Peebles. Two years of on-again, off-again preparations for a second expedition to West Africa, two years of pacifying Ailie and trying to overrule a multitude of objections, two years of the most tedious and thankless work he's ever done, tending the sick and cankered ingrates of Peebleshire. Two more years, two more children. Mungo junior came along in the fall of 1801, just after they got settled at Peebles; Elizabeth was born last spring.

All well and good. Healthy children, a loving wife. That's what life is all about. But already the size of his family has begun to worry him. Four years of marriage, three children. He tries to imagine himself in twenty years, his hair gone white, fifteen children clamoring for meat and milk and sugar buns, new suits and dresses, schoolbooks, dowries, university fees. "Three's enough," he tells Ailie, but she just looks at him out of the corner of her eye, sly and suggestive, fertile as Niger mud. "I want bairns to remember you by when you go off and leave me," she says, no trace of humor in her voice, each child a new link in the chain that binds him to her. At night she lights candles before the carved black statue that squats in the center of her dressing table like an icon, and once he caught her rubbing its swollen belly before climbing into bed. Touch her and she's pregnant again.

"I'm worried, Zander."

Zander squints up from his book.

"The way the family's grown and all. I feel responsible for them, I want to provide for them . . . but I just can't see going back to Peebles. This week down here at Fowlshiels has been heaven compared with the grind up there — heaven — and still I can't enjoy it. I feel like I'm wasting my life away. Every time I get on that horse and tramp out to some godforsaken cottage in the hills to watch some old gaffer wheeze to death I can't help thinking that's the way I'll wind up. Dying on my back. In bed. After forty years of boredom."

"So what does Ailie think?"

"You know what she thinks."

"No Africa."

"No Africa."

The explorer tugs indolently at his line for a moment, then shifts his gaze back to Ailie. He watches as she negotiates the current, cutting back against the flow, one arm suspended in a flash of foam, then the other, silver, luminous, clean and precise. She moves like a creature born to water. Moves with an easy fluid athletic grace, moves with a beauty that catches in his throat. He loses her momentarily in a shimmering crescent of reflected sun, only to watch her reemerge in an aureole of light, transfigured in that flashing instant to something beyond flesh and blood, something mythic and eternal. How could he ever leave her?

"Well," Zander is saying, "maybe there are greater duties than family duty. Maybe you owe something to science and civilization too."

Mungo turns to look him in the eye. "I got a letter this morning, Zander. Brought down by special messenger from Peebles. Early. Before she was up."

The news hits Alexander Anderson like an electric shock. Ten thousand volts. He kicks over the beer, drops the book and leaps to his feet. "From London?"

The explorer nods. "From the government. Lord Hobart. He wants to see me immediately . about heading up an expedition to determine the course of the Niger." The last few words are delivered in an almost reverential whisper.

Zander has been watching him, rapt, his eyes dilated, lips moving in silent accord with his every word. Suddenly he breaks into a grin and begins pumping the explorer's hand. "This is what we've been waiting for — this is it!"

"Shhhhh." Mungo looks like a weasel with an egg in its mouth. "I haven't told your sister yet."

"She won't like it."

"No."

Zander squats down beside him, balancing on toes and fingertips. He is twenty-nine and looks eighteen. "But surely she can see it's for a higher purpose — she's got to. She'll understand. I know she will."

Mungo snorts. "I wish I could share your optimism."

"Tell her. Go ahead — maybe you'll be surprised."

The explorer looks tentatively over his shoulder. Ailie and Thomas are wrapped in a blanket and roasting bits of meat over a fire. His mother is paring apples and rocking the baby, the two-year-old is screeching like a loon and running naked up and down the bank as if he'd been locked in the closet for a week. "You know, you may be right, Zander," Mungo says finally, rising to his feet. "I might as well have it out now." And then, less certain: "Though I hate to spoil the day."

But before he can take two steps, the whole question of the letter, Africa, ambition and Ailie is suddenly shunted to the back burner — because at that instant the tip of the cane pole begins to twitch. Very gingerly at first, but convincingly enough to catch Zander's eye. "Mungo!" he shouts, and the explorer, his reactions honed in the wilds of Africa, wheels round to appraise the situation in a flash, perceiving the pieces of the puzzle and its solution almost simultaneously (Zander's face, the pointed finger, the cane pole trembling along its length from the shock of a solid hit and careering for the water like a pilotless bobsled). He reacts without hesitation. One moment he's standing there looking down expectantly at his brother-in-law, the next he's throwing himself at the fast-receding pole, barely managing to catch hold of its last knobby deformation. He fights to his knees, staggers to his feet, the pole bent double in his hands, an incredible slashing force communicating with him at the far end of the line, silver in the depths, beating and rushing with the pulse of the river itself. "He's got one," Zander is shouting, "he's got a keltie!" And now Ailie and the boys are running toward him, excitement slapped across their faces like the first flush of winter.

Mungo strains against this fish with everything he's got, all his being focused on this thing extending from his fingertips to scrape the rocks and hug its belly to the deepest recesses of the deepest pools. He can feel every pebble, he can read the whole history of the river there, igneous pillars thrust through the surface, the flat scouring hand of the glaciers, the relentless buffeting of the watercourse, stream without end, draining into the sea and rising again in the clouds. Implacable, determined, he pulls at the mystery with every nerve and fiber of his body, with every ounce of blood and pound of flesh, he pulls.

And it pulls him, it pulls him.

✑ SIDI AMBAK BUBI

Mungo returns from London just before Christmas, the fringe of a tartan muffler peeping out from beneath his stovepipe hat, a small dark stranger at his side. If no one pays much attention to the explorer (familiarity breeds familiarity), the stranger is another story. No one in Peebleshire knows quite what to make of him. At first glance he seems ordinary enough — kneeboots, woollen trousers, greatcoat, cravat — but on closer inspection, the good people of Peebles find themselves confronted with a series of anomalies. For one thing, there is the question of the stranger's complexion, the hue of which seems to fall midway between the dun of barnyard muck and the cheesy yellow of goat's milk. For another, there is the question of his hat, which isn't a hat at all but a strip of linen wound round his head. Not to mention his ritually scarred cheeks, waist-length beard and the gold hoop piercing his lip in the most shamelessly barbaric way. All in all, considering that nothing has changed in Peebles in eight hundred years, the stranger's sudden appearance is every bit as extraordinary as the birth of a two-headed duck or the discovery of a new comet in the night sky.

They ride into Peebles at sunset, Mungo and his dark companion, the evidence of their dialogue hanging in the chill air like smoke. The denizens of Peebles — retiring types, quiet, half-asleep — are bent over their hearths as the horses clop past their windows, the puissant odors of neeps and potatoes, boiled beef and cockyleekie soup commanding their full attention. Even so, half of them are pressed to their windows or edging out into the street before the explorer has reached his front yard. They are in shirt-sleeves, aprons, slippers, some are even barefooted. All look as if they've just seen some prodigy, some freak of nature, some walking, talking, insidious illusion they can neither accept nor dismiss. "Did ye see what I seen?" says Angus M'Corkle to his neighbor, Mrs. Crimpie.

"Aye," she says, slowly shaking her head as if to unplug her ears, "and I'll be blessed if it wasn't one of the Magi himself come up for the Holy Day."

"Nay, nay. It's clear he's just some itinerant Jew . . . or maybe a Chinese Mongol."

"Ali Baba," says Festus Baillie, his jaw locked like a judge's. "Ali Baba himself."

◄§ ¿►

Sidi Ambak Bubi is neither Jew nor Mongol. Nor is he a freak of nature, a prodigy or an Arabian folkhero. He is, quite simply, a Moor: humble, unassuming, a trifle unctuous. A Moor from Mogador, well connected and educated, who originally came to London to serve as interpreter for Elphi Bey, Ambassador from Cairo. But when Elphi Bey expired suddenly after choking on a wedge of mutton and flushing a deep midnight blue, Sidi found himself out of a job. It would be months before Cairo could be informed of the Ambassador's death and arrange for a replacement. He began to feel concerned. It was at this point that Sir Joseph Banks stepped in. Would Mr. Bubi be so kind as to come round to No. 32, Soho Square? Sir Joseph had a proposition to make him.

When Sidi was shown into the library at Sir Joseph's townhouse, he found himself standing before two Englishmen: one elderly and squarish, with a cast of jaw that suggested a bulldog, the other young, fair-haired and muscular. The elderly man, as distinguished and formidable as a ship of the line, proved to be Sir Joseph Banks. He greeted Sidi with an outstretched hand, offered him a seat and a glass of claret (which Sidi, a devout Moslem, politely refused). And then turned to introduce him to his companion, Mungo Park.

Sidi flushed to his lip ring on hearing the explorer's name, rose awkwardly and stretched himself on the floor at his feet. "Oh Mr. Park, sir, I greatly admire your writings," he sang out in the high nasal whine of a muezzin at prayer, "and I applaud your efforts to open up our poor backward land to the civilizing influence of the Englishmans, I do, I do." By this time both Mungo and Sir Joseph were on their feet expostulating with the Moor to get up and behave himself, but apparently he hadn't yet finished what he intended to say. He lay there a full minute, nose buried in the carpet, before very hesitantly continuing. "But oh Mr. Park, Sir," he mumbled, "how heartily I deplore the shameful treatment you had from my co-religionists in Ludamar. They are sorry dogs." Apparently satisfied at having got this out, the Moor crept back to his seat on hands and knees, and perched at the edge of his chair, eyes averted, while Sir Joseph outlined his proposition.

Mr. Park, Sir Joseph explained, was in London for the second time in as many months for the purpose of organizing an expedition to the Niger Basin. The expedition was to have left within six weeks, but for an unforeseen reversal. The government of Mr. Addington had fallen, and the Colonial Secretary, Lord Hobart, had been replaced by Lord Camden. The new Secretary had informed Sir Joseph that the government could not possibly arrange for an expedition before September of the following year.

Mungo sipped moodily at his claret throughout this recitation. He was disappointed, disheartened, disgusted. In the fall, after that idyllic afternoon on the Yarrow, he'd spent two hellish days and nights trying to reassure Ailie that he had no intention of leaving her. She clung to him and screamed like a madwoman, threatened to drown herself, set the house afire, throttle the children in their sleep. He wasn't going to desert her again — she wouldn't allow it. She'd poison him first. He broke down under the pressure. "All right," he told her, "I'll run down to London and tell Hobart he'll have to find another man." She kissed his hands. They made love like newlyweds.

He was lying. Lying to buy time. In London he told Hobart: "I'm your man. Give me the supplies and manpower I need and I'll map the Niger for you, beginning to end." Hobart asked for two months to make the arrangements, and the explorer returned to Peebles, on edge, impatient, as guilt-racked as a sticky-fingered altar boy. "Did you tell him?" Ailie asked.

Mungo looked away. "Yes, but . . . but he's asked me to act as technical advisor for a new expedition to be headed up by some . . . some young Welshman Sir Joseph has dug up."

That was in October. In December there was another summons from Hobart and the explorer took the first coach for London. He stepped into the Colonial office, prepared to leave on the spot, already mentally drafting a letter to Ailie: *Dear Ailie, I love and cherish you and adore the children, but duty to my country and my God must come before even my sacred duty to my family. Africa awaits, the greatest adventure mankind has ever known, and I am the only man alive who* — Hobart's face stopped him cold. "I'm afraid I've got some bad news, Park," the Secretary said.

"Sir?"

"We're out."

Mungo stared at the older man in bewilderment. "Out?"

"Addington has resigned."

And so there he was, sitting in Sir Joseph's study and looking gloomily out the window when he should have been sailing for Goree. Nine months more. It seemed as if he was doomed to fritter away his talents in Peebles

forever, an overworked, underpaid, back-country sawbones. Lord Hobart,
Lord Camden, Addington, Pitt — what difference did it make? All he got
was excuses.

"Thus," Sir Joseph was saying, "I am prepared to offer you thirty
pounds sterling if you will accompany Mr. Park to Peebles and there tutor
him in Arabic in preparation for his forthcoming expedition."

The Moor looked around him as if he'd just been slapped. "T'irty pound
sterling?" he echoed, incredulous. "You give me?" Sir Joseph nodded, and
Sidi threw himself on the carpet. "*Ya galbi galbi!*" he sang, "*An' am Allah
ʿalaik!*"

⇥§ §⇤

Ailie is in the kitchen, fussing over a partan pie and boiling down the
snout, ears, cheeks, brains and feet of a freshly killed hog, when she is
suddenly arrested by a sound from the backyard. It's been going on for a
minute or two now, a sort of dull thumping, but she's been so absorbed in
her work she hasn't paid it any mind. There it is again. Viscous and
muffled, the sound of someone splitting wood in the distance — or leading
a horse around the corner of the house. Then it hits her: Mungo! In an
instant she's at the door, apron white with flour, the late sun spreading
butter over the stable, her husband, the manes of the horses, the pinched
dark stranger staring up at her out of his glittering, red-flecked eyes.
Who — ? she wonders, a vague unease settling in her stomach, but then
she's caught up in Mungo's arms and nothing else really matters.

Inside, Mungo and his guest settle down at the edge of the hearth,
warming their hands, while Ailie puts the kettle on and turns back to her
pie. Mungo had perfunctorily introduced the little man outside the stable
door, Seedy something-or-other, she didn't quite catch his name. Meanwhile, the small talk sifts down like a blizzard. Mungo asks how the
children have been, what the weather's been like, has she got enough wood
chopped, is that a cold she's caught? He expatiates on Sir Joseph's health,
the rigors of the trip, the new government, Dickson, Effie and Edwards,
but he hasn't yet gotten round to explaining Seedy. She takes the little man
to be an African, judging from the rag wrapped round his head and the
slashes dug into his dark cheeks and brow. A Moor? A Mandingo? And
what would Mungo be bringing him up here for? . . . Unless —

"So," she says, kneading her dough with a vengeance, "you've come to
visit Peebles . . . Mr. Seedy?"

The Moor looks up at her, as if surprised to hear his name spoken aloud
by such a person in such a place. He is huddled so close to the fire she's
afraid he'll burst into flame at any moment. "Oh my lady, yes, yes, I am

visiting Peebles." The look in his eye reminds her of Douce Davie when someone sets a ham out on the sideboard.

Mungo sighs, and gets up from the hearth. "God, that smells good," he says. "What are you fixing — brawn?"

"For Christmas," she says.

"No goose?"

She has the distinct sensation that he is trying to sidetrack her, that there is something about this Seedy he doesn't want her to know. "Goose, yes," she says, impatient, "goose too. But tell me," turning to the Moor, "will you be with us for the holidays, Mr. Seedy?"

The Moor looks puzzled. "Hollandaise?"

In an undertone, quick as a burst of gunfire, Mungo says something to him in a foreign language. Arabic?

Sidi grins. "I am a Moor, precious lady."

This is getting her nowhere. She turns to her husband, wiping her hands on her apron. "He'll be staying?"

But before Mungo can answer, the Moor leaps to his feet, as if by prearrangement. "Oh yes, kind lady, Mistress Park," he whines, rushing up to her and prostrating himself at her feet. "Wit' your permission, I am to stay two or t'ree mont'."

Ailie draws back as if she's been scorched. "Two or three — ?"

"Ailie," Mungo is saying, his voice low and deprecatory.

"Good lady, good lady," Sidi chants, pursuing her on all fours and making as if to kiss the hem of her dress. Suddenly he looks up at her and barks, "Tutor, tutor," with all the exhilaration of a lexicographer who's been searching out the word for a month.

"He's come to tutor me in Arabic, sweet."

"Arabic? Whatever for?" But she already knows the answer, her face draining, jaw gone rigid. "You're not — ?"

Mungo looks like a prisoner in the dock. "I uh — I've been meaning to tell you, uh, about what Sir Joseph — " he begins, only to be saved by the bell. At that instant Mungo junior pokes his head through the kitchen doorway, closely followed by Thomas. There is a moment of hesitation, and then they burst into the room, hugging at their father's legs, their shrill infantile voices rattling the windows with an ingenuous, radiant and all-consuming joy.

❧ FATHERS AND SONS

It's a long road to Hertfordshire. A road that goes by way of Enfield, various hayricks, an old virago's shack, the county jail and the hulks. But that's getting ahead of the story. Step back a pace and remember the winter of '02, blustery and bitter, and the two ragged figures shivering their way up the Hertfordshire road, starved, penniless and fearful, hounded out of town by the fanatical persistence of Claude Messenger Osprey, Jr.

They are disconsolate, these two, no longer certain that they've made the right choice, numbly wondering if freezing to death is really all that much better than hanging. Ned can barely lift his feet, so soporific is the cold. He wants to lie down in a ditch, pull the greatcoat over his ears and dream of steaming cauldrons and mugs of hot broth. And Boyles, poor flat-headed sot, is even worse off. He's long since fallen into a sort of trance, lurching up the road like a drunken automaton, pitching headlong into the bushes, flopping down in the road and embracing the rock-hard earth as if it were a featherbed. Each time he stumbles Ned turns back to exhort him him to get up and keep moving. "Come on, Billy, get up out of it now. You'll be dead in an hour if you lie there like that."

"Good."

"Come on now," tugging at the narrow shoulders as if at a harness, "we'll beg shelter at the next place we come to."

At that moment, the sound of hoof and wheel swells at them out of the penumbra of early morning. "Look out!" pipes a childish voice, closely followed by the screech of braking wheels and a man's basso shouting, "Whoa there, whoa!" The shadowy light reveals a farm wagon, its wheels skidded to a halt about half an inch from Boyles' angular head. The man at the reins is a rut-faced, graying farmer in his late thirties, his hands like blocks of granite and a soft salvationist's glint in his eye. "Well, brother, what seems to be the trouble here?" he booms, squinting down at Boyles' inert form.

Ned puts on his best lost-dog look and tells him that they're on their way to Hertford, but down on their luck. Without shelter they'll be dead of the cold before the day is out.

The farmer pauses to tamp the bowl of his pipe, the first long rays of the sun suddenly illuminating his face. "Can't have that," he grunts, smoke spewing from the corner of his mouth. "Climb aboard and make yourselves comfortable under the rug with my boys here."

Two sets of round black eyes peer from the shadows at the farmer's back. "Nahum and Joseph," the farmer says, as the boys make way for Ned and

Boyles in the back of the cart. Boyles is glassy-eyed from lack of sleep, warmth and drink. He stumbles twice, but manages to claw his way into the back of the wagon with an assist from Ned. "Under here," whispers the older boy, who looks to be about six or seven, and a moment later Ned and Boyles are nestled under a skin rug that must weigh eighty pounds, sipping at a jug of still-hot cider and pressing their feet to an iron bed warmer.

"Goin' as far as Enfield," the farmer says over his shoulder as the wagon lurches forward. "You're welcome to come along."

◦§ §◦

A lord in London — some distant, congenitally privileged, bewigged and besilked Member of the House, Knight of the Garter and hanger-on at White's Gaming Club — is responsible for the meticulously arranged gardens, stands of naked black trees and cultivated fields that engulf Nahum Pribble's one-room cottage. Nahum is merely a tenant. He owns two goats, a pig, a dozen hens and an ox. His wife is dead. She got into bed one night muttering something about a fat man sitting on her chest. In the morning there was blood on the pillow. Nahum buried her out back but the overseer made him dig her up and buy a plot for her in the parish cemetery. Ever since, Nahum has raised the boys on his own.

"Must be hard," says Ned over a cup of mulled wine. The windows are black. Boyles is snoring in front of the fireplace, a dog on either side of him. The boys are in bed.

"Hard? That's what Jesus must have thought when he was nailed to the cross and they stuck that spear in his side." Nahum is standing over a tub of water, his big hands scraping at the wooden supper plates. The firelight washes his features clean, lines and furrows softened, his face as smooth and timeless as a portrait in a darkened gallery.

"I mean raising the kids with no woman around."

The farmer turns to look Ned in the eye. "There's a father in Heaven that looks after Nahum Pribble, and Nahum Pribble is humbly thankful that he's been blessed to be a father on earth to look after them two boys there."

Ned glances over at the frame bed, the two forms in the shadows, the slow pacific rise and fall of the coverlet.

"That's the whole of my life," the farmer says, his voice so soft Ned can barely hear it over the hiss of the flames.

◦§ §◦

The next morning they're back on the road, provisioned with bread and cheese, a handful of dried apples and a jug of beer. Despite lowering skies, a stiff wind and temperatures in the teens, Ned is feeling optimistic. The farmer's hospitality has touched him, made him feel for the first time in years that the universe is not uniformly and actively malignant, that the milk of human kindness hasn't necessarily soured, that hope is in the cards though the deck may be stacked against you. He actually finds himself whistling — an air for the clarinet Barrenboyne had taught him years ago — as he ambles up the rutted road like a landowner out for a stroll.

Though Hertford is less than ten miles off, Boyles is so worked up about the beer he convinces Ned to stop and have a nip before they've passed the first milestone. Ned manages to get a fire going in the lee of a stone wall, and they have a chilly picnic of it, toasting the bread and cheese, burning the apples and washing the whole thing down with thirsty gulps of beer. The remainder of the journey is comfortless, a grim silent plodding against the wind, the road deserted, neither cottage nor inn in sight. By late afternoon they reach the outskirts of Hertford, and are summarily turned away from the first three cottages they approach. So much for the milk of human kindness.

"What'll we do now, Neddy?" Boyles stutters, hunched and trembling, blue in the face. The wind rattles the trees with a sound of bone on bone.

Ned is blowing into his fist, hugging himself, dancing. "Hit the next place," he puffs, "beg them to let us stand by the fire a minute and then point us the way to the Brunches'."

The next place is set back from the road in a grove of maple and yew. Numbed, they fight their way through thorns and nettles, over fallen trees and through the slush of a fetid stream, the thin coil of chimney smoke guiding their way, the first glimmerings of desperation pricking at fingers and toes. But when they come upon the house itself, they're stopped cold. The place is nothing more than a hovel, linked by means of a crumbling umbilical passage to an even smaller hovel in back. It looks like a Druid burial mound, or a reconverted sheepcote dating from the reign of William the Conqueror. There are no windows, stones have dropped from the walls and left gaps like missing teeth, the thatch of the roof is overgrown with weed, moss, brambles, saplings four or five feet high. "No use in wastin' your breath," Boyles sighs. "Nobody's lived here in a hunnert years."

But there it is, incontrovertible, the thin steady stream of smoke spinning from the chimney.

Ned goes down on his knees in the frozen muck and taps at the door, a tale of want and woe and sore distress on his lips, the story of how he and Boyles, on their way to their father's funeral in Cambridge — a wealthy man, their father, porcelain merchant, worth nearly two hundred thousand pounds at his death — were set upon by highwaymen, stripped of everything they owned and forced at gunpoint to change clothes with the heartless blackguards, and how they'd been wandering ever since, penniless, near dead with the cold and hunger, determinedly making their way to that distant seat of learning where a fat dazzling fortune awaits them . . .

As it turns out, there's no need for pretty speeches. The door wrenches back at the first tap, and before he can utter a word a wild shrick cauterizes the air and a wizened old crone is ushering them in the door. "Eeeeee-eeeee! Travelers, is it? Cold and 'ungry? Robbed on the road, no doubt? Well come on in and warm yerselfs round Mother's fire, come on now, don't be shy."

She is hunched low to the ground with some progressive deformity of the spine, this old woman, her squamate hands twisted into claws, the eyes keen as talons in a face as ravaged as the dimmest memories of the past. Boyles nearly knocks her flat in his rush to get at the fire, but Ned hangs back, alarmed, until she reaches out a withered claw and pulls him through the doorway.

Inside, it's a cave. Stone walls, earthen floor, a darkness meliorated only by the primeval light of the fire. Ned nearly trips over a shadow stretched across the floor, his heart racing like a quick little animal in a cage, something wrong, something dead wrong, all his senses strung to a pitch and that burned-once, twice-cautious voice gibbering in his head, look out, look out. He jerks back and the shadow snorts, rises from the dirt and materializes into a drooping, flap-eared sow.

" 'Ere!" shrieks the old woman, her voice as cracked and mad as a tortured violin, "come and warm yer bones. Eeeeee-eeeee!" Suddenly she wheels around on Boyles. "You, flattop — 'ow 'bout a snootful o' nippitatum, eh? Eh?"

She doesn't have to ask twice. Boyles has the jug to his mouth before she can lift it from the shelf, smacking his lips and gasping, running on with some nonsense about elixir of the gods, his lank legs thrust into the fire, his face red as an innkeeper's.

"And you, peachfuzz?"

Ned is backed up against the hearth, tense as a cat, half expecting to blink twice and discover a string of murdered children hanging from the ceiling or some nasty stinging thing coiled in the shadows. The sow shakes its ears and gives him a long slow look of utter disdain before collapsing in the corner, the scent of it hot in his nostrils, a fetor of decay and excrement about the place, a stink of life lived at the root and mired in every odious little event of the body. "No," he says, rubbing his hands. "No, we've really got to be going . . . just stopped to ask the way to Squire Trelawney's place — "

"Ah," the old woman breathes, "friends o' the Squire's, are ye?" Ned makes the mistake of nodding yes.

"Eeeeee-eeeee!" she caterwauls. "Well that's a good one, the divil and 'is dam it is. I took ye to be no-account, disreputable, vagabond, derelict bums, I did . . . but friends o' the Squire's, now that's a different story, yes," she cackles, "another story altogether." And then she cups her hands to her mouth and shouts down the passageway in a voice as raw and poisonous as a dish of toadstools: "Boy! Hallo, boy! Get yer lazy arse out 'ere and meet the fine gennemens wot's come a-callin'."

"Really, we just — " Ned stammers.

"Honored, I'm sure," the old woman shrieks, scraping the ground in an obscene parody of a curtsy. " 'Ere, 'ave a seat and give us peasants a minute o' yer precious time," thrusting a stool at him and calling out impatiently into the darkened passageway. "Boy!"

There is a movement on the far side of the room, furtive and shy, the form of a child emerging from the low rictus of the sheeprun. A boy, four or five, his face a dim white spot in the gloom. He stands there, uncertain, hanging his head.

"Well, ye young toad, stop yer loiterin' in the shadders and come over 'ere to yer old Mother — or don't ye ken the King's English no more?" The old woman, cocked and watchful, has stationed herself in the center of the room, at the pulse of things, playing to her audience like a demented actress in her most ominous role. What next? Ned is thinking, when suddenly she spins round on him, a leer on her face, the old gums working. " 'Ee's a littul pissant, that one, ain't 'ee? A reg'lar changeling. Why ye'd think 'ee was afraid of 'is own dear Mother the way 'ee acts."

Ned's face is locked like a vault. There is something familiar here, something sinister, something he doesn't want to know. And yet he looks on as if hypnotized, compelled despite himself, this grim inscrutable drama unfolding with a logic and momentum of its own. He looks on as the harridan writhes across the room and snatches the child to her breast like a greedy crow, her shriek of triumph like a razor drawn across a pane of glass. Looks on as she insinuates a withered hand under the boy's chin and twists his face to the light with a glittering malicious grin.

As the firelight falls across the boy's pinched features, illuminating the greasy wisps of hair and smudged face, the open sores on the chin and the steady patient gaze of a penned animal, Ned feels a panic rising in him.

Compelled, he stares at the boy as he might have stared at a bleeding
statue or his own epitaph etched in a gravestone, stares as he's never stared
before, Boyles turned from the fire to gawk at him, the only sound in the
room the hag's fierce rattling insuck of breath. And then he's up off the
stool, groping like a blind man, his mouth working in shock and incomprehension. He is looking at himself. Below the stark leering challenge of the
hag's eyes, he is looking into his own, the years stripped back, suffering in
ascendancy, the ragged orphan set loose on the streets. He is dreaming,
dying, going mad.

The harridan's shriek breaks the spell. " 'Andsome lad, wot?" she
cackles. "Though 'ee needs a bit of a cuff now and again, don't ye, boy?
Eh?" And as if to prove it, she spins him round and rakes his ear in a single
practiced movement. "Now get back to yer perch, ye dirty littul beast," she
spits, and the child vanishes into the passageway like a mirage.

It couldn't be, no, it couldn't. Look out, the voice shouts in his head.
"I — " Ned begins, but the noose is round his throat again, the hangman's
eyes like rare jewels glittering in their slits, and suddenly he has Boyles by
the arm. "Get up, Billy, get up."

Boyles has by this time turned his attention back to the jug, periodically
shaking it and holding it to his ear like a watchmaker inspecting a faulty
timepiece. He puts it aside momentarily and pokes the fire, happy as the
day he was born. "Wot?" he gasps, an edge of genuine shock to his voice.

"Eeeeee-eeeee!" the old woman keens.

Ned jerks Boyles to his feet. "Forget the jug, Billy — we got to go now.
Go now," he shouts, as if Boyles were brain-damaged or hard of hearing.

"Awwww," croaks the hag, picking at her ear. "So soon? But ye just got
'ere. Mother 'asn't 'ad time to get out the linen nor polish the silver,
eeeeee!"

Boyles' face is pained and confused. "I likes it here, Neddy," he whines,
but his companion is already pulling him toward the door in a desperate
trembling grip that pinches his arm — even through the coat — with all the
implacable urgency of a steel trap.

Ned hesitates at the door, his voice floating on a wave of adrenalin: "The
Brunch farm," he stammers, "old woman, which way is it?"

The semblance of a smile twists her lips. "Farmer Brunch? I thought you
boys was friends o' the Squire's?" The joke catches in her throat and she
begins to hack and wheeze like an overworked horse, but Ned is already
out the door, white-hot with terror and rage and confusion, fighting
through the brambles and jerking at Boyles' sleeve for all he's worth.

"Arf a mile . . . up the road, peach . . . peachfuzz," the old woman shrieks at his back. "At the fork. Just climb the fence and cut across the pasture. Stone cottage with a tumbledown barn . . . out back. 'Ear?"

Ned is running, panicked, every syllable an injection of fire and brimstone and the caustic salts of perdition, conscience rasping in his ear, Boyles forsaken, legs churning, arms parting the dead stalks and low-hanging branches as if they were waves and he a breaststroker making for shore, running for the cold hard road and the sanctuary of the Brunch farm like a filicide caught in the act.

∽ A TICKET TO GOREE

Half a mile up the road they come to a fork. A milestone on the right indicates the way into Hertford proper. On the left, a neck-high wall of interlocking stones, an empyrean expanse of greening pasture maculated with stubborn patches of ice, and in the distance, as the hag had indicated, the stone cottage flanked by the tumbledown barn.

Boyles stops short, puzzles over the milestone and then, scratching his head, crosses the road to the stone wall, hikes himself up on his elbows and takes a good hard squint at the distant farmhouse. After a minute or two of intense concentration, rapid lip movement and the ticking off of various sums on his fingers, he turns back to Ned. "This'll be it, Neddy, looks like."

Ned is only half listening. The encounter with the hag and her strange timid ward has anesthetized him, deadened him to the cold and the uncertainty alike, shut his ears to hope, calculation and the insipid chattering voice of his traveling companion. He can still see the child's eyes, hear the hag's squawks of triumph, feel that empty strangling sensation in his gut, the insidious cramp of a truth so unimaginable it can only be digested in the dark essential atmosphere of the bowels. When he looks up at Boyles, he can only nod.

A heave, a ho, and a thump, and they're in the pasture, looking half a dozen startled sheep in the eye. As they muck their way across the field, the farmhouse begins to look somewhat grander and more extensive than they'd been led to expect, the barn less tumbledown. Is this a tenant's cottage? With three chimneys and a second story?

Boyles is rubbing his hands with glee and Ned is on the verge of making the deductive leap between the unwonted sprawl of the farmhouse and the hag's ulterior motives, when the first shotgun blast knocks them flat. The second blast flings a fistful of mud in their faces and neatly threads the odd ball or two through their breeches and into the tender uncalloused flesh along the nether plane of their thighs and buttocks. An instant later a pair of wooden-faced gamekeepers are standing over them, guns smoking and boots glistening. Then there's a voice, deep as thunder along the spine of a mountain, righteous and indignant as the voice of God, barking out a terse command: "Off the ground, shitface."

Ned rises slowly, his buttocks on fire, staring into the mouth of the gun. The man behind the gun is as impassive as a weasel with a rat in its mouth, sallow and dead-eyed.

"But — but you don't — " Ned begins, but the man merely cuffs him with the stock of the gun in an automatic and exquisitely fluid snap of shoulder and elbow, and Ned finds himself face down in the mud again. Then there's the cold pressure of steel against the back of his neck, the cords drawn tight around his wrists, the quick itch of the burlap sack jerked over his head. The whole thing, from the initial shock of the report to the blind stuttering march across the fields, takes no more than five minutes. Through the pain in his flank and the throbbing of his jaw, Ned can make out the sniffling inebriate whimper of Boyles at his side, and in the distance, faint as the multifarious hissing of adders in a pit, the mad liquid screech of the hag.

⋇ ⋇

The rest is as predictable as rain in Rangoon. Squire Trelawney, determined to put a stop to the alarming incidence of poaching on his estate, sourly forgoes his dinner to sentence the pair to six hours of strappado followed by peine fort et dure, and if at that point still viable, strangulation unto death. The Squire's brother points out, as a matter of purely theoretical interest, that as the transgressors had neither fowling piece nor pelf about them, they should perhaps be sentenced for the less flagrant offense of trespassing. Not that he wishes to circumvent his brother's authority, mind, nor to in any way suggest that the guilty parties should be lightly dealt with, it is just that he finds the thought of torn sockets and crushed ribcages most distressing before dinner. The Squire, framed by the mounted heads of stag and boar and surrounded by his collection of seamen's knots, hesitates a moment, fiddling with his wig and staring off into space as if ruminating over his brother's objection. After a minute or so, his stomach rumbles mightily. "Oh, all right, Lewis, have it your way," he grunts finally. "Twenty years at hard labor."

There follow two months of close confinement at the base of an abandoned well, long since gone dry, but damp as a sink nonetheless. The food is poor, the incarcerees step on one another's toes, Boyles complains incessantly. "Wisht I'd never of been born," he groans, face to face with Ned in their cylindrical prison, barely able to move his arms without tangling them in his companion's. "And me feet — me feet's so wet the shoes is rotted off 'em. Besides which, I'm cold — spring, summer, winter — it's like the Arctic down 'ere."

In the daylight, Trelawney's overseer — a vicious psychopath with a spine so twisted his head lies flat against his left shoulder — lashes them to a plow beside an arthritic ox and drives them through the clods and mire of the fields from dawn till dusk. At night, they sleep in shifts. One of them climbs halfway up the well shaft and clings to the wet rocks, while the other hunches in the slime below, napping fitfully. As Ned clutches at a willow root one night, bracing himself against the far wall of the shaft with the cramped muscles of his legs, it begins to occur to him that he may have died after all, that his resurrection at St. Bartholomew's was nothing more than a waking in hell, and that everything that has transpired since — every ache, shin splints, stitch and cramp, every crack in the jaw and kick in the ass, every turnabout, disappointment and gut-wrenching loss — is no more than the tiniest link in the eternal concatenation of torments he must live through, moment by moment, muttering his soft savage imprecations over each, as if they were the devil's prayer beads.

It seems he's not far wrong.

Two months later a constable rides out from London to haul the prisoners from the well, chain them to the back of a wagon and march them into town, where they are remanded to the hulks in order to serve out the remaining nineteen years and ten months of their sentences, shoveling mud. The hulks, if anything, are closer and damper than Squire Trelawney's well, with the added liability of constant exposure to the reeking breath, runny bowels and festering phlegm of hundreds of hardened criminals, father rapers, generalized pederasts and blood drinkers alike. It's pretty rough. Packed in at night, three to a berth, in the leaking, creaking holds of rotted tubs perennially mothballed in the Thames and stinking of their slow transubstantiation to sawdust and mulch. Slopped like hogs on cabbage soup and gruel. Forced down into walled enclosures, thirty or forty feet beneath the level of the river, to ply the shovel, wield the pick and haul buckets of rich, reeking muck. Dredging, they call it. Backbreaking, spirit-crushing work. Lay the shovel down to wipe your brow and they lay open your back.

But just when things seem blackest, they get blacker still.

Sometime in the winter of '04, one of the higher-ups in the Admiralty is struck with an inspiration while staring into his eggcup. An inspiration that will directly exacerbate the sufferings of Ned Rise, Billy Boyles and hundreds like them. What with the war on and the shortage of able-bodied conscripts to man the ships and flesh out the infantry, it occurs to this lord and official that it is a shameful waste of manpower to garrison out-of-the-way-yet-still-vital posts with regular troops. Why not, he thinks, spooning up a neat crescent of soft-boiled egg, why not man those forts with convicts? They'd been used in the past for such purposes, why not conscript them again? Get some use out of the lazy vagabonds? Swear them in and put them to work? After all, they can always go back to dredging once the little Corsican has been run up a flagpole. The idea pleases this lord and official immensely. He takes it to his superiors, and they in turn take it to their superiors.

And so, in the early fall of that year, Ned and Billy are transferred from the black stinking hold of the *Cerberus* to the black stinking hold of the H.M.S. *Feckless,* and deposited, soaked in their own vomit, at Goree — Fort Goree, on the island of the same name off the coast of West Africa. Fort Goree, gateway to the Niger and bastion of rot.

⊷ NOLO CONTENDERE

"You've been lying to me. You're planning another adventure, aren't you? Well. Answer me."

"Not really."

"Not really? Then why bring this, this colored person into my house? Why jabber back and forth with him all day like some camel peddler at the bazaar, huh? . . . I said why bring this Seedy into my house? Don't you hear me?"

"I'm just brushing up."

"For what?"

"Listen: say the word and I'll stay."

"Stay."

⊷ LOOSENING THE BINDS

Sidi Ambak Bubi left Peebles after a stay of twenty-seven days, eighteen hours and six minutes. He was counting. Thirty pounds sterling or no, every minute under the slate roof in Peebleshire was like a week in Gehenna. It was Mistress Park. She was like a lioness with a cub, and he, Sidi, the slave sent out to bring back an infant lion for the Bashaw's zoo.

His assessment wasn't far off the mark. Ailie was fierce and defensive, strident, resentful, ungracious to the point of insult. She saw the Moor as an alien and divisive presence, a thief who'd come out of the dark fastness of Africa to steal her husband from her—and she responded in kind. Dogging his every movement, her bright suspicious eyes boring through his clothing, the door to his room, the very flesh and bone of his breast, always picking, insinuating, criticizing everything from the way he lit his *chibouk* to the condition of the turban wrapped round his head. She served him neeps and potatoes, bacon, ham, pig's feet. She spilled tea in his lap, swept Saharas of dust round him as he sat studying the Koran, encouraged the dog to nip at his heels and chew up his sandals. She was distressed, upset, sick unto death, and she took it out on the Moor from Mogador.

When Sidi finally packed up his bags and rode into Selkirk to catch the London coach, an uneasy peace settled over the Park household. Ailie held her breath, and drew back. Mungo was contrite. He had given his promise, finally and irrevocably. Yes, he had lied to her—he admitted it. His ambition had gotten the better of him and he had lied to her. But he would lie no more. Could she forgive him? She could. She clung to him, mad to demonstrate her love, ease his burden, show him how much she valued his sacrifice and the vow he'd given her. The subject of Africa lay buried—even if the grave was a shallow one.

Things were quiet for the next several months, though it became increasingly apparent that Mungo was restive and dissatisfied. He was short of temper. Uninterested in the children or the workings of the household. Reclusive, silent, morose. The stomach disorder he'd contracted in Ludamar came back with a vengeance, and half the time he merely picked at his food or sipped a cup of broth and barley and called it a meal. When he was free of the grind of tending his ignorant, carping, accident-prone patients, he sat brooding over his books and maps or handling the artifacts he'd brought back from Africa, almost in a trance, his fingers tracing the outlines of a bone knife or wooden mask as if it were a fetish or the relic of a saint. Each morning, at dawn, he mounted his horse and rode thirty-five or forty miles across the moors to oversee births and deaths, treat sore throats and imaginary discomforts, look on helpless as a leg dissolved in gangrene or a cancer ate out an old woman's intestines. This was his reward. This is what his daring and fame had got him. He was sick to death of it.

In May of 1804 he told Ailie he was selling everything — the house, the furniture, the practice. They would move in with his mother at Fowlshiels. He needed time to think.

"Think?" she echoed. "About what?"

He held her with his eyes. "About what I'm going to do with the rest of my life."

They were in the kitchen. Surrounded by potted herbs, crockery, wooden utensils, knives. A basket of freshly culled eggs, brown and white, sat on the table in a puddle of sunlight. Suddenly she pushed back her chair and swept the eggs onto the floor. "I know what you're doing," she said, her voice low, cracked with emotion. "You're loosening the binds."

"No, Ailie. Honey. I'm not. I've just got to have some time to think, that's all."

He was sincere. Or at least he felt he was. The confrontation over Sidi had left him feeling debased and low. He was a home-breaker, an irresponsible father, an egotist out to swell himself up at any expense — even if it meant lying to his wife like a common jack. This wasn't Mungo Park, hero, conqueror of Africa and unveiler of the Niger. This wasn't decent, clean and noble — it was despicable, and he despised himself for it.

There would be no more deceit. He was sure of it. The move to Fowlshiels was in no way connected with the expedition the government had promised him. It had nothing whatever to do with tying up his affairs, settling Ailie and the children comfortably and under the watchful eye of his mother, nothing whatever. No, it wasn't the sort of thing that made him feel free and untrammeled, ready to hop a coach for London at the drop of a hat. No, no, no. He just needed time to think. That's all.

✑ WATER MUSIC (SLIGHT RETURN)

There was a premonitory chill in the air the day Mungo left for Edinburgh, a foretaste of the bitter nights to come. It was mid-September, just after his birthday. The leaves were changing and in the mornings a cold gray mist fastened on the river like the spread claws of a cat or bear. There had been a party of course — Ailie had insisted on it, though the explorer seemed embarrassed by the whole thing, as if it were foolish or undignified, as if when you got down to it there was really no cause for celebration at all. "But Mungo, it's your thirty-third birthday," she'd argued. "Doesn't that

strike you as auspicious?" He looked up from his dog-eared copy of Leo
Africanus' geography. "Auspicious?" She was grinning like a clown.
"After all," she said, "it was a big year for Christ, wasn't it?"

Twenty-two guests turned out to drink the explorer's health, Walter
Scott, The Reverend MacNibbit and Thomas Cringletie among them. Scott
had just settled in at Ashestiel on the Tweed, though he'd been sheriff of
Ettrick Forest for the past five years and knew every farmer in the
area — including Mungo's brother Archibald. When Mungo moved down
from Peebles, Archie brought the two together, and by the end of the
summer Scott and the explorer had become fast friends. Mungo would
mount his horse, cross the ridge that separates Yarrow and Tweed, and
while away the long afternoons at Ashestiel, or Scott would show up
unannounced to spend the evening out on the porch at Fowlshiels or down
by the river, casting a fly and watching the midges hover over the shifting
surface. They took long walks together, heads down, rapt in conversation;
they fished, rode, drank and philosophized. Scott had published the
three-volume edition of the *Border Minstrelsy* the previous year, and
Mungo was drawn again and again to the old ballads, contrasting the poet's
versions and the ones he'd grown up with, pointing out inconsistencies,
delighting in correspondences. He was even moved to give his friend the
benefit of his own observations on the oral tradition among the Mandingoes and Moors. For his part, Scott never tired of hearing the details of
Mungo's travels — especially those the explorer had suppressed. He would
pour out a cup of claret and prod Mungo to tell him about Dassoud's
excesses, for instance, or Fatima's appetites and Aisha's soothing, supple
ways. About eating dog and groveling before Mansong, King of Bambarra.
About the strange rites he'd witnessed, the unspeakable acts and unnatural
practices.

Ailie was glad of the friendship. Scott was a man of culture and learning,
Mungo's coeval, and he seemed to have the ability to draw her husband
out, to cheer and energize him, keep him from mooning about the house
all day. But there were limits to everything. Mungo practically shut himself
off from the other guests at the party, cloistering in the corner with Scott
and Zander, their heads down, voices low. His mother and Archibald had
to jerk him by the arms before he would get up, blow out the candles and
start the dancing. And then it was right back to his corner, right back to
Scott and Zander. Their voices were lost in the skirl of the pipes, and from
time to time Ailie would glance across the room to see them mouthing
phrases, gesturing, debating something, their faces as flat and serious as
the faces of a clutch of ministers at tea.

That night, when they went to bed, Ailie gave him her present. It was a compass, set in cork. "So you can always find your way back to me," she smiled. "From Edinburgh or Ashestiel — or even London." She hesitated, her face lit with the glow of some burgeoning secret. "There's something else," she whispered, drawing close to him. He looked up at her, his face bland, the blond stubble of his cheeks transparent in the glare of the oil lamp. "We're going to have another baby," she said. "In the spring."

❧ ❧

Mungo left for Edinburgh the following morning. On business. He'd been in and out of town all summer, consulting with Saltoun, the solicitor, on matters relating to investment and contingency funds for his family. "Contingency funds?" Ailie had asked.

"One never knows," he said, solemn as the patriarch of the lost tribes.

"But you're a young man yet, Mungo — it's foolishness to think of, of such things at your age."

"I could be thrown from a horse tomorrow. Or tumble into the Yarrow and hit my head on a rock, or — "

She turned away. "I don't want to think about it," she said. "Do whatever you feel is right."

He kissed her in front of the house before he left. And then pressed her to him and kissed her again, stroking her hair and tracing the line of her jaw with trembling fingers. She was surprised at his passion.

"Give my love to the Macleods and Leasks," she said, "and to old Saltoun . . . You'll be back in four or five days?"

He was mounted now, looming high over the horse like a bronze statue frozen against the sky. She thought of the military, of the war with France, of Colin Raeburn and Oliphant Graham, dead at Copenhagen. And then suddenly, inexplicably, she thought of her mother. Mungo's face was impassive. She managed to smile. "Four or five days?" she repeated.

The sun was at his back and she had to squint to get a look at his eyes. They were the color of ice. The horse whinnied and she felt something shift in her stomach. He never answered her. Just drew back on the reins, swung the animal's head, and cantered off.

❧ ❧

The letter came two weeks later. From London. There was no return address:

19 September, 1804

My Dear Ailie:

Forgive me. I couldn't face a scene. As you will have guessed, or gathered from talking with your brother, I am off again for Africa. This time I will be at the head of an expedition financed by the government and consisting of some forty men. The opportunity is enormous. It is my patriotic duty to take it.

I will be in an agony until I return to you and the children, no doubt within the year. Our plan is to launch a boat at Segu and float it down to the sea. If the child is a boy, name him after Archie, could you?

Please try to understand me, Ailie, dearest Ailie. The Yarrow is tame, life is tame. There are wonders out there, wonders waiting for the right man to risk all to reveal them. I am that man, Ailie, I am that man.

Yours in love & Contrition,
Mungo

The letter pierced her like a bone spear flung by some black aborigine, some Seedy, straight from the stink and fear and incomprehensibility of Africa, straight from the black heart itself. She hadn't spoken a word to Zander: he'd been avoiding her. After the first week had gone by she knew the letter would come, knew what it would say before she opened it. She knew, but prayed to all the saints and archangels and powers in their spheres that she was wrong, that Mungo had been detained in Edinburgh, that he'd had a minor accident or gone out to the country with Robbie Macleod.

But no. He'd deceived her again. The son of a bitch. The cowardly, irresponsible, lying son of a bitch. To desert her like this, to lie to her, make it up, and lie to her again. To tell his innermost secrets to a stranger like Scott, and conceal them from her. Well she was through with him. He was no good, he was a liar and a cheat. He'd taken her love and trust, her faith and confidence, and stolen off under cover of a lie — like a thief.

She read through the letter again, flung it down in disgust. And then, almost as an afterthought, she picked up the envelope, turned it over in her hand and noticed that there was something scribbled inside the leaf — a postscript? The writing was cramped and hurried, so contorted it could almost have come from a different hand. She took the envelope to the window and squinted at the flailing loops and tight squiggles until she could make sense of them: *I can hear it in my dreams, hear it in the morning when I wake and the birds are in the trees — a rustling, a tinkling — a sound of music. You know what it is? The Niger. Rushing, falling, heaving toward its hidden mouth, toward the sea. That's what I hear Ailie, day and night. Music.*

The baby cried out. She dropped the envelope in the fireplace.

THREE

Niger Redux

"My son, you have now seen the temporal fire,
And that which is eternal; you have reached
A place where I myself can see no farther.
Thus far I have conducted you with skill;
Henceforth your own good sense must be your guide."

— VIRGIL TO DANTE, *The Divine Comedy*

⇜ GOREE (A HYMN
TO CONTAGION)

At the turn of the nineteenth century, the West Coast of Africa — from Dakar to the Bight of Benin — had a reputation for pestilence and rot unequaled anywhere in the world. With its heat and humidity, seasonal deluges and galaxies of insects, it was a sort of monumental Petri dish for the culture of exotic and frighteningly destructive diseases. *Beware and take care of the Bight of Benin,* went a sailor's ditty of the time, *There's one comes out for forty goes in.*

Spotted fever, yaws, typhus and trypanosomiasis throve here. Hookworm, cholera and plague. There was bilharzia and guinea worm in the drinking water, hydrophobia in the sharp incisors of bats and wolves, filariasis in the saliva of mosquitoes and horseflies. Step outside, take a bath, drink the water or put a scrap of food in your mouth and you've got them all — bacilli, spirilla and cocci, viruses, fungi, nematodes, trematodes and amoebae — all eating away at your marrow and organs, blurring your vision, sapping your fiber, eradicating your memory as neatly as an eraser moving over the scribbled wisdom of a blackboard.

From a cosmetic standpoint, the filarial diseases — elephantiasis and loiasis (also known as wriggle-eye) — were especially unfortunate. In elephantiasis, a mosquito-borne malady, teeming roundworms dam up the lymphatic system like insidious little beavers, causing the skin to erupt in granulomatous lesions and the legs and testicles to swell up like obscene fruits. Loiasis, on the other hand, focuses its ravages above the neck, and is transmitted by the bite of certain blood-sucking flies so abundant in the area that most mammals wear a sort of dark coat of them from dawn till dusk — when the mosquitoes take over. In its final stages the disease is characterized by the appearance of the adult worms beneath the conjunctiva of the eye. The worms pulse and writhe there, active little ribbons of flesh, quietly going about their business of feeding, mating and eliminating waste.

If one managed to survive such horrors, there was always kala azar or dumdum fever. A chronic disease, invariably fatal, kala azar makes its presence known by the appearance of pustulating epidermal ulcers, marasmus and enlargement of the spleen. And then there was leprosy, the most dreaded affliction of them all. Relentless in its gross deformation of the body, malignant and hideous in its gradual abrasion of the extremities and the slow but persistent degeneration of facial tissue that leaves its victims looking like pitted prunes. *Balla jou,* the locals called it: incurable.

And then of course there were the more prosaic diseases, the ones that were largely responsible for saving thousands of French, English, Dutch and Portuguese colonials the expense of cemetery plots back in Paris, London, Amsterdam or Lisbon. Malaria headed the list, closely followed by dysentery and yellow fever. Their victims — tradesmen, slavers and soldiers of fortune alike — would literally sweat and shit themselves to death, often within a week of their arrival on what had become popularly known as the Fever Coast.

There were no cures. Various quacks prescribed bloodletting, calomel, laxatives, and emetics to encourage "a gentle puke." Or Dr. James' Powder, a talc- and borax-based product no more effective in combating disease than candied orange peel or horsehair pillows. Jesuit's bark or cinchona had been known since the 1600's as effective in treating malaria, but the evidence current at the turn of the nineteenth century was against it, labeling it a quack remedy like all the rest. The poor blundering star-crossed soldiers and explorers of the day didn't have the vaguest conception of what caused the host of appalling disorders that decimated their ranks and crushed their hopes. It was generally believed that miasmata, "putrid exhalations from the earth," brought on the ravages of these fevers and digestive cataclysms. The mosquitoes, flies and sandfleas? Why bother even to swat them.

And so it was at Goree, the little blister of volcanic rock just off the coast of Senegal that was home to the Royal African Corps. Heat, filth and disease. Inadequate supplies, beggarly broken soldiers recruited from the hulks, a scarcity of drinking water, the sickly yellow wash of the sea. Degradation, debilitation, death. Things were so bad that the garrison commander (a career soldier by the name of Major T. W. Fitzwilliam Lloyd whose improprieties* had so alienated his superiors that he'd been given the choice of discreetly shooting himself or taking the post at Goree)

*The transcript of the official proceedings against the former colonel charged him with eighteen counts of conduct unbecoming an officer, including "the serving of tea to his staff while dressed in a lady's taffeta gown" and "the compelling of eight privates, under penalty of was forced to halve food rations, double the brandy allowance and issue the following standing orders: *Gang No. 1 to be employed digging graves as usual. Gang No. 2 making coffins until further notice.*

It was the winter of 1805. The dry, salubrious season, when there was a bloom in every wasted cheek and a faint fey smile on every pair of cracked lips. When insect populations were down and sun baked out your lungs and dried up your bowels. But already the eternal forces of meteorological change were at work, the earth spinning round the sun, tilting on its axis, winds hissing, clouds mounting in the south like celestial armies.

Before long, it would begin to rain.

⋖ OH MAMA, CAN THIS REALLY BE THE END?

Ned Rise wakes with a headache. Or no. Not a headache. A sort of generalized racking misery that makes him feel as if his pores are bleeding and his brain is leaking out his ears. Weak as a nonagenarian, he props himself on an elbow in the darkened dormitory and listens to the wheezing and moaning of the others as they toss on their sweaty pallets. He recognizes the racheting gasps of Jemmie Bird, one of his mates on the work crew, the oral flatulence of Samuel Purvey and the puling intermittent whistle of Boyles, hardly distinguishable from the whine of the mosquitoes. It is dark as the grave. Two o'clock? Three? Ned turns to reach for his gourd of rum and suddenly he's doubled up on the floor, that fiery demonic pain tearing at his guts until he can do nothing but stiffen and champ at the wooden bedpost until the spasm passes. But it doesn't pass. It mounts in waves like a storm hitting the beach until it leaves him rocking and moaning and clutching at his stomach like a woman laboring to deliver a monster.

When he wakes again, he finds himself in the middle of the floor. He is wet with his own perspiration and his trousers are crusted with the yellowish serum he's been evacuating these past few days. There is a stench of illness in the air — of catastrophic, all-devouring illness, of illness like a hungry, insatiable thing — and someone is whimpering softly at the far end of the room. It is then that the chill takes hold of him again, gently at first, like a dog with a rodent in its teeth. Then it comes on with a vengeance and Ned hugs his legs to his chest, teeth clacking, his head jittering at the tip of

---

court-martial, to rub down his naked body with dustmops while continuously rehearsing the phrase: 'O, I am a lowly snake in the grass, depravèd and despicable.' "

his spine like a jack-in-the-box. The cold is terrible, worse than the fire. He can feel the ice floes poking at him, the dark cold grip of the Thames, the tread of polar bears dancing on his chest, he looks up into the blackness and sees crystal igloos and Eskimos dead in the snow. He struggles to push himself up and stagger back to his pallet and the feeble warmth of his army-ration blanket. But he can't. He can only lie there, huddled, while all around him the darkness opens like a mouth.

✌ A LOAD OF ASSES

Pennants are flying, mainsails, topsails and jibs rattling in the breeze, the prow slicing the water as neatly as a scythe while whales spout and dolphins leap and a fine invigorating salt-sea spray fans out over the rails like a nimbus. Sea and sky are a matched set, blue as delftware, and the sun is nothing less than a stupendous spotlight fixed in the middle of it all — as if the world were a stage indeed and the ship and its crew approaching the denouement of some momentous command performance. The atmosphere rings with the joyous braying of the asses as their nostrils dilate round the rich and multifarious scents of landfall, with the huzzas of the sailors and the wild exuberant strains of Georgie Scott's clarinet as he soars through "Over the Sea to Skye," "Jolly Mortals, Fill Your Glasses" and "O An' Ye Were Dead, Guidmen." Bracing, is what it is.

Mungo Park stands at the rail of the *Crescent,* His Majesty's military transport, and looks out over the spanking blue waves to where the island of Goree heaves up out of the sea, crenellated battlements and great stone barracks scintillating in the sun like something out of a fairy tale. At his side, Zander, Georgie Scott, and the four carpenters he'd recruited from the hulks at Portsmouth. At his back, forty-five asses. Dun-colored, with stubborn, red-veined eyes. They razz and stink, lift their tails, spatter the decks. "This is it, Zander," the explorer shouts, throwing an arm round his brother-in-law. "There's no stopping us now!"

✌ ❧

Perhaps not. But they were very nearly stopped on the glossy conference tables of London and Portsmouth, the expedition ground down to nothing under the foot-dragging heels of Pitt's wartime government and Lord Camden's somnambulist's shuffle. Mungo had rushed down from Scotland in September — at Camden's urgent request — expecting to leave before the month was out. He'd dodged Ailie, briefed Zander on the sly, and drawn up a detailed list of supplies and equipment necessary for the expedition. He'd even come up with a proposal that would warm the cockles of the most mercenary bureaucratic heart. At Sir Joseph's suggestion, the explorer had emphasized the practical benefits of the proposed expedition rather than the purely scientific ones. There was gold in the Niger Valley, he asserted — more even than in Guinea or Ashanti — and a host of primitive black nations mad to trade massy lumps of it for a few beads, mirrors or pewter gravy boats. And if the British didn't claim it, the French would. To plumb the Niger was a mandate that went beyond science, beyond national pride even — it was good sound business sense.

The government went for it. Camden agreed to underwrite the whole thing and to give the explorer carte blanche in the selection of trade goods, pack animals, equipment and manpower. Mungo was to be assigned the rank of captain, and his brother-in-law commissioned a lieutenant. Georgie Scott, an old school chum and distant relation of the poet, would serve as draftsman and third in command. The explorer would be further authorized to choose four carpenters from among the prisoners confined to the hulks at Portsmouth, and to take one officer and thirty-five soldiers from the garrison at Goree. The carpenters would assemble the longboats in which the explorer planned to cruise down the Niger; the soldiers would protect him from the Moors. As far as beasts of burden were concerned, Mungo planned to stop in the Cape Verde Islands and purchase forty-five asses — this in addition to the fifteen or twenty negroes he would hire at Pisania.

"Fine, fine, fine," Camden had grinned from beneath his wig of office. "Splendid. Spare no expense, my son, we're behind you one hundred percent." He plucked a silver letter knife from his desk and began picking at his fingernails. "There is one small matter, though — how do you propose to get back?"

It was a good question. No one was quite certain where the Niger disembogued — there was even some doubt whether it gave onto the sea at all. One faction, led by Major Rennell, the most distinguished geographer of the day, insisted that the Niger either ran out of steam in the Great Desert or flowed into Lake Chad. If this were so, the entire expedition would be stranded in the middle of the continent, with no possibility of returning against the stream, and faced with a long perilous trek through uncharted territory — a prospect that smacked of death, disaster and a rotten investment. Others, however, felt that the Niger was in reality the upper tributary of the Nile or the Congo, in which case the expedition could safely — perhaps even merrily — float down to the sea. Mungo was certain that the latter was true, and he insisted that on reaching the mouth of the Congo it would be a simple matter to catch a slave boat bound for St. Helena or the West Indies. He looked Camden dead in the eye. "In any case, Sir, I am prepared to do what I must and suffer the consequences. Nothing ventured, nothing gained."

The Secretary for Colonial Affairs beamed at him like a doting grandfather, and poured out two glasses of claret from the decanter that stood on his desk. "Well," he grunted. "So be it, then. I'll just submit your proposal to the P.M., requisition the funds, and you'll be on your way in no time."

That was in September. In October the requisition was up for imminent consideration. By November the explorer was distraught. It was the same old story, a repeat of the previous year's debacle when he'd hurried down from Peebles and hung around with his hands in his pockets while Addington gave way to Pitt, Hobart to Camden, and Sir Joseph, with a face as long as a hound's, advised him to go back home and study Arabic. Criminal, is what it was. A damned shame, a pity and a waste. But what could he do? He was powerless.

November dripped by. Mungo sat in the darkened room and stared out the window. He pounded his head against the wall, juggled inkwells, shredded paper. Then he got angry. By God, they weren't going to do this to him again, he shouted, over and over, until the bare walls rang with it and his limbs began to twitch with purpose and determination. Action came like a release. By December the explorer was spending every waking moment lobbying for the expedition: scribbling off petitions, ingratiating himself with influence peddlers and power brokers, sprinting beside the carriages of dukes and earls like a common madman and sharing so many spots of sherry with so many officials that his brain flapped round like a windmill and his liver went into shock. All to no avail. The New Year came and went. Things seemed hopeless.

But the slow mechanism of bureaucratic process — that majestic civil clockwork that formulates what is and shall be through the accretion of accident, greed, intuition and influence — was busily at work, shaping events behind closed doors. Sir Joseph was campaigning vigorously, a nation of shopkeepers was howling for new markets, and Camden, moving with the speed and dispatch of a three-toed sloth, was finally beginning to attract Pitt's attention. The decisive moment came one night during an intermission at the theater. Camden plopped himself down beside the P.M., offered him a pinch of Araby Spice snuff, and presented his case. Yes, Pitt agreed, the Niger should be opened up to trade — British trade — and yes, gold was highly desirable. A day later the funds were made available, the commissions drawn up and the war sloop *Eugenia* dispatched to accompany the *Crescent* to Goree as a discouragement to French privateers. Mungo summoned Zander, packed his bags and set sail, better late than never, on January 29, 1805.

•◌§ ◌̂•

As the explorer stands now at the rail of the *Crescent,* gazing on the coast of Africa for the first time in over seven years and fired up by the cheering of the crew and the exultant braying of the asses, a disquieting thought begins to insinuate itself into the rosy reaches of his optimism. It is a meteorological thought, a thought deriving from his previous long and sorrowful association with the weather patterns in this part of the world. The date is March twenty-eighth. A date which falls very close to the end of March, which is already to say the beginning of April. The explorer thinks of Camden's whiskered cheeks and powdered handkerchiefs, of the dilatory two-fingered courtesy of all the lords and ladies in London, of the morass of polite society and sententious bureaucracy. He has beaten the system, yes, and here he is on the very stroke of his finest hour . . . but the sad fact remains that the long months of battling the government's inertia have consumed the dry season, day by balmy salubrious day. In May — June at the latest — it will begin to rain. Then what?

But as quickly as the thought enters his head — nasty and insinuating, like those sudden barbed little intimations of one's own mortality that well up to interrupt the progress of fork to mouth or arrest the ingenuous tapping of one's foot at the concert hall — he dismisses it. Why dwell on niggling little unpleasantries at a time like this? Here he is, after all, returned to the scene of his greatest triumph. Here he is with a boatload of provisions and trade goods, crates of arms and ammunition, the government behind him, bosom friends at his side. Here he is about to head up an expedition on the grand scale, with porters and armed guards and the rights and prerogatives of a captain in His Royal Majesty's service. Here he is on the deck of the *Crescent,* the wind in his hair, with a load of asses.

◌̃§GIVE ME SOME MEN
WHO ARE STOUT-HEARTED MEN

It is rumored round the backrooms and bunkhouses of the fort that a celebrity has appeared on the premises. Mungo Park, the renowned African explorer and best-selling author, the only European to lay eyes on the Niger and live to tell about it, has come into their midst. The news generates a flurry of excitement.

" 'Oo?"

"Mungo 'oo?"

"Nivir 'eard o' the bleeder."

"Is 'ee white?"

But as soon as the men lapse back into their customary apathy (a sort of listless downward spiral relieved only by drinking, gambling, whoring and dying), interest flares up anew: this visitor is looking for men. Men! To traipse over hill and dale with him, out in the clean open country — and at double pay! Truth. Jemmie Bird overheard the whole thing while he was waiting table for the Major. But that isn't the best of it. The explorer carries authorization from the Colonial Department to offer a discharge to any man accompanying him — a discharge that includes a full pardon for those convicted of crimes, and return passage to England. Great God in heaven be praised, here it is, plopped in their laps like the Holy Grail — a chance to get out of this hellhole!

The rumor spreads like a brushfire fanned by harmattan winds. By 9:00 P.M. the entire garrison — all three hundred seventy-two men (or rather, three sixty-eight, four having expired during the interval) — is massed outside the Major's quarters, each and every one — sick, debilitated, and walking dead alike — begging, wheedling, imploring, beseeching, adjuring and entreating to be taken on the mission. A tumult erupts when the Major, in full dress uniform and pressing a corsage of orchids and baby's breath to his bosom, steps out onto the veranda, the saintly and flaxen-haired newcomer at his side.

"Men!" he shouts above the crowd. "Stalwart fellows of the Royal African Corps: hear me out!"

The roar gradually subsides to the level of isolated cursing and frothing, then to a low vicious snarling as of a pack of dogs disemboweling one another, and then finally to disgruntled muttering and a sad species of terminal wheezing.

"As you have all no doubt heard," the Major cries, "this distinguished gentleman at my right, Captain Mungo Park — " (here he is interrupted by a boozy voice calling for three cheers for Mungo Park and by the crazed yabbering of " 'Ear, 'ear" that succeeds it). The Major takes advantage of the interval to lift Mungo's arm aloft in the victory salute before continuing. "Mungo Park has come among us with a mission — a mission as noble and challenging as the momentous campaigns of Caesar, Alexander and Horatio Nelson — "

"Fuck noble," shouts a man in the front of the crowd.

"Fuck speeches," shouts another. "Take me! Take me!"

Almost instantly the crowd picks up the refrain, sniveling and slobbering, flinging up their hands like schoolchildren: "Me, me, ooh, take me!" From here on it is chaos. The sick throw away their crutches and dance like coryphées, the enfeebled strain to lift logs and boulders, the fevered recite recipes and the lyrics of popular songs to demonstrate their perspicuity. Fights break out. Imprecations rake the sky, stones and clods of earth begin to rain down over the crowd like a judgment from above. Suddenly a torch flares out against the darkness — and then another, and another. The mob presses in on the Major's flimsy bamboo balustrade, chanting "me, me, me, me," crazed and dangerous, disaster in the air . . . and then the explorer clears his throat.

Intense and immediate, a silence falls over them The sound of shushing is universal, like the wash of distant seas. Mungo is stirred by the spectacle, by the energy, the need, the almost worshipful clamor he's aroused and silenced in the space of a few short moments. He steps forward with the confidence of a born orator. "Give me some men!" he rumbles, caught up in it, emotive taps open wide, every last histrionic fiber swelling him to heroic proportions, "Men who are stout-hearted men, stout-hearted men to the end!"

❧ NED THE OBSCURE

The sun scorches the sky as if it were newly created, as if it were flexing its muscle, hammering out the first link in a chain of megatonic nuclear events, flaring up with all the confidence of youth and all the promise of eternal combustion. Which is to say it is hot. Damnably hot. And as quiet as the surface of some uninhabitable and forbidden planet. No bird stutters from a dusty bush, no insect hums, whines or buzzes, no lizard rasps the back of its neck with a lazy hindleg. There isn't even a breeze to lift the vegetation and drop it back down again.

Slowly, oh so slowly, a human presence begins to obtrude on this scene of utter desolation — from over the hump of a slight incline, Gang No. 1 can be seen making its gradual way past the blinding facades of the fort's buildings and across a field strewn with igneous rubble. The members of the burial detail, some thirty in all, are staggering under the weight of picks and shovels and the four freshly hewn coffins balanced on their shoulders.

Half an hour and fourteen faintings later, they have managed to traverse
the hundred yards or so of broken ground that gives onto their destination:
a sandy knoll overlooking the sea and randomly disfigured with grave
markers. As they set their burdens down, a number of the men can be
heard to complain about the imposition of having to dig graves in the heat
of day. The usual practice is to let the deceased stink a day or two — or at
least until nightfall. But this morning the Major has ordered the previous
day's casualties removed for immediate burial, no doubt as a point of
etiquette with regard to the explorer's presence.

"All right, men," barks Lieutenant Martyn, "five minutes. And then I'll
expect you up on your feet and attacking this flinty earth like it was the
hide of the judge that sentenced you." Martyn is a nineteen-year-old
enthusiast. His uniform is impeccable, his posture rigid. He loves the army.

In response to his command the twenty-nine underlings fling themselves
down like so many wet rags, gasping and moaning, snatching for waterbags
and rum bottles. They are a sorry lot, these men, bearded and sunburned,
their uniforms a disgrace, soiled rags wrapped round their heads and feet
and parasite-riddled legs. They are untutored and unskilled, drunks and
brawlers, second-story men and murderers, incorrigible to the core. But
then, how necessary is a good attitude to the digging of a grave? How much
skill or enthusiasm does it really take? . . . Still, as in any large aggrega-
tion of men, there are those particularly suited to specific tasks, those who
over the years have developed special skills and inside knowledge. So too
at Goree. Among those assigned to the burial detail are two ex-
professionals schooled in the churchyards of Islington and Cheapside: Billy
Boyles and Ned Rise.

"Ah Neddy, it's a sorrowful hot day, init? And wot a bitch to have to be
out here bleedin' from the pores just because some fancy Lunnon monkey
is come round to tea with the Major, eh?" Boyles is peering slantwise at his
friend from beneath the shaggy brim of a Panama hat. To all outward
appearances he isn't appreciably different from the man who bamboozled
Osprey, drank Nahum Pribble's beer and lived at the bottom of Squire
Trelawney's well. Neither dysentery nor ague has touched him, so inured is
he to filth and deprivation, so hardened against the assault of microbes by a
lifetime of wallowing in the shit, scum and slime of London's foulest and
most putrid holes. Suddenly, the shadow of an inspiration lifts his lower lip
and depresses his nose. "Hey: you think he'd take us along wiff him?"

Ned's eyes are bloodshot. He has lost weight and is feeling light-headed.
For the past two nights he has been unable to sleep, racked with the chills
and fevers of dysentery. "You kidding?" he growls. "He'll be wanting your

spit-and-shine crew, the ones that can stand up straight and toddle off to sleep like babes. Shit. What would he want with a couple of walking corpses like us?"

Boyles' features rearrange themselves into a slow, stubborn pout. "I'm as good a man as any here," he says. And then immediately qualifies it. "If I gets my rum ration regular. Besides, if he don't take us, you know as well as I we'll be diggin' our own graves before long."

At that moment Martyn spins round, stamps his boot in the dust and barks out an order to the effect that the whole crew can haul their filthy lazy arses up off the ground and get to work, toot-sweet, or suffer a knock about the ears from his military-issue, one-and-three-quarters-inch parade baton.

Ned rises wearily and braces himself on the handle of his shovel. He looks at Boyles like an old streetdog pinned beneath the wheel of a cart. "That's right, Billy, that's right. I'll dig yours if you dig mine."

◄§ §►

Three hours later Boyles and Rise are propped up against the trunk of the sole acacia tree on the knoll, drinking up the bipinnate shade. Their shovels, planted to the haft, stand like sentinels over the half-filled grave before them. The heat distorts the horizon, lays a flat hand over the dead still sea. The others are long gone.

What has happened is this: too debilitated to ply his shovel, Ned stumbled to his knees and begged to be excused. Martyn accused him of shirking and rapped the small of his back with the baton. There was no response. Martyn rapped again, a little more vigorously, like a man locked out of his own house. Ned lost consciousness. As punishment for this flagrant dereliction of duty, Martyn ordered the revived Rise to remain on the knoll till the grave was filled — even if it took him till Christmas. Billy Boyles volunteered to stay on and watch over him.

So here they are, marshaling their strength to get up and complete the task. By way of refreshment, Boyles tips back a pint of rum while Ned drools into a waterbag. The heat is implacable. After awhile Ned lifts his head to scan the shore absently, splotches of color drifting before his eyes, a lone sorry gull picking at a spot of something in the sand. He is thinking of the past, of better times, of standing at the bar in the Pig & Pox and downing a long wet draught of beer, when he suddenly becomes aware of a movement down the beach. He can't be sure, a white rippling haze draining everything of color and dimension, but there seems to be a figure making its way toward them — two figures. He squints into the sun, shades his eyes. Yes, two figures, tall and short, ambling along the shore in this

dizzying heat like shell collectors out for a stroll at Brighton. Who in God's
name? And then it hits him.

Instantly Ned is on his feet, shovel in hand, flinging dirt like a prospector
on to the motherlode. Alarmed, Boyles drops the bottle and scrambles up
beside him. "Neddy: wot is it? An attack? Is that wot it is?" Ned neither
slows down nor glances up. His voice is as taut and urgent as a strung bow:
"Pick up the shovel, you idiot. Dig. Dig for your life." Bewildered, Boyles
takes up his shovel and begins pitching earth into the open hole.

A few minutes later, the work nearly complete, Boyles glances up and is
startled to see two strangers standing over him. The one is short, dark and
effeminately slight, a smile on his lips and a dimple creasing his chin. The
other is tall and wheat-haired, erect as a pillar, a three or four days' growth
of reddish beard furring his cheeks — but wait a minute. Isn't that — ?

Mungo Park stands there in his coruscating boots and nankeen trousers,
in shirt-sleeves and waistcoat, the peach-colored jacket flung carelessly
over his shoulder. His brother-in-law is beside him, leaning back on one
leg, arms akimbo, dressed up like the most insouciant beau on Bond
Street. "Well," the explorer says, "it's good to see that at least somebody
around here is capable of exertion." His voice is hearty as a handshake.

Ned, digging furiously, suddenly whirls round as if surprised, jerks to
attention and snaps a salute. "Sir!" he barks, the response as smooth and
automatic as if he were a trained seal and the explorer a man with a fish.
He makes an effort to hold the explorer's eyes and to control the hot/cold
tremors rattling his knees and snatching at his elbows. Still, he can't
suppress the surprise he feels at seeing the explorer up close for the first
time. He'd expected an older man — forty at least. After all, this fellow's a
celebrity, been to Africa and back, written books, hobnobbed with the
cream of society. And he can't be any older than Ned himself.

Mungo pushes a lock of hair out of his eye, barely sweating though the
heat is like a hammer. "No need to be so formal, friend," he says, and Ned
relaxes. "Alexander and I were beginning to think that nobody on this
island ever left sick bay."

"Well, Sir," Ned says, dredging up all the schooling in his voice, "the
Lord has blessed us with our health, and we feel duty-bound to do what we
can to repay Him by seeing that those less fortunate can at least have a
decent burial."

Mungo and Zander exchange glances, like men at a horse sale who've
just been quoted a price so preposterously low it makes their palms crawl.

"Yes, Sir, Billy and I have been out here for three hours, seeing to the

burial of the four unfortunates called to their reward yesterday in the
excitement of your arrival, Sir."

"Oh — then you men know why my brother-in-law and I have come to
Goree?"

Boyles, who has to this point stood by with his mouth hanging open,
begins to get the idea. "That we does, oh that we does," he sings, a silly
wet grin splitting his face in two. "It's a great and glorious mission you're
about, init? One that'll redound to the everlastin' glory o' King George
and the Queen and all the proud cityzens of Merry Old, am I royt?"

The explorer has already removed his hat to get at a notepad concealed
in the crown. He is beaming like a hero. "So," he says, pen poised over
paper, "I take it you fellows would like to come along with us, then?"

✑ CROSSING THE RUBICON

The thick sludge of tropical air — already pregnant with humidity — is
penetrated on this particular morning by the lusty jubilant cries of men
who consider themselves uncommonly fortunate, serendipitous even.
These are the cries of the elect, the chosen few, the lucky dogs who've just
kissed the beauty queen and tucked the turkey under their arms: these are
the cries of the winners. "Hoorah!" they cheer. "Pip-pip!" Intermingled
with these cheers is another sound, a sound like celestial static — brazen,
tinny, grating — the sound of musical instruments violated and abused.
The source of this secondary cacophony is the regimental band, which
consists of six bugles, two trumpets and a viola. Stationed just outside the
main gate, the band is hammering away at "Rule Britannia" and the
bourrée from the "Royal Fireworks Music." The occasion is momentous.
Rank upon rank of red-jacketed soldiers stand at attention, the Major
himself has deigned to rise early and straddle his dapple-gray, the band
rings out like a convocation of archangels: Mungo Park's second expedition
is under way.

The thirty-five men the explorer has chosen to accompany him are
prancing through the gates like peacocks, crowing out their good fortune,
looking almost dashing in the new uniforms provided for the occasion. And
why shouldn't they crow? They're escaping a hellhole, a pit, the very maw
of pestilence and death, and setting off on a jaunt that will lead them
through the countryside and back to England, free men and heroes to

boot. The rest of the garrison isn't so sanguine. The three hundred twenty-five men Mungo has left behind (eight more having expired in the interval) are cheering, true enough, but only for form's sake. They are dejected, jealous, fatally disappointed. Some have turned their heads and burst into tears. Others are sniveling openly or blowing their noses on shirttails or blackened rags.

The explorer, at the head of the van, is brimming with good cheer and optimism. He's got himself thirty-five good men, strong, stalwart and true — not to mention eager and stout of heart. He's got his asses, the government is behind him, Zander at his side, and the band is playing. What more auspicious way to launch the greatest adventure of his life? He is grinning, grinning till his lips crack, all the while saluting the crowd and thinking: this is it, finally and at long last, this is it. There's no turning back now, nothing to stop him. He'll track the Niger and capture the hearts and minds of the world. Nothing less than immortality awaits.

Fifteen minutes later, on board the *Crescent* again and sandwiched between his cap-waving men and the throng of blaring asses, he checks his roster and conducts a quick roll call. The solid Celtic and Anglo-Saxon surnames slip off his tongue like heavy syrup and the responses snap back at him, enthusiastic, this one pitched high, the next rasping and timbreless, the next scraping bottom. There are forty-five men in all: himself, Zander, Georgie Scott and Lieutenant Martyn, the four carpenters, two sailors recruited from the *Eugenia* for the purpose of piloting the boats on the Niger, and the thirty-five brave lads he's spirited away from the garrison. Of these last, he can barely match names and faces, though he does recognize Jemmie Bird, Jonas Watkins, Ned Rise and Billy Boyles, among others. Besides Martyn, all the men but one are privates first class. The exception is Sergeant M'Keal, an outstanding man, tried and true, and with a wealth of experience ranging over his thirty-one years of active service. Mungo could tell from his handshake and the look in his eye that here was a man — never mind his service record. Never mind that he'd been twelve times a corporal and nine times a sergeant and would have gone even higher but for the unfortunate attachment to the bottle that always returned him to the ranks. The man was true-blue. Any fool could see that.

Mungo looks up at the commotion on shore as the *Crescent* draws back from the dock. Every man in the garrison has tears of joy in his eyes. The band is blazing, the Major waving a white handkerchief, the sails bellying in the breeze. Mungo raises his clenched fists in salute, glorious moment, as the wind takes hold of the boat and the shore begins to slip away.

・§ ζ・

On the way up the Gambia to Pisania, Ned Rise leans back against a crate of trade goods, lights a cigarette and gazes out on the brown wash of the river, the flights of birds, the great grasping claws of the cypresses that line the banks like decapitated sphinxes. He is feeling better, on the mend from his bout with dysentery, exhilarated by his good luck and the prospect of returning to England within the year. The explorer is all right, he thinks. A little pompous and straightlaced maybe, but a man you can work around . . . yes, a man you can definitely work around. Ned closes his eyes and pictures the Thames, a clean riveting blue under the sun, the explorer beside him at the helm of the *Crescent,* the docks packed with grateful cheering mobs and loose women, the future secure. *Ned,* the explorer says, turning to him, *you've been invaluable to me on this expedition, invaluable. I couldn't have done it without you.* He takes Ned's hand, a soft saintly nimbus trembling round them both. *Name your reward, old boy — name it and it's yours.*

He wakes gently, some uncertain space of time slipped by — a minute? an hour? — the natter of river martins and hoopoes wafting across from the near bank, and from somewhere the crazed laughter of Boyles and Bird, drunk as loons. He rubs his eyes, looks out at the line of treetops slipping serenely across the rail, and begins to sense, in a vague and incremental way, that all is not as it should be. Case in point: the shadow that looms over him, bulky, stationary, unmistakably human. Ned squints up, momentarily blinded, unable to make out the face in silhouette. "Jonas?" he tries. "Billy?"

There is no answer. The stranger merely stands there gazing down at him, while Ned shades his eyes and tries to blink away the sunspots and shadow images. What he sees is not at all reassuring: a flexed jaw and dull porcine eyes, clumps of matted doggy hair randomly interspersed with swaths of naked scalp, the rutted face and thick ears of a born clod — and all of it set atop a tensed mass of bone, sinew and rib-cracking muscle. The composite somehow dredges up unpleasant associations — painful associations — and Ned is on the verge of making an intuitive leap to the dim worrisome past when the stranger breaks the silence.

"Well dammee, if it isn't Ned Rise."

In that instant, inexplicable, impossible, three thousand miles and seven long years away, Ned knows that it is Smirke standing before him. And instinctively covers himself. "The name's Rose, friend, Edward Hilary Rose."

The innkeeper goes down on one knee, his bristling sweaty face as struck with wonderment as a child's. "Why—it can't be. The divil take yer fingers if I didn't see ye strung up for a murderer . . ."

Ned gathers his feet under him and very gradually cocks his arm, wary of any sudden movement.

"But it's you, it is—look, there's the mark o' the 'angman on ye," Smirke rasps, breathing beer and onions in Ned's face and pointing a thick finger at the drooping neck of his shirt.

"No, friend," says Ned, inching off in a crabwalk, "you've got the wrong man. I'm a soldier, career man. Born and raised in Cornwall, never been to London in my life—"

"Lunnon? 'Oo said anything about Lunnon?" And suddenly Smirke's hand is at his throat, the big rippled forearm jerking him to his feet as easily as if he were a bundle of rags. The innkeeper holds him suspended there for a long nasty moment—his eyes reduced to slits, the rawboned face twisted with rage and hatred—before flinging him against a wall of packing crates. "And wot about them nubbins, then—'ey, Neddy?"

Ned thrusts his hand deep in his pocket, but Smirke, powerful and reeking, takes hold of his wrist and forces the hand up against a crate of lorgnettes, where he splays the fingers across the rough pine slats. Mute and incontrovertible, the ravaged fingers tell their tale.

Smirke says nothing, his breathing deep-chested and satisfied, almost a succession of snorts. He looks Ned in the eye, so close their noses are touching, his breath coming quicker now, as if he were approaching some sort of climax. "Ye've been the ruin of me, Ned Rise," he rasps, his voice as toneless as a defective's, "and now 'ear why."

Ned stands there, pinned against the crates, clutching Smirke so close they could be lovers, while the big man spits curses in his face and narrates a deranged and obsessive tale of loss and woe. "You shit," he breathes, so soft it could be a term of endearment. "You scum-suckin' prick. You stinkin', motherfuckin', faggot turd. I useter to be a respectable man," shouting now, "the proprietor of a respectable establishment—and now look at me." Ned is looking—no choice in the matter—and thinking only of how he can escape the madman's clutches, lure him over the rail and sink him in the festering ooze. But no such luck. Smirke tightens his hold and goes on.

He'd lost the Vole's Head nearly six years earlier—lost it—after it had been in the family for three generations. And all because of the humilation and loss of confidence he'd suffered over the Reamer Room incident. Trade fell off. The higher class of patron began to eat and drink elsewhere and Smirke was forced to auction some of the trappings to pay his bills. Inevitably he had to close down, and within the year he was wandering the streets, a broken man. It was about that time that he ran into Mendoza. Need a quid or two, old friend? Mendoza asked, plucking a note from a fat bankroll. As usual the ex-pugilist was dressed in style, looking as prosperous as a prince, though he hadn't had a fight in years. Down on yer luck, eh Smirke? he said with a grin. Come round and see me: I'll fix you up. Two nights later Smirke was climbing in the second story window of Lady Tuppenham's house, while Mendoza kept an eye out below. When Smirke backed down the ladder twenty minutes later, his arms laden and a sack of silver slung over his shoulder, the night watchman was steadying the ladder for him. Within the hour Smirke was in Newgate, and from there it was the hulks at Portsmouth. When the explorer came around looking for carpenters, Smirke, who'd done a bit of remodeling and whatnot at the Vole's Head, stepped forward and offered his services. And so here he is. In this pesthole. "And all because of ye, Ned Rise!" he shrieks suddenly. "When I seen ye danglin' there at the end of the 'angman's rope I says to myself it wasn't near bad enough for ye, not near. I wanted to kick that black-'ooded pansy aside and do it myself, twist the rope double tight, choke ye till ye wisht ye'd never seen the light of day!"

Desperate, the madman's breath in his face and hands at his throat, Ned opts for the elbow in the ribs, followed by a swift knee to the crotch. One, two: uff-uff. It has no effect. Smirke is leaning over him, breaking his back, wringing his neck as methodically as a butcher throttling a Christmas goose. Ned tries to cry out but his windpipe is choked off, there's nothing there, and he has to settle for a blind hopeless flailing while the life rushes out of him like water down a drain.

It is Lieutenant Martyn who saves him.

"Here!" the Lieutenant shouts. "You men!" And then the baton comes down across the back of the innkeeper's skull with a sound reminiscent of chestnuts popping on the open fire.

As Smirke goes limp in his arms, the great wet bulk of the man weighing on him like leviathan and forcing him to the deck while Martyn shouts commands and blasts on his whistle and footsteps come thundering up the planks, Ned Rise begins to reconsider his position, thinking with a certain regret of his pallet back at Goree, thinking that perhaps he's made a mistake, thinking that maybe, in the final analysis, this isn't all it's cracked up to be.

❧ DISAPPOINTMENT AT PISANIA

The initial disappointment is trifling — the result of a minor accident, unforeseeable, unavoidable — and yet for all that, something of an evil portent, a bringdown, a rotten and insipid way to launch so historic an adventure as this. Even worse, it involves the first death.

Leland Cahill, like most of the men recruited from the garrison, had been drinking heavily in celebration of his reprieve from the certain doom of Goree, drinking to the success of the expedition, the honor of Mungo Park, the courage of his companions and just about anything else he could think of. Cahill was an acne-scarred eighteen-year-old, somewhat below the median in intelligence, who presented an innocuous and winning front, and who had been sentenced to life imprisonment for sacrilege, public micturition and stealing woollen clothes from tenter grounds. Sober, he was a notch above worthless; drunk, he was no more capable of pulling his weight than a cross-eyed catatonic from Bethlehem Hospital. Nonetheless, when the *Crescent* came to anchor off Pisania it was his task — along with Mitchell Mewshaw — to secure the gangway.

Since the river was running low at this season, the ship's captain was forced to drop anchor some hundred and twenty yards offshore. Fortunately, Mungo had foreseen this eventuality and had sent ahead to have a raft constructed for the purpose of transporting men, animals and equipment from ship to shore. The raft was waiting for them as they rounded a bend in the river and drew within sight of the outbuildings of the factory.

By unanimous consent of the officers, the asses — whose stench was terrific in such close quarters and high temperatures — were to be evacuated first. As if aware of their prerogative, the asses became increasingly animated as the two sleek Pisanian negroes positioned the raft alongside the ship. Unfortunately, Cahill and Mewshaw, passing a bottle of gin and swapping dirty stories, took no notice of the situation. When the raft was properly secured they merely backed up a step or two, fastened the ropes and guided the wooden gangway over the side of the ship and into position. A mistake. As the gangway breached the bulwarks the asses began to stamp and snort, impatient with the crowding and the swaying of the ship; the instant it touched down they stampeded. A dun blur shot over the rail and down the narrow walkway in a fury of crashing hoofs, pandemonious braying and hellish kicking. Eighteen asses plunged directly into the water. The remainder managed to make the raft — shaken and wild-eyed — scrambling hard to escape the push from behind. Inevitably they spooked the negroes and capsized the raft. In all, six asses were lost. As for Leland

Cahill, private first class, he was last seen pitching headlong down the sloping ramp of the gangway, one hundred and eight individual hoofs making their separate imprints in his flesh.

•୨ ୧•

The second disappointment is less tangible, more a mental and spiritual letdown than the first. More a disappointment in the true sense of the word — a betrayal of expectation rather than a sudden tragic turn of events.

After the explorer had straightened out his men and asses and assigned a crew to grapple the river for Cahill's body, his first thought was of Dr. Laidley. It had been nearly eight years. And yet when he thought of Africa, he thought of Laidley. The old man had equipped and instructed him in preparation for that first mission — had taught him Mandingo, filled him in on native customs and introduced him to Johnson. While Mungo lay back in bed, nearly eviscerated from his first bout with jungle fever, Laidley had nursed him, brought him cup after cup of stiff, cleansing native tea, read to him from Donne, Milton and Shakespeare in a voice as serene and assured as the Bank of England. He was the last to see the explorer off and the first to congratulate him on his return — and the first white man to hear the historic news of the Niger. He was the center in a chaos of colors, dialects, tattoos and nose rings, the single fixed point in an ever-shifting pattern of bizarre needs, wants and practices. He was Mungo's mentor.

As the explorer made his way through the tumble of reed huts — each with its barking dog and naked children framed in the entranceway — and up the dusty street to the doctor's rambling residence cum fortress cum factory, he broke into an anticipatory grin as he thought of the pleasure of seeing him again, shaking his hand and introducing him to Zander, telling him of the phenomenal success of the book and the effect his discovery was having on the cartographers of Europe. He could already picture the congenitally flushed cheeks, the white tonsure, the nodding head and pursed lips, the sideways contemplative glance of the old man as he sat in his cane rocker absorbing all the news of England before exploding in a flurry of hospitality. "Yes, yes, yes," he'd say, fatherly, Franklinesque, trotting round the room till the tails of his jacket caught the wind, "but here, have some palm wine, some goat's cheese, a dish of kouskous. Or how about a steak? Cigar? Brandy?" Mungo would inscribe a copy of his *Travels* for him, and they'd sit back on the veranda and immerse themselves in a connoisseur's palaver about the countryside, the flow of words laving him, washing out the lint of seven years' absence, conjuring up half-forgotten truths about meteorology and geography, about royal succession and tribal boundaries. If the truth be known, the explorer was in sad need of a refresher course.

All this ran through his head as he and Zander ascended the familiar rough-hewn steps of the piazza, but a nagging question kept intruding itself as well: why hadn't the old man come out to greet them as they landed? Was he indisposed? Away in the bush?

The answer waited for him just behind the open door, in the lank-haired, unshaven person of D. K. Crump, the doctor's former assistant and temporary successor. Crump was slouched in a wicker chair, a bottle of gin on the desk before him and a reefer of *mutokuane* fuming in his hand. His eyes were latticed with red. Beside him, her heavy lids half shut in ecstasy or stupor, a black woman in a striped shift languidly rotated a fan while Crump, his hand thrust through the armhole of her dress, manipulated her breasts as if they were potatoes in a sack.

It took a moment for the explorer's eyes to adjust to all this. The factory was dark and immense, strewn with articles for barter. There were knives, muskets, kegs of powder, bolts of cloth, mirrors, demijohns of wine and brandy, kegs of nails, axes, saws, jacks-in-the-box and penny candies by the barrel. And up against these, a mountain of local products taken in exchange — elephant tusks, teeth and feet, amorphous mounds of bees-wax, birds' feathers of every hue and description, baskets of peppercorns and peanuts, great twisted tangles of ebony, the limp pelts of leopard, lion and zebra. It looked like the aftermath of some natural disaster, the leavings of a flood, driftwood and jetsam, piled in a dusty heap that lost itself in the dim reaches of the warehouse. The explorer took in the sweep of it, and then turned back to this bare-chested man with the stringy biceps who seemed to preside over it all.

"I'm Mungo Park," he said, bowing, "and this is Alexander Anderson, my second-in-command. Is Dr. Laidley about?"

The man looked up at him for a long moment, as insouciant as a lizard on a rock. He took a drag on his reefer, and then laughed, as short and sudden as the single bark of a dog.

Mungo shifted uneasily on his feet. Crump jiggled the black woman's breasts. Zander took a step forward. "See here," he said, "you've been asked a civil question — do you know the whereabouts of the factor here, or don't you?"

Crump's eyes were dead blue, emotionless to the core. He set the reefer on the edge of the desk and took a drink of gin. Then he laughed again. "Ha!" he growled finally. "The old geek's gone and kicked off then, near a month back."

Prying the details from him was like drawing splinters from flesh. But after ten minutes of patient questioning, the two geographical missionaries were able to establish that Laidley's death had been accidental. It seemed that the doctor had just returned from an extended collecting trip in the interior, during which he'd survived the onslaught of a dyspectic lion, the strike of a black mamba and a Foulah raid, when he strolled out into the courtyard to inspect his roses, was stung in the right nostril by a honeybee and died gasping twenty minutes later. Crump — Dirk Crump, a London lowlife and ne'er-do-well who'd convinced the company he was the man for the job — had been sent out a month earlier to replace Laidley's former assistant, who had succumbed to the climate. He supervised the funeral arrangements ("a bunch of bollocky wogs muckin' about in the earth"), said a few words over the mound of yellow clay that swallowed up the good doctor, and notified his superiors in London of the changed circumstances at the factory. It would take four months for the news to reach the offices of the West African Company in London, another six or seven before the company could act on it. Until then, Crump was in charge.

The explorer was deflated. There would be no reunion, no hospitality, no reassuring chitchat about the state of the surrounding countryside. There was only this grinning degenerate, this hyena with his feet propped up on the doctor's desk. Mungo turned to leave.

" 'Ere, Mr. Explorer, ain't you forgettin' somethin'?" Crump rasped, his eyes glittering. Some sort of weird excitement had come over him — he was on his feet now — swaying back and forth like a snake about to strike.

The explorer paused in the doorway. "Yes?"

"The raft. The bloody raft you ordered. Wot you think, they grows on trees?" Crump began to laugh — a sick, soughing sound — at his own joke.

"What of it?"

"Well we expects to be paid, we does. The West African Trading Company don't give no credit to nobody. As far as I'm concerned, pal, you're no different from any of these bush niggers out here." Crump was no more than a foot away now, hands folded under his biceps. "So pay up, Jack."

Mungo sighed. "All right, I'll write up a draft on the Colonial Department — "

"Uh-uh, friend — all transactions in cash. My boys — and you can see a few of 'em out there now — "

The explorer looked. Seven or eight wildly painted savages with spears, pistols, muskets and longswords slouched against the pillars of the veranda, looking as if they hadn't heard a good joke in years.

" — as I was saying, my boys worked their arses off on that raft, includin' three days' worth of overtime at time-and-a-half, and they expects their just deserts, if you see what I mean."

"Very well," Mungo said, all business. "What do we owe you?"

"Five hunnert guineas."

The explorer was stunned. "Five hundred — ?"

"We won't pay it," Zander snapped.

The little group stood there at the doorway for a moment, Zander's words sucked up in the humid sponge of the air as if they'd never been spoken. It was hot, and the explorer could feel the sweat coursing down his temples and salting the corners of his mouth. Suddenly, one of the painted men grunted and everyone turned to him. He was made up in black and white, the paint dividing his face in two, ribbing it like a xylophone. He pointed a finger at the oil palm on the far side of the clearing. A small colobus monkey was perched on one of the grooves, nibbling at something and periodically reaching over its shoulder to groom the even smaller monkey which clung to its back. Slowly and deliberately, with a total absence of emotion or flutter of concern, the xylophone man raised his musket and squeezed the trigger, pinning both animals to the tree for a single agonizing moment detached from time and process, before they fell like rags to the earth.

Mungo reached for his purse.

⇛ ⇝

The final disappointment is merely rankling — and puzzling. And yet at the same time it is somehow more deeply disturbing than the others, more a blow on the gut level, more the sort of thing that stalks dreams and tightens the bowels.

After a brief conference with his officers, Mungo determined to leave Pisania the morning following his confrontation with Crump. The new factor was clearly hostile, his associates potentially dangerous. There was nothing to be gained by extending their stay at Pisania, and each day brought them closer to the onset of the rainy season. The only essential matter of business — recruiting some eighteen or twenty blacks to serve as porters, guides and interpreters — would involve no more than an hour or two. The explorer was confident. From long experience, he knew only too well how to inflame the native heart with material lust. He would offer half a bolt of scarlet cloth and the price of a prime slave to any man willing to accompany him into the interior. All he need do was breathe the rumor and his tent would be inundated by eager volunteers, hordes of them, jabbering away like futures speculators, pushing forward to spit in their palms and shake hands with the white man to seal the bargain. He could sit back and take his pick.

But something went wrong.

Though he'd announced his offer just after noon, dusk came and went and still there were no takers. Had the headman kept the news to himself, hoping to fill all the available positions with his own relatives? Had the explorer, whose Mandingo was admittedly a bit rusty, failed to make himself clear? By eight o'clock he began to feel concerned. Without blacks to manage the asses and haul supplies and equipment, the onus would fall on the soldiers, who would be hard put looking out for themselves when the rains began. Even worse, there would be no one capable of communicating with distant tribes or even of searching out the right road. "No," the explorer finally said to his brother-in-law as they sat beside the oil lamp in his tent, "there's no way around it. We've got to have blacks, even if we have to offer them double pay, an estate in the Cotswolds and the King's underdrawers thrown into the bargain."

Outside, the air was thick with smoke from the men's cookfires. Largely unconcerned about such trifles as Leland Cahill, Dr. Laidley, the going rate for rafts and the availability of black porters, the men were instead applying themselves assiduously to the tasks at hand: roasting chickens, draining gourds of *sooloo* beer and introducing the native women to venereal disease. The explorer could hear them cursing softly in the bushes as he strode through the darkened little shanty town on his way to the headman's hut. From the river, faint but unmistakable, there was the eerie whine and wheeze of crocodiles mating in the muck.

The headman, a sinewy, middle-aged fellow in a beaver hat and a French cambric shirt with the sleeves removed, was just sitting down to his evening repast as the explorer stepped from the shadows and into the unsteady circle of light cast by the cookfire. The man's name was Damman Jumma. His hut, a triumph of contemporary mud-and-wattle architecture, shared a common wall with the stockade erected round the factory, and the firelight lit the tips of the pointed timbers till they glowed like a row of filed teeth. A number of stripped and blanched logs were arranged round the cookfire in front of the hut. Damman Jumma's wives, children, cousins, uncles and dogs were lounging on and against these logs as if they were so many sofas and loveseats, chattering and joking, spooning up bowls of hot kouskous and gnawing away at slabs of salt beef from the explorer's stores. When Mungo appeared, the group fell silent.

"Greetings," Mungo said, the Mandingo dialect thick and leaden on his tongue. There was no response. The explorer buttoned and unbuttoned his jacket, licked his lips and made a stab at conversation. "Enjoying the salt beef?"

A fat woman with stretched and knotted earlobes glanced up at him, her face smeared with grease. Bony children, suspicious-looking dogs and salt-haired old men stared up at him so fixedly he began to feel as if they expected him to start dancing or juggling or something. Damman Jumma said nothing, but looked up at the explorer out of eyes that rolled back on themselves till they looked like hard-cooked eggs.

Mungo cleared his throat. "Uh, Damman, uh the reason I've stopped by is to ask if you've uh, you know, spread the word about the expedition and the top wages I'm offering."

The headman inserted a slab of beef in the pocket of his cheek and began masticating noisily. Everyone watched him, silent. It took him three or four minutes to break down the rubbery meat, swallow it and lubricate his throat with a long pull at the calabash. When he looked up at the explorer again he was shaking his head. "*Babarram wo dodoto,*" he said. "No one will go."

The explorer was incredulous. "What do you mean no one will go? I'm offering half a bolt of red cotton cloth direct from Birmingham and the price of a prime slave. That's more than you'd make in two years sitting around here hauling crates for Doctor—I mean, Mr. Crump."

All eyes were on the headman. Using only his teeth and a splinter of wood, he was slowly prizing the cork from a bottle of Chateau Latour that Mungo recognized as having come from his own private stock. Damman Jumma spat out the cork and took a long swig before passing the bottle to his favorite wife. "Listen," he said finally, speaking in colloquial Mandingo, "you can offer this and that till you're blue in the face, but nobody is going to go with you. The feeling around here is that you're *kokoro kea,* a bad risk. And that's all she wrote."

Shaken, the explorer returned to his tent to talk things over with Zander. They decided to offer a bolt and a half of cloth, a case of Whitbread's beer and the value of two prime slaves to any able-bodied man who would accompany the expedition. The next morning they hired a *jilli kea* to canvas the countryside, singing out the offer at every village within an eight-mile radius. There was no response. The explorer waited two days more. Finally, on the morning of the third day he called in Zander, Martyn and Scott and told them that the men would just have to shoulder the load. The asses were packed, the troops inspected and provisioned, and the expedition set off on the road to the Niger.

As they marched out of Pisania, the overloaded asses already bucking and complaining, the locals watched wide-eyed, some shaking their heads, others clutching at *saphies* and scribbling in the dust. They watched with the sort of grim and dumbstruck fascination that might have welcomed the early Christians to the lion pit or assailed the barefooted children of the Middle Ages as they gathered in droves to march across Europe and drive the infidels from the Holy Land. They watched with prayers on their lips and a certain lurking prescience of man's mortality in their hearts. They watched, solemn as priests, as the crazed and stinking wild-eyed white men drove their asses through the gates and up the long tortuous road to nowhere.

ᕯ IN SADNESS

Ailie clenches her teeth, her breath torn in gasps. She is thinking, through a trembling pink delirium of pain, about things eschatological and generative, about childhood, adolescence and old age, about budding and parthenogenesis, about trees and sunlight, food for the body, decay. Her mind is suddenly blooming and philosophical, as if she were sitting at her desk reading Locke or Galileo or Saint John the Divine, instead of lying here on the verge of shouting out the filthiest epithets she knows. Meanwhile, the birds have started in again and the windows are beginning to soften with the light of dawn. She bites her finger. There is something inside her, vital and impetuous, crowding her bones, fighting to get out.

This is her fourth, and still the pain is enough to make her jump and writhe like a spider on a burning log. *In sadness shalt thou bring forth children,* she thinks, and then, more bitterly: *Thy desire shall be for thy husband, and he shall have dominion over thee.* From somewhere, as if through a haze and at a great distance, the voice of Dr. Dinwoodie, soothing and gentle. And then the answering murmur of Mary Ogilvie, the housemaid, and the clatter of spoon and cup. There is something in this simple domestic music, something that speaks of normalcy and release, something catalytic. Suddenly she finds herself bearing down, the flow and process growing familiar, natural and automatic, the pain on hold, her heart and lungs and muscles clicking along in conjunction, locked now in athletic fervor, pushing to win, break the tape, drive the ball home. There. She can feel the head between her thighs, Dinwoodie's fingers, the hitch of the shoulders and then the final purgative rush toward release. It comes like an explosion, with a sucking, scouring sound, as if the whole thing were the climax of a stupendous bowel movement. She swells her lungs. It is out.

Drained, she sinks back into the pillow and closes her eyes. There is the snip-snip of the doctor's scissors, a splash of water, the cry of an infant. From somewhere below she can hear her father berating his apprentice, something about poultices and plasters. Then, close at hand, Dinwoodie's voice, sussurant and reverential. "It's a boy, Ailie. A fine strapping laddie, feisty as his father."

And now it's in her arms, red and wet, stinking of inner secrets and the must of the womb. She doesn't care. Boy or girl, child or monster, she doesn't care. What does it matter? she thinks, something coppery and bitter in her throat. Her husband's deserted her. Tired and alone, she's given birth to an orphan.

◄§ SOMEBODY TO LEAN ON

She has visitors, people coming and going, grinners and well-wishers. What a darlin' bairn. Coochie-coo. Hello, goodbye. Through it all, she lies there propped up against the pillow like a suffering saint, feeling odd, odd to be the object of so much pity and admiration, odd to be back in her girlhood room, back in the bed she'd slept in alone for twenty-five long years. Odd to be alone again.

Almost from the beginning it had been clear that things weren't going to work out at Fowlshiels. Ailie saw the move back to her mother-in-law's as an implied criticism, as Mungo's way of telling her she'd failed at Peebles. Accustomed to managing her own household and making independent decisions regarding everything from the composition of the kitchen garden to how often the dog needed worming, she inevitably came into conflict with her mother-in-law. Things went from bad to worse when Mungo deserted her. It seemed almost as if the old woman blamed her for Mungo's rashness and irresponsibility, as if it was glaringly obvious that Ailie had failed as a homemaker and driven her man out into the wilds to face cannibals and ravening beasts. In the kitchen, on the porch, out at the well, Ailie could feel her mother-in-law's censorious eyes on her, and through each of the hundred little domestic motions of each day, she seethed with a growing resentment of her husband and the intolerable situation he'd forced her into. A month dragged by, then another. Ailie was pregnant, exhausted, the children ran around the cramped cottage like gypsies and red Indians, her mother-in-law retreated behind a wall of glacial and imperious silence. When her father invited her to move in with him at Selkirk, Ailie jumped at the chance.

And so, she's come home. Home to deliver her baby and lick her wounds, home to raise the children under her father's sheltering roof. Now, the baby asleep, her father out on his rounds, the children visiting at Fowlshiels till she can get her strength back, the house whispers with quiet. She's home all right, free from the turmoil at her mother-in-law's, but the hours hang on the face of the clock and the windows are perpetually gray. She is bored. Dispirited and anxious. She tries to read an article on asexual reproduction in the green hydra. She starts a letter to Mungo, then tears it up in frustration. What's the sense? He'll never see it anyway. Finally she gets up — painfully, slowly — to look at herself in the mirror. And is startled by what she sees: a woman of thirty, small-boned, with delicate features, snarled hair and a look of hurt and anger indelibly stamped across her face. A woman whose jaw is set, and whose eyes cut like a knife, fierce and unforgiving.

The day wears on. Katlin Gibbie, grown fat and matronly at twenty-six, comes to visit, her fidgeting grabby children in tow. Betty Deatcher stops by, the Reverend MacNibbit. Half the town it seems. And each one with an offering: something for the baby, a bundle of flowers, a loaf of bread, a cup of broth. But Zander isn't there. Nor Mungo either.

The thought of them is enough to makm her stomach go hollow with a dread that aches like hunger. She tries to focus their faces in her mind — husband and brother — but can picture only Seedy, grinning, licking his chops, a bone thrust through his nose. As she reaches for the miniature on the night table, her brain is suddenly swamped with evil recollections, images long suppressed springing up like toadstools out of the damp grist of her unconscious, images Mungo had conjured in the quiet of their bed, the darkness hanging over them like a blotter, his disembodied voice pushing, pushing, pushing, until she could see every line of Dassoud's face, smell the spoor of lion and hyena, taste the soothing muck of dried-up watercourses in her aching throat. Could they be in trouble? Sick? Injured? Something is tingling at the tips of her fingers and toes, playing round the periphery of her consciousness, something vague and unsteady, something like a premonition. But no, she's worked up, that's all. Just a morbid fantasy, thcy'll pull out of it, what can happen with a whole troop of armed soldiers there to protect them?

Sharp and sudden, the downstairs bell assaults the silence like a scream. More activity in the foyer. A murmur of voices, footsteps on the stairs. She doesn't want to see anyone. Not in this state. Mary's knock. "Who is it?"

"You've a visitor, ma'am."

"Send them away, I'm exhausted."

Sounds of shuffling in the hall, an importuning whisper.

"He says he's come a long way, ma'am—all the way out from Edinburgh."

Edinburgh? Who—?

At that moment the door cracks open and Mary sidles into the room, apologetic, as the visitor shows himself. A tall man, tall as the doorframe, hair combed back over his ears and gathered in a knot, silk stockings, buckled shoes—could it be?

"Ailie, I—" he stammers, and then steps forward with a package in his hands. "I mean, congratulations."

"Georgie Gleg?" She doesn't know what to say. Her first impulse is to pull the covers up over her head, so stricken is she with guilt and mortification. The last time she saw his face was that gray December morning seven winters ago, the morning they were to be married.

Uninvited, Gleg pulls a chair up to the bed and eases into it with a crack of his bony knees. "I was up at Galashiels," he says by way of explanation, "visiting my mother and stepfather, when I heard the good news—this is your fourth?"

Ailie nods.

"—and so I just had to stop round and, and pay my respects."

What can she say? Here he is, the man she's humiliated, the man she's abused worse than any slave, sitting before her twisting a gaudily wrapped package in his hands, looking as if he were to blame for the whole thing. She suddenly feels herself going out to him. "Would you care for some tea?"

Gleg stays for three hours that first day. Draining cup after cup of tea, as if he were taking part in some sort of contest, crossing and uncrossing his great gangling legs. He fills her in on his past, cocks a sympathetic ear as she tells him of her hopes and fears. "What, what happened between us," he says finally, and she can't look him in the eye, "was good for me in a way. I went out and tried to make something of myself. Edinburgh was an oyster waiting to be cracked, and with my uncle's help I've cracked it, Ailie, in these seven years and four months I've gone right to the top of my profession."

He had. After matriculating first in his class at Edinburgh University, he went to study at Surgeon's Hall under the second Alexander Monro. Driven by an obsessive need to prove himself worthy in some abstract way,

Gleg devoted himself slavishly to his studies, excelling at anatomy, chyma and materia medica, sacrificing social life and recreation for papers and books, hoarding his pennies to buy the finest French surgical instruments. He was rabbinical, monkish, withdrawn. He quoted Boerhaave and Morgagni verbatim, improved on Monro's paracentesical procedures, wrote treatises on the spleen and sphenoid bone, and for his M.D. thesis he definitively described the sphincter ani. Two years later he was appointed professor of anatomy, and at the same time set up a small private practice in a walk-up just off the Canongate High Road. He was soon driving a coach and sporting au courant London fashions. He'd even found time to take up fox hunting and golf, and to publish a series of articles in the Philosophical Society's journal.

All this he reveals gradually, over the course of the afternoon, while sucking at a sugar cube or flailing his geometrical elbows as if they were featherless wings. Finally, he comes to the end of his recitation, and the room falls silent. Ailie has brushed out her hair. The infant lies sleeping beside her, still as a portrait. Ailie clears her throat. "And your wife?" she asks.

Gleg looks down at the floor. "I've never married."

❧ ☙

During the course of the next two weeks, Gleg visits her daily. Ailie is glad for the company. Gleg amuses her — eternally ridiculous — and yet there's something else there too. She can't quite pin it down at first, but in a moment of revelation she realizes what it is: gratitude. Gratitude for the fact that he worships her. Still. After all these years and all that's happened, he worships her. And for her part, a little worship is just what she needs about now. She's been down in the dumps, hurt to the quick by Mungo's rejection of her, feeling worthless, unappealing, a woman who can't keep her man. And then along comes Gleg, almost like a pilgrim approaching a shrine. His eyes tell her that she's a goddess. That he's kept her portrait by his bedside through the long lonely years. That he has been, is now, and always will be her slave.

She can't help but feel guilty, leading him on, consenting to see him, accepting his gifts and attentions. But she's bored and lonely, and he makes her feel good. What's the harm in it?

"Listen," he tells her one day toward the end of his stay at Galashiels, "I know what you're going through and I'm sure things will work out . . . I mean, he's a fine man, Mungo, and as sure as he came back to you that first time he'll be back again — I know he will." Gleg has been turning a book over in his hands, a parting gift, *La Vie Réduit* by Pierre Menard. He is struggling with his emotions, the words backing up in his throat as if he were trying to speak and swallow dry saltines at the same time. "What I mean is, uh—"

Ailie is embarrassed. The look on his face as he stood outside her bedroom door on that fateful morning suddenly comes back to her. She tries to rise from the chair but he takes hold of her arm.

"—if anything should happen, you know, and you need help—money, emotional support, anything at all—you can always come to me, because I, I—"

She's touched. Who wouldn't be? "That's very kind of you, Georgie."

"You can lean on me," he says.

◄§ PUBLIC RELATIONS

No one really has any idea how much an ass can take.

A hundred pounds? Two hundred? Three? Half a dozen sacks of rice? Three kegs of gunpowder and a crate of walnut-framed mirrors in the Queen Anne style? A roll of baft the size of a giant redwood? There is no question that the creature is a beast of burden, that it exists to haul things as surely as a mosquito exists to draw blood. But then why is the animal so ill-tempered, so bristling and recalcitrant?

Even the Foulani assmasters would have to shake their heads over that one. And certainly no one connected with the coffle has even a passing acquaintance with the finer points of an ass's nature. Least of all Ned Rise. Born and raised in the city, what does he know of solipedous quadrupeds? Or blobber-lipped blackamoors for that matter? Or hundred-and-ten-degree temperatures that bake the brain inside your head as neatly as kidneys in a pie?

What he does know is that the expedition is a shambles. Already. Seven days out of Pisania and confusion is the order of the day: soldiers bitching, negroes pilfering, asses collapsing under the weight of panniers loaded with lead shot. Right from the beginning Ned has had his doubts. First off, they were forced to leave five hundred pounds of rice behind at Pisania because the asses couldn't handle it. Five hundred pounds. Of food. And yet they loaded up every last scrap of trade goods—red flannel nightcaps, beads and stones, India baft, glass marbles, linen napkins and French crystal—and dozens of sacks filled with tiny white seashells. Loaded it all up so the asses could barely stand. And then there was the curious little problem with the guides and porters: not a single wog, blind, beggared or lame, would go with them. Not for all the beads and baubles in the world. So who has to haul all the excess baggage and drive the asses? You guessed it. Add to that the fact that the great white hero has about as much idea where he's going as Jemmie Bird, and it's no wonder you've got men straggling all over the road, footsore and pissed through with their own sweat, hollering for double rum rations and red meat for dinner.

So it's gone ever since they left Pisania. Up at dawn, haggling with splay-nosed harridans over the water at this well or that, loading up the bucking, biting asses and hobbling off down the road, the heat like a fist in the face, like a prizefighter backpedaling and jabbing away at you every step you take. Walk till you drop, then get up and walk some more. When the sun goes down you pitch your tent outside the walls of some mud-and-wattle shithole, and boil up a blackened kettle of rice. If you're lucky, the white hero haggles with the local niggers and comes up with an emaciated goat or a couple of senile chickens. And then, before you know it, the sun is up and you're back on the road again.

Ned's chief responsibility in all this is ass #11. The number is painted in red on the animal's flank, and again on the double load of opera glasses and Birmingham knives lashed to its back. Across the dusty plains and through the drooping forests pullulating with biting, stinging insects, down ravines and up rises, through the baked and blasted streets of squalid little shanty towns — Samee, Jindey, Kootaconda, Tabajung — up to his neck in river mud, sweat and red dust, still light-headed from his bout with dysentery and keeping an eye out for Smirke, Ned Rise finds himself following ass #11, step for step and movement for movement, as if he were surgically attached to it, as if he were a suckling babe and this great hairy lop-eared beast were his mother. He plods along, his hand on the ass's flank, near to fainting with the heat, the stench and the exertion, dodging ass turds and swatting flies. Every once in a while he looks up through a film of sweat to see one of the officers riding by on a fine sturdy Arabian, uniform pressed, a canteen held to his lips.

On this particular day — the seventh day out — it looks as if there'll be a break in the routine. About four, a rumor goes up and down the length of the coffle: they're heading into a big town, Medina, capital of Wooli. A thousand huts, somebody whispers. Women, beer and meat. Park's going to give them a full-day stopover. Though the coffle is spread out in either direction as far as he can see, Ned can sense the effect this rumor has on the men. There's a lightness in their step, the ass switches fall with a studied regularity, somewhere up ahead someone laughs. Inspired, Ned

begins to drive his own ass with a vengeance, anxious to lay his bones down
in the shade of a mud-walled hut, take his shoes off and maybe find himself
a little negress to massage his feet and groin.

The trail at this juncture winds through a grove of thorn and fig. It is dry,
tinder dry, the wood brittle, a fine patina of dust spread over everything.
Lions cough in the bush, antelope skitter through the trees like a fall of
leaves. As Ned rounds a bend, he spots Boyles up ahead, halfheartedly
slapping at his ass's haunches and poking along like an errant schoolboy.
"Hey Billy," he calls, "wait up a minute, will you?"

Boyles turns to look over his shouder, squinting into the styptic sun, and
then flags a hand over his head. "Neddy, hey!" he shouts, subsiding into
the bush like a deflated balloon while his ass — #13 — pokes at the stiff
hastate leaves in the hope of finding something palatable. As Ned comes
up, Boyles reaches out a thin wrist to hand him a canteen of rum and
water. "Did you hear, Neddy?" he says. "Stick-up-the-arse is going to give
us a two-day layover at Medea. Five thousand huts. Cold springs bubbling
up out of the ground. And there's so much *sooloo* beer they slosh it into
the cattle troughs to fatten up their goats and bullocks and the like."

Sooloo is the only native word in Boyles' lexicon. But at each village they
pass — even if it consists of only three or four brittle bleached-out
shacks — he makes good use of it, repeating the word endlessly, in all its
permutations of pitch, timbre and syllabic emphasis, all the while panto-
miming the libatory sequence from first drink to elation, stupor and
collapse. Black faces crowd round him. Smiles break out on fleshy pink
lips, teeth flash in the sun. The white man is a traveling circus, a fool, a
zany. *Kakamamie kea,* they laugh. He's crazy. Before long someone
appears with a calabash of beer or mead or palm wine. Boyles puts it to his
lips, drains half of it at a gulp and then wobbles his legs and rolls his eyes.
The audience roars. Pretty soon a second calabash appears, and then a
third. Someone strums a *simbing* or raps out a rhythm on the *tabala,* the
women begin a shuffling dance, and Boyles helps himself to the liquor. No
matter where they are, Billy Boyles, like a thin taper guttering in the wind,
manages to stay lit.

During the course of the next two hours, impelled by high hope and
rising expectation, Rise and Boyles slowly succeed in passing one man after
another until they've made their way very nearly to the head of the coffle.
Immediately ahead of them is Sergeant M'Keal, striding alongside his ass
like a man half his age, stone drunk of course, and roaring out snatches of
some obscure regimental song or other. Beyond M'Keal are two other
eager beavers — Purvey, it looks like, and can it be? — yes, Shaddy

Walters, the cook. Neck and neck, their switches moving like metronomes across the buttocks of their respective asses, panting, wheezing and drooling, existing only for the promise of Medina, that obscure object of desire looming over the hill before them like a vision in a dream. And way up there, halfway to the high, baked, red walls, Park and Scott, drifting along on their chargers, the lovely liquid melodies of Scott's clarinet hanging in the air like an invitation.

Ned and Billy step up their pace, hungry for surcease. Thwack-thwack, echo the switches. Clotta-clot, answer the asses' hoofs. Down a long slow incline and into a basin of green, the road slicing through a cluster of cultivated plots sectioned off by rows of stakes driven into the ground. These are the early crops, nurtured drop by precious drop from the trickle of thirsty wells, emergent leaves pinned to the earth and waiting to burgeon in the driving rains of the monsoon — swaths of sprouting peanuts, yams and sorghum flanked by still, silent fields of maize. Here it is suddenly, a conspiracy of water, chlorophyll and cellulose standing erect and viridescent in the sun, here it is after all those interminable miles of yellowed grass and dehydrated forest, the sight of it reassuring, anodynic, as cool as a compress held to the eyes. Beaming, Boyles turns to his companion: "Pretty, ain't it, Neddy. Almost like — " He is about to say, "Almost like home," but doesn't have the opportunity to round out the sentiment because ass #13, perhaps as wistful and aesthetically gratified in its own asinine way as he himself is, has suddenly veered off the road and made a beeline for the green nirvana trembling before its aching eyes. The defection is duly registered by Ned's ass, which immediately kicks up its heels and dances round the road as if it's been stung in the flank. A moment later the animal throws back its bead, bucks off the double load of opera glasses and knives, and lurches after the first with a lusty bray.

"Hey!" Ned shouts. "You come back here!"

"Heel!" Boyles roars.

But to no avail. The asses are already two hundred yards off, up to their withers in greenery and munching away with as little thought or compunction as milch cows set out to pasture.

Mungo is there in a trice. As are about three hundred Medinan farmers with hoes, pitchforks and spears. There is a tumult of voices, hysterical shouts and vehement curses, a confusion of flying feet. The explorer is in the thick of it, lashing out at the errant asses with his riding crop, trampling row upon row of carefully nurtured, irreplaceable and life-sustaining plantlings. Ned and Billy too, running pell-mell through the wide slashing leaves, calling out hopelessly to their asses, frantic to put an end to it, exonerate themselves, pull the world up on its axis and crank it back to the composed misery of five short minutes ago.

But the line's been breached, the damage done. Swarming like insects, the farmers converge on the first of the asses, inundating the hapless animal in a flurry of flailing hoes and bloody spears. Killer bees, locusts, army ants, they break open the crates and fight over the trade goods, rip the ass's limbs from the sockets, strip off the skin and butcher it on the spot, already rising up in group frenzy to seek out the rest of the malefactors, equine and human alike. They make short work of the second ass, a thicket of spears sprouting from its hide like the quills of a porcupine, then turn their attention to the mounted explorer. He is thirty yards off, shouting out soothing phrases in Mandingo ("Forgive me for I know not what I do"; "Name your price"; "Looks like rain . . ."), while his horse stamps and whinnies. The immediate reaction is disappointing: a deluge of stones, spears and hoes clatters down around him.

By this time a number of the soldiers have come running up the road brandishing muskets and bayonets. M'Keal is roaring threats and racial slurs, and now Martyn is charging over the hill, his horse frothing, sword drawn. Ned manages to make it back to the road, where Walters and Purvey and some of the others have formed a protective circle, but Boyles is tackled and pinned to the earth by two irate little black men in baggy shorts and white toques. "Hold your fire!" Mungo bellows as his horse emerges from the ravaged field, leaves and tassels strewn across its back as if it's been decorated for a wedding parade.

Ultimately, it's a standoff. The gathering force of the Royal African Corps on one side, the enraged farmers on the other. Mungo's men hold their ground, worry written into their faces. The Medinans jeer and pelt them with clods of earth. One man waves a bloody ass haunch as if it were a weapon, while others sport red flannel caps confiscated from Boyles' baggage. The rest, to a man, are gesticulating with spears and hoes and middle fingers held aloft. "Up yours, white man!" someone shouts in Mandingo, and the whole crowd takes it up, a chant, a slogan, a promise and a platform.

The explorer sits astride his mount, looking out over the massed black heads, the swarms of reinforcements pouring from the city gates. He can't help feeling that somehow relations with the natives could have got off to a better start. Yes, something's gone wrong here, he thinks — definitely — as he watches the crowd swell like a blister, new arrivals taking up the chant, the pale flash of Boyles' face swallowed up in the black mass like a feather in an inkwell.

◄§ REQUIEM FOR A DRUNK

"Well, Zander, I guess this is the proof of the pudding, eh? — we've got to have a guide. If only to smooth things over. We certainly can't afford another unfortunate incident like this corn thing." Mungo draws on his pipe, contemplative. "That was a bad show," he says after awhile. "For a minute there I thought we were going to have a pitched battle on our hands."

Zander's eyes are rimmed with red. He looks worn out, emotionally as well as physically. "But what they did to him — it was worse than barbaric. It was, it was —"

"They're savages, Zander. No getting around it." The explorer is bent over a map, the wall of the tent pink with the setting sun, a dish of lentils and salt beef cooling in the dust beside him. "That's why we've got to get us a dependable black who knows these people and their habits and where the road goes and what village is next and who the headman is. I say we make for Dindikoo, Johnson's old village. They know me there. Maybe we'd even run across some relative of his — a cousin or a nephew maybe — who'd be willing to go with us."

Zander is staring down at the knot of his hands. He hasn't touched his food. "I don't know," he says. "I don't know."

◄§ §►

The coffle is camped at Barraconda, five miles up the road from Medina. Even by West African standards, Barraconda's a pretty sorry place. Forty or fifty huts huddled behind a wall of stakes and thorns, a grassless, shrubless, treeless perimeter pockmarked with the cloven hoofprints of kids and goats, a plethora of bloodsucking flies, a total absence of water. Having got word in advance from Medina, the Barracondans have mewed themselves up in their huts and drawn all the water from their wells. For the soldiers, it is pure hell. Nothing to cook with, nothing for the asses, not even a drop to moisten the lips. Worse: they've had to forgo *sooloo* beer, loose women and a holiday in Medina.

But nobody's complaining. Not after last night's sobering encounter and the gut-wrenching horror of the morning.

◄§ §►

Typically, things had gone from bad to worse in the cornfield the preceding evening. The ranks of the farmers had been almost immediately reinforced by platoons of snarling, frenzied women holding up their wasted infants and shrieking about hard times and loss of faith, the earth dried to powder, barren granaries and empty stomachs. Cripples slithered to the front of the press where they could shake their crutches in the white men's faces, while local orators set up bamboo platforms and began to denounce everything under the sun in shrill querulous tones. And through it all, the fearful doomsday howling of the town's dogs.

The combination was too much for Mungo's stout-hearted men: they were getting nervous. M'Keal was blustering, Martyn within a hair's breadth of spitting eight or nine skinny farmers on the point of his saber. And the asses, scenting ass blood and squinting out of their big flat eyes at the carcasses of their late companions, began to back off, ears pressed flat, on the verge of stampede. It was Scott who saved the day. He reined in his horse, bumped and jerked his way over to the beleaguered explorer and suggested that they withdraw to the hill behind them and worry about Boyles later. Under the circumstances, Mungo couldn't help but concur. He gave the order, his voice cracking, and the men fell back in a hail of sticks and stones.

They spent a miserable night, waterless and riceless, their stomachs growling, the sentries jumpy, hyenas stealing into camp to plague the asses and make off with two sacks of salt beef and M'Keal's leather hat. At eleven-thirty, Whulliri Jatta, the king of Wooli, sent out an emissary to discuss compensation and payment for the privilege of traversing his domain. The emissary was a shrewd-looking fellow of about forty-five, dressed in lion skins and a red-flannel nightcap. He strolled into the explorer's tent as if he owned it, sat down and refused to open his mouth until he had been presented with twenty-two hundred cowries, three yards of scarlet cloth, eighteen linen napkins, six knives, a pair of scissors and a mirror. Up to his neck in gifts, the emissary began to smile. "I be Sadoo Jatta," he said, "third son of Whulliri, and I am speak de King's English." Apparently satisfied at this, he clammed up and began sprinkling *mutokuane* leaves into a ceremonial pipe fashioned from the skull of a potto.

Mungo, Zander, Martyn and Scott leaned toward him. He gazed steadily at them, as relaxed and content as if he were sitting in his own bedroom. Finally Mungo cleared his throat, apologized at length for the damage to the cornfield, and asked what Sadoo's father might want in recompense.

Sadoo listened attentively to the explorer's recitation, from time to time nodding his head sagely. But when Mungo was finished the prince looked up at him blank as a wall. "Fadda?" he said.

The explorer repeated himself in Mandingo and Sadoo's features rushed with the joy of comprehension. He nodded furiously, then broke into a wide grin. "My fadda want," he said, "everyt'ing."

Six hours later the negotiations ended. Whulliri would get one third the party's amber and coral, forty thousand cowries, thirty yards of baft, a pair of silver-plated fowling pieces and Scott's tam o'shanter, in return for which the damages would be considered paid in full and the party would be allowed to traverse Wooli from border to border. No mention was made of Boyles. The explorer offered to ransom him for an additional forty thousand cowries and a portrait of King George III. Sadoo held up his hand. "No can do," he said, grinning amiably. And then in Mandingo: "You can come get him at dawn."

The prince's meaning became clear some two hours later when one of the sentries, awakened by the first rays of the sun, spotted something dangling from the wall beside the town's main gate. Something white against the red clay. Ever alert, the man screwed out his telescope and held it to his eye for a full fifteen seconds before dropping it with a startled cry. "My God," he gasped. "Cap'n Park! Leftenant!"

◆§ §◆

It was Ned Rise who cut Billy down.

The city was silent, the gates shut tight. While the men formed ranks and sighted down their muskets, Ned and Jemmie Bird approached the forbidding walls. A row of mute black faces looked down from above. Two vultures, suspended in the sky, began their descent in a slow wide helix. Somewhere a dog began to bay.

Boyles was dangling by one foot, about halfway down the wall, his arms hanging limp over his head. There was a silly grin on his face, as if the whole thing were the crowning moment of some superlative routine to hustle another drink. But he wasn't hustling another drink: he was dead. Ned could see the long purpling scar running from Billy's ribcage to his waist and disappearing into the folds of his trousers. They'd cut him open is what they'd done. Cut him open and stuffed him like a partridge. With sand.

Jemmie Bird cupped his hands and boosted Ned up the wall. Ned clung to the hard-baked clay like a cat, his fingers clawing for purchase, as he ground his pelvis into the wall and slowly made his way up. The sun was like a razor slash across the eyes. There was the low steady hum of swarming flies. In the silence and the heat, under the sky that fell back to the verges of deep black space and hid all that terror and emptiness beneath a specious screen of blue, Ned was undergoing a transformation.

With each inch he rose, each crease and depression his fingers and toes sought out, he felt it charging him, this new sense of himself and the bleak bitter universe, as if the wall were some oracle, some Grail, some radiator of cosmic reality.

He thought of Billy, poor flat-headed sot, poor innocent, come to this. He thought of Fanny, Barrenboyne, his own miserable childhood that was a joy compared to what he'd come to now, in this instant, creeping up a rough stinging rock face on the far side of the earth, surrounded by savages and criminals and mooncalves, risking his life to cut down the mutilated corpse of the only friend he'd ever known. At any moment one of the blacks could drop a stone or a spear. They could pin him to the wall like a cockroach. Stream out of the gates and massacre the lot of them. Well, good. Let them. He would welcome it.

Creeping, clinging, fifteen feet above the ground now. Billy's fingertips, curled in rigor mortis, brushing his face as he takes hold of his friend's cold rigid forearm and hefts himself higher, higher, the weird strained grin, blowflies creeping from the dead man's mouth and nostrils. What had Billy ever done to hurt anyone? For that matter, what had he, Ned Rise, ever done to hurt anyone? Who was keeping score? What did it matter? Ned reached out and hacked at the rope in a fury. I don't deserve this, I don't deserve this, I don't — he repeated over and over, as if he were praying. He wanted to die, he wanted to live. Then it came to him, hard and sudden, in a flash of recognition — he had a mission on earth. He could almost hear the trumpets of the archangels, the crackle of ancient scrolls. Ned Rise, elected in a burst of radiance. He had a mission and this was it: to eliminate Smirke, seduce Park and take charge of the expedition. Or they were all doomed. Like Billy.

The rope tore with a whisper, and Boyles' corpse, set free, fell to the earth like a side of beef. The black faces vanished over the lip of the wall. Dust rose. Ned didn't move a muscle, just clung there under the vicious sun with the stink of death and hopelessness in the air, his body slimed with sweat, sticky as some half-formed thing jerked from the womb. He clung there, a man with a purpose, a man who would fight and scratch, manipulate and maneuver — a man who would survive.

◄§ A.K.A. ISAACO

The road to Dindikoo is long, dusty and dry. It takes the expedition along a well-beaten route, through Wooli, Tenda and Sadadoo, across the rain-starved Nerico and Falemé rivers, from regions where white men are no cause for concern to vast territories where they are no more than rumor, chimeras to frighten children and subdue recalcitrant slaves. As they straggle into this village or that, footsore and weary, their tongues thick with dust, eyelids locked in a sun-blasted squint, Mungo and his geographical missionaries never know what to expect. Will the villagers turn tail and run as if they'd just seen the devil himself? Will they avert their eyes and go about their business as if oblivious to the fact that their front yards are congested with thirst-crazed asses and ragged white freaks just stepped down from another planet? Will they automatically reach for spears and quivers? Or will they come forward with a chicken or a goat, the women tall and bare-breasted and smelling of palm oil, the men as reassuring as parsons and squires? Each village is a cipher. Sometimes the explorer finds the key, sometimes he does not.

At any rate, he's been able to avoid a repetition of the incident that cost him Boyles, a pair of asses and a small fortune in trade goods and cowries. A little timely diplomacy — consisting largely in showering *Dooties* with gifts and compliments and keeping men and animals under a tight rein — has even allowed him to purchase water and provisions along the way, and to replace asses as they wear out. What's more, he's been lucky with the weather as well — thus far the rains have held off and the men seem relatively healthy. Though they gripe and moan ceaselessly. They want to turn round and head back, they're sick of rice, they want triple rum rations, immediate discharges, hazard pay. Their feet hurt, the heat is intolerable, their throats are dry, brains frying, stomachs rumbling, they have earaches, headaches and toothaches, they feel dizzy and don't want to turn out in the morning. The explorer has begun to wonder about some of his choices — especially Bird and M'Keal, both of whom have been consistently crapulent since they left Goree.

But if he's been disappointed in the majority of them, Ned Rise has been a godsend. Sober and industrious, looking out for his fellows' asses as well as his own, volunteering to scout ahead, palaver with the natives, strike tents, chop wood, haul water. He's the sort of man who's not afraid to step in and take charge when something goes wrong and the rest of them are milling around and wringing their hands like schoolgirls or seeking the solution in a bottle of rum, the sort of man who'll never say die, a scrapper who's out to conquer Africa rather than lie down and let it devour him. All this, and he's got a head on his shoulders too. He can read, write and do sums, and he's had some training in the Classics. Already he's picked up enough Mandingo to help smooth relations with the locals, sitting in on lengthy bargaining sessions over tolls, right of ingress, routes and distances, tokens, gifts and outright bribes. And there's no doubting his pluck — just look at the way he scaled that wall at Medina. No, if they were all like Ned Rise, Mungo could rest easy at night.

What with breakdowns of various sorts — asses expiring, soldiers shirking, missing the road and marching for half a day in the wrong direction — the expedition has fallen behind schedule. Held up and let down, it's taken them nearly a month to reach Dindikoo, gateway to the trackless waste of the Jallonka Wilderness. As they approach the village — a grid of shadow and light cut into a densely wooded hillside — the explorer becomes increasingly agitated. He repeatedly raises himself in his stirrups, fixing on the distant huts and granaries with an intense and exclusive concentration, as if he were afraid they might disappear if he were to look away. His heart is pounding at his ribcage. Superstitious, he crosses his fingers behind his back and utters a short prayer.

They've reached an impasse and he alone knows it. Up to this point they've been lucky — getting on without a guide, miraculously avoiding further conflict with the natives — but from here on it will be different. If they can't hire a guide at Dindikoo it's all over. Because Mungo has decided to trace a new route — along the ridge of the Konkadoo mountains — rather than bear north for the fanatical realms of Kaarta and Ludamar, or risk going south through the Jallonka Wilderness. At least to this point he's been traveling a familiar road, though it's been almost eight years and he's made his share of navigational errors. But to head due east over the mountains . . . Mungo doesn't even want to think about it.

Suddenly he's swinging round in his saddle and calling out to Zander. "I'm going ahead," he shouts. "Take charge and bring the coffle into that village in the glen."

◄§ §►

Dindikoo. It's just as he remembered it. Tilled fields jostling with deep umbrageous forests, shade trees spread like parasols over the neat thatched huts with their conical roofs and hard-baked circular walls. Wild begonias and ferns along the road, stumps choked with purple and white convolvuli, a kurrichane thrush massaging the shadows with long liquid glides and quick curt mordents. And the sweet sound of water, a trickle

nd a rush, from one of the rare magical springs that survives the dry
eason. Is that hibiscus he smells?

The first person Mungo encounters is a boy of ten or twelve, chubby,
dressed in a mini-toga and with a maddeningly familiar expression on his
ace. Could it be? "You, boy!" he shouts, but the child, surprisingly agile
despite his tendency toward endomorphic excess, has vanished into the
bush as nimbly as a chevrotain. Odd, the explorer thinks. Must have
rightened the bugger. And then dismisses it from his mind as he continues
on into town.

A moment later he's dismounting in a dusty courtyard strewn with palm
ronds and woodchips, amid a circle of naked children and broad-beamed
women. He smiles. Distributes beads and hard candy. "Remember me?"
he asks in his nicest Mandingo. "Mungo Park? The explorer?"

If they remember, no one gives the faintest sign of it. They just press
ound, hands extended, thirty or forty of them now. Patiently, grinning
and bowing to each matron and enthusiastically patting the head of each
child, he passes out another round of bead necklaces and all-day suckers.
After ten minutes or so his bag of tricks is just about depleted and the
women have already turned their backs on him, giggling and chattering
among themselves, trading a garnet necklace for a coral, dashing for their
huts to gauge the effect of their new jewelry against an old gown. The final
customer, Mungo realizes with a start, is the pudgy boy he'd seen on the
way in. The short blunt fingers dart out, envelop the sucker and neatly
deposit it in a dangling wrist *saphie,* the boy already glancing away as if to
duck a blow. "Wait," Mungo gasps, catching his arm. "*Kontong dentegi*
— what's your name, son?"

The boy stares down at his feet. Mungo can't get over how much he
looks like Johnson, right down to the cut and texture of his hair, the lay of
his ears, the pouting underlip and ironic eyes of the born comedian.
"Oyo," the boy says finally. "Woosaba Oyo."

Oyo. The name makes the explorer's blood race. "And your father?"

The boy points to a hut at the far end of the courtyard — yes, of course,
the explorer thinks with a sense of déjà vu — it's Johnson's hut. Just as he
left it. The neat baked half-wall, the high cone of thatched fronds like a
Chinaman's hat, and out back, the fenced alleyways of the wives' compound and the smaller cones, like a series of volcanic peaks in miniature,
that mark the roofs of their huts. Mungo shuffles toward Johnson's hut as if
in a daze, memories flooding back on him, something catching in the back
of his throat.

There's a woman out front, a slave, pounding millet with a pestle the size of a cricket bat. Beside her, splayed out in the dust, a dog the color of ripe banana, its whiskers gently rising and falling with each somnolent breath. The explorer pauses to feed his memory on the rich sensuous detail of the place — on the sights and sounds and especially the smells, isolate and distinct: wild honey, flowers in bloom, hasty pudding with shea butter, fish and oil and woodsmoke. Sodden togas flash on a hemp line, a gray parrot perches nonchalantly on a T bar beside the door. And there, in the shade of the raffia palm — isn't that Johnson's youngest wife? Yes. The one he broke the news to, couldn't have been more than fifteen at the time. He remembers the way she simply turned and ducked into the hut, no sign of emotion, and then kept the town awake through the night with her racking sobs of grief and incomprehension. And here she is, hardly a day older, sitting in the shade at her loom. "Amuta?" the explorer whispers at her back.

She turns to look up at him, no change whatever in her expression. Cicadas drone in the forest. A pair of hornbills clack and honk at one another in the branches overhead. "We've been expecting you," she says, saying it not as if it were a greeting, but a valediction, her voice weary and resigned, giving and taking at the same time. Mungo feels like an interloper, a criminal, bringer of bad tidings and blighter of crops.

Suddenly she's on her feet and motioning for him to follow. She pauses at the door of the hut, sad and beautiful, her hair bound up in tight corn-row plaits, her eyes like ripe olives. "Go ahead," she murmurs, and gestures for him to enter.

It is cool and dark inside, a funnel of milky light sifting down from the smoke hole at the top. The floor has been swept clean, the beaten earth smooth as tile. In the center of the hut, a circle of stones and three or four twists of the slow-burning liana the Mandingoes use in place of a lantern at night. To the left, a king-size bed consisting of a bamboo frame and a tightly-stretched bullock's hide. There are some wicker chairs and a bench, *saphies* and calabashes dangling from the center pole, a few earthenware vessels grouped in the corner. Just about what you'd expect from any native hut.

But what makes this one different, what makes it extraordinary and special, unlike any other hut in the whole of Africa, what makes it Johnson's hut, is the bookshelf, bathed in overhead light until it looks ghostly and illusory: the bookshelf neatly constructed of bamboo and hemp and lined with the complete works of Shakespeare, quarto volumes,

ǝound in leather. The sight of it somehow overloads the explorer's
ɡlandular system and he feels like crying, a deep ache in his throat and
ɔhest. He takes up one of the volumes at random — *Othello* — and reads:

> *If virtue no delighted beauty lack,*
> *Your son-in-law is far more fair than black.*

Iolly old Johnson, he thinks, shaking his head slowly and deliberately, as if
ɪt suddenly weighed two hundred pounds.

He replaces the volume and then notices Johnson's writing desk — no
more than a leaf really — squeezed up against a square shutter cut into the
thatch. Slips of papyrus paper, an earthenware jar of quills and a pot of
indigo ink: tools of the trade. *Never underestimate the power of the written
word, Mr. Park,* he would say if he were here now, grinning and shuffling
and holding up something for the pot. The explorer idly strokes the ink jar,
touches a sharpened quill to the tip of his tongue. Lost in reminiscence,
he's only vaguely aware that Amuta has left him alone in the hut, too
preoccupied to give much thought to her odd greeting ("We've been
expecting you." *We* who?), oblivious to everything but the sad sweet
sensation of fingering Johnson's artifacts and resurrecting the past.

When he turns round he is almost startled by the figure in the doorway.
Backlit, the face in shadow, too squat and wide for Amuta. A man. The
stranger steps forward, light on his feet for so squat a fellow, the botanical
fringe of his hair silhouetted in the light from the doorway, and for one
wild moment — trompe l'oeil — the explorer thinks it is Johnson himself
come back from the grave.

"*E ning somo, marhaba,*" Mungo says, the traditional greeting.

The voice that comes back at him is so hauntingly familiar it makes his
scalp creep and his throat go dry: "*E ning somo, marhaba Park.*"

Uncanny. The inflection, timbre, tone. But what with the size of the
village and all the inbreeding that goes on, who can say? The explorer
clears his throat. "Are . . . are you a relative of John — I mean of Katunga
Oyo's?"

Black in shadow, black in light, the figure steps deliberately forward
until bathed in the golden glow of the smoke hole, at once illuminated and
realized, the leading man gliding from the wings to a burst of applause.
Suddenly he's speaking in English: "Relative? No, I wooden say dat."

Mungo edges closer, the quill still clutched in his hand, blood pounding,
adrenalin up, all the voices of rationality, all the sonorous schoolteachers

and African Associates and pedantic scientists in safe and sane Great Britain shouting no, no, no. But it is. Yes, yes, yes: it is. Johnson. Johnson in the flesh.

The explorer's reaction is purely instinctual — he flings himself at the fat little man before him with all the enthusiasm of a freshman home for the holidays. "Johnson!" he cries, vigorously pounding his back and pinching the fleshy shoulders in a crushing embrace, "you should have written, you should have at least . . . but you don't know how good it is to see you, old boy, how good . . . but tell me," stepping back now, "how did you, I mean, I thought — ?"

The Mandingo remains perfectly rigid through all of this, making no effort to return the explorer's embrace, no effort at even the most rudimentary of social signals — he does not smile, he does not offer his hand. He seems so unmoved, so emotionless, that the explorer begins to doubt himself for a minute. Could this be a twin brother? First cousin? But no: it *is* Johnson. Unmistakably. Past sixty now but looking twenty years younger, his hair sprinkled with salt, fatter than ever. There's the gold straight pin through his nostril, and there, the look of mock dignity on his face, the look that says you've ruffled my feathers, friend, but I'll consider the case closed if you come up with a calabash of palm wine and maybe a leg of lamb to sweeten my kouskous. He's seen that look a thousand times. Of course it's Johnson. "Johnson," the explorer says, sharp and impatient, as if he were trying to wake someone from a deep sleep, "Johnson: don't you recognize me?"

The black man looks him dead in the eye. "The name's Isaaco."

"Isaaco? What do you mean? Johnson — it's me, Mungo." It is then that the explorer realizes what is lacking, the missing element in the composition of Johnson so permanently embedded in his memory: the toga. Spindly-legged and potbellied, his former guide is wearing nothing but a single piece of linen — immaculate as a buck's neckcloth — swaddled round his loins. Above it — and this is a shock — the great hard ball of his belly is seamed with two ragged horizontal scars, the first clamped across his ribcage like a high-waisted belt, the second obliterating his navel and then skewing off at an angle into the folds of his loincloth, only to reappear, pink and ugly, along the outside of his thigh. Toothy, angular, the scars could have been cut with a stupendous pair of pinking shears.

A wave of pity and revulsion washes over the explorer and he reaches out a tentative consolatory finger, as if to smooth the line of the upper scar. "I — I didn't know. I would have done anything, you know that."

The Mandingo's eyes are fixed on the smoke hole.

"Johnson—"

The eyes dropping, no hint of amusement, jaw set. "The name is Isaaco."

❧ FIRST EDITIONS

Johnson/Isaaco is seated on a bullock-hide stool. He is wearing a crimson and indigo toga patterned over with pairs of leering yellow eyes, and he has assumed the lotus position. A cap of the sort worn by British sailors perches on his head. It is made of silk and has been nattily embroidered with gold thread. At his side, Amuta and a steatopygous twelve-year-old in a striped shift. Ranged behind him, alike as bowling pins, a host of retainers and slaves. Johnson, world traveler, wise man and *saphie*-scribbler, has grown wealthy.

On the other side of the fire, seated in the dirt, are Mungo, Zander, Scott, Martyn—and Ned Rise. The remains of a feast—a rack of lamb, plantain leaves, empty calabashes and yam skins—are scattered round them. Insects and amphibians chirr in the darkness of the surrounding forest, many-voiced, an electric current, and then some higher form of life silences them with a sudden desolate howl. The fire leaps.

"Well, John—er, Isaaco," Mungo says, hearty as a solicitor with an investment portfolio in his lap, "just what *would* induce you to come along with us as guide and interpreter?" The explorer raises a cup of *hoona* tea to his lips. "You can name your price."

Johnson belches softly into his fist. "You know," he observes, either by way of non sequitur or homily—the explorer can't tell which, "when a man finds hisself in dire straits, let's say clamped 'tween the jaws of a crocodile like a prime chop . . ." (he pauses here to wave down Mungo's pained objection) ". . . he has two options, the way I see it. Abandoned like a worn-out shoe by his friend and employer and left entirely to his own devices, he can either sink or swim. I mean he can give it up and drift off to his eternal reward as a pile of crocodile shit or he can use his brain, know what I mean? Maybe, down there in the crawlin' ooze with blind grubs and leeches and things already sniffin' him out and the old croc thinkin' he got himself one tasty big piece of beef, maybe then he takes his two thumbs like this," viciously stabbing at the firelight with his erect thumbs, "and maybe he drives 'em deep into them lidless old eyes, thumbs like daggers, right down to the core of that tiny lizard brain, and then tears back like he was pickin' apples off a tree. Huh? Now what kind of crocodile is goin' to hold on after that?"

No one knows quite what to say. Mungo is red with shame and guilt and frustration, and the crocodile reference is too arcane for the others — nothing more than idiosyncratic gibberish, the crazed mutterings of an old black bushman. The fact that Isaaco speaks English is surprise enough — who would have thought to hear anything but mumbo jumbo this far into the interior? Ned Rise, in particular, is struck by it. There is something in the old savage's manner that brings the nasty buried past heaving to the surface of his consciousness like a moldering log belched up by an eddy in a placid river. That belly, those eyes, that voice. They make him think of a day years ago when he stood beside the Serpentine and watched his future bleeding into the turf. They make him think of Barrenboyne. They make him think of revenge. But no. It's absurd. A London dandy — the first negro he'd ever seen — translated out here into the asshole of nowhere? No. These blacks all look alike, that's all. Or do they?

"Johnson," the explorer is saying, and then immediately corrects himself — "Sorry: *Isaaco*. What's past is past. But this time we've nothing to worry about, not crocodiles or Moors — we've got an armed guard with us."

Without blinking Johnson throws it back at him. "You think a handful of men is goin' to intimidate Mansong or Ali? Or Tiggitty Sego for that matter? You think they goin' to sit still for a whole platoon of white men stormin' 'cross their borders and insultin' the populace? Hah. Armed guard. Mansong could raise three thousand men for every one you got."

Mungo looks down into his cup as if it contained some fascinating new species of animal life. He has nothing to say.

"And what about Dassoud? What happens when he gets wind of you traipsin' through Bambarra again?"

Scott and Zander have begun to eye one another uneasily. Martyn squats over his heels, unconcerned, picking at the leftovers with his knife. "For old time's sake, Johnson," Mungo pleads. "For friendship. For what we went through together."

Johnson's face seems to soften. He takes a long reflective sip of tea, then tips the cap back on his head and puckers up his lips as though stifling a grin. "It'll cost you dear," he says finally. "I want Milton, Dryden and Pope. Leather-bound, gilt titles."

It takes a moment for this to sink in. The explorer sits there, his mouth working, and then leaps to his feet so suddenly he startles two of Johnson's elderly retainers and sends a dog yipping off into the bushes. "You mean you'll go?"

The soul of decorum, Johnson rises with a sigh and holds out his hand. Amuta and the twelve-year-old have produced calabashes of palm wine and are busy pouring out healthy drams into the cupped hands of black and white alike. Everyone is smiling. The startled retainers have rejoined the group and the insects and amphibians have started up again, raucous and celebratory.

Johnson takes the explorer's wrists and pulls him forward. "Listen," he says, his voice low, confidential, "the Pope I want signed."

◆ THE BEGINNING OF SORROW (PLISH, PLASH)

This time of year, bleak, blistered and relentless, when the wells are dry, trees wilted and granaries barren, when the savanna is like a shaven cheek and the dust devils dance in your face, when you eat dirt till your tongue is thick with it and your tears run black, this time of year you pray for rain. Mandingo, Serawooli, Foulah, Moor, Maniana and Ibo, you pray for rain. In each parched village the witch doctor purses his lips, serious business, and sows the fields with rat embryos or sloshes buckets of fetal blood on the cracked blanched faces of graven idols. Dogs go hungry, goats pull up their stakes and attack bamboo, wicker and thatch. The villagers tighten their belts and cook up a paste made from the yellow powder of the nitta pod and then turn their expectant faces to the sky. At sundown, when the moon is a bloody eye on the horizon, the women gather to strip naked and haul plows through the crusted fields while the local hyetologist chants his rain song in a piercing clamorous falsetto:

> Burst heaven, bleed water,
>   Borongay.
> Swell melon, plump kernel,
>   Borongay.
> Hey-hey, hey-hey,
>   Borongay.

Born to the cycle, Johnson is as much attuned to it as the sheep of the field and the jackals panting in the bush. But this year, for the explorer's sake, he's hoping the rains will hold off just a bit longer — at least till they get through the mountains. Of course it's going to be bad whenever the clouds let loose, but up here pussyfooting along the perimeter of toothy cirques and dead drops of anywhere from eighty to three hundred feet, it would be a disaster. No two ways about it. Categorically a mess. And so, model of prudence and preparedness that he is, Johnson has taken measures to insure against an untimely deluge: that is, he has concocted a potent antipluvial fetish consisting of the chucked scales of a small dune-dwelling lizard, a square inch of camel tripe, a pinch of sulfur and six lines of Milton's "L'Allegro."

As he rides now at the head of the coffle, however, the *saphie* dangling from a cord round his neck and his four manservants following immediately behind on their respective asses, he is beginning to have misgivings about the efficacy of his charm. The reason is simple: he smells rain in the air, a scent as rich and unmistakable as the aura hanging over a lake at dawn. He sniffs twice more to be absolutely certain, then wheels his horse round and works his way down the line of the coffle in search of the explorer. He finds him at the base of a rock-strewn hill, bent over an expiring ass. The ass is lying on its side, ribs heaving, forelegs jactitating. Sacks of nails, a pair of two-man saws, a wadded canvas sail and barrels of pitch and oakum are scattered over the stiff yellow grass beside the dying animal, looking as if they'd been dropped from a great height. "Come on, twenty-one," the explorer coaches, "come on old girl. Get up. You can do it." Behind him, looking sheepish, arrogant and stupid all at once, is the massive ginger-haired carpenter, the one called Smirke, his nose and cheekbones sunblasted to a slick tender strawberry.

"Mr. Park," Johnson calls, his voice sharp and urgent, "I got to have a word with you."

The explorer straightens up, rubbing his hands together like a floury baker, and turns to his dragoman with a smile. "Why certainly . . . Isaaco. What's on your mind, old boy?"

"In private, Mr. Park, sir, if you don't mind."

Smirke looks up sharp, either glaring or shading his eyes, Johnson can't tell which. The ass moans like a bedridden grandmother.

"Carry on here, Smirke, will you?" the explorer says, slipping into his saddle and setting his horse in motion with an easy flick of his wrist.

As they amble off, Johnson's smooth silken bellies rippling under his toga, the explorer turns to him, amiable and expectant. "Well?"

"Well, it's just this, Mr. Park — "

"Call me Mungo, old boy."

"Mr. Park, I think it's goin' to blow up one hell of a fierce thunderstorm within the hour and I say you better give the order to pitch camp right here and now or half these white boys'll be puking bile before nightfall."

The explorer cranes his neck to scan the sky. It is a deep, transparent blue from horizon to horizon, no speck of moisture in sight. The heat is so intense it seems to lift him off the horse and hold him suspended, like a bit of ash floating on the thermal currents above an open furnace. "You've got to be joking."

"No joke. I can smell it. Rain. Within the hour."

"But there isn't a cloud in the sky."

"Listen, Mr. Park, I got no time and no energy to argue. Right this minute my boys are throwin' together a shelter up top of this hill, behind that granite outcrop up there — the one that looks like a duncecap. If you got a brain in your head, you'll do the same."

The explorer's face is tentative and quizzical, as if he's just been told a joke he doesn't get. "Don't be ridiculous, Johnson — Isaaco — whatever the hell you want me to call you. It's nine-thirty in the morning. We've got a full day's march ahead of us. If you think I'm going to stop the men in their tracks and set up camp because you've got a feeling it might rain, I'm sorry but you're a Banbury cheese."

Johnson has already turned his mare away. He pauses a moment to glance over his shoulder, fixing the explorer with a look of weary resignation, like a schoolteacher standing over a student who has just subtracted ten from twenty-five for the third time and come up with eighteen. "You know somethin', Mungo — you just as big a ass as you was eight years ago."

◄§ §►

Forty-five minutes later the sky is the color of oiled steel and the wind is gusting at sixty miles an hour, kicking up clouds of dust that obliterate the horizon, far and near. Thunderbolts shatter the swirling haze of the sky and steaming funnels of wind deracinate big-boled trees as if they were stalks of celery. And then the rain comes. Roaring like Niagara, stinging, drenching, diluvian, it rushes across the flatlands and up the valleys, bowing trees and bushes, spewing leaves, spattering dust, blasting the bare rocky slopes of the mountains like salvos from a man of war. In an instant every crate and sack is soaked through, the men bucket-drenched, the asses running water like drainspouts. Boiling and brown with tons of suspended dust, the water comes rushing down the slope at them, a brook, a stream, a river, the rain glancing off the hard-baked shingle and sucked downward with a terrifying *whoosh*.

Shaddy Walters is the first casualty. When the wind comes up, sudden and fierce, the expedition's chief cook is working his way over a slab of coarse reddish granite humped and huge as the back of a whale. To his immediate left, a drop of two hundred feet; to his right, a sheer wall going up another hundred. Almost immediately his wide-brimmed straw hat lifts off and vanishes over the upper wall as if it were a bit of cannon wadding, and the dust lashes his eyes like a cat-o'-nine-tails. Then, with a clatter of pot and pan, his ass sits back on its haunches, whinnying. A sack of rice tears under the pressure and the individual grains flail the cook's face like gunshot, caught up in a rattling gust and whirled into the troposphere to be sown on barren ground hundreds of miles to the north. He is suddenly alarmed. Frantic, he tugs at his ass's halter as Mungo thunders by on his charger, shouting something into the teeth of the wind. The ass is in a panic, the eyes rolling back into its head, its knees slipping toward the edge of the precipice, tail beating back on nothing.

"Every man for himself!" shrieks Jemmie Bird, scrambling past, slipping, running on all fours — up and over the granite hump and bolting for a clutch of withered leafless trees on the plateau ahead. Suddenly, with an electrifying clatter, one of the big regimental cookpots flies over the ass's back, tears its cord, rebounds off the upper wall and clangs back over the escarpment ringing and ringing and still faintly ringing like a cymbal tossed down the side of Ben Nevis. The thought of abandoning his ass as Jemmie had looms powerfully in the cook's mind, but he suppresses it. If nothing else, Shaddy Walters is a stubborn man. A man who'll serve rice and onions three times a day for a week. A man who'll boil India tea till it tastes like gunmetal. A man who'll clutch an obdurate ass's halter from now till doomsday.

Which is precisely what he does. Two minutes later the rain hits with a slap, turns the ledge into a skating pond, and Shaddy and ass #27 plunge to their eternal reward locked in terror and tenacity, bearing down on the scree below like stupendous hailstones. If they cry out, thin mortal voices in the howling void, no one hears them.

Meanwhile, of the forty-one men remaining, excluding Mungo, thirty-eight are on their knees vomiting within minutes after the rain commences. Yellow Jack, dysentery, rash, fever, black vomit. The explorer has seen them before. Clutching their stomachs as if they've been gutshot, the men come straggling into the little clutch of naked thorns about which Mungo is frantically trying to throw up some sort of canvas shelter for the gunpowder, rice and rust-prone muskets. Some have managed to hold on to their asses, others have not. Nearly all of them collapse, gasping and shivering,

on the puddled and puked-over patch of level ground the explorer has
managed to roughly enclose. One of them, an eighteen-year-old by the
name of Cecil Sparks, is crying. The sound of it is nearly lost in the
cacophony of flapping canvas, thunderous rainfall and bowel-wrenching
grunts and groans, but it is there all the same, a whimper in the interstices,
a full-throated sob, the sound of hopelessness, the sound of failure,
self-pity and annihilation.

⋐ DUMMULAFONG

"Told you so." Johnson says it without malice, flat and simple, no inflection
whatever, telling it like it is. He is stretched out sumptuously on a
bullock-hide recliner, à la Madame Récamier, in tarboosh and red silk
dressing gown, his feet nestled in a leopard-skin rug. His camp, half a mile
back from the explorer's, is tucked behind a monolithic slab of rock, facing
north. Though the rain has continued through the night, beating down with
such relentless ferocity that the explorer has begun to wonder if he should
build his boat here and float down to the Niger, Johnson's tent is as dry as
Benowm in February. The floor has been lined with acacia branches to take
up any creeping moisture and the canvas walls have been reinforced with
slats of the same. A hearty fire is licking at the thighs of six or seven
gamebirds — partridges? — as Mungo steps through the flap, soaked to the
skin, and Johnson delivers his apothegm.

The explorer hangs his head, shamefaced and repentant. His sodden
greatcoat tugs at him in a forlorn, round-shouldered sort of way. "I'll never
doubt you again," he chokes.

Johnson inserts a pinch of Virginia tobacco in the bowl of his pipe and
delicately tamps it with his thumb. "Buck up, Mr. Park — it was bound to
happen sooner or later. The rain, I mean." He gestures toward the fire.
"Sit yourself down and dry out a bit, have a bite of squab and a spot of hot
tea and tell me all about it." A snap of his fingers and one of the servants
emerges from the shadows to help the explorer to a piece of fowl and pluck
a yam from the coals, golden-brown and oozing sugary juices. Dark,
aromatic, the spiced tea hisses from the spout of a silver teapot. "So,"
Johnson says, a swell sitting down to dinner at his club and discussing a
trifle tossed away at cards or the track, "how many did you lose?"

Mungo stares down at the food in his lap. The toll over the course of the
last twenty-four hours has been high. Too high. And there's no one to

blame but himself. First, there was Cecil Sparks, poor kid — some sort of seizure took him off just before dawn. He thrashed round the floor for five minutes or so, like a fish hauled up on the dock, then bit off the front half of his tongue, locked his jaw and died. Then, when it was light, Martyn reported that Shaddy Walters had been found at the base of the precipice, crushed beneath the carcass of his ass, and that he had been partially eaten by wild beasts. The cookpots, battered but serviceable, and fifty pounds of rain-bloated rice were recovered. H. Hinton — the explorer never knew the man's first name — had disappeared, along with his ass.

After a moment Mungo raises his head and focuses on a dark spot in the canvas just over Johnson's left shoulder. "Three," he croaks, as miserable as if he'd pushed them over the ledge himself.

"Hey, it ain't the end of the world, Mr. Park. You still got what, forty left?"

"Thirty-nine, not counting myself. Or you."

"So you made it through with none last time, right?"

Mungo looks away, and then, despite himself — the aroma is driving him crazy — tears into a dripping drumstick.

"The way I figure it," Johnson is saying, blowing smoke rings, "the rain should let up about three or so. It'll probably drizzle itself out for awhile, but if we're lucky we can make it to Boontonkooran by dark, drizzle or no. It's just a hole in the wall, but the *Dooty*'s no fiend or anything, and if you willin' to put up a little scratch — say five thousand cowries or so — he might be able to find you a dry hut or two and you can get yourself back together. What do you say?"

Heartsick, his lips glistening with grease, the explorer is slowly nodding his head. "You're the boss," he says.

❦ ❧

Boontonkooran is a way station, unremarkable but vital, given the circumstances. For sixty-five hundred cowries the explorer is able to rent three leaking, bug-infested shacks and purchase two day's provisions — milk, corn and millet — for men and animals. For an additional sixty-five and three buttons from his greatcoat, he persuades a robust octogenarian woodcutter to give up a pair of matched asses and go into retirement. On the negative side, there is no meat available — at any price — and the rains, having set in with a vengeance, force the beleaguered explorer to extend their stay through three bleak days and nights, during which the soldiers — damp, yes, but not dripping — sprawl in ragged heaps on the earthen floors of the rented shacks, sniffling, scratching, huddled in mildewed blankets and dipping their snot-crusted tin cups into a bottom-less pot of broth concocted by the new cook, Jemmie Bird, from salt beef, rice and a handful of wilted native vegetables. It tastes exactly like seawater, something you'd gargle with eight fathoms down, but at least it warms the innards. Outside, the rain beats down with unremitting intensi-ty, like nothing in any man's experience, not M'Keal's, Mungo's or Johnson's. Even the sailors recruited from the *Eugenia* — the elder of whom once rode out a typhoon off the Marquesas — have to concede that this takes the cake.

The weather has the explorer concerned. It's not so much the immediate problems of impassable roads, swollen rivers and slick precipices that worry him, but the long-range effects of the damp air on the men's health. Well he knows how pernicious the climate can be, how the putrid exhalations from swamps, flooded streams and pools of standing water can undermine one's health in the blink of an eye, how a host of mysterious diseases can reduce a man from a bruiser to a death's head in a matter of days. He himself, long inured to it, has been feeling a bit under the weather lately. And if even he is affected, what of scarecrows like Bird or consumptives like Watkins? Will he have to carry them to the Niger? And if so, who'll drive the asses and haul the supplies? Worse: who'll fight off the Moors?

On the second night of their confinement at Boontonkooran, hunched in the command tent they've set up beneath the sievelike roof of one of the rented huts, he confides his fears to Zander.

At first his brother-in-law doesn't answer. Just sits there, an open book in his lap, staring vacantly at the cold canvas wall. The explorer is struck by how drawn and wasted he looks, the skin pulled tight as a mask over his cheekbones, feverish eyes fled to the dark recesses of their sockets as if they'd gone into hiding. "Zander," the explorer says, alarmed. "Are you all right?"

Zander sighs. "A little feverish, I guess. Runny stool. When I stand suddenly I feel light-headed, as if I'd had too much to drink. Nothing really." The explorer is staring at him, mouth agape, a look of dawning horror twisting his features askew. Zander snaps the book shut. "You were saying?"

"Are you sure?"

"Sure of what?"

"That you're all right? No sore throat, vomiting, pins and needles in the fingertips?"

Zander's laugh is feeble, tailed with a cough. "I may be a shrimp," he says, coughing still, "but I'm tough. After all," making a joke of it, "I come from good stock."

The explorer attempts a smile but manages only a weird grin.

"Don't you worry about me," Zander says, his voice breaking on the final vowel to suppress a cough, " — just a cold, that's all. Now: tell me what's on your mind. Go ahead, shoot."

Momentarily mollified, but with a new worry to add to the list, Mungo vents his fears and uncertainties, admits as he could admit to no one else but Ailie his self-doubt, the terrible burden that leadership has become, lives in his hands like grains of sand in an hourglass.

Zander's reassurance is bland, rote. "You've done it before," he sighs, "you'll do it again."

"But I haven't . . . don't you see that? Eight years ago I had no one but myself to look out for. If I didn't make it, so much the worse. But now I've got thirty-nine souls in my pocket, not to mention the horses and asses and thousands of pounds worth of supplies and equipment. My whole reputation's on the line." He is on his feet now, pacing. Suddenly he whirls round, almost shouting: "And the men — what if they can't make it? What if the climate gets to them and deadens their spirit — what if they can't go on?"

◦§ §◦

It is no rhetorical question.

Sure enough, when the time comes to roll out and hit the road under lowering skies and a hint of light so vague even the birds are uncertain whether they should be chirping or not, three of the men refuse to obey the order. Or rather they are unable to. Unable even to stand. Rome, Cartwright and Bloore. Martyn has gone so far as to beat a quick tattoo on the bare soles of each of the malingerers, but without success.

"Sir!" he snaps at Mungo as the explorer is puttering over the arrangement of his saddlebags and cinching a load to one of the command asses. "Three of the men refuse to obey a direct order to roll out, Sir!" Martyn clicks his heels and jabs a salute into his forehead.

Won't roll out? Damn. It's just what he was afraid of. Jolted into martial consciousness by the towel-snapping tones of Martyn's voice, the explorer throws back his shoulders and marches directly toward the hut in which the shirkers lie. Most of the asses have been loaded, and the men are standing about in the light drizzle, impatient, red-eyed, hawking up balls of vileness on the sodden earth. Mungo stalks into the hut, already bristling, ready to vent all his frustrations in a single outburst.

The words are on his lips — "How dare you, you slackers!" — when he is pulled up short by the sight of them — the sight of them, and the smell of them.

The three lie huddled in the corner of the hut, too far gone to lift their eyes or even to brush away the festering hordes of mosquitoes that have mysteriously appeared with the onset of the rains, blackening hands and faces and sun-scorched collars like smudges of dirt. Cartwright appears to be asleep, his cheek pressed flat to the ground in a puddle of his own vomit, Old Rome is gibbering away sotto voce, and Bloore, supine, staring at the thatch like a catatonic. The smell is worse than any sickroom . . . there is the disagreeable odor of human functions gone awry, disordered by illness, but something more too, something earthy and essential; the sad stink of mortality.

"Ask them if they're ready to turn out, go ahead," Martyn sneers from the doorway. And then adds, in a kind of yip: "Sir!"

Mungo kneels beside Bloore and flicks a hand over his face to unsettle the feasting insects. The man's eyes never blink. "Bloore," the explorer says, his voice subdued, "can you walk?"

Old Rome, a man in his fifties who claims to have seen action against the Yankees at Saratoga, has been muttering to himself since the explorer walked in the door. Now he raises his voice, as if he were desperate, as if he were trying to placate some unseen deity, the God of Gibberish or the Lord of Limericks: "There was a young lady of worth," he begins, his voice growing increasingly stronger with the roll of the syllables until he's shouting, "Excessively proud of her birth, / I crept up behind her, / As if to remind her, / That . . . that . . ."

"Bloore," the explorer shouts, raising his voice to compete with the madman's ravings, "Do you want me to fix up a litter for you?" The sick man stares at the ceiling, the breath racheting through his nostrils.

"That . . . that . . ." Old Rome roars.

The explorer takes Bloore's callused hand. "Is there anything I can do?"

Finally Bloore turns his unshaven cheek and wild eyes to the explorer. A cord stands out in his neck as his head lolls to the side: no other muscle stirs. He looks as if he's deliquescing, sinking into the earth. The explorer can feel the sick man's breath on his face, ghastly, meat left out to rot. Bloore's lips are working.

"Yes?" Mungo says, bending closer. "Yes?"

"That a goose don't always have to honk!" cries Old Rome triumphantly.

Bloore gasps. His voice is the rustle of a feather in a windstorm. "Ain't

you done enough as it is, Mr. Hexplorer?" he croaks. " 'Ave an 'eart and
leave us die in peace."

⋅◊ ◊⋅

So it goes. The steady wash of the rain, the tardigrade progress, the
inexorable attrition. Roger McMillan, soldier, and Wm. Ashton, seaman,
are drowned when a native canoe overturns while crossing the raging
Bafing River; J. Bowden, carpenter, falls behind and is stripped and
murdered by thieves; Christopher Baron is torn to pieces by wild dogs
while vomiting in the undergrowth. Each day men collapse by the side of
the road, asses are lost, equipment dumped in the bush or pilfered by
blacks.

That's the worst of it: the thievery. The rest Mungo could live with
— man against nature and all that — but this unremitting assault by the
natives — the very people who would most benefit by his opening the
region to British trade — it's exasperating, heartbreaking. Instead of
looking on each successive village with relief, as a place of refuge and
respite, the explorer has come to dread the approach to any civilized area.
The word has gone out: the coffle is *dummulafong,* fair game. Up and
down the road, from Doogikotta to Kandy, the rumor flies like something
on wings: a party of sick white men is on the way, men so debilitated they
can hardly hold up their weapons or drive their asses laden with beads and
gold and things so exotic and wondrous that no names exist for them in the
Mandingo tongue.

And so the villagers turn out like flies, like jackals, like hyenas. To steal
something from these pale, puking, shit-stinking white men becomes a
matter of honor with them, like counting coup on the Great Plains or
standing erect and motionless before the crashing onslaught of an enraged
bull in the Sierra Morena. They are ubiquitous, merciless. On one
occasion, having dismounted to assist a soldier whose ass was mired to the
whiskers in muck, Mungo turns back to his horse to watch a native built
like a greyhound streaking off with his saddlebags. Another time, two
reedlike old men emerge from the bush in front of him, and as he
cautiously raises his musket, the one leaps forward to jerk it from his hands
while the other snatches the greatcoat from his back. And all this in a
driving rain.

"The only way to put a stop to it," Johnson says, heaving along on his
mare in a pocket of mist, "is to shoot all thieves on sight. Listen to me, Mr.
Park: I know these people." The near trees are gray with haze; farther
back they recede into the belly of the clouds. Leaves drip, strange
creatures call out from the forest, frogs mount one another and sing about

it. "This is Africa, brother," Johnson says, echoing something he'd said a long time ago, when old Eboe peered into the explorer's palm and the heavens split open, fracturing the sky from pole to pole. "It's dog eat dog out here. If you weak, they goin' to knock you down and strip your ass bare."

The order goes out, up and down the coffle: shoot on sight.

•§ §•

The immediate result of the explorer's get-tough policy is that Martyn and M'Keal, self-appointed watchdogs of the van, enthusiastically cut down a pair of elderly egg women as they teeter up the road, their fragile burdens perched atop their heads in great coiled snake charmer's baskets. Mungo inspects the slack tangled bodies, arms and legs splayed, neat holes through chest and eye, the blood mingled with running yolk and albumen until it looks protoplasmic, ageless, some essential jell of life festering to the surface of an antediluvian swamp. "Bury them," he says.

Ten minutes later, while leading his horse through a maze of immense rounded boulders tumbled over the grass like heaps of dead elephants, the explorer suddenly becomes aware of a commotion up ahead. One of the men . . . it looks like Ned Rise . . . is struggling with a pair of blacks. Mungo drops the reins and charges through the narrow cleft between the boulders, crying "Stop thief!" as if he were on a crowded thoroughfare in London or Edinburgh. The black men, naked to the rain, glance up quickly, coolly gauging the distance between the explorer and themselves, and turn back to the business at hand. One of them is dancing round in circles with Rise, both hands locked on Ned's musket and jerking it back and forth as if it were a two-man saw, while the other methodically hacks at the leather-bound bundles lashed to Ned's ass. By the time the explorer arrives on the scene, the first man is sprinting away with Ned's hat, the second vanishing into the bush with a fifty-pound sack of rice. Ned, still clutching the musket, lies sprawled in the mud, a victim of his own momentum and the thief's unexpected release of the gun.

Cursing, Mungo draws a bead on the first man. "Take that!" he shouts, squeezing the trigger. Nothing happens. The thief stops in his tracks, hands on hips, no more than a hundred and fifty feet off. And then, incredibly, he begins wagging his hips and thrusting his pelvis forward, obscene, taunting, contemptuous.

Mungo flings down his musket in disgust (wet powder, no doubt, damn it) and snatches up Ned's. But the thief, like a rabbit on the lip of his warren, has disappeared. The explorer is about to explode, the multiple frustrations pricking at him until what's left of his composure is like some raw bleeding wound, when he whirls at Ned's shout. He cannot believe his eyes. Some nigger son of a bitch is scrambling atop the charger he left in the defile no more than thirty seconds ago. This has gone too far. Trembling with righteous indignation, he jerks the musket to his shoulder, sights down the muzzle and lets fly. BOOM! The blast of smoke, a quick piercing shriek and Ned's excited cry: "You got him!"

Sure enough, there he is, knocked to the ground like a winged partridge. Mungo drops his weapon and breaks into a run as he watches the little thief lift himself from the wet earth and skitter off between the boulders, his leg torn open, some small bright object clutched in his hand. "After him!" Mungo roars, the thrill of the chase on him. A moment later he's back in the saddle and hurtling off after the wounded man, his alerted lieutenants — Johnson, Martyn and Scott — hard on his heels. They burst through the rocks just in time to see the thief struggle into a thicket ahead. In an instant they're there: but where is he?

"Come out of there, you bleeder!" Martyn shouts.

The horses crash through the brush, shattering saplings, wheeling to and fro in confusion. "Where'd he go?" Scott cries, his voice nearly a whinny, eyes fixed on the ground like a fox hunter's.

The frustration is boiling over. Voices call out, the horses snort and blow, reinforcements rush up on foot. But again, magically, the thief seems to have eluded them. The explorer turns to Johnson with a shrug, but Johnson is paying no attention to him, merely sitting there astride his mare, silently pointing a stick at the baobab above them. There, like a treed animal, is the thief, cowering against a gouty limb some twenty-five feet from the ground. He hangs his head, trembling, and drops the object clenched in his fist. One of the men picks it up. It is a compass, set in cork, the compass Ailie had given Mungo when they parted. To help you find your way back to me, she'd said.

"Shoot, Mr. Park." Johnson's voice.

Martyn, his blood up, makes it a chant. "Shoot. Shoot."

Ever so slowly, inch by inch, the explorer raises his pistol until he is looking down the length of it at the wretched little man quaking in the tree. The moment seems eternal, predator and prey, winner and loser. Small and hungry-looking, his skin purple with wet, the thief gazes down at him out of hopeless eyes, eyes gone dead already, a milkiness, a glaze there, as of butchered calves or dogs run down in the road. The man's thigh looks no bigger around than Mungo's forearm. On the inside of it, just below the groin, the flesh is shredded as if it had been ground up in a machine, and there are bits of hair and dirt and leafmold clinging to the edges of the wound. The rain is playing a threnody in the leaves.

"Shoot!"

The explorer thinks of Sir Joseph Banks, of his book, of London and the whirl of celebrity, Ailie, the children, sun on the Yarrow.

What am I doing? he thinks. What in God's name am I doing?

Then he pulls the trigger.

❧ THE LAST SMIRK

The report is terrible, awesome, rebounding off the rainslick boulders like the boom of dynamite in a concert hall, like the angry blast of a mountain blowing its top. It is tailed almost immediately by a piteous screech and one, two, three more rumbling gunshots. Ned Rise, standing alone in the defile, thinks of men at attention, flags waving, ceremonial salvos you can feel in your feet, the ushering in of a new era. He listens to these gunshots with a mixture of aversion and relief. Aversion at the thought of some poor wog cut down in his tracks, relief that the great white hero has finally come to his senses. Because things have been bad, very bad. What with the men dropping from fever and shits, the rain bogging them down and the niggers robbing them blind, it's begun to look as if none of them will lay eyes on the Niger — not Park, not the Leftenant, not the little sap of a brother-in-law. And where does that leave Ned Rise, survivor? In a heap with the rest of them, stripped naked by the natives, vultures spinning overhead. Unless Park toughens up and shows a bit of muscle. The gunshots are a good start.

Ned has been standing there the whole while, motionless, listening to the last distant hue and cry, waiting for the echo of the coup de grace. Now he turns back to his ass, recinches the saddle and tightens the lashings on the various sacks and trunks strung over the animal's back. The rain, if anything, has begun to fall harder. As he stoops for the all but useless musket Mungo threw down in the mud, his eye catches a movement in the glade ahead. More thieves? Wild beasts with a taste for ass flesh — or human? Instinctively, Ned reaches for his knife.

There it is again. A movement in the undergrowth. "Hey!" Ned calls out, nervously fingering the hangman's welt under his collar. The trail ahead dips through the glade — a single massive baobab, a cluster of saplings, savanna grass, wildflowers, thick clots of briar — and then descends a long rocky path flanked by another tumble of gargantuan boulders. At Ned's shout the movement stops abruptly. There is something back there, no doubt about it, and there's no way in the world Ned is going to move within range of it. He'll just wait till the others come up, he's thinking, when the briars begin to quake violently, as though some large animal were trying to uproot them.

Losing patience, Ned bends to shy a stone into the bushes and is surprised to hear the soft unmistakable thud of stone on flesh, a sound he'd learned to distinguish while winging pigeons as a boy. An instant later a pair of black hands part the leaves, and a disgruntled face appears — but what a face! As black and wild as a gorilla's. No: blacker and wilder, because it is a human face. The eyes glaring out from sockets reddened with ochre, deep vertical scars like terrible wounds creasing forehead and cheeks, the hair pulled back in a topknot and a tight necklace of cobra heads drawn round the neck like a warning, as if to say I am venomous and I will not hesitate to bite. This fellow makes the local thieves look like babes — even the savages at Pisania pale by comparison. Hopelessly, Ned raises the dripping musket, the knife clenched under his arm, pis aller.

Nothing happens. For a long moment Ned and the wildman face one another at a distance of perhaps fifty feet, the rain slanting down, Ned trying his best to look formidable and self-possessed. Then, suddenly, inexplicably, the wildman is grinning. A wild wet obscene grimace of a grin, big lips distended, teeth filed to points. And then he's gone. Poof. Like a degenerate elf.

•§ §•

That night they camp in the open, rain beating on the tents like aboriginal drums. There are brilliant flashes of light, the hollow ghostly calls of animals wandering in the night. Around two the watchfire is doused by a sudden driving downpour, and a pack of hyenas — chinless, ears pinned back — slink into camp and eviscerate a pack ass.

The following night they are again camped in the open, and again it is raining. So too the next night, and the next. As near as Ned can figure, it is around mid-July, a month past the time the great white hero said they'd be coasting down the Niger. Two more weeks, he tells them. Another hundred fifty, hundred sixty miles. Hang in there men, he coaches.

Ha. Hang in there. This morning Ned watched Jonas Watkins cough his lungs up and then pitch face forward in the bloody muck. They got him to his feet, but he just reeled round and collapsed again. His face was splotched red and white and his eyes were like milk. Park came by and asked if he could go on. Jonas couldn't answer. After awhile the great white hero remounted and told Jemmie Bird to leave some salt beef and ammunition for Watkins. Come along when you feel better, Park said. Another joke. If the expedition was a man going bald, poor Jonas was just another hair fallen to the carpet. But what really rankles is that skinny little wimp of a leftenant — the brother-in-law. He gets dragged along on a litter like he was royalty or something while Jonas gets dumped beside the road for the vultures. Who does Park think he's kidding?

Ned grits his teeth — and hangs in there. The month wears on. They climb ridges, traverse plains, pass through a succession of identical shit-stinking villages. Strange birds fly up in their faces, carnivores rush out at the asses in a tawny blur, herds of huge lunging deer with striped flanks and twisted horns fly off at the sound of their voices. They eat honey badger and woodrat, bathe in puddles infested with leeches, bilharzia and guinea worm. The world stinks of humus and creeping mold.

In one miserable two-day period they ford three rain-whipped rivers: the Wonda, the Kinyaco and the Ba Lee. Each booms along like an angry god, prickling with uprooted trees and tangled nests of brush, hiding snags and snakes and crocodiles, the water brown as a turd, ribbed and rushing. At the first one — was it the first? — Jimmy M'Inelli, a decent sort who could handle a deck of cards better with one hand than most people could manipulate a knife and fork with two, was gobbled up by a crocodile as if he were a bit of cheese and cracker. Ned was standing right next to him at the time, waist-deep and not ten feet from the far bank, when the thing plowed into the poor fool like a log coming down a sluiceway, flipped open its jaws in an awesome mechanical way, and sank into the brown stew of the current. One second he was shouting to M'Inelli to take his hand, the next he was looking at a ripple in the water. Ned never hesitated. He was an acrobat, he was an eagle. As he shot through the air he let out a short sharp bark of surprise, and then found himself on the bank, dripping and shuddering, heaving for breath like a steam engine. His mind was racing. He saw Billy's face, Shaddy Walters', Jonas', M'Inelli's. Fear seized him like a pincer: somehow, by force or persuasion, he had to circumvent Park.

◦§

One night, just outside a town called Bangassi, Ned is crouched beside the watchfire drying his shirt on a stick and tootling dreamily on Scott's clarinet. (A note on the clarinet: the explorer thought a little music would be a good idea, sweet melodies to soothe the local negroes and beckon to the coffle's stragglers, guiding them in like lost sheep. When he found that Scott was too sick to stand, let alone tongue a reed or sustain a half note, he asked for volunteers. The men groaned. Ned, always on the lookout for a chance to ingratiate himself, stepped forward.) The night is dank, a light drizzle feathering down like the breath of fallen angels. Jemmie Bird, assigned to the second watch, is sleeping soundly at Ned's feet; the others are whimpering and snoring in their sodden tents.

It is preternaturally still. So still Ned fancies he can hear the individual droplets as they coast down through the haze. He has just finished a moving rendition of his old standby, *Greensleeves* — the last sad crystalline note still hanging in the air — when he is startled by a low insistent rasping, repeated at intervals, and coming from the direction of the tents. He turns his head, eyes straining: is someone calling him?

The firelight is unsteady, rising and falling like the slow chop of waves against a pier, but yes, there is someone back there, on the far side of the command tent. He rises to his feet and starts forward, silent and inquisitive. But wait. It could be Smirke, that son of a bitch, out to waylay him again. He brings his feet together and leans forward, searching the shadows. "Hello?" he calls, half-expecting one of the boys to spring out at him with a laugh . . . but then the boys are a bit too sapped to be playing games — they've got to save their energy for dying. He's about to call out again when in a sudden flash of apprehension he sees it — that face — the same one that had stared out at him from the briars a fortnight ago. But now there are two, no, three of them. And that sound again, a sort of *hsssst:* are they calling him?

"Jemmie," he whispers, kicking out at his sleeping companion.

"Ma!" Jemmie bellows suddenly, "Mama!"

When Ned glances up again the faces have vanished, and Jemmie Bird is rubbing his eyes, muttering "damnedest dream," over and over. "Thought I was back 'ome in Wapping, suckin' at me mum's tittie — frightenin' is wot it was." There is a moment of reflective silence, the flames snapping at the air, and then Bird laughs out loud — "Ha!" — as if he'd just played a joke on himself, his head already dipping back toward his chest, the first of a mounting series of snores catching in his throat.

Jittery, Ned lays down the instrument and picks up his musket. He's about to step into the shadows and confront his demons when suddenly someone lays a hand on his shoulder and he whirls round in a panic to find himself staring into the astonished face of Serenummo, one of the nigger guide's servants. But where'd he come from?

E ning somo, marhaba, the slave says.

Ned returns the greeting. He and Serenummo have become chums of a sort, sharing an occasional pipe and chatting in Mandingo, Ned to improve his command of the language, Serenummo to probe the cat-eyed white man about the wonders of Enga-lond and the great salt sea. But now, before the slave can settle himself beside the fire, Ned takes him by the elbow. "Did you see anything out there a minute ago?"

Serenummo is tall and rigidly muscled, the veins standing out in his arms like lianas choking a tree. His face is keen and inquisitive, and when he talks, he talks in spate, tugging at his right ear for emphasis. Like most Mandingos he has only a vague idea of how old he is, but Ned guesses he must be about thirty-five. "See anything?" Serenummo echoes.

"Faces. I'm not even sure if I saw them myself."

The black man eases down beside the fire and draws a calabash from the folds of his toga. He waves the stoppered neck vaguely, offering a drink.

"Wildmen," Ned says, ignoring the calabash. "Naked and painted, with filed teeth. I think they've been following us."

"Ah," says Serenummo, "you mean the Maniana."

"Maniana?"

The black man nods. "Nothing to fear," he says, "they're just hoping to conduct a little business with you."

Ned is stung to the bone with doubt and apprehension. Business? What kind of business could he possibly have with these kinky monsters? Garroting and transfixion? Rape, torture and dismemberment? Like a street cat he's always managed to land on his feet — whether as fisherman, entrepreneur, resurrected Christ, grave robber or convict — but this African nonsense has him stumped. The filth and savagery of it — sometimes he wishes he were back in London dodging Osprey, Banks and the hangman. At least they're not going to slit you open and fill you with sand. Before he realizes it, he's shouting: "Well why don't they come out and show themselves then? Why hide in the bushes like a bunch of painted devils?"

"Not their style. You see," Serenummo says, pausing to tip back the calabash and search Ned's face, "not many tribes will trade with them, so naturally they're a little shy. What they want is, well — they like to consume their fellow man: heart, kidney, brain. We call them Maniana."

"Cannibals," Ned whispers, breaking into English.

Serenummo is lecturing now, tugging at his ear, eyes bright: he hardly notices the interruption. "They live far off to the east along the Joliba. When they fight a war, they gather up the dead and wounded and consume them. In times of peace their king sends out parties to ambush solitary travelers along the road, or failing that, to purchase a slave or two for the pot."

Ned has crouched down beside the black man, as rapt and horrified as a child drinking in tales of witches and hobgoblins. He can't help thinking about the men left beside the road, about the stragglers out there now. In the night.

"Of course," Serenummo adds, a nervous smile on his lips, "no one would ever actually do business with them — I mean sell them a slave. That would be too cruel," he whispers, glancing sideways at Ned, "too cruel. A fate worse than death."

At that moment a sudden sharp clamor swoops at them out of the utter desolation of the night. It is immediately succeeded by a bitter curse, a burst of grumbling and tooth gnashing, the rattle of asses' hoofs. "Damn me if I didn't bust me fookin' leg just now. Goddamnit. Curse that son of a bitch Park and the cunt of a whore that give him suck."

Smirke's voice.

Serenummo rises quickly, pats Ned's arm and slips off toward his master's tent as the commotion draws nearer. A moment later Smirke staggers into the puddle of firelight, four hollow-cheeked stragglers beside him, their eyes narrowed with fever and fright. The flanks of their asses are stippled with blood, the muzzles white with foam. "Christ," one of the men barks as he flings himself down beside the fire, "we was nearly eat alive back there!" Ned recognizes the man as Frair, a sack of bones and tired complaints, a real blue-ribbon whiner.

"Couldn't go on no more," adds another, weaving on his feet. "So we laid up by this big black tree and soon as the sun goes down these slinkin' wolves come up — Jee-sus — sniffin' at me feet they was."

Smirke sits heavily beside Frair, glowering at Ned as if he were personally responsible for all their troubles, while the others — as drawn and dazed as survivors of a shipwreck — lurch off toward the tent, asses in tow. Without a word, Smirke leans forward and digs into the pot of rice and onions the explorer has put aside for latecomers. He eats with his hands, chewing noisily, grunting and belching, sucking the mucilaginous gop from his fingers like a big henna lion lapping at its paws. Frair ducks in behind him, a thin-faced little jackal snapping up the scraps.

Smirke has grown thinner over the past months, his bulk reduced by disease and exhaustion. Most of his twisted coppery hair has fallen out, and his skin, where it isn't burned, is the color of tallow. He is still big, brawny and stupid — and hence dangerous — but he hasn't given Ned much trouble in recent days. Ned, favored by Park with a lighter load, is generally near the front of the coffle, while Smirke, saddled with an extra ass and two thirds of the carpentry equipment, invariably brings up the rear. After a ten-hour march in the rain, Smirke just doesn't seem to have the energy to settle his accounts.

Which is as it should be — because the time has come for Ned to settle his own. Forget that Smirke had beaten him lustily, stolen his hard-earned cash and ruined his chance with Fanny. Forget that he'd perjured himself to see Ned sent to the gallows those long years ago. It's of no consequence. What matters is that the madman is here, waiting his chance: it's kill or be killed. Just three weeks back, as they were saddling their asses on a grim sodden morning, Smirke had come for him without provocation. It seemed the canvas girth had snapped in his hand as he attempted to tighten it, and his temper snapped along with it. Hulking and enraged, he kicked the ass, flung down the useless strap and threw himself on Ned. The attack was brutal, calculated to stun and kill. He hit Ned in the lower spine without warning, drove him forward into a shallow pool reeking of urine and forced his face down. If Park and Martyn hadn't been on them in an instant, Ned would have drowned. As it was he got a lungful of fluid and a deep bone bruise that kept him stooped over for days. Smirke, raving and gibbering, had to be bound up like a bale of hay and slung across an ass's back. "I'll kill you for this, Rise!" he bellowed, again and again, till someone put a sock in his mouth.

Looking at him now, hunched over his meal like a slobbering beast, the close-set pig's eyes gone dead with fatigue and malarial asthenia, Ned has an inspiration. He holds his breath till Smirke and Frair are snoring in unison, the two of them splayed out before the fire like hounds after a hunt, and then leans over Jemmie Bird to check for signs of consciousness. Bird is dead to the world. Heart slipping, throat dry, Ned checks the priming pan of his musket and slips Jemmie's pistol into his belt. Then tiptoes away from the campfire, gradually melding with the shadows back of the tents. "Hsssst," he calls. No response. He tries again. Still nothing. And then, thin as a bristle, the call comes back.

The Maniana are there, fragments of the darkness. He can smell them — sweat and grease and the musk of some wild animal — a smell that startles him with its pungency and pervasiveness, a smell that dredges up ancient racial memories, at once atavistic and sematic. Then he sees them, grinning, their teeth hanging in the emptiness as if independent of jaws and faces. As they draw closer he backs toward the circle of firelight, the musket leveled at the nearest set of sharp gleaming teeth.

They emerge from the shadows as if from a pool, the dark sucking back at them. There are five of them, young and lean and wild-eyed. The smell grabs at his stomach. He motions them forward, and the nearest savage, the one with the cobra-head necklace, edges closer. Ned points down at the sleeping Smirke. "Trade?" he says in Mandingo. The cannibal looks down appraisingly at the big sunburned man, and then glances up at Ned. His teeth seem to champ and he snatches at his shoulders to suppress a tremor of anticipation. Suddenly his face becomes a question, a prayer, and he holds up three fingers.

Ned is puzzled at first . . . and then it hits him. He's asking if all three are for sale — Bird and Frair as well as Smirke. One of the others has come forward now, lean and hungry-looking, peering down at the sleeping men like a housewife at the poulterer's. No, Ned motions emphatically, and holds up a single finger before pointing again to Smirke. The first man looks a bit disappointed, the wolfish grin flickering momentarily, but then the second says something, sharp and flat, and both nod their heads quickly, like carrion birds dipping into a carcass: it's a deal.

Ned watches from the shadows as the five silently bind the slumbering Smirke with hemp cords, wrapping him like a mummy. When they've got him secure, the man in the cobra-head necklace slaps the big whiskered face awake, simultaneously plugging the pink bud of the blooming mouth with a wedge of cotton and beeswax. Smirke struggles against the cords as they haul him off, trussed like a pig, a string of mad protestations and cries for help mired deep in his throat. "Mmmmmmmm," he grunts, "mmmmmmmmmm," as if he were sitting down to a candlelit supper.

Electrified, Ned has drifted closer, fatally drawn like moth to taper, until he catches himself with a jolt — if he doesn't watch it he'll wind up in the pot alongside Smirke. Suddenly Cobra-head whirls round, one eye twitching, lips pulled back in a lewd unholy grin, the grin of one conspirator to another. Ned flinches as the savage holds out his hand. The smell of him, this close, is unbearable: Ned wants to tear his clothes off, run whooping through the trees, drink blood. There is something in the Maniana's hand, a black leather purse, small and smooth as a pear. Take it, he gestures, dipping his head and extending his arm. Ned reaches out for the soft black bag, wondering, and then realizes with a rush of giddy joy that this is his payment — Judas Iscariot — and he laughs deep in his head as he slips the bag into his pocket. He feels evil, powerful, exhilarated. A partner to demons and devils and things of the night.

He steps forward and looks Smirke square in the eye. The big man lies there like a whiskered baby, his mouth squawling against the gag, neck craning, arms drawn tight to the body as if swaddled in linen. Tendons ripple in his jaw, his throat swells with wasted breath. And the eyes: beating wildly from face to face, stark and terrorized, until they settle on

Ned with a look of wrath and hatred and utter hopelessness. Ned responds with a wink, snapping a hand to the side of his head and waving a pair of fingers like an old maid seeing a crony off at the docks. And then, slow as the sun rising over the hills, the corners of his mouth begin to lift, in a smirk.

✍ FROM THE EXPLORER'S NOTEBOOK

Bambakoo on the Niger
19 August, 1805

At long last, after all our trials and tribulations, we've made it: thanking the Lord for His guidance and protection, I've lived to duck my head in the Niger a second time and thrill once again to the soft swirl of its music as it rushes past my ears. And what a glorious stream it is, bursting with the precious cargo of the monsoon, black with silt, as expansive and majestic as any river on earth — even here in its extreme upper reaches.

The one lesson this arduous trek has taught us is this: that a party of Europeans, bearing trade goods, can penetrate to the interior with a minimum of friction, thievery and native antipathy, and the loss of no more than three or four out of fifty men, if proper precautions are observed and seasonal vagaries taken into account. As it is we've made it through with six stout-hearted and brave lads from among the soldiers at Goree — Martyn, M'Keal, Bird, Rise, Frair and Bolton — and a fine skillful carpenter come all the way with me from Portsmouth, one Joshua Seed, who is currently delirious. Unhappily, we lost the big fellow, Smirke, to noctivagant predators some days back, and Mr. Scott, feeling a bit under the weather, was forced to stay behind at Koomikoomi — a picturesque alpine village not forty miles distant — until such time as he should feel well enough to rejoin us.

Johnson — i.e., Isaaco, as he now mysteriously prefers to be called — has proven as invaluable to the current expedition as he was to the first. Devoted, knowledgeable, humble and intelligent, this true-blue African homme des lettres who once plucked cotton in the Carolinas and ministered to Sir Reginald Durfeys' sartorial needs at Piltdown and in London, has devoted himself heart and soul to extending the boundaries of geographical knowledge, forsaking the comforts of home and family to help us forge a new road from the Gambia to the Niger. Just this morning he appeared outside my tent with the humble but politic suggestion that we send word ahead to Mansong of Bambarra to the effect that we have entered his realm and ask his blessing for our enterprise. "A capital idea!" I cried, and immediately dispatched two of Johnson's black servants for Segu, bearing gifts for Mansong and his son Da, along with a letter detailing our object in once again visiting his country. It is my fervent hope that this munificent potentate will provide us with the vessels to prosecute our endeavor, as without carpenters it may prove ticklish to construct our own craft.

In the meanwhile, I have decided—again at Johnson's suggestion—to float down the river past Segu to the city of Sansanding (conveyed by a curious tribe who make their living at transporting goods and people to and fro in their dugouts, rather like the gondoliers of Venice), where we would dispose of our trade goods in barter and launch the H.M.S. Joliba for parts unknown. I quite agree with my faithful dragoman that etiquette requires us to bypass Segu, so as not to force ourselves once again on the bountiful and truly Christian charity of Mansong, who was of course so concerned for our first expedition. And while Sansanding is said to be a predominantly Moorish town, we should be able to get a better price there for our wares, and in any case, should be well off in the broad lap of the Niger before the Moors' ingrained fanaticism and unreasoning prejudices might work us any harm. Once afloat, I have determined to have no truck whatever with the local tribes, in the event that they should prove hostile, especially as we follow the river northward into the heart of the Moorish domain. I shall bargain with no one till we have reached the sea. God willing, the journey will be as tranquil as it is revealing. I have heard no word of the devilish Dassoud. I trust he has long since paid the price for his sins.

River of Mystery, River of Legend, River of Gold! How good it is to be back under its spell, to gaze out over the broad back of its churning waters, to ladle up a long cooling draught of its health and invigoration. Alexander Anderson, my own dear brother-in-law and second in command, seems much heartened by the spectacle of it. This courageous Scotsman, struggling against the effects of the climate and the violent exertions of our march, has stood by me through thick and thin, a comfort and an example. His fever seems much abated, and the healing waters of the Niger have brought such a flush back to his pale cheeks that I find myself thinking invariably of roaring hearths and the brisk gentle snowfalls of the Borderlands. I have every hope of his imminent and complete recovery, and of Mr. Scott's rejoining us before the week is out. And then, our minds and bodies refreshed, we shall set forth to conquer the Niger.

ᵉᵍ O THE HEAVY CHANGE

He was a born dreamer. A born fool, his father would have said, a brattlin' gowk, a randie gangrel, good for nothing but drainin' whisky bottles and liftin' a fork to his face. Sent off to school at the age of six, he drew into himself, a devourer of mythologies and travelers' tales, a solipsist who found refuge from the harsh physical world of boarding school in the soothing pages of a book or a solitary walk through overgrown woods and abandoned churchyards. Home for the holidays, he wandered the hills round Selkirk, a stranger to the crofters' sons who ignored him in the streets and then called him a snob behind his back. His sister was his only friend.

He was a boy, slight and unathletic, and then he was a man. He hardly noticed the change. It was as rhythmic and unremarkable a process as the movement of the seasons, grass greening, leaves falling, snow, rain, sun, boarding school, public school, university. From the moment his mother left till the day he took his degree at Edinburgh, his existence was calibrated, the path clearly marked, the pace easy, and there was no reason to ask himself what he wanted to do in life — he knew, with the bland assurance of the untried, that whatever it was it would be spectacular.

But then, back under his father's roof, degree in hand, Alexander Anderson was at a loss. For the first time in his life he was free to make a choice, run where his legs took him, do as he pleased. The responsibility was crushing. Horace, Catullus, Aristotle's *Physiology* — what good did they do him now? He didn't want to go into medicine, despite his father's pressuring — too belittling, disgusting even. Nor would he practice law or take up the cloth like so many of his unsettled classmates. He toyed briefly with the idea of making a name for himself as a poet — the glorious Southey, intrepid Burns, astonishing Anderson — but gave it up after filling six or seven copybooks with lugubrious, self-pitying tripe after MacKenzie's *The Man of Feeling* and coming to realize in an equable and matter-of-fact way that he hadn't a shred of talent. The military occurred to him next — the flashing red jacket, the drum and fife, bringing the French to their knees and all that — but no, that was where all the athletes wound up — on the battlefield, their heads staved in — and how could he, at five feet four and nine stone on the nose, possibly hope to compete with them?

And so, halfheartedly making the rounds with his father, he stayed on at Selkirk, infused with vague yearnings, bowed down like a snow-covered sapling with anomie and self-contempt, eating and dressing well enough on the interest from his modest trust fund, drinking to kill time, and dreaming, always dreaming.

Then Mungo came home from the Niger, scintillating, heroic, huge with success, and Zander no longer doubted what he would do with his life. There would be a second expedition, and Zander would be part of it. What more daring occupation was there? Not Nelson, not Napoleon himself could match it. The thrill of pitting oneself against the unknown, the delicious risk, the heady exhilaration of victory over nature itself: it was too good to be true. How could he have thought of anything else these past few years? Of course, he thought to himself, of course, the idea of it sprouting in him like a tough clinging vine, like ivy, burgeoning till it sought out and filled every crack and crevice of his being. He would wade through bogs, hack his way through scrub and nettle, scouting out the trail for his brother-in-law, small and quick and lithe, probing at all the deep-buried secrets of the Dark Continent. It was a revelation. Alexander Anderson, explorer. This is what he'd been saving himself for.

Little did he realize he would have to wait seven years for his chance.

Seven long torturous years, years that wore on him like an indeterminate prison sentence, no time off for good behavior. He killed time with drink, riding, a flirtation here and there. He hunted, smoked cigars, took up boxing to build his endurance. And he shadowed Mungo. Made him repeat his stories over and over till he could quote them word for word, till they ran through his head like the stuff of legend. He puttered away at the only trade he knew — doctoring — as a way of distracting himself from this thing that had become an obsession. At night, or on the long gray afternoons when he couldn't muster the energy to lance a boil or apply a clyster, he devoured everything available on the subject of Africa and exploration. He read Moore and Bruce and Leo Africanus; he wore out three copies of his brother-in-law's *Travels,* carrying a battered volume with him at all times, muttering over the dog-eared pages, quoting it to startled patients and half-witted farmers as if it were a holy book. Then one afternoon Mungo took him aside and told him to get ready. He was elated. When the bottom fell out three months later he sank into despair. A year passed — the longest, bleakest year of his life — before Mungo came to him again. This time it was no false alarm. He packed his bags in a trance, all his hopes and dreams realized, all the years of waiting come to an end. He was going to Africa.

◄§ §►

Now, the rain lashing at the walls of the tent like a Biblical plague, his guts turned to ice and his face on fire, he lies back on a sweat-soaked litter suspended between a pair of battered crates while a raven caws in the distance and black beetles crawl up his legs and whir in his face. He is dying. Sapped, wasted, down to just over a hundred pounds, he cannot — will not — go on. In disgrace, he's allowed himself to be carried — carried like a woman or child — by men nearly as weak as he. Mungo has dosed him with calomel, let blood, hunted up snakes and tiny antelope and eyeless white grubs the size of a man's forearm so that he could have fresh meat. All to no avail. He is dying. And glad of it.

Suddenly the flap swishes back and Mungo slips into the tent. His eyes are pits of concern, raw with doubt and worry, his face as gaunt and yellow as a deflated football. A drop of water clings to the tip of his nose. "How you feeling?" he asks.

Zander wants to lift his own weight from the explorer's shoulders, wants to lie to him and say *It's all right — don't you worry about me*. But he can't. When he opens his mouth to release the words there's nothing there, no sound at all.

Mungo isn't listening for the reply. He strides across the room, turns his back and shrugs out of the drenched greatcoat, then flings himself down on a crate beside his bed. There's a whiff of sulfur as he lights a tallow candle, and then the rustle of paper. A moment later he's scribbling away in his notebook with an almost frantic urgency, as if the act of putting words on paper could soften a blow or breathe life into a corpse.

Outside, the rain-slick village of Bambakoo bows under the weight of the deluge: tamarind, mahogany, fig, a freckling of bright tropical birds in a huddled wall of green. Beyond the glistening huts and thick cluster of riverine forest, the Niger punishes its banks, flaying the earth to its metamorphic bones, vocalizing its authority, swishing and sucking as it drinks in the rainfall like a bottomless hole. Zander can hear it from his bed, rain falling in the hills behind him, rushing past the tent in a throbbing network of brown tentacles, driving, caroming, leaping, until finally it breaks through to enlist in the stream for the long inexorable drive to the sea.

"It's a pity," Mungo is saying over his shoulder. "The loss of life, I mean. If I had it to do over I wouldn't leave England till I was damned good and sure the rains were finished down here." He pauses, the quill pen scratching away in the interlude. "It was the weather that did it — no doubt about it. We Scots and English just don't have the constitution to take all this rotten air, this constant soaking, this — " He throws the pen down and presses his fingers to his eyes. Back turned, he begins again, his words choked with pain and disappointment, some fresh piece of bad news sticking in his teeth like gristle. "I may as well tell you now," he groans, swinging round in his seat. "Scott's dead. He — " The explorer glances up at his brother-in-law and then turns away again, as if ashamed to look him in the eye. "He gave in to the fever two nights ago. The *Dooty* just sent word by special messenger."

Zander says nothing in response. He's having trouble keeping his eyes open, and he can't quite catch his breath. It's like the first time he went into a football match at school and found himself in the dirt, his senses jarred, the wind knocked out of him.

There is a moment of silence, lingering and dull, underscored by the background hiss of the rain and the roar of the Niger. "Zander?" Mungo says. And then, almost a bark: "Zander!"

He's there in a flash, leaping across the room and snatching at his brother-in-law's wrist as if to prevent him from slipping over the edge of a precipice. The pulse is nothing, as faint and intermittent as the rattle of a broken pocketwatch. Panicked, the explorer grabs him up in his arms — a bundle of sticks in a sack — and fumbles a vinegar-soaked rag to his nostrils. Zander's eyes flutter twice, the irises fixed under the upper lids as if staring back into themselves. There's a red welt on his throat, and a cold flat pallor has crept into his face.

Dying, he looks like Ailie.

◀ THE END OF THE ROPE

The Spanish use a single verb, *esperar,* to express both waiting and hoping. So too in English: there is no wait without expectation. One waits for spring, a table, death.

> **wait,** to stay in a place or remain inactive or
> in anticipation until something expected
> takes place.

Ailie is waiting. Staying in Selkirk, at her father's house, remaining inactive and expecting — what? The letter that tells her to wait no more, that she'll never see husband or brother again? Or the hastily scrawled missive bringing news of Mungo's reemergence on the coast of Africa, alive and well and embarking that day, a hero a thousand times over? Neither. Both. At this point she hardly cares: she's at the end of her rope.

All her life she's waited for Mungo, waited for him to finish school, come home from Djakarta, Africa, London. She can wait no more. Really, sincerely, she'd rather know that they were dead — he and Zander both — than to live in this limbo of suspense, in this agony of living for someone else, out of one's body, drawing each breath, day by day, in morbid anticipation of events in a place so distant it could be mythical.

She's had three letters. One from Zander, addressed at Goree, and two from Mungo, addressed respectively from the Cape Verde Islands and Pisania. The Pisania letter came last week. It lay flat as a dagger in the postman's palm, and the sight of it, sharp-edged and white, nearly cut her heart out. She thrust the envelope into her bag and hurried up the street in a nervous little jog trot, blood singing in her ears. She went through the front gate in a daze, the stairs echoed under her feet with a hundred insinuating creaks and groans, and then she was alone in her room. For a long while she just sat there at the edge of her bed studying the familiar handwriting scrawled across the envelope, fighting the impulse to chuck the whole thing in the fire. A quarter of an hour passed. And then, calm and deliberate as the tax collector, she slit the envelope with a paper knife and extracted the folded letter.

It said nothing.

Like its predecessor it was full of bravado and self-congratulation, talk of sturdy asses and stout-hearted men. He would lay the Niger flat, Mungo would, tape-measure and chart it end to end and be home in plenty of time to carve the Christmas goose. There were a few words of solicitude for her and the children toward the end. He hoped that the new baby was healthy and happy and that it was a boy. The letter was dated April 29: nearly five months ago.

She is waiting for another. She is waiting for Mungo to come back to her. She is waiting to resume her life. In the meantime, there are the children. Thomas, child of the century, is five, Archibald, born in April, has been weaned to applesauce and oatmeal mush. Together with Mungo junior and little Euphemia, they raise a persistent whining clamor that either soothes her with its substance and immediacy or drives her to distraction, depending on her mood. She hasn't touched her microscope since spring. She is bored. It's the same old story.

With one exception: Georgie Gleg. He spent the summer at Galashiels, away from the university and his practice. Each day he called on her in Selkirk with some offering, a bundle of flowers, box of sweetmeats, a three-volume novel. He took her out into the country in his carriage, brought her to dinner at what was left of the family estate at Galashiels. He entertained her. Distracted her from her brooding, her waiting, the stark gut-wrenching fears that clouded her days and haunted her nights.

Eyebrows were raised around town. Her father lectured her. She was a married woman, after all, and married to a saint and hero at that. She knew it, and felt a prick of conscience. But she felt just as strongly that she no longer owed Mungo anything, that he'd deceived and betrayed her and that she would do as she pleased, propriety be damned. Besides, her seeing Georgie was simply a reflection of her need for companionship — at worst no more than an innocent flirtation. The very fishwives who were so ready to cluck their tongues could be found out back of the inn on a Saturday night rolling and grunting in the bushes like sows in heat. No: they could all be damned. They had no idea what she was going through, no idea what it was like to be at the end of your rope.

◄ THE LETTER

Segu. A rainy afternoon in mid-September, 1805. Beneath the high whitewashed walls of Mansong's compound, a huddled queue of suppli-cants awaits the call to enter and pay obeisance to the potentate. They are a motley crew: tribal officials from the west in soggy sarongs and limp feathers, petulant-looking Moors with slabs of salt wrapped in antelope skin, old men in rags crouched over sorry goats, bullocks and monkeys. There are lepers and wastrels, singing men, beggars, slaves. And then there are the women. Big, broad-beamed village scolds with rolls of spun cloth, wicker baskets, caged songbirds and serval cats on leashes, ancient hags clutching baskets of wild tamarind to their withered dugs, barefoot girls, bright and nubile in indigo gowns and copper bracelets, lined up for inspection like birds of paradise.

At the far end of the queue, footsore and soaked to the skin, stand the forlorn figures of Serenummo and Dosita Sanoo, servants of Isaaco the scribe and emissaries of the *tobaubo* Park. The asses beside them are laden with rare and exquisite gifts intended for Mansong and his son Da. Gifts that range from the purely practical (silver tureens, double-barreled guns and kegs of black powder), to the epicurean (a case of Whitbread's beer and a string of blood sausage), to the merely fanciful (six pairs of velvet gloves, a pince-nez on a gold chain and a music box that grinds out the first eight bars of the "Ombra mai fu" aria from *Xerxes*). More importantly, these humble envoys have been entrusted with a letter from explorer to potentate, a letter written and conveyed with the utmost secrecy, three slips of paper the explorer seemed to consider as precious as gold, as potent as a *saphie*.

This letter. It was to be delivered *only* into the hands of Mansong himself, the explorer had insisted, his pupils shrunk to pinpoints of furious intensity; under no circumstances were its contents to be revealed to anyone else — not Wokoko, not the towering praetorian guardsmen, especially not to the Moorish merchants of the bazaar and *most* especially not to Dassoud or any of his henchmen. There was a strange, almost mystical look on the white man's face as he handed over the letter and repeated his instructions for the fifty-seventh time. Serenummo will never forget it. The *tobaubo* looked like a tribal necromancer perched high above the trees on some stony pinnacle, his arms spread wide, steeling himself for the leap into faith. Or oblivion.

Bambakoo, the River Joliba
10 September, 1805

To Mansong the Magnificent, Liquidator of Lions and Tamer of Topi, Mansa of Bambarra, Waboo, M'butta-butta, Wonda, Etc.

Your Royal Highness:

I am that white man who nine years ago came into Bambarra. I then came to Segu, and requested Mansong's permission to pass to the eastwards; your Highness not only permitted me to pass, but magnanimously presented me with fifty thousand cowries to purchase provisions along the road. This generous conduct has made Mansong's name much respected and revered in the land of the white people. Accordingly, the king of that country has sent me again into Bambarra, as his ambassador in good will, and if your Highness is willing to again grant me a hearing, I shall outline my reasons for returning to your great country.

Viz., your Grace well knows that the white people are a trading people, and that all the articles of value which the Moors bring to Segu are made by us. If you speak of a good gun, who made it? The white people. If you speak of a good piece of scarlet or baft, or beads or gunpowder, who made them? The white people. We sell these goods to the Moors; the Moors bring them to Timbuctoo and sell them at a higher price. The people of Timbuctoo sell them to you at a still higher price. Now, the king of the white people wishes to find a way by which we may bring our own merchandise to you, and sell everything at a much cheaper rate than you now pay. For this purpose, if Mansong will permit me to pass, I propose sailing down the Joliba to the place where it mixes with the salt water; and if I find no rocks or danger in the way, the white men's vessels will come and trade at Segu, if Mansong so desires.

Mungo Park

P.S. I hope and trust that Your Majesty will not reveal what I have written herein except to your own counselors; for if the Moors should hear of it I shall certainly be stopped before I reach the sea.

After two interminable hours in the rain, Mungo Park's emissaries leap to attention as the enormous gate suddenly creaks back on its hinges and a short heavyset man in a scarlet toga emerges and begins making his way down the line, pausing now and again to question a dripping chieftain or banter with a giggling coquette. The ambassador is accompanied by a pair of feathered and breechclouted giants with nasty flat-headed spears, quivers of poisoned arrows and great slashing bows with pull enough to pin an elephant to a tree. *"Kokoro killi shirruka,"* Dosita whispers, lowering his eyes. "Savages from the east."

Serenummo steps back a pace when the ambassador stops before him. The fat man glances shrewdly at the bundles lashed to the sagging asses, then looks Serenummo in the eye. "You've been sent by the white men, no? Doing the bidding of demons, yes?" Serenummo nods. The giants stare off into the trees, as if contemplating some rarefied spectacle beyond the ken of mere earth dwellers. "Follow me," the ambassador snaps.

They are led into a central courtyard overshadowed by a rambling mud-and-timber structure, a sort of longhouse divided into individual dwellings, some neat and symmetrical and roofed with stone, others so misaligned as to suggest the full range of geometrical possibility. In the near distance they can see the ancient sycamore fig that presides over the place like a protective deity. "Wait here," the ambassador commands, at the same time motioning to a pair of cowering servants who come forward to lead the asses off for inspection. Then he ducks into a passageway that seems to open up before him like a mouth, and Serenummo and Dosita are left standing in the muddy courtyard under the watchful eyes of the two giants. They've come a long way, and they're hungry, thirsty, tired and wet. No one offers them food or drink. No one invites them in out of the rain or asks them to take a load off their feet.

Half an hour later the ambassador appears at the entrance of a dark twisting passage at the far end of the courtyard. He motions to them with his index finger, then turns and flaps off in his sandals. They have to hurry o keep up, turning first right and then left, heading east, west, north, outh, passing through room after room, courtyards, walkways, corrals nd stables, led by the red flash of the fat man's toga as if it were unraveling, thread by thread, the secrets of the labyrinth. Finally they are hown into a dark mud-walled room lit only by a brazier and smelling of weat and incense.

At the ambassador's command they go down on their knees, touch their oreheads to the earthen floor in submission. When Serenummo looks up, e sees that he is indeed in the throne room, in the presence of the potentate himself. Mansong is seated on his gilt stool, enormous, like a ark statue. He is wearing a dirty periwig and earrings fashioned from ilver spoons. Beside him, his son Da, a miniature version of the king; at is feet, a white dog. Wokoko, witch doctor and chief counselor, sits on Mansong's right hand, dressed in his hyena skins and ostrich plumes, and he shadows are swollen with the big shifting forms of the bodyguards. But vhat is surprising is the presence of the two Moors. A one-eyed man drawing on a pipe, and his companion, a big man, hard as stone, with black nessianic eyes and a hyphenated scar across the bridge of his nose. What vould Mansong be doing with Moors in his council room?

"Mansong the Magnificent finds your gifts acceptable," the ambassador nnounces. "Have you any message for the king?"

Serenummo rises slowly, loosening the strings of his *saphie* bag in order o extract the letter. But then he hesitates, remembering the explorer's njunction. He can feel the Moors' eyes on him.

"Well?" the ambassador snaps. "Mansong is waiting."

Serenummo fumbles in his pouch and produces the letter. He bows, and teps forward to hand it to the king, but suddenly the big Moor is on his eet, quick as some pouncing beast. The royal hand is outstretched, the etter raised and proferred, when the Moor intercedes. "I'll take that," he ;rowls in Arabic, brushing back the extended hand of Mansong the Puissant as if it were the importuning hand of a beggar, snatching the letter rom the air and depositing it in the folds of his *jubbah* with a look of rage nd contempt.

No one, not even the fiercest of the guards, says a word.

◄ DASSOUD'S STORY, PART II

A nobleman, as proud as he was fierce, representative of a culture light
years in advance of the *tabala*-thumping, goat-sucking Sahelian Moors, a
man who had gazed on the Mediterranean and traversed the Sahara,
Dassoud was not the sort to be long content in the role of henchman and
human jackal. Second fiddle might be all right for a young man, someone
footloose and untried, but as Dassoud matured he came to expect a bigger
slice of the pie. Where before he'd been content, now he began to chafe in
his subsidiary role. He found himself resenting Ali's authority, coveting his
prerogatives, criticizing his tactics on the battlefield and at the peace table
alike. But the real key to his dissatisfaction, if the truth be known, was
Fatima. As she grew in years, so she grew in bulk. She blossomed, tucking
away kouskous and seedcakes, twenty meals a day, waking in the night to
call for milk and honey. By the time she reached her late twenties, the
queen had put on another eighty pounds. At four-sixty, she was irresistible. Dassoud decided to make his move.

He came for Ali in the night, just as sixteen years earlier Ali had come
for his own predecessor. Dispatching the Nubian guard and separating
Ali's head from his body was nothing, the work of a minute — the real trick
had been locating Ali in the first place. For the Emir, reasoning that the
night would inevitably come when the new usurper would stalk Benowm
with scimitar or garrote, had made it his practice to postpone retiring until
the latest possible hour, and to tell no one — absolutely no one — whose
tent he would grace with his recumbent presence. One morning he might
emerge from Mohammed Gumsoo's tent, the next from Mahmud Imail's.
It was a game of musical tents, and a practice of such long standing that the
Emir's people found it as natural a part of waking as the smell of
cooksmoke.

For two weeks, Dassoud had quietly visited each of the tents from which
Ali had appeared in the morning, remarking the servants who bundled the
Emir's bedclothes, rolled up his rugs and carted off his hookah. The
servants varied from day to day, but one — an old woman whose *jubbah*
hung on her like a winding cloth — was there to clean up nearly every
morning. Dassoud took her aside and threatened her: betray Ali or he
would crush her like a dung beetle. She was a twisted thorn root, her skin
almost pale, one eye as cloudy as a puddle of semen. A tarnished ring
glinted on her lip as she threw her head back and laughed. "I'll betray
him," she hissed, "gladly." Later, after mounting Ali's head on a stake in

the center of camp, Dassoud went to his queen, the blood still wet on his hands.

With Fatima's support, Dassoud was able to establish a broad base of power. As the widow of Ali, she lent him legitimacy in the eyes of the Moors of Ludamar; as daughter to Boo Khaloom, she gave him a blood tie to the Al-Mu'ta tribe of Jafnoo. It was a beginning, and Dassoud pursued it for all it was worth. Where Ali had been satisfied with rapprochement, Dassoud pushed for an active alliance; where Ali had overlooked encroachment on his borders, Dassoud sought to extend them. He went to great lengths to assure himself of Boo Khaloom's allegiance, and then, dealing from a position of strength, he approached the fierce Il Braken and Trasart tribes of the northwest and challenged their leaders to single combat. Remorseless, mechanical, he hacked them down one after another.

Within the year Dassoud was able to command a force of some fifteen hundred horsemen; from among these he picked two hundred men to serve as his elite cavalry. They were the best the desert had to offer. From Jafnoo and Ludamar and Masina, from the Il Braken and Trasart and Al-Mu'ta tribes, they came to Dassoud's tent, savage and skillful, quick lithe athletes, crack shots, superlative horsemen. No one could stand up to them. With Dassoud in the van like some hellish apparition, like a black *shaitan,* they ranged the length and breadth of the western Sahel, from Gedumah to Timbuctoo, pounding the earth to dust and terrorizing Foulah, Mandingo and Wolof alike. Even the mighty Mansong was cowed.

Dassoud was content. He was Emir of Ludamar, lord and husband to Fatima, commander of a private army and conciliator of the desert tribes. He had consummated his dreams, achieved his ambitions. What more was there? Before long he had settled into a comfortable routine of aggression and extortion, of raiding to the east and west and south, raiding to pacify recalcitrant villages, to acquire slaves and cattle, raiding for the sheer joy of it. It was a good life. He was content.

Until the sleepy afternoon he was sequestered in Fatima's tent, awash in the rich ferment of her flesh, soft music playing, the harsh sun and the cries of the battlefield a distant memory, until that afternoon when his idyll was shattered by the news that white men — *Nazarini* — were back in the Sahel. It was Ahmed, the one-eyed *Bushreen,* who stood respectfully before the tent and called to him in a low urgent voice. Dassoud parted the flaps almost instantly, a scowl on his face, weapon in hand. Ahmed could barely catch his breath. White men, an army of them, had just entered

Bambarra at Bambakoo, he gasped. They had firearms, they were killing blacks, taking slaves, pillaging the countryside.

The news hit Dassoud like a quick savage blow from the hoof of a camel. He stood there, stupefied, until surprise turned to anger. White men: *Nazarini*. He hated them to the bottom of his soul, hated them as he had never hated anything in his life. The one white man he'd ever laid eyes on — that groveling sneak of a cat-eyed explorer — had escaped him. Outwitted him. Beaten him. It was the only contest Dassoud had ever lost, and the memory of it was an open sore, as wet and raw as the day it first erupted. He clenched his teeth, remembering the humiliation it had cost him, remembering how he'd ridden into camp, empty-handed, in rags, and how, though no one dared say a word, a thousand eyes told him what they were thinking. And then there was Fatima — the way she'd coddled the freak, sitting by the hour and listening to his gibberish as if he were a *marabout* or a sage or something, while he, Dassoud, son of a Berber sultan and terror of the battlefield, was nothing. The thought of it, even now, so many years later, galvanized him with rage and hatred. He turned to the nearest thing at hand — Ahmed's camel — and knocked it flat with a single blow of his balled fist. Then he sprang on his horse and thundered off for Segu.

Two weeks later he was the happiest man alive, giddy with joy. Of all the *Nazarini* in the world, it was Mungo Park himself who had come back within reach of the Emir's long arm. And the letter. He laughed to think of it, even then circulating among the tribes of the north, stirring them to blind and irrational peaks of fury, fanning up the sort of deadly, implacable, blood-lusting rage that no assault on religion, cattle — even women and children — could so instantaneously arouse: the *Nazarini* were striking at their pocketbooks. What could be more perfect? He didn't care how big the white man's army was — he, Dassoud, Scourge of the Sahel, would have fifteen hundred frenzied horsemen at his disposal before the month was out.

And then, at Sansanding, he would greet Mungo Park once again.

SANSANDING

There are faces in the night, grimacing, leering, the faces of naked savages with serpent coils for hair, staring eyes and filed teeth. They close in on him, incisors champing with a hiss, there's a wild shout, spears and stones and poison-tipped arrows raining down, the suck of the current, the roar of the rocks . . . and he wakes, sweating, beneath the fine mesh of mosquito netting and a splash of stars. The explorer is at Sansanding, and he has been delirious on and off for a fortnight, a month — who knows? There was the death of Zander — yes, that set it off — and then the letter to Mansong. Beyond that, he can't remember what was real and what phantasmagoric, what occurred in the eyes and memories of other men and what transpired only in his own. There was something with Jemmie Bird, something bad, an argument with Johnson, a period of drifting, floating on the river, it seemed, and then the whirling scents and colors of the marketplace at Sansanding and Mansong's delay about providing a canoe. Yes, the fever subsiding, it begins to come back to him.

◄§ §►

Walls collapsed and volcanoes erupted the night Zander died. The sky split asunder and the earth lashed to and fro like a runaway wagon, pitching and lurching until the explorer had to get down on his knees and turn his intestines inside out. He retched, eyes tearing, a torrent of rice, tamarind, half-digested fish and bitter yellow bile spewing from his lips, while Zander lay there on his litter, dead. Mungo cursed. Bit his tongue. Pounded the dirt floor with his fists. When the earth finally stopped trembling he found that he couldn't get up, there was no strength in his arms, his legs had gone dead — he was like an ocean-run salmon that frantically lashes its way up the Yarrow, impelled by some ancient implacable force, leap after coruscating leap, only to flounder in a shallow pool, its back out of water, tail twitching feebly. He was spent.

The night wore on. There was a cry like that of a nightjar, the sound of rushing wings. Why was he beating his way up the Niger? he asked himself. Why was he risking life, taking life? What kind of man was he, Mungo Park, to drag a narrow-shouldered little parlor-sitter like Zander out into the teeth of the wilderness? To desert a wife and four children? To lead thirty-six men to their deaths and blow a cringing old negro to Kingdom Come as if he were nothing more than an insect or toad? What had he come to? The answer was something he didn't want to face. Not now. Not ever. At dawn, he pushed himself up and uncorked a keg of rum.

He was drunk for three days. Blind drunk. Johnson took charge in the interval, arranging for Zander's burial, organizing the equipment for the trip to Sansanding, dispatching Serenummo and Dosita Sanoo with the letter for Mansong. When Mungo finally came around, he found himself in a pirogue, stretched out like a Viking on his way to Valhalla. It was night, starless and black as the void. He heard the swish of the paddles, a low murmur of voices. He heard the hooting and buzzing and gibbering of night things, a sound that rose in volume until it was as loud and undifferentiated as the boom of a heavy surf, and then he saw shapes in the night, faces and colors, animals with the heads of eagles and tails of serpents, and he knew the fever was on him. He'd been miraculously spared during the overland trek, but now, what with the drinking bout and the night he'd spent on the damp ground, it had stolen a march on him. Suddenly he sat up in the dark. "Zander!" he cried. "Johnson!"

A warm hand spread itself across his chest. "It's all right, Mr. Park. A touch of the fever, that's all. You on the river now. Hear it?"

He heard it. But he couldn't just lie there — he was head of this expedition, after all. He had to get up and lead his men, steer the canoes, spy out the landfalls and come up with names for all the salient geographical features. There were maps to be drawn up, whole regions to be charted, botanical specimens to be plucked and dried.

The hand lay on his chest like an enormous weight. It was pushing him down, firm and persuasive. "Lie back, Mr. Park — everything's under control," Johnson whispered. "We hit Sansanding in the morning."

What? Come into Sansanding flat out on his back? Never. Fever or no fever, Zander or no Zander, he had to get up and lead his men. He slapped the hand away like an irate child and jerked himself clumsily to his feet amid a tumult of cries, fore and aft. He heard the squawk of a startled bird somewhere up ahead, and then the canoe was lurching violently, left, right, left again, and he was pitched headlong into the inky soup of the night and the cold quick fastness of the Niger.

There were shouts and curses, some in English and some in the Somonie dialect of the boat people. The canoe in which Mungo had awakened was twenty-five feet long. It had contained bundles of equipment, two Somonies, Johnson, Ned Rise and Jemmie Bird. When it capsized, passengers and boatmen alike were flipped into the river. Jemmie, who had lashed himself to the cookpots, floated briefly, buoyed up by the big iron cauldrons; when moments later they tipped and filled with water, he sank like a stone. Ned, meanwhile, had managed to get hold of the explorer's shirt collar and dog-paddle him toward the denser blackness of the shoreline. Johnson, floundering, happened by purest chance to blunder into the canoe, and hang on while it spun downriver, the sopping Somonies attempting to swim it ashore.

An hour later, the whole thing was history. The other canoes had converged on the spot with a torch, and had picked up the floating paddles. The canoe was steered to shore and righted, the explorer and Ned Rise located by means of hoots and whistles, and the equipment — which had been firmly lashed round the hull of the canoe — saved. Two kegs of gunpowder were ruined by the soaking, and a sack of rice had split. As for Jemmie Bird, he too was history.

◄§ §►

At Sansanding, the explorer was alternately lucid and delirious. Against Johnson's advice, he set up a stall in the marketplace — the Mussulmen gathered around like dogs, snarling and baying, shouting about infidels, white demons and cut-rate prices — and sold off nearly all the excess beads, baft and baubles. The proceeds went into purchasing provisions for the great voyage downstream to the ocean. These mounted steadily in the dark recesses of the explorer's hut, *guerbas* of beer and calabashes of palm wine, chickens in wicker baskets, strings of onions, desiccated fish, eggs, yams, millet and maize. Bundles of dried figs peeked out from beneath his pillow and lumps of goat cheese depended from the ceiling struts, redolent as an entire regiment's unwashed socks. There was something in that smell that cleared his head, and waking in the midst of it one morning, the explorer shook off the fever long enough to write Mansong again, begging for his help in coming up with a seaworthy craft. The Munificent One's response was ambiguous. The King smiles upon your enterprise, his messenger said, and will protect you as Mansong's strangers in all territories under his jurisdiction, from west to east. But you must wait until the annual sacrifice to Chakalla before he can do anything for you. Wait, the messenger repeated, and Mansong will see that you are taken care of.

Mungo waited.

The days fell together, end to end, like dominoes. It was October already, and the rains had begun to slacken. Time was wasting. Finally, after repeated attempts to impress Mansong with the urgency of his request, the explorer decided to act on his own, and sent Johnson and Ned Rise down to the river to purchase the largest canoe they could find. But no one, it seemed, would provide them with a means of leaving the country unless Mansong himself gave the word. Johnson held up clicking sacks of cowries — a king's ransom — but the boatmen just ducked their heads and looked away.

The explorer was in a quandary. Should he wait on Mansong's pleasure while the river sank and the Muslim merchants agitated against him? Should he up the bribe? Hire the Somonies to take him to Djenné and try his luck there? Swim for it? Unfortunately, the strain of it all brought on the fever again and he was incoherent for two days, jabbering about the Baroness' cleavage and Lady Banks' pug, about the strength of his arm and the accuracy of his kick on goal, and how the name of Park would live on in history, greater than any other. When he came round again, he dosed himself so heavily with calomel he was unable to eat or sleep for a week. It was during this rushing, whirling period of acceleration and intense stimulation that he hit on the idea of reverting to the original plan and constructing his own vessel, despite the obvious limitations imposed on him by lack of materials and skilled artisans.

Seized by the idea, he sprang out of his bed like a mastiff and strode into the tent where the surviving carpenter lay in his delirium. "Joshua Seed," the explorer boomed like a god, "get up from your sickbed and build me a boat."

The sick man held out a little packet of bony knuckles and Mungo helped him from his cot. In the hulks at Portsmouth, Seed had impressed the explorer with his work-hardened frame and the clarity of his eye. Now he looked and moved like an elderly gentleman with bowel problems. Slack-shouldered, yellow of eye and drawn in the cheeks, Seed shuffled out of the tent and into the blistering sunshine that had succeeded the rains. He took a deep breath, squared his shoulders and hobbled resolutely to the mound of nails, rusted saw, hammers, adzes and chisels that had survived the trip, and began pounding away at the scraps of wood that were scattered about.

He was at it all afternoon, periodically calling for more lumber. The explorer was delighted. He returned to his tent, fed the chickens, scribbled in his notebook and spat on the floor. At six, he stepped outside to see how Seed was progressing and was surprised to see that the carpenter had attracted a sizable crowd of inquisitive natives with his hammering and sawing, his meticulous measuring and planing and fitting. Mungo elbowed his way through the crowd, careful to avoid trampling any native feet, and was about to call out cheerfully to Seed — something like 'How's it coming, old boy?' — when he stopped dead in his tracks, choked with incredulity. Seed was working all right, whistling away as if he didn't have a care in the world, smoothing a corner here, shaving back a splinter there. He was working, but he wasn't building a boat. He was building a coffin.

Seed was gone by sundown. The explorer eased the late carpenter into his casket, paid a pair of Kafir Mandingoes to dig a hole, and buried him without ceremony. Boatwise, things looked pretty bleak. But it was at that moment — that very moment when Mungo pitched the first spadeful of earth into the grave — that Ned Rise waltzed into camp preceded by the dark, glistening, water-burnished hulls of two sleek native canoes that seemed to float on the air like gifts from the gods. With a grunt, the eight black porters flipped the big dugouts from their shoulders and set them down on the ground as lightly as if they'd been made of pasteboard. The explorer was ecstatic. He embraced Ned as if he were a long-lost son, slapping his back with both hands and smothering him with praise and promises of medals, plaques, awards and pecuniary largesse on their return to England. Then he looked at the canoes.

They were rotted through, both of them. Mud, river plants and expiring minnows lined the insides of their hulls, and a gargantuan bite had been taken out of the gunwale of the smaller craft, testimony to some historical confrontation with an irate hippo. In sum, the canoes looked as if they'd been constructed sometime during the reign of Charles I, and had been left to rot ever since. The calomel twitched Mungo's salivary glands, his lower lip fell, and he began to drool. "What is this, Ned?" he choked, unable to contain his disappointment. "Any fool can see that these are worthless hulks."

Ned was grinning. He'd found the canoes in a heap of river-run lumber at the edge of town. They were half submerged, waterlogged and rotting. No one owned them. He dragged them from the river, inspected them closely and decided they were worth a try. For fifty cowries apiece, he was able to hire the eight local flaneurs who balanced the boats on their broad flat heads and hauled them into camp. "Maybe we could fix them," he said finally. The explorer looked doubtful. "No, I mean it," Ned said. "Look," bending now to the slippery green hull of the larger boat, "the front half of this one isn't all that bad . . . and take a look at that one with the toothmarks. The back of that one seems pretty sturdy, no?"

The explorer looked. He was wired and jumpy with the tasteless white powder he'd taken to scourge himself of the fever. A tentative leg snaked out to thump the hull of the smaller craft. He went down on his knees, smoothing his hand over the wood like a furniture appraiser. Then he turned to squint up at Ned. "You mean . . . we could join the two of them?"

Ned snapped a hand to his brow and clicked his heels. "Splendid idea, Captain."

◆§ §◆

The H.M.S. *Joliba,* flying the British colors, was loaded and ready to sail by the fifteenth of November. In a short month, the increasingly lucid explorer, aided by Ned Rise, Fred Frair and Abraham Bolton, had managed to put together a reasonably seaworthy craft, forty feet long by six wide, flat-bottomed and drawing no more than twelve inches of water when fully loaded (Martyn and M'Keal declined to help, reasoning that they'd signed on as military men — "men o' the sword" — rather than laborers). A rusted spike projected from the front of the *Joliba*'s bow like a rugbyman's stiff-arm, and a canopy constructed of bent branches and a double layer of tanned bullock hide stretched half the length of the craft. The canopy would provide shade and shelter, and the hide was impervious to any of the slings and arrows that might come Mungo's way as he cruised down the mighty Niger into the unknown and almost certainly hostile regions to the east.

In addition, the explorer had taken some offensive measures as well, ordering windows cut at intervals in the bullock hide so that his men could fire from cover if necessary, and providing each of his remaining soldiers with fifteen new Charleville muskets which were to be kept primed, cocked and loaded day and night. This time, Mungo Park would stop for no one — neither Moor nor Maniana, nor any other disagreeable characters he might encounter along the way. No, if the watchword of the first expedition was to turn the other cheek, the motto this time around would be *guerra cominciata, inferno scatenato:* war commenced, hell unchained.

It was at about this time, when the boat was caulked, battened and provisioned, and the explorer clearing up his affairs at Sansanding, that he had his falling out with Johnson.

⁓ YOUR OWN GOOD SENSE

"I don't like it," Johnson had said when they reached Sansanding. "You sure you want to go through with this?" he asked as the boat began to take shape. And finally, when the *Joliba* was ready to set sail, he took the explorer aside and said: "You're crazy."

Now, on the eve of their departure, he stepped into Mungo's tent and announced that he was turning back. "This is it," he said. "The last time I ever lay eyes on you. No more shit, Mungo. No more Isaaco, no more Mr. Park. This is Johnson speaking — your old friend and companion, your advisor — and I say you ought to reconsider. I say don't go."

The explorer was seated at his makeshift desk, a welter of half-written letters, journal extracts and crude maps heaped up around him. Apart from the clutter of the desk, the interior of the tent was arranged with an Essene precision. In the corner, packed and ready, was the knapsack containing the explorer's personal effects; beside it lay the leather-bound trunks that protected his sextant and thermometers and the sheafs of dried stems, leaves and buds he planned to bring back to England for classification. All the foodstuffs had been removed and stowed away neatly in the hull of the *Joliba,* a lingering odor of goat cheese and chicken excrement testimony to their recent removal. Even the floor had been swept clean.

A moment passed — eight hammering heartbeats. Johnson's hortatory words hung in the air like the memory of something dead, while the explorer, dressed only in his underwear, squinted through the eye of a needle and moistened a strand of thread with the tip of his tongue. He never even looked up.

"I mean it, brother," Johnson said. "I'm takin' Serenummo and Dosita and the two Dembas and headin' for Dindikoo — tomorrow. If you got any sense at all — and by now I'm pretty well convinced you don't — you'll come with me."

Mungo was trying to close up a six-inch tear in the seat of his nankeen trousers, but his hands shook so he couldn't seem to thread the needle. This was frustrating. It was bad enough that he had to run around and get the boat loaded and the men ready, not knowing whether he was going off to triumph or defeat, but this damned sewing took the cake. He flung the needle down in disgust and glared up at Johnson. "Listen," he said, his voice thick and harsh, "don't you come around here trying to pressure me at the last minute because it's just not going to work. You've been a naysayer all along, and I'll tell you, I don't need it. Just get your things together and climb into that boat. Period. End of discussion."

Johnson was slowly shaking his head. He looked a great deal older than he had just a few months earlier at Dindikoo, more worn and frayed. He'd lost one of his chins, and the great bulge of his abdomen seemed to have receded. With his hair getting progressively whiter and his limbs stiff, he'd begun to look like the sixty-two-year-old he was. "You don't need me," he said, "you got Amadi Fatoumi."

It was true. Johnson had never been farther east than Sansanding, and knew absolutely nothing of the geography, the peoples or the languages of the lower Niger. And Mungo had engaged a new guide — an itinerant merchant named Amadi Fatoumi, who'd been as far as Kong, Badoo, Gotto and Cape Coast Castle to the south, and Timbuctoo, Hausa, Maniana and Bornou eastward. But still, the idea of going on without Johnson was insupportable. It chilled Mungo to the bone, frightened him to the soles of his feet. Without Johnson he was totally on his own. "All right," he said, pushing himself up from the table. "I'll triple your wages, send you crateloads of books, paintings — anything you want."

"No," Johnson said, still shaking his head in that weary, resigned way.

"You'll never send me anythin', Mungo. Because if you launch that boat tomorrow you'll never live to see England again."

"Bullshit!" Mungo shouted, hammering his fist against the tent-pole until the canvas began to quake and billow.

"Turn back," Johnson whispered. "For me. For your wife and your children. Turn back now before it's too late."

The explorer was stalking up and down in his underwear, flailing his arms like some great waterbird lifting itself from the swamp. "You know I can't do that, old boy." He was trying to control his voice. "I've spent a fortune — all government money — and I've lost nine out of ten men that came with me. Georgie Scott is dead, and Zander. And you expect me to tuck my tail between my legs and turn back now? How would I face Sir Joseph? Camden? Even Ailie? No: it's impossible. I've got to go on."

"Hey," Johnson's voice was soft, still soft, as if he were whispering to Amuta in the night, "stuff your ego, swallow your pride. You made a mistake, let's face it. You dragged all these sick dogs and all this excess baggage out here with you in the middle of the monsoon — what do you expect? Go back. Go back now and mount another expedition. You're a young man. You can do it."

Self-doubt was something new to Mungo, something that had crept up on him like a growth, a malignancy, during the course of this second expedition. Self-doubt, and guilt. Every word out of Johnson's mouth struck him with all the force of his own convictions, every word jabbed him like a needle. But he was stubborn. He threw his head back. "I leave at dawn."

"I won't be there," Johnson said. It was a simple statement of fact. He held the explorer's eyes as he reached into his toga and produced a silver-plated pistol: sleek and long-nosed, it was engraved with the initials of the only man he'd ever killed, an Englishman like this one, with his fair hair and red face. "Take it," he said, his voice rumbling so low as to be barely audible. "It's brought me luck."

Lit by a late-afternoon shaft of light, the gun flashed in the explorer's hand as if it were charged, as if it were some magical instrument capable of hurling thunderbolts and spewing brimstone. He tucked it in his belt, confused, searching out his words. "Johnson," he began, "you mean there's nothing I — "

The older man cut him off. "Watch out for Amadi Fatoumi," he said. "I don't like him. I don't like what I hear about him."

In these last days of uncertainty and apprehension, the explorer had become as volatile as a case of Scots whisky. A moment ago he'd been moved; now, at the mention of Amadi's name, a hot sudden rage grabbed hold of him and shook him till he trembled. "What do you mean?" he demanded. "Because he isn't fat and old he's no good? Because he doesn't wear a gold straight pin through his nose he can't be trusted?"

Johnson merely looked into his eyes, cold and steady. What he meant was that Amadi Fatoumi was about as trustworthy as a cobra with a toothache, and that Mungo was no judge of character. Fatoumi was a merchant all right — he sold guns and drugs and West Indian rum to the tribes in the interior and brought back slaves in return. He was a Mandingo — from Kasson — but his head was shaved to the skin and he wore an oily black beard that fanned out to his shoulders after the Moorish fashion. There was an unfathomable blackness to his eyes — pupil and iris nearly indistinguishable — and he had a habit of rubbing his hands and ducking his head as he spoke.

He'd turned up one afternoon with Martyn and M'Keal. They'd found him in the marketplace — or rather he'd found them. They were drunk, as usual, on *sooloo* beer and a clear hard liquor distilled from tomberong berries and known to the natives as *fou,* when he sidled up to them with a grin. Amadi had about twenty-five words of English — words like *fouter* and *kill* and *whore* — and he regaled lieutenant and sergeant with them for half an hour, playing the fool, until he escorted them down a back alley, provided them with the services of two pliant females and a ball of black hashish. "Captain, Sir," Martyn had said to the explorer some hours later, "this is a capital fellow." Amadi stood between the drooping Martyn and the wild-eyed M'Keal, in sandals and *jubbah.* He took the explorer's hand and pumped it. "Please to see you," he murmured. Half an hour later he was signed on with the expedition at triple wages and the promise of one quarter of the stores remaining on reaching Hausaland.

It was obvious to Johnson that the man was a backstabber and a cheat, quite possibly a murderer, and certainly a consort of the Moors. But no matter what he said, the explorer dismissed it. "You're jealous, that's all," Mungo said, "because Amadi Fatoumi's half your age and he knows twice as much. He can speak Maniana, Hausa, Tuareg and Arabic, and he's been to Timbuctoo and back."

Now, at the eleventh hour, the red-faced explorer trembling before him as if he were ready to grapple to the death, Johnson felt it useless to press his case, useless to point out that his informants had told him that Amadi had been raised as a slave of the Il Braken tribe, had stabbed a man over a game of quoits and had cheated three quarters of the merchants in Sansanding. No, Mungo was half-sick with guilt and fear and uncertainty, and he clung to Amadi Fatoumi and his putative knowledge as he might have clung to a lifebuoy in a rough sea. There was no sense in arguing: Johnson could only plead. "Don't go," he said.

Mungo looked as if he were on the verge of a seizure. "Why the bloody hell not?" he roared.

Johnson took his arm, but Mungo jerked away and turned his back. "All right," Johnson said. "Don't go because I care about your pigheaded bones, don't go because you won't come back. Remember Eboe?"

Mungo whirled round as if he'd been stung. There was a look of pain and bewilderment on his face, a look of terror.

"Remember?" Johnson repeated. "And how about that old blind lady — the one at Silla — the one that sniffed the white man's smell of you and took hold of your hair? You remember what she said?"

He remembered. Johnson could see it in his face. The old woman had paused and turned her dead eyes to him, muttering the name of a far-off place, a name that hung on her lips like the secret name of the devil, a strange barbaric incantatory name: *Boussa. Beware of Boussa,* she'd croaked. *Beware.*

Mungo's face drained. For a long while he stood there facing Johnson, his arms raised, as if he were fighting some sort of ritual duel with him. Finally his lips began to move, in silence, as if he were praying.

"Don't go," Johnson repeated, and the spell was broken. Mungo's face contorted, ugly as a mask. Quick and violent, he took hold of Johnson's toga, bunching it under his chin and forcing his head back. "Traitor!" he shouted. "Filth, scum. You're the one who's evil, you're the one who's out to undermine me — not Amadi Fatoumi." Then, with a single explosive thrust of his arm, he shoved the older man down in the dirt. "Get out!" he screamed, his voice broken with rage. "Get out, nigger!"

Johnson's face showed nothing. He pushed himself up, brushed off his toga, and stepped out of Mungo Park's life. Forever.

✑ BON VOYAGE

Somewhere a cock is crowing and a muezzin yodeling out the morning prayers. There is the scrape and shuffle of sandals outside the tent as townswomen bend to collect dung for their breakfast fires, and from the wild tangle of bush at river's edge, birdsong. Already, with the first light, a fierce parching heat has set in, and the tumescent air pours over the explorer as if it were slag. Wearily, with a puff of resignation, he rises from his sweaty blankets and head-splitting dreams to stagger outside and micturate against a wall of baked clay. Overnight the weather has changed, the seasons turned: just after midnight the wind shifted to the north and the harmattan began to hiss in off the great desert, bringing with it a feeling of enervation and depression that settles over him like a lead blanket. Standing there, half-awake, pud in hand, he feels washed out and hungover, though he hasn't touched a drop in weeks.

The dark stain blossoms against the pale wall, now a winged dragon, now the head of a stag, and he is staring down at it in dull fascination when he suddenly becomes aware of a presence at his back, the muted sounds of foot shuffling and throat clearing. Turning his head with the slow abstraction of a sleepwalker, he discovers that the remnant of his army is lined up behind him, in rough formation, their tattered uniforms glowing in the pale light. Martyn and M'Keal, Ned Rise, Fred Frair and Abraham Bolton. Their bags are at their feet, muskets in hand. Behind them, Amadi Fatoumi and his three villainous-looking slaves, dressed in *jubbah* and *tagilmust,* like Moors. Looking over his shoulder he sees that all nine men are staring at him, silent, respectful, as if peeing against a wall in his underwear were comparable to consecrating the host or changing water to wine.

"Captain, Sir," Martyn barks, breaking the silence. "The crew of the *Joliba,* reporting for duty as ordered."

Of course. This is the morning of their departure, the morning they cast their fate to the wind — or rather the water. Yes, in the moment of waking it nearly slipped his mind, the air so heavy and oppressive, a touch of the fever creeping up on him again: yes, of course. The great adventure begins anew!

"All right, Leftenant," Mungo croaks, tucking himself in and swinging round on his men. "Break down this tent, stow away my gear and prepare to shove off." Woozy on his feet and bleary of eye, he scans the frightened, hopeful faces of the men and wants to tell them it'll be all right, that the Niger doesn't dry up in the middle of the desert or end in Lake Chad, that from here on in it's smooth sailing. But he can't. Because for all his hopes and prayers, suppositions and gut feelings, he can't be sure that he isn't leading them to a watery death in the godforsaken omphalos of a godforsaken continent. All he can add, by way of inspiration and comfort is a supererogatory order: "And be quick about it."

◄᠗ ᠗►

Unbeknownst to explorer, guide or crew, the hills outside Sansanding are at that very moment thundering with the sound of hoofbeats: the harmattan wind is not the only thing rumbling down out of the north. No: Dassoud, Scourge of the Sahel, is on his way into town with twelve hundred wild-eyed horsemen burning to engage the white men's army. His intention is to hack the *Nazarini* to pieces — no matter how many they are or how well armed — and to impale Mungo Park's head on the tip of his spear as an offering to his lady, Fatima of Jafnoo.

Dassoud, it will be observed, is some two and a half months behind schedule with his current campaign. He had planned to annihilate the explorer before the month of September was out, but during the long dilatory days of late September, October and early November, he came to discover that he was not quite the scourge he thought himself to be. The root of his troubles lay in internecine squabbling between the various tribes under his leadership. Though fanned to frenzy by the explorer's letter and the intentions expressed in it, they were nonetheless reluctant to unite under Dassoud's banner — or anyone's for that matter. It was as simple as this: the timing was bad.

First, a blood feud had erupted between the Trasart and the Al-Mu'ta of Jafnoo. Mubarak of the Trasart had executed three of Boo Khaloom's serfs for poaching at one of his wells; in retaliation, Boo Khaloom himself stole into the Trasart camp, pissed in Mubarak's porridge and made off with his prize charger, which he held for ransom. After the ransom was paid in full, Boo Khaloom sent the horse back — in eight pieces, each neatly bundled in goat hide. Meanwhile, Mahmud Bari of the Il Braken had forgotten his chastising at the hands of Dassoud, and refused to participate in the *jihad* against the *Nazarini* unless he himself were to lead it. Exasperated, Dassoud was forced to waste two precious weeks in riding out to Gedumah, splitting Mahmud Bari open like a sausage and quelling the incipient rebellion. And then, as if this weren't enough, the Foulahs chose that precise moment for a sneak attack on Jafnoo.

Dassoud had met each of these challenges in his own fierce and summary way, but in the process he had lost valuable time. Each distraction maddened him to the point of frenzy as it deflected him from his goal. Each annoyance — whether it was the obligation to turn aside and slaughter three hundred Foulah men, women and children or the fact that his goat was overcooked and his kouskous mushy — so enraged him he felt his skull would burst, and he chalked up another strike against the explorer. To eradicate the *Nazarini* became a seething obsession, an obsession that broiled his soul day and night with a fire that burned all the hotter for each obstacle thrown in his way. But now, after two and a half months of maddening delays, Dassoud was on his way, roaring through the streets of Sansanding like a demon possessed.

⋅§ §⋅

There are coots on the water, and spur-winged plover. The surface heaves and boils with the last furious runoff from the monsoon, and a few attenuated native dugouts glide like the wind through lingering patches of morning fog. "Is everybody in?" Mungo shouts, feeling like a boy on the Yarrow, as he and Ned Rise wade into the current, their shoulders flush with the hull of the H.M.S. *Joliba*. And then, merry as a bridegroom proposing a toast, he breaks a calabash of *fou* over the prow and gives the order to shove off.

Martyn, looking twice his nineteen years with his beard and drink-debauched eyes, is at the tiller; the rest, including Amadi Fatoumi and his three retainers, are lounging about, their paddles in a casual heap. With the river in flood, propulsion should be no problem: heavily laden though it is, the *Joliba* bobs like a twig and maneuvers like a sailor's dream.

Ned Rise hops nimbly aboard as the current catches the elongated craft and swings it round, but Mungo lingers a moment, officious, the water to his chest, steadying the boat after it is no longer necessary. It is at that moment that the first gunshot echoes over the water. Startled and confused, the explorer looks first at Martyn — the lieutenant's mouth is hanging open, gaping as if to swallow an orange or an egg — and then over his shoulder at the dusty roadway leading down to the river's edge. The sight rivets him like a nightmare come to life. Bearing down on him, weapons held aloft, *jubbahs* flapping, is a countless host of Moors, their sweat-slicked horses pounding over the earth in furious stampede.

None of this has been lost on the others. Whereas a moment previous they'd been lounging about like hemophiliac princes, they are suddenly up and working furiously at the paddles, as the explorer, feet streaming in the wake, clambers aboard. Inspired by the grim prospect of their own imminent demise, the men have burst into swift, concentrated action — even the whiskery M'Keal, slick Fatoumi and frail Frair stroking away as if they were trying out for the Oxford crew. Mungo has suddenly caught fire too. Unable to locate a paddle in the confusion, he crouches low to the water and begins churning at it with his cupped hands, as if he were trying to part the waves or dig a watery burrow. "Heave!" Ned shouts beside him, and the *Joliba* begins to pick up speed.

They are less than a hundred yards out when the first Moor hits the water, a big fellow in black, lashing at his charger's muzzle and shrieking obscenities in Arabic. Within seconds the water is alive with Moors, hundreds of them, firing the odd musket, flinging spears and yabbering their war cry. Mungo, splashing wildly, risks a look over his shoulder at his arch enemies, their horses swimming like seals, their eyes on fire and nostrils dilated with the scent of blood, weapons flashing red in the rich meaty light of dawn. And then suddenly the strength goes out of his arms. The nearest Moor — sixty yards off, his horse nearly exploding with exertion — he knows him. He knows the blocky shoulders straining at the seams of the *jubbah,* he knows those eyes, that scar, that maniacal leering mask of hatred . . .

Dassoud's pistol is extended, his horse flailing, the *Joliba* drawing away. Desperately, the Moor sights down the gun barrel and fires, one more puff of smoke in the confusion of whirling *jubbahs,* clattering spears, shouts and billows of dust rising from the shore behind him. The smoke and dust are so thick and the noise so all-enveloping that the explorer can't be sure whether the Moor has fired or not, until all at once there is something warm and wet on his arm and a weight forcing itself down on him. Whirling round, he looks up into the stricken face of Abraham Bolton, who had been making his way to him with the missing paddle. Now, his right eye shot away, the private lurches over him, wagging the paddle in mid-air and fighting for balance. Mungo's reaction is instinctive: he ducks his shoulder, and Bolton, poor sot, tumbles past him and into the river like a sack of stones dropped from a bridge.

When Mungo looks up again he's staring into Dassoud's eyes across an ever-narrowing stretch of water, the Moor gaining, so close now his charger's agonized gasps tear at the explorer's lungs until he can barely catch his breath. Vaguely — as if in a dream — Mungo reaches for Bolton's paddle, but the Moor's eyes lock on him like grappling hooks and he can feel the walls of his throat constricting, all he can do to keep from bursting into tears at the unfairness of it all. Mesmerized, he cannot think of the ninety loaded muskets beneath the canopy or the silver-plated pistol tucked inside his shirt. He can only think of failure, ignominy and death.

But then Ned Rise's voice sweeps up out of the din, muscular and hortatory — "Pull boys! Pull!" — and the tableau begins to dissolve. Dassoud drops back and the *Joliba* is suddenly rushing with the current, far out into the cleansing river, far from the blood and terror and the grim grasping fingers of captivity, far out onto the broad back of the Niger. Transfixed, Mungo kneels there like a supplicant, unable to move or think, as he watches his bitterest enemy recede in the distance until the black spot of his head is lost in the pulse of the waters.

◄§ AND QUIET FLOWS THE NIGER

It is like descending into the body, this penetration of the river, like passing through veins and arteries and great dripping organs, like exploring the chambers of the heart or reaching out for the impalpable soul. Earth, forest, sky, water: the river thrums with the beat of life. Mungo feels it — as steady and pervasive as the ticking of a supernal clock — feels it through the searing windless days and the utter nights that fall back to the rim of the void. Ned Rise feels it, and even M'Keal. A presence. A mystery. A sense of communing with the eternal that drops a pall over everything, silencing the long-necked birds, the river horses, cicadas, crocodiles, coots, kingfishers and snipe, the great silver fish that leap clear of the water and fall back again without a splash. It is almost as if they've fallen under a spell, the explorer and his men, as if their blood were flowing in sympathetic confluence with the river and the river washing them clean of all the guilt and horror and hardship of the overland journey. Persuasive, gentle, the current pulls them through those first hushed weeks with a force and logic all its own.

But then the crew wake one morning under a sky like dried blood and it is as if their ears have been newly opened. Sounds boom at them, unbearable, from the squeak of the tiller to the rattle of the bullock hides in the cruel hot wind that seems to have snuck up on them during the night. Great Nubian and griffon vultures wheel overhead, and the men can hear the flutter of the wings. Hippos snort like blaring cannon and crocodiles bark like dogs. Suddenly the whole universe is shouting at them.

Mungo rolls out of his damp blankets, wincing at the roar, and is shocked to see that they are no longer gliding through the endless tangled groves of arching trees and clawing vines that have walled in both banks of the river since they left Sansanding. Stunned, he looks round him full circle, then pulls out his telescope and looks again. There is no hint of green over the water, no vegetation, no shoreline in fact. Then it hits him: during the night they must have passed into Lake Dibbie, that vast inland sea reputed to lie between Djenné and Kabara. He gazes out over the shifting surface, happy in his surmise. Immense, shoreless, the lake slaps at the hull beneath his feet, its waters churned to brown sudsing waves in the hot wind.

The explorer consults his compass. They are heading north by northeast. Toward Timbuctoo — and the great desert. He swallows hard, hoping that what old Djanna-geo and Amadi told him is true, that thereafter the river loops toward the south. But he looks down at the insistent needle of his compass, and doubts assail him. Could Rennell and the others have been right? Does the river in fact run out of steam in the Sahara? Does it roar down an endless hole in the earth? Evaporate in Lake Chad?

Disturbed by these reflections, Mungo makes his way toward the front of the canoe, where Amadi Fatoumi and his retainers are seated. The four men are hunched down over their ankles, feet splayed, tossing bits of carved bone against the concave hull of the canoe and redistributing piles of cowries according to the outcome. As the explorer comes up, Amadi ceremoniously pours a thin stream of black tea into a cup the size of a thimble and hands it to him with a nod and a smile.

"So," Mungo says, swaying with the boat, "we've made Dibbie, have we?" Hunched in the prow, Fred Frair fixes him with a brief vacant look and then gazes dolefully out over the water. Amadi looks up at the explorer as if he hasn't heard.

"I say: Dibbie, isn't it?" All at once the explorer realizes he's shouting. He can't help himself, what with all this noise. There is the maddening tinkle of spoon and plate somewhere in the rear of the boat, M'Keal's drunken snores booming out from beneath the canopy, the screech of distant gulls, hum of gnats — all of it as loud as if it had been amplified a hundred times. Exasperated, he bends to his guide. "What is all this bloody racket?"

Amadi looks surprised. He points to the sky. "The wind," he says. "Very dry." In answer to the explorer's next question — a rhetorical one: does the Niger move southward past Timbuctoo and is he quite certain? — the guide merely points again, but this time to a spot just off starboard.

It must be said that the attack at Sansanding — led as it was by his archenemy — has had an unsettling influence on the explorer. He's been jittery, his stomach has gone sour on him, a mysterious nervous rash has settled in his groin and between his toes. Like the hypochondriac who discovers a tumor under his arm with a surge of fatalistic joy, he has had his worst suspicions confirmed: they *are* out there, lurking behind every tree, camouflaged by the meanest village hut, out there lying in wait, just as he always knew they would be. And so, more than ever and with a single-mindedness that verges on monomania, he has determined to avoid any and all human contact. Against the protestations of his crew, he eschewed the cities of Silla and Djenné as if they were the abode of demons and basilisks, coming to anchor just above the farthest cluster of outlying huts and coasting down under cover of darkness. The men wanted to stop for fresh supplies — milk, produce, bread — but he wouldn't hear of it. No: he wouldn't stop at even the rudest native village hacked out of the bush, wouldn't stop for beer, fresh meat, to feel solid ground under his feet for five precious minutes. He wouldn't stop for anything.

Now, the sight of this spot on the horizon, this black speck, this nothing, fills him with terror. Out here in the middle of this oceanic lake, it can mean only one thing: people. Renegades, fanatics, murdering Moors. His first cry is stifled by the shock and disavowal that catches in his throat like a ball of phlegm. But then he shouts out like a sentry taken by surprise in a cold black night: "Attack! We're under attack!"

The response is instantaneous. Amadi and his men leap up from their piles of cowries, and Fred Frair, languishing just a moment before, springs to his feet as if someone had spilled a bowl of hot soup in his lap. Martyn is there in an instant, and M'Keal, in boots and underwear, is up and cursing. "Moors!" Mungo cries, raising the telescope to his eye at the very moment that Fred Frair, galvanized by the first terrible call to arms, shoots past him howling like a dog. The result, viewed in scientific terms, is as simple as action and reaction, force and counterforce: the explorer's elbow is jostled and the telescope flies from his hand to vanish instantly in the brown murk at his feet.

No matter. It doesn't require magnification to see that that blemish on the horizon is a party of hostile Moors. The men, their faces flat with panic, are ready to take their leader at his word. Martyn and M'Keal are already counting out the muskets — twenty-five, thirty, thirty-five — while Frair scuttles back and forth from the enclosure with barrels of powder, ramrods and wadding in the event that reloading should be necessary. Only Ned Rise, at the tiller, seems composed. With sextant and compass, and the makeshift sail he'd rigged up during the night, he steadies the *Joliba* in the slackening current, running for Timbuctoo, Hausa and beyond, running for London.

The explorer, meanwhile, has gone rigid, poised in the bow like a prize pointer. Dripping sweat, squinting till his facial muscles begin to quiver, he stares off at the horizon as if he could set it afire from the sheer force of ocular concentration. A long moment ticks by, then another. And then, in a sudden dark moment of revelation, he realizes that a fearful conjugation is taking place out there on the perimeter: *not one dot but three!* Three slick and swift native canoes packed to the waterline with bloodthirsty Moors!

"Three of them," Martyn says at his shoulder, and his voice is cold as a lancet.

Yes. Bloodthirsty Moors. Savages. Animals. He can see them now — can't he? — their headgear flashing in the sun. Suddenly a feeling of calm comes over him, the feeling ascribed to soldiers in the heat of battle. Firm and fatalistic, he lifts the musket to his shoulder and sights down the tapering barrel. "Prepare to fire," he hisses.

Twenty minutes he stands there, a drawing-room actor in a tableau vivant. The three canoes, in formation, draw closer, closer, cutting an angle that will inexorably intersect the path of the *Joliba*. He can see them quite clearly now, their black hulls in relief against the great ball of the sun rising like a tired old beast from the lake behind them. When they drift within range, he gives the order to fire.

The first barrage overturns the lead canoe with a sudden sharp slap. Distant arms flail in the air, there are confused cries, shrieks of pain. Eight muskets fire, are flung down and replaced by eight more. Another roar, another flash of light, and the second canoe is blasted from the water. What with the sun and the smoke the explorer can barely make them out, but certainly they're Moors — in *jubbahs* and baggy trousers — little matter that their faces are black and the cries those of women and children.

After the second barrage, the occupants of the final canoe take to the water, abandoning their craft to its fate. It is then that the crew — Amadi Fatoumi and his blacks included — begin firing at random, blazing away at a featureless head in the glitter of sun on water, cutting loose at the merest suggestion of a swimmer's wake. In the heat of it, the explorer draws a bead on a dark form clinging to the side of an overturned canoe, only to have his arm arrested as he squeezes the trigger. He whirls round on Ned Rise. Guns pop and roar, smoke hangs over the *Joliba* like a thunderhead touching down. "Tell them to hold their fire," Ned shouts, "it's a mistake — can't you see that?"

It is as if Mungo has been wakened from a dream. He drops the musket and looks up and down the line of men, shocked by the transformation in their faces. Even Frair, feeble though he is, looks like some sort of ravening beast, every muscle strung tight, his mouth twisted and teeth bared. Amadi's eyes are glazed and the tip of his tongue protrudes from the corner of his mouth, while his slaves are rapt as bumpkins at a shooting gallery. And the career men — Martyn and M'Keal — are in their glory. This is what they were born to, trained for, this is the moment for which they keep their bayonets honed and muskets oiled. Faces blackened with smoke, they take aim, fire, and snatch up the next weapon in a single fluid motion, merciless and implacable as machines. In his distraction, the explorer follows the line of Martyn's rifle over the chop and past the foundering canoes, to where a woman's head shows above the surface. A woman? — no, it can't be. But it can, and is. A woman, her *jubbah* billowing around her, copper earrings catching the sun, a woman struggling to tread water and keep an infant afloat at the same time. "Cease fire!" Mungo shouts. "Desist!"

But the command goes unheeded. For the next fifteen minutes Dibbie rings with excited shouts and the frenzied popping of gunfire till the canoes are splintered, the muskets emptied and the atmosphere is still but for the wash of the waves, the hell's breath of the wind and the slowly diffusing pools of gore that well up to darken the dull sudsing surface.

◦§ §◦

Two days later, having left the vacant immensity of the lake and returned to the main channel of the river, the crew of the *Joliba* is witness to a very foolish act on the part of Fred Frair. Suffering from a multiplicity of unspecified ailments, suppurating infections and mysterious tropical diseases, Frair has been languishing for the past several days, dispirited and dull, his wasted form pressed flat to the hull as if at any moment he might subside into the slick dark wood like some sort of insect. No one likes to see him there, but what can they do? M'Keal, the old veteran, white beard against a plum-red face, sits watching him by the hour, now and again offering him a slug of rum or palm wine as a cure for what ails him. Martyn, having watched forty companions kick off already, is unconcerned. He squats beneath the canopy, cleaning the muskets, reloading them, whistling. Ned never cared much for the little man anyway — he was a pal of Smirke's — and is too busy keeping an eye on the explorer, the compass, maps and tiller to worry about it in any case. And Mungo, brooding over the prospect of failure and the nasty character and habits of the Sahelian Moor, has no time for any of them. Still, no one wishes Frair any harm — they'd love to see him pull through. After all, if he goes, who's next?

On this particular afternoon — sometime in mid-December of 1805 — they are drifting with the current down a broad flat stretch of water under an incinerating equatorial sun, birds loud in the trees, insects in their ears, their eyes, their nostrils, when suddenly Frair sits up and begins shrieking like a drunk in delirium tremens. He can take it no more, he shouts. The heat, the fever, the stink of death. Amadi and his men look away. M'Keal bends over the thrashing private and tries to quiet him. But to no avail.

Of all the horrors he's experienced, in prison, at Goree, along the road, and all the diseases that gnaw away at him, what has finally pushed Frair over the line is an infestation of guinea worm, *Dracunculus medinensis*. Painful, nauseating, but normally no big deal. The explorer himself is currently suffering through his second infection, and Martyn worked one out of his leg two weeks earlier. But to Frair, the thought of this blind living thing — this worm — thriving inside him, eating away at his flesh, crapping and pissing in his blood, is insupportable.

The previous day a blister had broken in the hollow of his left knee and the explorer, after bracing him with a killing dose of *fou,* cleaned the wound and treated it. Within the moist bud of the sore, pale as the flesh of a man's belly, was the nether end of a female guinea worm, doing what nature expected of her: swelling, breeding, releasing millions of minuscule larvae with the amniotic wash of pus. Mungo carefully took hold of the visible portion of the parasite and wound a bit of it round a twig; then he bent to wash his hands in the river. And that was that: he'd done all he could to ease Frair's predicament. He could neither remove the worm, nor eliminate it. Two to four feet in length, it was embedded deep in the connective tissue of Frair's lower leg, wound tight as thread on a spool. Slowly, day by day, the worm had to be withdrawn by reeling it up on the twig, an inch or two at a time. If it were to break off and die in the leg, it would rot there, inextractable, and Frair would die of gangrene.

In his misery, in his loathing, in his horror, the foolish thing that Frair does is to tear back the little finger of wood fixed to his knee, thereby severing the worm. For a moment, no one reacts, and the din that has assailed them since Lake Dibbie screams through the silence. Then M'Keal whistles — sharp and sudden, as if he were calling a dog or exclaiming over the size of a fish — and one of Amadi's men spits into his hands for luck. Mungo, drawn by Frair's outburst, merely stands over him, watching the open sore glisten like a mouth. Then he shakes his head and turns his back.

There is of course no question of stopping to bury him. On Christmas Day (or thereabout: the explorer has lost track of the exact date in the haphazard jumble of his notebooks) Frair, swathed head to toe in a blanket of flies, is declared officially dead. As captain and head of the expedition, Mungo murmurs a few words over the corpse before committing it to the yellow ripples of the Niger, to the tiger fish, the turtles and the crocodiles.

That night, as he consults his watch by moonlight, the explorer finds that it has unaccountably stopped. German-made and set in an initialed silver case, the watch was a gift from Ailie's father in another age and another lifetime, when the young explorer first packed his bags and set off for the East Indies, a wellspring of hope and ambition. Now, sweeping along on the dark flood, that time seems as remote as the Age of Dinosaurs. He slaps the watch in his palm, holds it up to his ear. Raucous, derisive, the invisible forest howls at him with a thousand voices. Mungo looks up at the sky, at the shifting stars and the planets in their loops, and drops the silent timepiece into the flat black soup of the river.

◈ THE NETHER REGIONS

Days flit past, strung tight as a crossbow through the long sere afternoons, and then released, in the shank of the evening, with a whoosh of falling sun and rising mist. The New Year comes and goes, undocumented, in a blanket of sameness and a stench of decay. Silent and inevitable, the *Joliba* drifts past deserted villages, sandbars heaped with sunning reptiles, flocks of birds so numerous their plucked feathers could stuff every pillow in Europe. The river is always the same, never the same.

At Kabara, port of Timbuctoo, the explorer makes a miscalculation. He comes to anchor too early, and instead of hanging back to skulk past this most ominous of all obstacles in the dead of night, finds himself drawing even with its congested banks and mobbed water lanes in the broad gaze of mid-morning. His first reaction, as the city draws into sight round a bend in the river, is to fault his eyes. It's an illusion, that's all. A phantasm bred of an overtaxed mind, of fever and anxiety. But there it is, undeniable, clustered mudhuts and open warehouses, a spill of canoes clinging to the distant surface like a black film. Suddenly he turns on Amadi and begins berating him in bad Arabic, shrill as a dowager scolding her pug. The guide merely shrugs.

Mungo knows one thing only: that they must avoid Kabara at all costs. Timbuctoo is the nexus of the Moorish trade, the hub that links Sahara, Sahel and Sudan. If they'll resist him anywhere, they'll resist him here. He turns his back on Amadi in disgust and orders the men to their paddles, snatching the tiller from Ned Rise and swinging the canoe round 180°. "Dig!" he exhorts through his clenched teeth, and slowly, painfully, the overloaded *Joliba* begins to crawl upstream. After an hour, however, Kabara is still in sight, the men are sapped, and the canoe, at full steam, can merely hang in the current like an obstruction. M'Keal is the first to see the futility of it. "Cor, Cap'n," he calls over his shoulder to where the explorer sits at the tiller, "you expects us to 'old the barge 'ere till Gabriel blows 'is trumpet or wot?" The old soldier's words chuff from his lips: he's breathing hard, his hands tremble at the paddle, he glows with his own juices like a suckling pig over the spit. Mungo considers a moment, and then, hardening as he had on Lake Dibbie, he pulls the tiller full right and the *Joliba* swings back round on Kabara. "Prepare to repel any boat that approaches within fifty yards," he hisses. Bluebeard couldn't have put it any better.

This time, canoes do come out to intercept them. Long, whippet-like dugouts full of irate Mussulmen, Mussulmen who want to behead and dismember *Nazarini* for the glory of Allah, to avenge the failure at Sansanding and the slaughter on Dibbie, to reassert their born and sworn right to a trade monopoly and to sorely chastise these whey-faced infidels who have neither asked nor paid for the privilege of traversing their borders. Hopping mad, the Moors fill eighteen canoes with beards, teeth and spears.

What the Moors lack, however, is firepower. Though their canoes, craftily piloted by Somonies and riparian Soorka, fan out to converge on the *Joliba* from all directions, they are unable to make even the darkest of dark-horse approaches to spear-chucking range. Mungo and his boys, each armed with fifteen single-shot muskets, are blazing away like an army, sending a screaming sheet of lead out over the water to strip the flesh from Moorish bones and convert *jubbahs* to perforated winding sheets. Cursing through their beards, the Moors retire from the field and the *Joliba* whirls on down the river, uncontested.

◈ ◈

A week later the explorer observes that while they have passed Timbuctoo, they are still heading north — into the desert. The riverine vegetation, always lush, has begun to thin out a bit, and beyond the trees the hills are sparse and arid, prickling with euphorbia, desert rose and whistling thorn. The heat is profound, appalling, all-consuming. There is no escape from it. Beneath the canopy, as enervated as gutshot survivors of Austerlitz, Martyn and M'Keal play cards, doze, sip *fou* from a gourd, occasionally snaking out a hand to splash their shirts and faces with tepid river water. Ned Rise has erected a sunscreen over the tiller, and Amadi and his men, stripped to loincloths, squat in the shade of the canopy, rolling their bones and counting up their cowries. There is no thought of swimming. Not when crocodiles — some of them half as long as the boat — line the bank like spectators at a parade, or river horses beat the surface to a froth with a thundering, sucking, splashing display of pique or playfulness or whatever.

The sun rises and sets, time uncharted and undocumented, days strung together until another week is gone and still the river carries them north. There is no more beer or fruit or butter or bread, and the men are grumbling over a diet of salt beef, rice, yams and onions. Mungo looks at his compass forty times a day. He is concerned. So is Ned Rise. Ned questions the explorer, the explorer questions Amadi, Amadi shrugs. The suspense is killing. Not to mention the heat, the boredom, the doomed hopeless stir-craziness of men eternally at sea. This is what Columbus must have felt like, teetering on the rim of the world.

At a place identified by Amadi as Gouroumo, seven canoes dart out in pursuit of them, and the men, stripped down to shorts now like Amadi and his slaves, snap out of their lethargy long enough to pot a few luckless natives and strike terror in the hearts of the rest. Given the sameness of their days, given the boredom, the exercise is almost welcome, it is almost fun. What else have they got to do but lie around and sizzle like so many strips of bacon? Besides, cutting down the odd nigger or two keeps the old reflexes honed, steadies the hand and sharpens the eye against the day when some real trouble crops up. And it's not as if they were going out of their way to pick a fight or anything. No, these naked cannibals put out after them like crocodiles, just drooling for the chance to pop a white man in the pot. After all the black crow they've been eating, it'd probably be like veal or something.

The explorer doesn't like it. The people who attacked him at Gouroumo were negroes, and he's got no quarrel with negroes. But they really leave him little choice. Whether they've been put up to it by the Moors, or whether they're rankled because he hasn't followed protocol with regard to gifts and permissions, he can't say. All he knows is that they come out on the attack like a prizefighter lurching out of his corner, belligerent and determined, all he knows is that they want to stop him. And once he stops, he's at their mercy. He can picture them rifling his stores, breathing in his face, punching at his breastbone with their blunt cracked forefingers, all the while chattering away in some muddled troglodytic language that's like a barnyard flatulence, like pigs wheezing and kine passing wind. They could extort food and weapons, they could rob him, burn his notebooks, hand him over to the Moors. The thought of it throws a switch in his mind, case closed. Negroes will die, but he will not stop, come hell or high water. Repercussions be damned.

Unfortunately, the repercussions come sooner than he might have imagined, and in the form of canoes — sixty of them — just off a place called Gotoijege. It is late in the afternoon, two days after the incident at Gouroumo, and the *Joliba* is hugging a sheer rock wall that juts out into the river like a crooked elbow. Everything is still, stultified by the heat. The men are drowsing, caloric waves ripple over the rocky promontory, a lone vulture rides the convection currents high overhead. Gradually, like a waterborne leaf or twig, the *Joliba* works its way around the point and into the open river beyond. It is at this juncture that the explorer has his first intimation that all is not well: there seems to be something out there, obscured in the deep shadow of the promontory. Half a second later, which is to say half a second too late, he gets the picture.

It is a trap.

So many canoes crowd the cove it looks like a logjam. Up ahead, stretched across the river like a Stone Age armada, twenty more canoes hold the current. Hundreds of angry black faces, painted in various configurations of doom. Bulging black arms at the paddles, grids of swollen black vein and flexed muscle, flinty black hands clenched round bows and quivers, the nasty tapered shafts of long-nosed spears. No doubt about it: the word is out. Someone has let these people know that there are white men on the river, strange pale ghostly creatures running amok, creating havoc, murdering tribesmen up and down the shoreline, refusing to pay tolls or tribute or even to prostrate themselves before the high and mighty, the lordly and god-chosen, to plead for permission to pass through tribal lands. White men, begging to be chastised.

Suddenly, with a shout that could bring down all the snowfields in the Alps, the tableau erupts in violence. Where an instant before there had been sun and silence and the slow drowse of the drifting boat, there is now a frenetic seething wash of hostile humanity up and down both banks of the river. The promontory behind them is like a trampled anthill, swarming with stirred-up naked savages yabbering threats and insults and jabbing their pigstickers at the sky. Troops of women have emerged from nowhere, big-boned and bottom-heavy, cutting the air with calliope shrieks and pounding at great booming kettle drums as if they were flailing the hides of hapless explorers. Men and boys — hundreds of them — rush to the water's edge flinging spears and stones and flaming torches, riddling the ship with poisoned arrows and crude iron knives. At the same time the canoes shoot into action, slipping behind the *Joliba* as snugly as shadows, big black athletes at the paddles, painted warriors crouching down behind them to hone their spears and limber up their thrusting muscles. And all of them — men, women, children, paddlers, thrusters, bowmen, spear-chuckers and chiefs — hooting like butchers on a three-day drunk.

It is awesome. Terrifying. Overwhelming.

Could this be the end? the explorer is thinking, his vital organs curling up like hedgehogs, while Martyn reaches for his musket and Ned Rise rams the tiller hard right to send the canoe angling out from the spit. Arrows hit the canopy with a thunk-thunk-thunk, a rock cuts Martyn's cheek. They are staring into the faces of five hundred enraged savages, and another two hundred are hurtling toward them in quick low-slung canoes. They've been caught with their pants down, and it looks bad, looks as if they're whipped before they started.

But then things begin to fall into place: Ned gives them some breathing room, the sweet stink of the gunpowder fires their nostrils and before you know it they're rising to the occasion. Snatching up their weapons like the true-blue stout-hearted fighting men they are, saturated to the very clefts of their chins with true grit, blazing away like champions, like murderers. Once the boat is out of arrow range, it is easy. A shooting party. Potting ducks in the Cotswolds. They fire on their adversaries with a modulated rage, with the no-quarter-given, absolutely merciless absorption that possessed them on Lake Dibbie; they fire until the flotilla is destroyed, and then turn on the line of dugouts blocking their path downriver.

The blacks hold their ground. A hundred yards out, Ned swings the *Joliba* broadside and the men line up like a firing squad — Mungo, Amadi and the slaves on one end, Martyn, M'Keal and Ned on the other — and pour volley after volley into the dark line ahead of them as they drift down to meet it. One of their antagonists, in ostrich plumes and coral, looks to be a chief or a king maybe. He stands firm in the bow of the foremost canoe, a scepter clenched in one hand, the other solemnly raised in a commanding gesture, a gesture that says lay down your weapons and give up hope, lay down your weapons and surrender in the face of royal omnipotence and superior numbers. When Martyn knocks him flat with a single shot, it seems to take the heart out of the opposition. A moment later Ned brings the *Joliba* round again, rams the final canoe barring their way, and that's that. Child's play.

The only casualty is M'Keal. In the heat of the action, someone fired a musket at him — yes, a musket. A Moor, it looked like, seated in the prow of one of the pirogues — "a big sucker, in black." The ball excised the upper portion of his left ear and trimmed back his hoary locks an inch or two. A minor wound, by all accounts. But when he was hit, something snapped. He went berserk. Frothed like a rabid dog, wrote a new book of racial epithets, stamped and stammered and shook his fist. Then, muttering all the while, he began to fling things at the astonished black faces across the water. First he flung muskets, six or eight of them, then a keg of powder. The battle raged round him: no one noticed. He heaved a sack of rice overboard, a regimental sword, the sextant. The bloody aborigine buggers, he'd show them. Next to go was a box of ammunition, and then the explorer's duffel bag: compass, notebooks, half-finished letters to Ailie and all. Cursing, growling, beating his breast, the red-faced old soldier chucked over his shoes, his underwear, his Panama hat, the teapot, a barrel of salt beef and a crate of rotting yams. By the time the danger was past and they were able to subdue him, the stringy old veteran of the West Indian campaign had lightened their load by half, and put an end to any further plotting of latitude and longitude or worries about alignment with magnetic poles.

It hardly seemed to matter.

◄§ §►

Without chronometer, without compass, without sextant, the geographical missionaries of the H.M.S. *Joliba* look at the sun and know it is noon, forever, and that they are heading north, into the desert, into the glare, into the very maw of mystery. Their hair, thick with grease and dust, trails down their shoulders, their beards reach their waists. The proud red uniforms have long since degenerated to tatters — to loincloths — and the once-glistening boots have fallen to pieces. Unwashed, undisciplined, underfed, thin of rib and cloudy of eye, their skin blotched and sun-scorched, their bare feet blistered, they could be the last remnant of some ancient tribe emigrating to a new homeland, they could be cave dwellers, scavengers, eaters of offal and raw flesh. Only Amadi and his three slaves are unchanged. Alert and watchful, they sit beneath their broad-brimmed hats and throw their carved bones. They are not men of the nineteenth century, they are men of the millennia, men whose gait and gaze and quick clever hands prefigure Europe and all of written history. They know the river will bend. They know that maps and trousers and salt beef are irrelevant, and that white men are fools. They are patient. They are content. Their eyes are open.

Meanwhile, the big black canoe drifts with the current. By day there is the blinding flash of sun on water, the whole earth set ablaze, white-hot, the hills consumed in flame. At night the banks reverberate with ghostly echoes — muffled snarls, startled cries, the eerie gloating snigger of hyenas — and the water boils with heart-stopping explosions as of strange gargantuan beasts cavorting in the deeps or stretching their great horny tails across the river to trap the unwary.

One night, under a moon so brilliant it varnishes the surface of the river and throws a cool dispersed glimmer over trees and shrubs and broken tumbles of rock, they are awakened by a sudden shattering burst of shrieks

and growls somewhere up ahead. Primordial, cacophonous, chilling, it is
the sound of pack frenzy, of snarling snapping furious jaws, the sound of
wolves fighting over scraps of meat. But not only that: there is the hint of
something else too, something far more excruciating. As they draw closer,
they begin to realize what it is: human voices crying out over the clamor.

Everyone is awake now — even M'Keal — staring off into the darkness,
transfixed with horror. The sounds of tearing flesh, bones cracking, the
garbled cries for help: they flay the nerves like salt and nettles, unbearable,
as inadmissible as the image of one's own death and mutilation. Ned turns
away, the explorer's stomach churns. They can see nothing. A terrible
minute passes, then another, the night enveloped in demonic snarls and
torn gasping sobs, as if somehow, poor sinners, they'd passed the invisible
barrier and descended the long swirling tributaries of Acheron and Lethe.
Suddenly one of the men cries out: "There! On the right bank, just
ahead!"

The moon shifts, everything indefinite and insubstantial, there and not
here. Then the shadows begin to take on motion and life and the snarling
swells to a raging crescendo that ebbs in a single breath and a sudden
explosion of light: a torch flaring out against the darkness. Flickering and
unsteady, it illuminates the black humped forms of a hundred frothing,
toothy demons: hyenas. Claws and shoulders and raging black mouths,
hyenas, kid killers, graverobbers, choking on their own spittle. Against
them, a single man — a traveling merchant perhaps — backing away from
the gutted carcass of his camel, flailing the torch like an archangel's sword,
while a woman and child cower at his back, caught up in a bad dream.

Hunched low, the graverobbers close in, foaming at the carcass like fish
after chum, snapping down glistening gray loops of intestine, jockeying for
position, while others lumber in out of the shadows, their eyes bright with
greed and a hunger no amount of feeding can satisfy. The man backs off,
circling, while the woman, clutching the child as if it were already in pieces,
feints with a length of firewood. For a moment, the contest looks even. But
then in a sudden unforgiving instant, the torch dies out and the seething
wave of muzzle and mane closes over them, their torn shrieks already lost
in the rising volume of contentious growls and the percussive clash of jaws.

The *Joliba* sails on, amidst the gnashing of teeth and the crunch of bone,
heading north, into the nether regions.

◄§ THE BEAST WITH TWO BACKS

The Reverend MacNibbit's voice is disembodied, a deep, sure, mellifluous presence suffusing the clerestory with power and promise, with a prick of foreboding and a balm of reassurance. "And yea, though I walk through the valley of the shadow of death," he rumbles, shaking his great shaggy head and wagging his jowls, an admonitory tremolo creeping into his voice to underscore just how black and hopeless things can be . . . but Ailie isn't listening. Nor watching. Her head is bowed, as if in prayer, but her thoughts are elsewhere. Specifically, they are on Georgie Gleg — and the trip, the jaunt, the *adventure* she's about to embark on. This very afternoon. The preparations have been made, her bags are packed. She can think of nothing else.

Georgie had invited her to accompany him on a six-week tour of the Highlands, through Fife, Angus, Aberdeen, Banff and Moray, culminating in a week's stay at Avis House in Drumnadrochit, within sight of Urquhart Castle and one of the great deep churning lochs every schoolgirl knew so well in song and legend, the grandest loch of them all, Loch Ness. Avis House was the ancestral home of the Highland Glegs, currently tenanted by Georgie's second cousin, Fiona Gleg, a spinster in her early fifties. During her recent stay in Edinburgh, Georgie had treated her for peripractitis and gout, and to show her gratitude she'd invited him to pay her a visit and "ken the glories o'the grand old loch." Georgie immediately thought of Ailie. How a tour such as this would lift her spirits, allow her to live her own life for a change, take the onus of the patient wife, mother and housekeeper off her shoulders for a bit. It would be just the thing for her.

It would. She's never in her life been farther than Edinburgh, and she's only been there twice. Never been to London, the Continent, never even been to Glasgow. Mungo just packs his bags, takes her brother by the arm and tramps off halfway round the world. Any time he pleases. And she's stuck at home with the children like some drudge in a fairy tale. Well this is her chance, and by God she's going to take it.

Oh, everything will be very proper of course. Both Georgie's mother and Betty Deatcher are coming along as chaperones, and she's decided to bring her five-year-old with her as well. There'll be no hanky-panky, nothing scandalous. Still, her father is violently opposed to her going. He sees it as an affront to her husband, whether she's chaperoned or not. "And what if he comes home while you're away, lass — what'll I tell him?" the old man had demanded, his voice raw with anger and a stinging edge of accusation.

"Tell him I'll be back the second week in April."

"But Ailie, ye can't do that to the mon — he's your husband." In her
ather's own personal hagiography, Mungo ranked right up there with
aint Columba and Bonnie Prince Charlie.

Her eyes widened till there was nothing left of them but an angry splash
f green, cold and brilliant as the Firth of Forth, and her voice trembled
vith the effort to keep it under control. "He did it to me."

Now, sitting beside her father on the long hard pew, his breathing harsh
nd righteous, the children fidgeting, she can think only of release, of
scape, of turning her back on MacNibbit's fire and brimstone and stepping
nto Georgie's carriage. Above her, the stained glass is suffused with sun,
adiant, bright as blood, and it seems to pulse with the quick breathless
adence beating in her veins. The Highlands! Inverness! Loch Ness! She
an barely contain herself, she wants to jump up and dance round the
oom, shout out the news. Suddenly, the minister's words are playing in
er ears, refreshing, resuscitant, a breath of air in a drowning girl's lungs.
Surely," he exclaims, his voice rich with piety and exaltation, the good
vord melting on his tongue like a thick pat of butter, "surely goodness and
nercy shall follow me all the days of my life . . ."

Ailie looks up, as if the promise were meant for her alone, as if it were a
lessing for the road, a sign that she's made the right choice. The sermon is
ver, the parishioners rustling in their seats. She can't help smiling. Amen,
he thinks. Amen.

◆§ ॐ◆

Georgie's diligence carries them as far as Leith, where they take ship for
Linghorn and pick up the post chaise. From there they work their way up
ne east coast, through Cupar, St. Andrews, Ellen, Fochabers and Cawdor,
opping at inns and country houses for refreshment, taking time out to
flect on such curiosities as Dunbuy Rock and Gordon's Castle. Ailie
resses her face to the window, rapt, gazing on the windswept coast with its
unted spruce and fir and heaps of rounded boulders. Thomas, child of the
entury, is almost six. He clings to his mother's sleeve and whines, uneasy
ith the pitch and yaw of the coach, or interrupts Georgie's delirious
nonologue with aboriginal screams and resounding raspberries. He looks,
solutely, precisely, and in every detail, the image of his father. Mrs.
uaggus, in widow's weeds ("Poor Tyrone: his heart failed him as he was
ssin' off a sillabub with Archbishop Oughten one night — it was a sort of
ntest, a wager, you know — and Tyrone he woulda won it hands down
cause the Archbishop dinna have the stomach for more than six or seven
d my dear departed was already into his twelfth — his *twelfth* — when

the good Lord called him to his reward . . ." [a sigh] "I guess he shoulda
knowed better than to bait an Archbishop."), sits against the far window,
erect as a hatrack. From time to time she bathes her son in a smoldering
look of maternal regard, as if he were nothing short of Molière for wit and
a veritable Hippocrates for skill and accomplishment. Betty, in her late
twenties now, still unmarried and with a nose like a garden implement,
tries her best to be gracious and to respond to Georgie's nonstop barrage of
words, while Georgie, for his part, is so exhilarated by the very fact of
Ailie's presence that he is unable to shut his mouth, even when it's stuffed
full of onion and oatcake, all the long way from Selkirk to Drumnadrochit.

At Inverness, like Boswell and Johnson before them, they put up at
Mackenzie's Inn, and Ailie is in such a state of anticipation she hardly
notices the rough-hewn furniture and the desiccated flies in the corners, or
that the haggis tastes like stewed leather. All she knows is that the loch, the
glorious loch, is no more than three miles off. She tucks her son in, then
throws open the windows and looks out on the darkening treetrunks, the
raw wet smell of the loch in her nostrils. There is the distant cry of an
embergoose, and then the moon slips up out of the grasp of the trees.
Pocked and scoured, it is the very same moon that squats over Selkirk, but
here it looks different somehow, as if it were newly created, as if it were
something magical, a sign in the sky. She sleeps like a drugged princess.

In the morning they take the road for Drumnadrochit, winding through
stands of birch and scotch pine, the loch stretched out below them like a
great glittering arm of the sea. Ailie feasts her eyes, a strange sense of
fulfillment, of rightness, coming over her. Finally she's making her own
expedition, doing a bit of exploring for herself. She laughs out loud at the
thought of it — the explorer's wife exploring — and Mrs. Quaggus lifts her
eyebrows, as if she too would like to be let in on the joke. Ailie can't
remember a happier moment.

At Avis House they are greeted by an ebullient and talk-starved Fiona
Gleg, a red-haired woman in a bulky wool cardigan who sweeps past her
servants to embrace them, one by one, on the front steps. They've barely
had time to catch their breath before she knots them up in a concatenation
of questions, opinions, observations and suppositions, touching on every
thing from Uncle Silas' eczema to the egregious food at Mackenzie's, from
the stonework at Cawdor Castle — shoddy, isn't it? — to the disappointing
size of Dunbuy Rock and the odd color of little Thomas' eyes. In the
wainscoted vestibule, servants scuttling to and fro with trunks and bags
and hatboxes, Cousin Fiona turns to Ailie with a wide wet motherly smile:
"Mrs. Park," she says (it sounds as if she's saying Mrs. *Paddock*), "I've

heard so much about you — it seems the young physician here can talk of nothing else — and I'd like to say it's a pleasure, it is, and that ye're unco welcome at Avis House."

The red-haired woman has taken her hand. Georgie Gleg, distinguished professor and doctor of medicine, is shuffling his feet and looking down at his shoes. "And of course," Fiona adds, "I've enjoyed your husband's book."

◅§ §►

During the next few days, Avis House hums, roars and squeaks with activity, as if someone had loaded it on a colossal wagon and set the wheels rolling. The doors are wide open, the groaning board groaning, and every ambulatory, morally unobjectionable, semi-rational soul up and down both sides of the loch has been invited to pay a visit. Kilted men and women in tartan shawls show up for tea, for dinner, for cards or quoits. The Reverend this, the Doctor that, the Honorable Mister and odd Sir. Ailie can hardly keep track of the faces. There are Macdonalds in the parlor and Dinsdales on the lawn, beaming Camerons come for a look at the Edinburgh physician and the wife of the renowned explorer, sober-faced Ramsays eager to discuss Cave's *Lives of the Fathers* and Ogden's *Sermons*. Evenings are consecrated with vast bowls of punch and cider and bottles of port wine, nourished with mutton, herrings, fricasseed moor-hens, beef collops, frothed milk, tongue and bread pudding, and consummated with conversation and tobacco, music, dancing and parlor games. It could be Christmas, Michaelmas, the harvest feast. The whole county seems to have gone on holiday.

Ailie can't get enough of it. She feels like a girl of sixteen, light on her feet, witty, attractive, appreciated. For the first time in years she's the center of attention, whether jigging round the parlor with a young buck in kilt and argyles or talking fashion with the ladies or horses and dogs with a cross-eyed country doctor. Despite the odd position she's been placed in — wife to Mungo, jilter of Georgie — she couldn't feel more relaxed — or more welcome. She'd thought at first that Fiona's reference to Mungo was a subtle dig at her — and God knows Georgie's cousin and mother and all the rest of his clan had a right to resent her — but now she's certain the remark was innocent, a way of making conversation and nothing more. If anything, in fact, Fiona and Mrs. Quaggus have gone out of their way to foster a relationship between her and Georgie. They've taken Thomas off her hands, occupying him with Erse songs and tales of taibhs and goblins and the beastie that lives in the loch, stuffing him with cake, running him round the meadows. And Betty too. Less than an hour after their arrival a young, smooth-faced clergyman sat down to tea with them and hasn't left her side since. The whole thing is very strange. It's almost as if the two older women were matchmaking, as if Ailie were truly sixteen, free and unattached, the chosen mate for an exemplary son and sterling cousin. Either that . . . or a widow.

A widow. The thought comes to her, cold and insidious, as she's dressing for tea one afternoon, and it stops her dead for a moment. Do they really think — ? No. She's a married woman, mother of four . . . her husband's gone away for a bit. On business. Like a traveling solicitor or a circuit judge. And then suddenly, as if a wet sheet had been thrown over her, the truth of the matter strikes her. Mungo is out there somewhere, suffering, injured maybe, racked with disease, beleaguered by hideous grinning black faces and howling beasts, and here she is running around as if he didn't exist, like a schoolgirl or something, like a widow. Widow. The two evil syllables box round her head, insupportable, unacceptable: Ailie Anderson Park, Widow of the Late Great Explorer.

That's it. That's what this thing is all about, that's why old Quaggus and simpering Fiona are knocking themselves out to be so gracious. They've buried Mungo already, and they're softening her up — like a piece of meat — for Georgie. For a moment she just sits there, staring down at the shoe in her lap, humiliated, frightened, resentful of the scheming old biddies, resentful of Georgie. But then she leaps up off the bed and flings the shoe at the wall, as sore and hurt and angry as she's ever been. It's not Georgie's fault — he's been a saint, a savior — nor Mrs. Quaggus's or Fiona's. It's Mungo — Mungo's the one to blame. Would she be up here at the loch if he hadn't deserted her? Would she so much as look at another man if he hadn't broken his marital vows? No. Dead or alive, he's made her a widow, condemned her to solitary confinement. Well, he's asked for it. He has. And she'll be damned if she'll sit at home and wait for him till her hair's turned gray.

Ten minutes later she's sitting over a cup of tea, laughing till her sides hurt over some little joke Georgie's made. Her son, barely able to see over the edge of the table, glances up at her with Mungo's startled eyes and the laugh catches in her throat. There is a moment of silence, awkward, Betty and her preacher, Fiona and an assortment of Macdonalds and Ramsays staring down at their cups, until Mrs. Quaggus shoots out a hand to tickle the boy, and he subsides in giggles.

Fiona is tapping the edge of her saucer with a spoon, grinning broadly. "Ahem," clearing her throat, fluffing her hair. "If I can get a word in amidst all this hilarity, I thought perhaps you and Georgie might want to take a

ride out to one o' my tenants, Ailie — see some o' the quaint side o'
Highland life. Very picturesque, I assure you."

"Yes, let's." Georgie meets her eyes, then looks away.

"We'd be more than happy to look after the young gentleman," Mrs.
Quaggus adds.

"To be sure." Fiona is still smiling, lips drawn back to show her teeth.

❧ ❧

Outside, the sky presses down on them like a weight. Clouds obliterate
the hilltops, mist creeps up the glens. Where before there were early
flowers, ferns, leafing bushes, there is now only a low band of fog billowing
upward to join earth and sky. Ailie and Gleg lead the way, mounted on a
matched pair of chestnuts, while Thomas — he threw a tantrum until Ailie
relented and agreed to take him along — brings up the rear on a pony led
by Rorie Macphoon, Cousin Fiona's bailiff. They pause at the top of a rise
to watch a lone collie work his flock down the slope, white paws blurred as
he dashes in and out of a bank of mist after strays. A big broad-faced ewe,
just in front of them, glances over her shoulder like a nervous grandmother, hurriedly tearing up great streaming mouthfuls of heather and grass
before the dog can discover her. Georgie, in rare form, quotes from
Macbeth: "By the pricking of my thumbs, / Something wicked this way
comes," and old Rorie laughs as if his head would split.

The sky has darkened perceptibly and a light drizzle begun to thicken the
air by the time they reach the little cottage on the hillside. Quaint, Ailie
thinks, oh yes indeed, and then calls to Thomas to hurry and come have a
look. The boy wears a rapt expression, awestruck by the romance of the
scene, something out of the pages of a storybook. The hut is of turf, with a
crude, blistered wooden door and a square cut out of the front wall to
serve as a window. A stream courses through the yard with a sound of
gargling fish and mermen, the naked black trunks of pines reach up into the
smoking atmosphere like great solid beanstalks, there is a delicious
frightening cackle of voices mingled with the smoke rising from the
chimney. Georgie, riding crop in hand, raps at the door.

After a moment the door swings back and a bewildered-looking old man
pokes his head out. He gapes at Georgie as if he'd just dropped down from
another planet, inclining his cross-hatched face to one side and squinting
an eye shut to get a better look at him. Georgie is holding out his hand,
hearty and condescending at the same time. "Gleg," he says. "Georgie
Gleg. We've stopped by to pay you a visit."

If the words register they have no visible effect, except that the old fellow
tilts his head to the opposite side, as if he were contemplating a listing ship

or chinning an invisible violin. His lips are compressed, his eyes shuttered windows. Slowly, hesitantly, like a man who's answered a knock only to find no one there, he begins to pull the door closed. To this point, Rorie Macphoon has remained in the background, holding the pony's bridle; when he steps forward, the old cottager's face undergoes a transformation: where before he'd looked puzzled or merely obtuse, now a whole range of human emotions plays across his features. Ailie watches his initial look of enlightenment realign itself into something harder, an expression of anger and resentment, which is in turn succeeded by a sly glimmer of avarice and finally a sort of hangdog look of obsequious resignation. Georgie Gleg, the Edinburgh physician, presses half a crown into the old man's palm, and they enter the cottage.

Inside, an enormous brindled cat gazes up at them from the hearth, its eyes the color of cheddar cheese. Beside the animal, so still she could be made of wax, an old woman dozes in a chair carved from a treestump. A slab of oak balanced on two piles of paving stones serves as a bench, and a bedframe, set on the floor and heaped with heather, sags against the far wall. There is no other furniture in the room. In the glimmer from the hearth and the bleak gray light of the window Ailie can make out the shabby accouterments of the place: a crutch and a rusted hoe in the corner, sheaves of barley stacked on the floor, a mound of peat, string of onions, wooden washbasin. A wicker curtain cordons off the low cavelike back room, from which emanates a caustic stench of urine and the occasional unsteady caprine bleat. Sad, Ailie thinks. Pitiful. Better call it sordid than quaint. She shifts uneasily from foot to foot, listening to the goats make water and wondering why in God's name Fiona sent them to this hole.

"So," Georgie booms, warming his hands over the peat fire and turning to the old man, "you live here, do you?"

Startled, the cottager dips his head and steps back a pace. The turkey flesh under his neck has begun to quiver and Rorie is attempting some sort of explanation beginning with the phrase "Mr. Gleg" repeated three or four times and interspersed with "ums" and "ahs" and a good deal of foot shuffling and trouser tugging, when suddenly a discordant stream of language is washing over them from down below. The old woman, hunched and crippled, one eye dead, has come to life, treating them to a disquisition in Erse, the native tongue of the Highlands. And disquisition it is — she goes on and on, wound up like a mechanical gargoyle, her good eye leaping about its socket, delivering a regular lecture, every last word of which is entirely unintelligible. Finally, after what seems like a good five minutes, she ends with a wild stinging laugh like wind in the gutter, and then subsides in a spasm of coughing.

"What was that?" Georgie asks, turning to Macphoon.

Thomas, intimidated by the whole scene — the dimness, the stink, the unspoken threat — clings to his mother's skirts, while Ailie bites her lip to keep from laughing. The idea of it: Fiona thinks this *quaint*?

Rorie, hat in hand and shy as a sinner at the gates of heaven, clears his throat and looks at the ground. "She says she's the happiest woman in the world."

That does it. She can't hold it any longer. Suddenly Ailie loses control, laughing out loud, beginning with a barely suppressed titter and building to a series of breastbone-pounding whoops. Nodding and grinning, the old housewife takes a pinch of snuff and laughs along with her, hysterical, high and keening, a laugh like knives grating against a whetstone. "Happiest . . ." Ailie gasps, holding her sides, unable to complete the phrase.

And then the old woman is jabbering away again, her voice rasping and harsh, the strange musical language like something inexpressibly ancient and exotic, some Ur language, something you'd expect to find in Mesopotamia or Luxor or in the crumbling leaves of a faded parchment. When she falls silent, Ailie turns to Macphoon with an anticipatory grin: "Well? What did she say this time — more words of wisdom?"

Rorie goes through the same routine again — the foot shuffling, tugging at his trousers, turning the hat over in his hands — and then looks Ailie dead in the eye. "She says she's got her husband right here by her side, and that's all a woman could ever want."

The words drive home like separate blows from a mallet, a stake sinking into her heart. The old man is nodding his head and smiling — an obscene, wet-lipped parody of a smile that shows his yellowed teeth and the dead white tip of his tongue. And his wife, the old hag, is cackling like an overworked clock and struggling to get up out of the chair. Ailie feels as if she's caught in a dream, feels as if someone's played a bad joke on her, feels the bad breath of the universe whistling in her face and is frightened. The smile is gone.

Georgie, sensing that something has gone wrong, takes her arm and leads her to the door, nodding to the old man and pressing another coin into his hand. Alarmed, Thomas clings to his mother as if someone were trying to snatch him away, and Rorie, flushing, concentrates on his shoes. Shaken, angry, bewildered, Ailie steps out into the rinsed gray air and takes a deep breath, wondering just what is going on and why she's let an old crone's banter upset her so.

All at once there's a tug at her elbow. She turns. The old woman, bent over her crutch like an errant question mark, is looking up at her out of a sharp sly raptor's face. The dull light is blinding. Something wrong with the hag's lip, scarred, as if . . . as if had once been pierced through, like Seedy's. Ailie draws back instinctively, and the woman's hand snakes out to pat Thomas' head, pinch his cheeks, the cracked grating voice having its final say.

Ailie's face is burning. She looks at Rorie framed in the doorway, the white bulb of the old man's head at his shoulder.

The bailiff wets his fingertips, smooths the cap across his crown. "She had a boy like him once, she says. Run off on her." There are no trees, no bushes, the sky gone dark, the invisible loch in the deep glen roaring with a thousand voices. The old woman is rocking on her crutch, leering, rubbing the white bristle of her chin. "She says you ought to keep a watch on him."

For a long while, wending their way through the darkening forest, saddles creaking, the silent mist tugging at their elbows and knees, they can hear the knife edge of the old woman's laugh, cutting the night in two.

-◦§ ᴈ◦-

The final day of their sojourn at Avis House dawns like an intimation of July, bright and cloudless, the air gravid with a slow penetrating warmth, as if somehow the seasons had advanced, the earth pitched forward on its axis, the sun flared up like a bundle of twigs set atop a mound of glowing coals. Ailie is up at first light, intoxicated by the texture of the air, by the odor of daffodils and the sound of honeybees. Standing at her window and looking out over the loch, she can't help feeling a tug of regret, a resistance to the idea of leaving, of going back to the humdrum and the quotidian. Certainly she misses the children, and her father, and even in a way the staid domesticity of day-to-day life in Selkirk — but she's not ready to go back yet. This is adventure, this is living, this is what she's been looking for all her life. At home she has only her duty to husband, children, father, and her role as the constant wife of the absent saint and martyr.

There are sparrows and starlings on the lawn. Out over the loch a golden eagle coasts in the high thin air, luminous in the morning sun. She wants to go, she wants to stay. Wants to look into her children's faces, and at the same time she wants to travel farther, to the Hebrides, the Arctic, up over Russia and down to Tibet. At that moment she comes closer to understanding her husband than she ever will: the adventure, the surprise, the frisson of chasing down the permutations of possibility, the purity of doing and experiencing — how could looking on the same bit of yard, the same black mare, the same four walls even touch it? It is the sixth of April. Mungo has been gone a year and a half. Today is hers and hers alone.

At breakfast, Fiona throws open the windows to birdsong, golden light, an early hatch of mayflies. Tim Dinsdale is there, Donald MacDonald, half a dozen repentant Ramsays, Ewan Murchison, Sir Adolphus Beattie, Miss Mary Ogilvie, Betty and her preacher, Mrs. Quaggus, Fiona and Georgie. Everyone — even Reelaiah Ramsay — seems to be smiling, feeling chipper, talking about a ride or a walk around the grounds, a picnic or a match of croquet. The only topic of general concern is the weather. "Oh, it's a real pippin of a day," Mrs. Quaggus says, buttering her bannocks. "Wally," offers Sir Adolphus, looking up from his eggs and rashers, "really first-rate." Tim Dinsdale says he hasn't seen it this warm in April since '81, the year it snowed in July. "It's a blessing, is what it is," Fiona sighs. Ailie couldn't agree more.

Afterward, Georgie takes a seat beside her on the porch. In his simple brown suit, silk shirt and riding boots he almost looks elegant, uncoiling his long frame, throwing back his head and crossing his legs with an easy, self-confident air, proprietary and unassuming at the same time. His ears still stick out, his wrists insist on protruding from the jacket sleeves, his nose is like something you'd carry into battle — but does it matter anymore? Aren't those the things that a child would notice?

Georgie shifts in his chair. "Well, Ailie," he says after a moment, "it's your last day. Would you like to take a turn on the loch?"

"Rowing?"

He nods.

Fiona and Thomas are marching around the parlor, beating on kitchen pots and singing *Haytin foam, foam eri* at the top of their lungs, Betty and her preacher are strolling through the garden arm in arm, and Mrs. Quaggus, surrounded by Ramsays, is eulogizing her late husband over her sixth cup of tea.

Georgie is studying the side of Ailie's face. She turns to look him in the eye. "There's nothing I'd rather do."

◈ ◈

Beached at the mouth of Divach Burn, oars poised in the locks, the rowboat could be the remains of some fantastic form of life, a colossal insect washed ashore or the hollow exoskeleton of a prehistoric crab — but for the fact that Fiona has painted it cherry red — for visibility — and

whimsically christened it *The Kelpie.* The boat lies there in the undergrowth, an advertisement for civilization, while birds flit in and out of the
reeds and midges hover over the water. Georgie hops from one leg to the
other to remove his boots, drags the boat into the whisky-stained water and
gallantly hands Ailie into the stern. Then he lifts in the picnic hamper
(three bottles of wine, smoked salmon, sliced tongue, cheese, bread,
radishes and linen napkins), gives the boat a reasonably athletic shove and
they're off.

There's barely a breeze, and the air — it must be seventy-five or eighty
degrees — melts over them like butter. Ailie throws off her scarf and hat,
loosens her collar, and watches the reeds fall back in the distance and the
great battered tower of Urquhart Castle loom up on her right. It's glorious.
The day, the scenery, the company. She feels girlish and silly, the blood
gone light in her veins. Georgie strains at the oars. She wants to reach out
and tweak his nose.

"Shall we move in close for a look at the ruins from down here?" he
puffs, swinging the boat toward the castle promontory. He is facing her,
three feet away. Their legs are touching.

"Yes," she laughs, everything funny, everything perfect. She's drunk
already and they haven't even uncorked the wine. "Yes," she repeats, and
then, just as quickly, "no." Georgie, obedient as a dray horse, drops the
oars. "I mean, we've seen the castle. Let's strike out for the middle of the
loch, make the shore a speck, have an adventure. We could just drift along
out there, drift all day."

He grins a big horsey pleased grin. There is nothing he'd rather do than
ferry her around the lake — take her anywhere she pleases, drift till the sun
goes down. He leans into the oars with a vengeance, gobbling up the feast
of her eyes.

The boat rides out over the waves, the sound of the oars rippling like
wind chimes, and Ailie throws back her head, eyes closed, feeling like the
heroine of a medieval romance, like Una or Iseult the Fair. Here's
Georgie, the sweating hero, there's the castle and here the lady in distress:
all they need is a dragon. She laughs out loud at the thought of it and
Georgie joins in, his grin as wide as the horizon.

An hour later they're riding the loose abdomen of the lake, dead center,
shore to shore, the boat gently lifting and swaying with the almost
imperceptible breath of the great still body of water. The sun falls over
them like eiderdown, hot and luxurious. Georgie's jacket is draped over
the bow seat, his shirt has fallen open to the waist; Ailie has removed her

shoes and stockings, trailing her feet in the water like a country maid. Tongue and bread and radishes are spread out on the perfect blanched field of the linen tablecloth, and two empty wine bottles lie on the floor, softly rocking with the rise and fall of the loch. They are laughing, Ailie and Georgie, over old times.

"Those poems you used to write me! 'The Blushing Morn of your Cheeks / The Foaming Billows of your Breasts' . . . they were so, so ridiculous." She chokes on her laughter, gasping for breath, the mechanism gone autonomous, laughter like hiccoughs.

Georgie is laughing too. He *was* ridiculous. He admits it.

"And, and — the way you used to play that recorder, and, and sing — " Her face is flushed with wine and blood, two points in the back of her skull throbbing from the force of her laughter.

"I admit it," Georgie laughs. "I was preposterous, pimply-faced, a moonstruck adolescent." Suddenly he's not laughing anymore. "But I mean it, Ailie. I loved you. I loved you then and I love you now."

It is as though someone has suddenly dropped the curtain, changed the script. She was laughing half an instant before, in control, the joke on Georgie; now she's tense and riveted. His words dig at her like fingers in clay, softening her, making her blood beat like a parade of drums. Stop, she thinks, stop. And then: go on, go on.

He's on his knees now, between her legs, his lank knuckly hands rubbing fitfully at her thighs as if she'd drowned and he was trying to revive her. "From the first time," he says, "I swear — " but she puts a hand over his mouth, cradles his head, strokes the stiff yellow spectacle of his ears. The sun, the wine, the romance of the loch, the hoary castle, *a year and a half of celibacy*: she is on fire.

Worshipful, reverential, without a hint of clumsiness or uncertainty, he presses himself to her, a votary, the secret ceremony as smooth and proper as if it had been rehearsed. Her skirts, the undergarments, the buttons of his trousers. And Ailie: her mind has gone dead on her, she's a creature of sensation, of electricity, of stroking and smoothing and caressing, her eyes closed, caught up in the rhythm of it, the boat swaying, Georgie's shoulders trapped in her palms, his face in hers, his tongue . . .

Her eyes blink open, close, open again. Over his shoulder: what is that? Screened by his hair, the stiff geography of his ear. She's delirious. Delirious. He moves in her, but her eyes are open, she's craning her neck. It arches over the boat, rearing up, slick and muscular and wet — impossible, it can't be — a face at the tip of it, serpent's eyes,

the shadow falling across her flushed cheeks like a swift stinging slap.
No. It can't be.
She shuts her eyes and holds on tight — as if her life depended on it.

⊷ WATER MUSIC (REPRISE)

It is sometime in early April — the fifth? the sixth? — he can't be sure.
Time has become an irrelevance. There is only the sun and the inexorable
slide of the river, the long running slope to resurrection. And resurrection
it will be: he is certain of it. Forget despair, futility, self-doubt. The cards
are on the table, and they're all aces: the Niger has swung southward. Just
as he'd hoped and prayed it would, just as Amadi had predicted. For two
months now they've been heading south, and it's like an inoculation of
confidence. South. To the Atlantic. To vindication. To glory.

A simple turn of the river. It's done wonders for everyone's attitude.
Ned Rise has loosened his grip on the tiller, Martyn has begun to talk and
even smile a bit, and M'Keal — though still troubled in his mind — has
shown signs of coming around. And why not? They're like prisoners on
death row whose sentences have suddenly been commuted. Two months
ago they were staring doom in the face; now they're home free. All they
have to do is hold on a bit longer — and who knows, it could be no more
than a month, a week even — hold on and bask in a hero's welcome in
London, maybe even pick up a government pension. They'll be drinking
porter and punch before you know it, diddling the girls, sinking their teeth
into great dripping pots of bubble and squeak, wheels of Cheshire cheese
and craggy mounds of oysters. Oh yes: they're going home.

Of course, it hasn't been all singing around the campfire and Pollyanna
at the dress shop. Even after the river began pulling them southward they
had scare after scare, crisis on top of crisis. Hostile tribes lined the
riverbanks — the Juli, the Ulotrichi, the Songhai and Mahinga — and
squadrons of canoes regularly shot out to intercept them. One morning
they woke to see an army of Tuareg — kissing cousins to the Moors
— gazing down on them from a bluff. There must have been three
thousand of them, mounted on camels, their indigo *jubbahs* rattling in the
wind, beards bristling, double-edged swords glinting in the sun. They never
moved. Not a one of them. It was as though they'd been carved from stone.
And yet how terrible this silent presence was, how heinous, how
insupportable — what were they doing there, what did they want? Another

time, after a skirmish with a flotilla of native canoes, two black fanatics managed to board the *Joliba* in the confusion, and were about to rupture the blond bulb of the explorer's skull when Martyn wheeled round and dispatched them with a flurry of saber strokes. For days afterward Mungo went round fingering his head as tentatively as a man stacking eggs in a basket.

But by far the most disturbing event of the meridional leg of the journey was the defection of Amadi Fatoumi. It had been agreed that Amadi was to be released from any further obligation on reaching Yaour in Hausaland. There he would be given the balance of his wages in muskets, powder and tradegoods (he'd been paid the first half, in cowries, at Sansanding), and he would attempt to hire a Hausa tribesman to guide the expedition the rest of the way. Fine. That was the agreement. No one liked it — what if they couldn't find another guide? how could they land Amadi at Yaour without exposing themselves to attack? — but they would just have to live with it. That he would leave them was a given, but it was the way in which he was to do it that left them cold.

One evening four weeks back, Amadi and his slaves rose in a group, tucked away their carved bones, cowries, teapots and pipes, and shuffled their way to the stern, where Mungo stood beside Ned Rise, reminiscing about Bond Street and Drury Lane. Amadi spoke in Mandingo. They were three days out of Yaour, he said, but they would have to anchor for the night because there was a dangerous rapids just ahead. He would guide them through the rapids in the morning, and then begin making preparations for a landing at Yaour. Could he, he wondered, look through the things the explorer meant to give him in payment?

The slaves watched Mungo's face as if it were something to eat. He didn't want to think about Amadi's leaving him, didn't want to deal with it. He even thought of welshing, of holding a pistol to the guide's head and forcing him to go on. But no, he couldn't do that. His relations with the natives — insofar as he had any — had always been based on mutual trust. Amadi had fulfilled his part of the bargain, Mungo would stick by his. "All right," he said finally, "we'll hate to see you go, but I suppose there's nothing to be done about it." He looked at the guide hopefully, but Amadi's face was signed, sealed and delivered. "Well. There's no harm in your picking out what you want now — but remember, when we get to Yaour you've promised to find us a guide. Right?"

Amadi made a sign of obeisance, and then, shadowed by his slaves, ducked beneath the canopy to sort through the things that had survived M'Keal's fit at Gotoijege. For a long while the explorer could hear them mumbling over this object or that, whistling in awe, debating in a low murmurous dialect he couldn't understand. After an hour or so Mungo ordered Ned to drop anchor, and Amadi and his men retired to their customary spot in the bow of the boat. As it grew dark, the slaves huddled beneath their *jubbahs* and dozed off, but Amadi sat there, still as a corpse, his eyes scanning the shore, the glowing bowl of his pipe like a beacon in the gathering night.

In the morning he was gone.

Mungo couldn't believe it. He awoke to mist, the discourse of birds, M'Keal's snores, and made his way to the front of the boat to heat some water for tea over the brazier they'd erected there. But something was wrong. The bow of the boat was empty, the curled black forms that had been propped there these past four and a half months until they seemed a part of the ship—knots in the wood, human anchors, furled sails—were gone. Vanished. As if someone had taken an eraser to the corner of a familiar portrait. It was disturbing. Deeply disturbing. Frantic, Mungo roused the men and hurriedly inventoried the supplies.

Three-quarters of the muskets had disappeared. Kegs of powder, bullets, every last scrap of broadcloth, every trinket and trifle—about the only thing they hadn't taken was the clarinet Ned had inherited from Scott. Martyn was seething. "Damned aborigines, black coon Hottentot nigger thieves. They've swum off with it all, haven't they?"

They had. Crocodiles or no crocodiles. And now the men of the *Joliba* were left without a guide, without goods for barter, and very nearly defenseless, their arsenal decimated and their number reduced by half. It looked bleak, but not so bleak as it would look five minutes later. Because by then a carefully orchestrated attack would be under way, an attack that would feature tooth-champing Maniana cannibals and weapons rendered useless by sabotage (Amadi had wet the powder in each of the muskets he was unable to carry off, and had almost certainly made some sort of nefarious compact with the Maniana). Later, Mungo would think back on the incident and realize that the guide must have planned it from the first, must have been communicating with the ghouls all along, must have sold them out as casually as one might auction off goats or chickens. Amadi was cold-blooded. Wicked. He'd stabbed them in the back.

Fortunately, however, at the first gastronomic howl from the bush, Ned Rise had had the presence of mind to sever the anchor rope, and the *Joliba*—wet muskets and all—was able to drift down out of danger just as the ochre-painted savages stormed out of the bushes with their skewers and carving knives.

And so, here they are — guideless, cowryless, goodsless, anchorless, their clothes in rags and bodies devastated with disease, sunburn and culinary fatigue, the current carrying them where it will, the water level dropping as the dry season advances, sandbanks lapping at them like tongues, humped white rocks protruding from the sickly wash of the current like picked ribs, mites, flies, ticks, chiggers and mosquitoes biting, the odor of dead fish and exposed muck so rancid and oppressive they can hardly breathe — here they are, overjoyed, celebrating, heading south. Perhaps Amadi's betrayal has been good for them in a way, the explorer is thinking as he holds a match to his pipe and gazes out over the coruscating surface of the river. It's brought them together as nothing else could — four stalwart never-say-die Britishers rallying to confront a slippery treacherous world of blackamoors, cannibals and backstabbing, two-timing negro lackeys. And they've done it. They've succeeded. Amadi's treachery was the straw that didn't break the camel's back, didn't even bow it. They can handle anything, they know that now. Rain, disease, open warfare, perfidy, the loss of friends and brothers and companions at arms, the heart-sinking uncertainty of following the river northward into the desert — they've been through it all. The rest will be nothing, a piece of cake.

It is at this juncture that the first shadow drifts across the explorer's face — skirting the periphery of his consciousness like an insect hovering over a plate of pudding, and yet not quite intruding on it. His mind has made the associative leap from *heading south* to *piece of cake* to *London, glory, Selkirk* and *Ailie,* and he is scratching meditatively at his ankles, stuck on this last little imaginative nugget. Ailie. He wonders what she's doing with herself, if she's bored, angry, disappointed. She has every right to be disappointed, he'll admit that. It's been twenty months already, and how many more only God can tell. Poor thing. He can picture her pining away for him, haunting the post office, reading and rereading his *Travels* till the leaves dissolve. Well he'll make it up to her. He will. She can come down to London while he writes the new book — dedicated to Zander, and to her of course — and he'll give her anything she wants: a coach, jewelry, gowns, menservants, microscopes . . . It is then that the second, third and fourth shadows flit across his face and he raises his eyes reflexively to scan the sky.

Ned has already seen them. Vultures. Eight, ten, twelve of them already, and more coming. Dispersed like leaves, they hang in the still air, wings stiff and mute, gliding, rocking, spinning over the boat as if they were part of some towering mobile. It is a convocation, a synod of scavengers. Black wings against white torsos, eyes like talons, the pedestrian Egyptian vultures circle beneath the big regal griffons, wings spread seven and a half feet across, and the even bigger Nubians that scrape the roof of the world like something left over from the age of reptiles. And now, rushing to them like remoras to sharks, like flying hyenas, are flocks of crows and kites and great gangling marabou storks with their beaks like butcher's knives. In ten minutes the sky is dark with them, wheeling, silent, dozens upon dozens of hot yellow eyes intent on the blistered canopy and chiseled hull of the *Joliba.*

Ned cranes his neck to watch them. And Martyn, stiff-backed as ever though girded in rags and pockmarked with insect bites, has emerged from his nest beneath the canopy to shield his eyes and gaze solemnly at the black suspended forms, at the rigid wings and clamped beaks. Even M'Keal, sodden with drink and still half-crazed from the loss of his ear, the heat, fever, monotony or whatever, is standing there motionless, gawking up at the sky like a rube at the big top. The shadows swoop over them, eclipse them. Ned is uneasy. Whatever it means, it can't be good. He grits his teeth and spits into the river in disgust. Since they passed Yaour things have been looking up. There's been no rough water, they've seen no one, and the river, as far as he can tell from his observation of sun, moon and stars, is taking them due south. It's a pity something like this has to come along and spoil it. A real pity.

These last three weeks or so have been peaceful, pleasant, the steady wash of the river like the pulse of the womb, eternal, lulling, reassuring. He's begun, in a perverse way, to wish it would go on forever. London. What's London to him anyway? A place where he's been hounded, abused, persecuted, condemned. He has no relatives, no friends, nothing but enemies — Ospreys, Mendozas, Bankses. Billy's dead, Fanny's a memory. What's the use? Though the others talk of nothing else, Ned has begun to lose interest in going back — why kid himself? Medals, rewards: what a joke. It'll be the same old story. Pain and sorrow, loss and deprivation. Would the high and mighty Mungo Park even give him a second glance on the streets of London?

Homeless, fatherless, with neither prospects nor hope, Ned has begun to see this bleak, stinking, oppressive continent in a new light, as a place of beginnings as well as endings. All he's been through these past two years, all the heat and stink and disease, all the suffering and strangeness — it must have some purpose, some hidden meaning, some link to his life. He is thinking that maybe he won't return to London when they reach the coast. He'll stay on as a trader, or maybe he'll rest up and then work his way back into the interior, explore on his own, search for whatever it is he's been spared to find . . .

Of course the whole thing is just wishful thinking, daydreaming, mystic and elusive. The important thing — the bottom line — is still survival. He hasn't given up his post at the tiller, hasn't stopped battling the explorer for control of his own destiny, though the battle is as masked and subtle as it's been from the beginning, from the blistering day he and the blond hero first crossed paths over an open grave at Goree. No, he hasn't given an inch, and yet the issue is almost dead at this point. Perhaps it's the sun, the vestiges of fever, the lulling serenity of the past three weeks, but Ned has softened a bit toward his employer and fellow traveler. He is certain now that he will survive, that the worst is over, that there is nothing more this mad ass of an explorer can do to endanger him — and that certainty takes the defensive edge off his relationship with the man. Besides, Mungo trusts him so implicitly he's begun to confide in him, just as Ned had dreamed back at Goree; for what it's worth, he *has* become the right-hand man — superseding Martyn, Johnson, Amadi or any of them — as close to the great white hero as the puny brother-in-law had been.

They've talked, man to man. Still nights, mist on the water, forty-one men dead and the equatorial moon sitting on their shoulders like an immovable weight, they've talked. Mungo bared his heart, told him of his marriage, his children, of the pain of separation, of his ambitions. He talked as if he were talking to himself, for hours at a time, and then, apropos of nothing, he would turn to Ned and ask him how he'd lost his fingers or acquired the scar at his neck — "You know," he'd say, "it almost looks like a rope burn." Ned, his face frank and open, his gaze steady, would lie. "Butcher shop," he'd say, "cutting out steaks." Or, fingering the scar at his throat, "Oh, this. Nothing really. Got my head caught in an iron fence when I was a kid. No more than five or six. They had to fetch the blacksmith to loosen the bars."

No, worming his way into the explorer's confidence was barely a challenge. The man was easy, a self-centered fool. If Ned hadn't got a grip on the reins long ago they'd all be dead by now. Still, he bears the man no malice. In fact, he's all right in his own way — at least he's committed himself to something. That's more than Ned can say for himself. Mungo Park may be conceited, mad with ambition, selfish, blind, incompetent, fatuous — but at least he's got a focus for his life, a reason for living. That's the kernel of truth Ned has dug out of the motherlode of the past three weeks of drifting in the sun: there must be a reason, an organizing principle, to each man's life. For M'Keal it's booze, for Martyn weapons and bloodshed, for Park it's risking his fool hide to open up the map and get his name inscribed in history books. And for himself, Ned Rise? Mere survival isn't enough. A dog can survive, a flea. There must be something more.

But these birds. They cloud the picture, they complicate things. Suddenly a gunshot snaps out behind him, and he wheels round at the quick sharp surprise of it. It is Martyn, nearly on top of him, a musket smoking in one hand, the other clenched in a fist. Almost instantaneously a vulture slaps down on the deck. Stunned, bleeding, one wing askew, the bird scrambles to its feet and lifts its gleaming beak with a hiss. The lieutenant is grinning. He closes in, swinging the stock of his gun like an executioner's axe, M'Keal cheering him on. The bird leaps once, twice, like a rooster dodging a cart, and then Martyn catches it across the back. Bones crack, the claws rake reflexively at the floor of the canoe, and Martyn hits it again. There is a moment of silence, the bird motionless, and then M'Keal plucks up the carcass, a splash of feathers, blood and excrement, and presses it to his chin. "Look at me," he crows, "look at me. I've sprouted feathers!"

No one is looking. Something far more arresting than a swarm of carrion birds has suddenly caught their attention. A distant, moaning roar, the sound of white water beating at rock, the sound of waves and surf and the dead man's tide. Rapids. Mungo glances down at the crude map Amadi had etched for him in the burnished wood of the hull, then looks up at Ned with a cold flat helpless expression, the expression of a fettered prisoner in the hands of his enemies. His voice is hushed, barely audible over the approaching roar — one word, a whisper: "Boussa."

◀◦§   §◦▶

It closes in on them, this din, it boxes them in, booming with a hollow deep-throated resonance, exploding with sudden startling claps and peals, until it seems as if they're being swept into a battle at sea. Within minutes the river's surface has begun to tilt forward, stretching its neck, tapering, while the high-walled banks are suddenly askew, out of plumb, rearing back at a crazy angle. Ahead the channel is seething and white, great strips of rock moving beneath the surface like bone under skin. And almost imperceptibly, a new sound has begun to emerge from the muddled roar, a sucking, rushing sound, as of some unfathomable volume of water — a lake, a sea — sucked down a drain.

There is no time to fight it. No question of easing into shore, no hope of backing out. The only recourse is to lash down the movables — guns, powderkegs, foodstuffs — and ride the chute. Meanwhile, the river gets rougher by the second, tearing at them from every direction, tossing the boat like a twig, hauling it back down as if it were petrified. Ned jerks the tiller right and left, impossible to see over the bow, the flimsy stick all but useless in his hands, while Mungo scrambles up and down the deck, lashing things across the gunwales, muttering to himself, shouting out unheeded commands. Martyn, the tough and unshakable twenty-year-old, the blood-spiller, looks frightened, and M'Keal — buffoon, drunkard, madman — has flung down the dead bird in favor of lashing himself to the nearest canopy strut. High above, safe, placid, patient, the vultures hover like a swarm of monstrous gnats, like harpies, keeping watch.

"The paddles!" Mungo shouts. "Take up your paddles, men!" The men ignore him, the banks grow higher, the Niger heaves and bucks like a furious animal. They hold on, spray flying, the ceaseless racket of water impacting on rock all but swallowing them, the river pitching dizzily, snags and riprap raking like claws at the bottom of the boat. And now — in a quick running blur — the clay banks give way to walls, sheer rock faces pocked with geologic acne, rough as sandpaper above, smooth as the mythic glass mountain below. The canoe angles right past a single boulder big as an atoll, then jerks left again around a pair of scoured pillars, and there, up ahead — what is it? The glancing light, the froth and mist, the roar — it could be anything from a series of riffles to a second Niagara. "Hold on!" someone shouts, and they lock their jaws, bracing for a quick flight into eternity.

But once again the Niger defies their expectations: the roar derives from neither falls nor rapids. Six hundred yards ahead the river seems to stop cold, cut off by a monolithic wall of rock that stretches across the horizon like a felled giant. The banks pull back, the current slows a notch or two, and then they see the passage — a single channel gaping like a mouth in the center of the wall. The explorer goes cold at the sight of it — they'll be swept down like rats in a sewer, dashed against the rocks and drowned . . . but no, wait . . . that tunnel must be thirty feet high, forty! A sudden heady rush of elation sweeps over him: spared, spared yet again! "Look!" he calls back to Ned, "it's big as the portals under London Bridge — we'll clear it easy!" Yes, of course. And isn't that daylight on the far side?

It is. And in fact the great arched vault of the tunnel, abraded through the eons, is easily lofty enough to accommodate the *Joliba* — or a ship twice its height for that matter. But there is another factor involved here, a crucial and perhaps decisive factor that the explorer has not yet had an opportunity to take into account. It is this: what appears at this distance to be some sort of exotic growth darkening the rock wall ahead — it could be a dense thicket, fur bristling along the spine of some Mesozoic beast, clots of algae like skin — is in fact something very different, something animate, intelligent, hostile.

"Wait a minute!" Martyn is perched in the bow of the canoe now, straining his eyes toward the oncoming monolith like a lookout in a crow's nest. "There's . . . there's people on those rocks!"

People indeed. Mungo looks, M'Keal looks, Ned — his heart sinking: new life, purpose — hah! — it's Rise's Law all over again — Ned looks. As the river bowls them closer, everything becomes clear, as clear as a verdict of guilty, a sentence of death. An army is deployed along the cliff — so thick in places that the individual warriors seem to congeal in solid black masses like lumps of tar — an army big as the Czar's, big as Napoleon's, endless, as if all of Holborn had turned out in blackface and armed with spears and bows and hammered knives. All along the Africans have known this moment must inevitably come, all along they've assuaged their disappointments, nursed their stepped-upon toes, swallowed their ravaged pride in the certainty that ultimately they would have their revenge.

Check and mate.

The river pushes them, irresistible. Paddles are useless against it, the anchor lost. As sure as gravity exerts its force and planets tug round the sun, they will be pulled through that grim stone mouth ahead, pulled — like filings to a magnet — onto the spears of their enemies, fatal appetency. The explorer can see them clearly now — the Tuareg army that had looked down on them from the bluff, the Hausa tribesmen in their *jubbahs* and turbans, a contingent of Maniana, ocher limbs and filed teeth. There — those are the Soorka, and there, the nameless savages from Gotoijege, hot to avenge their king. Every prerogative ignored, every snub, every wound given and drop of blood spilled, has come back to haunt them. It is a day of ironies. Even sitting here now, watching his own death played out like a pageant, Mungo can see the bleached high-water mark of a second passage that neatly skirts the cliff ahead, wide and unencumbered and dry as a bone — navigable only during the monsoon.

Dreamlike, this moment before death. Fame, glory, wife, family, ambition — they're equally irrelevant. He is some big-horned buck in the grip of a predator, stunned beyond pain, his guts spilled in the grass, eyes glazing, the crack and drool of mastication like a dirge. He looks around him, detached, absent. Martyn is fooling with the weapons, Rise frozen at the useless tiller, M'Keal crossing himself. One hundred yards, the water sucking and seething. What can he do? Shoot one of a thousand? Take yet another life? No. Better to sit here and wait for the forest of spears, the jagged boulders, the cauldrons of bubbling oil.

But then something jolts him upright, something like anger, rage, a towering fury fed with adrenalin and hate: in all that crowd, through the thicket of weapons and limbs and jockeying torsos, he has suddenly, startlingly, isolated a single face. The face of the one man in all the fathomless universe he can hate with something approaching purity, with an absolute, implacable, merciless hatred, the one man who has thwarted him and barred his way like some cousin of the devil, unreasoning, cold and deadly, the one man he would have strangled in the cradle had he been given the chance: *Dassoud*. The two hissing syllables catch in his throat, slap at his face, and all at once Mungo is on his feet, lurching with the boat, dipping into the bright tatters of his shirt for the smooth ivory grip of his secret weapon, his *pis aller*, the gleaming silver-plated pistol Johnson had pressed on him with a parting benediction.

He's saved it, pressed close, through all these months. The hoarder's secret, tucked deep in the waistband of his ragged breechclout, concealed in the folds of the silly spangled shirt he's fashioned from the tatters of the Union Jack. If it came to the worst, if the river evaporated beneath his feet or he fell into the hands of the Moors, he planned to use it on himself. One bullet, one only. The bridge of the mouth, the soft pocket of the ear. But now, in a moment arranged in heaven, he sees what that bullet has been designed for, understands why it was dug from the ground, melted down, cast and hardened, appreciates why Johnson — salt of the earth — forced the pistol on him. In three minutes he will be dead. So will Dassoud.

Seventy-five yards. Fifty. The rabble is shouting now, pink mouths like wounds in the dark pinguid faces. Ten thousand pairs of lungs, plangent, a roar that for one fraction of a second crashes over the otherworldly din of the river, only to subside almost immediately into mute gesture.

Dassoud is there, waiting, perched not over the archway with the others, but clinging to a ledge at water level, out front, the single nearest man to the onrushing canoe. A knife is clamped between his teeth, a musket leveled in his hands. The *tagilmust* dangles at his throat, as if he has purposely exposed his face for the occasion, a tight triumphant smile drawn across his lips, his eyes a conflagration, bridges burned behind him. He has given up everything for this moment — his elite cavalry, his hegemony over the desert tribes, the soft fecund wash of Fatima's flesh. For four and a half months — since the day he failed at Sansanding — he has driven himself, obsessed, horses dying under him, his skin blistered and throat parched, to reach this spot. Haunting the land of the Kafirs, killing strange chattering things and sucking at the raw meat as he rode — no time to stop — inflaming the local chieftains with his news of the white men, the

Nazarini, waking, eating, drawing breath for this moment, this place, this Boussa.

Twenty-five yards. Martyn firing a musket into the sea of faces, spears like a forest in motion, M'Keal down, the boulders tipped back on their fulcrums. Mungo dips into his shirt and whips out the pistol in a fluid burst of light, the weapon flashing like a sword drawn from stone. He levels it at Dassoud's face, both arms steady, but the boat is lurching, difficult to draw a bead, swirling closer, the roar . . . a stone grazes his cheek, spears begin to sprout from the deck, somewhere behind him Martyn cries out over the thunder in his private agony . . .

In the rear of the boat, stunned and disbelieving, Ned Rise is frantically turning over the alternatives: should he jump and risk the current or wait to be battered to death, squashed like an insect against the hull? Breathing hard, his eyes dissolved in his head, he clings to the tiller out of habit, postponing the moment, staring up into the massed black faces and seeing the hangman all over again. Jump! he shouts to himself. Jump! But he can't, the water like the teeth of a saw, chopping and grinding at the rocks with a fierce frenzied buzz . . and then the first arrows begin to strike the canoe, M'Keal hit again and again, mouth open in a silent scream, blood like a surprise . . . and still Ned sits there. Milliseconds tick by, the boat heaving and rocking: Ned Rise, former clarinetist, ne'er-do-well, hangee and African explorer, dead man. He is fevered, panicky, in the mouth of the beast, every muscle frozen. And then he sees Mungo in the bow of the boat. Mungo, drawing something from his shirt in a storm of spears, arrows and stones. Long-nosed, slender, silver barrel, something out of a distant nightmare: a dueling pistol. Tumblers click in his mind. Barrenboyne. Johnson. His wasted life. And then, in a daze, he's up and dodging the spears and arrows, rushing for the bow of the boat, mad, mad, mad, struggling into the thick of it.

Fifteen yards. The boat dips violently and then rides up clear of the water, suspended for one giddy lingering instant, and Mungo has it, a clear shot, Dassoud's face big as a wagon wheel — but suddenly his hand is arrested, the pistol jerked from his grip. Ned Rise is there, soaked, insane, spear-grazed, clutching at the pistol as if it were the key to the universe, the Holy Grail, the deus ex machina that could lift him up out of the doomed boat and hurtle him to safety. "Give it to me!" Mungo shrieks over the pounding furious roar of the river, frantic, a fraction of a second left. He snatches the pistol, Ned wrestles it back, the boaʟ spinning for the abutment, the world coming down round their ears . . . "Barrenboyne!" Ned shouts, as if it were a battlecry, his features contorted, wet hair splayed across his face. Ten yards, five, all the explorer's hopes riveted on a silver cylinder, a fragment of lead: "Give it to me!"

"Poison!" Ned cries. "Anathema! A bad joke, it's a bad joke!"

"Eeeeee!" call the vultures, swooping low. "Eeeeeeee-eeeeeee!"

"What?" The explorer is shouting — bawling — a damp dismal wind howling through the tunnel in breathless sobs. "What?"

And then they're over the side.

It is like leaping into the teeth of a hurricane, dancing with an avalanche. They are buried, instantly, under the crashing countless tons of water, the very rocks quaking with the force of it. Dassoud's shot goes wild, the *Joliba* founders and in the next instant is dashed to splinters on the near abutment, Martyn and M'Keal, corpses already, are tossed briefly into the air and then sucked down the throat of the gorge as if they'd never existed.

Above, on the rocks, ten thousand voices whoop in triumph and exaltation. Barefooted, naked, their faces disfigured with ritual scars and gashes of paint, black faces, black bodies, the tribesmen embrace, kiss their sworn enemies, dance in one another's arms. The shout goes up, again and again, and the bonfires burn late into the night.

And the Niger, the Niger flows on, past the tumult of Boussa, past Baro and Lokoja, through rolling hills and treeless plains, playing over the shallows like fingers on a keyboard, stirring the reeds with a strange unearthly music, flowing on, all the way to the sea.

GODA

Disquieting rumors began to trickle back to the coast toward the end of 1806, rumors of Mungo Park's demise and the disintegration of his expedition. By January of 1807 they reached England, and shortly thereafter — like wind-borne microbes — they began to spread through Scotland. Ailie confronted these rumors — every last wild word — and refused to believe them. Mungo dead? It was impossible. A mistake, that's all, the upshot of giving the least particle of credence to the irresponsible jabber of those black aborigines, those abhorrent little Seedys with their disfigured faces and rotten teeth: what would they know of her husband's courage and resilience? After all, he'd been gone nearly three years the first time, and no one — not even her father, not even Zander — had believed he would survive. No. The rumors were foundless, ridiculous.

But as 1807 became 1808, and there was still no conclusive word of husband or brother, she began to hunger for rumors, rumors that might reinforce what she so passionately believed: somehow, somewhere, Mungo was out there. In 1810 the Colonial Department contacted the guide Isaaco through Lieutenant Colonel Maxwell, Governor of Senegal, and delegated him to look into the circumstances surrounding the explorer's disappearance. Twenty months later the elderly Mandingo emerged from the bush with a document inscribed in Arabic: it was the journal of Amadi Fatoumi. The white men, Fatoumi wrote, had been killed at Boussa, though he had done all he could to prevent it. Mungo Park was dead. He had drowned when the H.M.S. *Joliba* capsized in the rapids while under native attack.

Ailie repudiated the document. It was a lie. Mungo was alive — certainly he was — and Zander too. Her father tried to reason with her: "It's a sad fact, but ye maun face it, gull. Ye're a widow, and as much as it gars me to say it, ye're bereft of a brother too." His words had no effect. She'd heard it all before — fifteen long years ago, when the whole world was crying in its beer for the "daring young Scotsman swallowed up in the shadow of the Dark Continent," when her friends and relations flocked round to pat her back and her own father tried to force her into a marriage she didn't want. And now it was the same thing all over again. Each new rumor brought them to her door like crows. Betty Deatcher with her brimming eyes, the Reverend MacNibbit with a face like a gravestone. Poor thing, they said, watching her greedily, watching her with something like hunger in their eyes. Is there anything we can do?

Georgie Gleg wrote her from Edinburgh just after Amadi Fatoumi's journal was released. The letter was long and exhaustive — some thirty pages of exquisitely formed characters and precisely ruled margins — offering consolation, hope, money, a shoulder to cry on, a proposal of marriage. She never answered it. Instead, she gathered together all the mementos of Mungo's first expedition — the battered top hat, the ebony figurine with its cruelly distorted belly and limbs, the three editions of his *Travels* — and set up a sort of shrine in the corner of the parlor. Five chairs were ranged round the display, and she spent long hours sitting in one or another of them, the children at her feet, reading aloud from the *Travels* or from Mungo's letters, or just staring off into space, hoping, praying, waiting for the next rumor to make its way to her.

Oh yes, there were fresh rumors. Still. Six years after the fact and better than eight months since the Colonial Department had officially closed the case. They worked their tortuous way to her ears as if drawn by some mysterious irrepressible force. Through the Bight of Benin to the Antilles and Carolina, through Badagri to the Canaries to Lisbon, Gravesend, London and Edinburgh, from savages to slavers, from slavers to diplomats to the man in the street, the rumors persisted: white men were alive in the interior of Africa.

In fact, though no European would ever know it, there was a grain of truth in these reports. If they erred, it was an error of degree, not of substance — it was not white *men* who lived on in the deeps of Africa, but a single white *man*. A survivor. A man totally unknown to the public, a pariah of sorts, a man who had been born to poverty and experienced the miracle of resurrection.

⋅◦⃰ ◦⃰⋅

Some thirty-six hours after the disaster at Boussa, Ned Rise opened his eyes on nirvana for the third time in his life. But this time paradise was neither a dank, fish-stinking shanty on the banks of the Thames nor an operating theater off Newgate Street . . . it was brighter, far brighter, glaring with all the intensity of the tropical sun. The last thing he remembered was the grim leering face of his own death, the rock wall hurtling at him, the mob howling for blood, the struggle with Park . . .

And now what? He was disoriented. His body ached. There was a fire in every joint, his kneecaps felt shattered, a deep intransigent pain stabbed at his lower back. If he could summon the will to sit up and take stock of things, he would discover that he was as naked and unencumbered as the day he was born, the straw hat and tattered loincloth swept away in the flood, the silver dueling pistol buried forever in the muck of the riverbed. But he couldn't. He merely lay there, inert, the sun spread across his back like a blanket of flame.

His vision blurred, steadied. His temples pounded. He lay in a pile of rubble — leaves, branches, fragments of wood and bone — amidst the humped pastel forms of water-smoothed boulders, boulders strewn across the landscape like the eggs of antediluvian monsters. The air was as hot and still as the breath of a sleeping dragon, no sound, no movement, and then suddenly — violent contrast — it exploded with the stiff harsh rattle of beating wings. Ned looked up into the inevitable skewed face of a carrion bird, a vulture, splayed talons, wings spread like a canopy. Bold, combative, the great ugly graverobber hissed at him and took a tentative step forward. It begins again, Ned thought.

But then the bird leaped back, swiveled the flat plane of its neck in alarm, and lurched up out of his field of vision. Something had frightened it off. Hyena? Lion? Maniana? Ned could barely muster the will to care. He stared at the polished surface of the rock before him, a trickle of water washing his legs and groin, the clatter of wings echoing in the silence. Then there was another sound, breathy and melodic, no mere birdsong, no illusion created by rubbing branches or mimetic streams — it was the sound of music, the sound of civilization and humanity. Had he died after all? Was this the afterlife — purgatory — a steaming stinking groundless place where devils and angels vied for his soul? He closed his eyes. Perhaps he slept.

The music played on — flutes, it seemed, three or four of them, melodies intertwined like vines. He was lulled, he was comforted. By the time he pushed himself up the sun was low in the sky and only the convex crowns of the rocks were illuminated, suffused with a pinkish glow, as if each were about to hatch. The music had suddenly stopped. He looked round him: there was no sign of the Boussa rapids, no sign of music-makers, no sign of life. Nothing but smoothed boulders, tumbled to the horizon like melons or beachballs or great hairless heads, and the river at his back. Had he imagined flutes?

Shakily, the pain driving like spikes through his hands and feet, he pulled himself erect and then almost immediately collapsed against the nearest rock. He was bruised, torn and battered. Welts rose along his collarbone, and so many discolored abrasions spangled his legs, buttocks and ribcage he looked like a clown in motley. He'd taken quite a beating. But he was alive and breathing, and so fa. as he could tell nothing was broken. It was almost as an afterthought that he realized he was hungry.

Then — it was unmistakable — something moved. Out there, in the confusion of rocks. And then again: jostling elbows, hunched shoulders. "Hello?" Ned called. Nothing. He tried again — in Mandingo, Soorka and Arabic. There was a long moment of silence, and then, as if in response, the music started up again. No fool, Ned leaned back against the rock and tried to look appreciative. After a moment, he began to clap in time with the unseen musicians, while somewhere off to his left a drum started up, steady and sonorous, pulsing like a heartbeat.

Timid, skittish as deer, they began to show themselves. A head here, a torso there: hide and seek. Then they became bolder, and he saw that the rocks were full of them, little people, no bigger than children, standing out in the open now and gazing at him out of their placid umber eyes. They were naked, these people, their limbs bundles of fiber, their abdomens swollen like the rounded pouting bellies of infants. And they weren't black — not exactly — they were more the color of acorns or hazelnuts.

Ned waited. He could count eighteen of them now, including a pair of children. The musicians — four grizzled, splay-footed homunculi with nose flutes — kept up their piping, and the hidden drummer flailed at his hides. The whole troop was swaying to the music, and Ned, despite a nagging throb in his elbow, continued to clap along. It was at this point that one of the men separated himself from the others and began to make his way forward, feet shuffling in the dirt, head and shoulders undulating to the insistent pulse of the rhythm. He clutched a tiny bow to his breast — it looked like a toy — and wore a quiver looped over his shoulder. His nipples were dark rosettes, scarred from some ancient mishap — fire? war? rites of initiation? — clavicle and ribs protruded, his pubic hair was a snarl of white wire from which the rutted gray penis hung like a badge. An aureole of canescent hair fanned out round his head, and his jaws collapsed on toothless gums: he could have been the first man on earth, father of us all. Ned studied his face, trying to gauge the appropriate response, but the patriarch's expression was blank.

They were singing now, all of them, a bizarre high-pitched whining interspersed with clicks and grunts. For the first time Ned began to feel apprehensive — maybe they weren't so harmless after all. And then he saw it. Something glinting in the old man's hand: a knife? a gun? Was this it, was this what he'd been saved for? But then suddenly he knew what that refulgent, light-gathering object was, knew why they were offering it to him knew what he would do and how he would survive. All at once he could see into the future He was no outcast, no criminal, no orphan — he was a messiah.

The old man handed him the clarinet. It was still damp from its soaking but the pads were clear, the keys undamaged. The drum thumped, the flutes skirled. He put it to his lips — they were smiling now, ranged round him like precocious children — he put it to his lips, and played.

꿎 ꙮ

The years peeled back like the skin of an onion, layer on top of layer Beau Brummell fled to Calais in disgrace, De Quincey swallowed opium, Sir Joseph Banks and George III gave up the ghost. There were riots in Manchester, Portugal and Greece. Beethoven went deaf, Napoleon fell and rose and fell again, Sir Walter Scott was shattered by the crash of 1826 Feathered bonnets came back into fashion and furbelows were all the rage The Niger remained a mystery.

War, peace, Hapsburg, Hanover, décolleté bodices and cotton chemisettes, the fall of an empire, the restoration of a dynasty, Metternich, Byron, Beethoven, Keats — all of it passed Ailie by. She might as well have been living in another world. From the moment she succumbed to Georgie Gleg and had her hellish vision on the breast of Loch Ness, she was a changed woman. The vision — was it a vision? — had come as a warning, as a castigation. She had gone too far. Jealous and bitter, rebelling against the terrible emptiness of the camp follower's life, she had turned her back on Mungo in his time of need. She was an adulteress, an apostate, she was a sinner.

She spent the rest of her life making up for it. When she got home to Selkirk she set up the shrine in the parlor and gathered the children around to inculcate the legend of the father they hardly knew. He was a hero, she told them, one of the greatest men Scotland had ever seen, a man who faced danger in the way ordinary people sat down to breakfast. Where was he? they asked. In Africa, she told them. When will he be coming home? Soon, she said.

This was her penance. The shrine, the legend, the burden of raising the children alone. Gifts would come for her from Edinburgh: combs, dresses, perfumes, toys for the children. She returned them unused. Gleg sent letter after letter. She never answered them. And when he came to the door, the hurt and anguish ironed into his face, the servant girl turned him away. What have I done? he shouted at the windows, over and over. What have I done? he shouted, till her father threatened to call the constable.

The children grew. Her father died. She spent hours at the window looking out across the hills, waiting, hoping. And when she felt blackest, when she knew in her heart she'd never see either Mungo or Zander again, that's when the fresh rumor would whisper in her ear, that's when some trader would appear in Edinburgh with a story he had from a factor on the Gambia who had it from a native slaver who had it from a Mandingo priest: there was a white man in the Sahel, humble, saintly, living like a black. And it would start all over again. He was out there, she knew it.

Meanwhile, there were the children. Thomas, child of the century, was both a curse and a consolation. Like his father he was physically precocious, an athlete, the best footballer in Selkirkshire by the time he was fourteen. Tall, heavy in the chest and shoulders, hair like sand, he was the image of Mungo. She looked at him, and the past rose to haunt her like some sad unmentionable thing risen from the depths of a cold, dark loch. Mungo junior and Archie were like their father too — especially in the cast of their eyes — but Thomas was an exact replica, the hammered shape, the cast die. And more than any of the others he nurtured the legend of his father, pored over the books and maps in the explorer's library, repeated the litany of the rumors until the words were cut like glass.

By 1827 Ailie was in her early fifties, a tiny woman, prematurely aged, worn down by the accumulation of fruitless hours and the futility of her life: it was twenty-two years since she'd laid eyes on her husband. Her daughter was married, Archibald was off in the army, Mungo junior had succumbed to the wanderlust — dead of the fever in India, where he'd been sent with his regiment. Thomas never married. He lived on in Selkirk, close to his mother, sharing with her the onus of his father's disappearance, fostering the hope that he would one day return, hoary and triumphant, from the windswept hills, from the dunes and the jungles.

It was a cold clear morning in early autumn when he left. He had made his plans in secret, seeing no reason to alarm his mother. When she found him gone, she knew precisely what had happened: husband, brother, son. He wrote her from Accra, on the Gold Coast. It was simple, he had it all figured out. He would travel alone, as his father had done on the first expedition, living like the natives, making his way northeast through Ashanti-land and Ibo, striking the Niger at Boussa. The harmattans were blowing. Conditions were perfect. As soon as he could engage a guide he'd be on his way.

She studied the seal of the letter before she opened it. There was hardly any reason to read it: she knew what it said, could have written it herself. She was fifty-three. Mrs. Mungo Park. It was almost funny

She sat by the window a long while, the envelope heavy in her hand, a pale alien light blanching the shrubs, the rooftops, the trees, until even the distant hills were drained of color and life. On the shelf behind her, oiled and black, sat the ebony figurine: gravid, obscene, another artifact.

There were no more letters.